Quest for the Fallen Star

TOR BOOKS BY PIERS ANTHONY

Alien Plot
Anthonology
But What of Earth?
Demons Don't Dream
Faun & Games
Geis of the Gargoyle
Ghost
Harpy Thyme
Hasan
Hope of Earth
Isle of Woman
Letters to Jenny
Prostho Plus
Race Against Time
Roc and a Hard Place
Shade of the Tree
Shame of Man
Steppe
Triple Detente
Yon Ill Wind

WITH ROBERT E. MARGROFF

Dragon's Gold
Serpent's Silver
Chimaera's Copper
Mouvar's Magic
Orc's Opal
The E.S.P. Worm
The Ring

WITH FRANCES HALL

Pretender

WITH RICHARD GILLIAM

Tales from the Great Turtle (Anthology)

WITH ALFRED TELLA

The Willing Spirit

WITH JAMES RICHEY AND ALAN RIGGS

Quest for the Fallen Star

QUEST FOR THE
FALLEN STAR

PIERS ANTHONY
JAMES RICHEY
AND ALAN RIGGS

TOR®

A Tom Doherty Associates Book / New York

QUEST FOR THE FALLEN STAR

Copyright © 1998 by Piers Anthony Jacob, James Richey Goolsby, and Alan Riggs

A Tor Book
Published by Tom Doherty Associates, Inc.
175 Fifth Avenue
New York, NY 10010

Tor Books on the World Wide Web:
http://www.tor.com

Tor® is a registered trademark of Tom Doherty Associates, Inc.

Library of Congress Cataloging-in-Publication Data

Anthony, Piers.
    Quest for the fallen star / Piers Anthony, James Richey & Alan
Riggs. — 1st ed.
        p.   cm.
    "A Tom Doherty Associates book."
    ISBN 0-312-86409-4
    I. Richey, James.   II. Riggs, Alan.   III. Title.
PS3551.N73Q45   1998
813'.54—dc21   98-14560
                                                         CIP

First Edition: July 1998

Printed in the United States of America

0 9 8 7 6 5 4 3 2 1

❧

Mom, Kimmy, Cheryl
For all the beautiful enchantresses in my life
—JR

CONTENTS

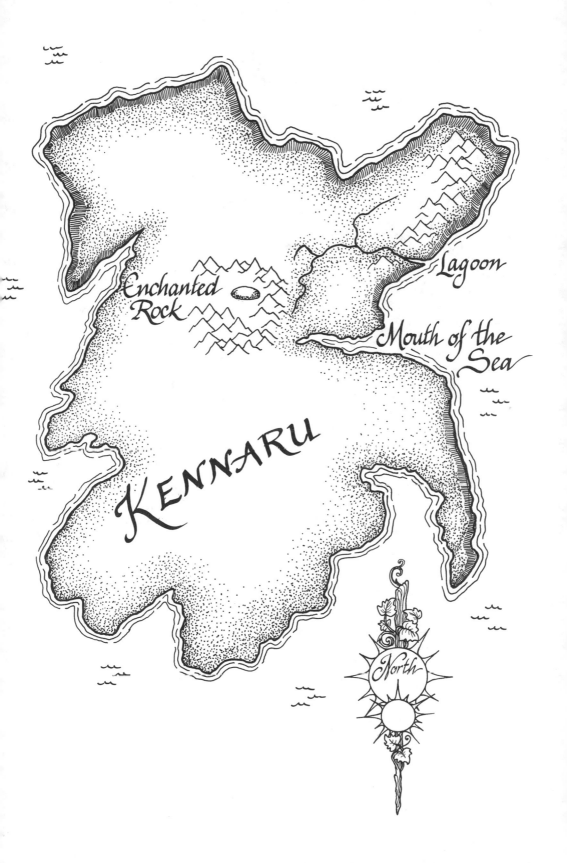

Barrier Peaks

Barrier Ridge

Long Lake

Marble Falls

Mts. of Time

ERIETOPH FOREST

Highlands of Balt

River

Pretgard Mts.

Rushvault

DESECRATION FAULT

Mossenmauve FOREST

Silver Flow River

Tranquil River

Sylvandale

Tel Adartak-Skysoar

WESTLANDS

Shane River

Bay of Peace

MOURY SWAMP

the Great Sea

Chentelle felt the dream surround her.

She walks along a rocky beach, approaching a small camp. The human huddles near the fire, working a marionette that looks exactly like himself. He dances the puppet at the edge of the fire, moving it closer and closer until the figure catches fire. Then he throws it in the sand and stamps out the flames. Chentelle reaches out to him, but he whirls away from her. With a bitter snarl, he picks up the puppet and starts to make it dance.

Again, she thinks. *Always the same.*

A star flares brightly overhead. It rips through the night sky, leaving a jagged scar in its wake. As the star disappears in the west, darkness bleeds through the tear: deep, cold, absolute. It spreads inevitably, swallowing everything in its path. One by one, the stars are extinguished.

Chentelle watches the emptiness grow, waiting to wake. But this time the dream doesn't end.

Mirroring the sky, blackness swells and swirls on the ground. Shadows deepen and coalesce, and shapes emerge from the darkness: twisted, grotesque figures with pale yellow eyes. They move forward, surrounding Chentelle, pressing her back closer to the flames.

She turns, looking for the human. But he's gone. The fire seems tiny now, near death. Chentelle feels a wave of cold as the eyes move closer. Suddenly she is not alone.

A man encased in metal armor stands beside her, his shield decorated with twin suns. He draws a glowing sword and walks calmly forward. He attacks, driving the shadows back. Each time his sword strikes, a creature falls.

But there are too many of them. They swarm over him, tearing at him with icy claws. He fights back valiantly, but Chentelle knows he cannot prevail.

Then, the human is back. He stands in the middle of the fire, wearing a wizard's cloak and clutching a gnarled staff. Beside him is an old man dressed in robes of the Holy Order. An aura of peace surrounds the priest. He rests one hand on the wizard's shoulder and holds the other out to Chentelle.

She takes his hand, and the world explodes in thunder and flames.

The sound still echoed in Chentelle's ears as she woke. It took her a second to identify the sound of wings: a gray dove had landed on her windowsill. Surprised but not frightened, she put her hand out to it. It came to her, as creatures did, even when not tame. A small parchment was tied to one of its legs.

~ 1 ~

ENCHANTRESS

Chentelle hurried through the forest. Her elven eyes had no trouble following the narrow path in the faint red glow of first-light. She saw the forest's edge in the distance and picked up speed, hoping to be out of Lone Valley before truedawn. But as she passed the final line of trees, a branch reached down and snared her arm.

"And where do you think you are going?"

Chentelle started to scream, but cut it off when she recognized the rough, womanly voice. She twisted her arm free of the branch, struggling to regain her calm.

"Willow," she said, keeping her voice to a loud whisper. "You scared me."

Willow leaned her trunk closer to Chentelle. Her hollow eyes glowered discouragingly from beneath an axe-hacked frown.

"Answer the question, little one," she said. "Why are you sneaking out of the forest this early in the morning?"

"Well, I—ah—"

The dendrifaun reached out a limb and brushed the pack slung over Chentelle's shoulder. "Taking a trip, I see."

The sight of the open plains danced tantalizingly between Willow's branches. Chentelle was so close! But already Deneob was fully risen over the eastern hills; Ellistar would not be far behind. She saw that the dendrifaun's roots were still firmly buried; it was too early for the living tree to be fully active. Chentelle could run for it, but Willow would only rouse the elders and tell them where Chentelle was headed. She had to convince the dendrifaun to let her pass.

"Please, old one," she said, adopting the formal mode of address. "You have to let me by. I've told you about the dream, the one that has come to me every night since I saw that falling star. Well, it came again last night. Only, it was different this time. It was telling me something, leading me somewhere. I can't explain it, but I know I have to follow it."

"Have you spoken of this to the elders?" Willow asked.

"No," Chentelle said. "You know what would happen if I did. They would debate the matter for several weeks and ponder it for a few more. Then Mother would convince the others that I am too young, too precious, too important to be allowed to go. Ever since—ever since Father died, she's been afraid to let me out of her sight. But I have to go, and I can't afford to wait."

Chentelle shifted guiltily in the silence. Her mother would be so worried when she found the note pinned to her child's bed. But it had to be this way; the dream demanded it.

Willow reached out and brushed her leaves across Chentelle's hair. "Mothers worry. It is their nature. Besides, you are a special child, and not just for your golden hair."

"I know, I know." The elf girl deepened her voice until it mimicked her mother's rich tone. "You are an enchantress, Chentelle, the first born in Lone Valley for five generations. You have a responsibility to yourself and to the village."

"Exactly," Willow agreed without mockery.

"But don't you see?" Chentelle said, returning to her normal voice. "I do have a responsibility. I have to find out what the dream means. And I'm not a child. I'm nearly two hundred."

Willow's branches swayed with amusement. "You are one hundred and sixty-three, and I have told you stories and watched you grow through each of those years. Tell me, did I ever share with you the story of Fizzfaldt the Wanderer?"

"Yes, old one, many times."

"Hmmph, well, then you see my point. Fizzfaldt, too, felt the need to leave the forest, to taste the soil of other lands. But he never returned. His stories are lost to us."

"Yes. That is too bad." Chentelle did feel the loss, for the stories of the dendrifauns were good ones. But she mistrusted Willow's point in this case.

"I will let you go, little one, for I sense that you are caught in the middle of a great tale. When your mother comes to me, full of worry, I will try to comfort her. And when she asks where you are, I will conceal the direction of your travel. But you must be careful, Chentelle. And when your story is done, you must promise to return here and share it with the forest. It would be a sad thing for us to lose another story."

Chentelle threw her arms around the old dendrifaun's trunk. "Thank you," she said. "I'll bring back a special story just for you. I promise." Then she turned and sprinted out of the forest.

"My dear," Willow murmured to her retreating form, "I am sure you will."

↷

Chentelle paused once she reached the open plain. Gently rolling hills glowed like copper in Deneob's soft light, stretching into the horizon. The emerald wall of the forest, with all of its seclusion, all of its protection, lay behind her. Far to the east, the first glow of truedawn heralded the rise of Ellistar, the Golden Sun. This was the point of no return.

Deliberately, Chentelle pulled off her pack and undid its ties. She reached inside and pulled out the dove. The bird slept comfortably, still reassured by the spell she had placed upon it last night. She unrolled the note and read it one last time.

> *Wizard A'mond, find the apprentice to A'pon Boemarre. Bring the Staff to the Holy City.*

It was signed with the seal of Marcus Alanda, High Bishop of the Holy Order.

Again, Chentelle pondered the message, and again she felt the twinge of an old sadness. A'mond had been wizard to the elves of Lone Valley for centuries, one of the few wizards to escape death at the Desecration Fault. The High Bishop had no way of knowing that A'mond had been killed in a freak accident last winter. So the dove had come to Chentelle, drawn by her magic. It was up to her to find this apprentice of A'pon Boemarre.

A'pon Boemarre! That was a name well known to every inhabitant of the Realm: Boemarre the Mighty, greatest of wizards; Boemarre the Hero, champion of the Wizard's War, slayer of the Dark One; Boemarre the Genocide, whose Desecration Fault swallowed entire races of giants and trolls.

A'pon Boemarre—oh, yes, Chentelle knew that name. The man who had saved the Realm by unleashing death on thousands, numbers that included Chentelle's own father.

Chentelle fought back tears at the memory. It was the first time her Gift had manifested. She had felt the dreadful power shaking under the roots of the forest, the echo of the world's pain when that force was unleashed. And she had felt the terrible emptiness of her father's death.

Chentelle shook her head, trying to clear the memory. She flipped the note over and scrawled a quick reply across its back.

Wizard A'mond has died, but your wishes will be carried through.

She signed the note and wrapped it back around the dove's leg. Then she softly stroked its head, waking it from the slumber she had induced. "Time to fly, little one," she said, tossing the bird into the air.

As the messenger dove disappeared to the south, Chentelle regarded the plain ahead. It stretched two score leagues between here and the Quiet Sea. A long way to travel to the beach she had seen in her dream. She would need help to get there.

She closed her eyes and inhaled slowly. As the air of the plain filled her lungs, the spirit of the land touched her soul. She felt the quiet rhythm of the grass, the rich life of the soil, the soft power of the wind. She felt the passionate harmony of nature and understood her own place within it.

When the reality of the plain was complete within her, she sang. Her voice was music and magic. Her song captured perfectly the harmony she sensed. Her voice radiated across the plain, a surge of peace and joy begging to be shared. This was Chentelle's Gift.

Slowly, she altered her song. She began to sing not only of what was, but of what she wished to be. Her voice shaped an emptiness in the plain, and she filled that void with her desire, with her need, but most of all with her love. She crafted a song of beckoning and backed it with the full force of her Gift, letting it flow beyond the world of men and into the Realm of Dream and Fairy.

Chentelle ended her song and waited. With her Gift, she could still hear her tune echo in the Fairy Realm. Soon, it was joined by another song. The empty places in Chentelle's call were being filled. But where her song was one of harmony and melody, the new music was one of rhythm and percussion and driving, unrelenting beat.

Chentelle snapped open her eyes, letting go of her Gift. Her face lit with a smile of undiluted happiness as she saw the unicorn herd charging across the plain.

They ran as if it were their sole purpose in existence. They flowed across the land with a speed no ordinary steed could match. In moments they were surrounding Chentelle, prancing playfully and nodding their heads in greeting.

As always, Chentelle was awed by the unicorns' appearance. She admired their graceful white bodies, their flowing manes, the ivory horns that spiraled outward from their foreheads. They were beyond words of beauty.

She stepped forward, careful to keep her movements slow and smooth. She knew that unicorns became nervous around mortal creatures.

The herd parted at her advance, creating a channel through which one beast approached and bowed deeply. Chentelle immediately recognized Kah, the stallion of this herd and her friend. She returned his bow and then continued her walk. She hummed softly as she moved, reassuring Kah with the melody of her voice.

The stallion tensed as she came near, but he did not run. Chentelle delicately caressed the unicorn's cheek and mane. Then she ran her fingers down his horn, sensing the pure magic contained within. "I am glad you came," she said. "It is a joy to see you again."

Kah danced away from her, nodding broadly. Then he stepped forward and laid his horn softly on her shoulder.

"Your trust honors me," Chentelle said. "I need to travel far and fast. Will you carry me to the Quiet Sea?"

The stallion backed away from her, nodding once again. Then he knelt in the grass, indicating with his horn that Chentelle should mount. She slid smoothly onto his back; then he rose easily, accepting her weight as if it were of no concern. She got a good grip on his flaring mane, knowing what was coming.

Kah trotted gently until they were beyond the circle of the herd. Then he neighed loudly and reared, pawing the air with his hooves. He was telling them to remain here. The other unicorns neighed in response and began grazing on the tender spring shoots. Kah spun eastward and took off with a surge of speed that stole Chentelle's breath. She loved the sensation.

The unicorn glided tirelessly through the rushing wind. Chentelle huddled close against the beast's broad back, riding the music of his stride. She buried her face in his rich mane and reveled in the smooth rhythm beneath her. Kah used his horn to draw strength from the Dream Realm. He could run for days without stopping, but she was only mortal.

A scent of wild strawberries in the wind forced Chentelle to recognize her hunger. She whispered into Kah's ear, and the fairy beast pulled to a stop. Quickly, she gathered the berries, still wet with dew. But she couldn't bring herself to rush the meal; the tangy-sweet morsels deserved to be savored. She satisfied her hunger and then picked a few more handfuls, adding them to her pack for later.

Then she climbed a second time on Kah's back, and they were on their way again. The leagues passed rapidly beneath the unicorn's thundering hooves. Chentelle was forced to call occasional stops to ease her tired muscles or sate her appetite, but they still made steady progress.

By the time Deneob disappeared into the west, Chentelle could smell salt in the air. Buoyed by the scent, she started to sing softly, matching her song to

Kah's beat. In response, the unicorn ran even faster. Soon, grassy plains disappeared into sandy hills. As Ellistar dipped below the horizon, they crested one final hill and looked out on the wide, calm waters of the Quiet Sea.

As Kah slowed to a walk, Chentelle reached out with her Gift. She felt the shifting spirit of the sand and the sharp awareness of the birds. And she felt the sea: vast, patient, incredibly powerful, and teeming with life. So much life! She felt fish and crabs and creatures whose names she did not know, all locked in an immense dance of survival.

And she heard a song, an intricate, beautiful theme weaving its way through the waves: whalesong, she realized. But there was something wrong. The song was full of fear and distress. Chentelle tried to sense the cause of the fear, but it was too distant.

"The water," she said. "I have to get to the water, Kah."

With a fierce snort the unicorn galloped ahead. He ran headlong across the beach and pulled up just at the water's edge.

Chentelle vaulted from his back and ran into the sea. When the waves reached her waist she took a deep breath and plunged her head into the water. The whalesong rang in her ears, and she answered it with her Gift. She poured her emotions into her song: her caring, her concern, her hope.

The whales answered. They sang of wrongness and of fear. They sang of something in the waters to the north, something that did not belong in the sea, something evil.

Chentelle pulled her head above water and gasped for breath. The threat she felt in the whalesong was so wrong, so unnatural. She had to do something.

She pushed herself back toward the beach and reached for Kah. "Something terrible is happening," she said. "It's just north of here. We have to hurry."

The unicorn reared powerfully and took off, hugging the coastline. He left the wind behind. Even so, Chentelle begged Kah to hurry. She sensed that someone or something was in great danger. In response to her words, the stallion raced even faster, yet Chentelle still worried.

"I fear we may be too late," she said. "We must get there *now*, Kah."

The unicorn neighed in response and summoned his magic. The color drained from his horn as the ivory became first translucent and then transparent. There was a sudden flash of light, and they were no longer on the beach.

They floated through a void of light. A dreamlike silence suffused her, as if she were on the edge of sleep. The possible danger ahead seemed unimportant; the urgency of her quest, an illusion. Kah's magic transported them through the Realm of Dreams, where concerns of the physical world had little weight. A moment of eternity passed; then the beach reappeared around them.

The unicorn skidded to an abrupt halt, weakened from the exertion. Chentelle, still disoriented from the transition, was nearly thrown. Only a firm grip on the stallion's mane saved her. She struggled for a moment to regain her senses.

They stood just beyond the waves on a wide stretch of sandy beach. Jagged rocks jutted out into the water before and behind them, forming natural jetties. Just past the rocks, moonlight illuminated a vision out of nightmare.

A hideous creature lay partially submerged in the dark sea. Its mouth was a great circular maw surrounded by curved fangs. Thick tentacles protruded from either side of the head, flailing about like tendrils of living vine. The body was covered with smooth armor plating, and the lobsterlike tail churned the shallow water as the creature chased a small sailboat. The foulness of the creature screamed at Chentelle's senses, and she knew that this was an Ill-creature, a spirit of evil summoned from the Abyss.

The monster quickly closed on the small craft and latched several of its tentacles onto the stern. The boat shuddered, caught between the pull of the wind and the creature's grip. More tentacles emerged from the water, reaching for the lone figure standing on deck.

Helpless, Chentelle watched while the man drew a sword and slashed at the attacking tentacles. But it was no use. The blade bounced harmlessly off the monster's flesh. It was a magical creature—only a magical weapon could harm it.

The Ill-creature tugged furiously at the boat, trying to pull it underwater. The man wedged his sword under a tentacle and pried it off of the boat. Then he started to work on the others. But whenever he succeeded in levering a tendril loose, the creature tried to reattach it. The man wielded his sword with a desperate frenzy. When he wasn't prying a tentacle from the boat, he was slashing at one trying to gain purchase. He couldn't hurt the creature, but he could push the tentacles away from their targets.

Finally he managed to pry the last tendril loose. The boat shot forward on the sea wind. But there was no control. Without steering, the boat raced toward the rocky shoreline. It crashed into the rocks, throwing the man into the water. The wind and the waves continued to drive the craft forward until its hull splintered against the stone.

The Ill-creature was momentarily confused, and continued to attack the remains of the boat. The man took advantage of his respite to swim toward shore, but on this particular stretch of beach the Quiet Sea gave the lie to its name. The wind-driven waves crashed and swirled around rocky outcroppings, punishing the man for every stroke. He was still a dozen cubits from the sand when the creature turned from the wreckage and lunged after its prey.

Kah reared in alarm at the monster's charge. Chentelle tried to calm him, but the unicorn backed skittishly away from the abomination.

Chentelle could feel the unicorn's terror. She knew he overcame the instinct to run only because of her urging. But she couldn't leave the man to die. She sang to Kah softly, using her Gift to calm his fear. Finally, she was able to guide him back toward the water, but what she saw there made the song catch in her throat.

The monster was balked, unable to move its bulk through the shallow water, and only this was saving the man's life. The beast had grabbed hold of the man with several tentacles and battled to pull him into deeper water. Somehow the man had reached a jagged spar of rock, and he clung desperately to it.

The intensity of his struggle struck Chentelle as if it were a physical force. She felt his anger, his determination, his indomitable will. His entire being was focused into the effort of his chest and hands and arms, into the extraordinary contest between human muscle and Ill-creature might. But it was hopeless. The monster was too large, too powerful. Slowly, inevitably, the man's hands slid across the surface of the rock.

Chentelle jumped from Kah's back and raced to the edge of the water. She had no idea how to help the man, but she felt she had to do something. Her

Gift was one of harmony and understanding, not combat, but it was the only thing she had. So she sang.

She gathered the magic around her and cast it outward to the Ill-creature. She bombarded it with images of peace and tranquillity. She showed the creature the harmony of nature and the joy of life. She sang—and the creature screamed.

The monster thrashed the water in agony. It released its grip on the human and whipped its tentacles wildly in the air. The purity of Chentelle's magic was more than it could cope with, and it retreated quickly into deeper waters.

She ended her song and stared at the churning water where the beast had been. "Thank you, Creator," she said.

She ran to the human. He had sunk beneath the waves as soon as the creature released him, but his hands still clung to the rock. Chentelle dropped her pack and jumped into the water. She tried to pull the man to shore, but his hands would not release their grip. She had to brace her legs against the rock and push with her whole body to pry them loose.

Without the support of the rock, the man's weight pulled Chentelle under the water. He massed far more than she did; even with the buoyancy of the water, he was hard to handle. She struggled to regain her footing, but the currents were too strong. She groped about wildly. Then her hand came to rest on something solid.

Kah! She recognized him through her Gift, and wrapped her arm tightly around the unicorn's leg. She wound her other hand in the human's hair and held on firmly while Kah pulled them out of the water.

Once on shore, Chentelle let go of the stallion and gasped for breath. She had been close to drowning herself, she realized belatedly. "Thank you, friend!"

Kah whinnied in response and danced back away from the water. He would not have approached it without compelling reason.

Chentelle turned to check on the human. He wasn't breathing. Quickly, she placed a hand on his chest, reaching out with her Gift. A swirl of emotions assaulted her senses, but she pushed through them, concentrating on his physical being. She felt a potent vitality about the man, but it was fading quickly, sinking under the weight of the seawater in his lungs.

Chentelle concentrated on her sense of the human's body and started to sing. She shaped her song in the image of the man, but without the intrusion of water. Then she reached out to the sea and took hold of its wholeness. She balanced her song of the man with a rhythm of water, ever moving but always returning to its proper place.

Her song took hold of the man, and he convulsed. Water jetted from his mouth and ran in thick rivulets back to the sea. He coughed spasmodically and collapsed, breathing heavily but evenly.

Chentelle also collapsed, exhausted. She lay facedown in the sand, sobbing. Her magic was good, but it put a physical strain on her.

A nudge from Kah's muzzle brought her back to awareness. There was a surge of anxiety coming from the unicorn stallion. She shouldn't have left him in doubt, thinking only of herself. "It's all right," she said. "He'll live. We'll both live, thanks to you."

The unicorn nodded his head in response, but continued to shift about nervously.

"I understand," Chentelle said. "You've been away from your herd for too long. I apologize for imposing on you. Go in peace, friend. I'll be fine, now."

Kah reared once in salute, and then raced into the west.

Chentelle examined the man more closely. She winced as she saw the bloody gashes left on his chest and arms by the jagged stone. He was partially bare, his shirt and boots having been lost during the battle. His face was broad and flat, but not unhandsome. His jet-black hair was matted and tangled, but she could see that it normally hung straight to his shoulders. He was much larger than an elf, at least four cubits tall, and seemed to be covered everywhere in lean, hard muscle. He slept soundly, but was shivering in the cool wind.

Chentelle could do something about that. She was cold herself. She set about gathering material for a fire. She found driftwood in abundance, much of it from the man's ruined sailboat. She found an area sheltered from the wind and piled her wood carefully. Then she spoke to it, using the words of power entrusted to all elves. The words took life in the center of the wood and filled it with warmth. The warmth turned to heat and then to flame. Soon Chentelle sat before a strong fire.

She went back to where the human lay and fought to pull him to the fire. Without the buoyancy of the water, she could barely move him. He must weigh more than twice her six stone. She had to do it piecemeal, hauling his legs forward, then moving his upper section. It was slow and clumsy and surely not kind to his sleeping dignity, but she did make progress. After much effort, she managed to get him close enough to benefit from the fire's warmth. Worn out again, she collapsed on the sand next to him.

"Blessed Creator," she gasped, "did you have to make humans so heavy?"

Blood pooled in the sand next to her. The man's arm wounds had been reopened by the drag across the beach. She chided herself for not realizing that this would happen. She shifted his arms so she could examine the cuts—and froze.

On the inside of the man's right forearm was a tattoo: a dragon, black as midnight. And it was moving.

Chentelle felt dizzy. Her stomach churned and bile burned the back of her throat. This was no trick of the light; the dragon *was* moving, shifting sinuously around the man's arm. And the hatred that it radiated pounded against her senses.

Chentelle scurried away from the man. Could it be? Was the one she had saved as evil as the creature that chased him? But if so, why hadn't she sensed it before, when she kept him from drowning? He didn't look evil. But the tattoo, that was evil. The malice it generated was unmistakable.

Cautiously, Chentelle crawled back to the human. There was only one way to be sure. She took a deep breath and laid her hand on the man's left arm, the one without the tattoo.

The evil hit her immediately. It pervaded the man's being, stretching to every corner of his soul. But there was more. Chentelle sensed passion, loyalty, trust, honor, need, compassion, anger, pain, resignation: a tumult of emotion surrounding a basic core of goodness. This was the man. The evil came from the tattoo; it was in the man but not *of* the man.

The complexity of the man's spirit was fascinating. Deep inside the furor of his surface emotions was a center of absolute calm. And within that center were secrets and wonders that glittered like gems at the bottom of a still pool. Chentelle extended her Gift to that core of tranquillity and—

She snatched her hand away, breaking the contact. She had no right delving into the man's innermost secrets. He was not evil. That was all she needed to know.

Chentelle took a cloth and water pouch from her pack and began cleaning the caked blood and sand from the man's wounds. When she passed it across the tattoo she felt the malignant heat of that region; the dragon didn't like being touched. Not by the likes of her. It snapped at her finger, but she jerked her hand away. The action roused the man momentarily, and he moaned softly before losing consciousness again.

"My sword," he said, speaking in the Tengarian tongue. "My—"

His sword. Chentelle brushed her fingers along his right palm, keeping a sharp eye on the tattoo. Of course the Black Dragon couldn't actually reach her; it was only a drawing. But she feared it anyway; malignant magic was not limited to the physical plane.

On the skin of his hand she found the trace of a thick-bladed black sword. Then she turned to the sea, searching. The image of the sword pulled her awareness under the surface, near the rocks, deeper, there. The sword lay safely on the sea floor.

She turned back to the man. The language he spoke gave away his origin, Tengarian. She should have guessed from his appearance. But the Tengarians were a mountain people, who remained isolated by their rigid codes of behavior. She had never heard of one sailing alone on a lowland sea. In fact, she had never heard of a Tengarian leaving his rugged homeland for any reason other than to fight a war or settle territorial disputes with the dwarves.

She finished cleaning the man's wounds and covered him with her bedroll. Then she examined her own condition. She was exhausted and filthy, and her gown was soaked, and her boots were filled with seawater. But otherwise she felt adequate.

With a sigh, she pulled off her boots and poured the water out of them. They were made from leatherbark and fully waterproof, but there were limits. Then she stripped off her gown and washed it in the sea. The dirt and blood rinsed easily off the spidersilk threads, and she laid it by the fire. Once dry, it would glisten as sublimely as on the day her mother wove it.

A muffled groan warned her that the human was awake again. He raised himself onto his elbows and glanced furtively around. Finally his eyes rested on Chentelle. He stared at her, unblinking, and Chentelle could feel the tension in his gaze. Slowly, never taking his eyes off her, he slid from under the blanket and got to his feet. Despite his obvious fatigue and disorientation, there was a certain professional competence to his actions.

Chentelle knew that humans had difficulty seeing in the dark, so she stepped into the firelight. She wanted him to understand that she posed no threat to him.

"You are elven," he said.

"My name is Chentelle," she answered, using his own tongue. "You are safe. The Ill-creature is gone."

The Tengarian's hand twitched at his side, but still his gaze never shifted. It was the mark of a warrior, never to take his eyes from a potential enemy. His hand was questing for his sword, but she knew that he could dispatch her quite readily without it. But she also knew he wouldn't, because he was a man of honor. She had not had to explore his inner being at all deeply to learn that. All he needed was reassurance.

"Your sword is in the water," she said, pointing. "It will wait until morning."

He reacted with horror. He turned to walk in the direction she pointed. He managed two trembling steps before he overbalanced and fell to his knees. The jolt caused one of his cuts to start bleeding again, and Chentelle could hear his sharp inhalation.

"Your sword is safe," she said. "I can feel it. I know where it is. Now, please come back to the fire. Your wounds need care."

He looked all around again, then back at her, assessing the situation. He nodded.

Chentelle moved forward and took his arm to help him stand, but he shrugged her off. Without help, he pressed himself upright and staggered back to the fire. Chentelle stayed close, ready to lend assistance, but the Tengarian shrank away from her touch. He managed to make it back to the blankets before falling to the ground once more.

"Water," he said. "I need water."

She handed him the leatherbark pouch and he drank from it in large gulps. Then he poured some water on his wounds.

"Save some," Chentelle said. "I have some herbs which will speed your healing, but they have to be mixed with water."

The Tengarian nodded and handed her back the pouch, but now he kept his eyes turned carefully away from her. Suddenly she understood. Humans almost always wore clothes when in groups, and her gown was still drying by the fire. For reasons she did not fathom, they seemed to feel that nudity was socially indiscreet. She pulled the travel cloak out of her pack and wrapped it around her shoulders. Then she mixed her herbs with water, using a seashell and her fingers as a mortar and pestle.

"This will heal your wounds quickly," she said. "But you have to let me touch you to apply it."

The Tengarian said nothing, but nodded once to show his assent.

"The herbs sting at first," she said, "but they will soon bring comfort and healing."

She sat beside him and rubbed the medicine lightly into his wounds. His pain was obvious to her Gift. She could feel the deep ache of his injuries and the sharp sting of the herbs. But he made no outward sign beyond a tensing of the muscles where she touched.

"How does it feel?" she asked, and received a nod in reply. "Do you feel well enough to eat?"

Again, the Tengarian made one nod in response.

Chentelle took out the rest of her food and divided it with him. It was a meager supper for two: two hard rolls, some cheese, an apple, and a few of the wild strawberries. "I am sorry that I do not have more to offer," she said. "I did not expect to have a guest."

Wordlessly, he accepted his share. They ate in silence. It was infuriating.

"Look," Chentelle said, exasperated, "will you at least tell me your name?"

"I am Sulmar," he said.

"And you are from Tengar," she said. "I come from Lone Valley forty leagues to the west. Will you tell me about your homeland and your people?"

"I no longer have a homeland," he said, "or a people."

Chentelle felt the bitterness behind his words. No people; he was an outcast. She tried to imagine being cut off from her community, but the thought was too horrible. She understood, now, the source of the pain she had felt in his heart. "I am sorry," she said. "What happened?"

The Tengarian didn't answer. Chentelle felt the anger and sorrow boiling inside him. The feelings were dauntingly powerful, but Sulmar's expression was unchanged. He locked his emotions behind an iron wall of discipline.

Then, slowly, he raised his arm, displaying his tattoo. The dark scar shifted eerily on the firelight. "This is the mark of the Black Dragon. It is a curse, an invitation for the powers of evil to consume my soul. So long as I wear it I am corrupted. I have no rank, no clan, no identity. To return to Tengar would mean my death."

"But why?" Chentelle asked. "What could make your people treat you so cruelly?"

"No," he said, "it was not the people. It was—" Sulmar's voice faltered and he lowered his head. "It does not matter. There is no returning."

"But surely—"

He raised a hand, cutting off Chentelle's reply. "Do not ask. I will speak of this no more."

She nodded. It was no more right to pry with questions than with her Gift, when the matter was truly private.

The Tengarian stood and shuffled to the far side of the fire. "See to your own comfort, girl," he said, pointing at the bedroll. "I will sleep uncovered."

The man's manner left no room for debate. Chentelle settled herself on the blankets and closed her eyes, listening to the crackle of the fire and the steady rhythm of the waves. Almost immediately the excitement of the day yielded to exhaustion, and she fell asleep.

☙

The dream did not come. That was the first thing Chentelle realized when she woke. The second thing was that Sulmar was not by the fire. She jumped up quickly, trying to ignore the pain in her legs and back. Ellistar was already rising over the water, and she squinted into the glare. There he was, standing near the shattered remains of his sailboat, staring at the waves. The tide was higher than it had been last night, but the waves crashed against the rocks with no less force.

Chentelle reached for her dress, then reconsidered. She wrapped the cloak around her body and walked down to join the Tengarian. "Good morning," she said. "How are your wounds?"

"Nearly healed." But Chentelle could see that rough scabs remained on his hands and arms.

She rested a hand on his shoulder and touched him with her Gift. Sulmar tensed, then relaxed. He was healing quickly, and there was no infection, but the cuts had been deep. It would be days before he recovered completely, and he would have to be careful lest he reopen the wounds. "You still need rest," she said.

"I must retrieve my sword."

"In your condition? Do you think I would let you drown again, or contaminate your wounds with salt water? I will get your precious sword."

Sulmar glanced at the pounding surf. "Girl, I cannot let you—"

"What?" she said. "You cannot let me face the perilous waves? Who do you think saved you from the Ill-creature last night? Speaking of which, you might at least say 'Thank you.' " She pulled the cloak off her shoulders and thrust it into his arms. "Now stand back."

The Tengarian stepped backward, eyes widening. Then he regained his composure and bowed smoothly from the waist. "I must ask your forgiveness."

"Oh, *must* you," Chentelle retorted.

Sulmar snapped stiffly back to attention.

Chentelle realized she had made a mistake. It was the first sign of openness he had shown, and she had punished him for it. She laid a hand on his arm.

"Now I must ask for your forgiveness," she said. "I understand what you meant, and I have felt the goodness and honor in your heart. I would like to call you friend."

Sulmar did not answer, but she could feel the softening of his ire. He was clearly not accustomed to independent or assertive women, and she surely resembled a child in his eyes, despite her maturity of body. He had thought of her first as a potential enemy, then as a helpless creature. Now, perhaps, he was ready to accept her as the elf she was.

She turned back to the sea. "Now I will get your sword." This time Sulmar did not protest.

Chentelle reached out with her Gift and started to sing. Her song reached out, spreading peace and harmony. Violent waves subsided to gentle swells and then stillness. For as far as her voice carried the Quiet Sea lived up to its name. Without stopping her song she stepped easily into the placid water.

She altered her serenade slightly, adding a note of playful beckoning. Almost immediately, her call was answered. A pod of dolphins danced over the water, joining in her song. Their clicks and whistles blended seamlessly with her melody. Chentelle spoke to them with her Gift, sharing her need.

The dolphins disappeared under the surface. Soon one of them reappeared with Sulmar's sword gripped between its teeth. Others followed bearing boots, a short knife, a scabbard hanging from a frayed belt, and a burlap sack filled with spoiled food. They deposited the items in Chentelle's arms, then rejoined their fellows.

She heard a splash behind her as Sulmar rushed forward. "Be careful," she said, letting her song fade. "Don't get your cuts wet."

"How is this possible?" he asked, taking the sword and setting it carefully on a rock at the shore. Then he took the other things from her hands and waded back and forth to set them on the dry beach.

Chentelle smiled. "It is my Gift," she said, absently patting one of the dolphins. "I am an enchantress. The magic of nature touches me deeply. It speaks to me, and when I sing, I can speak to it."

"I have heard legends of such people," he said. "It is said that only one is born in each millennium."

"I'm not sure whether that's true. There has not been another in Lone Valley for five generations, but one may have been born elsewhere."

A dolphin surfaced next to Sulmar, carrying a seashell in its mouth.

"How sweet," Chentelle said. "She's giving you a gift."

Sulmar shrugged and accepted the shell. Then he nearly lost his balance when the dolphin bumped into his legs. "What is she doing?" he asked.

"She wants you to pet her," Chentelle explained. "They are very affectionate creatures. She also wants you to know that she is the one who found your sword."

Sulmar ran his hand tentatively down the dolphin's side. She whistled happily and spit water into his face. Then she rolled away and splashed water at him with her tail.

"Watch out," Chentelle cried, laughing. "Don't get your cuts—" Then she became aware of something else. "Oh, no! Hurry, get out of the water."

Sulmar bolted into action. Before she even realized he was moving, the Tengarian snatched her into his arms. He carried her to shore in a half-dozen powerful strides and dropped her protectively behind him. He whirled to face the sea, sweeping his sword from its rock, raising it, and dropping into a balanced crouch.

"No, Sulmar," she said, gasping for breath. "It's not that kind of threat."

She pointed to the water splashing with renewed vigor against the rocky shore. "It's just the sea. Without my song to hold it back, the waves will become agitated again. I didn't want your wounds to get wet."

She felt the tension ease once more from the Tengarian. He even smiled when he reached down to help her stand. "I apologize for overreacting. I am not yet accustomed to—"

"I understand. I thank you for the gesture." For had the danger been to her, and immediate, he might well have saved her life. His action had indicated a readiness to do just that. Now, however, he was steadying himself, evidently having used more energy than was wise in his present state.

Chentelle called a brief farewell to the dolphins, then returned to the campsite.

She retrieved her cloak and used it to dry herself, conscious of the man's careful aversion of gaze. Would he have done that if he really saw her as a child? Then she dressed and put on her boots.

She saw that Sulmar had discarded the ruined food and laid the rest of his belongings by the fire to dry. He turned and met her eyes. "My lady, thank you for returning my sword. And—thank you for saving my life."

She smiled. "I was happy to help. But I am on an urgent errand, and I am afraid I must leave you now." She was privately pleased, however, that he was no longer calling her "girl."

"If I may ask—where is it that you go, my lady?"

She paused. Her Gift had shown her that the man could be trusted, but the dream had convinced her that secrecy was vital. "I am—seeking someone."

"Is it possible that you would need a companion?"

Chentelle started to decline, but Sulmar interrupted her. "My lady, I have lived all of my years according to the Oath of Discipline and the teachings of the Noble Path, but in the days of my suffering I lost even that. My anger and my bitterness threatened to consume me, and I wandered with no true destiny. My life was finished, my soul destined for the Abyss. But you intervened.

"There is a law within the Oath of Discipline that demands repayment for the gift of a life. You may demand any service from me that you wish. You may also choose your reward from among my lands, my offices, or my marriageable children. Alas, your options there are few."

Sulmar knelt before her. "My lady," he said. "I offer you my service. I beg you to make me as your liegeman. I am without destiny. If you do not accept, my disgrace will be complete."

"You don't understand," Chentelle said, taken aback. The man had swung from helplessness to seeming contempt, and now to—what? "I can't ask you to do this. There may be great dangers involved."

"Then you have more reason to accept my vow," the Tengarian said. "I am a warrior. Once I have sworn my loyalty, no danger will reach you without overcoming my sword. I beg you, my lady, accept my service."

Chentelle's Gift showed her the depth of his sincerity, of his determination, of his need. How could she accept such service? The man had no way of knowing the terrors they might face. But how could she refuse the longing she sensed in his plea? It was true that as he mended, he could become a formidable protector. And it would be good to have the company. "All right," she said. "I accept you as my liegeman, but only until I finish my journey."

Sulmar touched his head to the sand. "I swear myself to your service," he said. "You are my liege, and I will accept no other duty until you release me from my vow."

Chentelle reached down and helped him to his feet. "Fine," she said, "but no more bowing. I just want someone to travel with me."

"Until the journey's end," he said.

"Until the journey's end," she repeated, feeling a strange power within the words.

He smiled. "But I hope any formidable threats have the grace to wait a few days, as I regain my strength. I wouldn't want you to be obliged to rescue me again."

She laughed. "I hope so, too." Then she reconsidered her decision not to tell him her mission. Surely he needed to know it, to best serve her welfare. "I seek the apprentice of the wizard A'pon Boemarre," she said. "We must locate him and deliver a message from the High Bishop of Norivika. We will find him south of here, along a rocky coast."

Sulmar nodded. "Allow me a moment to prepare."

He sifted through the wreckage of his boat, salvaging some canvas from the sail and a length of rope. He used his knife to shape the canvas into a rough tunic, using the rope to secure the waist. He sheathed his sword and secured the scabbard and the small knife to his makeshift belt. Then he pulled on his still-soggy boots and kicked sand over the fire. He lifted his burlap sack over one shoulder and her pack over the other.

"Very creative, liegeman," Chentelle teased. "It may be that you will become a tailor in your later years."

"This will be adequate for now," he said flatly.

ॐ

They walked through the day, taking only brief stops to share the last of Chentelle's drinking water. Luckily, the day was pleasant and the sea breeze kept them cool. As they moved south, the coast became a thin strip bordering a rocky cliff dotted with small caves. They investigated these but found no sign of human presence.

As evening approached, Chentelle began to worry. The sky to the south was filled with storm clouds, and there was still no sign of the wizard's apprentice. Sulmar was bearing up well, but she knew he needed to get a good night's rest so that his healing could proceed. As it was, only the healing of her Gift had made him able to travel without soon tiring. Also, she was hungry. Sulmar could always catch some fish or crabs once they stopped, but the rocky coast offered little forage for an elven appetite.

There was a rumble of thunder in the distance, and something else. "Did you hear that?" Chentelle asked.

"Yes, lady. We should find shelter before the storm hits."

"No, not the thunder. I thought I heard a rooster crow. Did you hear it?"

"No, lady. But they say elven ears are more keen than human."

"If it was a yardbird, then there should be people nearby." She looked back at the storm front. "We should hurry."

As they continued south, Chentelle kept her ears alert. She heard the rooster again, and this time Sulmar heard it, too. They picked up their pace, all but running over the uneven shore. Soon, they sighted a small flock of chickens grazing on the sparse greenery that clung to the cliffs. A narrow crevice ran between two large slabs of rock, leading into the cliff's face.

They slid through the crevice and into a gap surrounded by gray rock. The dark mouth of a cave opening beckoned from the far side of the clearing. Chentelle started across, but stopped at the touch of Sulmar's hand.

"Be wary, my lady," he said, sliding in front of her. "There may be danger."

There might indeed be danger. Her awareness was mixed. Cautiously, they worked their way toward the cave.

"Be off with you!" called a harsh voice from deep within the cave.

Had they found him? "My name is Chentelle," she called back. "I am looking for—"

A blinding flash cut off her words. A billowing sphere of flame erupted from the cave. Sulmar grabbed her and pulled her into the shelter of some rocks as the fireball struck the boulder behind them. There was a deafening explosion, and a cascade of rock fragments showered down on them. Chentelle pressed her hands to her ears, trying to shut out the echoes of the blast.

"I want none of your talk," said the voice. "I said be off!"

The presence of such magic suggested that they were getting close to their objective. "Please," Chentelle said. "You have to help me find the apprentice of A'pon Boemarre."

There was no reply.

Chentelle waited. The silence stretched out interminably. Finally she had had enough. She stood and brushed the dust from her dress. "You don't have to be so rude!" she said indignantly.

Sulmar jumped to his feet beside her, sword poised, though it would surely be useless against the kind of magic they had just seen. "My lady! Do not expose yourself!"

She set her little jaw. "I must accomplish my mission."

"Why do you seek the wizard's apprentice?" the voice called. It was closer, now, just beyond the mouth of the cave.

"I carry a message for him," Chentelle said, "from the High Bishop of No-rivika."

A figure detached itself from the darkness of the cave. The man, if it was a man, was covered completely in a dark gray cloak. The face was shadowed by a deep cowl. Even the hands were concealed by voluminous sleeves. A thin wooden rod extended from one of the sleeves. It was a *mandril* wand, used to focus the powers of Wood Lore, and it was aimed directly at Chentelle and her liegeman. The figure halted a half-dozen paces away.

"Speak your message," it said.

"How can we," Chentelle demanded, "until we know to whom we speak? I will not risk delivering it to a minion of evil."

"Lady," Sulmar breathed, as if in pain. He clearly feared that her sharp tongue was about to get them both blasted by fire.

The wand wavered slightly, then dropped to the figure's side. A hand came up and pulled back the cowl, revealing a lean, unhandsome countenance: the face she had seen in her dream. The man was tall, taller even than Sulmar, but thin to the point of gauntness. He stared back at her with eyes full of bitterness and sorrow.

"I am A'stoc," he said, "onetime apprentice to the Great Destroyer."

ᐁ 2 ᐅ

LEGION LORD

Lord Dacius Gemine's heavy footfalls echoed off the marble floor. He paused briefly before one of the finely carved chairs which lined the hallway, but he did not sit. Charmaine would have a fit if he scratched the furniture. With a sigh, he pulled off his gauntlets and dropped them into his basinet. There was a fresh dent near the helm's visor; testimony either to his skill as a teacher or to the fatigue of his shield arm. Wearily, he headed for the stairway that led to his private chambers.

"My lord."

Dacius turned, recognizing the voice of his elderly seneschal. "What is it, Charmaine?" he asked.

The seneschal shifted to her most official voice. "Lord Gemine, the elven lord Alka Shara, Vice-marshal of the Legion, Warden of Inarr, seventeenth in succession to the throne of Essienkal, begs an audience."

"Lord Shara is here?" Dacius said, smiling delightfully. "But how? No Legion ship has arrived at the docks. I would have been notified."

"I believe he came to the front door, lord," Charmaine said. "Shall I send him away?"

"What?" Dacius said. "Of course not. Where is he?"

"I told him to wait in your private study, lord," she answered.

"Perfect," said Dacius, handing her his helm and gauntlets. "Send the basinet to the armorer for repair. I'll go see what Alka wants."

"Shall I draw a bath, lord?"

"By all means," he said, bounding up the stairs. "And send some food to the study. Elven fare."

"Already sent," the seneschal said somewhat disapprovingly. She rolled her eyes. "Like I don't know my job."

Dacius reached the door to the study and threw it open. Lord Shara stood silhouetted against the far window. He was tall for an elf, nearly three and a half cubits, and he possessed a full measure of the lean grace which characterized his race. The green eyes, fine bone structure, and distinctly pointed ears were also classic elf features, but there was more gray than brown in his full head of hair. He wore the green and white leatherbark of the Inarr Regiment, with the crossed swords badge of the Legion over the heart.

"Alka," Dacius said. "It has been too long."

"Dacius, you look well. Keeping in shape I see," the elf said, pointing to his armor.

"Squire training," Dacius explained, somewhat ruefully, "for Lord Wyrle's niece."

The elf raised an eyebrow. "His *niece?*"

"She is a very independent lady."

"There are few who accept such an honor," Alka said, "even from the Duke of Norden West."

"I assure you, it was not by choice." Dacius motioned for Alka to help him remove his platemail. The armor came off piece by piece, and they piled it beside the large desk which dominated the room.

"So how did you come to sponsor this remarkable young woman?" the elf inquired after a decent interval.

"Did I ever tell you how His Grace saved my life?"

Alka shook his head.

"Twice, in one day?"

"No, I do not believe you have."

Dacius smiled. "It was during my first posting to the Hordelands, not six months after I earned my pendant and was accepted to wear the crossed swords. I became separated from my company during a goblin attack. I was surrounded. Lord Wyrle cut through the lines and broke me free. Then, on the way back to camp, he rescued me when I stumbled into a goblin pitfall." He sighed. "My mistake came in the way I expressed my gratitude. I said to him, 'If there is any way to repay you, I shall, by my honor.' "

"An oath!" Alka said, not even trying to contain his laughter. "You gave him an oath in exchange for a mere duty of battle."

"The Duke," Dacius said quietly, "considers it two separate oaths."

"Two!" Alka slapped the desk in amusement. "Oh, that is a heavy price, but tell me, Dacius. Is she any good?"

"She nearly won her pendant this afternoon."

"Oh," Alka said, "that is something I would like to see."

"I'm sure you would, just to watch me struck down by a squire."

Alka smiled. "If she is this close to her pendant, I am sure it would be a worthy match. And this was in full armor?"

Dacius nodded, feeling a sense of pride. He felt immediately at ease with the elf, as if it had been only hours or days since they had last been together. "By the Creator," he said. "Can it really have been two years? So much has happened since you left for Essienkal."

Some hint of pain must have shown in his face or his voice, because Alka's manner became suddenly serious. "I heard about your family."

His family. The memories swarmed over him: his mother, his father, Cinder, just three more casualties in a long and bloody war, three more victims of goblin treachery, three more stones to cast shadows on a quiet hill.

The war had gone well for Odenal. The human armies scored great victories in the Hordelands, forcing the goblin Heresiarchs to sue for peace. But on the day the treaty was signed a trio of goblin warships attacked the Isle of Rennock. Norden West was decimated by fire and steel. On his return, Dacius was greeted by the graves of his parents and his lover. Of course, the Heresiarchs denied knowledge of the raid, calling the attackers pirates and outcasts.

"I am told—I am told they died well," Dacius said. "My parents defending their lands and Cinder trying to shield a small child."

"Cinder?" said Alka.

"My betrothed. You would have liked her. She had eyes that glowed like the sea mist. She—"

Dacius pressed his eyes shut, fighting against the tears. He felt Alka's hand come to rest on his shoulder. The touch was featherlight, but there was a quiet assurance in the grip that seemed to lend him strength. Dacius squeezed the elf's hand with his own. "It is good to be together again."

"It is indeed. And we may stay together for quite some time."

"You mean you will be staying for a while?" said Dacius. "That's wonderful."

The elf glanced around the room quickly before answering. "No, my friend, I mean you will be leaving with me. I am here to take you to the Holy City."

"Norivika?" Dacius did not try to conceal his astonishment. "But why?"

"Forgive me, friend," Alka said, "but now is not the time for explanations. We leave at sunrise, but no one must know our destination. If any ask, tell them we travel to Infiniterium on business for the Realm."

"Tomorrow! But that's impossible. I can't leave now. The repairs to the main hall are just under way. Plus, I'm still bartering for a decent shipment of new seed grain for the local farmers. And what about my responsibility as overseer of the new defenses and my obligation to Lord Wyrle's niece? She's almost ready, I tell you. How can I abandon her now? Give me a month, five weeks at the latest, and I'll meet you at the Holy City."

Alka reached into his tunic and removed a carefully folded parchment. He handed it to Dacius. The letter simply stated that Lord Dacius Gemine was required to obey the instructions of Alka Shara in all matters pertaining to his quest. It was sealed with the personal signet of Cyrus, King of Odenal.

"But why?" Dacius asked. "Why me?"

"Because I know I can trust you. And because you are one of the finest Legionnaires I know."

"Oh, come on! There are many who—" He broke off, realizing that Alka was not trying to flatter him.

The elf crossed the room to the fireplace. Two shields decorated the mantle: the crossed swords of the Legion, and the twin suns of House Gemine. Between the shields hung a straight, double-edged sword with a well-worn handle. "Is this your grandfather's sword?"

"You know it is."

Alka nodded. "A worthy blade. I think it would be a good idea for you to bring it along."

"Bring the vorpal sword? Why? Surely you don't expect—"

"Call it sentimentality," the elf said. "I well remember the songs this blade sang in your grandfather's hand." He paused, staring at Dacius with his intense green eyes. "My friend, there are so many questions within you, but the answers must wait. I must have your trust in this, and I must have your word that you will do exactly as I have said. This is important, Dacius."

There was an edge in his friend's voice that Dacius had never heard before, an edge that demanded respect. Alka would not ask if the need were not real.

"You have my pledge, Alka," Dacius said. "And with or without the King's command, you have always had my trust. I will do as you instruct."

A knock at the door interrupted them.

"Come in," Dacius said.

A serving maid entered, bearing a large platter of fresh fruit and roasted vegetables.

Alka smiled. "Such a feast, and I must play the poor guest and turn down your hospitality. The hour is late and there are preparations to be made. I will call for you at first-light, my friend. Good night."

"Creator keep you."

As the elf strode quietly out of the room, the serving maid turned to follow.

"Wait," Dacius beckoned the maid. "Leave the food. And tell Charmaine I won't be needing that bath after all. I want to see her, the marshal, and the steward in the main hall one hour from now. And tell the cooks to start some fresh bread; it's going to be a long night."

"Yes, lord."

Dacius walked to the fireplace and took down the sword which had belonged to his father and his father's father. The leather-wrapped hilt fit easily into his hand, as if his own fingers had worn the grooves in the grip. He pulled the blade from its metal sheath, admiring the perfect balance. Mystic runes seemed to flow like water across the blue-hued steel, proclaiming this as a weapon of power.

The vorpal weapons were artifacts of the Wizards' War, forged expressly to combat the Ill-creatures. That war was more than six decades gone, and no Ill-creatures had been seen in all those years. But now Alka wanted him to take up a sword which had been unused for generations, and Alka had never stopped carrying his own vorpal blade.

Dacius sheathed the sword and rested it against the desk. He sat down, grabbing a quill and some blank paper. With a sigh, he began composing a letter to Lord Wyrle's niece. It was, indeed, going to be a long night.

Dacius lifted his sea chest onto the ceiling of the carriage. He had packed sparingly, but the trunk was still heavy with the weight of his armor and weapons. He made sure the chest was strapped securely in place. He had ordered Charmaine to stay in bed until truedawn, but he suspected she was watching anyway. He waved toward the window of the upstairs parlor and joined Alka in the cab.

The elf sat alertly on the padded bench, looking as if he had both slept fully and been awake for hours. His bright green eyes showed no trace of fatigue. "Good morning," he said.

Dacius stretched, groaning softly at the stiffness in his back and shoulders. "I'll suspend judgment, for now."

The driver cracked his whip and the horses started forward, hooves clacking rhythmically on the cobblestone drive. They passed the gatehouse and turned onto the gravel roadway, heading down the long slope into Norden West.

The fields were red under Deneob's feeble light, a hue that Dacius suspected was more than mirrored in his own bloodshot eyes. Most of the town was still asleep, though a few merchants on Market Square were already opening shop. The few people they did pass greeted them cheerily.

Dacius loved that about Norden West. The Isle of Rennock lay outside the main trade routes, so its towns remained small and friendly. When Legion business took him to Infiniterium or Thyatius, the crowdedness and unruliness of the city always left him deeply disturbed. Norden West was his home in a sense that no busy city could ever match.

They arrived at the docks, and the carriage pulled to a stop before an elven merchant ship. A proud three-masted vessel made of the finest trees from the Inarr. The name of the ship was inscribed on the bow in flowing elven script: *Otan Stin*.

"Now I know why I had not heard of any Legion ships reaching port," he said.

"Secrecy, my friend," said Alka.

Alka paid the coachman and helped Dacius pull down his chest. They crossed the wharf and stopped at the foot of the trader's gangplank. A pair of elves watched their approach from the ship's deck.

"Permission to come aboard, Captain," Alka called out.

"Aye, and welcome aboard, Lord Shara," said the shorter of the two.

"Captain Rone," said Alka as they reached the top of the gangplank, "may I present Lord Dacius Gemine. Dacius, this is Captain Rone and his shipsage Vagen."

The two were a study in contrast. Vagen stood as tall as Alka and was so thin he appeared almost ephemeral. His skin was pale and unlined, but his hair was pure white. The captain was barely three cubits tall, but stocky for an elf. His tanned face carried deep wrinkles around the eyes and mouth, but there was no gray in the long brown hair which he wore braided and wrapped around his neck like a scarf.

"Lord Gemine," Captain Rone said, in the harshest rasp Dacius had ever heard from an elf, "you are welcome aboard the *Otan Stin*."

Then he turned and started bellowing to his crew. "Zubec, show Lord Gemine to his bunk and help him stow his gear. Everyone else, prepare for departure. Vagen, assume your post."

The elves scrambled to make ready as Captain Rone headed for the wheeldeck. One sailor detached himself from the activity and approached Dacius.

"Shall we go below, lord?" he asked. Such a question, on ship or in battle, was never really a question, but a strong suggestion relayed from a superior.

Dacius hesitated. He would prefer to stay on deck for the departure, but he didn't want to make the sailor's job more difficult.

"It's all right," Alka said, bridging the silence. "You stay and watch, I'll stow your gear."

The sailor nodded and picked up the gear; Alka had cleared it for the foreigner.

Dacius thanked him and turned back to observe the crew. Some elves scurried through the rigging, preparing the sails, while others used long poles to push the ship away from the dock. The shipsage stood at the bow, leaning heavily on his oak staff.

Captain Rone stood at the wheel, checking the clearance from the dock. "Mark!" he said. "Vagen, the ship is yours."

Vagen turned to face over the prow. He raised his staff and began chanting softly. Then he lowered one end of the staff and touched it to the deck. There was a moment of stillness as the oak of the staff fused with the wood of the deck. Then sagewind filled the sails and the ship began to move.

Dacius felt the smooth acceleration, and listened to Vagen's chanting. He inhaled deeply, savoring the smell of the sagewind. It was an aroma that was never encountered elsewhere, a mixture of salt and sea and the will of the sage.

He knew sailors who swore they could identify a shipsage by the scent of his wind.

Dacius felt an old longing rise within him, a longing for the sea, a longing which had been missing since his return from the Hordelands. "A good morning, indeed," he said.

The *Otan Stin* moved swiftly through the quiet waters of Norden Bay. As they cleared the natural harbor, Vagen released his control of the wood and the wind, yielding the ship to the natural currents. The shipsage looked spent from his efforts, but his steps were steady as he headed belowdecks to rest.

Captain Rone shouted orders as the crew jumped to take control of the vessel. The *Otan Stin* caught the wind and turned north into the Great Sea. Off the starboard bow, Ellistar's golden face was just rising over the Isle of Rennock.

Dacius turned away from the rail and jumped when he saw Alka at his shoulder; he hadn't heard the elf approach. He saw that several other elves were now on deck. Almost all wore the crossed swords of the Legion over their hearts, though their uniforms came from several different regiments. Dacius noted that the elves were all armed. Even Alka wore his vorpal sword, though the chances of piracy were slight this far from goblin lands.

An old elf wearing undyed leatherbark sat on the steps to the wheeldeck, tuning a lute. His hair hung past his shoulders like strands of gray iron, restrained only by a headband of red silk. A sword rested on the elf's left hip and a pair of ironwood rods hung from his right.

Dacius was surprised; most elves had adopted steel weapons during the Wizard's War. He had heard of elven fighting batons, but never seen them used.

A crowd formed about the elf as he began to play. As Dacius and Alka moved closer, a strange look passed over his face. He shut his eyes and subtly altered the timbre of his music, slowing the tempo and moving down the scale. Then he started singing in the common tongue of the Realm, his slight accent giving the words a strange, lilting quality.

> Wrapped in armor, shining clear,
> A gallant knight who knows no fear.
> Horse hooves beat the ground with pride,
> As man and steed ride forth to cheer.
>
> Truth and honor are his guide
> Through devastated countryside.
> His battle cries, his solemn oaths:
> The beast that plagues this land defied.
>
> From darkest pit, flies forth the ghost,
> A dragon, black as Hel's own host.
> He sounds his challenge to the knight,
> And spews his curse upon the coast.
>
> The hero charges to the fight,
> Pitting courage against might.

The ring of steel, the dragon's roar,
The dance of death in cold twilight.

The red sun falls beneath the shore.
The dragon spreads his wings to soar.
The golden star shines on the gear
Of one brave knight who fights no more.

The crowd of sailors and Legionnaires shifted uneasily. The elf played and sang marvelously, but the melancholy nature of his song had caught them off guard.

"A beautiful song, Thildemar," said Alka, "but such a grim ending. I do not believe I have heard it before. Is it an old tale?"

"No, Alka Shara," Thildemar said. "It came to me just now as I watched you and your friend approach."

The words hung in the air for several seconds before a call from above interrupted the silence.

"Begging your pardon, Lord Shara," said Captain Rone, "but if your man there is through depressing everyone, I was wondering if he could play something a little more cheerful for my crew. We don't get to hear so fine a voice very often."

There was a general murmur of assent, and the aged elf started strumming a lively melody. He sang a ribald ballad of a dancing warrior and three enchanted maidens that soon lightened everyone's mood.

Dacius felt a tap on his shoulder. Alka motioned with his head, and the two of them disengaged from the crowd. Alka led him below deck and took him to the cabin that they would share for the voyage.

"That was a disturbing song," Alka said.

"Indeed," Dacius agreed. "And a strange singer, for all his talent."

"Thildemar? Do not worry, Dacius. I trust few men in this world, and none more than you, but I would gladly trust Thildemar with my life. In fact, I have done so on many occasions."

"But who is he? He isn't Legion."

"No, but he was," Alka said. "He was my commander during the Wizards' War. He resigned his commission after the Desecration."

Dacius's mind reeled. To him, the Wizards' War was military history, a battle fought generations ago by men like his grandfather. But Alka and Thildemar were there, witness to the greatest conflict in recorded history.

"Thildemar was at the final battle?" Dacius asked, still finding this hard to credit.

"No, Dacius. No one who went to that final battle returned alive. Your grandfather and I survived because our wounds kept us away from the front; Thildemar survived because of his dreams. In the weeks before the battle, he suffered from terrible visions. They robbed him of sleep, threatened his sanity. Finally, he was forced to remove himself from command. He sent his troops to final confrontation while he returned to Essienkal."

In such a case, there could be those to whom the word "cowardice" occurred. But Dacius remained silent.

"It is said that time heals all wounds, Dacius, but elven memory is long. I lost a brother on that day, whose image haunts me still. Thildemar lost every man in his regiment. On that day, he swore that never again would he order a man to his death."

Dacius had heard stories of the Desecration Fault, of the vast wasteland which marked the spot of A'pon Boemarre's confrontation with the Dark One. He tried to imagine the guilt of sending good men into such a slaughter. No wonder the elf's songs were grim.

"What kind of threat," Dacius asked, "could inspire him to take up arms again?"

"The gravest. Ill-creatures have been spotted in the Realm. It is rumored the Dark One has returned."

"The Dark One!" Dacius experienced an ugly chill. "He survived the Desecration?"

Then realization came as he looked at the sword hanging at Alka's side. "The weapons—you are collecting men who possess vorpal weapons."

"Very intuitive, my young friend," Alka said. "With us on this ship are fourteen of the finest elven Legionnaires living, each armed with a vorpal sword. We are under orders to serve and protect the High Bishop of Norivika in whatever manner he requires."

The High Bishop. Not since the Wizard's War had he called upon the Legion's protection. He did not need to; the power of the Holy Land kept him safe. This could only mean that the High Bishop meant to leave Talan.

Dacius opened his sea chest and pulled out his grandfather's sword. His jaw tightened as he strapped the harness around his waist. He was beginning to understand his friend's caution.

ᐁ

The *Otan Stin* struggled northward in faint winds for three days. Whenever the wind died altogether, Vagen would summon the sagewind to fill the sails. But the effort tired him quickly. Slowly, the ship made its way up the coast.

Dacius stood at the portside railing, watching the white foam wash against the distant shoreline. Sometime in the night they had passed the jagged mountain range that formed the boundary between Odenal and the desert plains of Larama. Now Dacius searched that bleak coast for the next landmark which would indicate their progress—the port city of Atbok.

Dacius was eager to reach Norivika. The tales of the Holy City were fantastic. It was said to be a paradise in which no evil could exist, a center of worship which radiated peace and turned the land of Talan into haven for all peoples. The capital of a country which had no government and no army, a country whose citizens were devoted to the arts of healing and meditation. Dacius found himself eager to experience the truth of the Holy City for himself.

An angry shout called Dacius's attention to the wheeldeck. Captain Rone was screaming at Alka over the carved stone pieces of a castle game.

"Damn it all," he yelled. "I have never met a man who can win so many damned games in a row."

Dacius smiled. Alka played at the King's Court in Essienkal, and he had not lost a game of castle outside of that elven city for more years than Dacius had been alive. Rone grumbled some more, but he was already setting up the pieces for another game.

Some sailors called for music, and Dacius heard the answer of Thildemar's lute coming from the stern. Dacius turned back to the rail, idly listening to songs of love and courage and the deep longings that drive men's souls.

As evening approached, the lookout cried, "Atbok, ahead to port."

Dacius looked, but the city was still too distant for human eyes to see. To the south, though, he could see dark clouds forming above the horizon. He headed back to the wheeldeck.

The wind picked up, and Captain Rone shouted for all sails. The *Otan Stin* ran with the wind, making good speed at last. But lightning flashed to the south and the seas were becoming rough.

Captain Rone squinted into the wind. "This is a good omen, as well as bad. The storm has brought us much needed wind, but I cannot say how long it will remain at our backs. This is a rare storm, to blow up so quickly this late in the season."

"Atbok fast approaching," cried the lookout.

"And now I must decide," said Rone, "whether to draw her in to dock or to try and outrun the storm. Which do you favor, Lord Shara?"

Alka rose an eyebrow. "I am no seaman, Captain, but I would always consider safety as a first priority."

"Indeed," the captain agreed. "But which path leads to safety? The storm won't stop before it hits Atbok, that much is obvious, but how far north will it reach? We are better off riding the edge of a storm in open water than suffering the brunt of one tied to a dock. And you tell me your mission is one of great urgency. Who knows how long we would be delayed in Larama? And of course there are docking fees to consider, and cargo taxes."

"You need not worry yourself about fees, Captain," Alka said. "Your vessel is chartered and we are your only cargo. The expense of your trip has already been well covered."

"That it has, Lord Shara," Rone said. "So the question lies entirely in the behavior of the storm. I have sailed these waters countless times, and I have never seen a storm blow into the Quiet Sea this time of year. We run."

"I can only be assured by your words," Alka said.

Dacius nodded, trying to ignore the persistent rumble of thunder. He could only hope that Captain Rone's experience proved true.

The *Otan Stin* sped northward, leaving Atbok far behind. But the storm continued to advance upon them. By the time Ellistar set in the west, dark clouds had completely surrounded them.

The wind whipped the sea into a frenzy, and driving rain weighed down their sails. Lightning flashes struck the blackened ocean all around them, and the roar of thunder was constant. The *Otan Stin* pitched in the waves as if it were the plaything of an angry child. Captain Rone ordered all passengers secure belowdecks.

Dacius' hammock swung wildly with the ship's rocking. He tried to rest, but he was afraid he would be thrown to the floor if he slept.

"It would seem Rone's judgment of the weather was incorrect," he remarked, half hoping to be refuted.

"I fear this storm may be more than Rone can manage," Alka said. "But there is little we can do, now. I suggest we sleep while we are able."

"Sure," Dacius said, though he was anything but certain that he could sleep.

In fact, the constant rolling was making him nauseated. Luckily, he had not eaten anything since early that afternoon. He forced his hands to release their grip on the hammock. He closed his eyes and concentrated on his breathing, willing himself to relax.

Suddenly the cabin seemed to turn on its side. The lantern hanging from the ceiling flew against the wall and went out. Dacius tumbled from his hammock. His sense of direction was distorted, but he seemed to hit the wall of the cabin first and then slide to the floor.

"Dacius," Alka called, "are you all right?"

"Yes, but confused," he replied. Then strong fingers wrapped around Dacius' arms and helped him to his feet. "What happened?" he asked.

"I do not know," Alka said, above the howling of the wind. "But surely the storm is worse."

Dacius heard faint cries and the pounding footfalls of men running on the deck above their heads. Then the door flew open and dim light filtered in. A young Legionnaire stuck his head through the opening.

"Lord Shara," he said. "We are under attack!"

There was a flash as Alka used his elven Lore to relight the lantern. He grabbed his sword belt and handed the lamp to Dacius. "Follow me," he said, racing out the cabin door.

Dacius paused only long enough to secure his own blade, but when he reached the corridor Alka and the other Legionnaire were already gone. He ran for the nearest ladder and climbed to the main deck.

As soon as he threw open the hatch, the storm assaulted him. Rain blasted his face, and the wind threatened to tear him from the ladder. His lantern died immediately, and he dropped it to the deck.

Dacius pulled himself onto secure footing, crouching low against the gale. He heard men shouting, but the wind made it impossible to determine the direction from which the sound came. He searched the darkness and spotted a flash of blue light coming from the prow. He headed in that direction.

As he came nearer, he saw several patches of dim blue radiance, each one centered around a sword. *The vorpal swords*, he realized. They were giving off light as the elves wielded them in battle. But what were they fighting?

A flash of lightning gave him the answer.

A huge black form crouched near the foremast. Its legs were bent backward like a bird's and ended in immense three-clawed talons. The body was manlike, though twice the size of any man Dacius had seen, and great bat wings spread behind it, anchored to immensely muscled shoulders. Set deeply in the brow of a huge hyena head, the monster's eyes glowed with the pale yellow of an infected wound. This was no natural animal; it was an Ill-creature, a twisted servant of the Dark One.

Dacius' eyes were slowly adjusting to the darkness. He struggled to make out a handful of sailors and Legionnaires. They surrounded the creature but seemed unwilling to close. He saw that several bodies already cluttered the deck around the monster's feet, evidence of what happened to those who closed too quickly.

The beast rose to its full height and threw its head back, showing wickedly curved fangs. It lashed out, striking the foremast with one massive arm. Wood shattered as the pole tore loose from its support. Elves scrambled out of the way as mast and sail crashed to the deck.

By the Creator, the beast meant to destroy the *Otan Stin*! Dacius froze, unable to move. The sound of the storm filled his ears, but mocking laughter echoed inside his skull. It was hopeless. No man could fight against such power. How could flesh and blood stand where stout wood had fallen? The Ill-creature would strike them down as easily as it had severed the mast.

Captain Rone leaped forward, lashing out at the Ill-creature with his cutlass. He landed heavy blows on the monster's legs and chest, but he might as well have been striking a stone statue. The blade bounced ineffectually off the beast's skin.

The Ill-creature struck out with a wing, lifting the captain from the deck and tossing him contemptuously into the sea.

But the captain's charge had broken the paralysis. Dacius drew his sword. He was a knight, a Legionnaire; he would not give in to fear.

The vorpal blade radiated with fierce blue light. The pommel was warm in his hand, and Dacius felt a surge of power and clarity. The rage of the storm, the chaos of battle, the incapacitating fear, they all seemed distant now.

The crew of the *Otan Stin* had rushed forward to avenge their captain, but their weapons were useless against the Ill-creature's magic. As the sailors fell back in futility, Dacius could see a lone figure protecting their retreat, balking the monster's counterattack with a wall of brightly glowing steel. There could be no doubt about the identity of that one. But one was enough only to foil the monster, not to slay it. Calmly, Dacius moved forward to Alka's aid.

The Ill-creature hesitated for a moment, backing away from the vorpal swords. One taloned leg slid forward, kicking a crumpled shape into the light of their weapons. It was the young Legionnaire who had come to their cabin, the vorpal blade still clutched uselessly in his hand. The beast moved forward, driving a clawed foot easily through the fallen elf's body as it advanced.

YOUR WEAPONS WILL NOT SAVE YOU, MORTALS. I WILL KILL YOU ALL AS EASILY AS I KILLED THIS FOOL.

The voice thundered inside Dacius's head, threatening to swamp his mind in terror. But this time he cast off the beast's influence. Because he knew it *was* the beast, and not his own cowardice. And that his weapon could hurt the thing. That was why it was so eager to make him believe otherwise.

Alka Shara shouted defiantly at his side. "I have felt your kind before, Ill-creature! Your powers do not deceive me. Go back to the pits of Firesta—go back to your master. Your powers are nothing, here! Leave before I send your foul soul back to the Abyss."

ARROGANT FOOL, I WILL TEACH YOU ABOUT POWER. The Ill-creature raised a hand and pointed at Alka. Lightning danced around its claws and then shot forward, driving the elf backward.

Dacius screamed and jumped forward. His vorpal sword came down on the outstretched arm, cutting it to the core and ending the lightning barrage. Armed with this blade, he could bring his fencing skill into play. Nothing but an opposing weapon could prevent him from scoring. He feinted, making the creature react, drawing it into vulnerability. Then a second, lesser stroke sliced into the monster's belly. Blue tracers of light were left in the wounds, as if fire bled into them. Dacius leaped sideways, avoiding the beast's vicious counterstroke.

The monster's rage pounded against his mind. It advanced swiftly, trying to overwhelm his defense. Huge claws struck again and again, and his parries became more and more desperate. This thing did know how to fight when vulnerable; there was a calculating quality to the mental barrage. There was little room to maneuver, and the rocking of the ship's deck made footing treacherous. Dacius counterattacked cautiously, seeking an opening to attack the Ill-creature's chest or neck. But the opening never came.

The ship lurched violently, throwing Dacius to the deck.

The Ill-creature was also caught off guard, but huge beats of its wings kept it from falling. Hissing triumphantly, it lunged forward.

Dacius brought his weapon up—too late. A monstrous claw closed around his wrist like a shackle. Bones snapped, and the vorpal sword fell from limp fingers. He was lifted off the ground and dangled helplessly before the creature's face. The huge jaws opened and a long, snakelike tongue darted against Dacius's face.

The stench was unbelievable. Dacius struck out with his free hand, groping for one of the hideously glowing eyes. But the Ill-creature deflected the attack, snapping at his fingers with needlelike fangs.

YOUR DEATH IS JUST THE BEGINNING, LITTLE MORTAL. SOON, ALL OF INFINITERA SHALL BOW BEFORE THE DARK ONE.

Suddenly, a shaft of blue light erupted from the monster's shoulder.

Dacius fell to the deck, struggling to remain conscious. Pain shot through his arm. He looked down and saw a jagged edge of white pushing through the flesh of his wrist. Pain was good; it helped him fight off the dizziness. Where was his sword? There, a flash of blue against the deck. He scrambled forward, grabbing the weapon with his left hand.

Strength flowed into him from the blade. Pain receded. The world stopped spinning. Good; now he had to gauge the situation, plan a reaction.

Alka clung to the Ill-creature's back, seeming oblivious to the terrible burns which covered much of his face and chest. He had driven his sword through the beast's shoulder from behind. He had one arm wrapped around a wing for purchase and was using his body weight to drive the blade deeper into the monster's body.

The Ill-creature thrashed violently, trying to dislodge the elven warrior. It blasted the air with its wings and carved through the wooden deck with its talons, but Alka would not let go. The gleaming blue blade inched slowly toward the monster's heart.

Dacius moved forward, raising his sword for a left-handed strike, but the Ill-creature shot into the air, wings beating furiously against the added drag. He watched the beast's progress, following the glowing shard of Alka's sword against the night sky. It lifted higher and higher, gaining height slowly. Then suddenly it reversed direction and shot back toward the ship.

The mocking laughter sounded again in Dacius' skull as the Ill-creature came into sight. It dived without slowing, crashing through the weakened planks of the deck and through the hull below.

Alka's body smashed against the wood. He lacked the toughness of the Ill-creature. His spine bent horribly and the vorpal blade slid from his grasp.

Water poured through the ruptured hull. Dacius had time to scream his friend's name only once in despair before being thrown into the crashing waves.

❧ 3 ❧

Holy Man

Marcus Alanda watched the storm rise over the Quiet Sea. The fury of the tempest and the suddenness of its approach made him wary. The thick black thunderheads rolled steadily northward. Then the leading edge of dark clouds dissipated, turning into gentle mists. It was the sign. If the storm had been natural, the Barrier would have had no effect. Evil was active in the Realm.

For the third time in his life, the High Bishop felt a quiet summons in the back of his mind. Marcus turned away from the window and headed for the tower stairs. He descended the steps with a vigor that belied his three score years. Indeed, only the slate gray color of his short hair and the worry lines which surrounded his clear blue eyes gave any hint to his age. Living within the harmony of the Holy Land did much to keep a man young.

His acolyte waited at the base of the tower.

"Brother Ethnan," Marcus said, "find Bishop Sarra and tell her to meet me at the docks in fifteen minutes. Then fetch the ferryman on duty. We will need his services tonight."

"Yes, Father Marcus," Ethnan said, already departing.

Marcus crossed to a small alcove. Every hall in the Cathedral of Light had such an alcove, and every alcove contained a reading pedestal and two books. The larger book contained the Scriptures of Jediah, written by the first High Bishop of the Holy Lands. The smaller book had many names: the Book of Truths, the Creation Codex, the Revelation of the Sphere. But most people simply called it the Old Book. Marcus opened it and read the first paragraph.

In the perfect emptiness, a Sphere was formed. And within the Sphere, the races were born. The Creation was perfect, and the Creator was perfection. The Sphere existed in balance, in harmony, and for the eyes of the Creator. For its existence was Beauty. Its purpose was Beauty.

Marcus' heart ached with the truth of those words, a truth that no longer existed. The Creation had a Flaw. A crack had appeared in the structure of Creation, giving birth to the Abyss. And the Abyss had given birth to Evil.

Marcus closed the book. The truths in its pages spoke of an earlier age, of a time before the Flaw. There was no mention of evil in the Old Book, for there was no evil in the world when the Old Book was written. The truths of the Old Book were beauty, harmony, peace: perfection which once was and perfection which must come again. This was the faith of the Holy Order. Evil could be overcome, if the Flaw were healed. The Creation could be made whole once more.

As always, reading from the Old Book invigorated Marcus's faith. The Dark One was alive. Evil worked to extend its power into the Realm. But it would not do so unopposed.

෨

The others were waiting at the dock when he arrived. Marcus could sense their curiosity, but no one questioned him as they boarded the skiff. The ferryman poled away from the dock, then raised the sail to catch the evening breeze. In a few minutes, the telltale glow over the bow augured their approach to Atablicryon Island.

Marcus smiled as the glow slowly resolved itself into the temple which gave the island its name. The Atablicryon by night was one his favorite sights in all the Realm. Unlike the bright, flickering radiance which shone from the Cathedral of Light, the Atablicryon glowed with a gentle, cool white light. The glow was absolutely even in intensity, as if the stones merely reflected some outside radiance. As a student, Marcus had taken part in numerous debates on the source of the Atablicryon's illumination. Now he knew, but he kept the knowledge to himself.

The design of the temple was elegantly simple. Four colonnades ran through tiered gardens, converging at the foot of a vaulted stone dome. The dome was supported by a ring of eight columns and open on all sides. Eight sets of stairs led to the dome, four from the colonnades and four from smaller paths through the gardens. The entire structure was constructed of a smooth white stone that had never been found elsewhere in the Realm.

There were no docks on Atablicryon Island, and no one had ever suggested building one. The ferryman guided the skiff onto the beach near the end of one of the rows of columns. Once the craft was firmly beached, the passengers climbed out.

Marcus rested a hand on one of the pillars. As always, the surface matched the temperature of his skin and was perfectly smooth. The Atablicryon had stood on this island for at least eleven thousand years, but there was not a single imperfection to be found on any of its stones. Marcus led the others down the pathway of light to the central dome.

A feeling of deep peace filled him as he walked the familiar corridor. Many were the days he had spent wandering these paths, finding solace in the peace of the gardens. Marcus climbed the steps to the dome, and walked to the center of the floor. He sat on down, motioning for the others to join him.

"You are no doubt curious," he said, "as to why I called you here. But I ask you to be patient a moment longer. What I have to discuss with you tonight is of vital importance to the Holy Order, to the Realm, and to all of Infinitera. Before we begin, I suggest we make use of the peace which the Atablicryon provides." He glanced at an assistant. "Please lead us in the First Meditation of Jediah."

The young priest smiled in appreciation of the honor Marcus gave him, showing even teeth. "Yes, Lord High Bishop."

The priest closed his eyes and began humming a simple, four-scale progression. As the others joined their voices with his, he chanted softly:

"*In peace, there is harmony.*
In harmony, there is unity.
In unity, there is healing.
In healing, there is peace."

Here, at the center of the Order's power, the familiar meditation gained special force. Marcus's spirit touched the beauty of Creation and was filled by it. The Perfection of Unity was not lost; it still lived in the Atablicryon. And it could live again in the Realm.

Marcus opened his eyes; his course was clear. "Thank you. Let us keep this peace in mind as we prepare for the coming days." He turned to face his acolyte. "Brother Ethnan, how long have you served as my acolyte?"

"Two years and ten months, Father Marcus."

"Then explain to me," Marcus said, "what the First Meditation means."

"It was Jediah's greatest revelation," Ethnan said. "In the Age Before, the Holy Order was dedicated to the Great Truth, the Perfection of Creation. But the Flaw made that truth an illusion. Jediah's vision showed him that the purpose of the Holy Order had to be transformed. The meditation teaches us that healing is possible, that Creation can be restored."

"And how does that relate to the Final Prophecy?"

"The prophecy also comes from Jediah," the acolyte said. "He recognized that corruption was growing, infecting the souls of man. Beyond the influence of the Holy Order, the races of man were becoming hateful, selfish, separated from community. Harmony was lost, sacrificed to the Flaw in Creation. The prophecy outlines two possible outcomes for Infinitera. Either Creation will be healed and the Abyss unmade, or the Holy Order will fail and the world will fall to despair and be destroyed."

"Yes," Marcus said, "and the prophecy is not false. Two weeks ago, a falling star fell into the western sky. Did any of you notice it?"

Bishop Sarra met his gaze with eyes as blue as his own. "I saw the star," she said. "It has entered my meditations several times since that night. I also saw the storm that blew over the Quiet Sea this evening. Was the star an omen?"

"Yes, an omen of great evil. The Dark One did not die at the Desecration Fault. He still exists, and his Ill-creatures are active in the Realm. That is why I have called you here."

There was a murmur of dismay. The others had known that the occasion was serious, but could hardly have anticipated this. Now they understood that they faced a siege of historic significance.

"I will be leaving Talan at some time after the Ceremony of Light," Marcus continued. "In my absence, Sarra, you will function as High Bishop. Brother Ethnan will assist you with any administrative details that might come up. In the event of my death, I have prepared an official proclamation naming you as my successor. Should it need to be used, your first duty is to return to this spot and spend the night in meditation."

"I do not understand," Sarra said, troubled. "The Dark One is alive, and you are leaving? What about the kingdoms? Have you called for the Legion? Do the wizards—" She paused, then continued in a hushed tone. "Marcus, have you received a revelation?"

"No, Sarra, or perhaps yes, though I am not a prophet. One day, you will come to know the source of this knowledge, but not today. For now, you must rely on your faith. And I must rely on your trust."

Sarra smiled. "Marcus, I have known you since we were both acolytes to

Father Serdonis. I shall do as you ask, though I pray it will not become necessary. Where will you be going?"

"I must find another Atablicryon."

"Another? But the temple is unique. In all the histories of the elves there is no mention of another like it."

"So we have been taught," Marcus agreed. "But the second Atablicryon exists. It lies on an island far to the south, an island that no human or elf or dwarf of the Realm has ever seen. No chart in any library shows this island. Yet it exists."

"And you know where it is?" Sarra asked.

"No, but Gorin does. He is a special priest, with expertise we shall need. His people know of that place, though I think they do not know it contains an Atablicryon. They call the site *Kennaru*, the Dread Island. It is taboo. Powerful curses punish anyone who goes there." Marcus shrugged. "I shall nevertheless be obliged to make trial of that curse." He looked up, meeting each of the others' eyes in turn. "We must all pass this test."

Sarra made a gesture of resignation. "I think none of us enjoy curses, but they cannot be allowed to daunt us."

Marcus put his hands to his lips and then extended them in the sign of harmony. "The whole of Creation," he said.

The others mirrored his gesture.

"Harmony," Ethnan said.

"Unity," the young assistant said.

"Healing," Sarra said.

"Perfection," Marcus said, finishing the ritual. "Thank you, my friends. That is all. Please tell the boatman to return in the morning. I will spend the night here in meditation."

They nodded, deeply troubled. Marcus watched them file out.

Sarra paused at the head of the stairs. "Follow your own advice, Marcus. Trust in your faith. The Creator grants us strength."

And we will need it, Marcus thought, watching her leave.

When he was certain that he was alone, Marcus opened his mind in meditation. He felt the power of the Atablicryon suffuse him. Beneath his feet, a circle of stone began to glow brightly, shining like a polished diamond. The light surrounded him, and the world disappeared.

Marcus floated in an ocean of harmony, a place without substance, full of radiant light and subtle music. He felt comforted—as if he were a child again, sleeping in his mother's arms. He rested in the wellspring of the Holy Order, the fount from which its healing power flowed. His soul sang in absolute harmony with the Creation.

The music that filled him sounded like quiet chimes and flowing water and the singing of nightingales. As he listened, the music resolved itself into a beatific voice. It was a voice he had heard twice before, once on the day he had become High Bishop and again on the day of the Fallen Star: a voice that he knew only as the Protector.

"Welcome, High Bishop Marcus Alanda," said the Protector.

"I have witnessed the sign," Marcus said. "Evil moves against the Realm."

"Is the way prepared for your quest?"

"Yes. I have sent for the Bearer of the Staff and summoned the Legion for protection. Gorin will guide us to the lost island, though he fears the test of crossing the Barrier. I plan to travel during the Season of Light, when the powers of the Dark One are at their weakest."

"You have done well," the Protector said. "Now it is time to prepare you for the true purpose of your journey."

"True purpose? Am I not seeking the second Atablicryon?"

"That is the beginning," the Protector answered. "But not the end. At the Atablicryon you will find an artifact, the Sphere of Ohnn. With the Sphere in your possession, you will be able to destroy the Fallen Star."

"Destroy the omen? Why?"

"It is more than an omen. The Fallen Star came through the Abyss and has reached Infinitera. It holds a power of evil more dangerous than the Dark One himself: a power that will defile all of Creation. The Ill-creatures search for this power. If they find it, then Infinitera will die."

"By the Creator," Marcus exclaimed. "They must not succeed. But if the Star came from the Abyss, why doesn't the Dark One know where it is?"

"It did not come from the Abyss. It fell through the Abyss from Beyond. I can sense its presence by the disharmony with Creation, but the Dark One has no way of tracking it. This is to our advantage."

"Then you know where it is?"

As soon as he said the words, an image formed in his mind: a desolate, frozen plain. Somehow, he knew that it lay far to the west. A huge crater scarred the tundra, and within it Marcus sensed a presence even colder than the surrounding ice.

"I understand," he said. "And with the Sphere of Ohnn I can destroy this evil."

"Yes," the Protector said, "but not with the Sphere alone. The Sphere of Ohnn is a core fragment of pure Earthpower: the primal force which binds Creation and makes life possible. It contains the power needed to destroy the Fallen Star, but only the Thunderwood Staff has the power to ignite the Sphere."

"The Bearer of the Staff," murmured Marcus.

"And you will need one more thing. To face this evil, you must understand it. I must implant the *knowledge* of this evil in your mind, as I have planted its location. Only when the evil has become a part of you will you be able to destroy it."

Marcus felt suddenly alone, isolated from the sea of harmony. "But submitting to evil is wrong. The Scripture of Jediah expressly forbids the acceptance of evil in any form."

"I know the Scripture," the Protector said. "I am the one who gave the words to Jediah. You must trust in your faith, Marcus Alanda. The knowledge by itself is no threat to your soul, so long as you do not pursue the course of evil. Only, you must decide now whether you will accept this burden, for once given, the knowledge cannot be taken away. And the knowledge must never be shared, lest the evil spread. You must take it with you to your grave."

"But how am I to decide, unless I know what the knowledge is?"

"You must ask yourself whether you are capable of this trial, whether you can risk your soul for the sake of Creation—and win. But know, Marcus Alanda, that there is no other who carries the faith of the Holy Order woven so strongly into his being. You are the best hope for Infinitera."

"Then my choice is clear. I must accept my own counsel. Give me the knowledge, Protector. The Creator will help me carry it."

The music that surrounded Marcus faded, leaving a profound silence. The voice of the Protector became a faint whisper in his mind. "Hold on to your faith. There will be pain."

Marcus braced himself. Even so, it was awful. A thousand needles pierced his skull, driving into his brain. The needles unleashed a torrent of morbid visions. Each image was a dark tendril, so cold that it burned. Marcus screamed as the tendrils worked their way into his mind, into his soul. The darkness coalesced, forming a dense pit in the center of his being. The seething mass multiplied and expanded, threatening to consume him. It spoke to him, with sinister persuasion.

Such power, I could rule Infinitera.

No! Marcus tried to reject the thought, to cast it out of his mind. But pain lanced through him. The evil was now part of him. He could no more expel it than he could throw away his heart.

I could do such good. The people would sing my name in praise.

The thoughts were coming faster now, with more detail, more clarity, and insidious logic.

The world would find unity again, under my direction.

The Scriptures of Jediah taught members of the Holy Order how to summon sanctuary, an aura of protection that surrounded the priest's body. Marcus used that technique now, but he focused the sanctuary into his mind, his soul. He found the core of evil within him and surrounded it with layers of harmony and peace. He built a barrier around it, a buffer that protected his conscious mind from the knowledge he bore.

Slowly, the pain receded. The darkness was still there, but it was dormant. The corrupt suggestions became mere whispers, then faded out. For the time being.

Marcus collapsed on the floor of the Atablicryon. Tears ran down his cheeks, and his body trembled against the stone. He pulled himself into a ball and waited for sleep to come.

~ 4 ~

APPRENTICE

A'stoc led Sulmar and Chentelle into the cave. The rock closed in around them until they were forced to walk in single file. Finally they came to a dead end at a bare stone wall.

A'stoc spoke a word of command, and the rock face swung inward, exposing a small, dark passageway. He spoke again, and a line of crystal orbs began to glow, lighting the narrow tunnel. He stepped forward, motioning for his guests to follow.

Chentelle paused at the doorway. She laid her hand on the rock, reaching out with her Gift. She felt power within the stone, ripples of warmth and vibration. The forces were delicately balanced, supporting the weight of the door with their equilibrium.

"Tell me, elf girl," A'stoc said gruffly, "how did you know where to find me?"

Chentelle whispered softly to the power in the rock, pulling at it gently with her Gift. The stone door swung silently shut.

"I had a dr—" Chentelle cut off her reply, for she had lost her audience. A'stoc had whirled and walked away, covering the hallway with long, heavy steps. She hurried to catch up with him, and Sulmar followed at her side. She kept her peace, for her mission was almost done. But it occurred to her that rudeness must be this man's way of life.

They emerged from the tunnel into a large, dark chamber. Chentelle felt a gentle throb of power as A'stoc called for light. All through the walls of the cavern, natural crystal formations started to shine with gentle, white light. The floor had been worked into three circular tiers, sinking down to a central pool. A steep stairway connected the three levels.

"This is my home," A'stoc said, descending the first flight of stairs. "As you can see, it contains natural deposits of adartak, an effective focus for Crystal Lore."

The second tier appeared to be kitchen and living quarters. A sagging cot lay buried underneath piles of clothes and books. A small dresser served to separate the bedroom and the kitchen, which held a stove, a large cupboard, and a breakfast table with two chairs. A healthy fire burned in the stove.

A'stoc tossed the debris off of the chairs. "I apologize for not having a parlor, but I do not often have visitors." The sarcasm in his voice was palpable, but it softened. "Rest yourselves. You look weary."

Chentelle lowered herself onto a chair, grateful for the relief from hard days of walking and riding.

A'stoc pulled off his cloak and tossed it onto the cot. Underneath, he wore a faded robe which might have been silk. It had been sky blue once, but now was stained and worn nearly to rags. He had no leggings or trousers, and his long feet were protected only by leather-and-rope sandals.

He slid the bed over to the end of the table and sat down on its edge. "So tell me your message, elf girl," he said.

Chentelle studied the man who sat before her. She knew that wizards used their power to prolong their lives, but A'stoc seemed both ancient and young, both proud and defeated. His tanned skin was unlined save for the deep crease of his perpetual frown, but his unkempt hair was the color of sun-bleached bone. There was fire in his pale gray eyes, but there was also the look of a caged animal. He was definitely the man in her dream, but there was something else. She felt as if she had known him long before that.

Then it came to her. After the war, a human had come to Lone Valley, seeking Wizard A'mond. He had been a pitiful creature, consumed by pain and despair. His emotions called out to Chentelle, to the grief she felt at her father's passing. She had never spoken to him, but somehow touching his sorrow had helped her deal with her own. This was that man, different but unchanged.

"Well," said A'stoc, "are you going to tell me the message, or did you come all this way just to stare?"

"Sorry," Chentelle said. "I'll give you the message. But first you should know how I came to bear it. I intercepted a dove sent to Wizard A'mond. The High Bishop was unaware that the wizard had died during the winter."

A'stoc closed his eyes and rested his head on long fingers. "A'mond," he whispered, "I remember him. A master of Wood Lore. I went to him after the war, looking for knowledge or perhaps comfort. He was ancient, even then. You bear sad news, elf girl."

"And there is more. The High Bishop wanted A'mond to seek you out. You are supposed to take the Staff to the Holy City of Norivika. And on the way here, Sulmar and I encountered an Ill-creature. It is clear that the High Bishop needs your help to deal with their threat."

"No!" A'stoc slammed his palms against the table and lurched to his feet.

The movement startled Chentelle and caused Sulmar to jump to his own feet, hand resting on the hilt of his sword. But the wizard only stalked off into the kitchen area.

"I cannot help you," he said. "There is nothing I can do for the High Bishop. Nothing."

"I—I don't understand," Chentelle said. "You are going to ignore the message?"

"There is nothing to understand, elf girl. I cannot go, and the two of you must leave."

A'stoc turned his back, dismissing them. He pulled open the large cupboard and grabbed a wine flask and a clay goblet. He sucked a large swallow directly from the flask and then filled the goblet, simultaneously wiping his chin clean against his sleeve.

"He is a coward, mistress," Sulmar said, not taking his eyes off the wizard. "He would hide in a wine bottle rather than take a stand against evil."

A'stoc pulled himself to his full height and glared at Sulmar. The wine flask trembled as his grip tightened. The tension between the two men was palpable, but then the wizard laughed and took another swallow of wine. "Bloodthirsty Tengarian!" he said. "You are Tengarian, aren't you?"

Sulmar's posture remained rigid. "No," he said, "though I was once."

A'stoc continued as if he hadn't heard the response. "I know your people:

barbarous savages. You spend your lives looking for an opportunity to die, for a hopeless cause to make your own. And now you've found one, haven't you?"

He pointed at Chentelle. "Look at her, Tengarian. She wants us to fight the Dark One. And you stand by her side like a loyal puppy, wagging your tail at her folly. I'm sure it will be a glorious death. You are welcome to it."

Sulmar's knuckles grew white on the pommel of his sword, but his voice remained even. "My mistress sets her own path. I stand beside her, as is my duty. When I see evil, I fight against it. When I see something precious, I strive to protect it. I do not know what you do." He turned his back to the wizard and returned to his seat.

A'stoc turned to Chentelle. "Listen to me. There is no use in me going. Tell the Bishop that the power he searches for is lost. Tell him, elf girl, that I do not have what he seeks." He drained the goblet in one smooth motion and started to fill it again.

"But my mission was merely to inform you of your mission," she protested. "I have nothing to tell anyone else. I shall be going home."

He peered sourly at her with some discomfiting insight. "I think not."

"But—"

"No! We do not talk. We eat, we drink, we sleep, and then you leave."

So his dismissal had become a surly invitation. "Thank you, wizard," Chentelle said politely.

A'stoc started to say something, but stifled it. He grabbed two more goblets and set them on the table along with the flask. Then he started chopping vegetables into a large stew pot. He went up the stairs and came back with an already slaughtered and cleaned chicken. He roasted this separately from the stew and finished the meal preparations by warming some hard biscuits over the fire.

Chentelle was famished, but the smell of roasting flesh was making her ill. She understood that humans felt the need to eat animals, but her empty stomach could not bear the stench. A few sips of the strong wine only made her queasiness worse. She got up and wandered away from the table.

What did A'stoc mean by negating her intention to return home now? He had magical sources of information, but he obviously did not care about her. What did he know?

Huge stalactites were hanging from the cave's ceiling, glittering like a beetle's wings. She went to one and brushed her fingers against a shard of shining crystal, reaching out with her Gift. The adartak glowed with power. It was a web of fire running through the cold strength of the stone. And at the center of the web, there was something else, another power. But it was shielded from her. She reached for it with her Gift but felt only a cold, hard wall.

Chentelle pulled back into herself, keeping only a hint of the extended awareness that was her Gift. The pool—the power she felt was centered at the pool.

She walked down the stairs to the third tier. This was apparently A'stoc's workshop. The large stone tables and desk were covered with scrolls and experimental apparatus. Long bookshelves rested awkwardly against the curved walls, and the floor was littered with glass shards and loose parchments. In the center of the workshop, the silvery surface of the pool was surrounded by a ring of rune-carved stones.

Drops of fluid fell from stalactites thirty cubits above, striking the pool with a muffled *plunk, plunk, plunk.* It didn't sound like water, and the surface remained absolutely still. Not a single ripple marked where the drops passed. Chentelle moved to the pool's edge and peered in, but she saw only her own somewhat disheveled image reflected in the water. Whatever lay below the surface was hidden.

She knelt down and touched the surface, searching with her Gift. Shallow ripples marked the passage of her hand. It was water, cool and pure but unnaturally still. Fields of power hummed through it, pulling it taut. And there, below the tension of the surface waters, was the other power she had felt. It pulsed with vitality, a core of fire burning in an ocean of ice. Chentelle reached for it with her Gift.

An electric shock coursed through her fingers, knocking her back from the water. The pool began churning violently, as if it were boiling. Streamers of mist poured from the surface, swirling about in a wind which seemed to spring from nowhere.

Chentelle turned to flee, but a gust of wind blasted her to the floor. The gale twisted around her, pressing her against the rough stone and then changing direction, forcing her back toward the pool. Her finger tore at the rock, trying to find purchase, but it was no use. The wind was too strong.

The mists coalesced above the water, taking form. A thick, sinuous body ended in a massive, square-jawed head. Long forelimbs led to wicked claws of vapor. The thing reached for Chentelle, opening its jaws to reveal a pit of absolute darkness within.

She screamed.

Suddenly, Sulmar was there, his black sword striking at the mists. The blade seemed to pass harmlessly through the vapor, but the thing shied away from the attack.

"*Nalchea! Mig Noka!*"

A'stoc's shout brought instant calm. The wind died, the water quieted, the mist faded to nothingness.

The mage stood rigidly, glaring at Chentelle. He said nothing for a long moment. Then, with a visible effort, he turned away and walked back up the stairs.

"Dinner is ready," he called contemptuously over his shoulder.

Sulmar appeared, reaching down to help her to her feet. "Are you all right, my liege?"

"Fine," she said, trembling. "Thank you for your help."

"I did only my duty, liege," he said. "I should have been here in time to prevent the threat."

"And I expressed only my feelings," Chentelle replied. "I should not have interfered in what was not my business. Now let's go eat. I'm famished."

They ate in silence. A'stoc drained his wine goblet with amazing frequency and refused all openings to conversation. The stew was bland, but filling. And Sulmar seemed to be enjoying his roast chicken.

Once Chentelle's belly was full, her mind started racing. Why did A'stoc refuse to go to Norivika? And what was it she had sensed in the water? The wizard said he did not have the power to help the High Bishop, but there was something puissant in that pool. A'stoc was hiding something.

Chentelle inhaled slowly, steeling herself to face the mage's anger. "Wizard, what was it I disturbed in the pool?"

A'stoc glared at her over the rim of his goblet. "Do you know anything about wizardry?" he asked, with particular calmness.

Chentelle shook her head.

"No?" he said. "I suppose there are not many who do. That is a magepool, elf girl. You must never disturb the surface of such a pool. *Wizards* are notoriously paranoid about such things, they protect them with powerful wards."

He put a strange inflection on the word 'wizards.' Chentelle could not tell if it was mockery or awe.

"But, wizard," she said, trying to guide him back to the subject, "I sensed another power in the well. Something separate from the spells on the water. You said that you did not have the power the High Bishop seeks, but what I felt was great power. Why is it that you refuse the High Bishop's call?"

A'stoc drained his goblet and slammed it against the table. "Jester tricks! The power you felt is nothing compared to the power of the Dark One. I told you—"

The mage cut himself off. A thoughtful look passed over his face and he turned to face Chentelle. "How did you close my doorway?" he asked quietly.

"It is my Gift," she said. "I am an enchantress. I can sense the forces of life and magic that—"

"I know what an enchantress is, elf girl," he said sharply. He upended the flask over his cup, but no wine poured out. He set the empty flask on the floor and started to rise, but he lurched unsteadily and fell back in his seat.

"I will get it for you," Chentelle said. She did not approve of the way he was imbibing, but she knew that it was pointless to aggravate him further. She went to the cupboard and found two shelves full of bottled wine. She selected a dark burgundy that seemed identical to what they had been drinking and brought it back to the table. She filled A'stoc's glass and set the flask down within his reach. Then she returned to her chair.

A'stoc said nothing.

"Wizard," she said, laying a hand on his wrist.

He jerked his arm away from her, nearly toppling the wine flask in the process. She realized that while touching was natural to her, it was not necessarily so to humans. "You want to know why I don't jump at the High Bishop's call?" he asked.

"Please," she said. "I need to understand."

"Then you have to understand the Wizards' War," he said, reaching out and sandwiching her hand between both of his own. "Use your Gift, little enchantress. I have something to show you."

Chentelle's hand felt tiny in his grasp. Now he was touching her, and that was perhaps good. The intensity of his need struck her even before she called on her power. Part of her wanted to recoil from him, but she knew that she could not. She would not, even if she were capable. She had to understand. She opened herself to the Gift.

A'stoc was a wall, a barrier that resisted all attempts at penetration. Then the shield dissolved, lowered from within, and Chentelle sensed a diamond-hard core of power: shining, multifaceted, sharp-edged.

Then the emotions hit her. She tossed in a maelstrom of bitterness and despair, of suffering and sadness. The power, the depth of the feelings overwhelmed her. It was too strong to fight. She surrendered, letting the current of anguish wash over her, through her. A'stoc's pain, A'stoc's memories, became hers. Slowly, the tide of emotions resolved itself into a progression of images.

She watched the Dark One emerge from the Abyss, building his strength for the assault. He seduced the trolls with promises of power and wealth. Then he created an army of Ill-creatures, breeding them in foul pits deep beneath the surface. As his power grew, others flocked to his banner: first the gnomes, then the goblins.

In Norivika, the High Bishop moved to counter the threat. He called upon the separate kingdoms of human, elf, and dwarf to unite their forces under one command. And he summoned the Lore Masters of the Collegium. A'pon Boemarre answered that call. And Chentelle—A'stoc—had followed her master.

Some wizards joined in battle against the Ill-creatures, others worked in laboratories, filling volumes with mystic rune-writing. A'pon Boemarre locked himself away in Norivika. Chentelle waited impotently while her master studied in seclusion. Then after more than a year, A'pon Boemarre emerged bearing the mightiest weapon ever known: the Thunderwood Staff. He had created it from the Tree of Life—the Tree which binds the Earth and Sky. And it frightened him.

She had seen his fear, though he hid it from all others. The Thunderwood Staff held power over life itself. Its power was unimaginable, perhaps uncontrollable. But that power was needed.

The forces of evil slowly crushed the Legion armies. The power of the Ill-creatures was too great. Slowly, inexorably the Dark One advanced into the Realm. Then A'pon Boemarre took the field. The Thunderwood Staff was in his hand, and she was at his side.

Chentelle recoiled as memories of blood and death filled her mind. Battle after battle played out in her thoughts as the war continued. For four years, the tide of war swept across the Realm. Thousands died; even the giants were caught up in the struggle as their homeland became a center for the conflict. Again and again, the armies clashed. Again and again, the Staff proved too much for the Ill-creatures. And victory increased the confidence of A'pon Boemarre.

The Legion pressed its attack to the heart of the Dark One's power, the breeding pits where he spawned his Ill-creatures. The armies met in the Western Mountains, near the homelands of the giants and the trolls. Neither side held back its reserves; everyone knew the war would be decided here. War banners covered a dozen mountainsides, but the true battle took place beneath their feet.

In a cave under the mountains, beside molten pits that led to the Abyss, A'pon Boemarre confronted the Dark One. He raised the Thunderwood Staff and summoned its power, surrounding himself with a corona of green flame.

The Dark One emerged from the pit. Shadows danced around his body, obscuring him from sight, but slowly a face became clear: her face, A'stoc's face. The face smiled and paralysis gripped her. She was unable to speak, unable to move, unable even to look away.

Boemarre lashed out with the power of the Staff. Green flames enveloped the Dark One, burning brighter than the Golden Sun. But they could not penetrate his shield of shadow.

The Dark One moved forward, grabbing at the Staff. Bolts of emerald and ebony shot through the cavern as he tried to wrestle it away from the wizard. Power throbbed around the battling figures. The ground trembled, and deep cracks appeared in the floor. The fire pits erupted in molten geysers. A fireball began forming around the staff: not green, not black, but pure white. The intensity of the light was too much too bear. It burned her eyes, blinding her, but somehow she could still see.

A crevice opened up beneath Boemarre and the Dark One. They dropped through the crack, and the Thunderwood Staff flew from their hands. It fell in Chentelle's direction. One end landed in her palm; the other struck against the stone floor. The fireball exploded.

The Earth screamed in her mind. The wall of flames expanded outward, leaving destruction in its wake. Every blade of grass, every shrub, every insect, every being in its path caught fire. The flames passed through the assembled armies. Elves burst into flames; knights burned inside their armor; goblins were reduced to piles of ash; and the fire kept going. Village after village of peace-loving giants were consumed by flame, and the fire kept going. The entire race of trolls died as their marshes boiled around them, and still the fire kept going. The Earth itself burned and twisted in the conflagration. Then, at last, the holocaust stopped.

Only she was left alive. The wasteland stretched around her as far as she could see, a vast panorama of death. And she walked. She walked through fields littered with the corpses of men she might once have known. She walked over twisted landscapes of dust and rock and soot. She walked until she couldn't walk anymore. Then she slept. And all the while she never let go of the Thunderwood Staff.

When she woke, she started walking again. She came across the corpse of an animal that still had some flesh on its bones, and she attacked it in hunger. The burned meat made her thirsty, but there was no water. She walked. At some point it rained, and then she could catch water in her mouth or lick it from depressions in the rock. And she walked.

She walked for leagues. She walked for days. But the wasteland kept going. It stretched before her, vast, seemingly without end. But she couldn't stop. She kept walk—

"My liege?"

Chentelle lay curled in a ball on the floor, trembling. Tears poured down her cheeks, and she had difficulty breathing. Sulmar was tapping gently on her wrist. He must have broken the contact.

She forced herself to uncurl, fighting the wave of nausea that accompanied motion. She was Chentelle, not A'stoc. She had never been to the Desecration Fault, never walked through the desolation. Never eaten the flesh of a corpse of an animal. They were A'stoc's memories, not hers. It hadn't happened to her.

She managed to stop crying and bring her breath under control. By the Creator, she had never imagined such horror was possible! And A'stoc had lived through it. She searched for the wizard, and saw him slumped across the table, hiding his face in his hands and crying softly.

"My liege? Can you speak?"

"Sulmar," she said, clutching at the stability of his arm. "I'm all right, Sulmar. At least, I will be soon. Will you help me up?"

The Tengarian lifted her easily off the floor and set her gently back in her chair. "I was worried for you," he said. "Almost as soon as the wizard touched you, you cried out in pain. I knocked his hands away from yours, but still you fell to the floor."

Chentelle followed Sulmar's gaze to the slumped figure of the wizard. He was no longer crying, but he still hid his face in his hands.

"Do not trust him, mistress," Sulmar said. "He lives without honor."

"It was not his fault, Sulmar," she said, going to the wizard.

She placed a hand on A'stoc's shoulder, being careful not to reach out with her Gift. "I am sorry. I did not know that anyone had survived the Desecration."

A'stoc looked up, staring past her with bloodshot eyes. "No one did," he said. "No one did."

Chentelle wanted to reach out to him, to comfort him. But his pain was too deep, too powerful. She didn't know how to help him, so she just sat with him. The silence stretched for long moments.

"And it was all for nothing," he said, finally. "So much destruction. So much death. And for what? The Dark One has returned, and we have no magic to oppose him. The great wizards are gone forever, and their knowledge died with them."

"What do you mean?" Chentelle asked.

"The old wizards recorded their spells in rune-writing," he explained. "A magic script, indecipherable to the untrained. It was part of their paranoia, their jealousy. The Masters guarded their secrets well, especially after the necromancers appeared. And when a wizard dies, his spells die with him. The old Lore books are filled with blank pages. Only a few handwritten documents survive."

"But what about the Collegium?" she asked. "The Lore Masters of Tel Adartak-Skysoar?"

"Fools!" A'stoc said. "And worse than fools. There are no true Masters there, no wizards to rival A'kalendane or A'pon Boemarre. The knowledge is lost. They struggle to relearn the most basic spells. They are children, lost in the wilderness and pretending to be guides. In time, they might find their way home. But if Ill-creatures move in the Realm, then time runs short."

"Then we must act now," Chentelle said. "Don't you see? The High Bishop wouldn't send for you if he didn't have a plan. We must have hope. The Creator will not abandon his Creation."

"Hope!" the mage bellowed. "Hope is a road that leads only to despair. The High Bishop does not know what he asks. I am powerless to stop what is happening."

"Apparently the High Bishop thinks otherwise," she said, struggling to keep her frustration in check.

"That does not change the fact."

Was he just going to sit and watch while the world suffered, while the Dark One destroyed Creation? No, Chentelle had to convince him to act.

"Please, wizard," she said. "You know what will happen if the Dark One triumphs. More than any man alive, you know the horrors that his victory will bring. You *must* help us."

"No." He lurched to his feet and staggered one step.

"If you do not even try," she said desperately, "then you have already decided the fate of the world."

A'stoc started as if she had slapped him. "Enough!" He drained the last of his wine and collapsed onto the bed beside him. "I will think about what you have said," he mumbled. "But you leave in the morning."

The lights began to dim as A'stoc drifted to sleep. Chentelle removed the wizard's shoes and tucked a thin blanket around him. Then she and Sulmar hurriedly set up their beds for the night. Soon, loud snoring filled the chamber and the glow of the adartak died completely.

Chentelle's mind raced. She had to convince A'stoc to answer the High Bishop's call. But how? She couldn't force his cooperation. And he had suffered so much. She shuddered at the memory of his pain. No wonder he was bitter, afraid to hope. But he had to help.

The questions continued, but she had no answers. Finally the exhaustion of the day took its toll, and sleep claimed her.

ठ

She is home, walking among the familiar trees of Lone Valley. Slanted shafts of light penetrate the ceiling of branches, lacing the pathway with bright white patches. The trees whisper to each other, but she can't understand their words. Something feels wrong; there is a strange presence in the forest.

The forest moves into darkness. Deep shadows fall between the trees, covering her path. Something is moving just beyond the field of her vision. She whirls, but she sees nothing. Her skin tingles. She can feel it, watching, stalking. The whispers start again. *Doom. Doom.*

She runs. The trees close in on her, channeling her down a narrow path. Branches tear at her face and her clothes, but she keeps running.

She emerges into a black void, empty of trees, empty of light, empty of sound. She stumbles into the clearing, groping her way through the darkness. The shadows are cold. Her skin shivers at their touch. She moves forward, but the void seems to stretch forever.

Suddenly, cruel laughter echoes in the gloom. A figure flows out of the darkness. A hideous creature with taloned legs and huge wings.

The demon's pallid stare paralyzes her. She can only watch in horror as a great clawed fist extends toward her. The hand uncurls, and the broken, lifeless form of a dove falls by her feet.

ठ

Chentelle woke to the sound of her own screaming. Sweat ran down her face and her breathing was fast and heavy.

There was the sound of a sword being drawn from its scabbard. "Mistress, are you in danger?"

"It's all right, Sulmar," she said. "It was a dream, a dream of evil." But she knew that it had been a dream of truth. The Ill-creatures knew about her mission.

Was it morning? It was impossible to tell. The darkness of the cave was absolute. But she felt rested, as if she had slept several hours.

"A'stoc," she yelled into the darkness. "Wizard, wake up. They know. The Dark One knows that the High Bishop has sent for you. A'stoc!"

A muffled voice sounded from the direction of the cot, and dim light filled the chamber. A'stoc lay curled on his bed, clutching his head tightly in his hands.

"Hel's Maw," he grumbled. "Not so loud, girl."

Chentelle tossed off her blanket and hurried to his side. "Please, A'stoc, you must go to Norivika. You must!"

A'stoc rolled over, lowering his feet to the floor. "Aaah, where are my shoes? What did—"

He stopped suddenly, clutching his arms to his body. Then he stumbled to the kitchen and vomited in the nearest bowl. When he was finished, he slid slowly down the front of the cupboard and sat on the stone floor.

Chentelle felt a twinge of despair. This was the hope of the world? No, there was more to this man than the drunken spectacle before her. She had felt that last night. She had to figure out how to reach the strength inside the man.

She wet a cloth and handed it to the mage. "A'stoc, please. So much depends upon you."

"Quietly, please," A'stoc said, pressing the cloth to his face and staggering to his feet. "You have no idea the pain that you cause me."

"But, wizard—"

He silenced her with an upraised hand. "My wits were not so addled last night that I failed to consider your words. I have decided to go to the Holy Land."

He was going! "Thank you, wizard," Chentelle said. "You are truly wise."

"Then why do I feel like a fool, elf girl?" he demanded. "And stop calling me wizard. I never earned that title. I have only a fraction of the knowledge my master possessed. I cannot even call upon the Staff's power."

She was tempted to ask him similarly to stop calling her girl, but concluded that issue was pointless. "You can't use the Staff? Still, the High Bishop must have reason to call for your aid."

"The High Bishop has no idea what he asks. I go with you only to show him the truth of our situation."

"With me? But I am going home."

He looked at her. "I think not," he said, as he had before. "Consider my inadequacies. Do you think I would ever get there alone?"

Her mouth dropped open. It was true: this caustic, depressive, drunken caricature of a mage was unlikely to complete any journey of more than an hour, without help.

A'stoc forced a grim smile. "If I must suffer, so must you. Your task is not done until you get me there."

So it seemed. Because if she refused, so would he. And the fate of the world perhaps depended on him.

She made her decision. "Then we should leave now, wiz—A'stoc. I dreamed that the Ill-creatures know about the High Bishop's message. They want to stop you from reaching Norivika."

"You dreamed it," he said. "And I suppose all your dreams come true."

Chentelle felt the bitterness of his sarcasm. "No," she said. "But sometimes they do. Sometimes I can *feel* the truth of a dream. And this dream was true."

"Maybe," A'stoc said. "But we are safe for now. My home is not easy to find. And it is only two days travel to the Barrier."

"Then the sooner you leave, the better," Chentelle said. "Your home was not too difficult for me to find."

A'stoc threw the cloth to the ground in disgust. "Enough of your prodding, elf girl. I told you I would go." He glanced at her. "With you."

"With me," she agreed with resignation. She was committed, too.

"And me," Sulmar added. But he did not seem distressed. She realized that his motive differed: he wanted to travel and find adventure, but could do so only in her company. She hoped he did not succeed in finding more than any of them cared for. That winged monster of her dream . . .

A'stoc searched for his shoes, finally finding them at the end of the cot. After several tries he managed to slip them on his feet and stand up.

"Wait here," he said, working his way slowly down the stairs to the magepool.

Chentelle moved to the edge of the tier and watched.

A'stoc's steps became steadier as he neared the pool. The surface of the well glowed faintly, and the mage stood near its edge for a time, seeming to draw strength from the water. Then he spoke a single word. The water started churning, though not as violently as it had the night before. Mist rose from the pool, taking the shape of two giant, long-fingered hands.

The mage started chanting, and the hands reached down into the pool. Misty fingers pushed into the water and pulled it apart as if it were solid. A hollow channel formed, reaching down into the depths. Suddenly a shaft of brilliant light exploded from the opening. A wooden staff floated upward inside the light.

A'stoc gestured, and the staff drifted toward his hand. As soon as his fingers touched the wood, the light died, and the walls of water came crashing together.

The staff was gnarled like the root of an ancient oak. Magical runes were worked expertly into its surface, carved to blend smoothly with the natural contours of the wood. The tool radiated power, power similar to the magic of the unicorns but far stronger. It pulsed with *life*.

This was the Thunderwood Staff. It could be no other.

A'stoc held the Staff with both hands, his knuckles white with the force of his grip. "Well, then," he said. "Let us go see the High Bishop."

✑ 5 ✑

AFTERMATH

Dacius woke to the taste of sand and salt water. He spat, trying to clear his mouth, and pushed himself upright. Pain shot through his right wrist. The world spun and he fell back to the ground.

His vision contracted into a haze of darkness. No! He had to stay conscious. He bit down hard on the edge of his tongue, using the sharp pain to counteract the ache in his wrist. Blood mixed with the grit in his mouth, but his vision cleared.

He was on a beach. Deneob was in the sky, casting everything in a reddish hue. Debris from the *Otan Stin* decorated the shoreline. He remembered kicking off his boots, fighting desperately to stay above the waves. He must have latched on to some timbers and floated out the storm. He rolled carefully onto his back and sat up. Except for his boots, he did not seem to have lost—

His left hand leaped to his side. Thank the Creator, the vorpal sword hung safely in its scabbard. He had managed to save it from the storm.

Slowly, Dacius got to his feet. His arm throbbed, and he risked a quick glance. A small, jagged spur of bone poked through the skin just above his wrist. Congealed blood and sand kept the wound from bleeding anymore. He laid the wrist against his chest and braced it with his other arm. Now he could travel.

He weaved his way down the beach, searching for survivors. His balance was off, and it was difficult to make his legs move properly. He shivered in the ocean breeze. It was cold. His skull pounded, and he lifted his hand to his forehead: sweat. He was feverish.

Flotsam littered the shore. He spotted a patch of color: part of a uniform. He worked his way closer. There were bodies, three of them. Two were sailors; the third wore the green and white of the Inarr Regiment.

The Legionnaire lay facedown, his head canted at an alarming angle. Dacius knelt in the sand and rolled the body over. Graying hair fell around a face that he had known all his life. Alka! The elf's eyes stared blankly into the sky.

Tears ran freely down Dacius's face as he reached down and closed his friend's eyes. "Watch for this one, Creator," he said. "He has served you well."

Dacius wanted to stay and bury his friend, but it was impossible. Even if he were capable of the action, his first duty was to find other survivors. He forced himself back to his feet and continued down the beach. The world seemed desolate, lifeless. Clumps of wreckage loomed toward him through a haze of fever. Often, there were bodies mixed with the debris. Some were sailors, and some were Legionnaires, but all were dead. The sand tantalized him with promises of rest, but Dacius kept walking.

Smoke rose from behind a small cluster of rocks. Someone was waving to him. There were a half-dozen figures, maybe more. Two of them headed toward him. As they neared, Dacius recognized Captain Rone and Thildemar. The old musician appeared unhurt, but Rone had one arm slung in a makeshift splint, and a mass of bruises covered the left side of his face.

"Lord Gemine," Thildemar said, "my heart is gladdened to see you alive."

Something within Dacius relaxed at the sight of the elves. The world started to spin, and he dropped to his knees in the sand. "Alka," he said. "My friend—dead."

"By the creator!" Rone cried. "Be damned that hideous creature! Where is he?"

Dacius gestured back. "I saw him. He—" But he could not continue. He fell forward.

Arms wrapped about his shoulders and a slim hand pressed against his forehead. "He is hot with fever," Thildemar said.

The captain shouted instructions, and more elves appeared. Dacius was soon being carried gently toward the shelter of the rocks. A Legionnaire was carefully feeding deadwood into the fire, using his elven Lore to prepare the wet timbers for the flame. The elves laid Dacius beside the fire and covered him with a heavy cloak.

Thildemar poured water over Dacius' wrist, cleaning the wound. "This needs to be set. Prepare yourself. There will be a great deal of pain."

Someone pushed a thick layer of cloth into Dacius's mouth. He bit down hard while Thildemar pulled and twisted his wrist. Bones ground against each other, and Dacius screamed. Pain shot through his arm, burning, throbbing, piercing. When the tide of darkness washed across his vision, heralding unconsciousness, he welcomed the relief.

The faces of Thildemar and Captain Rone appeared above him. "Lord Gemine," Thildemar said, "are you rational?"

Dacius took a moment to consider. He was exhausted, feverish, probably in shock. But he did not seem to be delirious. His wrist was strapped to his chest. It ached severely, but the pain was manageable. "Yes," he replied evenly.

The old elf smiled. "Good."

"How long have I been out?"

"Only a short while," the elf replied. "Just long enough to splint your arm. Now, if you are able, then as the ranking Legion officer present command falls to you."

"Me?" Dacius asked. "What about you?" Then he remembered what Alka had told him about Thildemar. "Or, Captain Rone?"

"I'm no Legion Lord," Rone said. "Besides, how could I ask men to follow my lead, when my last decision was so disastrous? Good men died for my arrogance. And I lost the finest ship I've ever sailed."

Thildemar placed a comforting hand on the captain's shoulder. "The blame is not yours alone, captain. You based your decision on sound judgment of these waters. Had the storm been a natural one, your skill would have seen us through. It was the Ill-creature's magic that destroyed your vessel, and you had no way of anticipating that danger."

Captain Rone nodded at Thildemar's words, but the tension remained in his posture and his voice. "Nevertheless, this burden is not mine."

"All right," Dacius said, "I accept the command, for now. What is our situation?"

"I make our position to be on the northern reach of the Larama desert," said Rone. "We have to travel along the coast to reach the Holy Land. The Altan Noff mountains cut off all other routes until you reach the dwarven passes far to the west. The sand will slow us until we reach the foothills, but we should still reach Talan before nightfall."

"A Legion outpost used to sit at the border, just beyond the pass," said Thildemar. "If it has not been abandoned, they should be able to give us healing and provide us with horses until we reach Norivika."

"The monster that attacked us last night, will it be stalking us?" Dacius asked.

"They cannot travel in daytime," Thildemar replied. "Direct sunlight kills them. But we must assume that it, or another Ill-creature, will attack again once darkness comes."

"How did it find us?" Dacius said.

"I do not know," Thildemar answered. "Perhaps the Dark One intercepted a message to the High Bishop. Or maybe the Ill-creatures have a way to sense our presence. The powers of evil are not to be underestimated."

Dacius looked at the piles of debris that were his companions around the fire. "How many of us are there?"

"We have ten survivors," said Thildemar.

Ten. Pictures of broken bodies strewn along the beach ran through Dacius's mind. "What have you been able to salvage?" he asked.

"Primarily clothes and timber," Rone said. "The food was spoiled, but we did find some fresh water." He handed a flask to Dacius. "And we recovered vorpal blades from five of the fallen Legionnaires."

Dacius took the flask. The water stung as it washed across his tongue, but he swallowed it gratefully, quenching a thirst he hadn't even been aware of.

"Lord Gemine," Thildemar said. "Concerning the dead, some of the men want to bury them before we leave, giving them at least some of the honors they deserve. Others fear that the delay will leave us short of safety when night falls; they counsel immediate departure. The outpost can send riders back tomorrow to recover the bodies and transport them home."

Dacius turned to Captain Rone. "How certain are you about our position?"

"I know this coast," Rone said. "I can see the Altan Noff range. We aren't far from the pass. We should have no trouble making it by evening." He paused, looking at Dacius. "Begging your pardon, lord, but that's assuming you can travel a steady pace."

"Of course I—" Dacius cut himself off. This was no time to let pride rule his mind. He was injured, feverish, weak with fatigue, and sore from the night's exertion. He faced a barefoot march over difficult terrain, and the lives of ten men might depend on his ability to keep up. He thought of Alka, remembering his friend's body lying crumpled in the sand, eyes staring blindly into nothingness. Rage began to burn within.

"Bury the bodies," Dacius told Thildemar. "And hurry. We must reach the outpost by dusk."

As the elves turned and left, Dacius took several more long swallows of water. His thirst satisfied, he lay down in the sand. The warmth of the fire worked its way into him, driving away his chill. And he slept.

❧

When Thildemar shook him awake, Ellistar was already fully risen over the horizon. Dacius squinted his eyes against the brightness, but he was glad for the heat. With Thildemar's help, he struggled to his feet. The sand felt warm under his toes.

He looked down. "The heat might be a problem. I'll need protection for my feet."

Thildemar nodded. "None of the dead had boots that would fit a human. Perhaps we can cut some material from one of the blankets and bind it around your feet."

"That will have to do," Dacius said. "Are the burials finished?"

"Yes, Lord Gemine," the elf said. "We wait only for the words of honor. As ranking officer, that duty falls to you."

Dacius nodded. He motioned for Thildemar to lead, and followed the elf to a clearing which contained a dozen shallow mounds. Each grave was marked by a small circle of stones, symbolizing the unity of Creation.

Dacius positioned himself so that his shadow fell across the grave marked as Alka Shara's. "Most of these men," he said, "I did not know. One, I have called friend ever since I learned what that word meant. But all of them died for the same reason."

Dacius drew his sword with his left hand. "This blade has hung in my hall for generations. I heard stories about the magic it held, the sacred trust it was created to uphold. But not until last night did I understand the meaning of those stories.

"The Dark One, the evil we thought ended forever, returns to threaten the Realm. During the Wizards' War, the Legion fought against the Ill-creatures with the greatest of Lore Masters at our side. Those wizards, and the magic they commanded, are gone. During the Wizards' War, every Legionnaire was armed with a vorpal weapon. Now there are only these few that we carry with us. None of that matters. The High Bishop has called us, and we answer that call.

"Last night, we saw the face of evil. We saw the reason this weapon was crafted. We saw the purpose for which the Legion was created. And these men, our comrades, our friends, gave their lives. Some of these men did not wear the crossed swords, and are not listed in the Legion's rolls. But I name them now. They were Legionnaires. They died fighting our fight. They died defending our cause.

"The Creator will be watching these souls, will welcome them into the Unity of the Sphere. They have earned that right. They are Legionnaires, and they served in honor."

Dacius looked down at the simple marker by his feet. "Good-bye, my friend. I will miss you."

He shut his eyes against his tears. When he looked again, he saw that many of the elves were weeping openly. "We will wait fifteen minutes," he said, "so that each of you can say his private farewells. Then we march."

⤳

Dacius paused as he crested the bluff. Before him, the hills of the sea pass gave way to a broad, rocky plain. In the distance, perhaps a league from the final hills, the dusty brown of the plain transformed abruptly into a verdant green. The change was crisp, sharp, as if one could begin a step in the barren plain and end it in a lush garden.

Thildemar came up beside him. "An amazing sight, is it not, Lord Gemine?"

Dacius nodded. The pounding in his head kept perfect time to the throbbing ache in his wrist. His feet suffered from a dozen cuts and bruises inflicted by the rocky ground, and he leaned heavily on the makeshift staff that Thildemar had provided from the wreckage of the *Otan Stin.* He was hungry, thirsty, and exhausted.

He looked to the west and smiled. Deneob was just beginning to set, and Ellistar was still well above the horizon. He could see the dark outline of a Legion outpost sitting just in front of the boundary line. He pointed at it with his staff. "Let's go. We don't want to be late for supper."

An hour of hiking brought them to the gates of the outpost. It was an imposing structure of steel and gray stone. The fortification was small, but sturdy. The ramparts were high and capped with impressive parapets. The gate was fronted by two steel portcullises and protected by thick stone towers. Arrow slits and artillery casements were placed to provide covering fire for all main avenues of attack. When properly manned, Dacius judged that the fort could withstand a large assault force for several days, but he was curious about its placement.

The sentries at the gate responded quickly to their presence. A quick check of their uniforms and condition insured that the party was ushered through the gates and settled into a large visitor's hall. Cooks hastened to prepare food and drink, and healers were called to tend to their wounds.

Dacius settled himself wearily onto a bench near the hearth and waited. Soon, two bearded humans wearing white robes of the Holy Order appeared. The priests glanced quickly around the room, then one of them went to Captain Rone while the other came to Dacius. He removed the makeshift sling that bound Dacius's arm and examined his wound. The man's touch was gentle, but Dacius still winced in pain as the wrist moved.

"Good," the man said. "It set well. That will make this easier." The priest covered the joint with his hands and started to chant.

Dacius felt a stillness move through his arm, a calmness. The pain disappeared as the feeling of harmony coursed through him. He felt rapturous, filled with love. The break in his arm made no sense; it was obviously incorrect. He considered it for a moment and felt the bones knit together and the wounded flesh heal. That was better.

The priest moved a hand to his forehead, and Dacius realized that he still burned with fever: how unnecessary. He opened himself to the priest's song, letting the harmony course through his spirit. The fever disappeared under its gentle soothing. The cuts and bruises disappeared from his battered feet. Even the aches of a long day's exertion vanished. He felt wonderful, perfect, at home in Creation. All was well.

The priest stopped his chant. Dacius felt the material world slowly take hold of him again. That was fine. It was where he belonged. He turned to thank the priest and suddenly realized that he was hungry. No, he was famished. A deep empty pit yawned where his belly should be. He placed a hand over his stomach.

The priest smiled. "It's all right. Food is coming. Eat heartily tonight. You need to regain the strength you have spent." He turned away to examine one of the other Legionnaires.

"Thank you," Dacius said, heading over to join the group at the dining table.

The food came almost immediately: large trays of steamed vegetables, fresh bread, and a thick corn soup. By unspoken consensus, no one attempted conversation until everyone had had a chance to satisfy their appetite. They devoured the food as if it were the finest meal from the courts of Essienkal.

After he had eaten, Dacius took a moment to examine his new command. There was Thildemar, of course. Already Dacius had gained a firm respect for the old elf's experience and insight. Perhaps he felt a special kinship to him because of their shared connection to Alka Shara.

Next, there was Simon: a dark, lean elf who seldom spoke. His hair was jet-black and twisted into dozens of tight braids which swung freely around his head. He carried a long vorpal dagger in addition to his sword, and his white uniform was decorated with the purple and gold of the elven King's personal guard.

Then came the brothers, Leth and Gerruth. They were unmistakably kin. Their sharp chins, round faces, and laughing green eyes were nearly identical. They both wore the green and white of Alka's Inarr Regiment.

The other two Legionnaires were youngsters, Drup and Alve. Drup wore the colors of the Endaleof Rangers, and Alve came from the Istagothe Regiment. Each was barely two hundred years old, and, like Dacius, they had inherited their weapons from their fathers.

Finally, there was Captain Rone and his two surviving crewmen: Zubec and Pardec.

They were a motley assortment. Ten men, counting himself, who might hold the fate of the Realm in the strength of their sword arms and their courage. He listened to the elves' conversation, trying to gauge their frame of mind.

"How can this be?" Gerruth asked. "The Ill-creatures were vanquished during the war, their breeding pits destroyed. How have they returned?"

"The power of evil is great," Thildemar said. "The Dark One was not destroyed, and he has discovered a way to bring his creatures back to the Realm. The how does not matter, only the what."

"That is right!" Gerruth said. "And we know the what we are up against. We served in the Wizards' War—at least some of us did. Ten men to turn back the Dark One's tide, it's impossible. What hope do we have?"

"We have the hope in our hearts," Thildemar replied. "The High Bishop knows our strength. He would not send for us if he did not believe we could succeed. Our duty is clear. We must go to Norivika and discover what must be done. We have no other option."

"He is right, Gerruth," Leth said, laying a hand on his brother's shoulder. "We must continue."

The others nodded agreement, though Dacius saw signs of nervousness in

Alve and the two seamen. It was a sentiment he understood all too well. If just one Ill-creature had destroyed their ship, what would a host of them do?

But Gerruth was not done. "During the war we had the power of the wizards at our side. Doesn't this concern you, Thildemar?"

"Of course it does," the old elf said evenly. "But it is not something I am able to control. All I have to offer is my courage and my loyalty, to the Realm and to the Holy Land."

Gerruth shook his head. "So many dead," he said. "Our brothers, our fathers, all lost for nothing. Must we fight the same war again, pay the same price?"

There was a long silence, broken finally by the voice of Simon. "Gerruth, if you tire of battle, then turn over your weapon to someone who will fight. The Realm needs defenders."

Gerruth started at the remark. He looked to his brother for support. "No," he said. "No, it's not that I am unable to fight—but my heart grows weary at the bloodshed. I had hoped that we would never have to suffer that cost again."

"As did we all," Thildemar said. "As did we all."

Silence hung in the air as each man considered what had been said. Now was the time to sway them.

Dacius stood. "None of us wants this," he said. "But we all understand what must be done. The Realm needs us. The High Bishop has summoned us. And we must not fail." He looked around, catching the eye of each. "Take heart. The Dark One does not move against us because he thinks we cannot succeed. He fears us. I don't know why, but he does. Already he has failed to keep us from reaching the Holy Land. Take heart, Legionnaires. This is what we were born for. We will not fail."

Dacius saw the men respond to his words. Even Gerruth nodded confidently.

Dacius turned to face Rone. "Captain," he said, "you and your men are free to choose your own course. We are at the border to the Holy Land. I consider your charter to be fulfilled, and will recommend that whatever payment you are owed be sent to whatever port you specify."

"Your pardon, Lord Gemine," Rone said, "but I never let anyone but myself decide when my job is done. I signed on to make sure your party arrived in Norivika, and that's what I aim to do."

"Excellent." Dacius walked over to where the party's supplies were stored and removed three of the spare vorpal blades. He went back to the table and set them down in front of the sailors. "Then arm yourselves. I will not have you go into battle again unprepared."

The seamen picked up the weapons carefully. "We can kill the monsters with these?" Pardec asked.

"No," Thildemar said. "It is impossible to kill them, because they are not alive. But powerful magic can break the connection to the flesh they animate. A mortal strike with a vorpal weapon drives their soul back to Firesta, or Hel as the humans name it. The weaker Ill-creatures may be destroyed by any substantial wound. Strong demons, like the one we faced last night, will fall only to the most deadly of strikes."

A knock at the door interrupted them. Dacius turned and saw a Legion officer walking through the open portal. "Greetings," the man said, "I am Commander Thean. I trust you have had time to recover from your ordeal?"

"Yes," said Dacius. "And we thank you for your gracious hospitality." He quickly introduced the other members of his party.

"Well met," Thean said. "My sentry tells me you have urgent business in the Holy City. Is there any assistance I can provide for your mission?"

Dacius glanced down at his bare feet. "Well," he said, "we could use re-provisioning and some fresh uniforms, and horses to speed our journey."

"Of course," Thean said. "Our primary function these days is to serve as a way station for travelers and caravans. We should be able to find clothes to fit all of you, though I doubt we can match your unit colors. Will you be leaving tonight or in the morning?"

Dacius considered. He felt strong and refreshed after the combined efforts of the healers and the cooks, but he was still tired. They were all drained from the stresses of the last day and night. "In the morning," he said.

"Wonderful," said Thean. "I'll have my quartermaster see to your provisioning. And, if you are interested, I would be honored to give you a tour of the garrison."

"That is kind of you," Dacius said. "I would like that very much, as soon as I find some boots."

Thean laughed. "I'll send in the quartermaster. Come by my office when you are ready."

Dacius made a quick list of supplies they would need and handed it to the quartermaster when he arrived. Almost immediately, a messenger returned bearing a pair of black leather boots. The fit was not perfect, but it would do. Dacius left to find the commander.

Thean was waiting for him, and the tour began immediately. It was dusk, and the darkness leached the color from the battlement, where silhouettes of sentries could be seen passing between the merlons. Torches and cauldrons illuminated the outer courtyard, throwing shadows into the empty niches of the wall. Dacius looked into the pools of darkness and tried not to think of the Ill-creatures.

"Your garrison is nearly a fortress," he said. "We should sleep safely tonight."

"Why thank you, Lord Gemine," Thean said, leading him around the perimeter of the outer courtyard. "I am proud to say that I had something to do with it; military construction is something of a hobby for me. The outer wall is entirely new. We completed it only three months ago. Much of the work was done by my own men, though engineers from the Holy Land gave us help on some of the more intricate details."

Thean pointed across the yard to the older and smaller stonework. "The inner wall was the garrison's original bulwark. As you can see, we are still working to extend its walls and connect it to the outer fortifications. We also plan to remodel its defensive emplacements and raise the battlements an additional three cubits. By the time we are finished, this will serve as a model garrison for future construction."

Thean beamed in obvious pride at his accomplishment, and Dacius had to admit that it was an impressive structure.

Thean led him through the gate to the inner courtyard. "You may have noticed that there is no outer wall on the north face. We built only two connecting catwalks to the walls of the previous fortification. This is because of the unique location of this garrison."

"Unique?" Dacius asked. "In a strategic sense?"

"The north wall coincides exactly with the Barrier which separates the Holy Land from the rest of the Realm. The protection of the Holy Land shields us from attack from the north. It also provides us with the perfect avenue of retreat if we are overrun. We simply walk through the north gate and the power of the Holy Land shelters us."

Dacius had heard of the sphere of protection that shielded the lands of Talan. "I am curious," he said. "Why is the garrison built outside of the Barrier?"

Thean laughed genially. "Let me guess, Lord Gemine. This the first time you have been to the Holy Land?"

"True," said Dacius. "This is my first visit."

"Then come with me." The commander led him to the north gate. Unlike the southern fortifications, this gate had no parapet to protect it, no portcullis to block its passage. In fact, there wasn't even a gate. It was simply an open portal in the stone wall. As a defense, it seemed ludicrous. Anyone could circle around to enter it.

A sentry saluted them sharply as they approached. He recorded their names in a logbook, and then waved them through the opening.

Dacius examined the boundary between Talan and the garrison. There was no visible wall, but the air on the other side looked different, as if he were looking through a glass or into a clear pool. He stepped through the portal—and his world changed.

His senses came alive, clearer than he had ever known was possible. Every nerve tingled with acute awareness. The vitality of the earth, the splendor of the sky; he saw it all as plainly as he saw his own hands. His nostrils filled with the mingled scents of wild grasses and the salty sea. A gentle breeze flowed across his face like a mother's touch. The wind, the birds, insects, even his own heartbeat combined to serenade his ears in perfect harmony.

They walked a short distance into the field. An easy power flowed into Dacius' legs, as if he were drawing strength from contact with the land. He felt relaxed, soothed. Fear and uncertainty fell from his mind. He did not need to worry about protecting himself; there was no danger here. If he had not known better, Dacius would have said he was being seduced by wine or strong ale—except that his consciousness was focused, precise.

Dacius knew that his jaw hung open in amazement, but that was fine. A man should be amazed to feel such beauty. He looked at Thean and smiled at the beatific look on the commander's face.

"Now you understand," Thean said. "There would be no point in building a garrison inside the Barrier. Violence is impossible here."

He was right. The land itself radiated harmony and preservation. There was no threat of evil in the Holy Land. Dacius *knew* that he was safe here. He looked down at the vorpal blade which hung at his side. What a useless object. He couldn't imagine drawing it, using it in battle: not here, not in the midst of such perfection.

Commander Thean followed his gaze. "Ah, you begin to feel the second reason for keeping the garrison outside of Talan. Legionnaires who are exposed to the bliss of the Holy Land for too long risk losing their fighting spirit. Some find that even after they return to the world outside they can no longer serve the Legion. They are unable to take up arms, even in defense. Some never leave the Holy Land at all."

He gestured back toward the gate. "Each of us makes his own decision whether to return or to stay. For myself, it is my family which keeps me wearing the crossed swords. My brother is a carpenter, my father, a farmer in the Tarim Valley. They live in a world where this harmony is just a dream. That world is out of balance, full of evil, greed, disharmony. But it has its own beauty, too, and it is worth protecting."

Family. Dacius thought of his own family, long buried under the warm hills of Norden West. Death was so cruel, so unnecessary. It unbalanced Creation. He had killed a score of goblins during the Hordeland Wars. Did one imbalance serve to correct the other? No, it was all disharmony. But beyond the Barrier, the world was disharmony. He thought of his homeland, pictured it overrun with Ill-creatures. Thean was right. That was something he would fight to prevent.

"This is what I fight for," Dacius said, "but I believe it could ruin a knight. I am amazed that your men can stay away."

"It requires true discipline," Thean said. "And it is another reason for my construction projects; keeps them too busy to think about what they're missing."

Dacius looked around, trying to take in the wonder of Creation. "Is this the way the world is supposed to be?"

"I believe so," said Thean. "The Old Book says that during Creation's beginnings the races were in balance with the world. Death was unknown and the harmony of the Sphere was perfect. Somehow, a Flaw was introduced to Creation, and the world drifted out of balance. But the Holy Land stayed pure. It is a reservoir of the original unity, an example of what the world should be: a place of sanctuary for the weak, healing for the injured, comfort for the troubled in spirit. It is, indeed, what we fight for."

Dacius felt the truth of the man's words, the truth of the harmony that surrounded him. As a boy, he had been taught the stories of Creation and the Creator, but they had seemed abstract, unimportant. Now, the reality behind those stories filled him. This was how the world was meant to be, how it could be again.

Suddenly, a scream tore through the night air. It was discordant, abrasive. More screams. They were coming from the gateway. The garrison! It was under attack.

Commander Thean was already running for the gate. The pacifism of this region did not mean a person could not be aware of danger, or that he could not hurry.

Dacius drew his vorpal sword and followed, though at the moment he could not think of using it for any violent purpose. As soon as he passed through the Barrier, blue light shone forth from his blade, and the violence in his nature surged back. An Ill-creature was near. "Thean, order your men into the Holy Land! They do not have the weapons to fight this."

But the commander did not hear. He was far across the inner courtyard, heading for the sounds of combat.

Dacius ran for the inner gate. The outer courtyard was filled with chaos. Legionnaires poured from barracks and dining halls, rushing to man the defenses. A half-dozen officers were shouting orders, trying to organize their men, but with little success. Shouts of combat and the clash of arms sounded from the area of the front gates. Dacius pressed himself through the crowd, forcing his way to the visitor's hall. His men were arranged in a half circle around the entrance, weapons bared and glowing brightly.

"Thildemar, you're with me," Dacius said. "Simon, take the rest of the men and start organizing a retreat for the garrison personnel. They must fall back to the Holy Land. Then establish a defensive position at the inner gate. The outer wall is too long for the few of us to man."

Dacius and Thildemar worked their way toward the front gates. As they approached, details of the battle were clear. Four dark forms stood on the parapet near the gatehouse. Somehow they had scaled the battlements and established a position on the wall. They were covered head to foot in gleaming black armor, and the visors on their helms revealed glowing yellow eyes.

"By the Creation," Thildemar exclaimed. "Tenebrites." He shouted at the Legionnaires on the wall. "Fall back! They are shadow knights; you can't fight them! Fall back to the Holy Land!"

But the guardsmen stood their ground. Commander Thean was rallying a defense around the upper entrance to the gatehouse. Another group of guardsmen threatened the Tenebrites' rear, but their attack was useless.

Two of the shadow knights turned to face the attack from the rear. The others advanced steadily on the gatehouse. The sword and arrows of the Legionnaires bounced ineffectually off their armor. Methodically, they moved through the defenders, cutting down man after man with their dark gray blades.

Dacius and Thildemar sprinted for the nearest stairs. They pushed their way through the defenders, shouting for the guardsmen to fall back. They broke through the front ranks and came face-to-face with the shadow knights.

Thildemar sprang forward in a lightning attack. His sword slashed across one Tenebrite's chest, carving a tracer of blue flame in his armor. The shadow knight made no sound, but he staggered away from the attack. The elf pressed his advantage, driving the monster backward.

Dacius had no more time to admire Thildemar's technique. He moved forward to engage the second Tenebrite. This close, he could see that there were no joints in the Ill-creature's armor; it was a single piece, like the smooth shell of a beetle. Dacius struck toward the Tenebrite's head, but the creature parried. When their blades met, some of the blue light faded from Dacius' sword, and the shadow knight's weapon started to shine with dim red light. The Tenebrite was leaching magic from his vorpal blade!

The realization threw Dacius off balance, destroying the rhythm of his attack. The shadow knight counterattacked with a series of heavy strikes, and Dacius was forced to give ground. The creature's technique was basic, but it had incredible power. It was all Dacius could do to parry the cuts without being driven from the wall. And with each clash of steel, the light of his sword dimmed and the red blade grew brighter.

Suddenly, Thildemar appeared behind the shadow knight. The elf's vorpal blade carved a deep gouge in the Tenebrite's side, and then swung upward and struck through the monster's neck. The Ill-creature burst into flame, reducing itself to ashes in the span of a few heartbeats, and the glow of Dacius' sword regained its intensity.

"Do not fight them with power," the elf said. "Use speed. It is too dangerous to cross swords with them repeatedly."

Dacius nodded his understanding, and they both raced to cross the span of the gate.

The battle at the other tower had not gone well. A dozen corpses decorated the battlement, all wearing Legion colors. Thean stood alone at the steps to the gatehouse, fighting a desperate delaying action. He launched no attacks of his own, but merely tried to stand his ground, parrying the shadow knights' attacks and keeping them from advancing. But they were too powerful. One of the Tenebrites forced him away from the stairwell, and the other headed down into the gatehouse.

"Cover!"

The shout from behind caused Dacius and Thildemar to drop immediately to the ground. Someone had brought a ballista to bear from the tower behind them. A loud thrum announced its firing, and the heavy volt flashed above their heads.

The missile struck the shadow knight full in the back. A tremendous crack thundered in the air as it shattered against the Tenebrite's armor. Shards of wood filled the air around it—but the creature was unaffected. It took advantage of the momentary confusion to drive through Thean's guard and separate the commander's head from his body with a single stroke.

A rumble from below betrayed the raising of a portcullis. Dacius jumped up and saw that Thildemar was already on his feet, running for the stairs. The Tenebrite who had killed Commander Thean was moving to intercept the elf. "Secure the gate!" Dacius shouted, taking up a guarding position at the top of the stairs. "This one is mine."

Dacius faced the shadow knight, feeling the rage rise within him. His face was hot with blood, and a scream came, unbidden, to his lips. He had to channel the anger, control it, use it to fuel his attack.

He feinted toward the Tenebrite's head. When the creature moved to block, Dacius dived to the ground, redirecting his slash toward the creature's leg. The vorpal sword bit deeply, dropping the shadow knight to the ground. Dacius continued his roll, coming to his feet behind the crippled monster. With a powerful lunge, he drove the tip of his blade into the Tenebrite's back. The Ill-creature exploded into flames and smoke.

Dacius ran down the stairs. There was no one in the gatehouse, but a quick glance showed that both portcullises had been jammed open. Sounds of combat rang from outside the open door to the main gate. Dacius charged through the portal.

Thildemar fought the final Tenebrite just inside the main gate. The shadow knight had a dozen scars of blue fire decorating his armor, but his sword was a brilliant flame, far brighter than the faint blue ember of the elf's sword. The Tenebrite pressed the attack, and Thildemar was forced to retreat, dodging whenever possible rather than meeting the monster's sword.

Dacius rushed at the shadow knight's flank, forcing it to abandon its attack. He planned to force the Tenebrite to face him, giving Thildemar a chance to finish from behind.

But the Ill-creature did not meet his charge. Instead, it ran backward, creating a cushion of space between itself and the Legionnaires. The creature's legs blurred, dissolving into shadow. The darkness swelled and transformed, re-solving itself into a long chitinous trunk, flanked by six segmented legs. The Tenebrite loomed above them, a distorted hybrid of mounted knight and giant insect. It whirled and ran toward the front gate, giving its back to the Legion-naires.

Dacius jumped forward, but surprise had delayed his reaction by a heartbeat. The creature reached the gate before he could close the distance. The Tene-brite's glowing red sword rose high in the air and shot down like a bolt of lightning. The bar which secured the gates was a beam of oak, nearly a cubit deep and a half cubit wide, but it shattered like dry kindling under the impact.

An instant later, Dacius's vorpal sword sliced through the shadow knight's spine. The Ill-creature flared and dissolved into ash, but already the gates were being forced open. Dozens of grotesque black forms pushed through the opening. The creatures were twisted horribly, as if some madman had randomly assembled body parts from a dozen species of man and animal. The Ill-creatures rushed through the gate, overrunning the outer courtyard.

Dacius and Thildemar retreated into the gatehouse and barred the door.

"What are those?" Dacius asked.

"Vikhors," the elf said. "Too many for us to fight in the open."

Dacius nodded. "We need to reach the inner fortifications. The courtyard is impassable, so we'll have to use the catwalk."

They climbed the stairs. On the battlements, they were joined by a handful of guardsmen who had been on the wall when the gates opened. Dacius took the lead, guiding them toward the west tower. Thildemar assumed a position in the rear, guarding against any Ill-creatures who climbed onto the parapets be-hind them.

The courtyard below was filled with turmoil. A dozen or more Legionnaires had been trapped in the courtyard. The vikhors had surrounded them and were slowly tearing them apart with sharp claws and jagged fangs. Scattered among the vikhors, Dacius spotted two more shadow knights, towering above the chaos in their grotesque centaur forms.

The Legionnaires made the tower without being spotted. But as they headed north along the west wall, a dark figure crawled out of the shadows ahead of them. Drool glistened on the vikhor's fangs as it advanced on Dacius. It reached out for him with an oversized claw.

Dacius sprang forward, driving the point of his blade through the creature's heart. The vikhor screamed horribly as its body dried up and crumbled like burnt charcoal.

Dacius cursed his luck. The scream called attention to their position. Al-ready, a dozen vikhors were howling in answer as they raced for the tower stairs. They moved much faster than a man could run.

"Run for the catwalk!" Dacius screamed, standing aside and pushing the first of the guardsmen ahead of him. He let all of the garrison personnel file past, and then joined Thildemar in the rear.

Dacius and the elf moved backward in unison. Before they had gone a dozen steps, the first vikhors were upon them. The Legionnaires fought a retreating action, giving ground steadily but not letting the vikhors force them out of position. The narrow parapet was their ally. It kept the vikhors from flanking them or overrunning them with numbers. Their swords built a web of deadly light that held the Ill-creatures at bay.

They retreated until the catwalk to the inner fortifications appeared at Dacius' left side. He started to move onto it, but there was no way to do so without breaking the solidarity of the joint defense.

"Run for it," Thildemar yelled. "I will hold them off."

"No, we go together or not at all." Dacius lunged forward in attack. The move caught the lead vikhors by surprise. He pierced one through the neck, and hamstrung another as he disengaged. "Now!" he cried.

Thildemar leaped nimbly sideways, taking a secure stance on the catwalk. Dacius dropped back into position next to the elf, and they continued their retreat.

Dacius heard the ring of metal on metal from behind him. Good, the guardsmen were hammering out the pins which secured the end of the walkway. As they drew closer to the sound a voice called out to them.

"Lord Gemine, on three! One! Two! . . ."

As one, Dacius and Thildemar jumped backward, clearing the end of the catwalk and landing amid steadying hands on the inner wall. The catwalk collapsed, dropping the vikhors a dozen cubits or more to the floor of the courtyard.

One of the monsters managed to leap forward, catching the top of the wall with a single hand. It pulled itself upward with incredible strength, but Thildemar was there. A single stroke of his sword severed the vikhor's hand, sending the creature falling to the ground below. The separated claw burst into blue flames, but retained its hold on the wall until Thildemar kicked it loose.

One of the vikhors still standing on the far wall threw itself into the air, but the distance was too great. It plummeted to the ground, striking with an impact that would have crippled any living creature. But the vikhor was unharmed. It rose to its feet and joined the mob attacking the inner gate. The other vikhors on the wall leaped to join it.

The Legionnaires ran down the spiraled stairs and through the archway that led to the inner courtyard. The field was nearly empty. Most of the guardsmen had already fled through the north gate, and Dacius' company, under Simon's charge, manned the battlements of the inner gate.

"Fall back!" Dacius shouted to his men. "The garrison is cleared. It serves no purpose to fight here."

The elves broke from the wall and ran for the north gate. As they reached the courtyard, vikhors swarmed over the top of the wall. Rather than be slowed by the stairs, the Ill-creatures jumped from the fortifications, crashing to the ground and then rising again to give chase.

Dacius and Thildemar took up guard positions to either side of the north gate, making sure it stayed clear for the retreat. The vikhors were still far behind when the last of the Legionnaires disappeared into the Holy Land.

"That's the last," Dacius said. "Time to leave."

As he turned to follow his men, Dacius saw a flash of black wing out of the corner of his eye. He lunged to the side, knocking Thildemar to the ground. Huge black talons ripped the air where the elf had stood just a moment before. Dacius rolled to his feet and stared into the eyes of the winged demon that had attacked the *Otan Stin*.

The creature crouched in front of the north gate, wings outstretched. Even hunched over, it towered over the Legionnaires.

I REMEMBER YOU, MORTAL. The demon extended its right claw. A dim blue stripe marked the spot where Dacius's sword had landed. A thinner scar marked the creature's belly, and a jagged line ran garishly through its left shoulder. **YOU ARE THE ONE WHO COULD NOT KEEP ME FROM KILLING HIS FRIEND.**

The voice pounded into Dacius's mind. And with it came fear. Terror gripped his heart, froze his limbs, the same terror he had felt aboard the *Otan Stin*. The Ill-creature did this, forced this upon him. And if the fear did not come from within, then he was not truly afraid.

Dacius lifted his vorpal sword, fighting to control the trembling in his arm. "I am the one who will bury his blade in your heart, demon."

His words broke the Ill-creature's spell. Thildemar moved forward, slashing at the monster's left side. The demon pulled away from the attack, placing his right side toward the elf. It was hurt. The wounds Alka had given it were not yet healed.

The demon blocked Thildemar's next strike and drove the elf to the ground with a slashing wing. **FOOLISH CHILD, IT IS TIME YOU LEARNED TO BOW BEFORE YOUR MASTERS.**

Dacius circled to attack the creature's vulnerable side, but the monster was ready for him. The clawed right hand shot out, unleashing a ball of pulsing flame. Dacius lunged out of the sphere's path, but the fire struck the wall behind him, causing it to explode. A fragment of stone drove into Dacius' skull, stunning him. He fell to the ground, his vorpal sword slipping from numbed fingers.

Laughter echoed in his mind, ringing through the pain. **IT IS OVER, MORTALS. YOUR LIVES ARE AS SHORT AS YOUR HOPE. BE ASSURED, I SHALL NOT MAKE IT PAINLESS.**

The demon raised its hand. Lightning coursed from its fingers, arcing downward to surround Dacius and Thildemar. It flowed over their bodies, burning them with a thousand tiny sparks.

Dacius writhed on the ground. Every inch of his body burned under the attack. His muscles spasmed uncontrollably, twisting his body into unnatural contortions. Blood seeped from his eye sockets, and his tongue swelled, closing his throat. By the Creator, he had never known there could be such agony!

Suddenly, the assault ended. There might have been a scream, but he couldn't be sure. Dacius struggled to his feet, trying to make his eyes focus.

The Ill-creature was staggering away from the gate. A glowing dagger protruded from its back, fitted precisely between the shoulder plates. It was Simon's knife; the elf must have thrown it from the other side of the Barrier.

Now they could finish it. Dacius grabbed for his sword. His fingers would not unclench, so he gripped it awkwardly between his wrists. He saw Thildemar struggling to his feet near the far side of the gate. But a horde of vikhors was charging; it would be disaster to dally here. "Run!" he shouted, lurching toward the portal.

The Legionnaires staggered through the portal together, just a few steps ahead of the charging monsters. Dacius felt the peace of the Holy Land take hold of him, soothing his pain. He turned back to look through the Barrier.

The demon had managed to remove the vorpal blade from its back. It cradled the blade in a massive claw, staring at it. Then it closed its hand. Red flames surrounded the fist, burning with blinding intensity for the space of three or four heartbeats. Then the monster opened its hand. The magical blade had been reduced to a pool of glowing slag. The Ill-creature let the liquid run through its fingers onto the ground, and then turned to face the Barrier.

The creature stared at them for a moment. Then it opened its jaws and hissed menacingly. When it spoke, it used a voice like steel grinding on stone, not the voice in the mind that Dacius had heard before. "Look at me, children, you who cower behind this wall of lies. Look at the face of your death. I know you. I know the doubts in your mind, the terror in your hearts. You are doomed. Your mission is hopeless. In the end, you will fail. And when you do, I will be there, waiting. I am Throm. We will meet again. Remember that, and pray to your Creator that I will be merciful, though it will do you no good."

The Ill-creature placed one claw on either side of the gate. Lightning shot through the stone. The wall exploded, collapsing into a pile of rubble that blocked their view of the courtyard.

Wearily, Dacius examined his fellow Legionnaires. He could feel the depth of their sorrow, the pain of their loss. The power of the Holy Land filled him, making their emotions plain to him. Dacius felt the security, the harmony, the beauty of Creation. But the comfort, the sense that all was right in the world, that was gone.

He turned to the north and started walking.

❦ 6 ❧

Holy Land

A'stoc rooted around in his laboratory, searching for some artifact or another that he thought they needed for the trip. It was infuriating; he seemed oblivious to the urgency of their mission. After the mage had retrieved the Staff, Chentelle thought they would leave immediately. But the man had spent hours collecting supplies, including a prodigious amount of wine for such a short journey. At least he had found a shirt for Sulmar to wear, though the sleeves had needed to be cut back.

"A'stoc—" Chentelle said.

"I told you before, elf girl," the mage snapped, "we'll leave when I have everything I—Hah! There it is." He held a small crystal globe in his hand.

"Is that the last?" Chentelle asked. "Are you ready to leave, now?"

"Yes, that's the last." A'stoc carried the crystal up the stairs and stowed it in his pack. He pointed to the far side of the cavern. "Those stairs lead up to the top of the cliff. A stone doorway blocks the exit; I'm sure you will have no difficulty opening it. Wait for me outside the cavern."

"Wait for you?" Chentelle said. "I've been waiting for you for hours. I thought you said you were ready."

"I am ready," he snarled. "But I will not leave my home without securing it from intrusion. Now go. The defenses I set will attack anyone other than myself who sets foot in the cavern."

Chentelle felt the blood rush to her face. "Oh, I'm sorry. I'll wait for you on the surface."

Sulmar waited for her at the base of the stairs. The Tengarian had her pack slung over his shoulder. He looked quite striking in A'stoc's black shirt, though it had taken some urging to convince him to accept the mage's gift. Chentelle smiled at the Tengarian as she passed.

A'stoc's voice followed them up the spiral stairs. At first, Chentelle could make out grumbles of complaint. Then the tone shifted as A'stoc started chanting his incantations. Finally, the sound died away completely, lost in the depths behind them.

Unfortunately, their light was also fading rapidly. The adartak crystals became fainter the farther they moved from the mage's power. Chentelle was forced to pick her way carefully over the uneven steps.

"Mistress?"

Sulmar's voice had an odd quality, an uncertainty that she had not heard from him before. She looked back and saw that he was many steps behind, almost out of view. Of course, human eyesight was notoriously poor in dim light. He was climbing blind. "I'm here, Sulmar, just a few steps above you. Hold still. I'll see if I can bring us more light."

Chentelle reached out with her Gift, intending to call more illumination from the adartak, but the air was filled with power. She could feel strands of energy shifting in the air all about her. It had to be part of A'stoc's warding spell. The balance of forces was delicate. If she interfered with it by channeling power into the adartak, she might disrupt the wards. She didn't even want to think about how A'stoc would react to that.

She walked back down the steps and took hold of her liegeman's hand. "I guess we'll have to do this the hard way."

Sulmar's arm was rock hard with tension. She could feel his unease, his sense of helplessness. Being led blindly through the dark destroyed the warrior's equilibrium. His skin was slick with sweat, and his breathing sounded thunderous in the cramped stairway.

Chentelle wanted to say something, to reassure him. But what could she say that he didn't already know? She couldn't even speed their journey. Whenever she tried to increase the pace, Sulmar stumbled or tripped on the stone stairs.

She pushed her sensitivity upward, feeling for the accumulation of power that she knew would mark the doorway. The energy of the wards made it confusing, and she had to keep some of her concentration to guide Sulmar, but there seemed to be—yes, there it was. "Almost there," she said. "Just a moment longer."

She sang out softly, sending her Gift upward, overturning the delicate equilibrium which held the doorway. Light poured into the tunnel, gently at first, but with increasing intensity as they circled upward to the doorway. Chentelle felt relief fill her liegeman as the pathway became clear to his sight. She released his hand and danced lightly up the remaining steps.

They emerged on the top of a high cliff. Chentelle shielded her eyes against the glare and looked around. Deneob was almost directly overhead, leading her brighter sister on their journey through the sky. The top of the bluff was covered by a rich garden. The main crop was grapes, but potatoes, carrots, onions, and various greens were also in evidence. Below them, the Quiet Sea whispered softly against the rocky shore.

The boulder behind them rolled back, sealing the entrance to the cave. A'stoc stood just beyond the doorway, the *mandril* wand in one hand and the Thunderwood Staff gripped tightly in the other. The mage passed the wand over the boulder, chanting liquid syllables in some arcane tongue. The door seemed to melt into the hillside, becoming an unbroken slab of rock.

"You have a beautiful garden," Chentelle said.

"I thought you were in a hurry to leave," the mage said, walking brusquely toward the southeast. "Let's get on with it."

Chentelle glanced at Sulmar and shrugged. They caught up with A'stoc easily, but the set of his shoulders discouraged any further attempts at conversation. In silence, they began their journey.

They walked through meadows richer and more varied than Chentelle had ever seen. She saw dozens of flowers for which she had no name, spread out under the twin suns like a carpet of rainbow. Insects were woven all through the tapestry, decorating it with the music of grasshoppers and the dance of butterflies. The trill of songbirds blended with the soft sigh of the wind, adding the perfect counterpoint to the natural harmony.

The loveliness of the land buoyed Chentelle. The perfumes of a dozen blossoms blended in the air, and every breath filled her with beauty. She walked lightly, effortlessly, as if her feet barely touched the ground. The cadence of her steps blended smoothly into the rhythm of the natural orchestra.

Hours passed, and still Chentelle felt no fatigue. The open plains gave way to rockier terrain, and the patches of flowers became smaller. But the air was still thick with their fragrance. Scattered oaks began to appear, proffering cool patches of shadow beneath their spreading leaves.

The trees reminded her of home. Though this was only her third day away, already she missed the familiar forests of Lone Valley, so full of life and warmth and comfort. Her mind filled with memories: resting against Willow's roots, listening to the dendrifaun tell the same story for the hundredth time; singing with her mother, blending voices in the special harmony that only they shared. Tears came to her eyes at the thought of her mother. She would be so worried. Chentelle had thought to be returning by now. She sighed deeply, trying to release her guilt.

"You must be tired, elf girl," A'stoc said. "We will find shade and rest."

She started to protest, but stopped when she saw the exhaustion on A'stoc's face. Rivulets of sweat ran from his forehead, and his mouth hung open as if he lacked the strength to keep it shut. His feet barely cleared the ground as he shuffled forward, but she knew the mage would not admit his own fatigue. "Thank you," she said. "A rest would be welcome."

They called a halt under a large, double-trunked oak. Dual shadows fell to the east of the tree: one long and faint, the other shorter and darker. A'stoc dropped heavily to the ground and slid off his pack. He pulled out a flask of wine and started drinking from it. After several large swallows, he stopped drinking long enough to slide to the tree and lean against its trunk. Then he took another drink.

Chentelle and Sulmar sat down in the grass across from him. They broke into the stores he had provided and set up a quick meal of cheese and hard bread. Chentelle looked around, gesturing at the wildflowers and the clear azure sky. "This land is so open," she said, "so beautiful."

A'stoc regarded her with a bitter gaze. When he spoke, his voice was raspy with dust, fatigue, and wine. "You are amazingly cheerful, enchantress, for a bearer of such dark news."

"Wizard, it is too early to fall prey to despair," she said. "We are protected by Sulmar's sword and the power of your own magic. We will make it to Norivika."

The mage's lips twisted into a sneer, but the look in his eyes was pure sadness. "I told you before, elf girl, I am no wizard. My name is A'stoc. If you must refer to me by a title, then 'woodright' is the appropriate term, though 'apprentice' is perhaps more accurate." He took a long, long drink of wine and tossed the empty flask into the grass.

"You should not drink so heavily."

A'stoc seemed confused for a moment, then he turned to face Sulmar. "Ah, the Tengarian speaks. Why do you give a damn how much I drink?"

"I do not want to carry you," Sulmar said flatly.

"Why you—" A'stoc started to jump up in anger, but stopped himself suddenly. He settled back against the tree. His face relaxed into a calm mask, but something burned in his eyes as he glanced from Sulmar to Chentelle and back again.

"What an unlikely pair you are," he said mockingly. "I wonder what it was that bound you to her service. Gold, perhaps? I have known many a Tengarian who believed honor and gold were two sides of the same coin. No, I think perhaps you seek something more precious, though less tangible. Tell me, when did you meet our innocent young enchantress?"

"Yesterday," Sulmar answered.

"Yesterday?" A'stoc snapped his head around to face Chentelle. "Is this true? You have known this man for one day and you make him privy to all our secrets? Have you not seen the brand on his arm? Even I can feel the evil it embodies. He is accursed, a servant of evil. Perhaps it is he who sets the Ill-creatures on our path."

Chentelle shook her head. "Sulmar is marked by evil, but he is not evil himself. I *know* this, just as I know that you are not evil, for all your bitterness and despair. Sulmar is not allied with the Dark One. It was he who was being attacked by an Ill-creature when I encountered him. I trust him with my life, A'stoc."

The mage closed his eyes and rolled away from her, onto his side. He kept the Thunderwood Staff clenched tightly to his chest. "You trust him with more than that, enchantress," he said softly.

Chentelle could see A'stoc's hands tremble with the effects of alcohol and exhaustion. She picked up her leatherbark waterskin and walked over to where he lay. "You need rest, A'stoc, for your mind and your body. We have a fair journey ahead, but we can wait a few minutes before continuing. And, please, drink water. It will help you more than wine."

A'stoc curled more tightly around the Staff. "If you would have me rest, elf girl, then leave me in peace."

"Let me touch you, wiz—A'stoc. I can ease your fatigue." She extended one hand toward his back.

"No!"

Chentelle could feel the man's fear. It was evident in the way he clutched the Staff. The inability to command the Thunderwood Staff mocked him. It was a symbol of the failure and frustration that were central to his world. In his heart, he felt that he was nothing but failure, and he was afraid that he would fail again. She set the water down gently beside him, and walked away from the tree.

She sat down on a granite outcrop surrounded by daisies and rested in the warm sun. A light breeze eddied across the field, tossing her hair about her shoulders and catching up the trees and the grass in its dance. She hummed softly, letting herself drift with the song of the prairie. A lone butterfly floated toward her over a sea of flowers. It landed gracefully on her outstretched hand, winking its large, orange wings in silent salutation. Then it took flight again, whirling merrily around Chentelle's head.

She laughed. "Okay, little fellow, as you wish."

She looked over to the shade tree where they had stopped. A'stoc lounged against the tree, holding the waterskin in one hand. Sulmar had apparently finished his meal; he stood off to the side of the tree, where he could easily watch both A'stoc and herself.

Chentelle smiled and sang out with her Gift. She used no words, only the magic of pure, harmonious sound. It was a summoning song, much like the one she had used to call the dolphins, but simpler. This song contained no sense of need, no holes that required filling. It was a song purely about joy, about life, about the beauty of being together. It was a song about play.

And it was answered. Thousands of butterflies came flocking to Chentelle's call. They filled the air around her with motion and color. She started dancing, twirling to the music of her song. And the butterflies danced with her. She felt the feather touches of a thousand wings brushing her face, her arms, her lips. Some of the insects landed in her hair, forming a jewel-colored crown. The rest formed currents of color that flowed through the breeze, keeping perfect time with her song and her movements.

She let the music grow, expanding the dance until it encompassed A'stoc and Sulmar too. The butterflies swirled happily within the shape of her song, circling around her companions and bringing them into the dance. Sulmar swayed slowly back and forth, letting his body drift to the music's rhythm. A'stoc sat motionlessly, slack-jawed, shifting only to brush away one insect that was crawling toward his mouth.

Chentelle let her song come to an end. Gradually, the butterflies drifted away, returning to the pursuits from which she called them. Soon, only one was left: the orange butterfly that had first come to rest on her hand. It spun excitedly before her face, wings glittering in Ellistar's light.

Chentelle smiled and nodded. "You are quite welcome."

The insect came to rest lightly on her lips, then fluttered away.

A'stoc had gotten to his feet. He and Sulmar just stared at her from under the shade of the tree, looks of awe and wonder on their faces.

"I have never seen—never felt anything so beautiful, any magic so graceful," A'stoc said.

She felt so happy, so proud of the beauty she had helped create. But something in the way they looked at her made her feel self-conscious, and she turned her eyes shyly to the ground. "Are we ready to go on?"

A'stoc nodded absently, handing her the water bag and picking up his pack. He started walking, leading the party directly south, now.

They walked until the red light of Deneob sank below the horizon, leaving Ellistar alone in the sky to cast her long shadows. The flowered meadows gave way to grassy hills decorated sporadically with clusters of oak and cottonwood. As Ellistar, too, began to set in the west, they passed into a narrow valley formed by a small stream.

A'stoc came to a halt, leaning heavily on the Staff. "We will stop here for the night," he said, indicating a circular clearing within a copse of trees.

The mage did not look well. He wheezed with every breath and his legs trembled, even with the support of the Staff. Chentelle and Sulmar took his arm and helped him get settled against a tree. It was a measure of A'stoc's exhaustion that he did not protest their help. Once A'stoc was settled, Sulmar left to inspect the area around their camp.

"You need rest and warm food," she said. "I will heat up the rest of the stew you brought."

His hand shot out to catch her wrist as she turned to leave. "No," he said weakly. "No fire."

Of course, the servants of the Dark One moved freely at night. If they were being sought, a fire would betray their presence. Chentelle remembered her dream of the Ill-creature. She was embarrassed to have forgotten such an obvious precaution.

A'stoc stared at the lengthening shadows. "I had forgotten what it was like."

A glance at his face told Chentelle what he meant. Fear. He was remembering the terrors brought on by darkness. Images flashed through her mind, grotesque shapes materializing out of the night, tearing at her with hideous fangs and malformed claws. No not her, A'stoc, it was A'stoc's memory she was reliving. It must be something she retained from their moment of communion.

She peered into the twilight. The hills around their clearing were still plain to her eyes, as was the slender creek to the west. She could see nothing threatening, but she was unsure. She had heard tales of Ill-creatures that could fool even elven vision.

When Sulmar returned, he reported finding nothing to threaten them in the immediate area. They unpacked rations and the three of them shared a cold supper of stew, cheese, dried fruit, and the remaining bread. By silent agreement, Chentelle and Sulmar gave A'stoc the lion's portion of the food, and he pretended not to notice.

The mage looked better by the time they had finished their meal. He rummaged through his pack and brought out the orb that he had retrieved from his laboratory. He set the melon-sized crystal in a depression at the center of the clearing and pulled the *mandril* wand from the folds of his cloak. Then he walked around the perimeter of the camp, gesturing with the wand.

Chentelle felt the threads of power A'stoc was weaving into his spell. He anchored each strand to the orb, and spread the other end through the surrounding terrain. He built a balanced web covering the camp and everything within a hundred cubits, including Chentelle and Sulmar.

As A'stoc moved around the camp, a pinpoint of light started growing inside the orb. He completed his circle and returned to the clearing. Still chanting, he passed the wand around Chentelle's head, and she felt the strands fall away from her. Then he repeated the procedure with Sulmar.

The crystal sphere glowed, now, with the strength of a small candle, though the light was mostly shielded within the depression. A'stoc tapped the orb once with his wand, sending a quiver of tension through his spell. "Now we can sleep in peace. Anything larger than a raccoon that enters the detection spell will trigger the orb-light."

They spread their bedding under the trees and settled down for the night, serenaded by the rhythmic songs of crickets and nightbirds. Chentelle was spent from the long hike. She knew that as soon as she closed her eyes and relaxed she would fall asleep. But her mind refused to quiet down. She glanced at her companions.

Sulmar on his back, sleeping easily. His sword rested across his belly and both arms were outside the covering of his blanket: one on the hilt of the weapon, the other on its sheath.

A'stoc seemed to be asleep, but he was tossing fitfully. As Chentelle watched, his eyes snapped open, and he sat bolt upright. His breathing was heavy and sweat covered his face. After a moment, he realized that Chentelle was awake, too. He met her gaze and spoke to her in near whisper. "You said that you saw the threat of the Ill-creatures in your dreams. What else can your Gift show you?"

"I can sometimes see hints about the future," she answered. "Usually my dreams are of good things, not evil. Like the time my friend Erina fell in love with—"

"I get the idea," A'stoc interrupted, "but what about the past? Do you ever see into the past?"

It was nice to have him ask her questions for a change. "Well, when I touch an object that belonged to someone, I can sometimes get a sense of occurrences with strong emotional content. But most of the time what I discover is not very helpful."

A'stoc nodded thoughtfully, but did not speak. He seemed to be waging a silent debate with himself. Finally, he turned back to Chentelle. Slowly, he lifted the Thunderwood Staff and extended it to her. "Perhaps you can help me, enchantress. I must know whether you can unlock the Staff's power."

Chentelle was amazed. That A'stoc would allow her to touch it showed how much his trust, and his desperation, had grown. She could not refuse such a gesture.

She took the Staff in her hands, cradling it carefully. The wood felt warm to her touch, and she could almost swear she felt a pulse. She met A'stoc's eyes, seeing the mix of yearning and despair that warred on his face. "I will try."

She ran her hands along the Staff, introducing her fingers to the wood. Even without her Gift, the power of the Staff was obvious. It was solid in her hands yet somehow yielding, as if it were at one time both harder than rock and softer than her own skin. The carved runes blended perfectly with the natural curves of the timber, forming an impossibly smooth surface. Closing her eyes and taking a deep breath, Chentelle reached into the wood with her Gift.

Instantly, a barrage of emotions swept over her: hope, anger, frustration, despair. The feeling had the taste of A'stoc about them. In the long years he had possessed the Staff, his presence had become strong within it. Images formed, visions of bitterness and hopelessness. A'stoc spent all his energy studying the Staff, at first with A'mond and then alone. She felt the anguish of decades of failure.

She had to go further back. She pushed through the long period of frustration, reaching for the feelings below. Jealousy, anger, mistrust, betrayal. She saw A'stoc at the Collegium of Tel Adartak-Skysoar. The Councilors there refused to help him, fearing his power if he gained control of the Staff. He felt the covetousness of their concern and left the crystal tower in secret. He soon learned that his mistrust was well placed. Assassins followed him from the Collegium, trying to kill him and steal the Staff. They failed, but the attempt left him deeply scarred.

The memories were still too recent. She went deeper, past the wall of numbness that she knew represented A'stoc's time in the wasteland. She sought the core of power deep inside the wood, the essence shaped by A'pon Boemarre.

Suddenly agony shot through her soul, pain more terrible than she had ever imagined. She screamed, and the Thunderwood Staff fell from her lifeless fingers.

ॐ

Cold. That was the first thing she felt, cold that issued from somewhere deep inside of her. She couldn't stop shivering. Gradually, she became aware of other things. She was crying. Tears ran uncontrollably down her face, forming tiny pools in the earth. People were shouting in the distance. No, not in the distance, right above her. It was Sulmar.

". . . do not know what you have done, apprentice, but you will follow her into death."

Death? But she wasn't dead. Was she?

"It wasn't me," another voice said. A'stoc. It was A'stoc's voice, but it sounded strange, vulnerable. "Let me go. I may be able to help her."

Suddenly Chentelle remembered. She had been examining the Staff, trying to unlock its secrets, and she had felt— By the Creator, so much pain!

"Sulmar," her voice sounded weak, impossibly faint, but she had to make him hear. "Sulmar, it's all right. Don't hurt him."

The Tengarian was at her side in an instant, cradling her in his arms. "Mistress, you are alive! But how? I saw the way you lay. There was no life in your body."

His body was warm and Chentelle huddled against it, trembling. She tried to answer him, but she could not. Her tears came with renewed vigor, choking off her voice.

She was dimly aware of A'stoc rising to his feet and retrieving the Staff. "Enchantress?" he said.

She forced her body to unclench, releasing her death grip on Sulmar's warmth. But she couldn't make herself leave the comfort of his strength and surety. She wiped her eyes clear with his shirt and turned to face the mage. "I—I touched the spirit of A'pon Boemarre. I felt him unleash the Desecration. Oh, A'stoc, I felt his death. I am sorry. I can't find what you need. I can't reach past that wall of agony."

"No, enchantress, it is I who am sorry. Once again I let myself fall into the trap of hope, and this time it was you who paid the price." He turned to Sulmar. "I am going to sleep, now. If anything trips the orb-light, I trust that you will respond with your usual brutality and thoroughness."

Sulmar's body tensed at A'stoc's insult, but he did not respond. Instead he settled himself on the ground next to Chentelle, resheathing his sword. He seemed so strong, though she knew he was still recovering from his injuries. He wrapped his warmth gently around her, and they drifted into sleep.

Chentelle woke with a sense of wrongness. She lay still, listening, but she heard nothing. Then she understood. She heard nothing, not even the sound of insects. She called upon her Gift, stretching her awareness. A'stoc's spell still covered the camp, so she reached out to the hills farther away. Her mind felt the cool presence of the river and the quiet life of the grass and something else, something cold and terrible.

She sat up, waking Sulmar with her movement. She warned him to silence with a gentle finger on his lips, then slid quietly over to A'stoc's bedroll. She shook the mage gently by the shoulder and whispered into his ear. "A'stoc."

As soon as her hand touched him, she felt herself pulled into a dream.

৵

A'stoc is surrounded. Gnarled hands grapple with him, trying to wrest the Thunderwood Staff from his grip. Desperately, he pulls the Staff free from his attackers, but the wood shrivels and dies. Finally, it snaps like kindling in his hands. The world begins to wither all around him. Every creature calls his name with its last breath. "A'stoc. A'stoc. A'stoc!"

৵

The mage started, breaking contact with Chentelle. He blinked and rubbed his eyes in confusion. "What—?"

Chentelle placed her fingers over his lips. She put her own lips very close to his ear, so that they touched it when she spoke. "We must be quiet," she whispered. "Something comes."

She pointed across the river. A hunched figure could be seen silhouetted against the waning moon. It shambled down the hillside toward the water. At first, she thought it might be a misshapen old man, but the arms were too long, hanging nearly to the ground. The head was wrong, too, with brutish jaws and a squat, thick skull. The figure was naked but covered all over with coarse reddish hair.

"Hel's Pits," A'stoc muttered tersely. "A vikhor."

He rolled silently to his feet and started to gather up his things. "Hurry. Their senses are not sharp. We may be able to hide from it."

Chentelle and Sulmar quickly moved to help him. They removed everything from the clearing and hid behind the shelter of the trees.

"What did you call it?" Chentelle whispered softly.

"A vikhor. Animated flesh without a true soul. When vikhors kill, they take a fraction of that person's spirit for their own. If they kill enough to gain a soul, then they leave their bodies behind, becoming wraiths. So they have a nigh insatiable appetite for mayhem."

Chentelle started to ask what a wraith was, for she was not versed in the Lore of Ill-creatures, but stopped herself at the sound of splashing water.

The vikhor was crossing the river, padding easily through the shallow current. It emerged downstream of them, ambling along sometimes on two legs, or on three, or four. On occasion it even seemed to use its head as an appendage. No natural creature, certainly. It picked up speed scurrying into the east at an impressive pace.

"Thank the Creator," Chentelle whispered. She turned back to A'stoc and froze. The wizard stared past her shoulder, his face twisted into a mask of rage. She spun back around and had to stifle the urge to scream.

The vikhor had stopped running. It paused, cocking its head and looking about. Then it started walking directly toward their camp.

But why? How did it know where they were? Then Chentelle saw it, the orb-light. "A'stoc," she whispered frantically, "the crystal."

"I know," he said, barely managing to keep his voice to a whisper. "But I cannot deactivate the spell from here, and if I move into the clearing the vikhor will spot me anyway."

Chentelle wanted to cry out, to jump up and run, to do anything other than just sit there as the Ill-creature moved closer. Her body quivered with fear and blood hammered in her ears as the glowing yellow eyes approached the limit of A'stoc's wards.

Brilliant light flashed through the clearing. The vikhor yelped in pain, covering its eyes and shaking its head in surprise.

A'stoc leaped to his feet, aimed the *mandril* wand and shouted a spell. The wand flared, and a magic fireball flew from its tip. Flames engulfed the Ill-creature before it could react.

The vikhor vanished into a pile of ash, but in its death it gave a sudden, ferocious roar. The sound was horrible, deafening. It echoed through the narrow valley before fading into the distance.

Then it was answered. A chorus of howls came from the low hills on the other side of the river.

A'stoc raced into the clearing and grabbed the crystal sphere. He slipped it into his pack and hefted the weight onto his back. He looked at the sky for a moment, then turned to Chentelle. "We cannot risk a light. You will have to guide us to the high hills east of here."

Chentelle hesitated, unsure of what the mage wanted.

"Hurry," he growled. "If we keep moving we have a chance."

Chentelle scooped up her pack and started running east, staying close to the cover of trees whenever possible. She kept her pace slow and tried to use the most even paths, but still the humans had difficulty keeping up. A'stoc's labored wheezing was loud in her ears, and even Sulmar stumbled occasionally in the dim light. She eased her pace slightly so her companions would not hurt themselves.

"No," A'stoc gasped. "Do not slow. We will keep up."

As they moved away from the riverbed, the terrain became rougher and there were fewer trees to provide concealment. The hills were still half a league away, and they were all weakening. She pulled to a halt near the final cluster of trees. "A'stoc, we will lose our cover if we continue."

The mage did not stop running. He grabbed her pack as he passed, forcing her to stumble along with him. "Do as I say, elf girl! Make for the top of the nearest hill."

Chentelle pulled herself loose, fighting to keep her balance. "Fine," she said, but she felt terribly exposed as she led the way onto the open plain. As they neared the foot of the hill, she suddenly realized the mage's plan. A faint red glow in the sky promised that first-light was not far off. They scrambled up the hill.

It seemed more like a mountain. The slope was steep and the surface wet with dew, making purchase difficult. But they crawled with ragged determination, digging fingers into the hard dirt to pull themselves up the hillside. Finally, they reached the top. Staggering with exhaustion, they discarded their packs and faced back to check their trail.

At first, Chentelle thought maybe they had escaped detection. But then she saw a half-dozen riders emerge from the trees. For a moment she thought they might be a Legion patrol, but as they neared she saw that their armor was completely black, even to the horse's barding. No, not horses, the rhythm of their gallop was wrong—the beasts had too many legs. By the Creator, they weren't riding the beasts; they were a part of them!

"Shadow knights." A'stoc almost spit the words.

The creatures pulled to a halt at the base of the hill. Chentelle could see them clearly now. The upper body of an armored knight perched disgustingly on the body of a huge, black beetle. As she watched, one of the Ill-creatures lifted its two back legs off the ground and rubbed them together with blinding speed.

Chentelle clapped her hands over her ears. The shrill whine seemed to pierce her skull and scrape down the length of her spine. It was answered almost immediately by a series of howls from the surrounding countryside.

"They're coming," she cried. "What can we do?" But she knew the answer: nothing. They were exposed on the hilltop, with no avenues of escape.

A'stoc was not even looking at the Ill-creatures. He still scanned the horizon to the east. He turned to face her, shaking his head grimly. "I will have to fight them."

He removed the orb from his pack and set it on the ground. A quick spell called forth light from the crystal, illuminating the hilltop. A'stoc turned to face Sulmar. "Your sword is useless against these creatures. Stay behind me when they attack. You can't fight them, and I do not want you getting in my way."

A horde of vikhors converged at the bottom of the hill, arriving from all directions. Apparently they had been spread out to search, but now the search was done. The shadow knights stayed inhumanly still as the pack of vikhors swarming about them grew. Then, when perhaps a dozen of the twisted creatures were present, one of the knights lifted an arm. That slight motion sent the vikhors charging up the hill.

A'stoc moved to intercept them, *mandril* wand raised in one hand, Thunderwood Staff held uselessly in the other. He incanted a spell, and a fireball shot from the wand, engulfing the lead vikhor.

The Ill-creature howled in agony as the mystic flames reduced it to ash. Its fellows ignored the flames, continuing their charge. But the blaze did not die after it had consumed the vikhor.

Chentelle let her awareness expand, sensing the complex lines of force that still bound the mage to the fire. Now she understood. A'stoc hadn't just called forth fire from the wand, he had bound the fire to his will.

He gestured with the wand, never stopping his chant. The flames swirled into a whirlwind of fire. The cyclone shot up the hill, burning its way through a chain of vikhors before coming to a halt in front of the pack. Then it stopped spinning and spread itself into a wall of fire.

Now the vikhors had to acknowledge the mage's flame. It blocked their path up the hill. They scattered, circling the wall on both sides.

Sweat ran down A'stoc's face. He gestured with the *mandril*, and the wall divided into twin plumes of flame. One flare struck a group of four vikhors, igniting two of them and sending the others diving for cover. But the other flare wavered in the air and missed its mark. It set fire to some bushes but did nothing to stop the charge of the four vikhors on that flank. They circled around the hill, out of the mage's sight, and came up behind him.

"A'stoc, look out!" shouted Chentelle.

But the mage was exhausted, unable to sustain his spell. Both plumes of flame went out. The mage was chanting rapidly, trying to invoke another spell, but his attention was on the two Ill-creatures in front of him. He didn't notice the four closing from behind.

Chentelle reached out with her Gift and started to sing. She had no idea if it would have the same effect on the vikhors that it had on the sea creature, but she had to try. She filled her voice with harmony and tranquillity, and projected it at the vikhors.

The twisted Ill-creatures howled and writhed in pain. But then something happened. Their howling was so loud that it drowned out Chentelle's song. The Ill-creatures recovered and lunged toward her, never stopping their deafening roar.

Chentelle stumbled backward. One of the vikhors was almost upon her, its claws reaching out for her throat. She tripped over something and fell, screaming in fear.

But the vikhor did not reach her. Sulmar met its charge with a leaping kick, driving it backward into its packmates. The Tengarian landed in a balanced stance, hands held open before him. He kept himself between the vikhor and Chentelle, dodging and deflecting their attacks with uncanny precision.

He swept the feet from under one vikhor, and sent another tumbling over the fallen creature in one smooth motion. It would have been comical if the stakes were not so high. Sulmar kept three of the monsters tangled up with each other, but the fourth one disengaged, turning back to attack A'stoc from behind.

Chentelle shouted another warning.

The mage turned, lifting the *mandril* wand, but he was too slow. The vikhor was already on him. He dodged a vicious swipe at his face, stepping sideways and trying to bring his wand to bear. But the vikhor's elbow caught him on the backswing, slamming into the side of his head. A'stoc crumpled to the ground, wand and Staff falling from limp fingers.

The vikhor snatched up the Staff, holding it high above its head and bellowing in triumph.

A'stoc struggled to regain his feet. He lunged toward the vikhor, trying to pull the Staff from its hands. But the Ill-creature was too strong. It struck the mage in the face, knocking him contemptuously to the ground.

"No!" Chentelle cried. "Sulmar, help him!"

But the Tengarian was trapped in his own struggle, unable to break free of the three vikhors that attacked him. And more Ill-creatures were climbing the hill, soon to overwhelm them with numbers.

The vikhor attacking A'stoc suddenly moved toward Chentelle, raising the Thunderwood Staff high overhead, gripping it like a club. To it, the Staff was no more than a handy length of wood. It smiled horribly at Chentelle, pausing to relish her reaction before unleashing its killing blow. It savored the fragment of her spirit it would possess when she died.

Chentelle sang. She did not know what else to do. She gathered her power and sang, focusing the harmony of her music at the creature holding the Staff. If she could catch him by surprise, he might drop the weapon. But it was no use. The vikhor countered the song with his own howl. She had failed.

Then, the timbre of his howl suddenly changed. Shafts of red light burned through the vikhor's flesh. It screamed in agony and melted into nothingness. The Thunderwood Staff dropped harmlessly to the ground.

First-light. It was first-light, and Deneob's red rays were falling on the hill-top.

The vikhors fighting Sulmar were trapped by the light as well. The other Ill-creatures scrambled hurriedly down the slope, running to find shelter from the sun. The light pursued them, illuminating more of the hill. At the bottom, the shadow knights wheeled as one and galloped into the west.

They were safe. Chentelle wanted to collapse on the ground in relief, but she had to check on A'stoc.

The mage lay unconscious, blood pouring from his mouth and nose. A large bruise showed plainly on the side of his head. Chentelle reached out with her Gift, examining the wounds. Fortunately, the damage to the side of his head was mostly superficial. The skull was not cracked, though there was some minor swelling in the tissue around the brain. The cuts on his face were also not serious, though his nose was broken. Chentelle grabbed a bandage from A'stoc's pack and pressed it to his nose, stopping the bleeding. That was all she could do for now.

"Are his wounds serious?" Sulmar asked.

Chentelle poured water over a clean cloth and used it to wipe A'stoc's face. "I don't think so, but he might have a concussion."

"He's a cantankerous lout, but no coward, and he fought well. I have not before encountered enemies as tough as these Ill-creatures."

"He's no lout. He has suffered in ways we have not." Chentelle finished cleaning the mage's face, then looked up at Sulmar. "You saved my life—both of our lives. Thank you."

"A warrior does not expect gratitude for performing his duty, my lady," the Tengarian said. "But you are welcome."

Chentelle stared at Sulmar, trying to guess the emotions that lay underneath his impassive facade. But he remained a mystery. In many ways, the barriers of duty and service that the Tengarian surrounded himself with were as formidable as the walls of anger and frustration behind which A'stoc hid.

A soft moan from the ground ended her reverie. A'stoc was waking up.

The mage groaned and lifted a hand to his head. Then he glanced around in sudden panic, relaxing only when he saw the Staff lying on the ground beside him. He wrapped a hand reflexively around the wood and glanced up at Chentelle. "How long have I been unconscious?"

"Only a few minutes," she said. "Just long enough to clean your wounds."

The mage sat up, his face twisting in pain. "We must be on our way."

Chentelle laid a hand on his chest. "You need to rest awhile longer. That was not a slight blow."

"No." A'stoc pushed her hand aside and struggled to his feet, leaning heavily on the Staff for support. "They know where we are, elf girl. We must reach the Holy Land before nightfall. We can rest after we are safe inside the Barrier."

Sulmar grabbed the mage's pack, lifting it onto his own shoulders. A'stoc started to protest, but the Tengarian cut him off brusquely. "You are injured. We will make better time if you do not otherwise encumber yourself."

They worked their way carefully down the hill and retraced the path of their flight. When they reached the river, they followed its course to the south. A'stoc was unsteady on his feet, but he drove himself adamantly forward, refusing all of Chentelle's suggestions to pause and rest. Finally, when Deneob was already low in the west, he relented and called a short stop for food.

Quickly, Chentelle and Sulmar prepared a meal of fruit, nuts, and cheese. The small meal seemed like a feast after so many hours of walking. They ate hurriedly, but Chentelle took the opportunity to broach a subject that had been worrying her all day.

"A'stoc," she said, "what if the Ill-creatures go into Lone Valley? They might attack my home, my family."

The mage swallowed the last of his meal and washed it down with a mouthful of wine. "Your home is safe for now. The Ill-creatures' only concern is the Thunderwood Staff. They know where we are and where we head. They will not turn aside to attack an insignificant village. The Dark One still gathers his strength; he will not launch the war until he is certain of victory. Then none of us will be safe."

Chentelle was perplexed. "But the vikhor held the Staff, knowing nothing of its power."

"The vikhors are the least of Ill-creatures, the idiot hounds. A shadow knight would have taken the Staff and galloped instantly away, bearing it to the Dark One. We were lucky."

"Lucky!" Sulmar echoed ironically.

A'stoc heaved himself to his feet and they started walking again. They continued following the river until Deneob disappeared below the horizon, and still there was no sign of the Holy Land. Chentelle felt fear rising within her. What if they didn't make it? A'stoc could barely keep himself upright, and Sulmar was visibly fatigued. They didn't stand a chance of fighting back the Ill-creatures again.

Then, she saw something in the distance. A small wooden bridge spanned the river ahead of them. "A'stoc, I see a bridge. Is that the entrance to the Holy Land?"

The mage paused, looking to where Ellistar hung above the horizon. "Thank the Creator. No, it is not the border, but it means we are close. We just might make it."

They pushed their pace, moving as fast as A'stoc was able to manage. A dirt road connected to the other side of the bridge, leading southwest. The even surface allowed them to increase their speed again. As the Golden Sun started to set, Chentelle sensed the Holy Land beckoning to her.

She felt it before she saw it: a presence at the edge of her awareness, a promise of peace and tranquillity. Then it came into view. A line of change ran across the land in front of them. The prairie through which they walked was rich and fertile, but it seemed a desert compared to what she saw on the other side. The earth there seemed to glow with life. The grass was thicker, the air crisper. "A'stoc?"

"Yes," he said. "Welcome to the Holy Land."

They crossed through the Barrier, and stopped abruptly.

Chentelle was amazed. The serenity of this place was absolute, perfect. It washed over her and through her. Her spirit sang with it. It was as if she had called upon her Gift, but it required no effort. It was natural for her to feel in harmony with the world. She extended her awareness toward her companions.

A'stoc stood in awe, evidently surprised at the power of the feelings that infused him, and amused at his own surprise. The tension that was so much a part of him disappeared. His face lost its perpetual scowl, relaxing into an easy smile. Even his hands loosened their grip on the Staff.

Chentelle smiled. She had always felt bad that other people could never feel the harmony of nature the way she did. It was so wonderful that her friends could share in this awareness, so much more natural than the isolation of the outside world.

"My liege, look," Sulmar said, a rare smile on his face. He felt it, too. He extended his bared right arm. Nothing but smoothly muscled flesh showed on the fading light. The mark of the dragon was gone!

"It is the power of the Holy Land," A'stoc said. "No evil may exist here."

Chentelle nodded in agreement. It was only right. "The curse is broken. You can go back to Tengar, now, if you wish. I will excuse you from your vow of service."

"No," he said. "Your journey has not ended. My service is not complete."

"How did you come to wear that curse, anyway?" A'stoc asked. There was no challenge or disparagement in his tone, and could be none, here; he was merely curious.

"It was a matter of honor," Sulmar said. "One whose details I do not wish to share with you." There was no insult in his tone, only caution. Chentelle understood. There was no need for secrets in the Holy Land, but they would not remain here forever.

"Perhaps you are wise not to," A'stoc agreed. He moved off to the side of the road and slumped to the grass. "Let us rest here. I am too tired and too hungry to keep walking."

Chentelle wanted to disagree. Her own body felt strong, invigorated by the power of the Holy Land. But she was well aware of the mage's fatigue. The day's travel had taxed him to his limit, and his energy had been further depleted by the cost of healing. The Holy Land replenished the spirit but not the physical body. A positive attitude was not enough to counter exhaustion.

She and Sulmar set up their camp and prepared a hearty supper from the last of their supplies. They ate quickly but without haste. There was no sense of urgency; they were safe here. When they finished, they dropped into peaceful slumber, wrapped in the protection of the Holy Land.

Chentelle woke once in the night, or thought she did. The Ill-creature from her dream stood just beyond the Barrier, glaring at them through jaundiced eyes. Chentelle felt no fear. There was no danger, here. She met the creature's eyes and smiled.

The demon leaped into the air, perhaps insulted, extending huge bat-like wings. It disappeared quickly into the night sky.

In the morning, Chentelle could not be certain whether she had truly awakened or only dreamed the encounter. Either way, the experience seemed distant and unimportant. She gathered up her gear and made ready for the day's journey.

Both Sulmar and A'stoc seemed much restored. The wonderful ambience might not instantly abate fatigue, but it did enable sleep to do that job.

They walked through natural prairie for perhaps an hour before finding cultivated land. Rich fields of grain lined the road, broken occasionally by a dense orchard or open pasture. The people greeted them openly and warmly.

Around noon they met a merchant hauling goods from the scattered farms into the city for sale. He offered to let them ride on his wagon in exchange for news from outside the Barrier, and they hastily agreed. The pace of the wagon was not great, but it was both faster and less wearing than walking. The merchant also shared his food with them, understanding their need. He reacted to their news of the Dark One's resurgence with quiet faith.

"The High Bishop will know what to do," he said. "It is wise of you to seek his guidance."

They traveled with the merchant for two days, halting on the evening of the second at a small farming community. The laughter of children at play filled the air, mingling with the easy conversation of neighbors who knew and loved each other. The village reminded Chentelle of her own home in Lone Valley. The construction was nothing alike; the people here lived in squat rectangular houses built upon open land. But there was the same sense of comfort and belonging.

"We will spend the night here," the merchant said. "Sleeping in soft beds and sharing a warm meal with one of the farmers."

Chentelle smiled at the thought. She breathed deeply, taking in the aromas of fresh grain and wood smoke in the salty breeze. "Wait. I smell the sea. It must be Norivika Bay. Are we that close?"

"The bay lies just beyond this village," the merchant said. "If you can convince one of the boatmen to ferry you across, then you would reach the city tonight."

Chentelle turned to look at A'stoc. Their sense of urgency was gone, but intellectually they remained aware that time was critical. He nodded, and they quickly gathered their belongings and thanked the merchant for his kindness. They walked briskly through the village and followed the road through a series of gentle hills on the other side. As they cleared one of the hillocks, Norivika Bay came into view. Though the far shore could not be seen, a spire of light was visible, floating above the water.

"Is that the Cathedral of Light?" Chentelle asked.

A'stoc nodded. "It is made entirely of adartak. The crystal refracts and magnifies the light within."

"It shines like a jewel," she said, admiringly.

The road wound downward to the water, passing through thickets of tangled cedars and oaks. Then it turned west, following the shoreline a short distance to a long wooden pier. Several small craft were moored here, rocking gently in the waves. A row of small cottages faced the pier, and three figures sat talking on the porch of the nearest one.

As they neared, one of the figures called out to them: an extremely tall human with chiseled features and a stiff mustache. "Evening, travelers. If you're looking for the inn, it's back the way you came, about half a league. Of course, if you're looking for the innkeeper, he's right here beside me, enjoying the sunset."

The squat figure next to him nodded amiably.

"Thank you, kind sir," Chentelle said, "but we are hoping to find a way across the bay. Is it possible that one of you gentlemen is the captain of one of those vessels?"

The man laughed. "Captain, eh—why yes, I am Captain Johan, master of the finest sailing skiff to ever brave the treacherous waters of Norivika Bay." He laughed again, and this time his friends joined in.

"Wonderful," Chentelle said. "Then, will you give us passage?"

"Of course," he answered. "Burney and I are going to the city tomorrow, midmorning. You are welcome to join us, though you will have to share space with several barrels of fine ale."

"Tomorrow? But we must reach the city tonight."

"Tonight! No, I do not think that is possible. Burney and I have spent the long day ferrying goods back and forth, and this is our first chance to relax. Still, perhaps you should explain your need. Burney, fetch a light and some chairs for our guests."

The third man stood up and went into the cottage, returning in a moment with two small chairs and a lamp. "We only got these two extra chairs, Johan."

Chentelle moved forward, into the circle of illumination. "That's all right. Really, sir, we can't stay. We have to get to the High Bishop tonight."

"Why, you're an elf," Johan said. "I wondered why a little girl was speaking for two grown men. Well, gentle elf, tell me what this need of yours is that it should take precedence over a well-deserved rest for my brother and me."

Chentelle examined the man. She could sense the fatigue in his muscles, the soreness in his back and shoulders. He was not being lazy. He truly did feel the need for rest. But she had to convince him. She knew that he could feel her own urgency, the power of her need. He just wanted to know what caused the feeling, so he could evaluate the need for himself.

She opened herself up to his scrutiny, pulling down any barriers to her thoughts and emotions. She let him feel the terror, the horror, the desperation that she had experienced over the last five days. "The Dark One is alive," she said. "Ill-creatures are abroad in the Realm."

Johan cried out. "Such *evil*! How is it possible? The Dark One alive, Ill-creatures moving freely in the kingdoms. You were right, gentle elf, your mission must not be delayed."

The huge man stood up, revealing a frame at least four and a half cubits tall. "Daniel, return to your inn. You must spread this news among the villages. Burney, take these chairs back inside and make sure all of the fires are damped. I'll go ahead and start rigging the sails."

Johan picked up the lantern and started for the pier, his long strides leaving Chentelle and the others behind.

As she rushed to catch up, Chentelle heard a resigned whisper come from A'stoc.

"Yet another step on the road to despair."

⊰ 7 ⊱

ENLIGHTENMENTS

Johan guided the sailboat smoothly over the obsidian waters. Waves lapped gently against the bow, driven by the same steady breeze that filled their sails. The moon had not yet risen, but the boatman seemed completely confident in his knowledge of the bay. The Cathedral of Light was a beacon, both a mark of their destination and a sign that urged them forward. As they drew nearer, other lights could be seen. The small flickerings that dotted the far shore were obviously the city lights of Norivika. But there was also a haunting glow radiating from a small island to their south.

Chentelle turned to their pilot. "Captain, what is that glow?"

He laughed gently. "Please, call me Johan. The light you see is from the Atablicryon, the most sacred temple in the Holy Land. The most dedicated members of the Holy Order are often drawn to the island as a center of prayer and meditation, but the rest of us avoid it. It would be disrespectful to go there without strong reason."

"The Atablicryon," Chentelle said. "A'stoc, have you ever been there?"

The mage looked sad, suddenly, as if he were remembering something painful. "No, but my master did. It was from the gardens of the Atablicryon that he plucked the Tree of Life and shaped it with his magic into a weapon of destruction."

The bitterness in his voice saddened Chentelle. It was so unnecessary in this place of perfect harmony. "But the Staff isn't just a weapon, is it? Surely its power can be used for other things."

"I have no way of knowing," he said. "For me, it is useful only as a walking stick."

Again, Chentelle felt the pain in his voice. She searched for some words to ease that pain, but she found none. The silence stretched between them.

A'stoc dropped his eyes. "I apologize. I should not take my anger out on you, even muted as it is in this region. You are right; the Staff can be used for other things. My master used it to prove that the Fundamental Law of Wizardry was incorrect."

"The Fundamental Law?"

"You are familiar with the elven Lore of wood-shaping?"

"Of course," she answered. "*Rillandef* and *rillanmor*, they are used to shape dead wood or live trees into useful items."

A'stoc nodded encouragingly. "And what happens when the shaper of an item dies?"

"Then another has to renew the enchantment, or else the wood will return to its original form."

"Exactly," A'stoc said. "That is the Fundamental Law, the belief that all magic dies with its maker. Whether the common Lore of elves and dwarves or the finest spells of the old masters, all powers were subject to this law. Or so everyone thought. During the Wizards' War, my master and A'kalendane discovered the spells of Earthpower. With Earthpower, a wizard can tap into the energy of Creation itself. He can cast spells that survive his own destruction. A'kalendane used this power to create powerful weapons for the Legion; my master used it to shape the Thunderwood Staff."

The mage's eyes became unfocused, as if he were staring at something far away. "I remember the first days after A'pon learned to control the Staff. He dreamed that its power could be used to affect the Creation itself, to heal the Flaw that destroyed the Time of Perfection."

Suddenly, the bitterness was back in his voice. "Instead, he used it to create yet another scar for this world to endure. Thus runs the road called hope."

Chentelle sat helplessly as A'stoc's pain washed over her. The mage was tortured by demons that not even the Holy Land could wash away completely. She wanted to reach out to him, to ease his burden, but she did not know how. Finally, she turned away and watched the lights of the Holy City flicker above the bow.

Johan steered the skiff expertly into an empty docking space. He dropped the sails, and Burney jumped onto the pier to tie them off. "Well, here we are. Good luck in your journey, gentle elf. Put your trust in the High Bishop. He is close to the Creator; he will know what to do."

"Thank you," Chentelle said. "And thank you for the passage; we appreciate your sacrifice."

"I did only what was necessary," Johan said, dismissing her compliment with a shrug. "Burney, get back on board, brother. There's a soft bed calling for me, and I don't aim to keep it waiting."

A'stoc started down the dock before the boat had even pulled away. "We will not find a carriage this late. We must walk."

Chentelle followed him down the deserted pier and into the city streets. It was so different than she had imagined. In Lone Valley, they told stories of human cities, stories of dirty streets and cramped alleys filled with people. But Norivika was beautiful. Wide avenues ran between rows of well-kept townhouses. Gardens were common, and nearly every intersection was decorated with a park or a fountain. Crystal orb-lights illuminated every corner, and the soft music of wind chimes floated in the night air.

They turned onto a wide boulevard that headed straight for the radiant spire of the Cathedral of Light. The road climbed a long, gentle hill. Gradually, the townhouses thinned and then disappeared altogether, replaced by a vast park which surrounded the foot of the Cathedral.

As they reached the park, more details became clear. The main body of the Cathedral consisted of four large halls with curved facades. The halls formed a great circle surrounding a tall central spire, which rose above the park like a bejeweled mountain. Huge orb-lights were located at the junctures of the halls and underneath the base of the spire, spreading their illumination through the entire crystal structure.

They passed through a large portal and into the antechamber of the temple.

Chentelle noted that there were no gates guarding the way, no doors which could be barred against entrance. That was proper. The Cathedral was the meeting place for the races of man and their Creator. It had to remain open to all.

A young human in white robes came forward to greet them. "May I help you, travelers?"

Chentelle started to speak, but A'stoc answered first. "I am A'stoc, Bearer of the Thunderwood Staff. My companions are the Enchantress Chentelle—the Messenger—and her liegeman, Sulmar. We are here to answer the High Bishop's call."

The young man bowed respectfully. "This is a great honor, Bearer. You and your fellowship are most welcome to our hospitality. We have been eagerly awaiting you, especially since the others arrived. I am Brother Ethnan, personal acolyte to the High Bishop. Chambers have been set aside for your use. If you are amenable, I will take you to them."

"Please do."

"The High Bishop will be informed of your presence," the acolyte said. "I feel certain that he will want to meet with you in the morning."

Brother Ethnan led them into the body of the Cathedral and up to the second floor of one of the main halls. The translucent walls, floors, and ceiling were disorienting. Chentelle's feet were secure in the solidity of the crystal, but her eyes kept telling her she was hanging in the air without support. Some of the chambers they passed were screened with tapestries and rugs, giving their occupants privacy. It was to a collection of these rooms that they were taken.

"These are your chambers," Brother Ethnan said. "Breakfast will be served upon the rising of the Golden Sun. Is there anything else you require?"

A'stoc shook his head.

"Then I bid you all a good night. Sleep well; the Creator is near."

The acolyte left, and they each entered one of the shielded sleeping rooms.

Chentelle was exhausted, but she was not so tired that she failed to notice the beauty of her surroundings. The floor was covered completely by a thick rug, and rich tapestries concealed the walls of the chamber, decorated with flowing scenes showing the Sphere of Creation as it was during the Time of Perfection. A large wardrobe sat open and empty next to a bed that would easily sleep six of her. Beside the wardrobe was a chest of drawers with a pitcher of fresh water and a basin. On the wall across from the bed, an open window let in the cool sea breeze.

Chentelle slipped her boots off and ran her toes luxuriously through the carpet. Quickly, she stowed her gear and poured water into the basin. She washed herself thoroughly, and then, after a moment's thought, washed her robe as well. If they were going to meet the High Bishop tomorrow, she should look her best. After she finished, she hung the dress in the wardrobe to dry. Then she brushed her hair, working out the kinks and tangles of several days on the road. Finally, she collapsed gratefully onto the bed.

She slid between the cool linen sheets, letting the soft mattress soothe her into sleep. Her muscles ached from the long hours of walking, but she felt a deep sense of satisfaction. She had followed her dream, and brought A'stoc to the Holy City. Still, she was haunted by a feeling that her part in this fight was not over. She tried to figure out the source of her premonition, but the call of sleep was too strong to be denied. Her eyes closed, and she did not dream.

ᔆ

Chentelle awoke to the smell of blueberry muffins. She glanced around her in confusion. Was it morning already? Her sheets and blankets were still neatly tucked, and she felt as if she had only just closed her eyes. But even if the aroma of breakfast didn't convince her, the golden light coming through the window was conclusive.

She slid out of bed and splashed water on her face, trying to wash away her lethargy. She did not remember the last time she had slept so deeply and dreamlessly. She dressed herself quickly and headed for the assembly chamber where Brother Ethnan had indicated that breakfast would be served.

The large table that dominated the room was crowded with food and people. Sulmar sat on his own at one end of the table, but Chentelle had no idea who the others were. Most of them were elves and wore Legion uniforms. But one of the Legionnaires was human, and several of the elves wore civilian clothing. All of them were heartily attacking the delicious-smelling breakfast.

As Chentelle moved to take a seat near Sulmar, a silver-haired elf in unmarked leathers stood and faced her. "Greetings, lady, I am Thildemar, from the forest of Inarr. My companions are Legionnaires under the command of Lord Dacius Gemine." He nodded his head toward the human, a heavily muscled warrior whose fierce red hair and beard were offset by gentle blue eyes and a kind smile. "Also with us—"

"Captain Jack Rone," interrupted a stocky and deeply tanned elf, "and I make my own introductions, thank you." He bowed deeply over Chentelle's hand. "At your service, my lady. I have been telling my mates that this Cathedral of Light was the most beautiful sight in the wide Realm. I see now that my judgment was hasty."

Chentelle blushed, both flattered and embarrassed by his words. "I am Chentelle, from Lone Valley. I see you have met my liegeman, Sulmar. We travel with Wizard A'stoc, who comes at the request of the High Bishop."

Captain Rone guided her to a seat at the table near his own. "We, too, travel on the High Bishop's business. Though it has been two days since we arrived, and His Eminence has yet to tell us what that business might be."

"Captain Rone!" the human lord shouted, but his voice held more amusement than anger. "You know the High Bishop has only been waiting for the arrival of these brave souls. He wishes to brief all of us at once."

"Of course, Lord Gemine," the captain said. "You must forgive me, lady. I lost a fine ship and crew to a vile creature from Firesta's deepest pit. Why, the Ill-creature would have killed us all if not for my own bravery. And the strong arm of Lord Gemine, of course."

"You were attacked, too?" Chentelle asked. "What happened?"

Lord Gemine laughed. "Perhaps I should tell the story, lady elf. The good captain chafes when he is forced to chain his imagination to the truth, and this story has enough pain."

The human's tone turned serious as he related the Legionnaires' battles on board the *Otan Stin* and at the border garrison. In the heightened atmosphere of the Holy Land, his tale carried them along as if they lived the events with him. Grief filled the room as he spoke of the deaths of Commander Thean and his good friend, Alka Shara.

Tears ran freely down Chentelle's face. It was so terrible. She stood and went to Lord Gemine. The human sat silently, still lost in the sadness of his tale. Chentelle wrapped her arms around the man, hugging him tightly. It was a small comfort, but it was all she could do. "Do not blame yourself, Lord Gemine. You did all that anyone could."

The human squeezed her tightly for a moment and then released her. "Thank you, lady. I feel your special healing power. But do not let my sorrow color your own heart. I mourn my friend's death, but be assured, I know where to lay the blame for his demise. And please, my name is Dacius."

"And I am Chentelle."

"Lady," Thildemar said. "You said that you and your companions were also attacked."

"Yes." Chentelle told them about the journey from A'stoc's cave and the battle on the hilltop. As she spoke, she could feel the iron resolve of these men. They understood the horror she was describing, and they were determined to defeat it. When she described how the vikhor had wrested the Staff from A'stoc's hands, she heard a gasp of surprise.

"The Thunderwood Staff," said Thildemar. "I believed that it had been destroyed in the Desecration."

Chentelle heard a strange note of longing in his voice. "No. It survived, as did A'stoc himself." She remembered the scenes of destruction she had experienced in the mage's mind. "But nothing else."

"No," Thildemar agreed, "nothing else."

"That was a terrible time," Dacius said. "And so will this one become, unless we stop it. It seems clear that the High Bishop has called us together to stop the Ill-creatures."

There were murmurs of agreement from the other Legionnaires.

As Chentelle returned to her seat, she again noticed Sulmar seated at the table's far end. There was no feeling of isolation or rejection about him, only a sense of detached readiness. She nodded toward him and smiled. "How are you this morning?"

He glanced down at his bare right arm and returned her smile. "I am well, mistress."

"He speaks!" Captain Rone exclaimed. "You are a miracle worker, young beauty of Lone Valley. I plied the man for an hour with the finest food and conversation this side of Essienkal and received only a greeting edgewise for my trouble."

Chentelle glanced at her liegeman, who remained silent. "Why do you not speak to them?"

"Mistress, you are my liege," he said. "I divulge no information unless you express otherwise."

Chentelle understood. The Tengarian's Oath of Discipline apparently had little room for ambiguities. He was an instrument of her will. He did nothing without her consent. She was a little intimidated. Such service was a frightful responsibility.

"Sulmar," she said. "These men are here for the same reason that we are. Please speak freely with them." She turned to the others. "Do not be offended. It is his way."

Captain Rone spoke quickly. "Oh, we weren't offended, fair lady. We understand the need for discipline and secrecy. Why, I remember once when I was sailing off the—"

The captain's story was interrupted by the sound of Brother Ethnan clearing his throat. "Forgive the intrusion. But if you have all finished eating, the High Bishop would like to speak with you all in the meeting hall. If everyone—" He stopped and looked about. "Where is the Bearer?"

Chentelle looked at the still-closed door to the mage's sleeping room. "I will get him," she said, rising from the table.

The heavy crystal door swung open easily at her touch. Curtains were drawn across the chamber's window, and the screening tapestries blocked out the light which suffused the Cathedral. A'stoc lay fully clothed on the bed, clutching the Staff to his chest. He stared in dread at the darkened ceiling, as if the building were about to collapse and crush them all.

"A'stoc," she called softly.

He snapped his head around, glaring at her as if she had struck him. But he did not speak.

"The High Bishop wants to see us," she said.

"Of course," he said. "We might as well get this over with." He jumped quickly to his feet and followed Chentelle back to the assembly chamber.

Brother Ethnan spoke to A'stoc as they entered. "If you wish to break fast before the meeting, Bearer, we will wait."

"No. I have no wish to delay."

The acolyte bowed and indicated that they should follow. A'stoc and the others did, but Chentelle, and therefore Sulmar, held back.

A'stoc paused. "What's the matter?"

"I am not part of this meeting," Chentelle said. "I came only to see you here. I do not wish to intrude where I do not belong."

He snorted. "You aren't done yet, lady elf. I can still balk."

"But—"

Brother Ethnan smiled. "You are on the list, Lady Chentelle. Please do accompany us, with your liegeman."

She was supposed to join the meeting? This was a courtesy she could not decline. She nodded acquiescently.

He led them through the outer hall to the stairs of the central spire. They ascended several levels and then followed a corridor which curved along the outer wall of the tower. The busy streets of the Holy City were clearly visible far below them.

Chentelle felt a twinge of dizziness and eased away from the transparent outer wall. She looked down at the floor, hoping to steady herself. There was nothing there. A hundred cubits below her feet, the ground beckoned to her. "Oh, no!" she cried, stumbling in vertigo. Only Sulmar's supporting arm kept her from falling.

"Thank you," she said. "This walking on air takes some getting used to."

Brother Ethnan laughed gently. "I know what you mean. It took me several weeks to stop bumping into walls, and even longer to walk without my hands spread in front of me. I look upon it as an act of faith."

They continued down the corridor until it ended in a huge set of crystal doors. Brother Ethnan threw these open and led them into a vast hall, filled with hundreds of paintings and sculptures. All of the artworks were dedicated to the Creation and the Time of Perfection. A huge table commanded the center of the room, surrounded by chairs for at least fifty people.

"Please make yourselves comfortable," the acolyte said. "The High Bishop will be here in a moment."

Chentelle ran her hand over the smooth surface of the table, feeling the love and care that went into its crafting. It was obviously the product of *rillandef*. The wood from a dozen oaks had been seamlessly blended by a true master of the art. No carvings decorated the table, but the natural grains of the wood had been highlighted and enhanced. The graceful swirls hinted at a dozen designs and elegantly evoked the flowing harmony of the Creation.

The company seated themselves around the table. Almost immediately, the doors opened again, and two figures came striding through. The first was an elderly human wearing a white robe identical to Brother Ethnan's. The other was shorter, the size of a dwarf or a small elf. He, or she, was completely masked by a voluminous, cowled white robe. Even the hands were hidden inside long, bell-shaped sleeves.

Both figures marched quickly to the head of the table, and the human spoke. "Greeting to you all. I am Father Marcus Alanda, High Bishop of the Holy Order in Talan."

Everyone stood and bowed their heads in respect.

"Please join hands," the High Bishop said. "I would like to call the Creator's blessing to our gathering."

The company linked hands, except for the cowled figure, who extended the folds of its robe in lieu of them. Chentelle wondered at this, but obligingly took a fold in her hand, as did the person on the other side. In this manner they formed the circle, which represented the Sphere. But there was a problem. The table was too wide for the members on the end to reach across. Brother Ethnan overcame the difficulty smoothly, climbing onto the polished surface and sitting respectfully with crossed legs. From there, he could easily grasp hands with the people on either side.

When the circle was whole, the High Bishop spoke. "In the name of the Creator, I called for you to come. In your love of the Creation, you answered that call. In the circle of worship, we come together. In the circle of worship, we create the Perfection of the Sphere. In the circle of worship, we find harmony with Creation. In the harmony of Creation, we find all. The Creator blesses us with this gift."

"Bless the Creator," they responded.

The High Bishop motioned for them to sit. "To start with, I think some brief introductions would be helpful." He nodded toward A'stoc. "Wizard, will you begin?"

A'stoc stood. "I am A'stoc, apprentice to A'pon Boemarre, Bearer of the Thunderwood Staff." Then he sat.

Now, it was Chentelle's turn, but she wasn't really sure how to announce herself. Finally, she decided on the title that A'stoc had given her at the gate. "I am Chentelle, the Messenger. And this is my liegeman, Sulmar."

Thildemar went next, naming himself and his homeland. Then each of the Legionnaires declared himself by name and regiment. Finally, Captain Rone introduced himself and his two crewmen, Zubec and Pardec.

The High Bishop listened to them all. Then he turned to Chentelle. "I am curious. You announced yourself as the Messenger. What became of the Wizard A'mond?"

"Your Eminence, he died during the winter," Chentelle said. "The dove you sent came to me, and I carried your message to A'stoc."

The High Bishop made the sign of harmony and closed his eyes in prayer. "A'mond, yours was a brave and gentle soul. Your passing leaves us all poorer for your absence. I will pray that you find peace with the Creator. But in my heart, in my faith, I know that you have already done so. Be whole in the Creation, my friend. When the time comes, we will be together again."

The words were charged with a power of faith and reverence that called to something deep within Chentelle's spirit. Tears rolled down her face as she was overcome by a grief she hadn't realized was still within her. The pain of A'mond's death came upon her anew. Then it faded into nothingness as the grief was lifted from her. Joy and understanding filled her, for as she let go of A'mond in death, her heart sang with memories of A'mond in life.

Suddenly, Chentelle realized that the High Bishop had spoken to her again. He looked at her expectantly, as if waiting for an answer. "Um, I'm sorry, Your Eminence. What did you say?"

He smiled reassuringly. "Please, call me Father Marcus. 'Eminence' is too proud a title, especially for this brave company. I asked how it was the dove came to you. Are you a student of the High Lore?"

Chentelle tried not to blush. There was nothing intimidating about Father Marcus' manner. But he had such a serenity about him, such a sense of *presence*, that she was nervous anyway. "No, Your E—no, Father Marcus. I think the dove came to me because of my Gift. I am an enchantress."

Amazement showed on his face. "You surprise me, my dear. I did not know an enchantress existed in the Realm. Why did you not introduce yourself with the title?"

Chentelle shrugged, embarrassed at her mistake. "I am not used to announcing myself as one. And in any event, I do not belong in this company. I merely sought to deliver the message, because A'mond could not, and—"

A'stoc broke in. "She is young, for an elf, High Bishop, and unfamiliar with the protocol for meetings such as this. But if not for her Gift, your message would never have reached me. And if not for her passion and persistence, I would never have been persuaded to come."

"Then all of Norivika owes her a great debt," Father Marcus said gravely.

Chentelle released a tense breath, grateful that the mage was speaking for her. And he was saying such kind things. Maybe Father Marcus' blessing had affected A'stoc, too. Maybe it had allowed him to release some of his own grief. She looked at the mage, letting herself see him with the vision of the Holy Land.

There was a calmness about him, now. A sense of acceptance and forgiveness that softened his thorny nature. But she realized that the hard core of anger remained. The deep pit of bitterness and self-doubt which plagued A'stoc still resisted the peace of the Holy Order.

She turned back to the High Bishop. "Father Marcus, did the dove ever return to you?"

"No," he answered. "It has not returned. Do you know what has become of her?"

Chentelle remembered her vivid dream of the Ill-creature dropping the lifeless bird at her feet. Sadly, she nodded her head. "She is dead."

The High Bishop's face seemed to mirror her own pain. Tears welled in his clear blue eyes as he whispered a quiet prayer. Then he looked up and spoke to the company. "I know of the evil that roams beyond the Barrier, but I would hear also of your own experiences. Lord Gemine, will you share your tale first?"

"As you will, High Bishop." The human lord stood and drew in a deep breath, and a remarkable change moved through him. Deep, almost uncontrollable energy filled his body. His face and hands seemed to animate of their own accord. His eyes reached out to his audience, and he began to speak, pulling them into his tale with subtle gestures of hand and expression. His rough voice turned every word into a rasp, which he used to carve out the fine details of his saga.

Chentelle realized that Dacius' earlier telling, for all its power, had been restrained. He had a flair for telling that even Willow would envy. Though scarcely an hour had passed since Chentelle last heard the story, it hit her with undiminished force. She felt herself carried along with the joy of the human's reunion with Alka Shara, and her tears fell again at the telling of his valiant sacrifice. Finally, the tale brought them back to the Holy Land. Lord Gemine stopped speaking, his gruff tones deepening slowly into silence. But it was not an empty silence. The charge of battle, the pain of lost comrades, the determination and courage of the Legionnaires, these things and more echoed through the quiet hall.

Dacius spoke again. His voice was steady, forceful, but empty now of the rough power that had driven his narrative. "High Bishop, I understand that you have called on the Legion to counter this threat, and we stand ready to answer that call. But you see how many men are here. We do not even fill this table. Without more weapons, I do not see how we can stem the Dark One's tide."

"Patience, Lord Gemine," Father Marcus answered softly. "I will answer your concerns, but first I would hear the wizard's tale. If you would be so kind, Wizard A'stoc."

A'stoc shrugged and then spoke without rising. "The enchantress brought me your summons. I decided to answer it. Ill-creatures attacked us on the way here. We escaped."

Father Marcus waited, but A'stoc said no more. The priest gave a soft sigh and turned to face the company. "I have called you here for a purpose, but perhaps not for the one which you expect. The Dark One and his minions are a grave threat to the Realm, but they are not the only threat. There is another evil loose on Infinitera, a power more terrible than the Dark One himself, one that threatens to destroy the Creation. That is the reason I have brought you all here."

"But I am here only incidentally," Chentelle protested. "Because the dove found me instead of the one it sought. Now I must return home."

Father Marcus paused, seeming surprised. He glanced at A'stoc.

"She is a truly innocent creature," A'stoc said dryly.

Father Marcus smiled. "So I see." He turned to Chentelle. "My dear, you greatly underestimate your importance. The dove sought not merely a person, but a figure of power sufficient to do the necessary job. You were that figure, and you confirmed it by forcing the attendance of this curmudgeon." His gaze flicked to A'stoc, who grimaced. "Your potency is great, enchantress, though subtle, and we do need your participation in this most vital mission. I beg you not to desert us in this critical hour."

Chentelle was astounded. "But I'm only an elf girl who—"

"Have you not seen signs? Dreams? Signals that this is your destiny?"

There he had her. "I have dreamed," she agreed. "If it is truly your wish—"

"It truly is my wish, enchantress," he agreed. "For the sake of the salvation of our Realm."

She was overwhelmed. "Then of course I agree."

Father Marcus nodded, as if she had just confirmed the obvious. Then he addressed the full group. "Before I continue, I must make one thing clear. In this matter, I do not act as an official of the Realm. No oath or onus of duty compels any of you to join my quest. Any man, or woman, who wishes may leave now without bearing dishonor. I ask only that you remain in the Holy Land and speak to no one of what you have learned until the quest has been completed."

As the High Bishop paused to examine the faces of his company, Chentelle felt the weight behind his words. An evil more terrible than the Dark One, it was almost beyond belief. She felt suddenly small and insignificant. What could she do? She had been helpless even against the foul power of the vikhors. How could she fight a power greater than the mightiest of Ill-creatures? But how could she not? The Creation needed her, and she could not refuse. When Father Marcus' gaze fell on her, she just smiled and tried to nod resolutely. After all, she had just agreed.

Then the High Bishop's eyes turned to A'stoc. "I will wait to decide until I hear the object of this quest," the mage said.

He was not yet committed? And they expected her to see that he did commit. Chentelle sighed inwardly.

"Very well," Father Marcus said, turning back to face the company. "We will sail south, deep into the reaches of the Great Sea. There is an island there, the remnant of a lost continent. In the eleven thousand years of elven history, no mention is made of this land, but it exists. On the island is a second Atablicryon, a companion to our own Holy Temple. And in this temple we will find an artifact to aid us in our mission, the Sphere of Ohnn."

"The Sphere of Ohnn," A'stoc exclaimed, a look of amazement on his face.

"Do you know of the Sphere?" Father Marcus asked him.

A'stoc shook his head in confusion. "Yes—I mean no. I mean, the Sphere of Ohnn is a theoretical construct. My master and some of his colleagues speculated that an artifact might exist which served as a gateway to Earthpower through the inanimate, just as the Tree of Life functioned as a bridge through the living. But it was only a conjecture."

"It is more than conjecture," Marcus said. "The Sphere of Ohnn holds a fragment of pure Earthpower, the primal force which binds the Creation. Retrieving the Sphere is the first step of our quest." He paused, waiting patiently for A'stoc to speak.

Chentelle could feel the mage's excitement. His curiosity was aroused by the prospect of finding an object his master had only imagined. But something within the man held back. Years of bitterness and disappointment refused to release him from their grip.

"I am intrigued," he said. "Please continue."

The High Bishop nodded. "First, I would like to introduce my companion, Gorin, another follower of the Holy Order."

The cowled figure walked to Father Marcus' side and pulled back his cowl, revealing a pale round head, devoid of hair and far too large for his small body. Large black pupils floated in bloodred eyeballs, covered occasionally by a transparent lid that did nothing to interrupt his eerie stare. The ears were catlike and perched far back on the skull, and the pointed nose was partly covered by two flaps of skin which opened and closed in rhythm to his breathing. The thin black lips parted, revealing multiple rows of teeth. "Greetings."

"RRRAAAHHHH!"

Chentelle snapped her head around at the incoherent growl of rage. She saw Dacius jumping to his feet and reaching for his sword. Anger poured from the man in hot waves. His hand closed around the hilt of his weapon, and a bout of terrible trembling seized his body. A look of confusion crossed his face as he realized that he could not draw the blade.

"It—it's a goblin," he said, struggling to regain control of his voice.

Chentelle saw that several of the other Legionnaires had also gotten to their feet. They, too, were staring at the goblin as if ready for violence.

"Peace," said Father Marcus softly. "There will be no fighting here. Nor is there any need."

He was right, of course. The aura of the Holy Land made violence impossible. And it was equally impossible for the goblin to pose any threat to them here. Quickly, the Legionnaires returned to their seats, looking almost embarrassed for their reaction. Only Dacius remained standing.

The goblin reached out his hands in the sign of harmony, revealing long dexterous fingers tipped with gleaming ivory claws filed neatly into blunted nails. He met Dacius' eyes and spoke to him in a soft, impossibly deep voice. "I understand that you have reason to hate and mistrust many of my race. But I am not they. I have dedicated my life to the teachings of the Holy Order. The Lord High Bishop has graced me with this opportunity to serve the Creation, and I am going to be accompanying him on this quest. I hope that you will be able to overcome your prejudices for the time which we will be together."

A chastened look came to Dacius' face as he dropped his hand to his side. He bowed to the goblin. "You are correct. If you work to assist the High Bishop, then you are not my enemy. I apologize for my outburst."

As Dacius returned to his seat, the goblin spoke again. "The island the Lord High Bishop seeks is known to my people. It lies far to the south of the lands of the Realm, well beyond any of your trade routes. In order to reach it quickly, we will have to follow the southern current. Do any of you understand what that means?"

"Aye," Captain Rone said. "It means hugging the coast of the Hordelands all the way. It means traveling for weeks within reach of goblins raiders."

"That is right," said Gorin. "We have to travel close to the lands of my people. That means danger, both from piracy and from Ill-creatures, for the Heresiarchs have always been open to the servants of evil. Therefore, it is to our benefit to travel discreetly."

The goblin bowed to Father Marcus, yielding the floor.

"Captain Rone," said the High Bishop, "have you ever sailed a goblinship?"

The elf raised one eyebrow. "Can't say I have, Father."

Marcus nodded toward his fellow priest. "Brother Gorin was once a sailor. The vessel he sailed on is still here in the Holy City. If you think you are able to pilot it, then we shall use that ship to avoid challenge as we pass through goblin waters."

"If I can handle it?" said Rone. "Beggin' your pardon, Your Worship, but there's not a sailing ship been built or dreamt that I can't handle with a willing crew, especially with a former hand there to help me learn the ropes. If you need a captain for your goblinship, then I'm your man."

"Excellent. Now, I propose to travel during the First Season of Light in order to avoid detection by the Ill-creatures. That should give Captain Rone time to familiarize himself with his new vessel and the rest of you time to make whatever preparations you deem necessary. Are there any other questions?"

Chentelle's mind was spinning. A secret mission aboard a goblinship, traveling to an uncharted island to retrieve an artifact that no one else even knew existed, battling the Dark One's creatures to fulfill a quest to stop an evil even more terrible than the Dark One himself—it was almost too much to comprehend. She had to follow where her dream led, but she never dreamt that it would lead her to this. She wondered what Willow would think, or her mother. Would her mother understand? Would she ever forgive Chentelle for leaving? Memories of Lone Valley filled Chentelle's thoughts, but even in her mind it seemed very small and very far away.

Dacius' voice brought her attention back to the present. "Your pardon, Father Marcus, but if we all sail off into the Great Sea, who will defend the Realm from the Ill-creatures?"

A flicker of sadness seemed to cross the High Bishop's face, but it was soon replaced by the quiet surety that seemed to surround him like an aura. "For that, we must depend on the Wizards' Collegium at Tel Adartak-Skysoar. Our own mission calls us elsewhere, to face a more dangerous threat."

"But must we leave the Realm without protectors?" Dacius asked, dismayed. "I know that you say this other threat is more dangerous, but how certain are you of that knowledge? And how do you know we will find this island? Are we to abandon the defense of the Realm based solely on the word of one goblin?"

Father Marcus sat silently for a while, as if weighing a decision. "Forgive me. I have told you what I may. Gorin is not the source of my knowledge. It is another, one who I trust implicitly and absolutely. And now I must ask you to place a similar trust in me. I have no wish to keep secrets, but the knowledge I have been given carries a terrible price, a price I alone must pay. You must believe me: if our quest fails, then Infinitera will be destroyed by an evil more terrible than anything the races of man have ever known."

As the High Bishop spoke, Chentelle's mind was filled with images from her dream, visions of darkness spreading through the world. Unbidden, the words came to her lips. "The Fallen Star."

Father Marcus turned to her in amazement. "How do you know of this?"

"My dream. I've seen it in my dream."

The High Bishop nodded. "Yes, it is the Fallen Star of which I speak."

A'stoc's voice broke in. "What is this Fallen Star? Chentelle, why did you keep this from me?" There was a resonance of pain in his voice, almost betrayal.

Chentelle didn't know what to do, how to answer him. "I didn't—that is, you never—"

"Wizard A'stoc," Father Marcus inserted smoothly into her awkward pause. "It was not her duty to inform you of this. It is mine. The Fallen Star is the evil that I have asked you here to defeat. It has come from beyond the Abyss and threatens the very existence of the Creation. It is powerful beyond measure; neither the power of the Holy Order nor the Lore of the Collegium can affect it. Only with the primal force of Earthpower can we hope to destroy it."

"So that is why," A'stoc said, "you seek the Sphere of Ohnn."

"Yes. And that is why I need you. I have the knowledge to destroy the Fallen Star, and the Sphere of Ohnn has the power. But only you can unlock that power."

A strange look came over A'stoc, as if he were listening to a distant sound. "Me? Why me?"

"You bear the Staff," Father Marcus said. "Only the Thunderwood Staff can free the Earthpower from the Sphere."

A'stoc stood and picked up the Staff from where it lay beside him. Slowly, in one hand, he raised it high over the table. When he spoke, it was in a voice filled with vitriol. "Then the world is dead."

A clamor of questions filled the chamber as the company tried to understand the meaning behind A'stoc's words.

With a sudden motion, the mage slammed the end of the Thunderwood Staff down on the table. The loud clap reverberated through the quiet hall. When the echoes died, he spoke again, the words grating slowly between his clenched teeth.

"The knowledge of this power," he said, shaking the Staff in the air, "died with my master. I have spent a lifetime trying to unlock its secrets, a lifetime of failure and futility. I cannot summon orb-light through this stick, much less break open the Sphere of Ohnn and unleash the Earthpower! You must accept reality, Father Marcus. I cannot help you."

There was stunned silence. Chentelle saw the confusion as the others tried to digest A'stoc's words.

Only Father Marcus remained unperturbed. The iron foundation of the priest's faith seemed unassailable. "Nevertheless," he said, "we must try for the Sphere of Ohnn. It is our only hope. The Creator has not abandoned us. Perhaps on our quest we will uncover the means to unlock the Staff as well. Possibly the Wizards' Council at Tel Adartak-Skysoar will know how to help."

Chentelle cringed. The High Bishop had unwittingly said exactly the wrong thing. She remembered the visions she had gained when she touched the Thunderwood Staff, the deep pain A'stoc had felt at the Collegium's covetousness and betrayal. She prepared herself for the mage's furious retort, but it never came.

A'stoc only dropped his face into his hand and shook his head sadly. "You have no idea. You place your faith in fools and failures, then follow blindly down the inevitable path. The Council knows nothing. Your hope is misplaced."

Father Marcus rested a hand on the mage's shoulder. "I do not place my hope in such fragile hands, Wizard A'stoc. My faith lies in the Creator himself, and in the tools he has given us to protect his work. If the wizards of the Collegium have no answers, then perhaps you will find some clue in A'pon Boemarre's workshop."

A'stoc's head snapped upward as if he had been slapped. "What are you saying? My master's workshop in Odenal revealed nothing of his work."

The High Bishop nodded. "But surely you know he had a workshop here in the Cathedral, as well. It was here that he carved the Thunderwood Staff."

A'stoc's eyes were suddenly alert, almost manic in their intensity. "And this workshop remains intact?"

"It is untouched since his departure. The seals on the chamber have not diminished through the decades. It has resisted all of our attempts to enter. If you can open the door, then perhaps you will find something useful."

A'stoc slammed his hand against the table. "I am a fool! Sixty years of failure and frustration, and I never guessed that this workshop might still exist. Perhaps A'valman was right about me." He started to stand. "Father Marcus, where exactly is the laboratory?"

The High Bishop stopped him with an upraised hand. "A moment, Wizard A'stoc. I will take you there once this meeting is adjourned."

He turned to face the assembled company. "You all have an understanding, now, of the task that lies before us. I say again, if anyone here does not wish to take part in this quest, they may decline freely." He paused, but no one spoke. Chentelle knew why: the others could not deny the effort to save Infin-itera, any more than she could.

"Then this meeting is concluded. I suggest that we all use the weeks until the Ceremony of Light to prepare ourselves. If you require anything from the Cathedral staff, please make your needs known to Brother Ethnan."

Father Marcus left the table, motioning for A'stoc to follow. Chentelle moved quickly to the mage's side. "Wait for me."

"Lady Chentelle," Father Marcus said, "I would like to have this time alone with Wizard A'stoc, so that we may acquaint ourselves. I am sure you can understand."

She couldn't go? After all this business about how important she was to the mission? Chentelle looked helplessly to A'stoc, but the mage avoided her eyes. Fine. If that was how he felt she would find something else to do. She spun around, almost running into Sulmar, who had fallen noiselessly into step behind her.

"One moment." A'stoc's voice made her stop and turn again. "Perhaps it would be best for the enchantress to accompany us. I seem to recall she has an interest in magical laboratories, and I would never have learned of this one if not for her. I am sure you understand, Father Marcus. We will have many opportunities to come to know each other."

"Of course," the High Bishop said, smoothly reversing himself. He seemed quietly pleased, as if he had proved a point. "Please join us, Chentelle. We may all benefit from your insight."

"Thank you," Chentelle said. But she wanted to make a gesture of conces-sion as well, so that the High Bishop would not be offended. "Sulmar, will you stay with the others so that we can keep abreast of their preparations?"

The Tengarian started to protest, but she silenced him with a gesture. "Please, Sulmar. I am in no danger here. The Holy Land protects us all."

Sulmar nodded, unable to argue against such an obvious truth. "As you wish, liege."

ᐁ

Father Marcus led them deep into the heart of the Cathedral. They descended flight after flight of crystal stairs until the transparent walls gave way to solid bedrock. They entered a hallway which led through a maze of wine vaults and underground storage rooms. The construction was granite, now, instead of adartak crystal, but the stone was highly polished and intricately fashioned.

The passage took them to a portal guarded by two massive wooden doors. A small shelf was carved into the stone beside the door, and in this shelf were several wooden rods, each carved in the shape of an open hand. Inside each hand was a large, polished crystal.

Father Marcus lifted out one of the rods. *"The light of the Creation shines within you. Share your light with us."* He passed his hand over the crystal and a steady glow of orb-light grew within it.

Chentelle was amazed. She had felt none of the outpouring of power that A'stoc used to fuel his spells. Neither had she felt the kind of union and communion with the stone that was her own Gift. The stone seemed to be glowing in the light of its own power. "How did you do that?"

Father Marcus called light from another rod, smiling at her curiosity. "We follow the wisdom of Jediah, who learned that through faith and devotion it is possible for us to recapture a small part of the original Creation. In the Time Before, all adartak glowed with the light of Perfection. I have merely reminded these crystals of their true form."

The High Bishop pushed open one of the doors and led them down into the catacombs. The stonework here was much rougher than in the cellars above, and a thick coat of dust swirled around their feet. They weaved their way through a dozen twists and turns, following intersections that seemed to materialize from out of the shadows. Always the High Bishop seemed to choose the narrowest and most uneven of hallways, and always their path sloped deeper into the earth.

"I believe that Wizard A'pon was jealous of his privacy," Father Marcus remarked, "so he chose a location that would deter visitors."

"Indeed," A'stoc said. "He gave orders that no one was to come near during his experiments, not even his apprentice."

The pain in those quiet words was almost too much to bear. Chentelle wanted to reach out, to reassure A'stoc that he was not the failure he believed. But the bitterness that surrounded him held her at bay. It was a wall without gates, impregnable, unbreachable.

"Of course, I forgot that you were there," said Father Marcus. "I was only a child at the time. But you never came back to the Holy City, did you? So Father Serdonis never had a chance to tell you about the workshop."

"No," A'stoc agreed. "I never returned."

"We're close," Chentelle said. She could feel it. The air down here was cold and damp, but it hummed with an almost audible energy. She could feel a great concentration of magic ahead.

"Why, yes," Father Marcus said. "We are close. It is just around this last bend."

They turned the corner and entered a long, straight passageway. At the far end, just before the hallway ended in blank stone, a large wrought-iron door hung on the left wall. The stone of that wall was alive with power. It pulsed in

Chentelle's mind, beating with a slow, steady rhythm like the heart of the world. It surrounded not only the door, but the very walls of the chamber within.

"There it is," Father Marcus said. "But that door has resisted all attempts to access the chamber within. Neither tools nor spells nor the prayers of my brethren have been sufficient to the task."

A'stoc ran fingers slowly over the iron lock. "I have some Lore in magical locks. Perhaps that will be enough." But there was little hope in his voice.

Chentelle felt the mage reach out with his power. Sweat beaded on A'stoc's brow as he reached his mind through the metal, exerting his will on the bars and tumblers. Slowly, straining against decades of disuse, the lock clicked open. But the magic ward was unaffected. A'stoc pulled at the ring, but the door did not move.

"What is wrong?" Father Marcus asked. "I heard the lock open."

"There must be another lock somewhere," A'stoc said. "But I did not sense it with my magic. Perhaps it is in the wall."

Another lock? "Wait," Chentelle said. "It isn't another lock. It's a spell. There's a magic ward that covers the whole chamber."

"What? Are you sure?"

"Of course I'm sure," she said. "I can feel it. It's very powerful. And it flows with its own rhythm, almost like a living thing."

A'stoc's eyes widened in understanding. "Of course, he used the Staff. I didn't think to check for a magical ward; all of A'pon's spells should have died with him. But with the Staff he could fuel his ward with Earthpower."

"And you have the Staff," Chentelle said. Then realized her mistake. He had not mastered the Staff.

The excitement in A'stoc's eyes died suddenly, replaced by a look of absolute defeat. "Then we are lost. No wizard alive has Lore which can counter such magic."

"I could send for some engineers," Father Marcus said. "We could remove a section of the wall."

"No. The stone would not give way. It will hold to the shape of the ward until the spell is broken. And the spell will not fade until the power of Creation is broken. We are lost."

A'stoc turned and started marching furiously back and forth in front of the doorway. The thick air vibrated with his anger and despair. With every second step he brought the Thunderwood Staff down hard against the stone floor, sending deep echoes of sound through the narrow passage.

Chentelle looked to Father Marcus, but the High Bishop just shook his head helplessly. They settled in and watched the mage pace.

Eight steps. Turn. Eight steps. Turn. And all the while beating his tattoo against the stone floor. *Boom.* Pause. *Boom.* Pause. The corridor shook with the rhythm. Even the throbbing of the mystic ward adjusted itself to the mage's cadence.

"A—A'stoc," Chentelle said tentatively.

"WHAT?"

"The ward," she said. "It's responding to the Staff."

"What?" This time the mage stopped pacing.

"The pulsing," Chentelle said. "When you beat the floor with the Staff, the ward pulsed in response."

A'stoc looked at the Staff in his hand, as if seeing it for the first time. Slowly, he reached a hand out and placed it against the stone wall. "I think it would be best if you both sought shelter around the corner."

He was going to try it!

Father Marcus glanced quickly at the Staff and the door. "I understand."

Chentelle could feel A'stoc's tension and determination. She pressed a hand softly against his arm. "You can do this," she said, and then joined Father Marcus in the walk down the corridor. She was halfway to the corner before she heard the mage's reply, barely audible even to elven ears.

"Or die trying."

Chentelle huddled against the stone wall while A'stoc prepared to attack the ward. Effortlessly, she invoked her Gift, letting herself flow naturally into expanded awareness of the Holy Land. She felt the quiet presence of Father Marcus beside her, wrapped in a peace and serenity that was almost inhumanly beautiful. The steady power of the ward burned like a sun, and the rock of the catacombs glowed in its reflection. And beside the ward, a tiny moth hovering near the holocaust, stood A'stoc.

The mage was summoning his power, using the steady mantra of his incantation to coat himself in thin shields of magic. As each layer was completed, A'stoc's presence seemed to solidify, to become clearer, more distinct. He wove his own identity into the spell, forging himself into an anchor of reality.

Without stopping his chant, A'stoc raised the Thunderwood Staff and placed it against the ward. Immediately, the Staff flared into life, pulsing in unison to the ward's rhythm. Magic flared through the hallway, igniting the very air in a maelstrom of power. And in the center of it all, standing like a rock against the hurricane, was A'stoc.

The mage increased the urgency of his chant, stressing the rhythm, hammering out the beat with his voice and his will. He drove his power into the Staff. And, slowly, the Staff responded. The throbbing of the wood changed, adjusting itself to the tempo of A'stoc's spell.

But the rhythm of the ward did not change. Where Staff and spell came together, there was conflict, disharmony. A shudder passed, as though the world held its breath. And chaos erupted in an explosion of violence.

Chentelle was thrown into the air. She fell, sliding against the floor and slamming into the far wall. Pain lanced through her head, and the world became hazy and indistinct. Darkness closed in around her vision.

"Chentelle? Enchantress, can you speak?"

Father Marcus' voice helped Chentelle to anchor herself. Slowly, everything came back into focus. Her face and arms burned from scraping across the rough stone, and the back of her head ached from impact with the wall, but she was not badly hurt. "I'm all right."

Father Marcus helped her struggle to her feet. The priest was unshaken, his robes as neat and unwrinkled as when he had entered the council chamber.

Chentelle tried to shake her head clear, but that only increased the throbbing. "What happ—"

"Aaahhhhh!" The scream of pure agony echoed through the narrow passage.

"A'stoc!" Chentelle pulled free of the priest's hands and ran around the corner. The walls of the hallway were blackened like the walls of a hearth, and dust clouds hovered over a small pile of rubble at the far end. A gaping hole in the left wall marked where the door had stood, but there was no sign of the mage. The mass of rubble and cloud of dust were not large enough to hide a body. As Chentelle came closer she saw another hole, scarring the wall opposite the doorway. A passage had been driven several cubits into the solid stone, and at the far end of the tunnel was A'stoc.

The mage sat sprawled on the floor, clutching his face in both hands. Tears ran down his arms, and his shoulders trembled violently. The Thunderwood Staff lay discarded by his side.

Chentelle rushed forward, almost losing her balance on the uneven ground. "A'stoc? Are you well?"

"Chentelle?" His head snapped up and his eyes locked on hers. "Chentelle!" With a sudden lurch, the mage jumped to his feet and grabbed her by the shoulders. He squeezed her tightly and ran his eyes up and down her body. "You're alive! I was afraid—I thought—"

"We are all alive, Wizard A'stoc," Father Marcus called from the hallway. "And you have succeeded where all others failed. The door is open."

A'stoc quickly dropped his hands. He swayed slightly, as if losing equilibrium, but soon righted himself. He bent and retrieved the Thunderwood Staff. "Well, then, let us discover what we have found."

A'stoc picked his way across the rubble and led them through the shattered doorway. The orb-lights revealed a square chamber, perhaps fifteen cubits on a side. The aroma of herbs and minerals filled the room, fresh as the day they were gathered. Four tables had once dominated the center of the room, stocked with vials and crucibles and a dozen other implements common to the wizard's workshop. All lay in ruin now, crushed under the impact of the twisted iron door, which had been torn from its hinges and thrown across the room. Partially obscured by the rubble, a narrow stone door in the far wall was still intact.

Only a desk and a small chest tucked into one corner had escaped destruction. A'stoc opened the chest and lifted out a pair of candlesticks, a silver place setting, and a red velvet tablecloth. A softness came over his features as he examined the items, then returned them gently to their places. An inkwell and a small red notebook rested neatly on the polished surface of the desk. A'stoc pulled the quill from the well, fresh ink dripping from the tip. He paused for a moment, watching the ink pool, then opened the notebook. A look of pure astonishment crossed his face as he scanned the handwritten pages.

"By the Creator!" The mage whirled suddenly around, orienting on the stone door. Frantically, he scrambled over the shattered tables, oblivious to the splinters of wood and glass. He slammed into the door, pressing furiously against it for a moment. Then, making a sudden realization, he pulled on the handle. The door swung readily open, revealing a small chamber dominated by several large bookshelves. Each shelf was filled with neatly bound red volumes.

From the doorway, Chentelle and Father Marcus watched as A'stoc leaned the Staff carefully against one of the shelves. Then he pulled down one of the books and examined it in the orb-light. "*A'gnivesa's Experiments with Fire.*"

He cradled the book reverently for a moment. Then he replaced it with a trembling hand and reached for another. "*The Codex of Cleansing Rites: Vol. I, minerals and salts.*"

The mage scuttled from shelf to shelf, calling out the titles of one book after another in childlike glee. Finally, he collapsed, sliding slowly to the floor with his back pressed against one shelf and a thick red volume clutched to his chest. "Bless you, Master," he said in a hushed voice. "Bless you."

Father Marcus cleared his throat. "May I take it that you find this discovery to be a cause for hope, Wizard A'stoc?" he asked softly.

A'stoc snapped a sharp look toward the priest, but then he threw back his head and smiled thinly. "You may take it as you wish, High Bishop. Thanks to the wisdom of A'pon Boemarre, the Lore of the great wizards has been preserved. Here, in the Holy Land where no evil could reach it, recorded by hand and ink, the legacy of my master is preserved. Whether that will be enough to save us, I cannot say."

Father Marcus stared. "All the Lore?" he asked, as if some impossible dream had come true, but was in danger of dissipating before it could be grasped.

"We must—" A'stoc paused, as if surprised at his own words. "We must share this discovery with the Collegium. But the originals must stay here, where they are safe. Can your scribes make copies of these volumes?"

"Of course," Father Marcus said. "I shall order the work to begin at once."

While the humans talked, Chentelle's attention was drawn to something at the end of the far shelf. Something about it just didn't look right. As she walked toward it, the impression disappeared. She tried to remember what it was that had seemed strange, but she couldn't. The shelf was identical to all the others. Wait, not quite identical. This shelf was shorter. It seemed to be missing a section.

She walked to the other end, where the missing section should be. But it didn't make sense. The ends of the shelves were all lined up. They must be the same length. Then it became clear. The room wasn't square. The walls and the shelves all slanted slightly, creating the illusion of square angles. But this end of the room was narrower.

Chentelle walked around behind the shelf, hoping to get a better perspective. She discovered two things. First, there was not enough space behind the shelf for even a slim elf girl to squeeze. And second, the walls in this corner did not actually meet. A small gap, obscured by shadow, opened into a hidden niche. Inside the niche was a pedestal on which rested a single red notebook.

"A'stoc," she called. "I think you should come look at this."

The mage hurried over. "What is it, Chentelle? What have you—"

He broke off as he saw the hidden niche and its contents. Slowly, he approached the pedestal, holding up his orb-light to examine the book. "*The Creation and Control of an Animate Manifestation of Earthpower as Extracted from the Living Gateway in Arboreal Form.*" He looked up, his eyes lighting. "By the Creator, enchantress, you found it!"

"Found what?"

"The powers of command for the Thunderwood Staff. This is where they're recorded. This lone volume is more valuable than all the others together. We're saved!" A'stoc flipped open the cover of the book—and a fine mist of soot billowed into the air.

The glow of the orb-light clearly illuminated the look of absolute horror on his face as he stared at the ashes which were all that remained of the book's pages.

ಌ 8 ೞ

QUEST

Chentelle lifted the tray of food from Sulmar's arms. "I think it would be better if I went the rest of the way alone."

"I am sworn to your service, mistress," the Tengarian said, "but it is difficult to protect you if you will not let me stay by your side."

"Please, Sulmar," she said. "You know he does not react well to your presence. Besides, I am in no danger here."

Sulmar looked down into her eyes, his expression absolutely blank. "Very well, mistress, I shall be exercising in the gardens. But be wary. The Holy Land is proof against evil, but it does not necessarily protect us from harm. Bear in mind that explosion when the mage opened the workshop."

"Of course," Chentelle agreed quickly. "I'll come and get you when I am done."

She pushed open the heavy door with her foot and descended the steps into the catacombs. Tracks in the dusty floor attested to the heavy traffic that this path had seen recently. Ever since the discovery of the Lore Books, the scribes of the Holy Order had been bustling about furiously. The job of organizing, indexing, and duplicating A'pon's library had them working day and night. Chentelle was a little nervous about intruding on their effort, but concern for A'stoc compelled her. The scribes worked in shifts, resting in turns, but A'stoc allowed no one access to the Lore books without his presence. He had been working without respite for three days.

A trail of orb-lights mounted hastily on the walls of the corridors marked Chentelle's path. She followed their trail, ignoring the myriad forks and side passages which seemed to have been constructed solely for the purpose of confusing travelers. As she neared her destination, she passed several newly opened rooms in which scribes were laboring. Finally she reached the workshop. The wreckage had been cleared from the room, but the twisted metal hinges still rested in the cracked stone of the doorway.

A long table had been placed just inside the door. A'stoc sat behind it, Thunderwood Staff propped carefully against the wall beside him. He had his face buried in one of the tomes that covered the table in a dozen haphazard stacks.

He did not look up as Chentelle pushed one of the stacks aside to make room for the tray of food. She lifted the cover off the tray, and the hearty aroma of hot stew filled the air. She even fanned the steam in the mage's direction, but still there was no response. "A'stoc! You have been working for three days. If you won't rest, then you must at least eat."

The mage snapped his head up from his book. "What have you got there?" he barked.

Chentelle jumped in surprise at his harsh tone. "Just dinner, A'stoc: stew and bread and some cheese and a tumbler of fresh water."

"What?" he said. "Oh, not you, Chentelle. Him."

Chentelle turned and saw a young scribe frozen in the doorway, clutching a large volume in his hands.

"The th-third volume of the metallurgy catalogue, wizard," he stammered.

"The third volume," A'stoc roared. "Then bring back the second volume."

"I-I h-haven't finished the second one, wizard. This one is for Lallas."

"Very well," said A'stoc, "but I'm holding you responsible for it." He scribbled a quick note onto a parchment and waved the scribe away, muttering about posting a guard. Then he looked up at Chentelle.

"And what do you want?" he asked.

"I want you to eat."

"Hel's Pits," he growled, slamming down his stylus in disgust. "Can I not have five minutes peace from these interruptions? I will eat when I am hungry."

"You will eat because you need to," Chentelle said, shoving the tray in his direction. "Now."

A'stoc glared at her, then lowered his eyes to the tray. "Well, perhaps some water. I am thirsty." He picked up the glass and drained half of it in several large swallows. Then he looked up at her, the ire now gone from his eyes. "All right, leave the food. I'll eat it as soon as I have finished with this chapter."

Chentelle yanked the book from his hands. She marked his place and carefully set the book at the far end of the table. Then she pushed the tray directly in front of him.

A'stoc pointed at the food. "Am I to assume that you will not leave until I have eaten this?"

Chentelle found another chair and removed the pile of books from its seat. Then she pulled it around the table and sat down across from him. "You are very perceptive, for an apprentice."

The mage inhaled deeply and slowly, as if he were about to explode. But he released the breath with only a snort and a self-mocking smile. "Father Marcus is right about who tames the curmudgeon," he muttered. He pulled the tray toward him and started to eat.

Chentelle was embarrassed but insistent. "It's just that you are so important to this effort. We can't let you starve yourself."

He glanced sharply at her. "No other reason, lady?"

Startled by the appellation, from him, she had no ready answer.

"If calling me 'wizard,' " he said between mouthfuls, "keeps these scribes in line, then I will not contradict them. Thanks to the Lore in these books, it may be that I will finally become worthy of that title."

Chentelle studied the mage, trying to see beyond the barriers he erected. The lean face and discontented eyes only hinted at the torments he inflicted upon himself. But she sensed something else, an excitement, an expectation. In anyone else, she would call it hope. The promise of the Lore Books called to him, drove him forward. Determination burned like molten steel in his soul. But even here, he was plagued by doubt, by fatalism, by the deep fear that his quest was doomed to failure.

Chentelle glanced at the books scattered across the table. The Lore they held was so different from her own Gift. Her talent worked in harmony with nature, finding the delicate balance of Creation and working with those rhythms. But the wizard's way was more cold, more calculating. The High Lore taught its practitioners to exert their will on Creation, reshaping it to their own desires. It was a strange philosophy, but she struggled to understand it.

"What were you studying?" she asked.

A'stoc gestured to the book she had taken from him. "That volume deals with some of the finer points of Wood Lore. It is number five in a set of twelve. Master A'pon taught me some of the Lore in this collection, but there are so many useful spells and experiments that he never shared. Given a decade or more, I could barely scratch the surface. If only he had told me of this library." He dropped his eyes and shook his head sadly. "Was I really so untrustworthy?"

Chentelle felt the pain of his question. "No," she said softly. "It's as you told me. The old Masters were afraid of their secrets being betrayed by necromancers. It wasn't just you. A'pon Boemarre was afraid to trust *anyone* with this Lore."

A'stoc nodded slowly. "Perhaps you are right, enchantress. Why else would he lock the books in the deepest basement of the holiest building in all the Realm?"

"Where they would be secure from all discovery," Chentelle said. "But you were able to overcome the spell on the door."

"Not me, the Staff. The Staff's magic was used to power the warding spell. When the two came in contact again, the Staff was activated and the power of the old spell was freed. All I had to do, all I could do, was redirect the power to another use."

Chentelle glanced pointedly at the empty doorway. "Well, to me it looked as if you dipped your hand into somebody else's magepool."

A'stoc stared at Chentelle with a look of astonishment on his face. Then he threw back his head and laughed.

It was a good laugh, one Chentelle was surprised to realize she had never heard before. There was fatigue in the sound, but the mirth was genuine, open. It pulled at her, coaxing her to join in the merriment. So she did. It felt good to share an honest emotion with the taciturn wizard. It felt right. The song of their laughter rang perfectly in the harmony of this place.

The mirth faded away gently, naturally, leaving an easy smile on A'stoc's face. "Well put, enchantress. An apt analogy, indeed."

The mage swallowed a few more bites of stew. Then he looked up and adopted a more serious tone. "Chentelle, I want to thank you. I would never have come here if it had not been for your persistence. I admire your courage and your determination." He lowered his head quickly, almost before he had finished speaking, as if he were ashamed to admit his gratitude.

"Thank you for those kind words. You are most welcome to any help I may have given you."

"You are as gracious as you are—" A'stoc turned away, not finishing. He mopped up the last of his stew with a bit of bread and popped it in his mouth. Then he washed it down with the last of the water. Finally, he turned back to Chentelle. "There, I am finished. May I return to my book, now, mistress elf?"

Chentelle sighed as she felt the man's barriers snap back into place. It was so senseless. This land was alive with the music of Creation, and for a moment they had shared in that song. But now he was pushing her away again. He had opened up before, when conversation had turned to the Staff. Maybe it would work twice.

She handed him the book. "Have you found out anything more about the Staff?"

A wave of pain washed over A'stoc's face. He reached into his robe and pulled out a bundled cloth. Carefully, he unwrapped the cloth, revealing the charred remains of the book they had discovered. "I cannot understand it. It was all here, the command words, the hierarchy of powers, the rituals of binding, all recorded in my master's own hand. But then he destroyed it. It had to have been him. No one else could have bypassed the warding spell. But why? Did he become so jealous of the Staff's power that he could not stand the thought of anyone else using it?"

He paused, shaking his head sadly. Then he looked up at Chentelle, a thin smile coming slowly to his face. "But perhaps I have learned something after all, despite A'pon's paranoia."

"That's wonderful," cried Chentelle. "But what? How?"

"As you said," the wizard replied, "I put my hand into someone else's magepool. But I am not a novice. When the Thunderwood Staff was activated, I was not just riding the wave of power, I was also learning from it."

The force of his excitement crashed over Chentelle, making her almost dizzy. "Does that mean you can activate the Staff? Oh, A'stoc, that's fantastic. Do you think you will be able to help the High Bishop?"

"The High Bishop?" A'stoc's face darkened, all signs of openness and excitement hidden behind a curtain of suspicion. "Did he send you down here to ferret information out of me?"

"No! I mean—Father Marcus did ask me to talk to you, but—"

"So he sent you to see if the old apprentice knows what he is doing," A'stoc growled. "So you come bearing food in kindness, but all the while you're spying for Marcus."

Chentelle jumped to her feet. "I am not so manipulative! I came here of my own will, urged only by concern for you. Though I'm hard-pressed to imagine why at just this moment. Do all wizards lead lives of mistrust and suspicion? Have you learned nothing from the beauty of this land? I came to you with friendship, A'stoc. How you receive it is up to you." Her words were bold, but there were tears in her eyes.

A'stoc turned away from her, shielding his eyes with one hand. "Your words are convincing, but how can I trust them? You are an enchantress, able to weave the fabric of a man's heart with the power of your voice."

He hesitated for a moment, rocking back and forth in inner turmoil. Then he shot out of his chair, grabbing the Staff with both hands. He towered over Chentelle, anger flaring in his eyes, but there was no threat of violence. In this place, anger could be turned only to resolve. "You are curious. And the High Bishop is curious. Well, perhaps it is time to show you what I can do. I would not have you worrying unduly."

With that, the wizard marched out of the chamber, moving quickly with long, purposeful steps.

"A'stoc, wait," Chentelle cried. "Where are you going?" But no answer came.

She hurried out the doorway and caught a glimpse of the wizard disappearing around the corner. She raced to catch up, having almost to run in order to keep pace with A'stoc's strides.

A'stoc ignored all questions about his destination or his purpose. In silence, he led her up from the depths of the catacombs. When they reached the ground level, he marched directly to the central stairway and started climbing again. The ground fell away as they mounted flight after flight of invisible stairs. The mage covered two or three steps with each stride, and Chentelle fought to keep up. By the time they reached the level of the main assembly hall, both were struggling for breath.

As they climbed to the next level, Chentelle saw that a large gathering was being held in the hall. Father Marcus addressed an assembly of priests and other clergy. Chentelle waved frantically, catching the High Bishop's eye. She pointed at A'stoc, shrugged her shoulders, and motioned upward with both hands.

Father Marcus stared up at her through the transparent ceiling, surprise and concern plain on his face. Then he nodded. He spoke briefly to his fellowship and then headed quickly for the door.

Chentelle turned back to the stairs and gasped in surprise. A'stoc was no-where in sight. She ran upward, almost slamming into the tapestry-covered door that marked the top of the stairs. She threw open the door and darted through. And paused in wonder.

She was in a huge circular room that seemed to occupy the entire top floor of the Cathedral. There was no roof, but high walls around the circumference shielded the room from the winds which whistled above her head. Another stairwell lay before her, leading into the central spire rising high above. Inside it, barely discernible through the glare of reflected light, was the dark figure of a climbing man. Chentelle pushed herself toward the steps.

The stairs wound their way around the tower, narrowing their spiral as they climbed. From here, Chentelle could see all of the Holy City, sprawled out peacefully around Norivika Bay. She passed a belfry filled with huge crystal spheres of various sizes. The balls looked hollow and hung from a central beam like large bells, but there were no pull cords or strikers. And the stairs kept leading higher.

Suddenly, a gust of wind blasted Chentelle's face. She slipped on the trans-parent stairs and nearly lost her balance. The ground taunted her from a hundred cubits below. Vertigo threatened to overwhelm her, but the cool wind helped her keep her mind clear. The top must be near, for the wind to be so strong. She forced herself onward.

Within a dozen steps, she passed through an open doorway onto a narrow observation platform. She stood at the very top of the Cathedral of Light, with no walls between her and the vast blue sky. The unobstructed wind screamed about her, nearly tearing her from the platform. Desperately she groped for support. Her hands found a narrow balustrade. She clung to it, steadying herself. The wind whipped her hair about her head, and her robe about her legs.

At the center of the platform, A'stoc rested his weight on the Thunderwood Staff, defying the gale that thrashed his tattered robes. He nodded to Chentelle, mouthing words which were lost to the wind. Then he lifted the Staff high above his head.

Immediately, Chentelle felt a surge of magic. A'stoc drove his will into the

Thunderwood Staff, trying to form a channel to the unimaginable power within. The wood remained inert, but still he poured his strength into it. Sweat beaded on his forehead and was ripped away by the wind. His arms trembled, exhausted by the strain, but his determination, his desperation, would not let him quit.

Suddenly, the Staff flared into life. A nimbus of deep green light erupted from the wood, permeating the wizard, sending a torrent of force coursing through his body.

A'stoc's laughter echoed through the air like thunder. He thrust the Staff into the air, and a blast of eldritch energy sliced into the cloudless sky. The azure calm churned and started to darken. Again and again, the wizard thrust his bolts of power into the air, and the sky turned black beneath a sorcerous storm.

Chentelle screamed. The harmony of the Holy Land was being twisted to A'stoc's will. With the Thunderwood Staff, he could bend Creation itself. Not even the peace of the Holy Land was inviolate. The aurora of light that surrounded the wizard was beautiful, magnificent, but the power it heralded was terrifying.

A'stoc shouted a command and the winds stopped. Overhead, the storm clouds hung in eerie stillness. The wizard stood with arms upraised to his accomplishment, strange shadows dancing across his face in the emerald glow of the Staff. His smile was one of pure rapture, but the wild gleam in his eyes spoke of other, darker emotions.

Soft footfalls marked the arrival of Father Marcus. The sound echoed strangely in the mystical silence. But when the High Bishop spoke, his words banished the emptiness, filling it with unshaken faith and calm concern. "Wizard A'stoc, why have you done this? The Dark One surely watches the Holy Land. He will sense this disturbance."

"Let the Dark One see!" A'stoc shouted. "Let him know the power that opposes him!" The wizard's body trembled with barely contained energy. "I have done it! I have unlocked the power of the Staff. Now I can avenge my master. If the Dark One stands against me, I will destroy him."

"Wizard A'stoc," Father Marcus said soothingly. "It is well that you have learned to wield the Tree of Life. We sorely need its power. But before you attack the Dark One, remember your master. Remember A'pon Boemarre. He, too, wielded the power you now feel. But he failed. Would you share his fate?"

Chentelle felt a softening in the wall of anger and energy that seethed about the wizard. But it was not enough. The song of the Staff was still too strong. "A'stoc." She pitched her words carefully, blending each syllable into the pattern of power and doubt. "Do not lose yourself. Do not let this power swallow you. Be true to your soul. Be true to your heart."

Slowly a change came over the wizard. The shadows faded from his face, and his eyes widened in dismay. "By the Creator, what have I done?" He let the Staff drop to his side, releasing his hold on the elements. The green radiance flickered into nothingness, and the wind returned in a sudden thunderclap, nearly unbalancing them all. A'stoc staggered to his knees, nearly losing his grip on the Staff as he struggled for support.

Chentelle leaned into the wind, forcing her way to the wizard's side. Father Marcus came up beside her, and together they struggled to help him rise. But the swirling winds turned every motion into a battle for equilibrium. They managed to get A'stoc to his feet, but a sudden gust made the human lurch violently. Chentelle overbalanced and lost her footing. She staggered sideways, crashing into the transparent railing. For a moment she teetered on the brink of falling. Then a strong hand caught her outflung wrist.

It was Sulmar. He pulled her back from the edge and lifted her easily to her feet. The Tengarian poised on the balls of his feet, shifting his balance almost instinctively to counter the force of the wind. He anchored Chentelle with one arm and used the other to help Father Marcus pull A'stoc into the shelter of the stairs. As they entered the spire, the first drops of warm rain washed over them.

❧

The weeks passed slowly as the two suns grew farther apart and the nights grew short. They passed the time making ready for the quest to come.

Dacius and the Legionnaires trained diligently, though it was a struggle for them to practice arms in this place of serenity. The human lord even had the smiths of Norivika work to replace the armor that had gone down with the *Otan Stin.* Word had reached him that the bodies of the others had been recovered and returned to their homelands for permanent burial, but none of the lost swords had been found. They would have to make do with the arms they had.

Father Marcus spent the time organizing and preparing the Holy Order for the trials they would face in his absence. The reports from beyond the Barrier, tales of Ill-creatures appearing in ever greater strength and confidence, caused him obvious pain, but his only response was to exhort the scribes to increase their effort. He remained adamant that none of the party leave the Holy Land to assist in the defense. For now, the defense of the Realm would have to be entrusted to the wizards of the Collegium.

A'stoc remained sequestered among the Lore Books. He took his meals in the workshop and had a cot installed next to his desk so that he would not have to climb the stairs to find sleep. He emerged only on those rare occasions when the need for cleanliness or a softer sleep became overwhelming.

Chentelle used the time to explore the Holy Land. With Sulmar always at her side, she wandered the city of Norivika and its outlying villages. Everywhere she was greeted by an open friendliness that woke echoes of home in her heart. With Brother Ethnan's permission, she even traveled to Atablicryon Island. The gardens there were very different from the wild beauty of Lone Valley, but somehow the tranquillity of the place eased her homesickness.

Finally, the First Season of Light came upon them. Sulmar had gone to the gardens to perform his afternoon exercises, and Chentelle was taking advantage of the rare solitude. She wandered the upper levels of the Cathedral, keeping only her thoughts for company. The transparent walls and floors no longer made her uneasy. Now, she took pleasure in the illusion of floating freely in the air, seeing the beauty of the world from the Creator's own perspective.

But today she felt unsettled, out of step, somehow, with the peacefulness of the Holy Land. It was nervousness, she realized, anticipation. Tomorrow they would leave the security of the Holy Land, and who could know what they would encounter?

Lost in her thoughts, she walked straight into Father Marcus as he rounded

a turn in the corridor. The High Bishop seemed to be as startled by the encounter as she was.

"Lady Chentelle," he said, "please excuse me. I did not see you."

"The fault is mine, Father Marcus," she said. "I'm afraid I wasn't paying
attention to where I was walking."

The old priest smiled at her warmly. "I understand. After so many weeks
of waiting, it is hard to believe that the time is here. Preparation and planning
are a poor substitute for reality, it seems."

"I know." His words described exactly what she felt. "Usually, the view
from up here calms me, gives me a sense of peace and belonging. But today,
everything seems different, somehow."

"We have a few hours before supper," he said. "I was going to spend part
of that time in meditation, to prepare myself for the Vespers tonight. Would
you care to join me?"

"Yes," said Chentelle. "I think I would. I am curious about the way your
devotions relate to my own Gift."

The High Bishop turned around and started walking back the way he had
come. "Then follow me. Perhaps we can help you find peace and satisfy your
curiosity at the same time."

He led her through a tapestry-shrouded door into a small room. With a
start, Chentelle realized that it was his own sleeping chamber. An elven-crafted
bed filled one corner, elegant without being luxurious. The opposite corner was
occupied by a small writing desk and a collection of books. The floor was car-
peted, wall to wall, in rich blue, and the wall opposite the bed was covered with
a magnificent tapestry depicting doves in flight through a rich garden. It was
one of the gardens of Atablicryon Island, but in the tapestry a huge tree dominated the center of the garden. The other walls were covered with plain drapes
of blue or white.

There were no chairs other than the small bench at the writing table, but
a pile of pillows lay against the far wall. Father Marcus settled himself on one
of these and motioned for her to choose one as well. The High Bishop reached
without looking into a shelf beside the bed and drew out two books.

"These are the foundation of the Holy Order," he said. "The texts upon
which all of our devotions are based. The Book of Truths tells us what the world
was like in the Time of Perfection, what the world was meant to be. The
Scriptures of Jediah tell us how we, as servants of the Creator, can act to restore
the Creation. Through these meditations we learn to return small parts of the
Creation to their true form. This is the truth behind the powers of the Holy
Order, the power to heal, to create sanctuary, to summon orb-light and warmth
from the earth, and, most importantly, to bring peace to the troubled spirit."

Father Marcus opened the Scriptures of Jediah. He flipped the pages with
a practiced hand, coming quickly to the passage he was seeking. He handed her
the book. "This is the Meditation on Darkness. I always review it before cele-
brating the Grand Vespers. Will you sing it with me?"

Chentelle glanced at the flowing script, reading the prayer silently. The
words seemed simple enough, and the meter was straightforward. She set the
book down in front of her and nodded to Father Marcus. He began singing in
a pleasant baritone, and she joined in, letting her voice flow easily into his.

"The world must turn away from Ellistar,
The world must turn from Deneob into night,
The song exists in silence, between notes,
In shadows do we learn to love the light."

They repeated the chant again and again. Each time they sang a little bit softer, until only the melody remained, kept alive by the music of their voices. But the words had not disappeared. They echoed softly in the quiet corners of Chentelle's mind.

She tried to follow their meaning. The meditation really didn't seem to be talking about darkness at all. It was about motion. The world turned away from the suns because it *had* to. And later it would turn out of darkness and back to the light. That was the rhythm of Creation. It was present in the change from day into night, and it was there in the progression of the seasons. Motion could not be denied.

She thought about her own life. She was in darkness now, traveling away from her home, her family. But she would return. That was the lesson of the meditation. The Creation was a sphere. The rhythms always brought you home again. And she had certainly learned to love Lone Valley in the time she had been away from it.

But what about the third line? How could a song exist in silence? If the meditation was talking about her own life, then the notes must be her experiences. Or maybe they were her. She would be a different person when she next saw Lone Valley, a different note. And if you could play all the notes of all the different Chentelle notes that she would become in her life, you would have a song. But the song didn't live in the notes. It lived in the experiences that made those notes different, in the process of growth and change.

It was all starting to make sense. The quest they were about to begin wasn't a journey into darkness. It was just part of the natural cycle of Creation. And they were not traveling alone. They were joining in the song of the world, fulfilling one small part of the Sphere of Perfection.

Chentelle realized that she had stopped singing some time ago, and she no longer heard the voice of Father Marcus. It didn't matter. The song of Creation was strong within her. It lifted her spirit, carrying her outward. She joined in the perfect harmony of the Holy Land, of the world, of the Sphere of Creation as it was meant to be. She spent a timeless interval lost in the wholeness of perfect union.

Eventually, she realized that it was time for her to return, to become separate again so that she could complete her own part of the great harmony. Gradually, she became aware of her body, of the floor beneath her legs, the rhythm of her breathing. Sound filled her ears, and she realized that she was singing again, humming the rhythm of Father Marcus' meditation.

The High Bishop sat across from her, eyes closed, humming the same tune. She let herself be drawn into the tranquil pool of his spirit. There was a peace and serenity about him that was perfectly in tune with the Holy Land. She drifted in that calmness for a time, and then she noticed something else, something deeper.

There were walls in his soul, walls as solid and impregnable as A'stoc's, except that these walls were turned inward. One part of Father Marcus' mind had been separated from the rest. And she could sense a presence behind those walls, something cold, something dark, something evil.

Suddenly, Chentelle was thrust back into her own awareness. She still felt the harmony of Talan, but the special communion with Father Marcus was gone.

The High Bishop had his eyes open, now, and he was staring at her in frank astonishment. He shook his head, slowly regaining his composure. He stood up, and offered a hand to Chentelle. "Once again, you have surprised me, enchantress. You are more sensitive to the Creation than I had realized."

Chentelle felt herself flush with embarrassment. "Thank you, Father Marcus. I found your meditation to be both helpful and enlightening."

He gave her a curious look, then nodded as if coming to a decision. "Lady Chentelle, I must know what you felt during our communion in the meditation."

"I felt the depth of your faith and serenity. It was truly beautiful." But she knew that his question had a deeper thrust. But what should she say? If he was really evil, then—No, he was not evil. She would have sensed that long ago. It had to be some type of curse or spell. "And I felt a hidden core of darkness, an evil that you keep locked away from the rest of your being. Is it a curse, Father Marcus? It's different from the taint on Sulmar's spirit, but I know you are not evil."

The High Bishop shook his head thoughtfully. "No, Chentelle, it is not a curse. Or perhaps it is, but it is also a hope. It is a burden that I have been chosen to carry."

"But what is it? And who chose you?"

"I will tell you what I may," he said, "but you must swear to keep all of this conversation secret, even from our companions."

Keep a secret from their friends and allies? But there was no flexibility in the High Bishop's eyes, and no arguing with the urgency she sensed in his voice. "I promise."

Father Marcus cupped one of her hands between his own. "What you felt within me is the knowledge of evil that will enable me to destroy the Fallen Star. I cannot tell you how I came to bear it, or even what the knowledge is. For now, it lies dormant within me, but when the time comes it will give me the understanding necessary to preserve Infinitera from destruction."

Chentelle felt the great weight of responsibility in Marcus' words. She also felt the unwavering strength of his faith. He was truly remarkable. "But wouldn't it be easier if you could share this knowledge? Then each of us could bear a part of the burden, and you wouldn't have to suffer it all."

He smiled and shook his head. "No, Chentelle, though your suggestion shows the strength of your heart. The knowledge I carry is as dangerous in its own way as the Fallen Star. This burden is for me alone to carry. When I die, I must be certain that this evil dies with me."

It wasn't fair, she thought. No one should have to endure such a trial without help. It was too much like the torment that A'stoc put himself through. But what could she do? "I understand," she said, closing her eyes against her tears.

And there was nothing more to say. They stood together in silence for a time. Then, by silent assent, they went to the dining hall to join the others for supper.

ॐ

Chentelle was surprised to see A'stoc sitting at the table with the others. But before she could say anything, a shout came from across the room.

"Mistress! Are you well? I have been searching for you."

"Sulmar!" she said, suddenly embarrassed. "Oh, I'm sorry. Father Marcus was teaching me about the meditations of the Holy Order. I lost track of the time."

The Tengarian gave Father Marcus a look that bordered on mistrust, but he fell into step beside Chentelle without another word.

"I do hope that you have not been waiting long," the High Bishop said to the company. An assortment of vegetable dishes, sauces, and freshly baked breads filled the air with delicious aromas. Marcus took his place at the head of the table and waited for Chentelle and Sulmar to find their seats. "The Creator has blessed us with this bounty. Let us be thankful and accept it in the spirit of service and unity."

As one, they brought their hands to their lips and extended them in the sign of harmony.

"It is good to see you, A'stoc," Chentelle said. "I thought we would have to drag you from your books when it was time to leave."

The wizard pointed at Sulmar with a spoon full of carrots. "Well, since your trained barbarian had interrupted my studies anyway, I decided this would be a good time to pack for our journey."

Chentelle turned a quizzical eye toward her liegeman.

"The mage dissembles, liege," Sulmar said. "When I told him that you had disappeared, he broke off his research to help me search."

Chentelle turned back to the wizard in amazement. She wasn't sure which surprised her more, A'stoc interrupting his studies or the note of respect in Sulmar's voice. "Why, A'stoc, thank you."

The wizard glanced about uncomfortably. Finally, his eyes came to rest on Rone. "Captain, how go the preparations for the ship?"

"Huh? Oh, fine, wizard," Rone said between mouthfuls. "The provisions have been stowed, and the hull is tight. I just wish I had been able to take her out and get the feel of her. But I guess a goblinship sailing around Norivika Bay would attract a bit too much attention, eh? Oh, but I have found a shipsage I can live with, so I guess we're as ready as we're likely to get. I've even settled on her new name."

The last comment caught everyone's attention, but the captain did not elaborate. Finally Dacius broke the silence. "Well I'll ask. What is this new name?"

"Well, Lord Gemine," said Rone. "Since our voyage will be shrouded in secrecy and deceit, I've christened her accordingly. Her new name is—*Treachery.*"

Dacius cocked an eyebrow in surprise. "Interesting choice."

After that, the meal proceeded with little conversation. There was an unusual tension in the air, generated by the closeness of their departure.

As the banquet drew to a close, Father Marcus addressed the company. "Friends, you all know that the quest we begin tomorrow will not be an easy one. I have told you before, and I will tell you again. If any of you wish to decline the danger, you may do so freely."

One of the Legionnaires stood up. It was Gerruth. "Lord High Bishop, we have sat here, safe in the protection of the Holy Land while the people we are sworn to protect suffer the Ill-creatures' attacks. We have stayed here because you told us it was necessary. Because your quest demanded secrecy, we have ignored the screams of our brothers. Because your quest may be the Realm's only hope, we have denied the cries for vengeance in our souls. Do not insult us by questioning our courage now."

"Gerruth!" Dacius snapped. "That's enough. Apologize to Father Marcus."

"No, Lord Gemine," the priest said. "It is I who should apologize." He turned to Gerruth. "This waiting has been difficult for all of us, but it has brought special pain to you, whose sense of duty cried out for action. Without intending to, I have made that pain worse. I ask for your forgiveness."

The stiffness melted from Gerruth's posture. "You have it, Lord High Bishop. As well as my own apology. I should not have taken out my anger on you. But have faith in this, the Creator himself could not stop me from being aboard that goblinship in the morning."

The Legionnaire's determination was quickly echoed by the rest of the company.

Father Marcus bowed his head in acknowledgment. "Your faith and courage are both a blessing and an inspiration. We leave in the morning, but tonight the Holy Order celebrates a Grand Vespers. It is an open ceremony, and I hope that you will all attend. I can think of no finer way to sanctify the beginning of our journey."

"Oh, yes," Chentelle said. "It will be beautiful."

Dacius nodded in agreement. "I think I can safely say that we will all be present, Father Marcus."

"Then you think incorrectly, Lord Gemine," A'stoc said.

"What?" Chentelle was astonished. "Aren't you coming?"

"No," the wizard answered flatly.

This was terrible. If anyone needed to feel the unity and communion of the Vespers, it was A'stoc. "Please, A'stoc, we won't be complete without you. And I think it would really do you good."

The wizard slammed his fist down on the table, scattering dishes and silverware. "Well, I do not!" He pushed himself away from the table and stood, grabbing hold of the Thunderwood Staff. "I am tired from my research. I think I will go to bed early. Good night." With that, he spun on his heels and marched out of the room.

"That's a man with fear in his heart," Captain Rone said after the wizard was out of earshot.

"He has reason to be afraid," Thildemar said.

"What reason?" returned the captain. "Every man here faces the same burden."

"Perhaps, or perhaps not." Thildemar's eyes sparkled as he turned to Chentelle. "What do you say, enchantress?"

Chentelle's face started to flush. Something about the old elf's attention made her feel suddenly young and unsophisticated. "Yes. I mean, no, it isn't the same burden."

Captain Rone gave her a puzzled look. "Far be it from me to contradict a lady as beautiful and talented as yourself, enchantress, but it seems to me that we're all going to be in the same boat, if you'll pardon the expression."

"You're right, captain, but only half right." Chentelle searched for the words to explain what she was feeling. "You see, I am sure you are a very fine seaman, but there are other men who could pilot the goblinship. If not as well as you, then at least well enough. And each of the Legionnaires knows that the strength and skill of his own sword is supported by that of his comrade's. But only A'stoc can use the Thunderwood Staff. If one of us falls, someone will step into our place. If A'stoc fails, the world dies. Only Father Marcus carries a burden like that."

"Father Marcus?" asked Rone.

"Yes, he—" Oh, no, she was about to give away Father Marcus' secret. She glanced quickly in his direction, but the priest's calm expression betrayed nothing. She looked away and cocked her head, hoping the others would interpret her pause as shyness. "Well, he's the guiding force behind our quest. It's his wisdom, his faith that will lead us to our goal. In many ways he, too, is indispensable."

"Thank you, Chentelle," the High Bishop said, "though I am not sure I deserve to be singled out. A similar case can be made for you, too. I believe we are all indispensable to the success of this mission. The Creator has not brought us together without reason. Perhaps the Vespers will help us all understand that reason a little more clearly." He closed his eyes and cocked his head, as if listening to a faint sound. "I believe it is time. Will you join me?"

He led them out of the dining hall and across to the central stairs. But rather than going down to the ground-level temples, he took them upward. As they climbed, they could see the solitary figure of A'stoc, pacing furiously through the hallways below.

"How is it," Dacius inquired, "that the wizard can hold such anger despite the influence of the Holy Land?"

"Anger is not evil," Thildemar said, "only foolish. Wouldn't you agree, Lady Chentelle?"

Again, something gleamed within the old elf's eyes, but this time it was a flash of sorrow, a glimpse of an old and heavy pain. It vanished as quickly as it had appeared, and Chentelle felt a surge of embarrassment, as if she had eavesdropped on a private conversation. "Yes, though I think I would call it sad, not foolish. Especially when a person directs the anger at himself."

Thildemar's only reply was a slim smile and a brief bow of his head.

They reached the top of the stairs and emerged onto the roof level of the main cathedral. Deneob had long ago disappeared from the sky, and Ellistar was just passing below the horizon. In the fading light, hundreds of people occupied the roof. It seemed as though all of the Holy City was here, arranged in a circle around the central spire.

Father Marcus and Gorin broke off and headed toward the center of the gathering, where a small platform had been erected. The rest of them found an open area around the perimeter. There were no ushers or officials directing traffic; every person just knew where he should be.

As they settled into their place, Dacius tapped Chentelle on the shoulder. "You seem to know something about this ceremony. Can you tell me what it's about?"

"Well, I have never been to one myself, but Father Marcus did share some of the concepts with me. The Vespers ceremony is a celebration of evening and the hours of darkness. It's something the Holy Order does in private ceremony every day. But because tonight is the last evening before the First Season of Light, when there is no darkness, it is an open ceremony and everybody takes part."

"So what do we do?" Dacius asked.

"We sing."

He frowned. "Sing? I can't sing. I never sing in public."

Chentelle smiled. "You do not have to sing. But maybe you will find it in your heart to do so anyway."

Before Dacius could question her further, the clear tones of a ringing bell called the crowd to silence. Then, the deep voice of the High Bishop washed over the assembly. "Thank you, friends, for coming to share this communion with us. We celebrate the Grand Vespers introducing the First Season of Light. It is a time of reflection and contemplation, a time when we reach out to the truth of Creation, a time when we refresh our spirits with the love of the Creator. With open hearts, let us begin this communion."

Father Marcus made the sign of harmony. Then, leaving his arms extended, he closed his eyes and began to sing. He wove his song without words, establishing a simple rhythmic hum of four notes. Deeply, slowly, smoothly, his voice resonated high through the assembly.

Bishop Sarra joined him on the center platform, taking hold of his right hand. She joined in Father Marcus' song, blending her own ethereal voice to his rich baritone. She varied the theme, wrapping her melody through and around his own, then brought it back to the original four notes. The harmony they created was flawless.

Then Gorin stepped up and took the High Bishop's other hand. He sung a deep bass note, punctuating the theme like a drum. Then other voices joined in. Slowly, the harmony took on new depth, new complexities. The air filled with power as the song took shape. Tenors sang out like chimes, while baritones carried the theme, and the deep bass gave power to the entire chorus.

The song spread outward, moving through the crowd. Chentelle felt it take hold of her, and she surrendered herself to the rapture. She joined one hand with Sulmar's and the other to Dacius', and she sang. The Gift poured out of her, effortlessly, inevitably. Her voice joined in the chorus of Creation, echoing the perfection of the Holy Land. The communion was complete. She was joined with every person here, with the birds in the air, the fish in the bay. Everywhere the song reached, there was harmony.

She felt the voice of Dacius rising next to her. The human's reticence had vanished at the song's touch. Like everyone else present, he was pulled blissfully into the perfect harmony.

As the last members of the assembly joined their voices to the chorus, the song changed. The notes took on a new timbre, a new fullness. What had seemed to be perfection became more. The walls of the Cathedral of Light resonated with the power of the song, and from high above, another sound joined the harmony: bells. The great crystal bells in the spire rang in response to the voices below, each sounding a single, flawless note that echoed in the heart and lifted the soul.

Chentelle swam in the union of the song, losing herself in the ecstasy. She let herself drift, touching the spirits of her fellow celebrants as they passed. The song filled Creation, and she could touch everything within it. She felt herself drawn in a particular direction, and followed the pull. She floated through the crystal walls and floors until she felt something strange, something *other*. It was a cold thing, hard and jagged. It didn't flow or sing or sway with the melody of Creation. But it had its own song, a sad and tragic hymn filled with bitterness and recrimination. Of course this was A'stoc.

The wizard's walls were as hard as ever, but even they could not be impervious to this music. The harmony touched him, echoing in his soul, but his anger would not let him submit to the rhythm. He stood rigidly, leaning on his Staff, fighting against the stirring in his heart.

It made Chentelle want to weep. His suffering was so unnecessary. If only she could make him see. She wrapped her song around A'stoc, letting the music flow into him. She could not penetrate the wizard's walls, but she could make those walls resonate with her own harmony.

A discordant note thrummed through her spirit. Conflict. A'stoc's own song resisted her. She could overpower it; her own rhythm echoed the tune of the Creation. But that was not the way of harmony. She altered her song, trying to blend into A'stoc's rhythm and create a new harmony. She felt the disharmony fade. Slowly, the walls in A'stoc's soul started to soften, as their songs melted together.

Suddenly, she was pulled away. By altering her song to match A'stoc's, she had slipped out of harmony with the song of the Vespers. Now, the union was broken, and the ceremony was coming to an end. As the song died away, the participants were drawn back to their isolated existences. The last thing she witnessed, before the physical world claimed her awareness, was A'stoc, tears in his eyes, turning away and running for the shelter of his room.

The night was short, the morning bright. By the time Ellistar crept over the horizon, Deneob was well past zenith. This was why Father Marcus had chosen to wait for the Season of Light, the time when Infinitera moved between the Two Sisters. For weeks, there would be almost no darkness as the world shifted into the hands of Deneob, the Winter Sun. That meant that for weeks the Ill-creatures would be unable to act, unable to move against the quest.

They traveled by carriage to a large, closed boathouse near the shipyards. There was an air of excitement about the company, an exultation and anticipation that filled the air. It was a feeling shared by all of the party except two. Chentelle still felt a twinge of guilt for having disrupted the Vespers, though Father Marcus had assured her that the song had ended only because it had been the correct time for it to do so. Her gloom was only deepened by A'stoc's complete withdrawal from any communication. The wizard had not spoken a word all morning, not even in answer to direct questions.

They made their way inside the boathouse. A single, stout craft was moored within. It could not be mistaken; it was the goblinship, now renamed *Treachery*. Just over fifty cubits in length, its dark black-oak frame looked stained with malice, and the twin masts had awkward lateen-rigged sails. The design looked crude in comparison to the smooth lines of elven vessels, with the only hint of sleekness coming from the elongated prow with its fanged serpent figurehead. A single ballista was mounted just behind the bowsprit. The sight sent a cold shiver down Chentelle's spine.

"Father Marcus," she asked, "how did such a ship come to be in the Holy Land?"

"I think Gorin can tell that story best," he said, nodding toward his acolyte.

All eyes turned toward the goblin priest.

Gorin flicked his nictitating eyelids several times at the sudden attention. "It was entirely by chance," he rumbled in deep, soft tones. "Which is to say, it was surely by the will of the Creator. I was the spell-weaver of this ship, what you would call a shipsage. In its day, it was a proud whaling ship. But during the human wars, the Heresiarch of Desecration ordered it refitted as a warship. The first time it met a battle at sea, we learned the folly of that decision." He winced, then continued.

"A human warship routed us, and we were forced to flee to the north. But a chance storm caught us in its arms. It may have saved our lives, for it blew the humans off our trail, but it also blew us off our course and damaged our hull. It took all of my Lore just to keep the ship afloat. When the storm died, we headed straight for the nearest harbor we could see. That harbor was Norivika Bay.

"As soon as we passed through the Barrier, the peace and tranquillity of the Holy Land filled me. For the first time in my existence, I felt the communion of life. The rest of the crew was similarly affected. All thoughts of war became impossible and we surrendered to the officials of the Holy Order. My brothers-in-arms chose to return to their homes and families, even though it meant forsaking the beauty of Creation, but I stayed. The Holy Land breathes truths into my soul that I had never before imagined. I have dedicated my life to understanding those truths. One day, when I have learned enough, I will return to the Hordelands and teach my people the truth of the Holy Order, show them that the Ill-Lore of the Heresiarchs is not the only way."

Determination and devotion rang behind Gorin's words like finely tempered steel. It made Chentelle want to reach out and hug the goblin priest. And she was not the only one affected.

"That is a brave dream," Dacius said, "a dream worthy of any man. May the Creator smile on it."

"He will," Gorin said. "It is his will that guides me."

Chentelle had no reason to doubt that, and felt a tinge of guilt for her fear that the mission was by no means assured of success.

Captain Rone led the way onto the ship, bounding up the gangplank with unrestrained enthusiasm. "Get a move on, lords and lady. You have my permission to board and be quick about it. There's a wide sea calling, and I don't plan on keeping her waiting."

The captain's energy infected them all. Chentelle could not help smiling as she carried her pack up the walkway and boarded the ship. But her smile vanished the instant she set foot on the deck. A lance of agony shot through her. The wood for these planks had been severed by axe blades, and it was done while the trees were still alive! She staggered dizzily, and only Sulmar's quick support and the closeness of the rail kept her from falling. Nausea twisted her stomach, and she vomited over the side.

"Mistress, what is wrong?"

Sulmar's concern washed over her like a wave of clean water, helping focus her thoughts. "The wood—" she gasped. "The ship—can't you feel it?"

"No, mistress," the Tengarian said. "What can I do?"

His presence was a rock, and Chentelle used it to steady herself. She drew back her perceptions, pulling away from the source of her pain. "I'm all right, Sulmar. Just help me to stand."

He eased her gently to her feet, hovering nervously nearby in case she should swoon again.

"It's okay, now," she said, taking in a deep breath. "I was only caught by surprise. This wood has suffered such terrible pain."

"And you feel that pain," Father Marcus said. "I am sorry. I had no idea it would affect you so. Will you be able to endure?"

"I have to," she said. "This is the ship we have to use." She straightened her robes and forced herself to smile through the pain. "The worst has passed. I can still feel the echoes of pain, but it won't overwhelm me again."

"Lady Chentelle," Captain Rone said. "Maybe you should go below. Some rest in your cabin might do you good."

Chentelle shuddered at the thought of surrounding herself with the cries of the wood, of lying down on a bed of butchered planks. "Thank you, Captain, but I think I'll stay up here. The fresh sea air will help me most."

"As you will, lady," he said, and then he set about readying the ship for departure. His crewmen, the cousins Zubec and Pardec, helped him in this, as did several of the Legionnaires. Gorin helped them adjust the lateen rigging, and soon the *Treachery* was ready to sail. They were just missing one thing.

"Shipsage!" bellowed Captain Rone. "Paun, where in Firesta's pits are you?"

"Down here," cried a voice from the dock, "waiting for permission to come aboard, captain."

Captain Rone shook his head and sputtered something incoherent. "Permission granted. Come aboard, and pull the gangway in after you. All hands, make ready to cast off."

A handsome young human with dark hair and bright eyes made his way aboard. He dropped a sea bag casually on the deck and took up a place near the prow, leaning on a long oaken staff. He cocked his head and gave the captain a questioning look.

Rone sniffed at the sea air and shook his head. "Not yet, shipsage. There's a good breeze. I think we'll take her out on our own. It'll give us all a chance to get to know her."

He started barking commands, and the crewman and Legionnaires leaped to obey. They floundered a little at first, hindered by the unfamiliar rigging and the inexperience of the Legionnaires. But with Gorin's help, they soon developed a feel for the *Treachery*. They practiced tacking and maneuvering procedures until Captain Rone was satisfied with their control of the goblinship. Then they headed for the mouth of Norivika Bay.

"Who would have believed that I could learn something new about sailing from a goblin!" Rone cackled, giving Gorin a friendly slap on the back.

The *Treachery* slid confidently toward the Quiet Sea. But long before she reached open water, the wind began to die. Soon it was obvious that they were going to be becalmed.

"Shipsage!" Rone bellowed from the afterdeck. "Paun! I need you up here now."

The young man emerged from below deck and headed for the bow. He planted his staff against the deck and began humming softly. After a moment he turned and shouted calmly toward the stern. "Master Rone, I am having difficulty adjusting to the ship. The wood resists me. It will not make contact with my sagestaff."

"What do you mean you can't make contact?" Rone yelled. "Do I have to turn back and find another shipsage?"

"Master Rone, there is no need for such hasty action," Paun yelled back, somehow managing to sound even calmer as his volume increased. "The wood of this vessel is not good for spell-current. It makes for poor sagecraft."

Chentelle understood why. The wind did not like the aura of pain in the wood.

"What good are you, then," growled Rone, "if you can't control the ship?"

"Please, Master Rone," Paun replied, "try to contain your anger."

"Anger? I have no anger. This is merely an emulation of what I know I *should* be feeling. Wait till we get beyond the Barrier. Then my true emotion will register!"

Even Father Marcus had to smile at that truth.

Paun tried again. "I did not say that I cannot control the ship. I said that I do not yet have the *feel* of her. You must allow me the opportunity to accustom myself to the wood."

"Then just call the wind!" Rone screamed, stamping impatiently toward the wheel. "I'll steer!"

Paun bowed his head slightly. "As you command, Master Rone."

The shipsage turned back to the bow and resumed his humming. This time, he didn't plant his staff against the deck. Instead, he held it vertically before him, lower end just slightly above the wooden planks. He started to sway back and forth in rhythm to his hum, and the staff weaved before him, a silent partner in his dance of power. As Paun's motions became more strident, the sagewind rode about them, filling the *Treachery*'s sails. They shot forward, cutting briskly through the quiet water.

Once the wind was established, Paun slowed his dance, settling into a slow, steady rhythm that sustained the summoned wind without taxing his strength. His movements were stately, graceful. He seemed almost to be a part of the wind, whistling back and forth on the deck, contained only by some trick of the air currents.

The hours passed, and still Paun maintained his wind. Finally, when Ellistar hung low in the western sky, they passed through the mouth of the bay and into the Quiet Sea. Paun released his spell, and the sails fluttered as the dying sagewind battled against the prevailing sea breeze. Captain Rone shouted adjustments, and the crew adjusted the trim of the canvas. Soon, the sails grew taut again.

Paun weaved his way wearily to the cabins. "With your permission, Master Rone, I will go below and rest."

"Of course," the captain said. "And shipsage, you did an excellent job."

"Yes," Paun agreed. Then he disappeared below deck.

They continued on their eastern course. Chentelle sat on the foredeck, watching the bow slide through the waves. The expanse of clear water was so beautiful, so immense. And it was so full of life. A thousand voices called out to her, joining in the ocean's song. The slow rhythm of it filled her with peace. The steady power of it helped counter the pain she felt from the tortured wood.

Then, the fullness of the song was interrupted. A wall seemed to block off part of the Quiet Sea, deadening that portion of the song. Slowly, the wall worked its way toward the *Treachery*. No, it was the *Treachery* that moved toward the wall, toward the Barrier. They were approaching the boundary of the Holy Land.

Chentelle searched the horizon. The Barrier was invisible, but not undetectable. The air beyond the Holy Land had a different quality, a cloudiness and lack of purity. Chentelle could see the line of change, shimmering like waves of heat before them.

She was not the only one. "The Barrier!" cried Zubec, from his post on the mainmast.

"Eh? Excellent," the captain said, making a notation in his log.

The company gathered on the foredeck. Only A'stoc remained apart, locked away in his cabin as he had been since the voyage began. The rest of them watched the boundary come ever closer. They had been in the Holy Land for so long, surrounded by its serenity and protection. Now, they were about to put that comfort behind them. Chentelle heard a quiet prayer coming from behind her. It was Gorin.

The goblin priest noticed her attention and smiled. "This will be the first time I have left the sanctuary of the Holy Land since my conversion. For me, this voyage is a test of faith."

"As it is for us all," Father Marcus said, coming up behind his fellow priest. "But it is one we must pass. Trust in yourself, Gorin; your faith is strong."

They passed through the Barrier.

Chentelle staggered against the rail. She felt as if a piece had been torn from her soul. She was incomplete, unbalanced, removed from the hand of the Creation. Desperately, she sang, trying to recapture with her voice the song that was absent from her heart.

The music filled some of the emptiness inside her, bringing peace. But she was still alone, cut off from her friends, from Creation. She reached out with her Gift, weaving her song into the emptiness of the broken world. She felt the uncertainty of her companions, their sadness and loss. She felt Gorin's fear and Dacius' sorrow and the strange melancholy that gripped Father Marcus. She felt the dark rage that burned in Sulmar's soul. She felt all the spaces that had been left empty by the passage through the Barrier, and she filled those places with her song.

The music was an anchor, an echo of Creation that reminded them all of what was possible, of the reason for their quest. It wove them together, banishing the loneliness and isolation for at least these few, precious moments. It was only a temporary measure, but it was enough. As Chentelle let her song come to an end, she felt renewed confidence course through the company. The fear and uncertainty had eased, for now.

"Thank you, Chentelle," Father Marcus said. "Your song is a true comfort in this difficult time."

The High Bishop turned and addressed the company. "Remember this feeling, friends. We lost something precious when we crossed through the Barrier. But the thing that we lost is the very thing that drives us onward. We struggle now to keep that fragment of the True Creation from vanishing forever, to keep evil from overrunning all of Infinitera. It is a difficult quest, but one which must be undertaken, one which we have the strength to fulfill. Do not doubt that. The Creator is with us still. We just have to look more closely to find him." He paused. "If anyone needs to voice their thoughts in private, Gorin or I will gladly lend an ear."

"What I think," Dacius said loudly, "is that we need another song. Thildemar, didn't I see you stowing a new lute in your pack?"

The old elf nodded, a thin smile growing on his face. "One moment, Lord Gemine. I will see if I can find it."

There was a general chuckle. A lutist never lost track of his instrument.

Thildemar disappeared below deck, and reappeared again almost immediately. He took up a position near the wheel and started tuning his instrument with a practiced hand. The rest of the company gathered around, anxious to take part in some merriment. Chentelle started to join them, but stopped when her eyes fell on Sulmar.

The Tengarian stood quietly, staring at the pale red light that already illuminated the eastern sky. His face was as impassive as stone, and his posture seemed relaxed. But his arms trembled with tension, and his knuckles were bone white against the rail.

Chentelle knew that underneath the fabric of his sleeve a black shadow writhed sinuously on his forearm.

Time passed, marked only by the fluctuating light of Deneob and Ellistar. The *Treachery* sailed out of the Quiet Sea and into the vast reaches of the Great Sea. Captain Rone charted their travel carefully, sighting along the path of the suns. He consulted Gorin frequently, checking their position against the priest's knowledge of *Kennaru*'s location. Several times they saw ships on the horizon, but none approached. Even so, Rone kept them in the western edge of the southern current, taking advantage of the water's speed while staying as far from the Hordelands as possible. The daylight kept them safe from Ill-creatures, but goblins were another matter.

They countered the tension by sharing long tales and merry songs together, and by pursuing their private interests when alone. A'stoc remained withdrawn in his studies, though he would now give monosyllabic answers to direct questions. He, alone of their number, seemed unchanged by their passage across the Barrier. Father Marcus and Gorin spent much of their time in meditation, though they willingly shared their knowledge of the Holy Texts when asked. Rone and Dacius took turns keeping the Legionnaires busy, the captain trying to turn them into sailors and the Legion commander leading them through sword drills and combat exercises. Dacius gave Sulmar a vorpal sword and invited him to join the drills, but the Tengarian declined. He preferred to keep his own schedule of exercises, and he never stopped carrying his own black sword in addition to the vorpal blade.

Chentelle spent most of her time sitting on the foredeck, singing softly to herself. It seemed that the farther she traveled from Lone Valley, the closer it became to her heart. She missed it so! Perhaps she had always been fated to make this long journey, but she had thought she would be home by now, and the adjustment was not easy. The First Season of Light was always a time of great joy at home, a time to gather the harvest and rejoice in the cycle of life. The forest would smell of autumn flowers and roasting grain, and the people would gather in the village circle to celebrate the Szygy. Her mother would surprise her with a newly spun dress, and they would sit together among their dearest friends to watch the contests of story and song and weaving and magic.

Only she wasn't at home. She was floating in a ship whose every board cried out to her in muted agony. She was following a dream she didn't understand to a place she had never seen, in order to destroy an evil she could not comprehend. She was traveling with good men touched by evil, an evil goblin transformed by good, and a wizard so full of bitterness and despair that he would not even talk to her. And only in the deep song of a strange sea could she find comfort for her troubled mind.

A voice from the main deck called out to her. "Lady Chentelle, we are about to begin. Will you join us?"

So soon? Chentelle looked up at the sky and saw only a deep red glow lighting each horizon. It *was* time. She hadn't been paying attention. "Coming," she called, waving to Father Marcus.

The High Bishop stood in the center of the deck, ringed by the assembled company. Captain Rone had fixed the wheel so no one would have to miss the ceremony. Even A'stoc was present, looking somewhat wild and unkempt. Chentelle took a place beside the wizard and greeted him with a smile which was not returned. She was trying to think of something properly piercing to say when Sulmar came from somewhere to squeeze in between them.

Once everyone was in place, Father Marcus made the sign of harmony and led them all in the First Meditation.

> *"In peace, there is harmony.*
> *In harmony, there is unity.*
> *In unity, there is healing.*
> *In healing, there is peace."*

"That is the First Meditation of Jediah," the High Bishop said. "Words that we all know, and perhaps do not think about often enough. But there is not a time of the year when they are more relevant than the Szygy. At this moment, Infinitera lies in perfect balance between the Two Sisters. We have completed our orbit of Ellistar, and are about to begin the journey around Deneob. It is a time of perfect harmony between the Golden Sun and the Winter Sun, a time of light when evil cannot reign, a time of unity when all things come together.

"Every race, every nation, every village has its own ceremony to celebrate this time, but all of these ceremonies celebrate the unity of family and community, the harmony between man and nature, the healing of old wounds and grievances, the peace of wholeness with the Creation. I wish that each of you could be with your families on this day, to join in those celebrations, but that is not possible. We are called to a different duty. I cannot change that, but there is one thing I can do.

"We of the Holy Order have our own ceremony for this day. It is a simple ritual, but one that has great meaning to us. At Szygy, the forces of Creation are in balance, all things are joined in unity, all days are one. At Szygy, it is possible to share in that rapport, to travel in the mind to anyplace, to relive in the mind any day of your life. On this day that is so often celebrated by the exchange of gifts, it is a gift I would like to share with you."

He paused. "Brother Gorin, are you ready?"

"Yes, Lord High Bishop." The goblin's voice came from outside the circle, opposite Captain Rone. Gorin stood the same distance behind the seaman as Father Marcus did in front.

While the company watched, uncertain what to expect, the two priests started to chant. The words were indecipherable, but somehow they rang with meaning. Light sprang up around the clerics. Father Marcus started to shine with a deep golden glow, and a crimson aura surrounded Gorin. They became the Two Sisters, and the company was Infinitera, circling around the Golden Sun.

As one, the priests extended their arms toward Rone. Light flowed from their fingertips, coming together to surround the captain in a shimmering rainbow.

A look of deep joy came over the seaman's face. His mouth hung open in surprise and laughter poured from deep inside him. The glow lasted for only a few seconds, but even after it faded the look of rapture remained. Rone bowed deeply, first to Father Marcus, then to Gorin. "Bless you, bless you both." Then he left the group, walking in a circle until he came to a point opposite Gorin.

Without needing to be told, the rest of them moved also. They followed the path of their orbit, rotating around Father Marcus until Zubec stood balanced between the two priests. Again the clerics reached out with their glow, and Zubec, too, was taken by rapture. The procession continued, and soon Chentelle was standing between the holy men, waiting for the light to wash over her.

The dress was beautiful. The silver-blue threads made her hair glow like spun gold, and the spidersilk shimmered in the sunlight, surrounding her with tiny rainbows. How did her mother make them more dazzling every year? And how could she possibly top this one?

Chentelle jumped into her mother's arms, thanking her, hugging her. Then she danced around the room, unable to contain herself. What were they waiting for? Already the rich smell of roasting nuts filled the forest. The first stories would begin any minute.

Finally, her mother nodded to Chentelle and headed for the door. They ran to the village circle. Well, Chentelle ran, her mother walked with grace and dignity and maddening slowness, and Chentelle had to circle back a half-dozen times to keep from leaving her behind. Nearly everyone was present when they arrived, but a place had been reserved for them under the great oak nearest the brook. They settled into place, returning the kind greetings of their neighbors.

The stories were wonderful, full of mystery and magic and love and sorrow. Old Willow's tale of Fizzfaldt the Wanderer brought tears to everyone's eyes, and she was again given the title of master storyteller. Ellissandra won the judgment for her weaving, though Chentelle privately thought that her mother would have won, if only she had entered. A'mond dazzled them all with his fire rings and dancing smoke, and Erina surprised everyone by winning the music competition.

The celebration lasted through the Long Day, the day that started when Ellistar rose but did not end until Deneob set. After the contests ended, the people gathered into small groups of family and cherished friends. That was when gifts were exchanged and the private stories were told, when the bonds of family and community were reforged in love and harmony. Chentelle basked in the warmth and love, wishing that it could last forever.

She blinked in confusion and discovered that her eyes were full with tears of love. She stood on the deck of the *Treachery*, smiling with a joy that filled her soul. The memory was fresh within her, and her whole body trembled with emotion. It was incredible. She had relived the entire day in those few moments of light. "Thank you," she whispered. Then she walked around the circle to join the others.

Only Sulmar and A'stoc were left in the circle around Father Marcus. The Tengarian moved into the point of balance, and the glow surrounded him. Almost immediately, tears streamed down his face. He dropped to his knees, sobbing loudly, and a moan of unbearable sadness escaped his lips. The glow faded, and the Tengarian lurched unsteadily to his feet. He clapped both hands to his face, hiding his tears. Then with a visible effort, he dropped his arms slowly to his side. The face he revealed was once again as impassive and un-readable as a stone wall. He bowed deeply to Father Marcus, spun about smoothly and bowed again to Gorin. Then he took his place at Chentelle's side.

Now A'stoc moved into position between the priests. Even before they reached out to him, the wizard was trembling violently. He clutched the Thun-derwood Staff with shaking hands, holding it before him like a wand. The priests waited, and slowly he lowered the Staff. Then they reached out to him, ex-tending their light. But just before the glow touched him, the wizard jumped out of the way. "No!" he screamed. "No. I—I cannot—I have to—I—"

He looked back and forth between Gorin and the High Bishop, eyes darting like those of a cornered animal. Then he settled his gaze on Chentelle. One hand released its grip on the Staff and reached slowly in her direction. Then it snapped back to the wood. "I'm sorry," he said, turning and bolting for the hatchway to the cabins below. "I'm sorry."

It was an unsettling end to the ceremony, but the spirit of Father Marcus's gift to them was too strong to be broken. Captain Rone had to return to the wheel, so the rest of them found places to settle themselves around the wheel-deck. They watched the Winter Sun take her place as the daystar, marking her passage with stories of their homes and songs of love and friendship. Leth and Gerruth taught them all a dance from the Inarr Forest, and the seamen regaled them with fanciful tales from foreign lands. The hours melted away, and only Sulmar remained apart from the sharing, A'stoc being absent.

Chentelle was worried. Sulmar had suffered such obvious pain during the ceremony. She took advantage of one of Rone's saltier stories to speak softly to her liegeman. "Sulmar, are you all right? I don't know what happened to you, but if you're in pain I want to try and help. Is there anything I can do?"

"No, mistress," he said evenly. "There is nothing anyone can do."

Chentelle waited, but he didn't say anything more. She couldn't think of anything else she could say, so she turned back to join the others.

"Mistress?"

Sulmar's voice was uncertain, almost shaky. She hadn't heard him speak so unevenly since the night she saved him from drowning. "Yes?"

"Mistress," he said again. "It is not a pain from which I want to be freed. I saw—I saw the woman who was once my wife. And I saw the children who once called me father. They—they are alive, my liege. They are alive."

The pain and joy in his voice made Chentelle want to cry out in sympathy. She wanted to reach out to him, to say something that would bring comfort or solace. But there was nothing to say. Finally, she threw herself against his chest and wrapped her arms around him, hugging him tightly.

The Tengarian froze in surprise. His entire body went rigid. He started to reach down and disengage her arms, but he stopped the motion almost immediately. Slowly, his tension faded and he let himself relax in the embrace. He even wrapped one of his own arms around Chentelle's shoulders, though the other remained by his side, unencumbered. They stood like that for several minutes, sharing their own private communion with the Creation. Then they rejoined the others.

The gathering lasted until Deneob's cool red glow began to disappear below the water. Then they started to drift apart, ready to ease the fatigue of so many hours awake. But as tired as they were, they also felt a sense of peace, of hope, of renewed strength. The power of the Szygy still lived within them.

Chentelle said good night to the others and started for the sea door. But as she turned, something off the port quarter caught her eye. Silhouetted against the rising disk of Ellistar was a ship, a big ship. "Captain Rone, look!"

The captain stared at the shape on the horizon. "Goblinship, looks like a four-master. And she's on an intercept course."

❧ 9 ❧

KENNARU

Dacius jumped to the captain's side. "A warship?"

"Most likely," Rone said.

"Fires of Hel," Dacius swore. "I thought we had destroyed them all during the Hordeland Wars."

"Apparently not," came Rone's dry reply. "All hands! All hands to the deck. Paun! Take your place. Give me all the wind you can muster. Zubec, Pardec, turn sail; we're heading for the deep. And keep it trim. I want no slack in those lines."

"Can we outrun them?" Chentelle asked.

"No," he said, spinning the wheel hard to starboard. "That ship is built for speed, but we can gain some time for as long as Paun's strength remains."

"Won't they have a shipsage, too?"

"Probably more than one," Rone said grimly. "But ours is better. They won't gain on us while his magic holds. And we might get lucky. The natural wind might die. Then the *Treachery* will have the advantage in maneuverability."

Father Marcus came hurrying up from his cabin. Fatigue was written in deep lines on the old priest's face, but his blue eyes shone as clearly and alertly as ever. He scanned the horizon, taking in the situation at a glance. "I take it we are discovered."

"Yes, High Bishop," Dacius said. "But how could they have known?"

"That does not matter," Marcus said. "What matters is that we escape. What are our chances, captain?"

"Not good, Eminence," Rone said. "We must go into the deep, or they will gain a favorable angle of approach. But we are already close to the edge of the southern current. Leaving it will cost us speed. If we are lucky, they will break off pursuit. They may only be trying to drive us away from the coast."

"And if they follow?" asked Marcus.

"Then we fight. Lord Gemine, I suggest you deploy your men in the cover of the foredeck. If we must fight, I will turn to face them."

Dacius turned to face his company of six. "Bows and shields, everyone. I want arrows planted and ready for rapid fire. Deploy in close order. Simon, you and I will be shieldmen, covering for the archers. Thildemar, I need you below for a moment. Everyone else, prepare your positions. I will inspect in twelve minutes. Move!"

The Legionnaires dispersed in a flurry of action. Some went below to secure weapons and equipment. Others used the time to turn the two longboats and several barrels of fresh water into a makeshift fortification. In minutes, the barrier was complete, and Simon was supervising the younger Legionnaires as they prepared their lines of fire and cover. They were all in position by the time Dacius emerged from his cabin.

All eyes turned to the human lord as he climbed to the deck. He was completely encased in the heavy armor of a knight of Odenal. A plumed helm dangled casually off of one arm, and a great shield, bearing the crest of twin suns rising, hung from the other.

"Lord Gemine," Rone said, "are you certain that's wise? Should you have to swim, the weight of that armor will bear you down intolerably."

Dacius smiled. "Captain, a goblin warship typically carries four companies of marines and two Ill-Lore masters. I have six men to stop them with. If we are boarded, drowning will be the least of my worries."

The human lord inspected the defensive position, making one or two minor adjustments. He placed Thildemar in a location near the wheel, ready to defend Captain Rone if it became necessary, then ordered the men to rest in position. Finally, he came back to the wheeldeck himself.

"How long can he hold out?" Dacius asked, nodding toward Paun.

The shipsage was visibly worn. The sagestaff trembled in his hands, and his tunic was covered in sweat. He seemed to be kept upright only by the momentum of his dance.

"Half an hour," Rone said, "if we're lucky."

Chentelle looked behind them. They were maintaining their lead on the warship, but that was all. Once Paun's spell faded, that distance would close rapidly. "Maybe I can help."

She moved forward to stand beside the shipsage. His humming was quiet, almost subvocal, but she could feel its rhythm. She started to dance, swaying gently in time to Paun's music. She had to make sure she was in perfect harmony, or else his delicate spell would be disrupted. Slowly, she let the song rise within her.

She sang softly at first, adding only a quiet harmony, an echo of melody behind Paun's own. She reached out with her Gift, using it to sense the fragile structure of Paun's spell. Then she poured herself into the song, using her own strength to support the shipsage's own. Everything else faded into the background as Chentelle and Paun joined in a union of song and motion. The world was a web of magic floating on a breeze of will. Time was an eight-beat progression, measured in swaying dance steps and sliding notes.

Suddenly, the spell unraveled. The song ended in midbeat, and Chentelle staggered to the deck. The sagewind slackened and dissolved into nothingness. People were yelling behind her, but Chentelle couldn't make out the words. She felt oddly dissociated. She looked around and saw Chentelle standing by the railing, leaning against Sulmar's arm.

Chentelle snapped back into awareness. It was Paun who was lying on the deck. She had been seeing through the shipsage's eyes, lost for a moment in the connection that she had forged. That had never happened before. Her head swam with vertigo, and she stayed on her feet only because of Sulmar's support. She looked up, trying to focus on her liegeman's impassive face. To her amazement, Ellistar was now high overhead. "I think I need to go below."

The Tengarian swept her smoothly into his arms and carried her away from the bow. Gorin and Father Marcus hurried past them, heading to the foredeck to check on Paun. She let herself be taken as far as the main hatchway and then asked to be let down. Already her head was clearing. Sulmar opened the sea door so that she could descend the ladder, but she headed for the wheeldeck instead.

Dacius and Captain Rone stood together by the wheel, staring at the eastern horizon. It was empty; the warship was nowhere in sight. Chentelle walked toward them and almost tripped over Thildemar, who lay sleeping in a small patch of shade near the rail. She blinked in amazement.

Dacius laughed softly. "A wise warrior rests whenever he can, lady. I just wish I could join him."

"Why don't you?" she asked.

He pointed toward the forward defenses, where the other Legionnaires were also resting. "The reason they can sleep peacefully is that they know I will not." He paused, a quick smile brightening his face. "It is the privilege of command."

Chentelle nodded toward the horizon. "Are they gone?"

It was Rone who answered. "No, lady enchantress. They're still out there. I can feel them hovering, just out of sight. They couldn't match our speed once you added your strength to Paun's, but they'll be closing fast, now that the sagewind has ended."

Chentelle winced with chagrin. If only she had been able to keep up her song. They might have escaped. "I'm sorry."

"Sorry?" Rone said. "Lady Chentelle, I've spent nearly three centuries sailing one sea or another, and I have never seen a sage summon so strong a wind for so long a time. It was a fine run, lady, a fine run. But we are overmatched. If only we had another shipsage."

Another—A'stoc! "But we do have another," Chentelle said. "Well, another wizard, at least. I'm sure A'stoc can summon another sagewind."

Captain Rone shook his head uncertainly. "I don't know, lady. A shipsage is no ordinary wizard. It takes more than raw power to summon a wind. It takes a special feel that grows over years of practice. And if you'll pardon my saying it, lady, you and Paun struggled for hours to keep that wind alive. If the wizard could have helped, why didn't he show his face above deck?"

"I—I don't know."

"Still," Dacius said, "we don't have any other options. I will go ask him if he can help."

"Wait," Chentelle said, "I'll go with you."

The wizard had installed himself in a small cabin near the stern. They hurried down the ladder and through the salon. Paun lay stretched on one of the tables, being tended by Father Marcus and his acolyte. The shipsage was still unconscious, and the priests were both deep in prayer. None of them stirred as Dacius and Chentelle sprinted past.

The wizard's door was barred. Chentelle called out, and almost immediately the door swung open. A'stoc stood in the opening, glaring at them with wild eyes. His hair was disheveled and several days' worth of stubble sprouted from his face. In the closed passageway, his body odor was almost overpowering. Lore books and parchments lay scattered about the cabin behind him. "What do you want?"

Dacius stepped forward to answer him. "We are being pursued by a goblin warship. If you are capable of summoning a sagewind, then we might be able to evade them."

"For how long?" A'stoc asked. "Surely, they have their own shipsages. They will catch us eventually. We should turn and fight."

Dacius looked stunned. "Wizard A'stoc, it is better if we evade them. They have a superior vessel and a much larger complement of warriors."

A'stoc sneered. "Do not be a coward. We will be boarded eventually. Why delay the inevitable?"

With a visible effort, Dacius held his temper in check. "Wizard A'stoc," he grated between clenched teeth, "are you able to summon the sagewind?"

"Yes."

The human lord took a deep breath, relaxing slightly. "Thank you. Then, will you please take Paun's place on the foredeck?"

"No. Let the goblins come to us."

"What!" Dacius shouted. "Are you insane? Are you going to sacrifice us all to—"

Chentelle put a hand to the human's lips. "Lord Gemine, Dacius, let me try."

She turned back to A'stoc. The wizard was surrounded by his usual wall of anger and bitterness, but there was something else, as well. A new confidence. "A'stoc, we want to understand. Is there a reason that you want to fight the goblins? Are you going to use the Staff?"

"I have to," the wizard said. "There is an Ill-creature aboard the goblin vessel."

"What?" Dacius cried. "Fires of Hel, why didn't you say something before?"

"The knowledge was useless to you. The Ill-creature can not assault us directly during the Season of Light. It will use its goblin slaves to fight the battle. And I will deal with them."

"You knew," said Chentelle. "You knew all along that the Ill-creature was there. That's why you didn't help with the sagewind."

A'stoc nodded. "I thought it best to conserve my strength for the battle."

"Then follow me," Dacius said, spinning on his heel. "We wouldn't want you to miss it."

By the time they reached the deck, the warship was only a few hundred cubits off their stern. It loomed above the small whaler, an evil shadow promising only death and destruction. Amazingly, Paun was back in his position at the foredeck. The shipsage looked as if he remained standing by force of will alone, but stand he did.

Dacius turned to Chentelle. "You should wait in the salon with Gorin and Father Marcus. We do not need anyone else exposed." He turned away, heading for the bow to take up a position at the ballista with Simon.

He was right. Chentelle was no warrior. She should go below where it was safe. But the warship's steady approach kept her mesmerized. She stood in the shadow of the sea door, watching death slide silently closer.

A flare of light caught her attention. Simon had used his elven Lore to create a small fire on the shaft of one of the harpoons.

"Stand by sails!" Captain Rone shouted. "Stand by sagewind! Harpoon, stand by to port!"

The warship bore down on them. A half-dozen ballistae were arranged on her deck, but none were manned. They meant to capture the *Treachery*, not sink her! Dozens of goblins pressed at the warship's bow, anxious to board their prey.

"Sagewind!" Rone yelled. "Hard to port! Draw those lines!"

The sails angled sharply as the captain spun the wheel. Sagewind filled them in a sudden gust, and the *Treachery* cut sharply across the warship's bow. It was a suicidal move. The warship's ram cleaved through the water, aimed directly at their midships.

"Fire!"

As one, the archers loosed their shafts, each finding a target among the massed goblin warriors. Simon whispered to the loaded harpoon, and violent flames burst into life along the entire shaft. Immediately, Dacius fired the ballista. The missile left a trail of smoke as it tore through the warship's mainsail and lodged in its deck. The goblin crew swarmed in alarm, trying to extinguish the blaze.

"Paun!" Rone shouted, angling them away from the warship. "I need more wind!"

Suddenly, the sagewind doubled in force. The sails snapped taut, and the *Treachery* shot forward. They passed barely in front of the deadly ram. On the foredeck, A'stoc's gravelly voice sang out in rhythm with Paun's spell.

A massed cry of rage erupted from the goblinship, and a hail of spears and crossbow bolts launched toward them. But their sudden move had ruined the goblins' aim. Most of the missiles fell wide or short of the mark. Those that did find the *Treachery* landed harmlessly among the fortifications or were caught by Legion shields. But where some of the bolts struck, dark vitriol splashed, burning into the wood with an evil hiss.

Then the warship was beyond them. Captain Rone adjusted their course, taking them away from the warship. "Ready another harpoon!"

Dacius loaded another shaft, laughing wildly. "You are a madman, captain, a thrice-blessed madman! Who else would cut across the ram of a ship that size?"

Rone plucked an arrow casually from the rail beside him and tossed it over the side. "Thank you, Lord Gemine, but we are not yet out of the woods."

As if responding to prophecy, the sagewind sputtered and died. Paun collapsed in a heap on the foredeck, exhausted beyond all endurance. The two priests were by his side in an instant, carrying him back to the safety of the salon. The *Treachery* slowed, winds flapping loose in the sudden calm.

"Wizard A'stoc!" Rone shouted. "Take his place. Call the sagewind!"

"No," A'stoc said, moving back toward the wheeldeck. "I will fight them."

"What?" Rone turned to Dacius. "Now we see who is really mad."

"Captain Rone," A'stoc snapped, "evil drives that ship. They are here to bring an end to our quest and to capture the Thunderwood Staff. They will not give up the pursuit. Do you truly believe that we can outrun them?"

The captain glared in anger, but he had no answer for the wizard's argument.

"Good," A'stoc said. "Then we are in agreement. Now, make no more wild maneuvers. Let them come alongside." Without waiting for a reply, he wheeled away, tattered robes billowing in the wind. The wizard took a position amidships and planted his Staff against the deck, waiting.

The *Treachery* swung back toward the south, moving slowly without the sagewind. The warship had come about, and the two ships sailed toward each other, prow to prow. The distance closed slowly. Apparently the goblins were being cautious, perhaps wary for another surprise maneuver.

"Mistress?"

Chentelle started at the sound of Sulmar's voice.

"Mistress," he said again. "Will you go below?"

"Oh," Chentelle said. She looked around the deck, then turned back to stare at the warship's ominous approach. "No, I think I should stay here. I'll be safe enough in the shelter of the companionway, and A'stoc might need our help."

The Tengarian looked at her for a moment, his face unreadable. Then he ran toward the bow, covering the distance in swift, sure steps. He grabbed a spare shield from the defensive barrier and took up a position amidships near A'stoc.

"What are you doing?" the wizard screamed. "I do not need your protection."

"He is protecting me," Chentelle called, "in the manner he feels is best."

A'stoc stared at her in surprise. "What are doing here? You should be below where it is safe."

"I am not a child," she snapped. "I may be able to help. Have you forgotten the battle against the vikhors?"

"No," A'stoc growled. "Have you?" He whirled and stabbed a finger at Sulmar's face. "Do what you must, but stay out of my way."

The ships grew steadily closer. "Hold your positions!" Dacius shouted. "Wait for the lull." He and Simon fired another flaming harpoon, then fell back to provide cover for the archers. The incendiary projectile landed near the warship's foremast, but did no serious damage.

In response, the goblin marines let loose with a mass volley. A volley of shafts rained down upon the *Treachery*, splashing acid across the deck. Wood hissed as the defenders absorbed the attack with shields and barriers. Sulmar darted in front of A'stoc, intercepting a shaft just before it pierced the wizard's chest.

A flicker of doubt flashed on the mage's face, but it vanished almost immediately, replaced by a glare of cold determination. Suddenly, the Staff blazed into life. With a roar of thunder, green flames engulfed the wizard. "Get out of my way!" he shouted.

"Now!" Dacius cried. The Legion bowmen jumped to their feet, firing into the lull as the goblins reloaded. They moved with uncanny precision—nocking, aiming, and loosing their shafts in a steady blur of motion. Flight after flight of elven wood sailed into the air, trying to counter numbers with speed and accuracy.

The goblins responded in kind, launching rotating volleys of crossbow fire toward the *Treachery*. Much of the first volley was directed at A'stoc, but the bolts disintegrated harmlessly against his fiery green aura. Sulmar dropped back to shield Chentelle from stray shots, and Thildemar performed the same service for Captain Rone. But the bulk of the remaining volleys fell against the forward position. Dacius and Simon worked furiously to ward off the attack while their fellows continued to return fire. The elf danced back and forth with a shield in each hand, trying to provide cover for as large an area as possible, and the human lord's armor smoked and sizzled in a dozen places.

The inferno around A'stoc grew larger and larger. His face contorted in rage and exultation as he gathered the Staff's power. He raised the Staff overhead, and a whirlwind of flame twisted into life above the *Treachery*.

But focusing the power took time, and the goblin barrage continued. A bolt struck the barricade next to Alve's face, splashing his eyes with acid. The young Legionnaire screamed and went down. Instantly, Simon was there. He pulled Alve into cover and flushed the wound with water from one of the barrels. It took only seconds for Simon to insure his comrade's safety, but for those seconds he was exposed. A goblin shaft found the hole in the defenses and lodged in Simon's back. He screamed and fell to the deck. His body spasmed violently as the dark fluid ate into his spine. Then he lay still.

"No!" Father Marcus burst through the sea door and rushed forward, Gorin following close at his heels. The priests began their healing chant as soon as they reached the fallen Legionnaire, but it was too late. Simon was dead. Marcus hung his head and mouthed a quiet prayer over the body while Gorin attended to Alve.

"Enough!" A'stoc shouted. Roaring incoherently he thrust the Thunderwood Staff toward the goblins' ship. The cyclone of power leaped into action, swirling over the distance between the two ships in the space of a heartbeat. It seethed above the deck of the warship, then descended to swallow soldiers and crew alike in a holocaust of death.

Only it never reached its goal. In the instant before the flames touched the first goblin, the whirlwind reversed itself. It shot back toward A'stoc and funneled back into the Staff. The wizard screamed in agony as magic coursed through his body. Power flared out of control, finding release in the nearest outlet available—the deck beneath his feet. The planks shattered, exploding downward in a shower of splinters. A'stoc was thrown a dozen feet into the air and slammed to the deck with bone-jarring force. He moaned softly as the Thunderwood Staff slipped from his numb fingers.

The *Treachery* lurched as if struck by a giant fist. The hull groaned in protest as it was wrenched tortuously and then snapped back into shape. A spar snapped under the strain, and the foresail flapped uselessly in the wind.

As the little whaler drifted helplessly, a strong wind suddenly rose—a sagewind. The warship shot toward them, sails full.

"Hard starboard!" Rone shouted. "Zubec, cut down that sail; it's only dragging, now."

The *Treachery* pulled sideways, turning sluggishly. Desperately, they tried to outreach the goblins, but the whaler was too slow. The warship bore down on them. At the last instant, she turned aside. The sagewind died, and the ships slammed into each other, hull to hull.

Both decks rocked under the impact, but the warship had the advantage of much greater mass. Grapples snaked out, binding the vessels together. Goblins swarmed over the rails, falling upon the still reeling defenders.

Captain Rone shouted orders to his crew. The *Treachery* turned, catching what she could of the natural wind in her mainsail. She struggled to separate from the warship, but it was no use; the grapples held them tight. More goblins poured onto the deck. The Legionnaires fought valiantly, but their line was too thin. The goblins forced them back from the barricade and rushed through the breach.

Father Marcus and Gorin saw the goblins break through and immediately started to chant. They picked up Simon's body and summoned the power of the Holy Order, surrounding themselves with a shimmering aura of sanctuary.

The goblins sped by them as if they were invisible. Three of them headed for the wheeldeck. The rest oriented on Sulmar, who stood guard over the fallen form of A'stoc.

HA HA HA HA HA. Mocking laughter echoed through the skulls of the defenders. *ARE YOU THERE, LITTLE HUMAN? ARE YOU ENJOYING WATCHING MORE OF YOUR FRIENDS DIE? DO NOT WORRY, YOU WILL JOIN THEM SOON, THOUGH YOU WILL BEG FOR IT TO BE SOONER.*

"Monster!" Dacius shouted. "Come fight me! Come and die on my sword!" He hurled himself at the charging goblins, ignoring the rain of blows that fell against his armor. He slammed into their ranks, forcing them backward by sheer mass and momentum. The human lord planted himself firmly in the breach, roaring madly and swinging his vorpal sword in heavy, vicious arcs. Leth, Gerruth, and Drup leaped forward to close ranks with their commander. The gap was sealed.

But for how long? Already, more goblins were forcing their way over the rail, pressing their brothers forward against the thin barricade. Nearly a score of the creatures seethed at the bow, and even more waited at the rails for their chance to cross. The Legionnaires were sure to be overrun.

Somehow, Chentelle had to stop more goblins from boarding. But how? There were too many of them for her to pacify with her Gift, even if she could reach them through the rage and chaos of combat. And as long as the ships were joined by the grapples, more goblins would cross.

That was it! She had to loose the grapples. But again, how? Even if she could get to them, she had no way to cut those cables. They were strong enough to hold the *Treachery* despite her full sail. Well, if she couldn't sever the cables, maybe she could loosen the claws.

Smiling, Chentelle sang out with her Gift. She reached out not to the goblins, not to the claws or the cables, but to the wooden rails and deck of the *Treachery*. The wood was in such pain. Not only had it suffered the agony of being butchered alive, it had been abused repeatedly during the battle. The uncontrolled fury of A'stoc's Staff, the force of the collision with the warship, the cruel tearing of the grapples' claws, and the strain of holding the whaler against the wind's pull, all combined to stress the wood nearly to the point of breaking. It took only a slight push from her Gift to push it past that point.

The tortured wood let go. Wherever the grapples touched, joints of wood ceased to hold. Pieces of railing flew from their neighbors. Planks pulled free of the deck. The metal claws held fast, but the wood to which they were joined did not. The grapples fell uselessly into the sea. The *Treachery* shot forward, pulling away from the warship.

Chentelle let her song end and turned back to see how the battle was going.

Thildemar moved to block the three goblins charging the wheeldeck. He waited calmly while his opponents approached, standing in a relaxed crouch, one ironwood baton raised in front of his chest and the other held tucked behind his ear. The goblins spread out in an arc, trying to surround him. The creature in front attacked, leaping forward and stabbing with a saw-edged dagger. A half beat later, the two on the flanks charged, slashing at the elf's legs with gleaming claws.

Calmly, Thildemar moved forward to meet the lead attack. He deflected the dagger with one baton. The second lashed out in a blur, striking the goblin twice, once on each temple. As the lead attacker crumpled, Thildemar jumped past him. The flank attackers clawed futilely at the air where he had been. As the elf spun to face the goblins again, one of them screamed and dropped to the ground.

"Who gave you permission to board?" Rone shouted, tossing aside his crossbow.

The last goblin turned to see where the new attack came from, and fell in a heap as Thildemar's batons struck him in the kidney and skull.

Near the mainmast, Sulmar and A'stoc were faced by a half-dozen goblins. The wizard was conscious, but too dazed to stand. The Tengarian stood in front of him, black sword and borrowed shield raised in readiness. On the deck, between Sulmar and the goblins, lay the Thunderwood Staff.

Sulmar did not wait for the goblins to attack or seize the Staff. He charged. His black blade knocked aside a dagger and pierced the chest of its owner. He deflected a blow with his shield and twisted away from a claw that sliced through the right side of his shirt. He pulled his sword free of the dead goblin's chest and continued the motion in a smooth arc, cutting through the knees of another attacker. As that goblin fell, the Tengarian sidestepped another attack, tripped another goblin, and used the motion of his spin to hurl his shield like a throwing disk.

The shield flew through the air, heading straight for Chentelle. She jumped to the side, ducking for cover, and the disk flew over her left shoulder. It crashed into the chest of a surprised goblin, knocking him off the roof of the companionway and into the water. She hadn't even seen him!

By the time she turned back, Sulmar was the only figure standing amidships. A small pile of goblins lay dead or dying at his feet. Freed of the shield, the Tengarian now wielded both a vorpal weapon and his own dark sword. He made a quick check to insure that none of the fallen were feigning injury, then ran to join the battle at the bow.

When Sulmar reached the barricade, he vaulted over it without hesitating. The twin swords lashed out, felling two goblins before his feet hit the deck. He became a blur of movement, his body flowing unerringly from one technique to the next. He seemed to react to every attack before it was launched, deflecting it with a smooth motion or sliding gracefully out of the way. The Tengarian danced among the goblins, sounding the rhythm of battle with the cries of his enemies. He was a whirlwind of destruction, cutting a swath of death through the goblin ranks.

The Legionnaires rallied around his assault. Dacius and his men drove into the confused and demoralized goblins. In moments, not a goblin remained standing. The rout was complete.

Chentelle realized that this was the first time she had seen Sulmar fight when he was at full strength. He had been injured when she met him, and weak from loss of blood. But the time in the Holy Land had enabled him to recover completely. That land of peace had, ironically, enabled him to become a terror in combat.

Sulmar remained in a crouch at the bow, swinging his twin swords slowly before him in a graceful, almost hypnotic pattern. Blood enveloped him. It matted his hair. It stained his clothes. It dripped from his blades and splashed in pools on the deck. But the Tengarian's face remained calm, impassive. His expression never wavered as he moved slowly among the mass of bodies. Occasionally, one of his blades would break from its pattern, striking out to nick a face or prick a hand. But each time, the caution proved unnecessary.

Chentelle watched in horror and fascination as Sulmar completed his inspection. As he came to the last body, he dropped to one knee and laid one of his swords across the figure's chest. He used the other to cut two strips of cloth from the goblin's tunic. With quiet efficiency he wiped his blades clean and returned them to their scabbards. Then he turned toward Chentelle.

"Mistress, the deck is safe."

Chentelle moved slowly away from the shelter of the companionway. She tried to absorb the scene before her. Everything was eerily quiet; even the wind was still. The Legionnaires seemed frozen in place, eyes glued to her liegeman. A'stoc knelt near the mast clutching the Staff to his chest and rocking silently back and forth. It felt dreamlike, unreal. She wondered for a moment whether it *was* a dream. But the planks creaked softly under her feet, and the air was thick with bile and sweat and a bitter odor she couldn't place. And Father Marcus held Simon's lifeless body in his arms.

"Man the sails!" Captain Rone's shout cut through the silence, sparking them into action. "Paun! Call the wind, man! We need the sagewind!"

But there was no answer.

Chentelle darted quickly below deck. The shipsage lay prone on one of the dining tables. His breath came in ragged gasps and a small pool of spittle had collected near the corner of his mouth. His eyes were open but unseeing. Chentelle put a hand to his forehead and felt the yawning pit of his fatigue. It would be a long time before Paun summoned another wind. She closed his eyes and slid a rolled blanket under his head. Then she ran back up the stairs.

"It's no use, captain," she said. "He can't respond."

Rone turned and looked behind them. The warship had come around and was gaining ground quickly, propelled by a goblin sagewind. "Wizard A'stoc, can you fill our sails?"

The mage looked up at them, but he did not answer. After a moment, he lowered his head and started rocking again.

"A'stoc!" Chentelle rushed to his side. His face and hands were covered with dozens of small cuts and scratches, but he did not seem to be seriously hurt. "A'stoc, what is wrong? Are you hurt?"

The wizard lurched to his feet. "Hel's Heart, enchantress, do you still not understand? It is over. We are doomed. The Ill-creature sustains their wizards. We cannot outrun them. And this"—he pounded the Staff against the deck—"this mightiest of weapons, is useless."

The wizard threw his head back and started laughing shrilly. "Don't you see? It is a fine joke, the final punctuation on my illustrious apprenticeship. The

Tree of Life, enchantress, the Staff was created from the Tree of Life. Its power cannot be used against living creatures."

He dropped back to the deck, shaking with laughter that bordered on tears. His words became soft, nearly inaudible. "Damn you, A'pon Boemarre. Why did you destroy the book? Why didn't you trust me?"

"Mistress." Sulmar placed a hand on her shoulder. "You should seek cover. They are nearly within bowshot."

She waved him off. "A'stoc, don't give up. We need you. If the Staff can't defeat them, then we'll think of something else. But you have to call the sage-wind. We need more time!"

Father Marcus came up beside them. The old priest managed to look serene despite the blood which stained his robes and hands. "She is right, wizard. It is not yet time to despair. The Creator has not forsaken us. Call the wind. We must not abandon hope."

"Hope!" A'stoc shouted. He slapped his hand against the torn planking. "Your hope is ashes, priest, like the dead wood of this floating coffin."

"Cover!"

The shout came from behind them. Chentelle was pressed to the deck as Sulmar tried to guard her from the missile barrage. The Tengarian caught most of the arrows on his shield, but several shafts landed on the deck around them, splashing vitriol across the planks. Chantelle cried out as the acid burned into her hand.

A'stoc, too, had been caught in the spray. His cheek sizzled and smoked hideously. The wizard's whole body trembled, but he made no move to wipe away the caustic liquid. In fact, he seemed to be almost smiling as it burned.

"A'stoc!" Chentelle tried to go to him, but Sulmar's grip kept her pressed to the deck. The deck!

"A'stoc, the wood!" she yelled. "Their ship is dead wood, too. Use the Staff on the wood!"

If he heard her at all, he made no sign.

"Steady," came Dacius' voice. "They're still at extreme range. The next flights will be worse."

"Let go!" Chentelle pulled herself free of Sulmar's grasp and scrambled over to the wizard. She grabbed his face and made him look at her while she repeated her words, but still there was no reaction.

"Ready shields!"

"A'stoc!" Chentelle reached out with her Gift. She didn't have the time to develop her song fully, to ease the wizard's pain and coax him back to reality. She just summoned all of her need, all of her desperation, and poured it into him. Her words rang into the human's soul. "A'stoc, you have to act. You have to save us."

The wizard's face went blank as her power flowed through him. He got to his feet, raising the Staff above his head. Almost instantly, the power of the Staff burst forth. Green flames poured from the wood, engulfing A'stoc and then leaping upward in a broad sheet of fire. The flames formed into a huge wall that hovered in the air between the *Treachery* and the goblin warship. Pinpricks of flashing light marked the impacts of the goblin bolts as they flared into nothingness.

As soon as the flight of missiles was over, the flames started to shift again. Power continued to pour from the Staff as the wall rose higher into the air and drifted toward the warship. It formed into a spinning disk of fire, hovering just above the warship's sails. Then it started to descend.

Shafts of power rose up from the deck as the goblin wizards tried to counter A'stoc's power, but they had no effect on the disk's motion. The fires pressed closer and closer to the warship. Her masts were blasted into shards, and her sails burst into flame like dry parchment. Goblin seamen leaped from the rigging, diving into the sea to escape the destruction. The disk continued its motion, destroying everything in its path until it hovered less than a dozen cubits above the warship's deck. Then it flashed violently and dissolved into nothingness.

"By the Creator," Father Marcus said. "Such power, I never dreamed—" He shook his head, bemused.

Captain Rone shouted orders to his crew. The *Treachery* eased forward on the little bit of natural wind. They were barely moving, but it was enough. The warship was crippled. They watched it fall slowly behind.

"Safe," A'stoc said. Then he fell to the deck.

Chentelle dropped to his side, reaching out with her Gift. The wizard's face was badly burned, and he had dozens of scrapes and bruises, but those injuries were minor. It was fatigue that had caused him to collapse. He had exhausted every reserve of strength to summon the Staff's power. Gently, Chentelle caressed the man with her own power, guiding him into a deep and restful sleep.

Suddenly, A'stoc's eyes snapped open. He shoved Chentelle aside and lurched to his feet, grabbing the Thunderwood Staff almost instinctively.

"Out!" he roared. "How dare you! I will not be your puppet, child! I will—"

A'stoc's eyes rolled backward and he staggered to the deck, Staff slipping once again from limp fingers.

Brother Gorin scurried past Chentelle and squatted by the wizard's side. His deep voice rumbled in quiet prayer, and he reached out with a bony claw and stroked the mage's cheek. The burns on A'stoc's face vanished, replaced by the soft pink of new skin.

"Is he all right?" Dacius asked. The human lord's armor was splashed with blood and dented in a dozen places, but he stood perfectly erect, and his face gave no hint of fatigue.

"He will be," Gorin said. "But he needs much rest."

"Fine." Dacius turned his head, taking a quick survey of the situation. "Drup, help Gorin and the enchantress move the wounded below, then assume a post outside the wizard's door. No one enters without my leave. Leth, Gerruth, clear those goblins off the deck, then dismantle the barricades. Thildemar, help Captain Rone's people with their repairs."

Dacius turned to Father Marcus and lowered his voice. "High Bishop, will you prepare Simon's body? We will have to bury him at sea."

"Of course," Father Marcus said, still cradling the elf's body in his arms.

"Thank you," Dacius said. Then, raising his voice again: "Move, Legionnaires! I want this ship secured."

"Your pardon, Lord Gemine." It was Gorin's deep voice interrupting the Legionnaires' motion. "When you say 'clear those goblins off the deck' surely you mean to prepare them for burial."

"What?" The shout came from Gerruth, who came lurching toward them from the bow. "Have you lost your mind? These monsters killed Simon! They deserve no honor."

"They are our enemies," Gorin agreed. "They killed Simon, and you killed them. And now they are no one's enemies. They lived their lives in ignorance of Creation's harmony. Would you deny it to them in death as well?"

"Yes!" Gerruth shouted. "Let them burn in Firesta. They—"

"Enough, Gerruth," Dacius interrupted. "Brother Gorin is right. We cannot defeat the Dark One by matching his cruelty. Prepare the goblins for burial at sea."

"Lord Gemine," Gerruth pleaded, "how can you say that? Don't you know what the goblins do to the bodies of their enemies?"

Dacius glared at the elf, his cheeks flushing in anger until they nearly matched the fiery red of his hair. "The one who slew my father carved a hole in his cheek and ate his tongue. The one who murdered my mother removed her hair and carved foul runes into her naked skull. The one who killed Cinder took—"

The human's voice choked off and he turned away, shaking his head as if to clear sweat from his eyes. "You have your orders, Legionnaire."

The human's pain was obvious, but so was his desire for solitude. Chentelle turned to the goblin priest. "Brother Gorin?"

"It is true," he answered. "Among my people, it is the custom to disfigure the bodies of our enemies. Each warrior has a unique method of mutilation, so that the clanbrothers will know who made the kill. It is thought to bring honor to the victor."

Chentelle shuddered.

"I agree," Gorin said. "It is an abominable practice, but it follows the teaching of the Heresiarchs. My people know no other way. Neither did I, before I found the Holy Land. My own ritual consisted of splitting the—"

"Please. I would rather not know."

Brother Gorin bowed and moved to help Alve descend the ladder to the salon. The elf had a bandage wrapped around his newly healed eyes to protect them from the intensity of the sun.

"Sulmar," Chentelle said, "will you help carry A'stoc to his cabin? I want to talk to Dacius."

The Tengarian nodded, and Chentelle wandered back to the wheeldeck, where Dacius was in conference with Captain Rone. Thildemar came up beside her as she approached the stairs.

"The Creator blessed us when he chose you as his messenger," he said. "Without your Gift, we would have been lost."

"Thank you," Chentelle said. "But I didn't really do that much."

Thildemar smiled. "No, only what was needed, only what no one else could have done."

Dacius and Captain Rone stopped talking as they approached. Chentelle took a deep breath, trying to organize her thoughts, but Thildemar spoke first.

"We have one more concern, Lord Gemine," he said. "Two of the goblins are still alive."

"Alive?" Dacius asked.

"Yes," Thildemar said, motioning to two of the forms lying at the foot of the wheeldeck, "they are only unconscious. I have enough deaths on my conscience for this life."

Dacius looked at the elf strangely, but nodded his head. "Still, they have little value as prisoners. I doubt the Dark One has shared his plans with them. Captain, can we turn one of the cabins into a brig? I hate to spare the manpower to mount a guard, but I don't see any other choice."

"Why not let them go?" Chentelle asked.

"What?"

"Let them go," she said, pointing across the stern to the diminishing silhouette of the goblin warship. "Their ship isn't going anyplace for a while. We could just put them in a longboat and let them row back to their comrades."

"Give them a longboat?" Rone repeated. "But we have only the two."

Dacius held up a hand. "No, the enchantress is right. The remaining boat will easily hold all of our company, if the need arises. Thildemar, bind them securely for now; we will release them after the funerals are complete. They should regain consciousness by then." He nodded his head slowly, as if considering another thought, but said nothing more.

"Dacius?" Chentelle said as Thildemar moved away. "I was wondering, you ordered a guard for A'stoc's cabin. What are you worried about? Is there some other danger?"

The human stroked his beard and regarded her with his clear blue eyes. "Perhaps, but I hope that I am worrying about nothing. Don't be concerned, enchantress; the matter will be decided soon enough."

She did not pursue it farther, though she was perplexed.

The funeral for the goblin marines was brief and uncomplicated. Brother Gorin chanted solemnly over each body in the goblin tongue. Then he marked the corpse with the circle of Creation and Sulmar and Thildemar tossed it into the sea. Chentelle and the rest of the company stood by in respectful silence, while the two bound prisoners cackled among themselves in their own harsh language.

After the last goblin was consigned to the waves, the company moved to the stern, where the body of Simon rested on a blanket decorated with the Great Tree of Essienkal. The elf's uniform was immaculate: the white, purple, and gold fairly glowing in Ellistar's light, and jet-black hair fell across his chest in two perfect braids. The Legionnaire's vorpal sword rested in the scabbard at his left side. Simon's face was passive, unlined, and the corners of his mouth turned upward with just the hint of a smile.

There was something terrible in that smile, something tragic. Chentelle wondered whether her father had smiled like that, after he died.

Dacius stepped forward and took one knee beside the body. He bowed, and slid Simon's sword from his scabbard with practiced precision. Then he stood and saluted the body. "The Legion honors you for your service. Your sacrifice brings honor to the Legion. Your arms will be passed on to your sons and to the sons of your sons. Your valor shall be sung of and remembered. Your presence will be missed."

Dacius stepped away, and Father Marcus came forward. The High Bishop rested a hand on Simon's forehead and closed his eyes in meditation. A halo of silver light formed around the priest's head. The glow spread, slowly moving down the priest's arm to envelop Simon's body in a glittering aura. The aura remained even after Father Marcus opened his eyes and turned to address the company.

"When a person dies," he said, "his soul is welcomed back into the Unity of Creation. The Harmony of Perfection, the Unity of the Sphere, the Peace of the Whole, all of these blessings await Simon, as they await all of us. Such is the love of the Creator. Such is the gift he has given to all of the races of men.

"But for an elf, there is a special bond to the land of his birth. He is bound to the glens and the glades that nurtured him. He is bound to the winds that filled his lungs and carried his songs. And he is bound to the trees, the trees that sheltered him, the trees that grew with him and gave him strength, the trees that touch his heart no matter how great the distance between them.

"When an elf dies, it is customary to bury him at the roots of the tree where he was born, so that, in death, he may be a part of the forest, as the forest was a part of him in life. But the Creator has saved a special blessing for an elf who dies at sea, for all the waters of this world are one. The water of the Quiet Sea runs also through the rivers of Inarr, and the waters of Istagothe fall as rain on the Mountains of Time. All are joined in the Circle of Creation.

"We leave Simon here, in the southern reaches of the Great Sea. But when we return to the Realm we will find that he is waiting for us. We will find him in the currents of the river Essien. We will hear his voice in the raindrops splashing against the Home Trees of the Inarr. We will discover the echo of his laughter in the fountains of Essienkal. And we will know. We will know that Simon rests easily in the embrace of his Creator. We will know that the pain we feel is for our loss, not His."

Father Marcus stepped back and raised his arms. He inhaled deeply and sang a single sustained note. The halo surrounding Simon's body responded to Marcus's voice, glowing more brightly as the Bishop strengthened his tone. Marcus sang louder, and the body rose into the air. It hung above the deck, surrounded in an almost blinding aura of silver light. The *Treachery* drifted forward on the gentle wind, and Simon's body fell behind them. As the High Bishop let his note trail off, the body slipped gently into the waves.

Chentelle leaned over the stern rail, watching the shimmering light fall deeper and deeper into the blue water. None of the company moved or spoke. The only sounds were the quiet hiss of the sea against the hull and the incessant chattering of the goblin prisoners.

"By the Creator," Gerruth growled, "is there no way to shut those fiends' mouths?"

"They are frightened," Gorin said. "They imagine that we have kept them alive only to visit some special torture upon them, some horrible vengeance for Simon's death. I have tried to reassure them, but they will not trust the word of a coward and a traitor."

Father Marcus rested a hand on the goblin's shoulder. "Keep faith, my friend. The judgment of the ignorant should be feared only when it flatters."

"Still," Dacius said, "I think it is time to be rid of our guests. Captain Rone, have you prepared the longboat?"

"Aye, Lord Gemine," the captain growled. "It'll take on a bit of water thanks to the goblin's raid, but they'll make it back to their ship."

Dacius nodded toward his men. Leth and Gerruth disappeared below while Thildemar herded the bound goblins into the waiting longboat. Leth and Gerruth returned with strung bows, which they kept trained on the goblins while Thildemar loosened their bonds. Then Zubec and Pardec started to crank the winches and lower the boat into the water.

"Wait," Dacius commanded. He nodded, and Leth and Gerruth spun sharply, aiming their arrows at Sulmar's heart.

"What are you doing?" Chentelle demanded. She started to move forward, but Sulmar's strong hand reached out and pushed her back.

"Stay behind me, mistress," he said.

Dacius moved forward and stood directly in front of the Tengarian. "Please bare your right arm, Sulmar."

So that was it. Sometime during the battle he must have seen Sulmar's brand.

The Tengarian remained motionless, meeting Dacius's hard stare impassively. Chentelle pressed his arm aside, and moved around him. Sulmar started to grab for her, but froze at a nervous twitch from one of the archers.

"Stop!" Chentelle said. "Everyone, just stop for a moment. This is all a misunderstanding. There's no need for this."

"Enchantress," Dacius said, "please stand aside. I pray that you are right, but if your liegeman does not comply with my request he will be shot."

"No, you can't," Chentelle said. This was insane. She wanted to lash out, to scream, to do something to make the human listen. But what? Any sudden move could push the whole situation irrevocably into violence.

"I'm sorry," she murmured. Then louder, "Show them."

Calmly, Sulmar pushed the sleeve of his tunic above his right elbow. A black shadow writhed sinuously on his forearm. The dragon seemed to be grinning, reveling in the Tengarian's predicament.

An audible gasp passed through the company. "A mark of evil!" Gerruth hissed.

"He's not evil!" Chentelle said.

"Enchantress," Dacius said. "I have seen your liegeman's arm many times, but I never saw that brand until Throm's minions attacked. We all saw how bravely and how devastatingly your man fought. If he has been cursed by the Ill-creature, then he is a danger to our quest."

"You can't kill him," Chentelle cried. "He's done nothing wrong."

"I have no wish to kill him, enchantress," Dacius replied. "He may go with the goblins in the longboat."

"But that's not fair!" she said. "Dacius, how can you do this?"

For a moment, the human's demeanor seemed to soften, but his eyes never left the Tengarian. "The safety of this quest is my sole concern, Chentelle. I must know that he presents no danger."

"But he doesn't," said Chentelle. "Sulmar, tell them."

"The mark is the curse of the Black Dragon," he said emotionlessly. "I have carried it for more than a year. It poses no threat to you, to your company, or to your quest."

"Why did we never see the mark before?" asked Dacius.

"The brand disappeared while I was in the Holy Land. It reappeared only after we passed through the Barrier."

"It must be a curse of great power," Father Marcus said. "May I examine it?"

"Please stay back, High Bishop," Dacius said as the priest moved forward.

Father Marcus smiled. "I appreciate your diligence and caution, Lord Gemine. But they are unnecessary in this case. This man is not evil." He winked at Sulmar and pointed toward the twisting dragon. "May I?"

The Tengarian nodded.

Father Marcus pressed his hand over the mark and closed his eyes. He hummed softly and a quiet glow surrounded Sulmar's forearm. As the glow intensified, the dragon mark faded into a light gray shadow. But as soon as the priest removed his hand, the curse regained its original virulence.

"A powerful curse," Father Marcus said. "It has insinuated itself deep into your spirit, far deeper than I can affect permanently. I suspect only the one who cast it can remove it."

"Not even he," Sulmar said. "For I willingly accepted this curse."

"What?" Chentelle looked at Sulmar in surprise. "Why?"

"It was the demand of the Noble Path," he said. "For breaking my Oath of Discipline I was given the choice of a traitor's death or exile and the burden of this curse. It was considered a proper balance for the act of murder."

Murder! It didn't seem possible. Chentelle had seen the quality of Sulmar's spirit. In battle, he could kill brutally and without mercy, but that was different. Battle wasn't the same as murder. And treason? Sulmar's honor was everything to him. How could he have broken his oath?

"I don't believe it," Chentelle said.

"Nevertheless, mistress, it is true."

"I know little of the laws of Tengar," Dacius said, "so I will make no judgment based upon your crimes there. The High Bishop finds no evil in you, so I have only one question more. Where do your loyalties lie now?"

"I have only one loyalty," Sulmar answered. "It is to my mistress, the elven enchantress."

Dacius nodded and motioned to his men. Leth and Gerruth relaxed their bows, and the sailors started lowering the longboat.

"Forgive me for doubting you," Dacius said to Sulmar, "but I had to be certain."

"There is no cause for apology," the Tengarian replied evenly. "You acted to protect your charge, as is your duty."

There seemed to be nothing else to say. They resumed winching the lifeboat and goblins down to the water.

◌

On the twenty-eighth day out from Norivika, the company spotted land. The jagged outline of a mountainous island rose against the southern sky. Chentelle stood near the bow, watching the shore take shape as Captain Rone guided the *Treachery* closer. The craggy coast was dark and forbidding in Deneob's fading light. The shadows of the rocks seemed to bleed into the sea, turning it black and hard.

"Drop anchor," Rone shouted. "Zubec, furl the sails."

Chentelle looked at the elven sailor in surprise.

Zubec motioned toward the eastern sky, where the first hints of light were appearing. "It's dangerous to approach an unfamiliar coast, particularly a coast like that one. The captain will wait until evenrise before trying to find a safe channel."

Chentelle nodded. It made sense. Though Ellistar was technically the night-time star, now, its light was still stronger than Deneob's. She looked into the sky. High in the darkness, the dim sparkle of Coldaria was visible. The Legends said that, like Infinitera, it was a world that circled the twin suns. But it traveled far from their warmth, in a great arc that took a century to complete. Somehow, the jagged shore in front of them seemed as if it could have been lifted from that distant star.

"The Dread Island, eh, enchantress." Captain Rone slipped into place beside her. "*Kennaru*, the goblins call it. And it's no wonder; just look at those rocks. I'll wager there are more just like them, hiding beneath the wave, just waiting to tear into the *Treachery*'s hull."

Chentelle shuddered at the thought. "I'm sure you will guide us through safely, captain."

"Eh? Of course I will," Rone replied. "Did I ever tell you how I guided the *Otan Stin* through the Crashing Rocks and into the heart of the Goblin Sea. Now, there was a test. And we did it at night, too. We had to; there were pirates laying in wait on the other side. Ah, but she was a fine ship, and she had a fine crew, a fine crew . . ."

The captain's voice faded into nothing. He and Chentelle stood by the rail, sharing the silence and watching the sky grow brighter. One by one, the other members of the company came to join them, as word of their arrival spread through the ship. Soon, everyone was present except A'stoc.

Chentelle sighed. The wizard had not left his cabin since the day of the battle. They left food outside his door every day. Sometimes the food would be gone when they returned; sometimes it would be untouched. A'stoc re-fused company and only growled through the door when asked a question. With Chentelle, he wouldn't even do that. He maintained an icy silence whenever she tried to talk about what had happened. Finally, she had given up trying.

Once Ellistar was full in the sky, Captain Rone ordered the *Treachery* under way. With Zubec at the bow sounding the depth, he guided them cautiously toward the Dread Island. The cliffs looked even more formidable in the light. Sheer rock rose hundreds of cubits above the waterline, and dozens of tiny islets formed a barrier between *Kennaru* and the open sea.

They worked their way slowly eastward, rounding the edge of the island and following the cliffs south. Leagues passed, marked only by the drone of Zubec's soundings and the grim sameness of the unapproachable coast. Chen-telle watched the rocks and tried not to fidget. They were so close! It would feel so good to be on solid ground again. But what if the whole island was like this? Where would they land?

"Look to starboard!" Pardec shouted from the rigging. "There's a break in the rocks."

He was right. A narrow draw in the cliffs opened onto a small lagoon. An atoll partially ringed the lagoon, shielding it from the chopping waves of the Great Sea. As they drew nearer, a thin stretch of beach became visible. Beyond the sand, dense foliage filled a valley that climbed steeply westward into the heights. A waterfall splashed against the rocks north of the beach, marking the endpoint of a mountain stream that flowed from the west.

Captain Rone turned to the High Bishop. "What say you, Your Eminence? The passage is navigable, but we may find better farther on. Do we stop here or sail on?"

Father Marcus stroked his chin thoughtfully. He glanced at the sky and nodded. "Take us in, captain."

Rone smiled broadly and shouted orders to his crew. He maneuvered the *Treachery* smoothly through the rocks and into the shelter of the lagoon. He let the wind carry them close to the shore, then had Paun use his sagecraft to face the goblinship back toward the open sea.

"So," the captain said, turning once more to Father Marcus, "what now?"

Propelled by Paun's craft, the longboat slid swiftly away from the beach. Chentelle's eyes followed the shipsage back to the *Treachery*, but she hardly noticed. She was on land! It felt so wonderful to be away from that awful ship, to be separated from the pain of the wood. Her Gift sang outward, almost of its own volition. After so many weeks of keeping herself shielded, she was finally free.

And everything was so alive here. The forest was thick with vines and undergrowth whose like she had never seen. A hundred flowers filled the air with perfumes that were both half-familiar and tantalizingly exotic. Strange birds called to each other from the branches of unfamiliar trees, and colorful insects danced in the air. Even the waves that tickled her ankles seemed to promise a thousand joyous tales of darting fish and scurrying crabs.

Chentelle laughed and splashed up to the beach. She felt weightless, as if her feet reached the ground only through some accident of circumstance. She felt a similar happiness in Sulmar and the Legionnaires, though their discipline would not let them express it. She felt a twinge of sadness for Captain Rone and his crew, who remained aboard the *Treachery* waiting for their return. She hoped that they felt at least some of the joy that filled her.

Of course, even among the company on land there were those who were untouched by relief. A'stoc, unshaven and unkempt, had emerged from his cabin and joined the company as they loaded the longboat. Wrapped in his pain, he stood silently in the exact spot where he had stepped from the longboat, as oblivious to the beauty of this place as he was to the water tugging at his robes.

"Friends." Father Marcus' voice was tinged with concern. "I need to speak with you."

Sparked from their private thoughts, the company gathered around the High Bishop. Even A'stoc shuffled up to shore.

"I am concerned," Marcus said. "There is no doubt that this is the correct island. The Atablicryon should be emanating spiritual light like a mighty beacon, but I cannot sense it."

"Hel's bile," A'stoc spat. "Do you mean to say that we have not the slightest idea where to search for the Sphere? Are we to tromp aimlessly over this entire godforsaken island until one of us accidentally trips over an icon of true Earthpower?"

"That's enough, wizard," Dacius snapped. "As I understand it, your presence is necessary only to activate the Sphere once we have found the Fallen Star. If you wish to wait aboard the ship while we conduct the search, I will happily summon the longboat."

A'stoc glared at the human lord. Though slightly taller, the lean wizard seemed dwarfed by the Legionnaire's solid bulk and wild red beard. "I think I will remain, Legionnaire. You will undoubtedly need my protection should the goblins come upon you in force."

"My people will not come here," Gorin said. "They fear this place more than death."

"Your people," A'stoc sneered, "are craven and weak-willed. They will be easily driven here if the Ill-creature who commands them so desires."

"Peace," Father Marcus said, holding up a hand to curtail Gorin's reply. "The long confinement and the stress of our journey have taken their toll on all of us. Wizard A'stoc, you in particular have faced heavy trials in these weeks. But take heart, friends, we have made *Kennaru*. The Creator guides our steps, and He will provide for our success. We need only recognize His blessings when they arrive. Lord Gemine, please organize a reconnaissance of the valley. I will meditate on our course while I await your report."

Dacius glanced up at the sun. "We'll travel in pairs: Leth and Gerruth, Drup with Thildemar; Alve, you're with me. We have maybe four hours of Ellistar's light left, but she'll fall quickly behind those mountains. Turn back as soon as her bottom edge disappears."

The Legionnaires secured their equipment and disappeared into the jungle moments later. Father Marcus and Gorin wandered off to perform their ritual of meditation, and A'stoc was slumped against a nearby tree with his eyes closed. Chentelle turned to Sulmar, but the Tengarian was deep into his 'watchful and alert' posture. She sighed. The joy of this night was fast disappearing, but all was not lost. The water of the lagoon was clear and inviting, and it had been weeks since she had a proper bath. Smiling, she stripped off her gown and dropped it on the sand next to her boots. Six long steps and a graceful dive carried her into the waves.

The water was clear and pure. It wrapped around her like a cool sheet, sending a tingle of excitement through her nipples and her toes. She felt cleaner almost immediately. It was wonderful. A school of tiny blue fish darted to and fro just beneath her. She swam downward and reached for them with her Gift. They flitted around her, dancing in and out of her hair and skittering across her skin. It tickled and she had to laugh, losing what was left of her breath. She let go of the fish and followed the bubbles to the surface.

Even the air felt cleaner in her lungs. She took several deep breaths and then headed back toward the bottom. The fish had moved on, so she explored for a while on her own. It would have been nice to have company, but she knew that Sulmar would never allow himself to relax and swim with her in unknown territory. Maybe A'stoc? She had a sudden image of the wizard trying to scowl while tiny blue fish tickled his ears, and lost her air to laughter again. Still, it was worth a try. He could certainly use a good dose of clean water.

She surfaced and swam toward the beach. A'stoc was watching her, but he started and turned away when she stood up in the shallow water. "Do you like to swim, A'stoc? You should come in. The water is wonderful."

"I—I think not, enchantress," he said. "I prefer to rest while I have the chance. Please let me sleep."

"But it is restful," she said. "It's better than sleep. Trust me."

"Trust you?" A'stoc growled, snapping his head around to glare at Chentelle. "How can you—I—"

The wizard stammered to a halt, a flush coming to his cheeks. Then he dropped his face into his hands. "Please, just let me be."

Chentelle winced at the sadness in his voice, but she did not know how to help. She remembered again how unnatural humans could be about naturalness. Maybe that was part of the problem. Wordlessly, she turned and dived back into the waves.

The Legionnaires returned just before dark. The valley near the beach showed no signs of habitation by men, but Thildemar had discovered signs of a partially overgrown trail on the south bank of the river. Father Marcus conferred briefly with Dacius, and they agreed to wait until Ellistar rose again before heading inland. The red daytime of Deneob would be spent in rest and preparation.

Chentelle lay under the shade of a tree and struggled to relax. It was hot and humid, and Deneob's red glare seemed inescapable. Finally, fatigue took her. She slept. And she dreamed of yellow eyes that followed her wherever she moved.

⮜

Once Ellistar rose, Thildemar led them into the rain forest. The old elf slid through the brush like a phantom, passing through gaps in the foliage that seemed to appear magically before him and vanish just as quickly behind. He kept them close to the river where possible, but in many places the undergrowth was too thick. Drup and Alve used cutlasses from the *Treachery*'s stores to widen the paths that Thildemar found, but progress was slow. The heat was oppressive, and only Chantelle's Gift prevented the insects from being the same.

Finally, they came to the trail. At first, it seemed no more passable than the bare jungle behind them, but gradually it widened into a true footpath. They wound their way single file through the forest for perhaps a league. Then the path opened up into a small clearing.

Thildemar signaled a halt. "I think we should rest here," he said, wiping sweat from his brow.

Dacius raised an eyebrow, but nodded his assent. They broke out some rations and ate a spare meal.

"We are being watched," Thildemar said in an even tone, spacing his words between mouthfuls.

"Are you certain?" Dacius asked.

Thildemar nodded. "He moves ahead of us."

"Goblin?"

Thildemar shrugged. "I do not think so, but the tracks are unclear."

"He is human," Sulmar said quietly. "Twice, I have seen him through the trees."

Dacius cocked his head and regarded the Tengarian. "Can you bring him in?"

Sulmar nodded.

"When we move on," said Dacius, "fall back and slip into the forest. Try to herd him closer to us. If we hear or see him, we'll try to cut off his escape. I want him alive. If we can't capture him without injury, let him go. We don't need to make unnecessary enemies."

He stood and shouldered his pack. "Break's over, Legionnaires."

Once more, Thildemar led them along the forest path, but this time he had one less follower.

Chentelle stayed close behind Dacius, resting a hand on his pack so that she could follow him without full alertness. Slowly, she let her awareness expand, reaching out into the forest to find the watcher. She kept just enough attention on her body to keep it moving. She drifted through the dense web of life that surrounded them, searching for the complex thoughts and feelings that would set the human apart.

It was hard to keep herself divided. She kept stumbling on the uneven path and getting distracted by the sheer volume of life in this place. Finally, she managed to orient on the steady presence of Sulmar, working his way through the brush. She knew that he would be headed toward the watcher, so she used his progress as a guide.

There! Nervousness, fear, excitement, curiosity: that had to be him. His emotions were a jumble. He was afraid, but thrilled by the fear. Who were they? Enemies? Strangers? Was there a difference? What should he do?

Wait. What was that? Oh, no! They've discovered him. Run! No, not that way. Have to lead them away. Run. Run. Aahh, another one. Hide. No, keep running. Wait. What—

"Ooof." Chentelle doubled over in pain. It felt as if someone had kicked her in the stomach.

"I have him," Sulmar called.

In a moment, the Tengarian stepped onto the path ahead of them, carrying a small human over one shoulder. He dropped the man onto the ground and stepped back.

The human scrambled into a crouch, but did not try to run. He was small and lean, not much larger than an elf. He was naked save for a loincloth and a leather pouch, but his dark hair and thin mustaches were neatly trimmed. His eyes darted through the company nervously while he struggled to breathe.

"Is he injured?" asked Father Marcus. "Gorin, you are closer. See to his wounds."

Gorin worked his way past the intervening Legionnaires, and laid a claw on the stranger's chest, searching for injury. The man jumped to his right, gurgling in fear. His eyes rolled backward, and he dropped to the ground, unconscious.

❧ 10 ᙍ

Village

Is he all right?" Dacius asked.

"I think so, Lord Gemine." Gorin rolled the stranger over and examined his chest. "I see no injuries. He has only fainted."

"He was frightened," Chentelle said. "Your appearance scared him."

"Perhaps he has never seen a goblin before," Gorin said.

"Or perhaps he has seen too many," A'stoc broke in.

The man on the ground moaned softly.

"He's waking up," Dacius said. "Gorin, perhaps your face should not be the first thing he sees."

The goblin nodded and slid back behind the Legionnaires.

The stranger opened his eyes. Slowly, he lifted himself onto one elbow and shook his head. Then his eyes snapped open, and he burst into action. He scrambled backward, trying to turn, jump to his feet, and start running simultaneously. Of course, since Sulmar was standing immediately behind him, he succeeded only in tripping over the Tengarian's leg and falling face first into the dirt.

"Please," he sputtered, "don't hurt me."

Chentelle felt the bitter tinge of his fear. It quivered against her Gift like a taut string, ready to snap at any moment. She let the music rise within her. Softly, ever so gently, she started to sing. Half-whispered words reached out, soothing the man's fear, easing the tension that jarred his spirit. She moved as she sang, inching closer to the human until she could sit close enough to touch him with her hands as well as her voice.

"Easy," she said, resting her fingers on his wrist. "It's all right. We won't hurt you."

The human's deep brown eyes locked on to hers. "Wha—What are you?"

"I am an enchantress," she said. "My friends and I just want to ask you a few questions. Why were you spying on us?"

"I wasn't spying," he said. "I just saw you in the forest when I was gathering food to take—" He stopped and glanced at Brother Gorin, barely visible between Drup and Alve. "No. I have never seen enchantresses before, but if you travel with goblins then I will not answer your questions."

Enchantresses? "Oh, I see. No, we are not all enchantresses." She ran a finger along one ear. "I am an elf. Some of my companions are elves, too, but only I am an enchantress. My name is Chentelle."

He nodded. "I understand. I am Kelmek. You are very beautiful, Enchantress Chentelle. Why do you travel with monsters?"

"Brother Gorin isn't a monster," she said. "He's kind and good. He's a member of the Holy Order."

"A priest?" the man said. "I don't believe you. Goblins are cruel and vicious. They slaughter my people and serve the demons under Hel's Crown."

"But Gorin is different," Chentelle protested.

"Chentelle is right," Darius said, stepping forward slowly. "I know how you feel. Goblins murdered my family and my betrothed. I have fought against them for most of my life. But Gorin is, indeed, different from other goblins. He serves the Holy Order faithfully, and he has risked everything to help us in our quest."

Kelmek frowned. "Your words sound true. I can hardly believe that Enchantress Chentelle would have evil companions, but how can I be sure?"

Chentelle squeezed his wrist gently. "I know it's hard, Kelmek. But you have to trust us. Look into your heart. It will show you that we are not your enemies."

"I don't know," Kelmek said, shaking his head. "It is true that you do not look like the other monsters, but what if you serve the same demons?"

Chentelle felt the man's fear starting to stir. "Kelmek, you ha—"

"One moment." Father Marcus squeezed past Dacius and squatted down next to Kelmek. "Please excuse the interruption, Chentelle, but I need to know something. Kelmek, my name is Father Marcus. I, too, am a member of the Holy Order. Please tell me, have you seen these demons that the goblins serve?"

"Well, no," he said. "But they say the demons live underneath Hel's Crown. That's why they summon the goblins from the Mouth of the Sea, to extend their power through the Sacred City."

"The Sacred City?" Marcus asked. "Where is that? Can you tell us how to find it?"

"You don't know?" Kelmek asked. "Then you must not serve the demons." He lifted himself to his feet. "This is too much for me to decide. Since you are not with the other monsters, I will take you to the village. Elihaz will know what to do."

"Elihaz?" Marcus asked.

"The Holy Priest," Kelmek said. "Come on. Follow me."

"Wait," said Dacius. "You said the goblins were coming from the Mouth of the Sea. Where is that?"

"The Mouth of Sea?" Kelmek said. "About three leagues to the south, where the Stone City used to be."

Dacius' hand drifted to the hilt of his sword. "Fires of Hel," he muttered, "three leagues."

ะค

Kelmek led them at a brisk pace. They climbed out of the jungle and onto rolling plains. High mountains rose to the south, but they continued westward, following the path of the river. Almost immediately, isolated farmsteads started to decorate the landscape. But the fields were all barren, and not a single building remained whole and undamaged. The trail of devastation continued until they came to a winding path, leading south into the foothills.

They climbed. After a few minutes, they reached a small plateau. Patches of cultivated land ringed the edge of the plateau and continued up and down the mountainside in terraced layers. The center of the plateau housed the village itself: a dozen crude stone buildings were arranged around a central square. A large building filled the far side of the square, extending backward until it met the rock walls of the mountain behind.

A few people were scattered through the fields and houses, but they ran for shelter as soon as they saw the company. A bell started to ring, and suddenly dozens of people were running for the large building. As the last person entered, large wooden doors slammed shut behind them. Finally, the bell stopped ringing.

"Your people are certainly fearful of strangers," A'stoc said.

"We have learned to be," Kelmek replied, leading them into the village square. "We have had to."

"But you don't need to be afraid of us," said Chentelle.

Kelmek came to a halt near a rock-lined well that filled the center of the village square. He smiled at Chentelle. "I am not, but my people have not heard you sing. They have not felt your beauty. They know only that I have brought strange monsters to the village, so they run to the temple. Wait here. I will go and talk to Elihaz."

As Kelmek approached the temple, a viewing portal opened in the middle of one of the great doors. The gate swung open quickly and Kelmek was ushered inside. Then the door crashed shut again.

"I wonder how this village survives," Dacius said, eyes shifting across the open plateau. "With proper fortifications this place could be defended, but as it is, even a moderate goblin patrol could overrun the village."

"Look around you, Lord Gemine," A'stoc said. "What purpose would there be to an attack? There is nothing of worth in this desolate hole."

"But there have been attacks," Chentelle protested. "Kelmek said so. Besides, I think you're wrong. There's something special about this place, something charming. I think the people will help us."

"You are naive. These people care nothing for our quest." The wizard shook his head. "Have you learned nothing since this quest began? Why are you even here? Your childish hopes will lead us all to ruin."

"Wizard," Dacius said stiffly, "you are out of line. Chentelle has proven herself again and again. Our quest may well have been lost without her courage and resourcefulness, and everyone but you recognizes how special she is. I do not pretend to understand the meaning of her visions, but it is clear that the Creator has chosen her for an important task. If you can't show her the respect she's earned, then at least show some common courtesy."

"Lord Gemine," A'stoc said coldly, "I require neither your spiritual conjectures nor your lessons in protocol." He turned to Chentelle. "You should at least have waited aboard the *Treachery*. You would have been safer there."

Chentelle blinked in surprise. He was worried about her! She started to frame a reply, but A'stoc had already spun on his heel and stalked out of the square.

"Do not fear, mistress," Sulmar said. "I will not let you come to harm."

Chentelle realized that her shoulders were trembling. She calmed herself with a deep breath and smiled at her liegeman. "Thank you, Sulmar. I know that."

Eventually, the wizard chose to rejoin the company, but the mood for conversation had passed. They waited in silence until the door to the temple opened again.

Villagers skittered through the portal, singly at first, then in twos and threes. Most of them gave the company a wide berth, skirting around the edge of the square, but a few approached and welcomed them to the village. One young boy even insisted on greeting each person with a kiss on the cheek and a boisterous hug.

After the exodus was complete, Kelmek beckoned to them from the doorway. "Enchantress Chentelle, please bring your companions into the temple. Elihaz will see you now."

Chentelle looked to Father Marcus, but the priest just smiled good-naturedly and bowed, indicating that she should lead the way. Blushing slightly, she walked toward the temple.

Three paces from the door, she staggered and nearly fell. Sulmar was at her side in an instant, but even before the Tengarian caught her, the concern on his face melted into understanding. The world had come alive.

Chentelle laughed in delight as bliss and security filled her spirit. The air was filled with harmony, with the presence of the Creator, with peace. It was like being in the Holy Land—but, no, it was not. The rock walls of the temple remained cold and inert, and the power barely permeated the earth under their feet. It was only an echo of the Holy Land, faint but no less precious for that weakness.

One by one the company entered the temple and felt its weak power. Even A'stoc smiled as he entered.

"Blessed Creator," Father Marcus said. "How is this possible?"

Kelmek smiled. "Elihaz," he said simply.

They followed Kelmek deeper into the temple. He led them into a large, dimly lit chamber. Benches were arranged in a circle around a raised dais that held a simple stone altar. An old man sat on the dais, his back to the altar and his legs hanging casually off the edge of the platform. Like Kelmek, he was dressed only in a leather loincloth, though he also wore a spherical pendant on a thong around his neck. Candles flickered on the altar, showing a deeply lined face and sparkling brown eyes.

The old man pointed at Father Marcus. "I sense evil within you."

Kelmek jumped as if he had been struck. "I didn't know, Elihaz. I—"

The Holy Priest held up a hand, silencing the villager. "It's all right, Kelmek. You may go."

The young man bowed and backed from the chamber. His eyes stayed locked on to Father Marcus until the door closed between them.

"Well?" Elihaz said, turning back to Father Marcus.

"I will not deceive you," the High Bishop said. "I carry the knowledge of evil within me, but I do not serve its cause. I am Marcus Alanda, High Bishop of the Holy Order in Norivika, leader of the Holy Land of Talan. I believe in the sanctity of the Creation, and I follow the will of the Creator as well as I am able."

"That is a very long title," Elihaz said. "My own is Elihaz the Elder, Holy Priest, Protector and Spiritual Guide for the village, but most people just call me Elihaz."

Father Marcus bowed his head politely. "It is an honor to meet you, Elihaz. Please, call me Father Marcus."

Elihaz motioned to the benches. "Have a seat, Father Marcus. I think we have much to talk about. First, though, please introduce me to your companions."

One by one, they were presented to the Holy Priest. The old man greeted each of them and bade them to sit. His manner was friendly, almost jovial, but there was a penetrating nature to his questions. The tranquillity that filled the temple paled in comparison to the harmony of the Holy Land, but it was enough to guide Elihaz in his inquiries. Chentelle had no doubt that he was passing judgment upon them. And the success of their quest could depend on the outcome of that judgment.

The old priest gave particular attention to each of the Legionnaires, asking about the nature of their lives and beliefs. He talked with Thildemar about the sanctity of life and discussed family and duty with Leth and Gerruth. Drup and Alve were questioned about duty and responsibility. Dacius he chose to ask about sorrow and lost comrades. But when he came to Gorin, he asked no questions. He simply walked over and embraced the goblin. "You have a strong spirit, Brother Gorin. The Creator is truly merciful, to bring you here now."

Then A'stoc came forward. He nodded his head politely as Father Marcus presented him to the Holy Priest.

"A wizard! How wonderful," Elihaz said. He ran his eyes up and down the mage's body. "You are very tall, but you need better posture. You slump over as if the whole of Creation rests on your shoulders. I think maybe you lean on your walking stick too much. Try standing up on your own, instead. It's better for the spine."

A'stoc reared up to his full height and jabbed a finger toward the old man's face. His mouth opened, but no words came out. The wizard's lips contorted wildly, and the knuckles of his right hand whitened against the Staff. But still no sound came from his mouth. He spun around and stalked to an empty bench.

Chentelle moved forward and was introduced.

"Ah, the enchantress," Elihaz said, smiling warmly. "No wonder Kelmek is stricken. The grace of your form is matched only by the beauty of your spirit. But please, do not sing for me. My ears have grown hard with age, and I fear they would make a poor audience for your charms."

Chentelle wasn't sure whether to be flattered or insulted. She settled on embarrassed. "Thank you," she murmured. She wandered over to one of the benches and sat down beside A'stoc. Somehow, the wizard's rigid presence was comforting.

Elihaz climbed back to his seat by the altar. "On behalf of myself and anyone foolish enough to let me speak for them, I welcome you all. Now, why have you appeared on my doorstep in the middle of the night?"

"We seek a temple called the Atablicryon," Father Marcus said. "We have learned of a great danger, one which threatens all of Infinitera. The only way to defeat this evil is to use the power of the Sphere of Ohnn, which lies hidden in your Atablicryon."

"I have never heard of this Sphere," Elihaz said. "How do you know it is there?"

"We are guided by vision and prophecy," Father Marcus said. "In the Holy Land, the power of the Creator still flows purely, untouched by the corruption of the Flaw. At the center of this harmony is the Atablicryon, the holiest shrine of the Holy Order. Until recently, we believed it was unique, but now we know that there is an Atablicryon on this island. In the same way, we know that the Sphere of Ohnn is held within. I cannot tell the source of this information, but it is true."

Elihaz pulled his pendant over his head and toyed with it thoughtfully. "Visions and prophecies—my father once told me he would rather suffer a thousand curses than one true vision. But he used to exaggerate terribly. Well, we can come back to that. Tell me about this Holy Land."

"It is the last remnant of the True Creation," Marcus said. "It is the way the Old Book tells us the world should be. The peace of your temple is a wondrous thing, a miracle whose provenance I would beg you to share, but it is only a candle to the Golden Sun next to the harmony of the Holy Land. No evil can exist there, and all wounds are healed."

Except certain emotional ones, Chentelle thought, glancing sidelong at A'stoc.

Elihaz smiled and closed his eyes. "In the perfect emptiness, a Sphere was formed. And within the Sphere, the races were born. The Creation was perfect, and the Creator was perfection. The Sphere existed in balance, in harmony, and for the eyes of the Creator. For its existence was Beauty. Its purpose was Beauty."

"The Old Book!" Marcus exclaimed. "Do you also know the Scriptures of Jediah?"

"Jediah?" said Elihaz.

"The first High Bishop," Marcus said. "He revolutionized the Holy Order. He realized that worshiping perfection without fighting to preserve it led only to despair. He believed that the races of man had a destiny to heal the Flaw and re-create the Time of Perfection, so he dedicated his life to perpetuating harmony and fighting corruption. His words form the core of our belief."

"I have never heard of him," Elihaz said. He held up his pendant. "This is the core of our belief. It symbolizes the Sphere of Creation: perfect, unchanging, immutable. These are the truths I learned when my father welcomed me into the Holy Order. Do you know what we call it? No?"

The old priest held up a finger for silence and moved quietly to the door of the chamber. His eyes met Chentelle's for an instant, and he winked conspiratorially. Then he yanked the door open and Kelmek fell inside. "Well, boy," Elihaz said, dangling the pendant in front of his face. "What would you call this?"

"It's a rock, Grandfather," Kelmek answered tentatively.

"Excellent!" Elihaz cried. "You have been diligent in your studies. Now tell me what you have learned while listening at the door."

Kelmek looked as if he wanted to crawl out of the room and hide, but there was no escape. He stood and brushed the dirt from his knees. "I do not understand this High Bishop, Grandfather. He knows things that he cannot know, but he will not tell us how. He speaks of miracles as though they were trifles but gapes in awe at the refuge of the temple."

"Do you believe him?" Elihaz asked.

"I don't know, Grandfather," Kelmek admitted.

"Then ask him a question," prodded the Holy Priest, "something that will satisfy your doubts."

Kelmek stared at Father Marcus, brow furrowed in concentration. "All right, tell me what the evil is that you carry inside your soul."

Father Marcus turned from the boy to Elihaz. He locked eyes with the old priest for a moment, then turned back to Kelmek. "It is the same evil that we fight against," he said calmly. "It is the evil that will consume Infinitera if it is not destroyed."

Kelmek's mouth dropped open. He turned to his grandfather and shrugged helplessly.

Elihaz grinned and led the boy into the center of the room. He hopped into his seat against the altar and motioned for Kelmek to sit next to him. "Your revelations have unnerved my grandson," he said to Marcus. "But what confuses him, reassures me. A deceitful man would be sure to claim an impressive source for his secret knowledge, but you maintain silence. And what need would you have to summon the pale refuge I use to fill this temple, when you dwell in the light of the True Creation? Still, the boy did not ask quite the right question. Why do you harbor evil in your soul?"

Father Marcus smiled and bowed his head respectfully. "The evil that we battle is new to Infinitera. It comes from beyond the Abyss, from outside the Sphere of Creation. In order to destroy it, I will have to understand it. That is the knowledge I carry."

"And so it is settled," said Elihaz, "I will help you. But first, I will tell you a story of a true vision."

Another true vision? Chentelle was having trouble assimilating this. But she listened intently.

"In the mountains south of the village lie the remains of an ancient city. No one knows how long it has been since the city died, but for countless generations we have held that land to be sacred. In the center of the dead city is the mountain we call Hel's Crown. In happier times, it had other names: Enchanted Rock, the Dome of Creation. But that was before the demons came. Now it is Hel's Crown."

Elihaz climbed to his feet and paced behind the altar. "We used to bury our dead in the catacombs beneath the mountain. All the peoples did: the men of the Stone City, the folk of the scattered farms, even the wild men of the coast. But during my father's father's time, a great cataclysm shook the land. Cracks appeared in the earth. Rivers changed their course. And strange creatures appeared under the mountain, black as Hel's heart and just as cruel.

"The demons drove the people from the catacombs. They would not let us bury our dead. They would not let us travel in the Sacred City. It was intolerable. The Four Holy Priests joined together to resist them. They were great men: Kolos of the Stone City, Silas the Pale, Lazy Tom, and my grandfather."

He paused in his narrative, focusing on Father Marcus. "Do you know the power of sanctuary? Good. The power of refuge is very much like that, but we turn it outward, filling a space with the peace of our spirit. The Holy Priests filled the catacombs with the power of refuge. The demons were forced to retreat deeper into the earth. But the refuge lasts only so long as a priest remains, feeding it with his spirit, so an agreement was made. Each priest remained in the catacombs for one season, maintaining the refuge, while the others returned to their homes. And so it stayed for through my father's time and my own.

"Two years ago, everything changed again. People from every community had gathered under the mountain for the ceremony of renewal. My daughter was Holy Priest then. She was there representing the village, as was her daughter. But something happened during the ceremony. Holdar of the Stone City went insane. He broke the ritual and allowed the refuge to collapse. Before the other priests could react, the demons attacked. Men, women, children: no one escaped the power of their magic. No one except Holdar. They left him alive.

"He staggered out of the mountains two days later, babbling like a madman about a holy vision. Before he died, we learned two things: the truth about the slaughter, and the nature of his vision. He had dreamed of an ancient temple, older than even the Sacred City. It was deep underneath the mountain, deeper than the catacombs. During his time as guardian of the refuge, he had followed the dream and discovered the temple. He called it the Atablicryon."

Elihaz leaned heavily against the altar, looking suddenly frail and haggard. "I was the only Holy Priest left alive. I went to the catacombs and raised the refuge once more. I drove the demons back into the depths, and my people were able to recover our dead. For three days we worked to give them a proper burial. Then the goblins came.

"I had to choose. I could not hold the demons at bay and protect the village. I came home. Now, the Stone City is destroyed. The scattered farms are empty, and only goblins roam the coast. Now the demons rule from under Hel's Crown, and I am old. I am very old."

The priest's sadness echoed in Chentelle's heart. She felt a great emptiness, a void that could never be filled. Tears gathered on her cheeks. "I'm sorry," she whispered. "I'm so sorry."

Elihaz must have heard. He turned to her and smiled. "Thank you, dear child, thank you. But please, do not cry for my sorrows."

"I don't understand," Dacius said. "Why didn't you fight? Your people could have forged weapons, driven the goblins back to the sea."

Elihaz shook his head. "That is not our way. We believe in the perfection of the Creator and his Creation. To take up arms would be a violation of that perfection. It would be a violation of our selves. We have always relied on the powers of refuge and sanctuary to protect us."

"But they killed your people," Dacius protested. "The perfection you believe in is a lie. The Creation is flawed. If it wasn't, then such evil could not exist."

"Years ago," said Elihaz, "I would have argued the point with you. I would have pointed out that by preparing for violence you perpetuate the need for it. I would have said that just by wearing your sword you support the idea of violence as acceptable behavior. Those are the truths I was taught by my father and my father's father. I believe in those truths, but I find little comfort in them, now."

"Maybe I can help," said Father Marcus. He reached into his pack and pulled out a well-worn volume. "These are the Scriptures of Jediah. Centuries ago, he wrestled with the same sorrows that trouble you now. Perhaps the answers he found will help you find your own."

"Thank you," said Elihaz, accepting the book gingerly. "This is a precious gift. And it deserves a fair return. You will need a guide to find the Atablicryon, someone who knows the catacombs and who is not afraid to try the demons' lair. That someone will be me."

"What?" Kelmek jumped to his feet. "Grandfather, no! You cannot be their guide. I will not permit it."

Elihaz cocked his head and raised one eyebrow. "And who are you to permit me or not?"

"I'm sorry," said Kelmek, momentarily cowed. "But you're in no condition to travel so far. Besides, you have a duty to the village. You have to stay here and protect our people."

"And how am I to do that," said Elihaz, "if all of Infinitera dies." He waved a hand at the company. "You heard their words. No one will be safe if they fail in their quest. And they will never find the temple without a guide. I must go with them."

"No, Grandfather," said Kelmek. "If they must have a guide, then I will go with them."

The old priest shook his head firmly. "That I will not permit. You are the only family I have left, and the only hope the village has to survive after I'm gone. I will not let you take such a risk. Besides, you do not know the catacombs as well as I do."

"No," said Kelmek, "I don't, but I know them well enough. And I will be at risk no matter who acts as guide. If you leave, the village will be helpless against the goblins. But if I go, then the village will be safe, and I will be protected by the stranger's weapons and magic."

Elihaz sighed and dropped his eyes. "It seems that you are a better student than I knew. You are right. I will stay. But be careful, Grandson, and come back alive. The village needs you. I need you." He pushed his pendant into Kelmek's hand. "Take this. It may give you some protection."

"But, Grandfather," Kelmek said, "only the Holy—" He paused, reconsidering. "Thank you, Grandfather. Don't worry. I will be fine."

Elihaz turned to Father Marcus. "Watch out for him, Marcus Alanda, High Bishop of the Holy Order in Norivika, leader of the Holy Land of Talan. He is my hope."

Marcus bowed to the old priest. "You honor us with your trust and your guidance. Do not fear. Our path is dangerous, but the Creator guides our steps. Your grandson will be safe."

"May the Creator watch you all," said Elihaz. "Now, if you will excuse me, I am going to try and track down some sleep. I suggest you do the same."

Chentelle woke to the ringing of a bell. She rolled out of bed and tried to get her bearing. She was in Kelmek's room. He had insisted that she use it while he stayed with his grandfather. She ran to the window. The first hints of Ellistar's light brightened the sky, and people from the village were running toward the temple doors.

"Goblins!" someone shouted. "To the temple! Goblins are coming."

"Blessed Creator, not again." Chentelle yanked on her boots and slid into her dress. She rushed out the door and nearly ran straight into Sulmar.

"Oh!" Chentelle stumbled to a halt. "You startled me. I thought you were down in the assembly hall with the Legionnaires."

"No, mistress."

She saw a thin pile of bedding on the floor of the hallway. He had slept outside her door. "Sulmar—"

The clanging of the bell interrupted her thought.

"Come on." She raced for the stairs, certain that Sulmar was only seconds behind.

The entry hall was clogged with people. Villagers from beyond the gate were scrambling to get in, but their way was impeded by Legionnaires trying to force their way outside. Father Marcus and Elihaz guided the villagers who were already inside deeper into the temple, trying to ease the logjam. Chentelle tried to join the Legionnaires, but the crowd pushed her back.

"Allow me, mistress." Sulmar slid around her. He grabbed the nearest villager on the hip and shoulder and applied slight pressure. The man stepped sideways as his balance shifted, leaving an opening. Sulmar moved into the vacancy and applied similar pressure to the next person. He neither threatened nor overpowered anyone, but he drove a clear path to the temple doors.

Dacius and the Legionnaires were already outside, surveying the situation.

Suddenly, Thildemar appeared, sprinting toward them from the village square. He came to a stop beside Dacius. Sweat ran freely down the old elf's brow, but his breathing was even and controlled. "I marked a score plus three, Lord Gemine, all mounted. None were obvious shamans or witches, but they are veteran troops. Nearly all carry blood trophies."

Dacius nodded. "How long?"

"Perhaps four minutes," Thildemar said. He paused, then spoke again. "Lord Gemine, they follow our trail."

Muscles corded along Dacius' jaw. "So be it." He pointed to the two houses nearest to the temple. "Leth, Gerruth, Thildemar, take the left. Drup, Alve, you're with me. Wizard—where's A'stoc? Never mind. We don't have time. Sulmar, will you fight with us?"

The Tengarian looked to Chentelle.

She nodded. "Go on. I'll be safe in the temple."

"Good," Dacius said. "You're on the left. Archers, three shots no more. We don't have the men to hold a defensive position. Use the houses for cover, but don't get cornered. Work in pairs or groups; an isolated man is fodder for cavalry. Move out, Legionnaires, and stay calm. No one fires until my signal."

Father Marcus came up behind them. "Lord Gemine, there is no need for this. We will be safe within the refuge."

Dacius spun about to face the priest. "They follow our trail, High Bishop. We have to take them."

The Legionnaire ran off to take his position, and Father Marcus turned to Chentelle, a puzzled expression on his face.

She shrugged. "I have to find A'stoc."

The gates of the temple boomed shut behind Chentelle. She ran to the assembly hall. The wizard should have been easy to spot; he stood at least a head taller than any of the villagers. But there was no sign of him. Where could he be? She raced up the stairs, checking each of the sleeping chambers in turn. Nothing. What could have happened to him? Chentelle took a deep breath. *Okay, relax.* There had to be a way to find him.

She closed her eyes, reaching out with her Gift. The power of the refuge made it easy. She let her awareness spread outward, until it filled the temple.

She drifted in a sea of peace and tranquillity. She sensed the villagers below her, secure in the embrace of the Holy Priest's power. And below them, she felt the hard core of guilt and anger that could only be A'stoc. He was in the cellar.

She bolted down the stairs, taking them three at a time. The door to the cellar was ajar, and a lamp flickered from the bottom of the stairs. Muffled snoring drifted up to meet her ears. "Unbelievable," Chentelle muttered, hurrying down the final stairs.

The wizard lay on the floor, curled around the Thunderwood Staff. The smell of wine filled the room, and an empty jug lay propped against the wall. "A'stoc!" she shouted. "Get up! Goblins are attacking."

"Wha—?" The wizard rolled to his feet, groaning loudly. He rubbed his eyes and shook his head. "Aah! That was a mistake."

"A'stoc, hurry," Chentelle pleaded. "The goblins are almost here. They need your help."

"Goblins?" A'stoc said. "And they attack the village?" He raised the Staff and shook it wildly in the air. "I shall smite them with the legacy of Boemarre!"

"What?" said Chentelle. "But they're living creatures. The power would backfire on us."

"I know that!" he snorted disgustedly. "But I thought perhaps the villagers would appreciate the irony."

"What are you talking about?" she asked.

"The Staff," he said, "the Desecration. What do you think *caused* the cataclysm that brought evil to this island?" He lifted the Staff and squeezed until his knuckles turned white. "So what do you think, enchantress? How many more deaths can we add to its total?"

"A'stoc!" Chentelle reached up and grabbed his face with both hands, forcing him to look at her. "We don't have time for this. The Legionnaires need your help now."

The wizard glared at her. Slowly, the red glaze cleared from his eyes. "You are right, Chentelle. I apologize. Show me what is happening."

By the time they reached the temple doors, the goblins were nearly to the village. They rode huge birds with gnarled, backward-bending legs and wickedly curved beaks. As they reached the first stone buildings, they spread out, enveloping the structures in a loose formation.

A'stoc slammed shut the viewport. "Open the gate."

A villager slid back the bar, but before they could move, a clawed hand came down on A'stoc's shoulder.

"Wait," said Gorin. "I will go." Without waiting for a reply, he opened the door and stepped into the courtyard.

They watched through the open gate as the priest walked openly toward the lead goblin. He walked straight ahead, ignoring the amazed stares and frantic gestures of Dacius and his Legionnaires.

The lead goblin halted in the center of the square, and his troops reined in behind him. He carried a barbed lance, which he leveled at Gorin's chest. A dozen finger bones dangled from cords near the tip of the lance, rattling in the breeze. He wore a hideous mask that resembled an insect with huge tusks and seven eyes, and the same design was tattooed over each of the goblin's hearts.

Brother Gorin walked forward until the tip of the chieftain's lance touched his chest. Then he started to talk. His deep voice filled the village square with the harsh sounds of the goblin tongue. He spoke for several minutes while the goblin chief remained motionless. Finally, he fell silent.

No one spoke. No one moved. How long could this last? Moments stretched into minutes, punctuated only by the occasional shifting of one of the great birds. Chentelle's legs started to ache with tension.

At last, the chieftain moved. The tip of his lance dipped toward the ground and he turned to yell something over his shoulder. Then he froze and sniffed the air audibly. Suddenly, he screamed and spurred his mount forward. His lance came up, ripping into Gorin's chest and lodging in his shoulder.

"Fire!" Dacius shouted.

Chaos erupted. Legion arrows filled the air, dropping several goblins before they could react. The rest scattered, darting through the buildings to avoid the barrage. The chieftain planted a foot on Gorin's chest and shoved, ripping his lance free in a great fountain of blood.

"No!" screamed A'stoc. He charged through the temple door, raising the *mandril* wand as he moved. A bolt of fire leaped from the wand. It passed through the stream of blood with an angry hiss of steam and engulfed the chieftain. The goblin burst into flame and fell screaming to the ground. His mount ran wildly from the blaze, spreading panic and confusion among the other birds.

The wizard screamed wildly and charged into the square.

Chentelle froze. This was insane. A goblin charged toward her, twirling a sling above his head. An arrow caught him in the side, and he fell from his bird. Something smacked into the door just above Chentelle's head, and she jumped backward. One of the villagers slammed the door shut and dropped the bar. She was safe.

But images of Brother Gorin filled her mind: the fountain of blood, the priest writhing on the ground, goblins and warbirds charging madly through the square. A muffled roar echoed through the temple, punctuated by screams of rage and terror. She turned to the villager. "Open the door."

Panic hit her the instant she left the temple's refuge. She stumbled, falling face first onto the rocky ground. What was she doing? She was no warrior, no priest. How could she help? She wanted to spin around and run back to the safety of the temple. She wanted to scream and curl up in a ball. She wanted to dig a hole and crawl in until it was all over.

Brother Gorin lay in a muddy pool on the other side of the well. Chentelle rolled onto her feet and moved forward in a crouch, keeping low to the ground.

A warbird staggered and fell in front of her, one of its legs nearly severed at the hip. The goblin rider jumped from the saddle and rolled neatly to his feet. He oriented on Chentelle and raised his scimitar to strike.

A screaming figure leaped over the fallen bird and crashed into the goblin's back. A vorpal sword drove through the creature's chest, splattering Chentelle with blood. The goblin fell to the ground, and Leth turned to find another foe.

Chentelle scrambled around the fallen bodies.

A burning warbird ran wildly through the square, heading straight for her. She dived to the side, barley avoiding the animal's huge claws. She jumped to her feet and came face-to-face with a dismounted goblin. He was unarmed, but his claws flashed toward her.

A strong hand grabbed her hair, yanking her backward. Gerruth stepped forward, sword raised. The goblin hesitated, and the vorpal blade slashed out. The goblin's head rolled off shoulders, connected to the body by only a thin strip of flesh.

A jet of fire blasted through an opening between buildings, immolating a pair of riders who were closing in from behind the elf.

Chentelle pulled free from Gerruth's hold. She ran forward. Something screamed from just behind her left shoulder, but she ignored it. She dropped to the ground beside Brother Gorin.

Blood poured from the priest's torn chest, collecting in puddles on the rocky ground. The goblin's right hand hovered just above the wound, fingers twitching uncontrollably. His crimson eyes stared at her blankly through their transparent lids, and his mouth hung open. The lips were slack, but a steady moan poured from his throat.

He was alive, but for how long? Chentelle closed her eyes. She had to block out the battle. She ignored the screams and the ringing steel. She ignored the smells of sweat and blood and fear. She closed her mind to everything except the pain and the courage and the need of Brother Gorin. And she reached out with her Gift.

A scream burned in her throat. Gorin floated in a maelstrom of agony, a whirlpool of pain that attacked his spirit, pulling him steadily downward into a dark center of oblivion. Life poured from the priest in a steady stream, flowing into the void. But still he fought. The core of his spirit remained strong, focused. A warm glow of peace and security pushed back against the darkness.

Chentelle understood. Gorin was trying to summon the power of sanctuary. But he was too weak, his wounds too terrible. Already, the glow was fading.

She started to sing. She sang of peace, of tranquillity. She sang of the beauty of the Holy Land and the security of Elihaz's refuge. She filled her song with the Harmony of Creation, and she fed it like kindling to the fire that was Gorin's will.

Slowly, the glow became stronger, steadier. It pulsed with life, driving back the currents of pain. It spread through Gorin's body, through his soul. And where it passed, it left a calm surface of perfect peace and calmness. Pain disappeared; wounds stopped bleeding. Chentelle felt the priest slide into sanctuary, and smiled.

Then something heavy slammed into her back. A sharp pain pierced her side, jarring her back into awareness.

One of the huge birds sprawled dead on the ground at her back. The creature's iron-tipped beak pressed against her side, and blood seeped from a shallow wound. It must have cut her when it fell.

Sulmar stood on the bird's carcass, using the added height to cross swords with a pair of mounted goblins. Scimitars slashed downward in vicious arcs, and warbirds lashed out with beak and claw. But the Tengarian stood firm. Twin swords surrounded him in a wall of weaving steel. He parried every strike and threatened deadly counters, preventing either goblin from advancing or disengaging.

Dacius appeared from the right flank. His vorpal sword swung in a great arc, severing one rider's leg and carving deep into the side of his mount. Bird and goblin fell together in a mass of blood and screams.

Sulmar used the opening to drive his vorpal blade into the other bird's face.

The creature reared, throwing its rider. The black sword shot forward in a blur, beheading the goblin before he hit the ground.

Chentelle clambered to her feet. A quick look assured her that Gorin was fine, shielded in the aura of sanctuary.

A geyser of flame splashed across the wall in front of her. A'stoc cursed as the goblin he had been aiming for charged forward. The rider slashed downward, and A'stoc raised the Thunderwood Staff to parry. He blocked the sword, but the impact forced him to the ground. He scrambled backward, barely avoiding a clawed foot. The scimitar struck again, only to be parried by a Legion blade.

Leth slammed his body into the side of the bird, unbalancing it. As the mount stumbled, he drove his blade into its heart. The bird thrashed wildly in its death throes. One of the great claws lashed out, tearing through Leth's jerkin and leaving a ragged slash across his ribs. The Legionnaire fell to the ground, clutching his side.

The goblin rolled to his feet and leaped for the helpless Legionnaire, only to fall screaming to the ground as a stream of flame caught him in the air.

A'stoc lowered the *mandril* wand and staggered to his feet.

"Leth!" Gerruth's shout carried from across the square. He ran forward, oblivious to everything but his fallen brother.

A goblin raced at the Legionnaire's back. Then he fell to the dirt, an arrow quivering in his skull.

Suddenly, everything was calm. Only the moans of the dying and injured broke the silence.

"Legionnaires!" Dacius shouted. "Stay sharp. Sound off by rank. Report!"

"Thildemar. All's well."

"Gerruth. All's well. But my brother—"

"Leth. Injured, it's only a scratch."

Chentelle looked and saw a spur of bone projecting from the Legionnaire's side. She felt suddenly faint.

". . . All's well."

"Report received," Dacius said. "Drup, Alve, Thildemar, sweep the village, house by house. I don't want any surprises."

The door to the temple flew open and Father Marcus came running out. Several villagers followed him, though they were more tentative in their approach. Marcus rushed to Gorin's side and dropped to his knees. "Thank the Creator, his sanctuary is holding. You two, move him into the temple. I don't dare heal him until he can safely drop the sanctuary. And be gentle, his wounds are serious."

The High Bishop's tone brooked no argument. The villagers jumped to obey.

Marcus moved on to examine Leth's wound.

"Hurry," Gerruth said. "He's losing too much blood!"

"Help me remove his corselet," Marcus said.

Leth groaned as they worked the leather jacket free from his body. "See to the others," he gasped. "I can make it to the temple."

"Hush," Marcus whispered. "You have been brave enough for one day. Now lie still. Let the love of the Creator make you well." He ran his hands slowly across Leth's side. The jagged spur of bone receded, melding back into the rib cage. Skin grew together and covered the wound, leaving not even a scar to mark where the wound had been.

Leth raised his head. "Thank you, High Bishop. I feel—" His eyes closed, and he slipped into a deep sleep.

"Let him sleep for at least six hours," Father Marcus said to Gerruth. "He should be fine when he awakens."

Gerruth nodded and lifted Leth gently from the ground. Stepping carefully around the debris of battle, he carried his brother to the temple.

"Is anyone else hurt?" Father Marcus asked. "No? Then I will see to Brother Gorin."

"Wait," Sulmar said. "My mistress is injured."

"Chentelle? Let me see."

"It's nothing, really," Chentelle protested.

"Please," the High Bishop said, "not you, too. Why must everyone equate suffering with virtue. The Creator does not wish us to endure pain. He wishes us to cure it." He placed a hand over Chentelle's wound.

She felt a delicious warmth. It filled her spirit, washing away all fear and pain. He was right, of course. There was no need to suffer. Her world flowed with love and rapture; pain was an unnecessary distraction. She repaired the cut in her side, returning her body to the wholeness that was proper.

Marcus' hand left her side, taking with it the bliss. In its wake, a wave of exhaustion swept through her. But that was all right. The warmth remained.

Chentelle staggered, and Sulmar's arm was instantly around her, providing support. "I'm all right," she said, regaining her balance. "I'm just tired."

"You should rest," Father Marcus said. "The healing draws much of its strength from your own energy." He took her by the arm and started to lead her toward the temple.

"Father Marcus!" Dacius' voice brought them to a halt. "We have a problem." He nodded to Thildemar.

"The village is clear," the elf said. "But we found signs that at least three of the goblins fled before the battle was over."

The High Bishop turned to Dacius. "I do not understand. Please explain your concern."

"The *Treachery*," Dacius said. "These goblins were following our trail. If we had taken them all, then there was a chance that the ship's location would stay a secret. But now, even if they haven't found her yet, all they will have to do is backtrack along the trail."

Father Marcus nodded. "What do you suggest, Lord Gemine? Neither Leth nor Brother Gorin is fit to travel, and we cannot abandon our search for the Sphere."

"I know," Dacius said. "We have to warn Captain Rone. I will go back to the lagoon. Thildemar, you will be in command. Give me two days. If I am not back by evenrise of the second day, continue without me."

"Your pardon, Lord Gemine," said Thildemar, "but I cannot."

"What?" said Dacius.

"I have resigned my Legion rank," said the elf. "And I have sworn an oath never to lead men into danger. But even if that were not the case, I would not accept. Your primary responsibility is to your command. This mission should fall to someone else."

Dacius gave the old elf a hard stare, but Thildemar stood his ground. It was the human who looked away first. "The lagoon is probably crawling with goblins. Be careful. You have two days."

"I shall leave immediately," Thildemar said. He turned and jogged toward the trail down the mountain.

"Ex-excuse me. Thildemar," Chentelle said. "Why don't you take one of the birds?"

"A *skethis!*" he asked. "The goblins train those birds from birth to attack elves and humans. I doubt one would let me get within ten cubits before it tried to disembowel me."

"But it would make the trip faster, wouldn't it?"

"Yes," Thildemar said. "If the bird would let me ride."

"Let me try," Chentelle said.

She took a deep breath and let herself expand through the village square. She was so tired; it was hard to keep herself focused. She pressed her Gift outward, searching, searching. There! The *skethis* had come together in one of the terraced fields. She touched them with her Gift, and almost recoiled in horror. The birds were on fire with anger, violence, the need to conquer their rivals.

She started to sing: a *skethis* song, full of fighting and rank and social dominance. She sang of ferocity and blood lust and the control of the flock. She sang, and the *skethis* answered. They swarmed down from the fields, racing toward the village square. Their cries of challenge reverberated against the stone walls, filling the space with echoes.

Chentelle took those echoes and built them into her music. She turned the birds' roars of challenge into their wails of submission. She surrounded each *skethis* with the song of her triumph, then the lamentation of its own defeat. By the time the birds reached the village square, she was their acknowledged leader.

Chentelle went to each bird, introducing herself and accepting its surrender. It was sad. She tried to shift her song into one of friendship and shared need, but the *skethis* just stared at her with unforgiving eyes. Such feelings had no meaning in their world. Chentelle returned to her song of conquest.

She selected one *skethis* and made it acknowledge Thildemar as its superior. She warned the other birds not to attack any villagers; then she let her song end.

Fatigue pressed down on her. She could barely remain standing. "This is Claws-that-flash-like-lightning," she told the elf. "She will carry you where you want to go."

She was hardly aware of Sulmar lifting her off the ground, and she was fast asleep long before they reached the temple.

∾ 11 ∾

HEL'S CROWN

Chentelle stared down at Brother Gorin. He had been asleep for more than a day. Father Marcus had healed his wounds, but the strain had been almost too much for the acolyte. She ran her fingers across the smooth skin of the goblin's chest and shoulder. It was hard to believe that this was the same body. The Creator truly blessed the Holy Order when he gave to them the power to heal.

Gorin's eyes twitched and oriented on Chentelle. He moaned softly.

"Shhh," Chentelle said. "You need to rest."

He reached up with a trembling hand. "No. I must—"

Chentelle took his hand in hers. "It's all right. I'm here. What do you need?"

"I know—" he rasped. "I know what you did. You saved my life. I will not forget."

Chentelle shook her head. "I only helped. You're the one who did the work. You and Father Marcus."

"No," Gorin said. "I would be dead if not for you. I was foolish to think I could reason with them."

"No, Gorin."

Chentelle jumped in surprise as Father Marcus entered the room.

The High Bishop took Gorin's other hand gently in both of his own. "Not foolish, brother, though perhaps not wise. You acted on your faith, which is strong, and your hope, which drives us all on this quest. It was a noble effort, but I beg you not to try it again. We walk a dangerous path, and the Creation hinges on our success. We do not need another martyr. Now rest, my friend, we will need your strength soon. I will have food and water brought up to you."

He set the goblin's hand back on the bed and motioned Chentelle to follow him out of the room. "Gorin was right," he said, once they were in the hallway. "The Creator truly blessed us when he chose you for his messenger."

The candid sincerity in his voice touched Chentelle. But she wasn't certain how to respond. She shrugged self-consciously. "Thank you, Father. I only hope I can fulfill my part in this quest, whatever it turns out to be."

He smiled at her reassuringly. "I have no doubts that you will. You are stronger than you realize."

Sulmar fell in behind them, and they headed down the stairs. A voice hailed them as they reached the bottom.

"Father Marcus, Enchantress Chentelle, I've been looking for you." Kelmek hurried over to them.

"What do you need?" asked Marcus.

"Not me," said Kelmek, "the large man with the beard. He wants everyone to meet him in the assembly hall."

"Dacius?" said Chentelle. "Why?"

"I don't know," Kelmek answered. "But the elf with the silver hair just rode in. Maybe that has something to do with it."

Chentelle exchanged a quick glance with Father Marcus. "Kelmek," she said, "Brother Gorin just woke up. He needs food. Will you make sure someone takes him some?"

"If you wish it," he said, bowing smoothly, "it will be done."

"Thank you." Then she hurried after Father Marcus.

They were the last to arrive. Dacius and Thildemar stood near the central dais, and the rest of the company sat on the nearby benches. As soon as they found seats of their own, Dacius nodded to Thildemar.

"The *Treachery*," the elf said evenly, "is gone."

"What?" A'stoc said. "Do you mean she has been destroyed?"

"No, wizard," Thildemar answered. "There is no debris, no sign of wreckage. I swam nearly every cubit of the lagoon and found no trace of her. She is gone."

"Were there signs of goblins?" Chentelle asked.

Thildemar nodded. "The band that attacked the village followed our trail all the way from the lagoon. No tracks led to the spot, so they must have disembarked from a goblinship."

"Could the *Treachery* have escaped the lagoon?" Father Marcus asked.

Thildemar turned to Dacius, and the human stepped forward to answer. "It is unlikely. The passage to the lagoon is narrow, and she was virtually unprotected. And if she had escaped, the goblinship would have given chase, not stopped to drop off troops."

He paused, but no more questions came. "We must assume that the goblins have captured the *Treachery*. Indeed, we must hope that they have. Otherwise, we have slim chance of ever returning to the Realm. I propose that we have Kelmek lead us to the Mouth of the Sea. If the goblins concentrate their landings there, it may also be where they took the *Treachery*."

"No," Father Marcus said. "We must continue to Hel's Crown."

Stunned silence greeted the High Bishop's words.

"Father Marcus," Dacius said. "What good will it do to find the Sphere if we lose our way back to the Realm?"

"What good will it do to regain the ship only to leave it defenseless again while we retrieve the Sphere of Ohnn? We do not have the men to search for the Sphere and defend the *Treachery* at the same time. We must complete the one before we attempt the other."

"What about the crew?" Dacius demanded. "They need our help now!"

Father Marcus stood and walked over to Dacius. "I understand your pain, Lord Gemine. More than any of us, you have reason to hate leaving them to the goblins' mercies. But think this through. If they are to be killed, then they are likely dead already. If they are to be kept alive, then they will be alive when we return from Hel's Crown."

"And if they are to be tortured?" said Dacius.

"We must pray their wills are strong," Father Marcus said. "And we must leave immediately. If the Ill-creatures learn of our destination, all may be lost."

"Immediately?" Dacius asked. "What about Brother Gorin?"

"He needs time to recover. But we may need his strength." Father Marcus paused. "Ellistar sets in less than three hours. We wait until tomorrow's evenrise. As the Creator is merciful, he will be ready to travel by then."

Chentelle steadied Eats-the-marrow-of-her-enemies while Brother Gorin mounted. The priest pulled himself laboriously into the saddle. The *skethis* twitched angrily, sensing the goblin's weakened condition. Immediately, Gorin reached out, covering the bird's eyes with one claw and wrapping the other around its throat. He squeezed, and the *skethis* became docile. "Thank you, enchantress. It has been a long time, but I think we will be fine now."

Chentelle laughed. "No doubt. She won't dare to challenge you again." She took a second to check that everyone else was secure on their mounts, then swung into her own saddle.

She nodded to Kelmek, and the villager prodded his bird tentatively. They traveled light, having left most of their supplies at the temple. Still, they moved slowly as they became accustomed to the strange mounts.

Kelmek led them down the trail from the village plateau for a few minutes, then turned back to the south. They entered a switchback trail that climbed higher into the mountains. The way was steep, and the footing was awkward. Several times they had to dismount and lead their birds over the rough ground. But as the trip progressed, so did their confidence as riders. By the time Ellistar hung directly overhead, they were cresting the winding path's final slope.

Below them, a desolate gray expanse opened into the south. Mountains ringed the plain, surrounding it on all sides. Dark clouds hovered ominously over the western horizon, a grim wall poised to swallow the Golden Sun's light. Perhaps three leagues to the south, a pinkish mound dominated the horizon. "There it is," Kelmek said, pointing, "Hel's Crown."

A short trail took them down to the plateau. Stone ruins extended for as far as they could see, pressing right up to the edge of the mountains. Centuries of wind and rain had reduced the buildings to ragged outlines, macabre shadows of a huge and ancient city. Gray sand swirled around their faces, driven by the hot wind. They urged their mounts into a trot.

Beak-that-rips-throats-and-entrails drove forward with powerful strides. She ran savagely, joyously. Her claws hammered the ground, sending the *skethis* and her rider bounding into the air. Chentelle's weight was barely a challenge, and the warbird shrieked, exulting in her strength. Her cry inflamed the flock, and the warbirds leaped forward into a vaulting run.

There was power in the Sacred City. The air was charged with it. It sparkled in the hot breeze and in the dust that tickled across Chentelle's skin. But there was no life. Not even weeds grew between the tumbled stones. The grit that collected on her lips spoke only of dry and ancient bones.

The *skethis* raced onward. Ground flew beneath their feet, and leagues melted into the distance. But eventually the great birds began to tire. The humans' mounts suffered the worst, but even Beak-that-rips-throats-and-entrails felt the burning in her legs. By the time they reached the foot of Hel's Crown, the birds had slowed to a loping walk.

The great dome of rock rose steeply from the plain, as if a huge sphere had been driven halfway into the flatland. The fleah-colored granite rose hundreds of cubits into the air. Bare of vegetation, the surface of the rock was colored only by occasional runnels of jet-black stone. A narrow ledge angled from the base of the rock, climbing upward for fifty cubits and then fading into a hodge-podge of hand and footholds.

They reined in their *skethis* and dismounted. The great birds would never be able to manage those slopes.

"I can't make the *skethis* wait here," Chentelle said. "They'll die if they don't get water and forage."

Dacius looked around at the unbroken wasteland that surrounded them. "Send them back to the mountains. But have them wait for us there, if you can. We will need to move quickly once we recover the Sphere."

Chentelle sang softly to Beak-that-rips-throats-and-entrails. She told the warbird about fresh mountain streams that ran with clear water. Fat rodents came to the rivers to drink, and long-bodied snakes stayed close to feed on the rodents. Chentelle felt anticipation build within her mount. She tried to convey the idea that the *skethis* should wait in the mountains for her return, but the birds had little concept of the future. The best she could manage was a vague equation of the mountains as good place. She released her song.

The warbird shuffled her feet and squawked with excitement. She danced around the other birds and screamed challenges into the air, reasserting her right to rule. The other *skethis* whined in submission. Beak-that-rips-throats-and-entrails roared in triumph and started running northward, leading her flock back to the mountains.

Kelmek led them onto the narrow ridge. Faces pressed to the rock, they inched sideways until the ledge was hardly wider than their own feet. Then they started climbing. Kelmek guided them up a channel of slim cracks and rock swells. Using these tenuous hand grips and footholds, they pulled their way slowly up the slope.

Chentelle's fingers scratched for a grip on the bald granite. She could feel Earthpower coursing through the surface of the stone, but something blocked her from sensing anything deeper. She found a crevice and wedged her hand into it, adding one more member to the legion of abrasions that decorated her arms and shins. She pulled, lifting herself up to the next foothold. Her arm ached from the effort. She paused for a moment, breathing deeply and trying to stop the trembling in her legs. Her pack pulled at her shoulders, threatening to overbalance her and send her tumbling backward. It seemed to become heavier the higher they climbed, as though it had some natural attraction to the ground.

She worried about Brother Gorin. How was his strength holding up? A quick look downward reassured her. The goblin climbed without effort. His hard claws gripped the rock face easily, and he pulled himself upward with surprising agility. Indeed, it was Father Marcus who seemed to be having the most difficulty. Sweat poured down the old priest's face, and his labored breathing was audible even above the warm wind.

They came at last to another ledge. It was no wider than the first and barely long enough to hold them all, but it couldn't have been more welcome if it had held all the delights of a king's palace.

"We can rest here," Kelmek said.

Gratefully, they leaned against the stone wall.

"By the Creator," Father Marcus gasped, "how do your people carry their dead up this slope?"

"We tie ropes to the burial sled," Kelmek said, "and the family pulls their loved one up after them. We believe that by taking this burden on ourselves, we make the rest of the journey easier on the departed. They are assured of a safe passage to the next world."

The villager slipped out of his pack and spun around on the narrow ridge. He sat down smoothly, keeping his back pressed to the rock. He kept the pack on his lap and dangled his feet in the air. "You should rest your legs," he told them. "The next part of the climb is difficult."

A chorus of groans answered the villager.

"Hel's Crown, indeed," A'stoc muttered. "This damnable rock is liable to do the Dark One's job for him."

One by one, they managed to turn themselves around and sit down. Only Sulmar and Gorin moved with anything approaching Kelmek's easy grace. It seemed that they had barely completed the process when Kelmek stood and announced that it was time to move again.

Minutes crept by like hours, and they forced their way up the mountain. More than once they found themselves relying on holds that were solid to their hands but impossible to see from below. At last, the slope began to level off. The climb became easier, and they were soon able to scramble forward on all fours.

The upper surface of the rock was decorated by a sparse covering of grass and weeds, sprouting outward from narrow cracks in the surface. By the time they could walk upright, the grass had become thick and a thin layer of soil was appearing. They continued to climb, and were soon met by an amazing sight: a gnarled oak perched at the apex of the mound. It was small and twisted, but its very existence screamed defiance to the wasteland around them.

Kelmek used the oak to gather his bearing and adjusted their course slightly. They descended a short distance down the south side and came to an abrupt cliff. The south face of the mountain was a shattered progression of steep cliffs and narrow terraces. Kelmek pointed to a stone that marked the top of a vertical crevice and led them over the side. They worked themselves down to the first terrace.

A thin layer of soil had collected in the flat tier, and more oaks grew here. Kelmek went to the largest of these and gasped. He looked about in momentary confusion, then hung his head over the side of the ledge.

"The cave entrance is below us," he said, climbing back to his feet. "There should be a ladder here. Without it we can't get down. The cliff below slopes back into the rock."

Dacius went to the ledge and looked over. "I make it a twelve-cubit drop. Leth, Alve, break out your ropes."

The Legionnaires quickly dropped their packs and went to work. They tied two ropes to the tree, one at the base and one just above the first branches. They dropped the free end of the lower rope over the ledge.

"Thildemar," Dacius said, "you're first. Make sure that landing is safe."

He tied the other end of the higher rope around the elf's chest and motioned to Sulmar. The two humans braced themselves against the far end of the tree. They lowered slack slowly from the safety line while Thildemar climbed down the other rope. Soon, the safety line jumped against the rock, and they pulled up the free end. A few moments later they heard Thildemar's whistled "all clear."

One by one they descended the rope. This terrace was broader than the one above, but devoid of vegetation. A dark opening in the wall led deeper into the mountain.

Dacius came last, lowering himself carefully. He untied the line around his chest and glared at the hanging cords. Then he shrugged and turned back to the company. "I don't like leaving sign of our passage, but we may need them on our trip back."

"I would not worry," A'stoc said. "If my suspicions are correct, the danger in front of us makes any fears of a goblin patrol superfluous."

"And what, exactly, are your suspicions?" Dacius asked.

"I prefer to keep them private, for now," A'stoc said. "I may be wrong."

"And you may be right," Dacius countered. "The safety of this quest is my responsibility. If you have some insight as to what awaits us, then tell me now so that I can prepare."

A'stoc sighed. "Very well. I listened carefully to the old man's story. I believe the tunnels are inhabited by demonspawn. Now, make whatever preparations you wish."

Dacius stared at the wizard, but said nothing. He turned to Kelmek. "Take us in."

They entered the cave. Ellistar's light penetrated only a few cubits into the passageway. Beyond was darkness. Father Marcus pulled a globe of adartak from his pack.

"No," A'stoc said. "Use no magic, not orb-light, not elf Lore, nothing. It could betray our presence."

Father Marcus put the globe away. "I assume you have made other preparations?" A'stoc nodded.

Dacius also nodded. "Kelmek," he said.

The villager pulled a bundle of thin torches from his pack. He used a flint to light one of them, then passed its flame on to a second. He handed one of the torches to Alve and started deeper into the cavern.

The wide passage angled slightly downward. The floor was smooth and even, and the ceiling tall enough for even A'stoc to stand erect. They came to an intersection and Kelmek led them down the left fork. He went left again at the next junction, then right. He paused for a long time at the next split, then decided on the left passage.

A few minutes later, the tunnel opened out into a large chamber. The walls formed an almost perfect circle, and four stone pillars rose in the center of the cavern. Each pillar had a brazier resting upon it, though all were unlit. The light of their torches was just enough to illuminate a ring of holes bored into the wall.

Kelmek gave a strangled cry and ran to one of the openings. "By the Holy," he gasped. He ran frantically to another hole, then another.

"What is it?" Dacius asked, his hand going to his sword. "What's wrong?"

Kelmek held his torch to one of the holes. It showed a cylindrical opening, about two cubits in diameter and four cubits deep. "Don't you see? This is the village chamber. These are our tombs! We've buried our dead here for generations, but the tombs are empty. They're gone! The demons have taken our dead."

"Let me see," Chentelle said. She made her way over to the tomb. Maybe her Gift could tell her what had happened. If she used it only passively, to gather information, it shouldn't give away their presence. She ran her fingers across the tomb. It was smooth and cold, more like ice than granite. She let her senses expand, opening herself to the stone. "Aahh—"

She jumped backward, stifling a cry. Her fingers clenched in sudden pain.

"What happened?" Kelmek asked. "What did you find?"

"It's dying," she said. "The stone is dying. A'stoc, can you feel it?"

The wizard moved to the wall. He paused for a moment, then hummed a quiet enchantment. He reached out and brushed his fingers lightly against the rock. "Fires of Hel, something is draining the Earthpower from these walls." He stooped and touched the floor. "Here, too, this entire mountain is being drained."

"Blessed Creator," Father Marcus breathed. "What could do such a thing?"

A'stoc shook his head. "I would be more concerned with why it was done. Only a working of great magnitude would require draining so much power."

"But what about the bodies?" Kelmek demanded, his voice becoming shrill. "Where are they?"

Father Marcus put a hand on the young man's shoulder. "We don't know, Kelmek, but it seems likely that they have been taken to the lower levels. I believe that the demons came here because of the presence of the Atablicryon. If we find it, I think we will discover the answer to all our mysteries. Now, how do we reach the temple?"

The priest's words seemed to calm the man. He took a deep breath and nodded resolutely. "This way."

He led them to the far side of the chamber. A narrow crevice near the floor opened into a slanting tunnel. They had to slide feetfirst through the hole and drop into the lower passageway.

This corridor was much more cramped than the catacombs above. It was barely tall enough for Kelmek to stand upright. The other humans had to move in a continuous crouch, a task made even more strenuous by the loose rocks which covered the uneven ground. The air grew stale as the path turned sharply down and to the left. The walls closed in until there was hardly room to walk between them. Breathing became more and more difficult as smoke from the torches gathered against the ceiling.

Suddenly, Kelmek stopped short. "Something's wrong."

"What is it?" Father Marcus asked. "Why have we stopped?"

"The passage is a dead end," Dacius called from his position just behind Kelmek. "We ran into a wall."

"Wonderful," A'stoc growled. "We walk halfway through the mountain and then discover we made a wrong turn."

"No," Kelmek said. "No, this is the right passage. I'm sure of it. But this wall shouldn't be here. It's new."

"What?" A'stoc said. "Hold on. Let me through." The wizard moved forward, forcing his way past the people between him and the wall.

"Uuhhh," Gerruth grunted as A'stoc squeezed by him. "Whatever you're going to do, be quick. There's already hardly enough air to breathe. We'll all suffocate if we stay here too long."

"The air will last longer," A'stoc said, "if we do not waste it with unnecessary speech."

The wizard's words brought silence to the company. Alve smothered his torch, leaving half of them in darkness. Minutes passed, and still no one spoke. The air grew thick with smoke, and Kelmek's torch fluttered erratically.

"The wall is false," A'stoc finally said. "There is an Ill-Lore spell worked into the stone. I can open it, but I do not know the intricacies of goblin spell-work. I will have to force it. Unfortunately, there is also a ward. We will be discovered the instant I break the spell. However, the warding will allow another Ill-Lore practitioner to pass."

"Perfect," said Gerruth. "So all we need to do is find a passing goblin wizard and—"

"We already have a goblin wizard," A'stoc said, "if he will do the job."

All eyes turned to Brother Gorin, but the goblin said nothing. He raised a hand plaintively to Father Marcus. The last torch went out.

"By the Creator," Gerruth said. "What's the problem? Open the door, Gorin."

"Brother Gorin has taken a vow," Father Marcus said. "He has renounced the Ill-Lore of his past, and the evil that it brought. Now he is afraid of what will happen if he breaks that vow." The priest's voice softened. "But your fear is unnecessary, my friend. The Creator understands the urgency of our need. The Ill-Lore is not evil in itself, only in the uses to which it is put. Your faith is strong. It will see you through this trial."

After a brief hesitation, Gorin's "Yes, High Bishop" rumbled through the tunnel.

"Wait," Chentelle said. "Maybe he doesn't have to break his vow." Moving by feel, she pressed her way forward. There was hardly room to pass between the cramped walls and the huddled bodies, but at last she reached the wall. She reached out with her Gift, sending it into the stone.

The spell felt very much like the one at A'stoc's cave, but instead of drawing on the natural power of the rock it was imposed from without. She felt the balanced power that must be the door spell and, pulsing behind that, the concentration of force that must be the alarm.

She started to sing, her voice barely a whisper in the fading air. She worked her song into the rock, wrapping it around the door spell in gossamer layers. Ever so gently, she tilted the balance of the spell, making sure that the strings that attached it to the ward remained undisturbed. She gave one final nudge, and the stone door swung open.

A blast of warm air hit their faces. It was dank and fetid, but whole, and they gulped it greedily into their lungs. Kelmek set spark to new torches, illuminating a dark shaft that plunged into the depths. Rough stone stairs began just on the other side of the door and spiraled down the inside of the pit. A steady breeze rose from the hole, carrying a sharp odor reminiscent of a charnel house.

"Goblins," Gerruth said. "There's no mistaking that stench."

Brother Gorin tilted his head back and sniffed the air. "At least two separate clan groups, maybe three. And there's something else, something—sweet."

"Sweet?" Dacius asked. "Any idea what?"

"No, Lord Gemine," the acolyte said. "I have never smelled it before."

"Well, we'll find out soon enough." Dacius took the torch from Kelmek. "This is as far as you lead, son. Fall in behind Chentelle." He nodded to Thildemar, and the elf preceded him down the stairway.

A reddish-yellow light glowed at the bottom of the shaft. As they wound toward it, the heat became oppressive. Sweat poured down their faces, and the air burned in their throats. After several spirals, they came to a short landing. The stairs wound farther, but there was also an ironshod door that led into the wall of the shaft. Thildemar stopped, and Dacius nodded toward the door.

The elf knelt and put his ear to the bottom of the door. He waited for perhaps a minute, then reached up to try the handle. It was locked. He looked at A'stoc, but the wizard shook his head. Thildemar shrugged and motioned for Alve to come forward.

The young Legionnaire pulled a small case from his pack and squatted down beside the door. He inspected the lock, then removed two small rods from the case. He pressed these into the keyhole and manipulated the tumblers with precise, delicate motions. There was a muffled click, and Alve smiled. He returned the tools to his pack and moved off to the side.

Thildemar put one hand on the door and pushed. The door swung open onto a hallway of polished black stone. It was wide enough for three elves to walk abreast and appeared to have been burned into the solid rock. The hallway curved away in both directions, each with a slight downward slope. Thildemar turned to Dacius and raised one eyebrow.

The human lord faced back to the party. "Any suggestions?" he whispered.

No one spoke. After a brief pause, Brother Gorin came forward. He stepped past Thildemar and moved a short distance down each tunnel, sniffing the air intently. Then he came back. "There are goblins down each passage," he said softly, "but the sweet smell comes only from the left."

Dacius nodded. "It's as good a place to start as any."

They marched down the sloping tunnel, staying away from the center of the hallway. The smells became stronger, until even the humans were detecting them. The passage branched, and again they followed the sweet odor.

Somewhere behind them, a door opened and the sound of marching troops reverberated through the tunnels. The men spun about, weapons sliding from their sheaths in lightning motions. They waited, poised for action, but the sounds moved away from them, receding into the distance. But even after the silence returned, the Legionnaires remained at the ready. Their vorpal blades glowed in the darkness with a pale blue light. The glow neither faded nor increased in intensity.

At last, Dacius stood up from his crouch and sheathed his weapon. The other Legionnaires followed his lead. But Chentelle knew that the danger remained; the vorpal swords glowed only in the presence of Ill-Lore.

They continued their trek, passing more doors and an occasional cross-passage. Always they followed the strange scent. Eventually, they came to a circular room. Four new passages led from the chamber, each blocked by a heavy wooden door.

Thildemar inspected each door in turn, sniffing along its base and listening for any sound from the other side. At the third door, he suddenly jumped backward, reaching over his shoulder to grab his fighting sticks.

Vorpal blades slid from a half-dozen sheaths an instant before the door swung open. A trio of goblins froze in the threshold, staring in amazement at the poised Legionnaires.

Dacius shot forward. His sword traced a clean arc through the air, and the first goblin slid to the floor with a bubbling red gash across his throat.

The second had better reactions. He managed to draw his blade and parry Thildemar's first strike. He even launched a counterthrust. His point made it within inches of the elf's chest before a fighting baton brushed it aside. A blur of motion followed in which the sticks struck him on wrist, kneecap, elbow, and base of skull. He fell to the ground in a heap.

The third goblin had been a pace behind his fellows. He turned and ran, screaming at the top of his lungs.

Gerruth darted forward. He hurdled the goblin that Dacius had struck and landed in a full run. Before the final goblin had taken more than a half-dozen steps, the vorpal blade thrust through his spine.

Dacius cursed as the echoes of the scream faded. He pointed to a door that stood a dozen paces into the branching tunnel. "Gerruth, check that."

Sword at the ready, Gerruth threw open the door. He stuck his head inside, then called back to the company. "It's empty, Lord Gemine."

Dacius lifted his goblin easily off the ground and headed down the hall. "Move quickly, people. We need to get this cleaned up."

They hid the two bodies and bound and gagged the surviving goblin. But there was little they could do about the blood staining the hallway. They had neither the time nor equipment to clean it properly.

"All right," Dacius said. "We don't have time to move cautiously anymore. They'll soon know we're here. Now, I can't smell that odor in this passage. Does anyone else? Okay, we head back and try another door."

The third tunnel they tried carried the odor. They ran down the hall, abandoning stealth in favor of speed. The floor angled sharply downward and curved back in the direction they had come. After a long descent, the passage ended in another doorway. They paused, catching their breaths and preparing for action. Then Thildemar pulled open the door.

A spiral stairway wound deeper into the earth. Light pulsed from below, and the air itself seemed to vibrate in time to the malevolent glow. The sickly sweet smell became so powerful it turned breathing into a burden. Dacius gestured, and Thildemar slid silently down the stairs. Moments later, the elf reappeared, motioning for them to follow.

The stairway opened into a huge underground chamber. Reddish-yellow light filled the room, so they extinguished their torches. Unlike the passages above, this cavity appeared natural. Stalagmites jutted from the rough floor, casting strange shadows in the pale illumination. Another stairway was barely visible on the wall to their left. Thildemar led them in the other direction, keeping to the edge of the cave. They crept up behind an outcropping of rock and had a clear view of the cavern beyond.

A horrendous rip in the floor of the cave glowed with unnatural light. Molten rock churned in the fissure, radiating fierce heat. A thin spout of water trickled down one wall into the tear, filling the air with foul-smelling steam.

Objects floated in the magma, bubbling occasionally to the surface and spitting into flame. They were bones! The pit was filled with bones and rotted flesh. The remains swirled around each other, burning but not consumed. Occasionally they would meld together, forming new shapes, twisted shapes covered in ebony hide. Jet-black arms and wings and claws and fanged skulls bobbed hideously in the pit, skulls with glowing yellow eyes.

Chentelle staggered and barely kept from crying out. It was Earthpower that fueled the fires in the cleft, but it was Earthpower horribly twisted. The stones cried out in agony at the rape they endured. She reached dizzily for Sulmar's arm, clinging to the Tengarian's solid presence for support.

Near the center of the cavern, where the rent was widest, four large figures towered over a group of cowering goblins. They stood at least six cubits tall, but their gnarled arms stretched nearly to the ground. The huge limbs ended in a circle of four vicious claws that sprouted directly from the wrist. Bony plates seemed to connect each head directly to the shoulders, and two curved tusks extended from the massive jaws. Each one carried an iron staff nearly as tall as itself.

One of the monsters snatched a goblin off the ground. It dangled the creature in the air, then tossed him into the fiery pit. The goblin's screams rang through the cave as he burst into pale yellow flames. The Ill-creature raised its staff, and a blast of vile energy lanced through the goblin. The flesh and sinew melted into nothing, leaving only a pile of bare bones to sink slowly into the magma. And the pit glowed momentarily brighter.

The remaining goblins jumped to their feet and ran for the second set of stairs.

"By the Holy," Kelmek gasped. Tears ran freely down the young man's face.

"A breeding pit!" A'stoc hissed. "The demonspawn have opened a portal into the Abyss!"

Thildemar pointed past the demonspawn to the far side of the cavern. A jumble of fallen stone lay piled against the wall. Barely discernible in the midst of the rubble was the outline of a circular stone roof. Reaching out from the roof were the remains of a row of columns. It was the same colonnade structure they had all seen in the Holy Land.

"Blessed Creator," Father Marcus said. "The Atablicryon. Lord Gemine, we must find a way past the demonspawn."

"Past?" Kelmek said. "Aren't you going to destroy them?"

Father Marcus turned to meet the villager's eyes. "I understand your anguish. But we must think first of the quest. If we do not retrieve the Sphere, all of Creation will—" He dropped his eyes and turned to look at the breeding pit. "No. You are right, Kelmek. We cannot allow this to continue. Lord Gemine, can you engage the demonspawn?"

Dacius examined the layout of the cavern. "Thildemar and I will follow this ridge to the juncture with the fissure. That will bring us within thirty cubits. The rest of you follow the edge of the cavern toward the rubble." He pointed to the far wall. "That point brings you closest to the demonspawn and provides adequate cover. Wait there. When everyone is in place Thildemar and I will launch an attack. You will be able to hit their flank while they orient on us."

"That is suicide," A'stoc said. "Any one of those creatures could destroy your entire force. Ask your men, the ones who fought in the Wizards' War."

"I will be happy to entertain alternatives," the Legionnaire growled, "if you have a better idea."

A'stoc planted the Thunderwood Staff resolutely in front of him. "I will take care of the demonspawn. You escort the High Bishop to the Atablicryon."

Chentelle put a hand on the wizard's arm. "But you can't use the Staff as a weapon, A'stoc. It will rebound on you as it did with the goblins."

"You forget the Staff was created to be a weapon. It was created to destroy Ill-creatures. They are not alive, Chentelle. They have no protection against me." He nodded to Dacius. "Stay close to the walls. I will attack when you near the rubble."

They slid away from the rocks and crept around the edge of the cavern. Thildemar led the way, darting from one area of concealment to the next. He paused before each stairwell, making sure it was clear, then motioned them onward. They became even more cautious when the curve of the wall sent them back toward the demonspawn. The roar of hot wind and the hissing steam helped cover their movement. But every footfall, every scrape of a loose stone, echoed ominously in their ears.

Suddenly the cavern rocked with thunder. The ground shook, and rocks tumbled from the walls to clatter across the floor. A pillar of green flame blazed into life near the edge of the rift. And A'stoc stepped out from behind the rocks, cloaked in a mantle of Earthpower.

Before the demonspawn could react, the wizard struck. A crackling lance of green lightning shot from the Thunderwood Staff. It danced around one of the Ill-creatures, gouging chunks of black flesh from a thousand pinpricks of fire. The monster's wailing scream filled the chamber as A'stoc's assault reduced it to smoldering ash.

The other demonspawn called in the power of their Ill-Lore. Two of them slammed their staves against the ground, surrounding themselves with spheres of pale yellow flame. The other thrust its staff at A'stoc, sending a jet of the same yellow fire arcing toward the wizard.

The mage thrust his own Staff toward the attack. The pillar of flame that surrounded him flowed down through his arms and through the Thunderwood. Green fire raged through the air, swallowing the Ill-creature's attack and tracing back along its path. The demonspawn disappeared in an inferno of Earthpower.

But now the others joined the assault. Twin jets of force blasted across the cavern. A'stoc was forced to the defensive. He raised the Staff in both hands, calling forth a protective nimbus of power. Green light surrounded him an instant before the eldritch bolts hit.

Ill-power crashed into his shield with an explosion of fire. The wizard flew backward, landing among the stalagmites. A tiny sun of yellow flames formed in the air as the demonspawn pressed their attack. A'stoc disappeared in a holocaust of power. Slabs of stone ripped loose from the floor. The walls trembled, and showers of rock fell from the ceiling. And the onslaught continued.

The company had rushed toward the Atablicryon when A'stoc had first appeared, but now they froze. The rubble surrounding the temple shifted treacherously under their feet, and falling stones clattered all around them. Thildemar dived for the cover of a still standing column, and the rest of them followed his lead.

At last, the demonspawn lowered their staves. The conflagration of power flickered into nothingness. Still surrounded by their blazing yellow auras, the Ill-creatures threw back their heads and laughed. It was a shrill, grating sound, like steel plates grinding on stone. It echoed wildly around the stone walls, then stopped suddenly.

A pale green light was visible through the cloud of debris near the rift.

A'stoc levered himself slowly to his feet. He grabbed one of the ends of the Thunderwood Staff in both hands and whirled it around his head. Earthpower coursed along the length of the wood. He swung the Staff down and pointed it toward the Ill-creatures. Once again, green lightning lanced across the cave, striking one of the demonspawn.

Only this time, the creature was prepared. Lightning ripped at the demon-spawn's shield, tearing through the sphere of flame. But before it penetrated fully, the Ill-creature thrust its staff toward the fissure. A stream of energy arced into the tear. The instant it touched the surface of the pit, A'stoc's assault was redirected. Earthpower poured from his Staff through the Ill-creature's staff and into the molten stone. The rock churned violently, spewing gouts of glowing magma into the air.

A'stoc was trapped. Energy drained from the Thunderwood, feeding the vile pit. He was unable to break the circuit and unable to defend himself. The second demonspawn stalked forward.

"Sulmar," Chentelle cried. "Help him!"

The Tengarian sprinted forward.

"Leth, guard the High Bishop!" Dacius and the other Legionnaires dropped their packs and followed mere steps behind the Tengarian.

As he approached the demonspawn, Sulmar drew his vorpal sword. The blade carved a fierce blue glow through the air as he drove it at the demon-spawn's back. The weapon struck the Ill-creature's protective aura and stopped dead in the air. Yellow fire streaked down the blade and surrounded the Ten-garian. Smoke rose from his body, and he dropped to his knees. But he held on to the sword. Blue light warred against yellow flame until both exploded in a fountain of radiance.

Sulmar flew through the air, crashing to the floor a dozen cubits from where he had stood. The vorpal sword slipped from his fingers, its blade a twisted knot of dull steel. The Tengarian groaned and struggled to stand.

The Ill-fires flickered into nothingness, leaving the demonspawn unpro-tected. It whirled around to face the new threat.

Dacius was the first Legionnaire to arrive. He swung a powerful cut toward the demonspawn's leg, but the creature brought its staff around in a lightning-quick parry. The force of the block ripped the sword from the Legionnaire's hand and sent it flying across the floor.

The Ill-creature reversed its grip and snapped the staff down in a vicious counter. Dacius dived out of the way, rolling in the direction of his sword. Yellow sparks flew from the iron rod as it slammed into the ground, scoring a deep gouge in the stone.

Thildemar stuck while the monster was extended. A line of blue fire ap-peared on the demonspawn's arm, running from claw to elbow. The Ill-creature's only response was to launch an attack at the elf's head.

Thildemar ducked under the swinging staff. But as soon as he moved, the demonspawn snapped its powerful arms. The other end of the staff screamed toward the elf's ribs, far too fast to avoid.

Gerruth stepped forward. He swung his sword in a two-handed stroke, intercepting the iron staff. The impact drove him several steps backward, but it gave Thildemar time to move out of range.

Alve moved in behind the demonspawn's swing. He lunged forward, driving the tip of his blade deep into the Ill-creature's side. Flames erupted from the wound, and the monster staggered. Alve withdrew his blade and lunged again.

The demonspawn lashed out. Its staff moved with blinding speed, catching the young Legionnaire full in the chest. The strike lifted Alve off the ground. Ill-magic crackled around his body and he burst into flame. By the time he hit the ground, charred flesh was already falling from his bones.

The demonspawn threw back its head and laughed, showing none of the weakness that had lured Alve into a second lunge. Chentelle, watching, stifled a groan. She had thought the Ill-creatures to be mostly mindless savages. Now it was clear they were not. They had cruel cunning.

A'stoc remained locked in the demonspawn's magical drain. Green Earthpower still flowed from the Thunderwood Staff, feeding the dark spells that controlled the breeding pit.

Suddenly, the stream of force doubled in intensity. "Do you want my power?" A'stoc screamed. "Then take it, demonspawn. Take it all!"

He whirled the Thunderwood above his head and drove it toward the creature. The flow of power continued unabated, describing a spiral as the weapon moved. Again and again he lifted the Staff and hammered it against the air. Again and again the mystic cord pulsed with energy. Raw Earthpower poured through the demonspawn's staff. The iron turned red, then white with heat. The Ill-creature's claws burst into flame. Now it was the one unable to break free. The staff melted into slag. But the liquid fragments floated in the air, still trapped in the circuit of power.

The torrent of force ripped through the demonspawn and into the breeding pit. The surface churned, sending geysers of molten rock into the air. The magma radiated power, glowing with a light that rivaled Ellistar's. But the color of that was shifting from yellow to pure white. A cleansing fire swept the surface of the pit, reducing both human bones and growing Ill-creatures to ash.

A'stoc dropped the Staff to his side, cutting off the current of power. Molten iron splashed to the ground at the demonspawn's feet. The Ill-creature staggered forward and collapsed, shattering into a cloud of dust when it hit the stone floor.

Dacius charged at the last demonspawn's flank. The gloating Ill-creature didn't see him until it was too late. He drove his point into the monster's chest, lodging it deeply. Blue fire screamed around the blade as he jumped away from a wild counterattack, leaving the weapon lodged.

The demonspawn howled in pain. The iron staff clattered to the floor as the creature grabbed for the sword. The massive claws smoldered and hissed wherever they touched the blade, but they did not let go. Inch by inch, the Ill-creature pulled the blade from its body. Roaring in triumph, the demonspawn tossed the glowing weapon into the distance.

Sulmar stepped forward. Alve's sword danced in his hand, weaving a deadly web of blue light.

The demonspawn backed away from the blade, moving toward the fissure. Suddenly, it clapped its claws together. A splash of weak yellow flame jumped out and struck Sulmar in the face. The Tengarian backed away, momentarily blinded.

Gerruth leaped to the attack. Using great, two-handed strokes he hammered at the demonspawn. The Ill-creature staggered backward, a crisscross of blue fire glowing in the armored plates of its head and shoulders. The Legionnaire pressed his advantage, driving into the assault with renewed fury, but the monster held its ground.

A claw shot out, breaking the rhythm of Gerruth's attack. The second claw swung, and the Legionnaire was forced to retreat.

Thildemar slid around the demonspawn's guard. He slashed downward, cutting deeply into the Ill-creature's thigh. The monster dropped to its knees as the leg buckled beneath it.

Sulmar's sword crashed through the demonspawn's tusks and into its face. The creature toppled backward and landed in the crevice. White flames wrapped around it, reducing it to ash in seconds.

Chentelle rushed forward. "Sulmar, are you all right?"

The Tengarian blinked his eyes. "My vision is blurred, mistress. But I believe it will clear soon."

Alve was not so lucky. They gathered the elf's body and cremated it in the pure Earthpower of the fissure. It was the best burial they could manage. Father Marcus said a quick prayer for the Legionnaire, but that was all Dacius would allow.

"We must keep moving," he said. "The goblins can't have missed the signs of that battle. It would be folly to invite more deaths by dallying over this one."

Father Marcus nodded grimly.

They rushed toward the Atablicryon. Rubble surrounded the building, blocking any access from the ground. But when they climbed the pile of fallen stone, a small gap was revealed. The hole opened near the temple's ceiling and was illuminated faintly from below. They lowered themselves through the cavity and dropped to the floor beneath.

Chentelle immediately experienced a feeling of peace and security. It was similar to the aura of the Holy Land, but much weaker. And it hinted more toward solitude than communion. Still, it must be what kept the Ill-creatures away from the temple. Its true power might show only in adversity.

The walls glowed faintly with a steady white light, illuminating a bare interior inhabited only by dust and debris. No doors or corridors led from the room. It was entirely encased by rock and rubble. The Sphere of Ohnn was nowhere to be seen.

Father Marcus walked to a point near the center of the floor. He turned to face the company. "I must ask each of you never to speak of anything that you see within this temple," he said.

Each of them nodded. They knew that some great mystery was associated with this structure. Then Father Marcus closed his eyes and started to chant.

Light flooded the room. It shone from a ring of stones beneath the High Bishop's feet. It radiated in equal intensity from the simple stone sphere of Kelmek's necklace. And it burst forth from Father Marcus' own body. The brilliance increased until it became almost blinding. Then it vanished. And Father Marcus vanished with it.

Minutes dragged past.

"How long will it take?" Dacius asked Brother Gorin.

"I do not know, Lord Gemine," the goblin answered. "I fear that something is wrong."

The Legionnaire nodded agreement. "What can we do? Do you know where he is?"

"No. I have never before seen this power."

"A'stoc?" Dacius inquired.

The wizard was slumped against a wall, recuperating from his battle. He looked up at Dacius' question and shook his head.

Dacius walked over and examined the spot where Father Marcus had been standing. "It looks just like the rest of the floor. I can't see any difference."

"Maybe it was only reacting to Father Marcus' song," Chentelle said. She turned to Brother Gorin. "What was he chanting?"

"It was one of the meditations," he said.

"All right," Dacius said. "Everybody come here. Lock your hands together. Good, now don't lose contact with the people next to you. Gorin, I want you to lead us in the meditation."

They gathered around the temple's center. Chentelle took a place between Sulmar and A'stoc. The wizard kept his hand on the Thunderwood Staff, so she grabbed his wrist.

The goblin waited while the others found their places in the circle. "Close your eyes. Breathe deeply and slowly. Let all tensions slide from your spirit." He paused, and then started to chant.

"Peace, in the Creation.
Harmony, of the Creation.
Unity, with the Creation.
Healing, for the Creation."

The simple chant filled the temple. The four-tone structure reminded Chentelle of the Grand Vespers. She felt the same spirit of union and community with her friends. The meditation continued. Chentelle felt relaxed and refreshed; fatigue and worry melted from her. But there was no blinding radiance, no miraculous transportation.

Then she felt something, a slight warmth against her cheek, a distant call. She opened her eyes. An ember of light burned in Kelmek's amulet, faint but steady. She reached for it with her Gift, but the radiance eluded her. Kelmek stood just on the other side of Sulmar, but the glow seemed a hundred leagues away. If she could only touch it . . .

Chentelle let go of A'stoc's arm. She reached across Sulmar and wrapped her hand around the amulet. The glow erupted through her Gift. Unity. All was oneness. All things were joined. All places were here. There was an explosion of light, and Chentelle was elsewhere.

She floated in an ocean of oneness, a place without substance, full of radiant light. Music surrounded her, a single note that enfolded and protected. She felt secure—as if she rested in her mother's womb. The oneness extended forever. She was alone. She was all.

Wait. That wasn't right. She was supposed to find something, someone. "Father Marcus!" she called.

Pain lanced through her. The music buffeted her, louder than before. It was a tone of isolation, of emptiness. It seeped into her, reverberating in her spirit. She felt herself dissipating, dissolving into the unending sameness.

No. She wouldn't surrender. She sang out with her Gift. The monotonous tone rang in her soul, but she countered it with the four-tone progression of the Vespers. She filled her song with the communion of the Holy Land, the diverse harmony of Creation. The oneness of unity clashed with the oneness of isolation.

"*Stop.*" A monotone voice materialized out of the ceaseless drone. "*This is beyond toleration.*"

Chentelle let her song end. The note of isolation no longer pressed in on her. "Who are you?" she asked.

"*I am the Creator, the Dreamer of All Things. The question is, why am I being disturbed?*"

The Creator? Chentelle felt a shudder of fear. Had the temple really sent her to the Creator? If so, why was everything so empty? "I'm looking for Father Marcus and the Sphere of Ohnn."

"*No. Those things do not exist. Nothing exists. You are all illusions, fragments of my imagination. But why have you manifested to plague me with your cacophony?*"

Illusions? "I don't believe you. The Creation is no illusion. It's real. It's beautiful."

"*Ah, now I understand. You are an aspect of doubt. I thought that I was beyond that.*"

"What are you talking about?" Chentelle asked.

"*I see I must purge you again. Very well, I am the Creator. I am alone. Creation is an illusion, dreamed by me to combat my isolation. But this is a trap. I am still alone. Only by letting go of all illusion can I be free.*"

"I don't understand," Chentelle said. "Free of what?"

"*Of isolation.*"

"But that doesn't make any sense."

"*Enough. I have affirmed my determination. You are dealt with. Now, disappear.*"

"But you haven't dealt with me," Chentelle said. "I still need to find Father Marcus."

There was no answer. The music of oneness swelled again, drowning out her voice.

"This is childish," she said. "I know you're still there."

Nothing. The empty note droned on. Then, it was interrupted.

"Enchantress, is that you?"

"Father Marcus!" She could not see the priest, but there was no mistaking the gentle power of his voice. "Are you all right?"

"I am now," the priest replied. "I was—lost for a time. Then I heard your song, the song of Vespers. It gave me the strength I needed to summon a sanctuary. Now, I—"

"Silence. This is unacceptable. I will not be disturbed by the chattering of my own dreams. I am your Creator. I demand that you vanish."

Chentelle opened herself to her Gift, searching beyond the voice, past the tone of isolation. She sensed a distant pocket of harmony, a small sphere that rang with the harmony of the True Creation. She touched it with her Gift, and she was there.

"Hello, Father Marcus."

The High Bishop blinked in surprise at her appearance. "Greetings, Chentelle." He reached out and touched her arm. The aura of sanctuary surrounded her, filling her with peace. The music of this place disappeared, unable to penetrate the harmony of the Holy Order.

Chentelle smiled gratefully. "Thank you. I was growing tired of that note. Do you know where we are?"

The priest nodded. "The Atablicryon in the Holy Land is home to a spirit. I call it the Protector. This spirit inhabits a realm that is no place but is connected to all places. We are in the realm of this Atablicryon's spirit."

"Then that is the voice we heard?" Chentelle said.

"I believe so," he said. "But I fear that the spirit is insane. Somehow this realm has become severed from the Sphere of Creation. The shock of isolation must have been too much for it."

Chentelle thought about the spirit's rambling. "I think you're right. Is there any way you can heal it?"

Father Marcus shook his head sadly. "No. The spirit rejects the power of the Holy Order, just as it recoils from the touch of your own Gift."

Chentelle felt the pain behind those words. She put her hand over the High Bishop's and squeezed. "I'm sorry. What should we do?"

"I am not certain. I can return us to the temple, but we must find the Sphere first. And to find the Sphere we must have the spirit's aid."

"But it won't help us," Chentelle said. "It just wants to be left alone with its—" Chentelle smiled. "Father Marcus, drop your sanctuary. I have an idea."

"If you are sure—"

"I can't be sure. But I think this will work. This spirit reminds me of A'stoc."

He nodded, almost smiling. The sanctuary faded.

The desolate note crashed against them. Together, they raised their voices in the song of Vespers, driving back the isolation.

"Stop it. Will I never know peace again?"

"You will," said Chentelle. "But first you have to understand your illusions."

"But I have done so already. You are a manifestation of doubt. I explained you away, but you didn't vanish. The other one is an expression of irrational hope. I dismissed it before, but now it is back."

"That's because you haven't dealt with the third element," Chentelle said.

"I know of no third element. You are the first thoughts to plague me in many centuries."

"The Sphere of Ohnn," Chentelle said. "It is the object of our designs. You have misinterpreted us. We aren't individual thoughts; we're a collection of symbolic images. Only by examining the three of us together can you understand our meaning."

"The Sphere of Ohnn does not exist. I unthought it long ago."

"Then you must think it again," Chentelle said. "Only when you examine the three elements together will you be able to fully comprehend and dismiss us."

"This is a dangerous precedent. It is unwise to willfully embrace illusion."

"But only by embracing us will you be freed of our presence," Chentelle said, a note of desperation creeping into her voice. She wasn't quite sure of the logic, but hoped it would register for a mad spirit.

"Of course, that is axiomatic. Very well, I think the Sphere of Ohnn."

An obsidian sphere appeared before them, perfectly smooth, featureless, dark. It was as if a globe of shadow had been given substance. It was no larger that a child's ball, and shed neither light nor heat, but the sensation of power was unmistakable.

Father Marcus reached out and took the Sphere. "Blessed Creator," he said, "thank you!" Then he started to chant. The sea of light and sound faded into nothingness.

"Interesting, I would never have bel . . ."

They reappeared in the center of the Atablicryon. Their friends pressed around them, faces filled with questions.

"Mistress," Sulmar said, his voice filled with uncharacteristic emotion. "Are you all right?"

"Yes," she said. "I'm fine. And look, we found it."

Father Marcus held up the Sphere so that all could see. Questions started to come, but he held up his hand, silencing them. "I must meditate long on today's events before I dare to share them with anyone." He looked at Chentelle. "I suggest you do the same, though you are free to act as your conscience decrees. For now, it is enough to know that we have the Sphere of Ohnn. The first leg of our quest is complete."

"In that case," Dacius said firmly, "I suggest that it is time to leave."

There was a general murmur of agreement. They returned to the hole through which they had entered the temple. Climbing up was more difficult than dropping down, but they accomplished the task easily with a little team-work. Sulmar and Dacius lifted the others through the opening, then jumped up and were pulled through by Gerruth and Leth. They climbed down the pile of rubble and moved cautiously onto the floor of the great cavern.

HA HA HA HA HA. The laughter that ripped through their minds was mocking and caustic. And it was familiar. High on one of the cavern walls, a dark figure perched on a rocky ledge. It leaped into the air, spreading great black wings and gliding to the center of the chamber.

"Throm!" Dacius growled.

❧ 12 ❧

ESCAPE

A wave of cold fear washed through Chentelle's mind. The monster towered over them, bat wings coiled around its massive shoulders. Smooth scales rippled along the muscles of its twisted legs, and huge talons ripped into the stone floor. The Ill-creature radiated power, personified menace. She froze, unable to look away, and taunting laughter echoed in her brain.

A strong hand touched her shoulder. "Do not fear, mistress. I will protect you." Sulmar moved forward, interposing himself between Chentelle and the Ill-creature. The vorpal blade glowed brightly in his hand, and a dark aura pulsed with equal force on his arm.

SO, YOUR SOUL IS ALREADY CLAIMED. VERY WELL, I CAN STILL DESTROY YOUR BODY. PERHAPS I WILL GIVE IT TO MY SERVANTS AS A PLAYTHING. Throm gestured with one claw and scores of goblins came charging from the nearest stairway. They massed in formations a few cubits behind the Ill-creature, but did not attack.

Sulmar's contact had lifted Chentelle's paralysis. She still felt the fear, but now she could move. A quick look told her that everyone else was still affected. Kelmek was huddled against the rocks, curled into a ball of terror. Father Marcus and Gorin seemed frozen in the middle of prayer. The goblin's face was knotted with concentration, and sweat beaded on his face. But the High Bishop looked calm, almost serene. The Legionnaires stood like statues, blank-eyed, inert. Only Dacius still moved.

The Legion commander's sword scraped slowly along its scabbard. Inch by inch, arm trembling with effort, he drew the blade. "Tthhhrrrrooooooooooooooommmmmmmmm!"

SUCH HATRED YOU HOLD. YOU WILL MAKE A FINE SERVANT. BUT WHAT IS THIS? I SEE YOU HARBOR ONE WHO IS ALREADY MY SERVANT. COME HERE, LITTLE TRAITOR. COME TO YOUR MASTER.

A tortured scream poured from Brother Gorin's mouth. The goblin priest jerked forward, moving in awkward, trembling steps.

"Gorin!" Chentelle cried. "You have to fight him. Resist!" She reached out to grab him, but a hand on her wrist stopped her.

"He must win this battle alone, enchantress," Father Marcus said. "Do not worry. His faith is strong enough." The High Bishop turned and spoke softly to his acolyte. "Trust in your faith, my friend. It is strong."

The High Bishop's words seemed to galvanize Gorin's resistance. His halting steps suddenly stopped. "I—serve—only—the—Creation." A beatific look swept across his face as an aura of sanctuary surrounded him.

A pulse of anger lashed through the mental contact. Then, the paralyzing fear screamed into Chentelle, even stronger than before.

NO MATTER. I WILL HAVE HIM SOON ENOUGH, AS I WILL HAVE THE SPHERE OF OHNN. AH, YOU ARE SURPRISED. YES, I KNOW THE OBJECT OF YOUR QUEST. IT WAS CHILD'S PLAY TO PULL IT FROM THE MINDS OF YOUR FRIENDS. I ALLOWED YOU TO REACH THE ATABLICRYON ONLY SO THAT YOU COULD RE-TRIEVE THE SPHERE. NOW, GIVE IT TO ME!

Pain lanced through Chentelle's mind. She recoiled from the force of the demon's demand. Her legs quivered and she nearly collapsed.

"I think not," Father Marcus said. The glow of sanctuary sprang into being around him, and he gazed calmly at the Ill-creature. "The Sphere is beyond your reach."

"Rrrraaahhhh!" Dacius' sword flashed free of its sheath.

The weight of Throm's mental grip slipped from their minds, broken by the human lord's act of defiance. Blue light danced in the air as more swords slid from their scabbards.

The goblins shifted in response. A score of crossbows snapped into the ready, trained on the company. Others in the horde shook spears or clashed scimitars against round, metal shields. But still they did not attack.

Dacius' legs coiled, ready to drive him forward, but he held his position. His eyes scanned the mass of goblins. "Back to the rocks. We'll make our stand there."

Cautiously, every move slow and deliberate, the company retreated.

A wave of excitement swept through the horde, but still they did not attack.

YOU AMUSE ME, CHILDREN. PERHAPS I SHALL MAKE YOU MY JESTERS. FLY TO THE ROCKS. FLY TO THE TEMPLE. IT ONLY PROLONGS MY PLEASURE. Throm waved one hand in the air. Lightning shot from the claw, blasting the wall above the Atablicryon. An avalanche of shattered stone swallowed the temple, burying it completely. The mocking laughter sounded again in their minds.

A'stoc stepped forward. Fatigue dragged down his shoulders, but he raised the Staff firmly above his head. Green fire blazed from the wood.

AH, BOEMARRE'S APPRENTICE. TELL ME, LITTLE APPREN-TICE, HAVE YOU COME TO REPEAT YOUR MASTER'S FOLLY? I SENSE THAT YOU HAVE LITTLE CONTROL OVER THE THUNDER-WOOD. THE POWER WEIGHS HEAVILY ON YOUR FRAGILE SPIRIT. PERHAPS YOU WOULD LIKE ME TO LIFT THE BURDEN FROM YOU.

"Your mind tricks will not work on me," A'stoc spat. "I know you for what you are, a mere puppet for your master."

The Ill-creature hissed malevolently. Saliva bubbled at its lips and dripped to the stone floor. *PERHAPS. BUT WHEN I WIELD BOTH TALISMANS OF POWER, WHO CAN SAY HOW FAR MY MIGHT WILL REACH? SURRENDER THE STAFF, LITTLE MORTAL. I WILL MAKE YOUR DEATH EASIER THAN YOUR MASTER'S.*

"Burn in Hel, monster." A'stoc thrust the Staff forward. Flames of Earth-power roared toward the Ill-creature.

Throm lifted both arms in front of its face. The flames deflected off its crossed claws and shot into the ceiling. The cavern shook violently and rocks crashed around them. A boulder half the size of a man crashed down on the Ill-creature's back, but it shrugged off the impact.

A'stoc staggered as his spell was broken, and his aura of power flickered into smoke. He was thrown from his feet and sent tumbling backward onto the floor.

"A'stoc!" Chentelle ran forward to help the wizard.

The cavern erupted in violence.

A hail of missiles flew through the air, sending the Legionnaires scrambling for cover among the rocks.

Sulmar bolted forward, a flat slab of stone clutched in his arms. He jumped between Chentelle and the goblins, using the makeshift shield to guard his mistress. He was aided by the fact that few of the goblins dared to aim so close to their master.

The mass of the barrage fell on the Legionnaires, far from Throm. One bolt left a shallow wound on Leth's neck, and a spear grazed Dacius' thigh. But most of the missiles bounced harmlessly off the rocks. The goblins rushed forward, filling the cavern with their screams.

Chentelle grabbed A'stoc's arm and shoulder. Struggling against his weight, she helped him to his feet.

FOOLS. YOU CANNOT STAND AGAINST ME.

Fire burned through Chentelle's mind. The world twisted madly around her. Strange emotions flooded through her. She felt her own hands gripping her arm. No, she had wood in her hands, wood that pulsed with life. Then she understood. It was similar to when A'stoc showed her the Wizards' War. She was living his thoughts, his experiences.

HA HA HA HA. YOU ARE SO WEAK, LITTLE WIZARDLING. HOW CAN YOU HOPE TO CONTROL WHAT YOUR MASTER UN-LEASHED?

The Staff! She had to hang on to the Staff. The wood throbbed in her hand. It bucked. Throm was right. It was too strong. The Earthpower wanted to be released, demanded to be released. Flame burst from the Thunderwood. It enfolded her, embraced her, stroked her with a lover's fiery touch. 'You can be strong,' it whispered. 'I can make you strong. Nothing will ever hurt you again.'

Yes! Blessed Creator, it felt so good! The world exploded in magic and joy. She *was* power. A hurricane of force whirled around her, obedient to her whim. She thought, and a blast of pure force swept her enemies into oblivion. Another thought, and the Earthpower drained from the raging fissure, absorbed into her storm.

The stone above her head annoyed her. It cut her off from the light, made her feel trapped. A torrent of force shot upward, ripping through a thousand cubits of stone like a sword through naked flesh. Rubble rained down everywhere, but nothing could touch her. Laughter rang in her ears. Was it hers?

The whirlwind of power lashed at the mountain, tearing free huge slabs of stone and reducing them to dust. Pain burned through her body as the Staff channeled more and more power through her mind. No, she had to stop it; she had to regain command. She drove her will into the Staff. The cyclone raged in her mind. She tried to wrap herself around it, contain it. But it was hopeless. The storm was beyond taming, beyond control.

The Staff reached out, and a hundred goblins fell to the ground. Their lives drained into the Staff, feeding the tempest of Earthpower. The Staff reached out, and her comrades shriveled into lifeless husks. She felt each one of their lives as it passed through her to sustain the fury: Dacius, Father Marcus, Chentelle. By the Creator, no! Not her! Not—

Hel's Crown exploded into dust and gravel. Raw Earthpower ripped through the world. *Kennaru* shattered. Great rifts tore the island asunder. Mountains vanished below the sea, and new islands broke through the surface a thousand leagues away. Tidal waves a thousand cubits high pressed outward, driven by an expanding wall of force. And, in the center of Armageddon, she survived unharmed. The power of the Staff shielded her.

Blessed Creator, what had she done? The Ill-creature had been right. She was too weak. She couldn't control the Staff; no one could. She had destroyed everything. It was her pride, her impotence, but the world had paid the price. Desolation surrounded her, but it paled beside the emptiness in her soul. She wasn't worthy of the Staff. She wasn't worthy of life.

LET GO. GIVE ME THE STAFF.

Yes. The Ill-creature was right. If she kept the Thunderwood, she would kill them all. It was better to let go, to stop trying, stop pretending. She was nothing. Everybody knew that, even Throm.

"No!" A'stoc slammed the Staff against the floor. Earthpower blazed around him in a protective aura.

Chentelle was hurled backward, her mental union with the wizard shattered. Memories writhed in her mind, spinning without thought or direction. A horrid void ached in her spirit, the echo of A'stoc's despair. By the Creator, where had he found the strength to resist?

Throm charged at the wizard, swallowing the distance between them in a single powerful stride. *THEN DIE, LITTLE WIZARD. DIE AND KNOW THAT I WILL DESTROY ALL THAT YOU HOLD DEAR.* The Ill-creature reached out, seizing the Staff in hideous claws. Green flames swept through Throm's body, but they did not consume him. The power yielded to his will, shifting color until it surrounded him in a shield of yellow flame.

Sulmar launched himself forward, but the inferno of Earthpower was unapproachable. He grabbed Chentelle and pulled her back to the shelter of the rocks.

The goblins, too, were driven back by the flames. Their attack dissolved into chaos, and they retreated across the cavern.

A pillar of warring flames surrounded A'stoc and his foe. Flares of emerald and topaz swirled and flowed in a frenzy of fire. Both opponents gripped the Staff with two hands. Throm strained to lift the wizard off the ground, but the Earthpower kept him anchored. This battle would be decided by strength of will alone. And A'stoc was losing.

Slowly, almost imperceptibly at first, the yellow flames gained ascendancy. A jet of golden force drove through the wizard's defense, nearly reaching him before dissipating into the green. Throm smiled, baring wolflike fangs. The demon lashed out again, and A'stoc was driven to his knees. This time, the Ill-creature's power did not fade. It hovered in front of the wizard, pushing through his shield, creeping inexorably toward his heart.

A'stoc wrenched to the side. The heel of the Staff touched the floor, and the stones exploded. The blast hurled both combatants into the air, still locked together by the Earthpower. They flew in the direction A'stoc had pulled, covering perhaps twelve cubits in the air and landing in the jagged rift that had been the breeding pit.

The molten stone surged at the touch of the Staff. Pure white Earthpower drained from the rock, adding its force to the inferno. Wherever it touched the green flames, they grew stronger. But where it touched the yellow, they destroyed each other.

In instants, Throm was stripped of the fiery shield. An eruption of power tore the Staff from its hands and sent the Ill-creature hurtling through the air once more. It crashed into the far wall of the cavern and dropped to the floor, unmoving.

A'stoc floated above the pit in a corona of magic. His hands clenched the Staff with manic intensity as the power seethed angrily around him. A flare shot from the Staff, striking the cave wall and burying Throm's body under a cascade of falling rock. Another blast ripped through the earth under the goblins' feet, showering them with shrapnel.

The horde broke. They ran for the stairs, fleeing back to the tunnels above.

A'stoc drifted back to solid ground, carried in an orb of coruscating light. He walked toward them, leaving a trail of footprints that burned briefly with emerald fire and left scorched impressions in the stone. The crackling globe grew brighter and louder and larger with each step. Pain contorted the wizard's face and his eyes were wide with fear. "Run!" he gasped. "I can't hold it much longer."

"The stairs!" Dacius shouted, pointing with his vorpal blade.

They ran. The Earthpower ballooned outward, keeping them pressed close to the walls. The floor bucked and shifted under their feet. Ribbons of energy flashed through the chamber, cutting dark swaths of destruction. The earth shifted and groaned in protest, unable to endure the sustained abuse. Thunder rolled in their ears as part of the ceiling collapsed, burying half of the cavern. The stairway disappeared under a mountain of debris.

Dacius shifted direction without slowing. He took them to the second stairway, the one the goblins had used. He shouted a command. Thildemar, Leth, and Gerruth started up the stairs, weapons at the ready.

Chentelle stopped running.

"Enchantress, hurry!" Dacius yelled over the roar. His eyes tracked frantically over the collapsing walls. "We must chance it. It's our only hope!"

"No," Chentelle said. She turned, and started back to the center of the cave.

Sulmar appeared suddenly before her. He grabbed both of her arms, preventing her from passing. "Mistress, it is too late. You cannot help him."

Concern radiated from the Tengarian. She felt his fear, not for himself, for her. But he was wrong. "Sulmar, let go. Please, you have to trust me."

His hands trembled on her arms. She felt herself start to rise as the Tengarian lifted her to carry her to safety. Then, he let her go. He let her pass. Then he fell in beside her, his face was locked in a mask of iron determination.

"What are you doing?" Dacius shouted. "You'll be killed!"

Chentelle ran for the heart of the storm. Earthpower blazed all around her, scorching the air and crashing in her ears. But it left her untouched. She squinted against the brilliance, searching for A'stoc. There he was, a shadow inside the radiant fury. She took Sulmar's arm and led him through the magic. Dust billowed around their feet, dry, lifeless, empty of Earthpower. They sank deeper into the ash with each step. By the time they neared the wizard, it reached nearly to Chentelle's knees.

A'stoc towered above them, held up by the Staff's power. His body shook with strain, and tears mingled with sweat on his face. His mouth moved. The words were swallowed up in the howl of Earthpower, but the pleading in his eyes was unmistakable.

Chentelle shook her head. She would not run. She took Sulmar's hand in hers. Then she stepped forward, holding her other hand out to A'stoc.

The wizard's eyes squeezed tightly closed. His mouth contorted in a sound-less scream, and he fell to his knees. The Thunderwood Staff drove into the ground, imbedded in the dust. The holocaust exploded outward in a sphere of destruction. It swept through air and stone alike, reducing everything in its path to lifeless cinders.

Chentelle and Sulmar existed in a pocket of stillness, a bubble of peace in an ocean of rage. They watched in horror as the wave of annihilation swelled outward. The cavern floor, the stalagmites, even the roiling magma of the breed-ing pit, flashed into dust. The desolation spread, irresistible, unstoppable. It surged through the chamber, catching Dacius at the foot of the stairs.

The Legion commander had no chance. The devastation was driven forward by a hurricane of power. He barely had time to scream before the wave hit.

Only it never reached him. The desecration froze, locked in stasis. Then it collapsed in on itself. A sharp crack of thunder resounded through the cave as the power imploded, absorbed back into the Thunderwood.

A'stoc's scream sounded raw and weak in the sudden silence that followed. The wizard's eyes rolled backward into white, and he dropped face first into the dust. The flames surrounding him disappeared. The darkness was absolute.

Chentelle pushed herself forward through the shifting ash. "Sulmar, help me!" Her searching hands found the wizard's body. It was impossible to find good purchase in the loose powder, but somehow she managed to pull him to the surface.

Light flickered behind her. Sulmar blew softly on the torch, nursing the flame. She had no idea when he had picked it up, nor did she care. She was just grateful for the light. She waved the Tengarian closer and bent down to examine A'stoc. He was not breathing.

Chentelle reached into him with her Gift. He was cold inside, gray and empty. A tiny ember of life burned deep in his spirit, but it was surrounded by walls of numbness. She fanned the ember with her song, trying to build its strength. But the numbness resisted her, blocking much of her magic. The flame pulsed only a fraction more brightly than before.

She focused on his heart, willing it to beat with the measure of her own heart. Reluctantly, it did. She breathed, willing her breath to be his, infused by her Gift. The wizard started to breathe, but the breaths were weak and rasping. She had made his body function, but not well enough to endure long.

Chentelle pried the Staff from his stiffened fingers. The wood throbbed warmly in her hand. She shuddered, remembering the nightmare she had shared in A'stoc's mind. "We have to get him to Father Marcus."

Sulmar handed her the torch. Then, he lifted the wizard and threw him across his shoulders. The extra weight pressed him downward, and he sank nearly to his hips in the fine dust. He turned back to the stairs and drove himself through the ash with powerful strides.

Dacius stood at the foot of the stairs, his eyes and mouth hanging open. "By all that's holy," he muttered as they approached. "I have seen death before. I've seen the destruction of war. But I never—I—"

Rock shifted loudly somewhere above them, and the human lord's eyes snapped back into focus. "We'd better move. These walls could give out any moment." He motioned them to the stairs, taking the rear position for himself.

They emerged into a huddle of concerned faces. "What has happened?" Father Marcus asked.

"Later," Chentelle gasped. "A'stoc is hurt." She motioned, and Sulmar set the wizard on the ground.

The High Bishop knelt. He handed the Sphere of Ohnn to Brother Gorin and examined the mage. He started chanting almost immediately, summoning the power to heal. He continued for a minute or more, then stopped.

Father Marcus rose to his feet, shaking his head. "There is little I can do for him. He has no wounds, but his essence is spent. I can provide him comfort and easy rest, but his recovery depends upon his will to live."

"Can he travel?" Dacius asked.

Father Marcus nodded. "His body is not damaged. It should not harm him to be carried."

"All right, then," the Legion commander said. "Thildemar, take the point: twenty-cubit lead, but no more than two intersections. Don't take chances. We know the goblins are close." He bent down to pick up A'stoc.

Sulmar waved him away. "I will carry the wizard."

Dacius shrugged. "Leth, Gerruth, you're with me. Drup, you have the rear. Stay sharp." He led them down the passage, following the route that Thildemar had taken a few moments before.

They wound their way through the tunnels. Every intersection meant an anxious delay while Thildemar scouted for a possible exit. Several times they had to double back as a promising passage terminated in a dead end or a barred door. Tension built with each false turn. It was only a matter of time before they were discovered.

Thildemar rounded a turn in the narrow hallway. He immediately reappeared, backing cautiously toward them.

They froze. Callused hands moved to their swords, but they did not draw. The crackling torch in Chentelle's hand sounded huge in the silence.

When Thildemar reached their position, he pointed backward. The whole party retreated down the tunnel, stopping only after they had retraced several turns.

"That was the exit," Thildemar whispered. "I could smell the open air. But it is guarded by at least two score goblins, two score very nervous goblins."

"Crossbows?" Dacius asked.

"Many."

Dacius ran his eyes across the company. "We cannot fight our way through them. We must find another exit."

"But there is no other exit," Kelmek protested. "The stairs to the catacombs are buried. The goblin tunnels are the only other way."

"Perhaps not." All eyes turned at Brother Gorin's gruff voice. "Follow me."

They backtracked through several passageways. Then the goblin led them down a short side tunnel. The hallway ended at the closed wooden door with a goblin rune carved into it. Gorin listened at the door, then pushed it open. Foul odors swept into the hall.

"A sewer?" Gerruth asked. "You want us to crawl into a cesspool?"

Gorin pointed to a small iron grate. "The water moves. That means it connects to an underground stream. That is the standard practice, where a natural water flow is available."

Dacius pried up the grate and examined the hole. His nose wrinkled in disgust, and his eyes watered uncontrollably. He backed away, shaking his head. He reached over his shoulder and pulled a field bandage out of his pack, locating it by feel with no apparent trouble. He tied the cloth around his mouth and nose, forming a makeshift mask. "Hand me that torch."

The human lowered himself into the dark hole. After a few moments, he stuck his head back out. "It's cramped but manageable. Come on down. However, I strongly suggest you cover your noses."

They needed no special urging. Cloths masking their faces, they crawled into the sewer. The tunnel was small, perhaps three cubits in diameter, and they were forced to lurch forward in an awkward crouch. The humans had it worst of all, especially Sulmar, who had the additional burden of carrying A'stoc. Making matters worse, the bent-over posture brought their faces closer to the reeking sewage that trickled around their feet.

Only Brother Gorin seemed unbothered by the drains. The goblin was small enough to walk upright, and he was the only one among them not to wear a mask.

"How do you stand it?" Gerruth asked the goblin. "I know that your nose is even keener than mine."

Gorin cocked his head and regarded the Legionnaire. "The smell is strong, but I do not find it particularly offensive. It is no worse than the scent of pine or incense or human blood."

Chentelle's stomach wrenched violently. Only the fact that it was empty saved her from vomiting. It seemed as though days had passed since they entered Hel's Crown. She was exhausted. Her head throbbed, and her legs ached from all of the climbing and running and crouching. By the Creator, how terrible it must be for Sulmar!

Brackish water pooled and eddied on the uneven floor, and the slick excrement made their footing treacherous. They passed several small branching tunnels, most of which drained additional putrescence onto their ankles. After what seemed hours of hunched walking, they found where the tunnel drained into a wide underground stream. The natural channel carved by the water was wider, but no higher, than the goblin sewer. Fortunately, the flow of clean water eased the stench considerably.

Dacius stopped when he hit the stream and looked over the company. "Upstream," he said, heading that direction. After a dozen cubits or so of sloshing against the current he stopped again. "We'll rest here. Split up whatever rations are salvageable. Sleep if you can. We need to be sharp when we hit the surface. There's no telling what may be waiting for us."

Chentelle sank gratefully against the wall. The water was cold but clean. It felt glorious on her skin. She bent over and took a long drink, reveling in the clear taste. Her stomach rumbled, reminded now that it had been long empty.

Sulmar propped A'stoc carefully against the wall and slid into the water beside her. For the first time since his recovery in the Holy Land, the Tengarian showed obvious signs of fatigue. His breath came in harsh gasps, and his movements were slow, almost awkward. He cupped water in his hands and splashed it against his face.

Most of the rations were spoiled, but Father Marcus and Gorin had both managed to keep their packs dry and clean. They passed their hard breads and fruit through the company, allowing each member to eat or not as his stomach dictated.

Despite her hunger, Chentelle found that she could not eat. The first bite she tried to swallow lodged in her throat with the miasma of the sewers. She gagged, regurgitating the water she had just swallowed. Suddenly embarrassed, she handed the bread to Sulmar.

The Tengarian ripped a large chunk from the loaf and passed the remainder on. He ate several bites, chewing and swallowing without trouble. When Chentelle had recovered from her spasms, he handed her the rest of his share. "Take small bites and hold them in your mouth," he said quietly. "Do not try to swallow. Let them dissolve in your saliva."

Chentelle took the offered food. "Thank you, Sulmar." She tore off a small piece and placed it tentatively in her mouth. It worked. Another bite followed as soon as the first disappeared. As her stomach filled, her fatigue became irresistible. By the time she finished the bread, her eyes were barely open. She fell into sleep almost immediately.

The dream came an hour later.

∾

Thunder is everywhere. It washes over her, tossing her about like a leaf in the storm. She screams, but can't hear her own voice over the roar.

It is cold. She shivers uncontrollably. She tries to wrap her arm around her body, but some other force is moving her limbs. It shakes them wildly, twisting them into unnatural angles.

Everything is dark. She can't see. She can't feel. She's floating in something—water. But she floats under the surface. She can't breathe! She swims for the surface, but there is no surface. Walls appear all around her. She's trapped! Her lungs burn with the need for air. But there is no air. The darkness becomes somehow blacker. She can't breathe! She can't breathe! She can't—

∾

"Aaaahh!" Chentelle's eyes snapped open. She gulped air desperately into her lungs. *A dream—it had been a dream.*

"Mistress!" A whisper of steel told her that Sulmar had drawn his weapon.

"I'm okay," she said between gasps. "I'm okay. It was a dream. It was—" She sat up straight. "Dacius! Father Marcus! We have to move. Hurry, we have to get out of the tunnels."

No one argued with the urgency in her voice. In seconds the party was on its way, slouching downstream to the opening they hoped would be there, the opening that *had* to be there. Water swirled around their legs. It wasn't long before they realized that the level was climbing. A deep rumbling sounded from somewhere above.

"Holy Creator," Dacius said. "The storm clouds! I'm a fool. How could I have forgotten?"

Desperation drove their pace. Their world became a contest between a distant roar and the rhythm of their steps. The roar grew steadily louder, and their steps grew more difficult. The water fought them: it was too shallow to carry them, but too deep to stride above. They were not going to make it.

"Squat down!" Dacius shouted over the roar. "Cover your heads with your arms. Take deep breaths, starting now. After the initial rush, try to follow the current. Look for air pockets near the ceiling, but only after the first wave has passed. BRACE YOURSELVES!"

Chentelle wrapped herself around the Staff, clinging to it as tightly as she was able. A wall slammed into her back, nearly driving the precious air from her lungs. Water lifted her and spun her about wildly. Things bumped against her in the stream: arms, legs, others she couldn't identify. She couldn't hold her tuck; the current was too strong. One arm flailed out, scraping against rock. Pain flared in her wrist and elbow. She squeezed the other arm even more tightly around the Staff.

"Uhhnn!" Her head screamed at the sudden impact. Dizziness washed over her. She latched on to the pain in her arm, using the sting to keep herself conscious. Only after her head cleared did she realize that she had let out her breath.

She needed air. The water pulled her forward, but the current was slowing. Air pockets—that's what Dacius had said. But which direction was up? She was completely disoriented. The Staff! She tucked the Staff into her legs and surrounded it with a loose circle of her arms. She let go with her legs and the Staff bumped against one of her arms. Okay, that direction should be up. She grabbed the Staff with her good hand and stretched out the other one to scrape the ceiling.

Chentelle let the current move her, kicking only gently with her legs. She had to conserve the little air she had left. Already her lungs burned with the desperate need to breathe. That was panic. Don't panic. Stay calm. She was a strong swimmer. She had been underwater longer than this before. She concentrated on her fingers, letting them trace the outlines of the ceiling. The rough surface actually helped; it made her hands more sensitive.

She had a horrible thought—what if the Thunderwood was heavier than water? She could be following the wrong surface. No—that was fear talking. She had to trust her instincts. All she had to do was relax, wait until—yes. Her hand felt air.

She stopped her motion. The current was still strong, but she could resist it. The air pocket was thin, barely the depth of her hand, but it was enough. She pressed her face to the roof and sucked greedily at the fresh oxygen. After a few breaths, she noticed the air getting stale. That was all right. She inhaled one more time and ducked back under the water.

She swam with the current. Kicking herself forward with powerful strokes but keeping her hands in front of her to ward off impacts. She heard a rushing sound from ahead. Good, that meant the water had found an outlet. If her luck held, it would be wide enough to let her escape, too. A pinprick of light appeared ahead. She clutched the Staff and kicked toward the tiny glow.

Chentelle burst through the hole and found herself in midair. She tumbled down in a stream of water and landed in a shallow pool. Sputtering for breath, she stood up. The water came only to her waist; she was lucky the fall had been brief.

It was dark. The red globe of Deneob was barely visible behind the wall of black clouds that dominated the sky. Warm rain slapped against Chentelle's skin, driven by a hard wind. A long bolt of lightning ripped across the sky, and she decided to get out of the water.

"Enchantress, over here."

She headed for the sound of Thildemar's voice. It led her to a small cave, just downstream of the waterfall. Thildemar waved her inside. Several figures huddled together in the center of the grotto, taking shelter from the storm. Father Marcus and Gorin were there, as were Kelmek and the other Legionnaires. Only Sulmar and A'stoc were missing. A heap of supplies rested against the far wall.

"Enchantress," the High Bishop said, squinting to see her in the dim light. "And you have the Staff. Bless the Creator for sending you to us. Are you well? Do you need healing?"

Did she? She took a quick inventory. Blood ran freely from a shallow gash on her right elbow. Her head throbbed, but a quick check failed to yield evidence of blood. She was scraped and bruised in a dozen places and generally beaten up. Otherwise, she was fine. "Nothing serious. Where's Sulmar?"

"He has not yet appeared, Chentelle," the priest answered. "It may have taken him longer because of A'stoc."

As if on cue, there was a loud splash. Chentelle dropped the Staff and ran back to the pool.

Sulmar stood in the water. His left arm hung limply by his side, and he struggled to hold A'stoc's head and shoulders out of the water using only his right.

"Oh!" Chentelle jumped into the water and grabbed the wizard around the chest. Thildemar was just behind her, and together they carried him to shore. Sulmar followed under his own power.

They set A'stoc down as soon as they were on dry ground. The wizard had stopped breathing again. She took a deep breath and reached into him with her Gift. Life still burned in the wizard's spirit. It seemed neither stronger nor weaker than it had been before. This time, the problem *was* his body. His lungs were full of water.

As she had with Sulmar, so many nights ago, Chentelle shaped her song to repel the water. She filled the wizard with the song of air, and pulled at the water with the call of the river. A'stoc's stomach heaved and the water shot from his lungs. Soon, he was breathing on his own, though the breaths were still very weak.

A hand came to rest on her shoulder. "How is he?" asked Thildemar.

"The same as before," she said. "But he won't drown. We need to get him to shelter."

The elf nodded and headed for the cave. "I will bring help."

Chentelle turned to Sulmar. "What happened to you?"

"When the flood hit," he said calmly, "I grabbed hold of A'stoc. The water pulled us in different directions and we struck some rocks. My shoulder dislocated, and I was forced to maneuver us through the tunnel with only one arm. Luckily, the wizard was unconscious, so he did not fight me."

She put a hand on Sulmar's chest, careful not to disturb his shoulder. "Thank you for saving A'stoc. I know that you do not care for him."

The Tengarian looked into her eyes. Then he smiled. It was a thin smile, but it was there. "My people have a saying, 'Trust your first impression, but do not marry it.' "

She laughed. "Well, I think maybe he's learned to respect you, too."

Thildemar returned, leading Leth and Gerruth. The Legionnaires picked up A'stoc, and they all headed back to the cave. Father Marcus was waiting for them at the entrance. He examined A'stoc and agreed that his condition was unchanged. Then he attended to Sulmar and Chentelle, healing their wounds. Soon, they were all huddled together in the shelter of the grotto.

"Kelmek," Dacius said. "Where are we?"

"The east face of Hel's Crown," the villager said, "near the base."

"We can't stay here," Dacius said. "We're too close to the goblin tunnels. How far away is the Mouth of the Sea?"

Kelmek shrugged. "One and a half leagues, maybe two."

"Wait," Chentelle said. "What about A'stoc? We have to get him back to the village."

The Legionnaire turned to Father Marcus. "Can he still be moved safely?"

"Yes," the High Bishop answered, "but we need to get him to a secure resting place. The village would be best. He might benefit from the atmosphere of refuge in the temple."

Dacius looked at A'stoc, then lifted his eyes to meet Chentelle's. "I'm sorry. We have to secure the *Treachery* before the goblins who guard her learn we escaped from the caverns. The wizard can rest aboard the ship. Now, can you call the *skethis?*"

The *skethis!* If Chentelle could summon the warbirds, she could take A'stoc back to the village while Dacius and the Legionnaires rescued Captain Rone and the *Treachery*. But there were so few of them; what if they needed her and Sulmar to help? What should she do?

"I'll try," she said.

Chentelle closed her eyes and sang into the storm. She blended her voice with the thunder and the splashing rain. She pressed outward, searching for the primal emotions that drove the warbirds' lives. She filled her song with challenge and the lust for battle, but there was no answer.

She shook her head. "I can't reach them."

"Then we'll have to march," Dacius said. He walked over to the pile of supplies and pulled out two lengths of rope. He tossed them to Thildemar and pointed to A'stoc. "Field stretcher—there's no wood in this wasteland. Make sure to brace his head."

As the elf went to work, Dacius inspected the rest of the supplies. He took two adartak globes and handed one to each of the priests. "The rest is useless. We'll leave it here. The trail will be difficult enough. Okay, let's move. If we're lucky, the rain will cover our tracks."

Rain battered them the instant they left the cave. The dusty plain of the Sacred City had turned to slick mud in the downpour, and everyone suffered in the treacherous footing. Kelmek led them toward the eastern edge of the plateau. Dacius and Sulmar carried the front of A'stoc's stretcher, while the elven Legionnaires alternated turns on the rear.

Chentelle paced along beside the wizard, bracing her steps with the Staff. It pulsed warmly in her hand but with much less force than after the battle with Throm. The wood remained dry despite the storm. Any rain falling on the Staff was instantly absorbed into the Thunderwood. She shuddered once more, remembering the holocaust A'stoc had barely managed to control.

They trudged slowly through the desolate plain. Luckily, the eastern mountains were closer to Hel's Crown than the northern range. Though their pace was slow, they were able to reach the concealment of the ridge before the storm broke. As the rain softened, Kelmek led them through a well-marked pass and down toward the Mouth of the Sea. The water stretched out in the distance, blending seamlessly with the gray clouds on the horizon.

This trail was wider and less rocky than the winding path from the village, but they still found the going difficult. Stress and fatigue dragged at their limbs, and water weighed down their clothes. Dacius and Sulmar suffered the worst, but the human lord drove them on relentlessly. Only when they reached the heavy forest of the foothills did he signal for a halt.

"How far?" he asked Kelmek.

"Half a league," the villager said, "maybe less. The trail meets up with Kolos' Burn and follows it to the bay."

Dacius took them a short way off the trail to a tiny clearing. "Stay here. Get what rest you can, but keep a watch. The goblins could be right behind us. Kelmek, you're with me."

The two humans disappeared into the jungle.

Chentelle knelt beside A'stoc. The wizard was pale and feverish. Sweat ran down his face, and he was shivering violently. "Father Marcus, he needs your help."

The High Bishop placed a hand on A'stoc's forehead. He chanted softly and the wizard stopped shaking. Color returned to his cheeks, and his temperature returned to normal. The old priest slunk to the ground with his back against a tree. "Call me if the fever returns," he said an instant before his eyes closed in sleep.

"Father Marcus?" Chentelle said. "Are you all right?"

Brother Gorin rested a claw on her shoulder. "He will be fine after he rests. The wizard had no strength to put into the healing, so Father Marcus used his own."

Chentelle nodded. They could all use sleep. Even Sulmar looked haggard. A quick look confirmed that Leth was standing guard alertly. She lay down and rested her head on A'stoc's chest. If his fever returned, the shivering would wake her.

∾

She jumped awake at the touch of a hand. Sulmar held a hand to her lips, cautioning her not to cry out. She looked around. Dacius and Kelmek were back, but there was no sense of alarm about the camp. "How long?" she whispered.

"An hour," he answered, speaking softly but in a normal voice. "Lord Gemine has just returned."

Dacius motioned for them all to listen. "The *Treachery* is here, but so are three goblin warships. One of them is moored at the pier; the other two are anchored near the mouth of the bay. The guards around the dock are not especially alert, but there are lots of them." He looked up. Deneob was just starting to drop toward the west. "We'll have about an hour of darkness after the Winter Sun sets. That's when we'll make our move."

"Did you see any sign of the crew?" Father Marcus asked.

The Legionnaire shook his head. "No."

Chentelle suddenly had a horrible thought. "What if they were taken to Hel's Crown?"

Dacius' fist clenched and he let out a hard breath. "Then we leave them. The quest has to come first. But I don't think they were taken away. Throm was aboard one of those ships. The demon took them at the lagoon; it had no reason to drag them to the mountain."

"Assuming they are still alive," said Gerruth.

"Yes," Dacius said, "I am."

They worked their way back to the trail and followed it eastward. The ground sloped steadily downward, and they soon came to a narrow stream. Kelmek led them along the water's edge for several minutes. Then he led them across a series of stepping stones to the opposite bank. A tiny footpath took them to a sheltered clearing that had become partially overgrown. A naked goblin lay unconscious in the center of the clearing, bound and gagged with thick vines. A uniform and weapons were piled beside it.

"The Stone City people used to use this place for picnics," Kelmek said. "But the goblins seem to avoid it."

"We wait here until dark," Dacius said. "Then, we'll enter the stream and swim to the *Treachery*. The guards at the pier are only watching for an approach by land." He looked at Brother Gorin and motioned to the goblin uniform. "We need to find out if Rone and the others are here. Will you do it?"

Brother Gorin hesitated, glancing at Father Marcus. Then he nodded. He pulled off his robe and slipped into the goblin clothing. He strapped on the sword belt and gripped the short halberd awkwardly. "I never imagined that I would be wearing such a uniform again. You understand, Lord Gemine, that I cannot use these weapons in combat. I am still bound by my oath to the Holy Order."

"I understand," Dacius said. "I don't want you to fight. Just scout the buildings. And abort the mission if it looks as if you are going to be discovered. We don't need you to be captured as well. Are you ready?"

Gorin nodded. "I will return within the hour if I am able."

As the goblin left the clearing, Dacius turned back to address the company. "We will need a raft to transport the wizard. There is plenty of deadwood in the forest, and we can use the ropes to bind it together. It won't be much, but it should hold until we reach the *Treachery*."

"I can make the raft," Chentelle said. "I can wood-shape."

"Good," Dacius said. "The rest of you start gathering wood, but be careful. Travel in pairs and make sure you range away from the harbor."

Chentelle set the Thunderwood Staff by her side and considered the craft she needed. As the others returned with wood, she set the pieces carefully into the pattern she envisioned. She worked with the shapes of wood, fitting them into the proper configuration. Some pieces she had to discard as unsuitable, but the raft still took shape quickly. Soon, the basic shape was complete.

Chentelle called upon the elven Lore of *rillandef*, deadwood shaping. She hummed softly, using the tune to concentrate her will. She picked up two pieces of wood and ran her fingers over them. Wherever she touched, the wood became soft and malleable. This was natural deadwood; no one had killed it. It had lived its time and expired, so there was no pain in it. Otherwise she could not have worked with it. She pressed the pieces together like wet clay and then reached for the next. She was aware of nothing but the wood and the raft. Her hands moved quickly and surely, following the plan she kept clear in her mind. And the wood shaped itself to her need.

It took her only moments to finish the outline. Once that was complete, she started to meld the internal structure into the frame. She touched and smoothed and molded until the driftwood and fallen branches became a solid mass. Then, she sculpted that mass. She gave it a back-sloped rim to keep A'stoc secure and a straight keel to drive smoothly through the water. She fashioned the prow into a delicate curve, reminiscent of a rolling wave, and brushed a similar swoop into the pattern of the wood grain. Finally, she added two circular braces to hold the Thunderwood Staff.

"Impressive," Thildemar said. "You have a rare talent, enchantress. I have never seen so young a wood master."

"But I'm not a master," Chentelle protested. "The Gift helps me. I can feel the wood—almost as if *it* tells me how to shape. Still, I'm only a novice. You can see how flawed the raft is."

Thildemar bowed gracefully. "I beg to disagree, Lady Chentelle. It is as elegant and charming as its shaper."

"Thank you," she said, smiling at both the compliment and the exaggerated manners. "I'm just glad I could do something to help."

Whatever reply Thildemar might have made was cut off by Brother Gorin's arrival. The priest was breathing heavily, as if he had run all the way from the Stone City. "I saw them," he managed to say between gasps. "They are alive."

"Where?" Dacius asked.

Gorin paused, regaining his breath. "The city is all ruins, but a dozen buildings near the pier have been repaired. Two have been made into barracks, but most are warehouses. Captain Rone and his men are in one of the warehouses."

"How many guards?"

"It is hard to say," the priest answered. "At least two inside the building. Others come and go. The outer door was not guarded, but it is impossible to enter without being seen by the sentries posted in the clearing."

Dacius turned to the company. "Recommendations?"

"We will need a diversion," Thildemar said. "I can take out one of the sentries and lead the pursuit away from the clearing. But the alarm will alert the guards at the pier."

"So we take the ship first," Gerruth said. "Then we use your diversion to rescue the crew and fight our way back to the ship."

"There are a score of goblins in each barracks," Brother Gorin said, "plus the marines still aboard the moored warship. You cannot fight through them all. But I can distract them without raising a general alarm." He turned to Thildemar and pulled at his goblin uniform. "I am better suited for this task than you."

"Agreed," Thildemar said. "But be careful. Remember what happened in the village."

"I am not likely to forget," Gorin said. "Do not worry. My tools this time will not be peace and reason."

"I don't like it," Dacius said, "but it's our best chance. We'll split into two teams. Thildemar, you and I will free the prisoners, moving on Gorin's distraction. Everyone else heads for the ship. Leth, you're in charge. You'll move as soon as Deneob drops behind the mountains. The *Treachery* has first priority. If possible, try to hamper or disable the warships, especially the two blocking the harbor, but secure the whaler first."

The elves nodded. He turned to the goblin. "Gorin, give them thirty minutes, then start your distraction. Thildemar and I will slip into the warehouse during the confusion. As soon as we're in, break off and head toward the *Treachery*. Don't wait; we'll make our own way back. That's all. There's still some time before dark. Rest if you're able."

"Excuse me, Lord Gemine?" Kelmek lifted a hand tentatively in the air.

"Yes," Dacius said gently.

"You don't seem to need me anymore," the villager said. "And I really should get back to the village. Grandfather will be worried."

"Of course," Dacius said. "But are you certain you want to travel on your own? There are probably goblin patrols about. If you stay with us we can drop you back at the lagoon before we leave the island."

"Thank you," Kelmek said, "but I know these paths. I can stay away from any patrols. Besides, if the goblin warships chase you, you won't be able to stop. I think I better head back on my own."

"As you will." Dacius stepped forward and clasped the man's arm. "We thank you for your help. Without your courage and guidance we could not have succeeded."

"Yes," Father Marcus said, placing a hand on the villager's shoulder. "Our gratitude is poor thanks for your service to the Creation, but it is all we have, and we offer it freely. Please tell your grandfather that I wish I had been able to see him again. There is much we could have shared with each other."

"I will tell him," Kelmek said. "But it is the village that owes you a debt. Thanks to you, our ancestors have the peace they deserve."

The villager disengaged himself from the two humans and walked over to Chentelle. "Enchantress, I hope your friend recovers. He has done a great service to all of my people. I will make sure his story is remembered. I—I have been honored to help you in your quest."

"Thank you," Chentelle said. "We have been honored to have your help. You're a good man."

Kelmek smiled broadly and bowed. Then, without another word, he vanished into the jungle.

Dacius, Thildemar, and Gorin headed toward the warehouse on foot, not bothering to rest.

Chentelle felt A'stoc's brow. The fever had not returned, and the wizard seemed to be resting peacefully. She felt a momentary pang of envy. She needed sleep, too. But unlike the Legionnaires, she couldn't overcome her anxiety and relax. She sat in silence, watching the shadows lengthen.

When Deneob's rim slid behind the mountains, Leth spurred them into action. The Legionnaires stripped off boots and armor, and everything was loaded into the raft with A'stoc. They settled the raft into the stream and waded in behind it. The water greeted them coolly.

"Grab hold of the raft," Leth said. "We'll let the current pull us out past the extension of the pier, then come back to the *Treachery* from behind. No splashing. Gerruth and I will guide the raft; everyone else just ride along quietly."

They waited until the last hints of red faded from the horizon; then Leth nodded and they let the current take them. The stream wound gently through the rain forest, then widened and emptied into a natural harbor. On their left, the trees yielded to the ruins of a small town. A fire burned in the center of the rubble, casting flickering shadows on the few buildings that still stood. A stone pier stretched into the bay. The silhouette of the *Treachery* was plainly visible at its end, as was the much larger outline of the goblin warship.

They drifted into the middle of the inlet, past the extension of the wharf. The grim shadows of two more warships loomed in front of them, blocking the mouth of the bay. Leth and Gerruth guided them in a slow curve back to the stern of the *Treachery*. The ship shielded them from both the shore and the warship moored on the other side of the pier. Guttural voices floated down from above. There were at least two sentries aboard the *Treachery* and one or two at the far end of the dock. Leth motioned to Gerruth, and they paddled silently toward the ship's anchor chain.

They were going to try to sneak up on the guards. Chentelle waved frantically, catching Leth's attention. "Wait," she mouthed. "Wait."

He looked at her curiously, but nodded in acquiescence.

Chentelle closed her eyes and focused her attention on her hearing. The goblin voices were unintelligible, but they seemed calm, even bored. Low waves slapped softly against the stones of the pier, and a slight wind whispered out from shore. Good, she could do this.

She started to sing. Softly at first, almost inaudibly, but with growing strength she reached out with her Gift. She blended her voice with the quiet sounds of the sea, never letting her words become louder than the lapping waves. She wrapped her song around the goblin sentries, embracing them in a soothing lullaby. The guards on the pier were too far away; she didn't dare raise her voice that loud. But she felt the presence of two more sentries on the warship. Chentelle extended her charm to wrap around them as well. She guided them all gently toward slumber, and they followed.

She opened her eyes and nodded to Leth. "The sentries on both ships are asleep," she whispered. "But I couldn't reach the ones on the pier."

The Legionnaire smiled and reached into the raft. He pulled out two sword belts, hanging one over his shoulder and handing the other to Gerruth. They climbed quietly up the chain and slipped over the railing onto the *Treachery's* deck. A moment later, two ropes came sliding over the side. Sulmar and Drup fixed them to the raft, and the brothers hauled it up to the deck.

The ropes came down again, and Chentelle climbed to the deck. She swung herself easily over the rail, then flinched as her feet touched the awful deadwood of the deck. There was no sign of Leth, Gerruth, or the raft, but the hatchway leading below deck was open. The goblin sentries were crumpled in a heap near the far rail. She tried not to notice the rivulet of dark fluid that trailed from beneath their bodies.

Sulmar slid over the rail to stand beside her, and Drup followed an instant later. Father Marcus had more trouble with the climb, but they were able to pull him up without difficulty. Leth and Gerruth returned just as the High Bishop reached the deck. Each of them carried a long, metal crowbar secured from the *Treachery's* hold.

"Stay low," Leth whispered. "We don't need the shore guards to spot any suspicious silhouettes. Make sure the rigging is prepared for a quick departure, but don't raise any sails. Gerruth and I will be right back."

Chentelle watched them crawl over the rail and lower themselves down the ropes. They ducked under the surface and reappeared a minute later near the stern of the warship. They crawled onto the rudder assembly, prying at something with their bars. Then, they slipped back into the water and paddled quietly toward the mouth of the bay.

Drup didn't need any help with the rigging, so Chentelle went below to check on A'stoc. The wizard was still in the raft, which was parked just at the foot of the stairs. Father Marcus was kneeling by his side.

"How is he?" Chentelle asked.

"Unchanged," Father Marcus said. "But we should take him to his cabin. He'll rest better there."

Sulmar lifted the wizard out of the raft and carried him down the hall. Chentelle followed with the Thunderwood Staff. They put A'stoc into his bunk and arranged him as comfortably as they were able.

Chentelle pulled a chair over to sit beside the bed. Then she froze. A goblin voice was calling from outside the porthole.

They hurried back to the stairs and climbed cautiously up to the deck. Drup was crouched behind the rail, naked sword in hand. He raised a finger to his lips and waved for them to stay where they were.

Chentelle peered around the side of the wheeldeck. Two goblins were walking toward them from the shore. It was the other sentries. They stopped on the far side of some cargo crates which were stacked on the wharf. One of them called out again, a little bit louder this time. It was not an alarm, but there was a sense of growing urgency to the tone.

A hacking cough sounded behind Chentelle. It was Sulmar! The Tengarian was creeping toward the rail, grumbling and croaking in a deep, throaty voice. It was a passing imitation of a goblin with a bad cough.

The sentries seemed confused. They came forward, moving almost to the edge of the gangway.

Sulmar leaped over the railing. One foot lashed out, catching a goblin in the side of the neck. The sentry fell limply to the stone, his neck twisted almost entirely about.

The Tengarian landed in a crouch. He pivoted smoothly and sheathed his black sword. The other goblin sank to his knees, hands clasped to his throat. Blood seeped around his clawed fingers, and he slumped to the dock.

Sulmar dragged the bodies behind the crates and crouched beside them, waiting. No one else came, and there were no more calls or challenges. He slipped quickly up the walkway and back on board the *Treachery*.

Leth and Gerruth returned a minute or two later. Their mission was a success. The *Treachery* was theirs, and the warships were temporarily crippled. Now, all they could do was wait and pray for Dacius and the others.

Chentelle glanced to the east. The dark horizon gave no hint of Ellistar's approach.

❧ 13 ❧

Tribulations

The shouting started just before first-light. It had to be the distraction. Chentelle searched the goblin camp, and saw Brother Gorin stalking back and forth near the fringes of the central fire.

The goblin priest weaved unsteadily and swung his arms wildly, as if he were very drunk. He beat his halberd against the round metal shield he carried, and shouted challenges at phantoms. Then he started swinging the weapon, battering the air with great sweeping strokes.

The camp sentries surrounded him in the clearing, but they did not stand too close. More goblins appeared, straggling slowly out of the barracks buildings and forming a crowd around the ranting priest. More shouting broke out; some of the goblins seemed to be yelling encouragement while others called angrily for silence.

Gorin's halberd crashed into the fire, sending flaming brands splashing through the air. The blaze roared higher for an instant, then faded into gray embers.

"What is happening?" Father Marcus asked.

"I don't know," Chentelle said. Without the firelight, she could no longer make out details. The clearing was filled with a mass of shadowy forms. Yelling still filled the air, becoming more angry and strident. Then a yell of a different type sounded from closer to the pier: a scream of pure agony.

"To the ship!" came Dacius' bellow. "Run for the pier!"

A half-dozen shapes ran along the rocky coast, the Legionnaire's huge outline plain among them. Two guards moved into their path, halberds rising to the ready. Dacius charged through them without slowing. His blade swept the goblin weapons aside and cut down one of the goblins on the backswing. He slammed the other to the ground with his shoulder and kept running. One of the trailing elves sliced downward with curved blade passed, finishing off the stunned sentry.

The goblins in the clearing screamed in rage as they realized what was happening. Dozens came charging toward the dock. Others disappeared into the barracks. But none of them could stop the escaping prisoners from reaching the pier.

Dacius scrambled to a stop halfway down the pier, near a pile of cargo. Thildemar took a stand next to him. "Keep moving!" he shouted to the others. "Get the *Treachery* ready to sail!" He waited until the crew was passed, then scattered the crates across the dock. "Bowmen—covering fire!"

"Please move back, Chentelle." Leth's hand gently pulled her away from the rail. He and his brother stepped forward, bows already in hand and nocked. Drup was hard at work, grinding the winch to raise anchor.

Rone and the others scrambled up the gangway. The captain waved a goblin scimitar frantically in one hand. "Raise the sheets! Make ready to sail! Move, you sluggards, move!"

Zubec and Pardec bolted for the rigging. Pulleys squealed in protest as the sails unfurled. The canvas flapped feebly in the light breeze.

Bowstrings thrummed as Leth and Gerruth loosed their shots. Two goblins dropped, falling to the ground in front of the onrushing mob.

The others didn't even slow. They trampled their brethren and charged onto the pier. Two more fell to well-placed arrows, but then the mass swarmed into Dacius and Thildemar.

The Legionnaires stood their ground. The makeshift barricade slowed the charge, forcing the goblins to climb over and around the scattered boxes. Vorpal sword and battle stave lashed out with uncanny speed and precision, wreaking havoc among the first rank of goblins and adding their fallen bodies to the obstacle. But the goblins kept pressing forward.

Chentelle could see a second line forming behind the first rush, a line both better organized and better armed. "Sulmar, help them."

The Tengarian jumped nimbly over the rail. Both swords rang out of their sheaths before his feet hit the dock. He landed in a soft crouch and was running almost instantly.

A glint of motion flashed above his right shoulder. "Look out!" Chentelle cried.

A crossbow bolt shot through the space where Gerruth's head had been a moment before. It shattered against the mast, splattering the deck with hissing fluid.

The Legionnaire turned and loosed in one motion, his own arrow finding its mark in the chest of the goblin sentry from the docked warship. The second sentry ducked back behind cover. "My thanks, enchantress," Gerruth said, nocking another arrow without taking his eyes off the goblin's position.

"Paun!" Captain Rone screamed. "Piss and rot, man, what are you waiting for? We need a sagewind!"

"I know that, Master Rone," Paun said. "But the goblins took my staff. I can't move the wind without it!"

"Of all the—A'stoc!" Rone shouted. "Where's the wizard? He can call the wind."

"No," Chentelle said. "He can't. He's unconscious, and we can't revive him."

"You must," Rone growled. "Or else Paun better whittle himself another sagestaff. We are doomed if we don't get wind."

Something large splashed into the water off their port.

"Arbalest," Rone said. "The other warships must have heard the commotion. They'll move in and cut us off."

"They can't move," Chentelle said. "Leth sabotaged their rudders."

A second splash threw water onto the deck.

"Well, damn me and bless that lad," Rone said. "But it'll do us no good if we can't get this lady under way. Paun! Now or never, man, it's now or never."

The shipsage had both hands wrapped around the mainmast. His face twisted with strain as he hummed stridently and rocked back and forth. His whole body trembled, and one of his legs gave way. He fell heavily, striking his head against the deck. "I'm sorry," he said hoarsely.

"Man the harpoon," Rone shouted. He slapped his scimitar angrily and stalked over to the rail.

The Legionnaires were retreating steadily toward the ship. Dacius held the center position, giving ground step by slow step. Thildemar was on his right, and Sulmar's two swords wove a deadly shield on his exposed left. More than a dozen goblin bodies littered the pier, but the tide kept coming.

A wheezing cry sounded from the deck of the goblin warship. The second sentry had finally exposed himself. He fell, and his crossbow clattered to the ground, spending the shot harmlessly.

Gerruth turned back to the dock and nocked another arrow. He loosed that missile and one more. Then he and Leth both dropped bows and drew their swords. Dacius' feet had almost reached the gangway.

"Cover!" Drup shouted.

A volley of bolts scattered across the *Treachery*'s deck, sent by a formation of goblins standing just off of the pier.

The whaler's harpoon jumped in response. The huge missile tore through the ground under the archers' feet, scattering their formation.

A door slammed open behind them. A'stoc stood at the top of the stairs, gripping the Staff in both hands. The wizard took a halting step forward, then another. Like a drunken marionette, he staggered toward the mainmast—eyes closed, legs twitching awkwardly, Thunderwood clutched rigidly to his chest.

And Father Marcus walked just behind him. The High Priest chanted slowly, his brow furrowed in concentration. His right hand rested on the back of A'stoc's neck and never strayed as he followed the wizard onto the deck.

As one, the pair stopped before the mast. A'stoc's arms wrenched into the air. Marcus shifted his chant, and words grated out of the wizard's throat. Emerald fire blazed to life, surrounding both mage and High Priest. The flames shot skyward, and a gale ripped into the *Treachery*'s sails.

The ship lurched forward, then snapped to a halt. Wooden planks groaned with strain as the mooring lines pulled tight. Sailors and Legionnaires grabbed for support against the blast. Chentelle staggered against the rail, driven to her knees by the screaming wind. Only A'stoc was unaffected, secure in his halo of power.

Captain Rone scampered for the aft line. "Time to go, Lord Gemine!" he bellowed above the wind. "Pardec, on my mark, cut loose the bow line."

The sudden squall had thrown Thildemar and the goblins off balance. Dacius and Sulmar pushed forward, taking advantage of their greater mass and stability. They drove the attackers backward, creating a brief cushion in front of the gangplank. Dacius grabbed Thildemar with a supporting arm, and the three men rushed up the ramp.

"Now!" Rone screamed, scimitar raised high overhead.

"Wait!" Chentelle cried, pointing down the pier.

A figure was pressing slowly through the mass of goblins. It was Gorin. The priest's head was bowed. His hands were raised before his chest, clawed fingers curled into a circle. And he was surrounded by the gentle glow of sanctuary.

The goblins near the priest screamed in rage. Several of them lifted weapons to attack him, but as soon as they drew close their weapons dropped harmlessly to their sides. They gazed around in sudden confusion, helpless against the Creator's peace. The goblins moved out of Brother Gorin's path, unable even to block his progress so long as the sanctuary held.

The *Treachery* bucked wildly against her restraints. The gangplank bounced in the air, scattering several goblins who had been trying to force their way aboard. The sails snapped furiously and the planks around the mast bent with strain.

"Hurry!" Rone yelled. "She can't hold much longer."

Brother Gorin reached the foot of the plank. The goblins surrounding him gave way, powerless to block him. He jumped nimbly onto the walkway, but another lurch twisted the board under his feet. He fell to the wood and was nearly thrown into the sea. Only his hard claws held him to the board. The jolt broke his concentration and he stopped chanting. The aura of sanctuary faded.

Sulmar leaped forward. Keeping one hand on the rail, he reached out with the other and grabbed Gorin's collar. With one great heave he lifted the goblin and threw him onto the deck of the *Treachery*. Then he dived back to find his own cover.

"Now!" Rone shouted. His goblin blade sliced through the thick mooring rope.

The *Treachery* bounded sideways, shuddering slightly as the bow rope snapped an instant later. Chentelle tumbled across the deck, slamming violently against the far rail. Water sloshed against her face. By the Creator, the ship was canted nearly horizontal. They were going down!

"Hard aport!" Rone screamed.

The *Treachery*'s hull groaned in protest as the captain and crew struggled to make her respond. Somehow, they managed to face her with the wind. The sails ruffled, then cracked full, yanking the goblinship forward. She plowed through the water, slowly righting herself as they gained speed. They ran with the gale toward the open seas.

"Sound off!" Dacius said. "Is everyone all right?"

One by one, the company checked in. Everyone was shaken and bruised, but no one was seriously hurt. Only A'stoc and the High Bishop failed to answer. They were both still wrapped in Earthpower, oblivious to their surroundings.

Dacius pointed toward the east. The shadows of the two warships loomed ominously against the brightening sky. "What's our course, captain?"

"Straight between 'em, Lord Gemine," Rone answered, shouting to be heard above the gale. "No other choice. We'll have to pray our speed pulls us through safely."

Dacius paused for a moment, eyes roaming the deck. "We'll have a crossfire from their bowmen. Drup, Leth, Gerruth—grab bows. Aim for their artillerists and sorcerers. Thildemar, you and I are shieldmen. Sulmar, will you man the harpoon?"

The Tengarian hesitated, looking to Chentelle.

Brother Gorin stepped forward. "I will watch over the enchantress. My sanctuary will shield us both."

"Mistress?" Sulmar inquired.

"Of course," Chentelle said.

Sulmar headed for the bow.

"Good," Dacius said. "Everyone else get below."

Chentelle felt Gorin's hard fingers grip her shoulder. A rhythm of deep peace and security flowed through her, pulsing in time to the priest's chant. With mild curiosity, she watched the Legionnaires scramble to their positions. They seemed strangely agitated.

A hail of arrows clattered across the deck. Several of them ripped through the sails, leaving tattered holes. Most of the missiles targeted A'stoc and Father Marcus. Flashes of red and yellow danced around the fiery shield. The effect blended curiously with the splashes of black acid that hissed across the boards. It was like a painting of a dream, rather pretty in composition and color.

The *Treachery* was directly between the two warships, now, and arrows buzzed furiously through the air. Their own bowmen were forced to huddle under cover while the goblin barrage was spent. A large stone slammed through one of the upper spars. Wood and rigging came crashing down, pinning Leth to the deck.

A goblin sorcerer stepped to the rail of one warship. Lightning crackled around his outstretched claws. Chentelle felt mild concern, realizing that this was real danger. Then an arrow quivered suddenly in his chest, and he fell backward. She felt moderate regret and relief.

The goblins started to shift the focus of their attack. Convinced that the flaming humans were beyond their power, they switched their aim to Captain Rone, exposed on the wheeldeck. But he, too, seemed beyond their reach.

Dacius and Thildemar crouched on either side of the captain, dozens of goblin missiles sprouting from the twin shields each wielded. Vitriol smoked and scarred the metal-wrapped wood, but the defense held. The *Treachery* plowed forward, leaving the warships quickly behind.

Then lightning blasted through the wheeldeck. Rone and his defenders were tossed into the air. Dacius and Thildemar landed heavily, but Rone used the wheel to steady himself. He fell to his knees, but the *Treachery* never strayed from the wind.

Then came the arrows. Most of the final salvo fell short, raising brief white splashes in the gray sea. A few of them found the deck. Thildemar danced away as acid sprayed across his leatherbark tunic, and a metal bolt pierced Dacius through the calf. Captain Rone toppled to his side, blood running from his open mouth.

"Captain!" Zubec's voice sliced through the howling wind.

The warm safety suddenly disappeared. Brother Gorin was rushing past her, close on the heels of Zubec. By the Creator, Captain Rone! She ran for the wheeldeck.

Gorin and Zubec were crouched beside Rone. The priest was already beginning to chant, and Zubec cradled the captain in his arms. The wheel spun free behind them.

The *Treachery*'s bow swung across the wind, and the ship tilted dangerously to port. Chentelle stumbled forward, nearly landing on top of Brother Gorin.

A barbed metal tip poked through the front of the captain's chest. Blood soaked the boards under his back. "The wheel," he gasped. "Take the—"

Rone's death shuddered through Chentelle's spine. She felt a terrible cold, then nothing. After a time, she realized that it was dark. She opened her eyes.

Brother Gorin was shaking his head. "The arrow pierced his heart. His spirit was loosed. I could not call it back." He lifted a clawed hand to the captain's face and gently closed the eyes. Then he moved over to inspect Dacius' leg.

Zubec didn't say anything. But his eyes were tightly clenched, and the wheel trembled in his grasp.

☙

The blasting sagewind carried them eastward until Ellistar was full over the horizon. Then, the flames around A'stoc and Father Marcus sputtered and died. Both men collapsed to the deck.

Chentelle was at their sides in an instant.

A'stoc burned with fever. Chentelle reached into him with her Gift, but his spirit was still walled off from the world.

She switched her touch to Father Marcus. Weariness and guilt swept through her in a massive tide. She jerked her hand away, spinning dizzily under the onslaught. Desperation burned in her throat. Failure. Pain. She stumbled to her feet, trying to comprehend the rush of emotion.

Strong hands steadied her balance. Sulmar. She latched on to the Tengarian, anchoring herself to his steadfastness.

"Mistress, are you all right?"

She nodded. "I think so. Yes. Yes, I'm fine."

"What about them?" Dacius asked. "What did you sense?"

"A'stoc is still the same," she said. "But he has a fever now, a bad one. Father Marcus—I don't know. I think he just needs rest. But he has terrible feelings of—something. It's difficult to sort out."

"We should take them below," Dacius said. "Leth, Gerruth—give them a hand. Brother Gorin, can you help the wizard's fever?"

"Perhaps," the priest said. "I will try."

"Fine," Dacius said. "But don't exhaust yourself. There's no telling how long we'll be in the clear. Zubec, what's our course?"

The sailor pointed to the tattered sails, hanging limp in the still air. "We have none, Lord Gemine. The sagewind pulled us much farther east than I would prefer, but we're stuck here until the wind picks up. I suggest we use the lull to repair the sails. There's not much we can do about the spars right now."

"Agreed," Dacius said. "Then set course for the Holy Land. Get us underway as soon as you can."

"Yes, Lord Gemine. But, with your permission, I would like to bury Captain Rone first."

Dacius stared over the stern rail. "No. Repair the sails first. I will make sure the body is prepared, but the safety of the quest must come first."

Zubec turned away and knelt beside Rone's body. He brushed his fingers lightly across the captain's ruined chest. "The ship first," he said softly. "Always, the ship first."

Zubec stood and squared his shoulders. "Pardec, lower the mainsail. I'll get the patch kit. You, Drup, untangle the spar from those lines. We may be able to reroute the rigging. Gerruth, take the wheel. Just keep her pointed ahead. If the wind comes, I'll relieve you."

The elves exploded into action, pouring themselves into the mundane tasks with an almost manic concentration.

Dacius walked to Captain Rone's body and rolled it to its side. He drew his dagger and started to use its pommel to hammer the barbed arrow through the elf's chest.

Chentelle's stomach churned. She whirled and ran for the stairs, suddenly unable to bear the horror of sharing the deck with Captain Rone's corpse. She stumbled down the stairs, catching herself against one of the dining tables. It wasn't fair. They had made it. Why did Rone have to die? Why was the price so high?

Tears drifted down her cheek. Despite the captain's sacrifice, she felt relief, even elation, at their escape. But guilt followed immediately. How could she be happy when Rone was dead? Not just Rone; Alve and Simon and the Legionnaires from the other ship—the quest had taken them all. Good men had given their lives, and all she could think about was her own safety. How could she be so selfish?

"Enchantress?" Brother Gorin's gruff voice startled her from her thoughts. "Chentelle, are you all right?"

She wiped her eyes clear and nodded. "I'm just—" She shrugged. "I wish so many people didn't have to die."

"As do I. As do we all. Sometimes the Creator leads us along difficult paths."

"But why? What does it all mean?"

"Death has no meaning, Chentelle," the priest answered. "It is only a silence in Creation's harmony. It is life that has meaning. We create that meaning, each of us individually and all of us together. Captain Rone's life was filled with meanings: the sea, his ship, his crew, his sense of duty and justice. He shaped these meanings with his life, and they shaped him. In the end, his path led to death, as will yours, as will mine. His life has ended, but the reasons for that life have not. If we would honor Captain Rone, then we must honor those principles."

It sounded so reasonable, so soothing. Chentelle tried to latch on to Gorin's words, to mimic the goblin's unwavering faith. But her grief was too fresh. She decided to change the subject, not because the matter was slight, but because she had to divert herself from it until she could better cope with it. "How is Father Marcus? When I touched him, I felt something—" She searched for the proper word. "Horrible."

"He needs rest and solitude," Brother Gorin said. "He has done a thing that causes him much grief."

"I don't understand. Do you mean how he revived A'stoc? What did he do?"

The goblin grimaced, displaying multiple rows of pointy teeth. "The High Bishop did not revive A'stoc. He animated him, took control of his mind. The technique is usually reserved for teaching. It allows a bishop to lead a student through a meditation or ritual. Sometimes it is also used to bring comfort to those near death, to allow them to complete a task they feel is vital. But it is never, *never* used without the consent of the subject."

Chentelle felt a terrible emptiness. A'stoc was unconscious, his spirit unreachable. He could not have given his assent. This had been a terrible violation. Father Marcus had saved them, but at what cost?

Someone knocked lightly on the frame of the hatchway. "Your pardon, Chentelle, Brother Gorin," Dacius said. "We are ready to bury Captain Rone. Has the High Bishop recovered?"

"No," Gorin said. "I will perform the ceremony."

~

The priest spoke briefly, consecrating the captain's remains and commending it to the unity of waters. Then they gave Rone's body back to the sea that he had loved so well. Despite Gorin's reassuring words, the faces of the company were bleak and lifeless. They were the faces of broken spirits, molded in gray ash.

Chentelle could hardly bear to look at them. Their pain was so sharp, their despondency so deep. Each face was an echo of her own guilt and despair. It had to end. She thought about the words Gorin had spoken to her, fixing their message in her mind. Then she sang.

It started as a wail, wordless, wrenching, filled with loss and suffering. She touched each of the company with it, letting her Gift resonate with their own anguish. The cry grew louder, more strident. Then, slowly, she softened it, blending it into the simple rhythm of the tide. She developed a song of sea, of salt, of motion and vibrant life. She sang of courage and honor, of compassion and hope. She sculpted Rone in tone and melody, highlighting his passions, his humor, his sense of duty.

She sang, and the spirits of the company followed her voice. They passed through their grief to celebration of the life they had been privileged to share. Tears ran freely down the cheeks of warrior and sailor alike. But the sadness no longer filled them. Their hearts were also home to laughter and resolve, to hope and determination. The song tapered off gradually, disappearing into the sighing breeze.

"Bless you, Chentelle," a quiet voice said from the stairs.

"Father Marcus!" she exclaimed. "I didn't know you were there. Are you all right?"

The High Bishop looked pale, but his back was straight and his voice steady. Only the shadows surrounding his cerulean eyes hinted at some hidden pain. "No. But I am far better than I was, thanks to your wondrous voice. You have helped to ease a burden I thought beyond bearing."

"She's done more than that," Zubec said. "She's brought us wind! Pardec, tighten the starboard lines. We'll reach across her."

"But I didn't call the wind," said Chentelle. "It's just a coincidence."

"As you like, enchantress," Zubec said, bowing deeply and then jumping up to the wheeldeck. "But my heart is lighter, and the sails are full. And I know who I'll thank in my prayers this night."

Father Marcus turned to Zubec. "I am sorry to learn about Captain Rone's sacrifice. May I assume that you are now captain?"

"No," Zubec said. "This ship has only one captain. But I'll sail her home."

"Fine," the High Bishop said. "How are you at charts and navigation?"

"Better than anyone else on board," said Zubec. "I'm no Captain Rone, but I can guide us safely to the Realm."

"Good," Father Marcus said. "But we are not returning to Talan. Set course for the Westlands. Our destination is Tel Adartak-Skysoar."

Dacius came up beside them. "High Bishop, there is one thing I do not understand. Why would the Dark One place a breeding pit on so distant an island? Why didn't he place it somewhere in the Realm?"

"I believe it has to do with the Atablicryon," Father Marcus said. "The temple sits on a concentration of Earthpower. Perhaps it gave him pleasure to twist that power to his own ends."

"Yes," Chentelle said. "And Elihaz said that the Ill-creatures had been active on the island for many years. So they couldn't have been put there just to stop our quest."

"True," Dacius said. "But those years of activity have me thinking. We thought the Ill-creatures had been banished from Infinitera after the Desecration. Now, I begin to wonder whether they've been influencing the Heresiarchs throughout the Hordeland Wars."

"I suspect you are right," the High Bishop said.

"They must be stopped!" Dacius barked with sudden ferocity. "They are a blight upon all of Infinitera. The Realm will never be safe while Ill-creatures exist."

"You are correct," Father Marcus said. "But ours is a different quest. We fight a more dangerous evil."

"I know. The Fallen Star. But it is hard to believe that any threat can be greater than the Dark One. I *know* his evil. The Fallen Star is just a name."

"Not to me," the High Bishop said. "I must have your trust in this, Lord Gemine. Destruction of the Fallen Star is our goal. There can be no other. The whole of the Creation depends on us."

"I do trust you," Dacius said. "But it is hard. I am used to thinking in more concrete terms. Ill-creatures I can comprehend. The end of the Creation—" He shrugged.

"Must not occur," Father Marcus finished. "And it will not, so long as we remain true to our purpose. That is the message of Rone's sacrifice. Now, if you will excuse me, I want to check on Wizard A'stoc."

Chentelle's own concern for the wizard almost drove her to join the priest, but his manner did not invite company. Instead, she went below deck and headed for the galley. The aroma of baking bread filled the air, seasoned with just a hint of roasted potatoes. Whistling rang through the small kitchen, punctuated by the staccato clicking of a knife against wood.

Drup looked up from his work without missing a beat. "Oh, hello Chentelle, Sulmar. I thought I would fix dinner, since Zubec is acting as captain. Have you come to work or sample?"

"I'll work," Chentelle said. She was surprised at how young the Legionnaire looked in his apron and cap. He wasn't much older than she, but he had always seemed much older. Maybe it was the uniform. "What should I do?"

Drup flipped his diced carrots into a waiting bowl with a practiced flair. "Salad or soup, your choice."

"Soup," she said. "I could never slice like that."

The Legionnaire bowed extravagantly. "So nice to be recognized for the rare talent that I am. Very well, soup you shall be. The base is prepared; it lacks only seasoning and a proper aesthetic presentation. I leave those in your able hands, while I"—he tossed a tomato into the air, quartered it with two quick strokes, and caught the pieces in his off hand—"teach these vegetables to fear the very name Drup."

Chentelle grinned happily. "You certainly are in a good mood. Is there some special reason?"

A deep smile lit his eyes. "We're headed *home*, Chentelle. I can feel Endaleof calling me. Already, I can smell the scent of the forest riding on this salty wind."

Chentelle basked in the young soldier's joy. She hummed quietly as she worked, matching her tune easily to Drup's whistle. The soup was delicious. A quick taste verified that it needed little help from her. It also reminded her of the emptiness of her stomach. She was soon doing as much tasting as cooking.

Despite her dallying, the meal was soon ready. They ferried the dishes into the dining salon, and the rich aroma proved to be more than sufficient as a dinner bell. Leth and Gerruth nearly beat them to the table.

The company ate in shifts, always keeping at least three men on deck. They devoured the meal with a relish that spoke volumes about both their hunger and the quality of the food. Praises were heaped upon the cooks, and Chentelle did her best to direct them toward Drup. The young Legionnaire's smile never faltered.

Chentelle watched the progression of diners with growing concern. One face was conspicuously absent. Father Marcus was still sequestered in A'stoc's cabin. She remembered Gorin's caution that the High Bishop needed solitude, but she was worried. Well, A'stoc would need food even if the priest didn't. No one could blame her for taking the wizard a bowl of soup.

No one answered her knock, so she pushed open the door. Luckily, it wasn't barred. Father Marcus knelt beside A'stoc's bed, hands resting on the wizard's chest. A shimmering aura surrounded the two humans. A'stoc's face was peaceful, even serene, but Father Marcus looked haggard. The flesh hung limply from his cheeks, and his skin was almost gray. His hands and arms trembled visibly.

"Oh, no," Chentelle murmured. "He's using his own strength to try to heal A'stoc." She set the bowl of soup on the desk and shook the High Bishop's shoulder. "Father Marcus. Father Marcus, that's enough! It won't help anyone if you kill yourself. Remember the quest!"

The healing glow faded. Father Marcus blinked his eyes and glanced about the room. "Chentelle?" He tried to stand, but his legs gave way and he toppled over.

Chentelle caught his arm and struggled to hold him up, but he was far too heavy. Only Sulmar's quick assistance kept both of them from hitting the floor. Together, they lifted the priest into the desk chair.

"Thank you," Father Marcus said. "My legs seem to have grown stiff."

Chentelle studied the human's face, trying to read his condition in the worn lines and unusually guarded eyes. "I thought that you said there was nothing you could do for him. His spirit has to find its own way back."

The High Bishop winced. "That was true, before. But when I—controlled A'stoc, when I forced him to summon the Staff's power, it put great strain on his weakened body. Touch him."

Chentelle placed a hand on A'stoc's forehead. It was cool and dry, at first, but she felt the heat rising. Sweat beaded on his brow as the fever returned, undiminished by Father Marcus' efforts.

"You see," the priest said. "I can suppress the fever, but it returns as soon as I relinquish the healing." He levered himself unsteadily to his feet.

Chentelle stepped between the priest and A'stoc's bunk. "You can't continue. You need rest."

Father Marcus looked as if he wanted to push past her, but his weakness prevented him. "You do not understand. I need to heal him. The quest cannot succeed without him."

"I do understand," Chentelle said. "And I know that you blame yourself for his condition. But you didn't have any choice. You did what you had to to save us all."

"No," he said sharply. "What I did was an abomination. There is always a choice. I should have found another way. It was my weakness, my lack of foresight, that threatened the quest. But A'stoc is paying the price." He took one shaky step forward.

Chentelle put a hand gently on his arm, feeling the weakness that still trembled there. "You have to stop this. Please, you're killing yourself. I know the wizard is vital to the quest, but so are you. Without your leadership, your guidance, we are all lost. Whatever mistakes you may have made were driven by the urgency of our need. Don't abandon us now. Rest, eat some dinner. I will watch over A'stoc."

The High Bishop opened his mouth to answer, but then closed it and nodded in resignation. "Call me if the fever worsens."

"I will," Chentelle said. "Sulmar, help him to the salon. Make sure he gets a full meal and some sleep."

Chentelle waited until the humans had left. Then she picked up the bowl of soup and sat down on the wizard's bed. She poured a few drops between his slack lips and was relieved to see his throat move in a reflexive swallow. Good, at least he wouldn't starve.

She alternated between spooning soup slowly into A'stoc's mouth and wiping clear the sweat that streamed down his face. When her bowl was half-empty, the perspiration stopped. That was bad. The wizard's fever raged hotter than ever, but his body was dehydrated. She stood up to go fetch some water, but froze at A'stoc's quiet moan.

He was awake! No, his eyes were still shut, and he didn't react to either her voice or her touch on his shoulder. But he was moving. His face shivered, and he tossed spasmodically on the wet sheets. She reached out with her Gift, trying to calm him.

Fever and pain assaulted her. She swirled in a chaos of rage and fear. Fire burned from within and without. Her limbs jerked madly, wrenched in directions she was helpless to control. Her hand flew away from the wizard. She tripped and scraped her face across the rough wooden planks.

"Sulmar!" she cried. "Come here."

The Tengarian burst through the door an instant later, one hand floating near the hilt of his black sword. His eyes swept the room, alert for any sign of danger. Seeing none, he crossed to Chentelle in three gliding steps. "Mistress, are you hurt?"

"No," she said, using his arm to pull herself upright. "I'm fine, but A'stoc's fever is worse than ever. He's coming back, but he needs help. Find Brother Gorin. Tell him and Father Marcus what's happening. And get some water. He needs water."

"Aaahh!" A'stoc's eyes snapped open and his body sprang from the bed. He fell to the floor in a heap, arms and legs flailing wildly.

"Oh, no," Chentelle said. "Help me get him back in bed." Together, she and Sulmar raised the wizard to his feet.

His wide eyes stared through them, seemingly oblivious to their presence. But when they tried to lead him back toward the bed, he resisted. His gaze snapped into focus on the Thunderwood Staff, resting casually in the cabin's corner.

"Marcus!" A'stoc exploded into motion. He pushed through Chentelle and her liegeman, catching them off guard with his sudden movement. They overbalanced against the side of the bed and fell in a tangle. The wizard snatched up the Staff and was out the door before they could recover.

Sulmar rolled to his feet and turned a worried glance to Chentelle.

"I'm fine," she said, scrambling off the bed. "Go on."

The Tengarian ran through the door, and she followed close behind. An angry bellow rang through the hallway as they reached the salon.

"Why?" A'stoc screamed. "What right did you have to possess me?" He stalked forward.

Brother Gorin and Father Marcus had been alone in the salon. The goblin stepped forward to bar the wizard's path. "Wizard A'stoc, please control yourself. We must—"

"NO!" A'stoc slammed the Staff against the deck.

The *Treachery* shuddered as Earthpower blazed into life. Gorin stumbled, driven backward by the explosion. Green fire licked at the floor and ceiling, filling the chamber with dark smoke. Sulmar tried to move forward, but the flames pushed him away.

"A'stoc!" Chentelle yelled. "Stop it. You're sick. You need to get back to bed."

The wizard jerked around at the sound of her voice. "Stay away from me, enchantress!" He snarled the title like a profanity, lips curled in anger and bitterness.

"Wizard A'stoc," Father Marcus said softly. "Please, release the Staff's power. You are endangering the ship."

A'stoc whirled, a bestial growl rising in his throat. His left arm shot out, grabbing the High Bishop's collar. Earthpower flared as he lifted the priest off the floor and slammed him into the bulkhead. *"What right?"*

Father Marcus hung limply in the wizard's grasp, his head bowed to the floor. "No right—only necessity, and my own weakness."

The wizard lifted the Thunderwood high overhead. A long, wordless scream tore from his mouth.

"No!" screamed Chentelle. "A'stoc, don't."

"Summon the sanctuary," Gorin yelled. "High Bishop, protect yourself!"

But Father Marcus just raised his head and locked eyes with A'stoc. He stretched out his arms, offering himself to whatever vengeance the wizard demanded.

The Staff flared, surrounding both men in a blinding globe of emerald fire. The light pulsed once, twice, then disappeared in a burst of radiance. When vision returned, the two men were standing face-to-face, neither one showing signs of injury.

A'stoc spun and walked away from the High Bishop. He managed three halting steps before collapsing in a heap. The Staff fell from his fingers and rolled across the deck.

Chentelle and Sulmar were at his side an instant before the two priests. His pale skin was still hot with fever, but there was a strangely peaceful quality to his pallid face.

A thunder of footsteps rushed down the stairs. "By the Creator," Dacius said. "What happened?"

"All is under control, now," Father Marcus said. "Will you please have your people extinguish the fires. I must see to A'stoc."

"Father Marcus—" Gorin started.

The High Bishop interrupted him with an upraised hand. "No, my friend. Thank you, but this is something that I must do myself. Sulmar, will you assist me?"

The Tengarian picked up the unconscious A'stoc and followed Father Marcus back to the wizard's cabin. Chentelle retrieved the Staff from the corner of the salon and hurried after them.

The High Bishop motioned for Sulmar to place A'stoc in the bed. Then he took the Staff from Chentelle and laid it beside the wizard. "Thank you both for your help and concern. I believe the worst has passed. The Creator is truly merciful. Now, I must ask you to leave us alone. A'stoc and I have delicate work to do."

Exhaustion hung heavily on the priest's face, but his smile was fresh and full of hope. Chentelle carried that smile with her as she returned to the salon.

Leth, Gerruth, and Drup were splashing buckets of water on the ceiling as she arrived. The last of the flames sputtered and died out, leaving only charred wood to show where they had been. Dacius stood by an open portal, fanning with a blanket to drive out the black smoke.

"Lord Gemine!" Zubec said, thrusting his head through the doorway at the top of the stairs. "What in Creation—?"

"It's a long story," Dacius said. "Or so I gather. But everything is fine now. There's no danger."

"Good," Zubec said. "Because I think the goblin warships provide more than enough."

"*What?*"

ᕽ

They stared down the line of Zubec's arm. Far astern, barely visible in the red light, three tall-masted silhouettes poked above the horizon.

"Are you certain?" Dacius asked, squinting against the glare.

"There is no mistake," Thildemar said. "Three warships, following directly on our course."

"All three?" Dacius said. "Blood and bone, how did they know? They didn't even split up. We could have taken any heading back to the Realm. How are they tracking us?"

"By the Creator, no." All eyes turned at Gorin's whisper. "The wailing crystal, they must be homing in on the wailing crystal."

"What?"

"A fragment of the Hordemaster's Heartstone," he said. "Every ship carries one. It allows the navigator to fix his position relative to the Horde. They must have some way to reverse the process, to zero in on our position. It never occurred to me. I am sorry."

"Never mind that," Dacius said. "Where's the crystal?"

"In the forepeak," Gorin said. "I think. It might be hidden in the captain's cabin."

"Search the hold," Dacius said. "Paun, you check the captain's quarters. Look everywhere. We need to find that crystal." He turned to Zubec. "Can you lose them?"

The sailor shouted some orders to his cousin and turned them across the south wind. The warships turned as a unit, matching their course and swallowing up the distance. Zubec eased them back to the northwest, squeezing all possible speed from the natural wind. The dark sails continued to close.

"Bows!" Dacius said. "Set up positions along the stern rail! Thildemar, you and I on shield duty."

Chentelle watched the Legionnaires rush into action, wishing there were something she could do. Helplessly, she watched the warships glide closer. The wind shifted to the southeast, and the *Treachery* was forced westward. The warships adjusted course to intercept her. Lightning flashed behind them.

"A storm," Chentelle cried. "Look." A wall of heavy clouds loomed in the eastern sky. Distant thunder rolled across the waves.

"Wonderful," Gerruth said. "Just in case the goblins weren't enough for us to deal with."

"No!" Zubec said. "This is our chance. Pardec, trim the mainsail! We're coming about. Leth, Gerruth, give him a hand. Hurry!"

"What are you doing?" Dacius asked.

"The storm," Zubec said. "It's our only chance to lose the warships. The rough water will keep them from closing to board, and the winds will force them to lower sails. If the tempest is strong enough, it may drive them away altogether."

"What about the *Treachery*?" Dacius asked. "Can we survive the storm if it's that powerful?"

"Have you got a better idea?" Zubec asked, spinning the wheel. "Those are three fully manned warships."

The human lord had no answer.

Sails luffed momentarily as the *Treachery* turned, then caught the wind again. They reversed direction, steering eastward on a long tack. The heading would take them into the storm's center. It also took them back across the warships' course.

The goblins charged forward on their sagewind, adjusting course to cut off the whaler's retreat. Huddled figures could be seen massing on the bows. Something splashed into the water off the starboard bow: ballistae, finding their range. A second splash was closer than the first, and the third missile sailed over their heads to splash off the port side.

"Steady," Dacius said. "Archers, fire only if you see a sorcerer. Otherwise, stay shielded. We can't afford to trade shots with them."

Chentelle huddled against the doorway below deck. They weren't going to make it. The warships were closing too fast. A thousand cubits, maybe less, already the lead ship was turning to match the *Treachery*'s course.

"Cover!" shouted Dacius.

A hail of arrows flew from the warship's broadside. Most splashed into the water or clattered against the hull, but several landed across the deck. Splashes of acid hissed angrily, but no one was hit. A flaming harpoon arced over the water. It passed miraculously between the masts and crashed through the port-side railing before disappearing into the sea.

Zubec steered them northward, away from the broadside. Then, when the warship shifted to match their course, he turned them sharply east again. It was a repeat of the maneuver Captain Rone had used against the first ship, but Zubec had less sail and no sagewind to drive them. The warship's ram cut through the water, aimed directly at the *Treachery*.

Suddenly, the sails flapped weakly and hung slack. The warship was blocking their wind! The *Treachery* drifted slowly forward, carried only by their momentum.

The warship shifted course, tracking their drift. The big ship flew toward them, water frothing around its pointed ram. But she was going *too* fast. She couldn't turn in time to compensate for their motion. The warship slid past the *Treachery*'s stern, rocking the smaller boat with her wake. A handful of bolts landed against the Legionnaire's shields, but the marines had not been prepared to fire another salvo.

Wind filling her sails once more, the *Treachery* shot toward the storm.

The other ships had been arcing out to encircle them. One was now well behind them, but the other lay directly in their path. Zubec turned them south-ward, closer into the wind. Two more arrow storms raked the deck, but they did damage only to Legion shields and the *Treachery*'s deck. The whaler cut through the warship's wake, passing behind it before the large ship could adjust course.

The wind picked up, driving them through the choppy surf. All three war-ships were in pursuit again, but the *Treachery* had a substantial lead. The goblins would close, of course, but already the first drops of rain were splattering against the deck.

Zubec took them into the heart of the storm. Thunder roared around them, and hard rain drove against the deck. The *Treachery* pitched perilously on the turbulent sea. Lines snapped taut as the sails whipped in the gale. Water sloshed across the deck as the whaler's bow dipped almost into the water.

Chentelle peered over the stern rail. The warships were barely discernible through the rain. Their topsails were lowered, and they were no longer closing distance. Still, their bulk gave them greater stability than the *Treachery*. The goblins held to their pursuit.

Brother Gorin came scrambling onto the deck, his right claw clutched tightly into a fist. "I have it! I found the wailing crystal. It was hidden under the floorboards of the forward hold."

"Give it here," Dacius said, holding out his hand. The teardrop crystal glowed red in the Legionnaire's palm before he closed his fingers around it. He moved to the stern rail and stared into the storm.

"Can anyone see the warships?" he screamed. "No? Good. That means they can't see us, either." He hurled the wailing crystal over the rail.

Lightning carved ribbons through the darkness, punctuating the howling wind with drumbeats of thunder. The *Treachery* bobbed in the water like a child's toy, her masts straining against the wind.

"Tie down the sails!" Zubec shouted. "She can't take much more!"

Pardec and the Legionnaires rushed to comply, fighting to move against the wind and the rain. Zubec started to lash the wheel into place.

"Go below!" he yelled. "We can't do anything more!"

They scrambled down the stairs into the salon. Zubec came last, straining to shut the sea door against the tempest. Dacius reached up to give the elf a hand, and together they pulled the door closed.

"Thank the Creator," Dacius said. "With any luck, they'll home in on the crystal and think we're at the bottom of the sea."

The deck lurched under their feet as the *Treachery* rocked with the storm. Thunder vibrated the cabin walls, and water poured around the edges of the closed porthole.

"With any luck," Gerruth said, "we won't be."

Chentelle's stomach churned in rhythm to the swaying deck. Drup's fine dinner bubbled and burned the back of her throat. She fought a wave of dizziness and gulped air through her mouth. She needed something else, anything else to think about.

The door to A'stoc's cabin swung open. The wizard staggered out, groping his way down the hallway. He lurched into the salon, nearly crashing into the table around which they were all huddled. He looked pale and weak, but his eyes held none of their earlier madness.

"A'stoc, are you all right?" Centelleh asked. "Where's Father Marcus? Here, let me help you." She hurried around the table and grabbed his arm, helping him to sit.

"If you want to help me," he croaked. "Find me something to drink." He cradled his head into his hands, clutching matted white hair between his fingers. "Hel's Bones, this is worse than any hangover."

Chentelle went into the galley and dipped a mug of drinking water from one of the barrels. She returned to find A'stoc hunched over the bench, wiping a trail of liquid from his mouth.

"By all that's holy," he muttered. "What does Rone think he's doing. We can't survive a storm like this."

Chentelle handed him the water. "Captain Rone died sailing us away from *Kennaru*. We needed to use the storm to escape the warships, and now we need to weather it as best we can."

"Wizard A'stoc," Gorin said. "Where is Father Marcus?"

"Sleeping," A'stoc said. "I left him in my bunk. We achieved an understanding. He did what was necessary." He took a sip from the cup without looking, and his eyes widened in surprise. He raised an eyebrow at Chentelle.

"It's all we have," she protested. "The goblins took all of the wine and mead."

"This is fine," he said. "I'm so dry I could swallow salt water." He drained the mug in one long swallow. "Now, someone tell me what has happened since Father Marcus possessed me."

Briefly, Chentelle outlined the events since their recapture of the *Treachery*. Pausing in her narration only to ask Sulmar to bring the wizard some more water.

A'stoc drained the second mug as quickly as the first. His complexion was still pallid, but he seemed to be regaining strength quickly. "I see," he said when Chentelle had finished. "And where are we headed now?"

"Tel Adartak-Skysoar," Zubec said.

"It was Father Marcus' order," Chentelle said hurriedly, remembering the wizard's distrust of the Collegium.

The wizard grunted and curled his lip in disgust. "He probably wants to make sure the children are not fighting over their new toys."

"Only we may never get there," Zubec said. "It may have been a mistake to enter the storm."

"We had no choice," Dacius said. "The warships would have destroyed us."

"And now the storm is going to do their work for them," Zubec said. "We can't survive much more."

As if on cue, the *Treachery* pitched violently to starboard. Chentelle and A'stoc tumbled across the floor in a stream of seawater. They came to rest against the bulkhead, and started to slide again when the ship rolled back to port. Only Sulmar's quick support let them regain their feet.

"Chentelle," A'stoc said softly. "Please get my Staff."

"Are you sure?" she asked. "You can barely stand. What if you can't control the power?"

A'stoc met her gaze with bloodshot eyes. Thunder echoed around them in the small salon. "Then we will find a quicker death than drowning."

Chentelle would have had more confidence in his resolve if his hands weren't trembling noticeably. But he was right. They had no choice. She went to get the Staff.

A'stoc was waiting by the sea door when she returned. Without a word, he took the Thunderwood from her hands and nodded to Sulmar.

The Tengarian pushed the door open, and the wizard was sucked out into the storm. Sulmar struggled to pull the door shut, but the wind ripped it from his grasp. Rain blasted through the salon.

Outside, Earthpower flared like a green beacon through the storm. The flames grew larger, brighter. They pulsed in rhythm to the thunder. Then, they started to swirl. The fiery whirlwind drove high into the air, piercing the center of the storm. The flames expanded outward, passing through the *Treachery* and into the air beyond. In their wake, the seas became calm, placid. The rain disappeared, and a steady breeze pushed from the southwest. The Earthpower rippled outward for several hundred cubits, then it flickered into nothingness. The bubble of tranquillity remained.

Slowly, almost reverently, the company filed onto the deck. A'stoc stood near the mainmast, resting on his Staff. Thunder rumbled in the distance, muted by the bubble of calm that surrounded them. No one spoke. They stood together, sharing the moment of peace.

Suddenly, Drup's laughter cut through the silence. It choked off quickly as the young Legionnaire realized he was the center of attention. He nudged Paun, who was standing next to him. "Tell them what you said."

The shipsage looked confused. He shrugged. "I only remarked that Wizard A'stoc would make a fine shipsage."

A'stoc slammed the Thunderwood Staff against the deck. "A *shipsage*!" he roared. Then his face softened into an easy smile. "I thank you. That is high praise, indeed. Perhaps one day we will find out if it is true."

Laughter and quiet smiles rippled through the company. The tension of the last hours melted away.

Zubec vaulted up to the wheeldeck. "Wizard A'stoc, will this wind last?"

A'stoc nodded. "The storm will continue northwest until it dissipates. The warded area will travel with it. It would be wise for us to keep the same pace."

"Agreed," Zubec said, smiling broadly. He tore through the bindings that locked down the wheel. "Raise sails, lubbers. We're going home."

Canvas unfurled and billowed full. The *Treachery* glided forward on the steady wind.

✥ 14 ✥

Tel Adartak-Skysoar

Chentelle leaned against the forward rail, basking in the warmth of Ellistar's light. The Golden Sun was hardly past zenith, but already the red glow of Deneob burned in the east. The chill wind shivered across her arms and shoulders, whispering promises of a cold autumn.

She suppressed a shudder and stared out over the bow. The vast expanse of blue water stretched into the distance, but, today, the expanse was not endless. A ridge of solid land rose defiantly on the horizon: home.

Chentelle smiled. Twenty-eight days on the Great Sea had finally brought them back to the Realm. She could feel the land calling to her, welcoming her. She longed to feel the earth under her feet once more, to hold the smell of the forest in her nostrils. She longed to be finally free of the *Treachery's* tormented planks.

She closed her eyes and imagined that she was on land already, that she was back in Lone Valley. Erina would be with her, and they would dance through the trees, playing tag with the butterflies. When they got tired, they would lie down among the autumn flowers and sing to the larks and the whippoorwills. They would sing the soft grass and the tall sky, the green wind and the gentle hill. They would sing home.

"Thank you, Chentelle."

Chentelle started, suddenly aware that she had been singing aloud. Dacius stood beside her, hands gripping the rail, tears glistening in his blue eyes.

"I could *smell* the harvest; I could feel the fire's warmth." He shook his head. "I didn't even know you had been to Norden West."

Chentelle squeezed one of his hands gently. "I haven't. I was only singing of home. The sight of land inspired me."

"Land?" He shaded his eyes and searched the horizon. "Are you sure?"

"Of course," she said. "You'll be able to see it soon."

Dacius turned and shouted to Zubec, who was manning the wheel. "Do you see it?"

"Yes, Lord Gemine," the sailor answered. "We're still too far away to make sure sighting, but that's the Westland Ridge or I'm no navigator."

"Thank the Creator," Dacius said. "How long until we reach Tel Adartak?"

Zubec gazed thoughtfully into the sky. The *Treachery* struggled forward against the north wind. "Another day at least, unless the wind turns bold. Of course, we might make it before nightfall if we had a sagewind to drive us."

"I'll go get A'stoc," Chentelle said. She did not intend to spend another night listening to the screaming wood, dreaming of axes and mutilated limbs. She dashed down the stairs and back to the wizard's cabin. The door was, of course, locked, but her persistent knocking called forth a muffled grumble.

"Hold on, hold on." The door swung open, and A'stoc glared down at her with bleary eyes. "Hel's bowels, enchantress, it's not dawn yet." He yawned extravagantly. "What do you want?"

"It is too dawn," she said, "Deneob's more than half risen. And we've sighted land. Only Zubec says we won't get there until tomorrow without a sagewind, and Paun still doesn't have a staff, so you're the only one who can do it. If you come now we can make it to Tel Adartak before nightfall, and we won't have to spend another night on board."

"What gall! So 'Captain Zubec' summons me to the deck. Once again I am pressed into service as if I were a common laborer." He stalked over to the basin and splashed fresh water onto his face. The weeks at sea had been good to him. He grew stronger with each day, standing taller, moving more resolutely. The open air and sun had banished the unhealthy pallor from his face. He had even trimmed his beard, and the stiff, gray hairs now jutted defiantly from his chin.

Chentelle shifted uneasily from foot to foot. "But—"

A'stoc silenced her with a glare. "I thought that the elves were a patient race." He wiped the water from his face and tossed the towel onto the bench. "All right, all right, tell Zubec I will be there momentarily. Just stop staring at me like that."

Chentelle smiled. "Thank you, A'stoc. Won't it be wonderful to be back on solid ground again!"

"Hah, I thought we were going to Tel Adartak-Skysoar." He grabbed the Thunderwood Staff and pressed past her and into the hallway. He marched to the stairs and slammed open the sea door with a thrust of the Staff.

"I have come," he shouted, walking stiffly toward the mainmast. He spun and faced back toward the wheel. "Once more, the apprentice of A'pon Boemarre will use the Thunderwood Staff, the True Root of the Tree of Life, to paddle your canoe upstream. Perhaps when I am finished you would like to borrow the Staff to prop up your table?"

Zubec laughed. "An excellent idea, but I fear it is too long. Perhaps you could cut it into sections for me?"

"Sacrilege!" A'stoc slammed the Staff against the deck, and Earthpower blazed around him. The *Treachery* lurched as if caught by a giant hand, then drove forward on a blast of wind from the south.

Chentelle and the Legionnaires staggered wildly. Even Zubec lost his balance, and the wheel spun wildly for a moment. Then he recovered and brought the goblinship under control.

"Full sails!" he yelled, laughter dancing behind his words. "Full sails! We'll have wine with dinner if the shipsage doesn't falter."

Chentelle steadied herself on the rail and looked at A'stoc. Power surged around the wizard, swirling and seething, but it was controlled, harnessed to the rhythm of wind and wave. He stood serenely in the center, letting it flow through the shape of his will, carrying them all gently toward land. A quiet smile rested easily on his face.

They sped northward on the strength of the sagewind. Gradually, the details of the land became clear. Zubec made minor course corrections, reacting to clues and landmarks that only he recognized. By midafternoon, the *Treachery* was sliding into the arms of a large natural harbor. Huge crystal towers rose from the projecting spurs of land, but neither beacon was lit.

"Drop sail!" Zubec shouted. "A'stoc, loose the wind!"

Earthpower faded into nothingness. Zubec held them close to the eastern spur, and they drifted forward slowly, carried by their momentum.

Chentelle stared in wonder at the tower. It was pure adartak. Even without a beacon, the crystal glowed fiercely in Deneob's light. Red flares twisted through the stone, shifting and twisting as the goblinship passed. The tower fell behind, seeming to recede more quickly the farther they traveled. That couldn't be right. Chentelle pulled her eyes away from the tower and gasped in surprise.

The harbor was huge. A crystal platform filled the center of the bay, and boats of every size and construction circled around it. A wide river pressed northward into the hills on the far side, and smaller craft bobbed in its current. The stone and brick buildings of Tel Adartak proper huddled together near the fresh water of the river, but the rolling woodlands near the shore were criss-crossed with roads and docks and sprawling warehouses. Splashes of orange and yellow told of autumn leaves already turning, and red light flashed in the center of the city.

The *Treachery* continued to drift around the edge of the bay, taking its place in the seaborne parade. The wind had died to a mere whisper, but a strong current pulled them forward. Chentelle reached out with her Gift and felt an immense power behind the tide, a great will which emanated from the crystal island. Shipsages, dozens of them, maybe hundreds, working in harmony to tame the waters of the bay. The circular current ferried ships into the waiting docks and carried them out again once their business was done, without the need for wind or oar or even a pilot.

"Incredible, isn't it?" A'stoc spread his arms, mimicking the great swirl of water. "It is called the Bay of Peace, though it had another name before the war." He pointed to the flickering glow. "Can you see Skysoar?"

Chentelle stared. As they drew nearer, she could make out the shape: a pentagonal tower, carved from adartak and much larger than the beacon houses. It shot straight up for at least five hundred cubits, then widened into a platform. A stone wall circled the platform, and the tops of tall buildings poked above its rim. The whole thing looked like a huge, symmetrical mushroom.

"You should close your mouth," A'stoc said, "before one of these gulls decides to build a nest."

Chentelle swallowed hard, searching for words. "What—I mean—how did they . . ."

The corners of his mouth twitched, though whether they smiled or grimaced was impossible to say. "Earthpower. During the war, hundreds of wizards made Tel Adartak their home, lending their power to the cause. The area was rich in crystal deposits, and my master used the Thunderwood to call it from the earth. Dwarven Crystal Masters gave it shape, and a dozen Lore Masters protected it with their strongest spells. Then Boemarre used the Staff to weave Earthpower through wards and rock alike. Skysoar is impervious to assault, and it will stand unchanged until the Creation is unmade."

Chentelle shook her head in awe. "But why? What was it used for?"

"The city was the staging area for the Realm's final offensive. The port was filled with ships, carrying troops and supplies to the massed armies. From here, we fought our way toward the Dark One's domain. Inside the safety of Skysoar, kings and warlords sent thousands to their deaths. Behind the shield of its walls, wizards played games of treachery and power. It was used for sanctuary and destruction, for glory and deceit. It was Skysoar!" He shook his head and laughed bitterly. "I am told that they call it a university now."

Chentelle tried to imagine A'stoc and his fellows marching to battle. All the strength of the Realm had been bent toward that final confrontation: wizard and soldier, human and elf, A'stoc and her father.

"Where?" she said. "Where did it happen?"

A'stoc raised a questioning eyebrow, then nodded in understanding. He pointed to a place beyond the western hills. "There. The breeding pits lay a hundred leagues from the mouth of the Rupthauh. That is where the Desecration was born, where good men died for a false hope."

The words rang in Chentelle's memory, calling forth bitter images: ashes swirling in a holocaust, abandoning the frail bones that had once been their home; screams of pain torn from the twisted earth; the taste of desolation, dusty and bitter and seasoned with guilt. These were A'stoc's, gleaned from the Staff when she had touched it with her Gift. To them was added another, a memory wholly her own: waking from nightmare; a scream echoing in ears and throat; tears burning in her eyes; and the knowledge, certain, unassailable, that her father was dead.

They watched in silence, alone in their thoughts, while the *Treachery* slid into dock on one of the long piers. Dockworkers stood by, waiting to catch lines and tie her down. They had hardly finished their task when a short, round-ish human carrying a writing board called for permission to board. Zubec nodded to his cousin, and the gangway was lowered.

"Greetings and welcome," the human recited without emotion. "You are granted permission to dock at the third pier of Eastside, and bid to avail your-selves of the hospitality of Tel Adartak. The dockmaster reserves the right to examine all cargo and expel any visitors who fail to comply with all local laws and customs. The fee for docking is five talents per sail per day with a surcharge of ten talents per hundredweight of cargo unloaded without use of local dock-workers. The docking fee shall be reduced by twenty-seven percent for ships with registry in . . ."

The monologue trailed off as the man became aware of the nature of the *Treachery* and her crew. "Is this—? Who are you? Why aren't you flying colors? This is highly irregular. Where is your registration?"

"Patience," Zubec said. "Patience, good man. You ask fast questions with long answers, answers which would be best shared over a bottle of wine in the comfort of a fine inn. For the short of it, we sail out of Norivika under the flag of the Legion, and we claim the right to free docking thereby."

"What?" the man sputtered. "Free docking! Out of the question. What will I tell the dockmaster? If you're a Legion ship, then where are your colors? And when did the Holy City start commissioning goblinships for her errands. I de-mand to see your registry. I warn you, piracy is not tolerated in these waters."

"Enough!" Dacius' deep growl cut through the conversation. In a half-dozen steps he closed the distance between himself and the official. He towered over the docking clerk, the Legion badge on his chest barely a cubit from the smaller man's face. "Here is your flag. I am Lord Dacius Gemine, Knight-Captain of Odenal, Legion Commander of the First Mark. This ship sails under my orders, and she and her crew have done service the equal of any galleass in the fleet.

You can tell the dockmaster whatever you like, but this ship and this crew are not to be bothered. Am I understood?"

"Yes, lord," the man answered quickly. He tried to bow, but was pressed too closely between Dacius and the rail, so only his head bobbed up and down. "Of course, your lordship. I'll see to it. I'll take care of everything, don't you worry." He spun about and hurried back to the dock, muttering assurances the whole way.

Chentelle found herself smiling. She almost felt sorry for the poor man.

The sea door opened and Father Marcus stepped onto the deck. He nodded to Dacius. "Thank you. I would have handled the dockmaster myself, but I do not wish to advertise my presence too broadly."

Dacius bowed slightly in acknowledgment. "I know. Now that we are here, what is your plan of action?"

"We will use today to acquire horses and supplies for the overland journey," Marcus said. "Tomorrow we ride north. But first, I shall go to the Wizard Council, to make sure that the Lore Books arrived safely. Any who do not wish to accompany me may remain here."

"No," Dacius said. "We should not become separated. This is a strange city, and we do not know the dangers."

"I appreciate your caution," the High Bishop said. "But the wizards of the Collegium have long been our allies. I will be fine. Besides, someone needs to procure supplies."

"No," A'stoc said. "Lord Gemine is correct. You trust too quickly in the constancy of children. We should all go. Besides, I, too, have business with the council."

Father Marcus sighed at the edge behind A'stoc's words, but he nodded acquiescence. "As you will. We will have to stop on our way to make travel arrangements."

Zubec suddenly cleared his throat and stepped forward. "Begging your pardon, Lord High Bishop, but Pardec and me can take care of that. We won't be going with you."

"What?" Chentelle asked, surprised. "Why not?"

The sailor met her question with a gaze full of sorrow and grief. "Captain Rone swore to carry your quest over the Great Sea and back, enchantress. Well, we're back. You need horses now, not sailors. And we have our own duties." He reached out and grabbed his cousin's hand. "When the *Otan Stin* left Inarr, she had a complement of twenty-three. A good ship, a good crew, both now swallowed by the Great Sea. Families need to be told; debts need to be paid. That was the captain's job. Now it's ours."

Raw emotion poured through Chentelle's Gift: pain, loss, love, guilt. They swept around her, carrying her forward. She crashed into Zubec, and clenched her arms around his chest. Her body shook, and tears ran freely down her face.

They stood together, locked in embrace, rocking with a shared feeling, until the storm passed.

Zubec stepped back and bowed, kissing Chentelle's hand. "I thank you, Chentelle. Once again, you bring relief from the darkness. I'd wish the blessings of the Creator upon you, but He has obviously anticipated my request."

He turned to Father Marcus. "I'll send the horses and your personal effects to the Collegium, along with the bill."

"Thank you," Marcus said. "And thank you for your service. The Creator truly smiled upon us when he guided us into your hands. Now, we should be on our way. Wait—where is A'stoc?"

"Here." The wizard stepped onto the deck. In the weeks since they had left *Kennaru* he had taken to wearing loose trousers and open shirts, but now he had once again donned his apprentice's robes. The light blue cloth hung in ragged tatters around his arms and shoulders, and only a rope belt seemed to be keeping it from disintegrating altogether. "If we are going to meet with the council, I thought that I should dress appropriately." Then, without waiting for comment, A'stoc stalked down the gangway and headed toward the city. The company scrambled quickly after, following the wizard into the streets of Tel Adartak.

Chentelle felt a surge of joy as soon as her feet hit the dock. No axe had ever bitten into this wood. Her toes tingled with renewed feeling, and it took all her self-control to keep from skipping.

A'stoc led them rapidly through a sparsely populated maze of unpaved streets and alleyways. Then they emerged suddenly onto a wide cobblestone thoroughfare. Humans and elves bustled to and fro on either side, while a wide center lane of gray stones seemed reserved for carriages and carts. Shops and inns lined the avenue, selling all manner of goods and services. A thousand odors filled the air, some familiar, some tantalizing, and some that caught bitterly in Chentelle's throat.

The road took them to the base of the hill from which the Collegium rose. As they grew close, the traffic thinned and the shops disappeared. When they entered the shadow of the city above, a chill shiver ran down Chentelle's spine. The street was still straight and true, but it seemed suddenly desolate and abandoned.

"What happened here?" she asked A'stoc.

He paused and pointed to the barren ground beside the road. "The light of the suns never shines here. No rain ever falls on this earth. It is said that the shadow of a wizard is cold, and a wise man lives not within its reach."

They followed the road until it passed through an open archway into the base of Tel Adartak-Skysoar. A metal tube hung from a pole near the entrance. A'stoc stroked the cylinder with one finger, and a clear tone rang out strongly.

"Who comes?" came a rasp of challenge from the passage. Then a withered old human shuffled toward them from the darkness. His beard hung well past his belt, and he was bent and gnarled with age, but he walked without staff or cane. His right hand was stretched out before him, and a clear crystal sphere rested in its palm. He wore robes similar to A'stoc's, but beige and in far better condition.

A'stoc stepped forward. "An initiate of the first rank, accepted into service and confirmed before the council."

"Eh?" the man said, waving the crystal in the air. "Then what is the nature of magic?"

"Earthpower is the raw state of magic," A'stoc answered, "molded by the minds of men. Fluid is the nature of power. Who shapes it, commands it. Who falters, is commanded by it."

"Ah! It is you. Well met, A'stoc, Bearer of the Tree. It is long since you have honored us with your knowledge. Enter and be welcome; you have been missed."

"Wizard A'truen." A'stoc reached out to clap the old man on the shoulder. "It is good to see you well—and still quizzing initiates on the concepts!"

"Of course," A'truen said. "I'm nowhere near ready to retire. There's a century or two left in these old bones, never you doubt it. Now, remember your manners and introduce me to your companions."

"Yes, wizard," A'stoc said solemnly.

One by one he presented the company to the gatekeeper. The old man's eyes were heavily clouded, and he squinted horribly in the dim light. But he seemed to see them all clearly enough through some property of the crystal sphere.

"Quite a collection," he said. "A strange group indeed, if I may say so. But we are honored; it is not every day that the High Bishop of Norivika comes to the Collegium, nor every century either. Enter, all of you, and be welcome. The council will surely be eager to meet with you."

"As we are eager to see them," Father Marcus said. "But tell me, please, did the Lore Books arrive safely?"

"Lore Books?" A'truen asked. "What Lore Books?"

A stricken look came over the High Bishop's face. "By the Creator, have they been lost? What could have happened?"

"Wizard A'truen." A'stoc's voice took on a quiet edge. "You are the gate-keeper. Try to remember, has a special shipment of any kind arrived from the Holy Land?"

"Of course," the old man answered. "There's nothing wrong with my mem-ory. Nearly six weeks ago, it came as a caravan of trade goods, but any fool could see that was a disguise. The Legionnaires who posed as guards would turn it over to none but the council itself."

"There is your answer." A'stoc turned to face the High Bishop. "The council has kept the Lore for themselves."

"But why?" asked Father Marcus. "Why would they keep the books from display?"

"Because they are fools!" A'stoc slammed the earth with his Staff. "Nothing has changed. They are paranoid children, still bound by the fears that doomed their masters."

"You are wrong," A'truen said evenly. "Things are not as they were when you left. I do not know what Lore you speak of, but if the council withholds it then I am sure they have a good reason."

A'stoc stared at the old wizard, amazement and disgust warring on his face. "Have you gone senile, old man? Those books hold all the Lore of my master, A'pon Boemarre, all the Lore that was lost after the war. The Dark One lives! Ill-creatures are loose in the Realm, and those covetous idiots you call a council choose to hoard the knowledge which might save us!"

"The Lore of A'pon Boemarre! Truly, this is a great gift." He pointed a crooked finger at A'stoc's face. "To that list of characteristics you bemoan as immutable, young man, you might add your own temperament. Now, if you can control yourself for a few moments, I'll take you to see the council. Then maybe we can straighten this out."

Without waiting for a response, he turned around and shuffled through the archway. The adartak here was not clear like that of the Cathedral of Light, but milky and laced with other elements. It bent and refracted the evening light, cloaking the corridor in misty gray shadows. They passed underneath a huge block of crystal that hovered above the tunnel, suspended by no visible support. In front of them, a heavy iron slab covered with glowing runes and symbols completely blocked the passage.

A'truen spoke softly on liquid syllables and tapped his sphere three times against the door. Then he blew softly, as if extinguishing a tiny flame. The door swirled and vanished like smoke from a dying candle.

The old wizard took them into a large, five-sided hall. Shafts of glowing crystal protruded from the ceiling, bathing the chamber in light. The floor was polished marble and covered with mystical wards. They entered from the center of one wall. Twin stairwells occupied the corners on either side, but A'truen ignored these and led them forward. As they moved into the center of the room, the iron door slammed into being once more.

Chentelle's feelings were mixed. The evidences of powerful magic both excited and alarmed her. So much power, to be used for good or ill: how could anyone guarantee that it would not be abused?

The corner directly across from the door was filled by a wide circular shaft. A'truen crossed to the shaft and stopped. He whispered into his crystal, and then touched the sphere to the adartak shaft. A flicker of light shot upward, disappearing through the ceiling.

Almost immediately, a steady breeze blew from the hollow tube. Soon after, a circular wooden platform drifted down to them. Two men stood on the disk. The older of them wore robes of deep brown and carried an oaken staff in the crook of his arm. The younger wore robes of light blue, the same color as A'stoc's. His staff was joined to the surface of the platform, and he was chanting steadily.

"Up you go," A'truen said after the disk settled lightly on the floor. "The council will be expecting you."

A'stoc exchanged a quick bow with the gatekeeper, and they boarded the platform. The brown-robed wizard nodded, and the apprentice resumed his chanting. The disk fluttered beneath their feet, then rose into the air.

"This is incredible," Chentelle said. There was hardly a cubit's leeway between the wood and the crystal walls, but they floated up smoothly. "Are there ever any accidents?"

"Rarely," the wizard replied. "And almost never unless an initiate is in control." He smiled briefly. "Or is not in control."

She glanced nervously at the apprentice, whose face was tense with strain.

"Do not let him frighten you," A'stoc said. "There are safeguards in place. We are perfectly safe."

Chentelle turned to the wizard, who shrugged and smiled cheerfully.

Suddenly the platform faltered and began to shake. It lurched suddenly and bumped into the wall. The apprentice cried out and lost his chant. Sweat poured from his forehead, and the staff trembled in his hands.

"Concentrate!" the Wood Lore wizard said. "There is no weight; there is only the mind."

"I—can't . . ." the apprentice gasped.

The wizard tapped the platform with his staff. Immediately, the tremors ceased. Staff and disk melded into one whole, and the wizard hummed softly. Once again, they started to float steadily upward.

The apprentice pulled his staff free of the wood and sank to his knees.

"Do not despair." The words came from the wizard, chanted in the tune and rhythm of his spell. "This is an unusually heavy load. You performed splendidly. In time, it will become easier."

The platform slowed to a halt near the top of the shaft. A small circular chamber opened before them. The walls and ceilings were milky-white crystal with hints of blue hovering like sky behind the clouds. The floor was adartak as well, but it was highly polished and glowed with soft silver light. Marble columns rose to the ceiling at regular intervals, marking the boundaries to four connecting passages.

They stepped into the room, and the platform continued its ascent without them. The brown-robed wizard waved farewell, staying with the platform and the apprentice.

Father Marcus turned to A'stoc. "Which one leads to the council?"

"All of them," the wizard answered. "But I—" He cut off suddenly, staring past the priest's shoulder.

A lone figure walked toward them, strolling down one of the corridors. He wore a robe of royal blue, trimmed with gold and shimmering like fine silk. He had lean, angular features, and his jet-black hair and beard were meticulously trimmed. He stopped a few paces away, glaring at A'stoc with dark eyes. "So, it is indeed the apprentice A'stoc. I thought that I sensed the presence of our master's weapon."

A'stoc drew himself to his full height. His mouth curled in disgust. "It has been long years since we served the same master, A'valman. Perhaps you remember the occasion of our parting. It was the day you betrayed your father's trust, the day he banished you from his service."

A hard breath hissed between A'valman's lips. "I see that time has not dulled the barbs of your tongue, nor has it taught you wisdom in where to apply them. But then, recognizing the wisdom of another was never a trait your master valued. How nice that such folly lives on in his chosen successor. I am certain that he would be pleased."

"How sad," A'stoc sneered. "All these years and still you are not worshiped for your sagacity. And you wear blue! I am shocked. I expected the purple at least, if not the key. Can it be that your fellows, too, share the folly of not endorsing your brilliance?"

A'valman smiled and bowed mockingly. "Ignorance will ever be heard. The council knows you are here. Report to the chamber immediately." He spun about sharply and returned the way he came.

"Who was that?" Chentelle asked.

She received no answer. A'stoc was already striding forward, choosing the passage opposite the one A'valman had taken. He took them through a series of winding passages before coming at last to a spiral stairway. They climbed upward and emerged into an open courtyard.

A blanket of thick grass covered the ground, crisscrossed by a meandering stone walkway. Trees and hedges had been planted in seemingly random patterns and locations. Three sides of the park were surrounded by tall buildings and towers, gracefully sculpted from marble and granite. The fourth was bounded by the high wall which ringed the upper city. A'stoc led them through the park, heading back in the direction from which they had come. He was obviously choosing a circuitous route to the council hall.

They passed through an archway that seemed carved from solid mist and turned immediately onto a small side street. The evening light was fading, but enough remained to mark their party for something strange and exotic. Men and women stopped their business to follow the party with their eyes, and curious whispers followed them. Chentelle was surprised to note that most of the people they saw seemed like ordinary townsfolk. Only a few wore the colored robes of the Collegium.

A'stoc pushed through an iridescent gate and came to a halt in a neatly kept garden. A domed tower loomed before them, easily the tallest building in the city. "Wait here. I will see the council alone."

"No!" Chentelle protested. "Don't go alone. There's something strange happening here. I don't trust them."

"She is correct." Father Marcus laid a hand gently on the wizard's shoulder. "I am certain that the council remains our ally, but until we understand the situation more fully, caution is warranted."

"I agree," Dacius said. "You should not go without protection."

A'stoc laughed. "Lord Gemine, inside that building are the greatest mages left to the Realm. If they wish me harm, then your sword will make little difference in the issue."

Dacius stiffened, but Father Marcus stepped in before he could answer.

"Nevertheless, I, too, have reason to address the council. I will go with you."

"And I," Chentelle said. "You may need me to keep you from getting into trouble."

Sulmar stepped forward beside his mistress, saying all that he needed to with his posture.

A'stoc stared at them angrily. Then his eyes focused briefly on Chentelle, and their hue seemed to shift. "All right, all right." He tossed his arms in disgust. "We four, but no more. The rest stay here."

Father Marcus unslung the small pack from his shoulder and handed it to Gorin. "Keep this for me, brother. I will return for it shortly."

The goblin did not need to ask what was in the pack. They all knew what it contained: the Sphere of Ohmn.

A'stoc led the way into the tower. They passed through an antechamber decorated with murals drawn from the elven histories. Double doors of gilded iron dominated the far wall. Two men wearing beige robes flanked the doors. As the party approached, each man made a sharp motion with one hand. The doors swung open noiselessly. They were expected.

They entered a small amphitheater, though it could have doubled as an arena. Five high walls surrounded them, surmounted by tiers of long benches. In the center of the room was a plain stone table, flanked by three wooden chairs. Beyond that, nestled into the apex of the pentagon, a C-shaped table rose above them on a marble pedestal. Five high-backed chairs faced the table. Four of them were occupied.

On one end sat an elven woman with silver hair bound in an intricate braid. Beside her was a dwarf wearing a headdress of twined gold and rubies.

The center chair held a balding human; a simple wooden key hung from a leatherbark thong around his neck. The fourth chair was empty, and the fifth held A'valman.

The wizard smiled at the shock on A'stoc's face. "As you can see, we have altered the colors since your last visit. The council wears blue, now, to remind us of humility."

"Order." The human in the center chair rose to his feet. "I am A'rullen, First Chair of the Collegium. We extend welcome to the Bearer of the Thunderwood and his companions." He turned to Father Marcus and bowed deeply. "And we are honored to receive the High Bishop of Norivika. I regret only that we did not have the notice to prepare a fitting reception. Please, be seated. I will send for another chair."

"That will not be necessary." A'stoc placed one foot on a chair and stepped onto the stone table. He planted the Staff by his side and glared at the council, his eyes now on a level with theirs.

Chentelle hesitated. She turned to Father Marcus, but the priest seemed as taken aback as herself. She shrugged. The table was large enough. She climbed up and took a place next to the wizard.

The High Bishop smiled and pulled one of the chairs to the side of the table. He sat down casually, as if settling into his favorite reading lounge. Sulmar remained standing on the floor, ready to catch Chentelle if she fell.

A'rullen cocked an eyebrow but said nothing. A tubular bell sat on the table in front of him. He stroked it with one finger, sending a clear tone ringing through the hall. "This council is seated. We formally express our gratitude to A'stoc, Bearer of the Tree, for the incomparable store of knowledge he has given us. The Lore Books of A'pon Boemarre will save us a thou—"

A'stoc slammed the Staff near his foot. Tiny fissures appeared in the stone, but the table held. "Why do you keep the books secret? Why has the knowledge not been shared with the Collegium body?"

A'valman started to speak, but the First Chair silenced him with a gesture. "We are copying the books even now, but there are concerns of safety. The council has voted to delay open distribution until the Lore can be examined and the more hazardous—"

"No!" Again the Staff slammed down, shaking loose a shower of gravel from the bottom of the table. "The power is not yours to hoard! The Lore is for everyone. It must be; we do not have time for your paranoid games. Display the books immediately—without censorship, or I will denounce this council as corrupt!"

"How dare you?" A'valman jumped to his feet, tipping his chair over backward. "Do you see, A'rullen? It is as I told you. He is consumed by rage and bitterness. He does not deserve to—"

"Hold your tongue!" A'stoc was shaking with anger. Flickers of green flame danced along the surface of the Staff. "By the blood of our master I—"

"Fool! You'll never—"

"A'stoc!" Chentelle felt rocked with the throb of Earthpower, barely contained beneath the wizard's fury.

"Ssssuuhh."

It was a whisper, barely audible, impossible to ignore. It washed through her like a mountain stream: cold, shocking, lucid. Her flesh tingled and emptiness echoed in her mind. The room fell silent.

A'rullen leaned forward, one hand still clutched around his wooden key. "There will be order," he said softly. "Councilor A'valman, you will not speak until recognized by this chair. A'stoc, outrage is understandable, violence is not. Am I to understand that the distribution of the Lore Books is the problem that brings you here?"

"Among other concerns."

Councilor A'rullen sat back in his chair and stared at his steepled fingers. The other councilors shifted in their seats, but no one spoke.

Finally, A'rullen broke the silence. "Is it fair to characterize the gift of the Lore Books as a bequest contingent upon our making the knowledge freely available within the Collegium?"

"And without," A'stoc said gravely. "The knowledge is not to be restricted in any way."

A'rullen nodded. "It shall be as you desire."

Chentelle could feel the tension rise, see it in the hard stares and clenched throats of the other councilors.

A'rullen reached out and tapped the bell, but no sound came forth.

"I must protest," the dwarf said suddenly. "The council has already voted on this matter."

"We voted," A'rullen said gently, "on the disposition of what we thought was an outright grant of knowledge. But as you have just heard, we were mistaken. The Lore is ours to administer only so long as we comply with the conditions of the bequest. Do any present wish to make a motion that we reject the strictures and return the books to Norivika?"

Silence.

"Then it is settled. We will follow A'stoc's wishes. The books will be available to the public, restrictions placed on access only to protect the material itself."

"If you do not mind," A'stoc said. "I would like my *wish* to be enacted immediately."

"Of course," A'rullen said. "I will make the arrangements personally. Now, I wish to make a request."

Again, the other councilors bristled. Chentelle felt a stab of bitterness and resentment. It echoed through her Gift, filling the chamber with bile. The source was unmistakable; A'valman quivered on the edge of explosion. But the target was less clear: A'stoc, A'rullen, someone else entirely? She couldn't be sure.

"What do you want?" A'stoc asked sternly.

"Your help," A'rullen answered. "For many years we have been trying to gain access to the laboratory at Covenant's Keep. We know that a stockpile of vorpal weapons are inside. Now, thanks to your discovery, we have begun to hope that the knowledge of A'kalendane is also preserved within. We excavated to the level of the vault without problem, but there is a powerful forbidding upon the workshop itself. It has defied all attempts at penetration."

"The Lore of A'kalendane," A'stoc whispered.

Chentelle heard the passion in his voice, a tremor of excitement, even awe. A'kalendane was a legend, a sorcerer as famous as A'pon Boemarre and perhaps more powerful. It was A'kalendane who first learned the secret of Earthpower, A'kalendane who harnessed that knowledge into the vorpal Lore, A'kalendane whose forges armed the Realm when the darkness seemed unstoppable. But he had perished during the war, his workshop consumed by the Desecration Fault. Could the knowledge really have survived?

"Tell me more," A'stoc said.

But A'rullen only ran his finger along the bell.

A'valman rose to his feet at the silent signal. "I protest this action. You place the power to crack continents in the hands of a neurotic failure. Look at him. Already he is strained beyond his capacity. No man should bear the weight he carries, but do we act to ease his burden? No, you suggest that we make it even greater. This is madness. I demand a poll of the chairs."

A'rullen nodded and stroked the bell once more. The metal rang out clearly, filling the hall with a two-note harmonic. "The vote is called. Shall we ask A'stoc to attempt the opening of Covenant's Keep?"

The female elf stood. "I am A'hemlin, the Fifth Chair. I say yes."

"I am A'valman, the Fourth Chair. I say no."

"I am A'grimmel," the dwarf said, "the Third Chair. I say no."

A'rullen stood. "The Second Chair is absent. A'trile does not sit. I take his voice. I am A'rullen, the First Chair. I say yes."

He turned to A'stoc. "The issue is decided. The Council asks you—I ask you—will you go to Covenant's Keep?"

A'stoc turned to A'valman. For long seconds their eyes locked in an icy glare. Then a slow smile spread across A'stoc's face. "I would be honored to help you."

"No!" Father Marcus jumped to his feet. "A'stoc, you must not. We have to—we have to be on our way."

He turned to face the council table. "I am sorry. A'stoc cannot help you. We are on a quest of utmost urgency, and he is under my charge. Perhaps he can return when our mission is complete, but I cannot permit this to delay us."

Chentelle felt A'stoc's ire rise at the priest's words. "Wait. He didn't mean to—"

But it was too late.

"Bishop! I am a free man. I have chosen to follow you thus far, but mark this clearly. If you balk me before this council, I will follow no more!"

Chentelle gasped. Could he really mean that? Without the Staff, Marcus had no way to activate the Sphere of Ohnn. The evil of the Fallen Star would spread and Infinitera would be destroyed.

"Gentlemen, please." A'rullen's calm voice drifted through the tension. "The question has been asked, but it need not be answered in haste. There are obviously issues that you need to decide among yourselves. I suggest we all retire to consider the matter in private. The Guesting House has been prepared for you. Do you remember the way, A'stoc?"

"I do."

"Excellent." He tapped the bell, and a clear note resounded through the hall. "This council is concluded."

❧

The Guesting House was luxurious, designed to make comfort not only possible but inevitable. The common room was filled with plush carpets and soft pillows. Couches and lounges were arranged meticulously around soothing plants and delicate sculptures. Murals of exquisite beauty graced the walls, and a fresh breeze was funneled through the doors to the terrace. Nevertheless, none of the company was relaxed.

"Why?" Father Marcus' voice trembled with barely contained emotion. "Why is this so important? You jeopardize everything."

"Did you not hear A'rullen? There are vorpal weapons in Covenant's Keep, and only I can unbar the door."

"He's right, High Bishop," Gerruth said. "The Legion needs those weapons."

"All the weapons in the world will not help us if the Fallen Star is not destroyed." His eyes searched the wizard's face. "But that is not the true reason, is it?"

A'stoc spun away from the priest's gaze. "Enough! My reasons are none of your concern. The decision is made. I will go."

"A'stoc." Chentelle reached a hand toward the wizard, not trying to touch him, just letting him see it. "Please, we aren't trying to make this harder for you. We know how angry you are. We see it, feel it, but we don't understand it. What did A'valman do that makes spiting him so important? Why do you hate him so?"

The wizard hovered on the edge of decision for a moment; then he turned away.

Chentelle let her hand fall to her side. She turned to Father Marcus, but the priest's eyes held no answers either.

"A'valman was Boemarre's chief apprentice," A'stoc said without turning around. "He was also his son. When Boemarre decided to harvest the Tree of Life and create the Thunderwood Staff, A'valman opposed him. He argued that the Staff was too powerful to be controlled, that it was a weapon too great for man to own. He accused his father of hubris, of coveting the Staff only for his own aggrandizement. But his words only served to strengthen Boemarre's resolve.

"A'valman refused to accept his father's decision. He went to Norivika and pleaded his case directly to Serdonis, Father Marcus' predecessor. He tried to convince the High Bishop that the risk was too great, that Boemarre was unfit to be given access to the Tree. He failed, but by trying he betrayed his oath as apprentice and his duty as a son. When Boemarre learned of this treachery, he exiled A'valman from his service, banished him from his family.

"I do not know where he went after that. But I know that his heart turned bitter. When I returned to Tel Adartak-Skysoar after the final battle, he was waiting for me. He tried to usurp the power of the council and seize the Staff. When I learned of his plans, I fled the city. I have no proof that the assassins who followed me were acting under his orders, but I have no doubt, either."

The wizard turned around. His face seemed calm, emotionless. But the resolution behind his eyes was unmistakable.

Father Marcus nodded. "Where is this keep?"

"To the west, within the Desecration Fault."

The priest sighed. "It is not the direction I was hoping to take, but it is not the worst. Very well, we will go to Covenant's Keep, but only long enough for the vault to be opened. After that we must return to the quest."

"Agreed."

As if on cue, there was a knock, and Councilor A'rullen walked through the door of the common room. The old wizard carried an ebony walking cane, but his steps were sure and steady. In his left hand, he carried a bundle of wrapped cloth. He set the package on a table and bowed respectfully, first to Father Marcus and then to A'stoc. "Welcome to Tel Adartak-Skysoar. I trust the quarters are adequate?"

"More than adequate," Father Marcus replied. "Please, make yourself comfortable."

"Thank you." A'rullen whispered a command and tapped his cane against the floor. The stick melded into the stone and stood upright. Then the wizard lowered himself onto one of the lounges. "Ah, that's better. When I was young, I thought paradise was a soft couch and a loving woman. I was half right . . ."

The wizard spoke on, making pleasant conversation, but Chentelle's attention was drawn to the cane. The air around it seemed to spark and swirl, churning with something just beyond the threshold of vision. She closed her eyes and let her awareness flow into the Gift.

Power swirled around the polished wood. It radiated waves of distortion, pulsing and swirling through the room. It made everything hazy, indistinct. She extended the Gift toward A'rullen, but it was like trying to catch hold of a shadow. The same was true when she reached for A'stoc or Father Marcus. The spell that flowed from the cane interfered with magical perception, even her own.

A sudden tone of urgency behind A'rullen's words pulled her attention back to the conversation.

". . . you decided to answer?"

"We will travel to Covenant's Keep," Father Marcus said. "But we will stay only long enough for A'stoc to attempt the spell of forbidding. We will be prepared to leave in the morning."

"Excellent; I have already made arrangements for an escort." A'rullen paused. "It is obvious that you have urgent concerns of your own. I thank you for taking the time to assist us. Perhaps there is a way I may return the favor."

"No," Father Marcus said gently. "This burden is one we must bear alone. Your own task lies in the Lore Books."

"Yes." A'rullen turned to A'stoc. "I can't tell you what a blessing your arrival has been. Not only for the task you undertake now, but also for giving me the opportunity to open the books of Boemarre to the public."

"Why did you not act before?" A'stoc asked, suspicion heavy in his voice.

"I could not. The whole of the council was against me. They could not see beyond their fears and suspicion. Skysoar lost much to the necromancers during the war, and the old mistrusts are still strong. But that's the very reason why we must share our knowledge openly. How else will we recover what was lost?" A'rullen paused and breathed deeply, calming himself. "They do not understand. Only your arrival gave me the leverage I needed to free the books."

"Then it is lucky I came when I did." The expression on A'stoc's face softened slightly, but the edge remained in his voice. "Now, what can you tell me of A'kalendane's vault."

"Wizard A'trile is in charge of the excavation. He has managed to locate the workshop and clear the tunnels to its door, but the forbidding still blocks us."

"A'trile?" A'stoc said. "The old hermit? But his specialty is Wood Lore. Why was he researching A'kalendane's Lore?"

"He has grown fluent in both schools. Only A'valman is his superior in Metal Lore. A'trile had seniority, so I placed the excavation under his care. I felt he was more—reliable." A look of concern settled on A'rullen's face. "But now I am worried. A'trile has been neglecting his responsibilities, missing council meetings. At first, I assumed that he was absorbed in his research, but now I fear that his health is suffering."

"Has he been seen by a healer?" Father Marcus asked.

"No," A'rullen said. "A'trile can be quite—independent. But I am going to see him tonight. I need to be sure he can travel with us tomorrow."

"I will come with you," Father Marcus announced, "if you do not object. Perhaps he will let me attend to his needs. It will be best if all our strength is bent to this errand."

"Well said, Your Eminence. Cooperation is our hope in these times. Let us go." He stood and retrieved his cane. Halfway to the door he stopped and spun about. He picked up the cloth bundle from the table and tossed it to A'stoc. "I almost forgot. I thought that you could use some new robes. Your present ones have seen hard service."

A'stoc looked down at the tatters he was wearing and grinned. He tore open the package and froze, stunned by its contents. Moving slowly, he pulled forth a robe of deep brown, its edges trimmed with golden embroidery—the robe of a Wood Lore Master. He stared at A'rullen, saying nothing.

"I hope I have not offended," the councilor said. "I thought that these would be more appropriate for the Bearer of the Thunderwood."

"No," A'stoc said quickly. "I am not offended, but I have not undergone the trial. I am not yet a wizard, much less a master."

A'rullen flicked his cane toward the Staff which never left A'stoc's hands. "You command the most powerful magic on the face of Infinitera. No Lore Master alive has accomplished the channeling of Earthpower. Only you have done that. We are not what we once were. Our magic is but the shadow of our Master's, but you have given us the means to regain what was lost. You tell me that you have not stood the trial, but I say there is more than one test of a man."

A'rullen grabbed the fabric of his own robe. "We no longer wear the purple on the Council. Some people say this is to remind us that we are less than our predecessors. They are wrong. We choose the openness of the sky rather than the exalted seclusion of royalty, but we are the wizards of Tel Adartak-Skysoar. There are none better. The First Chair of the Collegium names you Master. Who shall say otherwise?"

A'stoc bowed deeply. "Thank you."

A'rullen smiled. "You are welcome. It is long overdue." He turned to Father Marcus. "Shall we go?"

"One moment." Dacius gestured, and Leth and Gerruth moved to flank the High Bishop. "You shall have an escort."

The company had hardly settled into their seats after Marcus and A'rullen left when the door to the common room opened once more—this time without a knock.

"A'stoc." Councilor A'valman stood stiffly at the threshold. "I must speak with you. Alone."

The two wizards locked eyes, and a predatory smile spread slowly across A'stoc's face. "I—"

"A'stoc," Chentelle said softly. "I will not leave you alone with this man." She braced her ears for his outburst, but none came.

A'stoc only nodded and smiled more broadly. "If you wish to speak, *councilor*, then speak. Neither I nor my companions answer to your beck. Be thankful. Their presence greatly enhances your safety."

A'valman's body quivered with tension, but his voice remained calm. "As you will. I have come to warn you. Do not go to Covenant's Keep, and do not stay in Tel Adartak-Skysoar. Whatever mission guides you, follow it—tonight."

"Do you think to frighten me, A'valman, to chase me away from you precious little fiefdom?" A'stoc laughed coldly. "Do not worry, councilor, I have no interest in your place in the Collegium. You have your status; enjoy it— while you can."

"Fool!" A'valman nearly spat the word. "This is no game, A'stoc. We are not children, anymore, wrestling for my father's attention. There are evil forces working within the Collegium. The Staff is in danger as long as you remain!"

"Evil?" A'stoc's eyes grew wide in mocking amazement. "*Surely*, you are mistaken. No one here would try to wrest the Staff from its rightful owner. No one here would send assassins to stalk me in the night. But I thank you for the warning." Suddenly, all humor vanished from A'stoc's face. He planted the Staff against the floor, and thunder echoed behind his voice. "Have no doubts. Whatever comes this night, I will be prepared."

"Will you?" A'valman said, scowling in disgust. "You rage against shadows a half century gone and ignore the peril that surrounds you. Have you forgotten all caution? Look at your companions: a spawn of the Heresiarchs, a Tengarian with darkness woven into his very soul, even the High Bishop is touched by evil!"

"That isn't fair!" Chentelle stepped between the wizards. "You don't know anything about Sulmar or Brother Gorin. And how dare you slander the High Bishop of Norivika. You should be—uhhn."

A shaft of pain drove into Chentelle's mind. She staggered and fell to her knees, clutching her head.

"What is it?" A'stoc's words sounded faint and distant. "Damn you, A'valman. If this is your—"

"Wizard A'stoc!" Gorin's deep rumble cut through the room. "A'valman is not the source. There is Ill-Lore being used, very near."

"What? Are you certain? There is magic all around us."

"No," Chentelle said. "Gorin is right." Her pain had vanished as suddenly as it came, but the memory of it was still vivid. "Something terrible is happening."

"Where?" A'stoc said. "Can you locate the source?"

"I cannot," Brother Gorin said. "I sense only that it is near."

Chentelle concentrated on the echo of her pain. If she could track along it, follow it back to the source . . . But everything was so hazy. Spells and shadows swirled in her mind, writhing around each other, obscuring the trail. "I'm sorry. It's too faint."

"Everyone find cover." Dacius' sword flashed from its sheath. A pale blue glow shone faintly from the blade. "Legionnaires, ready bows. Sulmar, watch the terrace."

"Wait! Goblin, elf-girl, come here." A'valman reached into his robes and pulled out four golden bracelets. He muttered a brief incantation and tossed them into the air. The rings formed a diamond and hung in the air, spinning slowly. "Quickly, cast your thoughts into the center, between the rings."

Chentelle stared at the pattern. A tiny pinprick of light marked the center of the diamond. She reached into it with her Gift, and the light surrounded her. All was whiteness, and yet she was somehow aware that the rings were spinning much faster, now. She heard—no, felt A'valman chant another spell. The syllables vibrated through her world, casting shadows in the brilliance.

The shadows thickened and took on substance—a room, filled with books and cluttered shelves. Father Marcus was there. The priest stood absolutely still, his mouth hanging open in an expression of horror or surprise. A small, wrinkled old human paced before him, waving a long wand of twisted bone. He seemed to be carrying on a one-sided conversation with Father Marcus. Suddenly, he froze. He turned and looked straight at Chentelle. His eyes gleamed with reflected light, and his thin lips twisted into an evil smile. The bone wand shot out, scratching across the High Bishop's face.

Chentelle screamed. Her mind was ripped open, and a river of agony poured through her body, searing every nerve. Her muscles convulsed wildly, throwing her to the ground. She writhed helplessly, unable to breathe, unable to speak. A faint whimper quivered past her lips, but in her mind, in her mind she was screaming.

This time, the pain did not fade. The eyes burned through her soul, seeing every secret, fouling every dream. There was no escape from the eyes, no relief. She would carry them with her forever, and they would destroy her. Already, they taunted her with whispers of despair, whispers that found echoes within her own heart.

You are weak. Soon, you will do anything to end the pain. You will betray all that you serve, all that you love. And even then you will not be free.

If she could have spoken, she would have begged to die. But there was no death. There was only pain and fear and the eyes that never blinked.

Peace.

Chentelle floated in unending anguish. Deep in her spirit, she struggled to keep an ember of hope alive. She had to hold on. Her friends would rescue her, A'stoc or Father Marcus. She had to hold on. Help would come. But soon, Blessed Creator, let it be soon. A dull pain caused a brief ripple in the torment, and she realized that her body had just hit the ground. Hardly a second had passed since the eyes first touched her.

Peace.

A second! One second! It was hopeless. She could never endure. The pain was all. She would surrender to it, let it wash her soul away. It was so easy. She just had to let go, to open herself to the exquisite agony of the glowing eyes. It was easy. But something held her back. A single note that refused to blend into the song of pain.

Peace.

Sanctuary! She felt it—the hymn of sanctuary. Brother Gorin was trying to reach her. She hurled herself toward the sound. The pain closed around her, filling her mind with screams and fire. But she felt the rhythm now. She poured her will into the Gift, pressing it through the anguish.

Contact! Instantly, the harmony of the sanctuary enfolded her. She was lying on the floor, her head cradled in Sulmar's arms. Brother Gorin knelt beside her, chanting steadily, and A'stoc was crouched above them. The expression on his face was unreadable.

The pain was gone, banished by the peace of the Holy Order. But the memory remained. Tears streamed down her cheeks, and she could not stop trembling. The specter of those horrible eyes loomed in her mind. She grabbed Gorin and hugged him tightly. "Thank you. Blessed Creator, thank you so much."

"Enchantress?" Dacius touched her shoulder gently. "I'm sorry, Chentelle, but I have to know what happened. Did you find the source of the Ill-Lore."

"You didn't see?" Chentelle scrambled to her feet, struggling to make her body work. "We have to hurry. Father Marcus is being tortured."

Dacius turned to A'valman. "A'trile's house! Where is it?"

"Follow me." A'valman spun around and ran for the door. The four golden rings clattered to the ground behind him.

A'valman led them on a mad dash through the dark streets. Chentelle's legs were still unsteady, and even with Sulmar's assistance, she fell quickly behind. Luckily the Legionnaires' vorpal swords were glowing steadily. The blue light gave them an easy trail to follow.

After a short run, the procession of blades stopped before a tall tower. Chentelle could see the open grass of the park lying just beyond. Angry shouts drifted back to Chentelle and Sulmar. As they caught up to the party, Earth-power flared around A'stoc's Staff.

The wizard stepped forward and slammed the Thunderwood against the entrance to the tower. The metal doors burst inward, tearing loose from their hinges. Dust and rubble billowed from the broken archway.

Shouts of alarm sounded inside the tower, and there was the scrap of steel weapons being drawn.

"Move!"

Dacius charged through the opening, Drup and Thildemar following close at his flanks. All three held swords leveled and ready. Six eyes searched the darkness for enemies.

There was a scream, and a blur of light slashed through the dimness, arcing toward Dacius's head.

The human lord parried. Steel on steel as he turned the blow. His arm whipped around for a counterthrust, and he froze. "Gerruth!"

"Lord Gemine!" The elf's eyes widened in shock. He stared at his glowing sword. "But the vorpal—"

"Quickly, where is Father Marcus?"

"In the study with Councilor A'trile." Gerruth pointed toward the stairs. "They wanted to speak in—"

Dacius was already moving. He bolted up the stairs. Leth emerged from cover, holding an arrow nocked in his bow and a look of confusion on his face. Dacius ran past, motioning for him to follow.

Chentelle's steps were becoming surer, and she hardly lagged at all as they wound their way up the narrow stairs. Hollow cackling rang in her ears an instant before she emerged into a dusty chamber, the chamber she had seen through the rings.

"Stay where you are!" The voice was parched and grating like a desert wind. Across the room, the withered old man from her vision stared down Legionnaires and wizards alike. His twisted wand waved in the air, barely a cubit away from Father Marcus' throat. The High Bishop stood motionless, frozen in the same posture she had seen before. "He dies at your first attack!"

"Stand easy. No sudden moves." Dacius slid slowly to his left, keeping his voice calm. "It doesn't have to happen like this, Councilor A'trile."

"A'trile!" The old man laughed evilly. His skin began to bubble and melt. Flesh fell from his body and dissolved into ash, revealing a hideous caricature of life. Dull white skin was stretched taut over a human skeleton, every contour of bone visible beneath the thin covering. Pale yellow eyes glowed viciously from empty sockets. "Fool! I am Bone—Bone the necromancer, Bone the Dragon Lord, Bone the immortal."

The wand flicked in Bone's hand. Lightning danced through Father Marcus' body, glowing in his eyes and the hollow of his mouth. "You have one minute to leave this house. One second longer, and I boil the blood in his veins."

"I think not." Green fire blazed into life as A'stoc raised the Staff. "Look around you, Ill-creature. You have no escape. Release the High Bishop or suffer the consequences."

More laughter. "So confident! Does my hostage mean nothing? Perhaps I need another."

The eyes swept through the party, searching, finding. They drove into Chentelle's mind, piercing her, swallowing her. Her body moved forward, walking quickly across the room to stand next to the necromancer.

No! She fought back, driving her will against the eyes. She tried to stop her feet, flail her arms, anything. But it was no use. She was trapped, helpless to control her own body.

"Chentelle?" The Earthpower flickered and went out.

"Mistress!" Sulmar jumped forward, vorpal sword twitching in his hand. He crouched in the center of the room, muscles tensed for an explosion of action.

"Ah, the Tengarian." Bone grinned, thin lips drawing back to reveal toothless bone. "Have a care, lackey. Your mistress survives only at my whim."

Chentelle wanted to cry out, to tell Sulmar not to hold back. Instead, her body moved behind Bone and opened a door that led to more stairs.

"This is absurd." A'valman stepped forward. A five-pointed metal throwing blade glowed fiercely in his hand. He gestured, and the weapon hovered in the air, spinning fiercely. "Release them or die."

"Tengarian!" Bone hissed. "Protect your mistress."

Sulmar lashed out. His knuckle bounced off of A'valman's temple. The Councilor and his vorpal star hit the ground together. Continuing the motion, Sulmar pivoted and drove the edge of his hand into A'stoc's neck. The surprised wizard crumpled slowly to the floor.

"Sulmar!" Dacius spun on the Tengarian. The other Legionnaires spread out beside him. "Don't be a fool, man. He won't release them."

"But I will," said Bone. "The girl, at least. She is of no use to me. Now, since you would not leave, I guess we shall have to." He inched toward the door, pulling Father Marcus with him. "But first, bring me that pretty stick, Tengarian. I think I shall add it to my collection."

"No." The deep growl echoed through the small chamber. All eyes turned as Brother Gorin threw back his cowl and marched forward.

"The goblin!" Bone cackled. "Will you stop me, then, little priest? Do you think your faith will prevail where the master of your Order has failed?"

"No." Gorin raised his hand, and lightning blazed from his fingers. Ill-Lore! The goblin had called upon the Lore of the Heresiarchs!

Bone was caught by surprise. Gorin's barrage drove him backward into the wall and the wand fell from his fingers.

Chentelle staggered as the eyes released her. Almost instantly, strong arms wrapped around her, and Sulmar pulled her away from the battle.

Gorin and the newcromancer were locked in struggle. The little priest pushed forward, driven by rage and desperation. Lightning surrounded him, flashing from eyes and claws and gleaming fangs. Bone countered with a shield of glowing white. The goblin's assault rebounded from it, tearing through the study. Desks shattered. Books burst into flame. Great gouges ripped through the floor, filling the air with stone shrapnel.

The Legionnaires hovered near the edge of the combat, unable to approach. The field of destruction had one gap, a small circle of peace surrounding the frozen form of Father Marcus, but that was unreachable.

Slowly, Gorin drove forward. Cracks began to appear in Bone's shield. The necromancer cowered backward, pulling his wards in closer.

Gorin pressed his advantage. Ill-Lore screamed through his body, crashing against Bone's will in wave after wave of rage and power. The shield splintered and started to flicker. Gorin reached forward with a crackling claw.

Suddenly, Bone opened one hand. The wand leaped from the stones behind him and flew to his grasp. His arm shot forward, and the twisted bone stabbed into Gorin's skull.

Gorin's skeleton shattered at the touch. Splinters drove outward, ripping through flesh and skins. The priest didn't even have time to scream. He fell to the floor, brain and heart pierced with a thousand needles of bone. The shape of the corpse was only vaguely recognizable.

"Enough!" Green flames roared into life behind her. "Legionnaires, stand aside."

A'stoc! But hadn't Sulmar knocked him unconscious? Out of the corner of her eye, she saw the Tengarian smile. She realized that Sulmar must have pulled his blow, to deceive Bone.

The necromancer bolted up the stairs, rounding the corner barely ahead of a jet of green flame.

"After him!" Dacius ran for the stairs, and then jumped backward. A sheet of crackling fire sprang into life, blocking the passage. The human staggered back into the study, driven from the oppressive heat.

A'stoc waved the Staff. A cool green glow floated toward the stairs. It enveloped the flames, surrounding and smothering. The green flashed brightly and disappeared. A'stoc moved forward and froze in midstep. The flames were still there.

Heat drove through the room, pressing steadily against their faces. Chentelle stared at the flickering flames. Something wasn't right. Maybe magical fires gave perfectly even heat, but she had never noticed it before. She reached out with her Gift, searching for the flame. Searching, searching, but finding nothing.

Then she realized. "It's an illusion! There's nothing there."

"Of course! No wonder the counterspell failed." A'stoc marched forward, passing through the flames and continuing up the stairs.

Chentelle and the others hurried after.

They climbed to the top floor of the tower. An ornate wooden door lay open before them. Beyond it was a bedroom, furnished with ascetic simplicity. Glass doors on the far wall revealed Bone, standing on the rail of a narrow balcony.

The necromancer's arms were raised into the air, but he spun about when they entered the room. "Too late, fools!" He sprang backward, hanging in the air for an instant, then plummeting downward.

They ran to the balcony and looked over the edge. The ground was more than thirty cubits below, but Bone danced on the ground, unharmed.

"Your quest is doomed!" he called. "We will meet again, and I will destroy you all!"

A shadow passed above them, blacker than the night. It floated toward the park, gliding on leathery wings and coming to rest in a clearing between trees. The sinewy body was covered in dark scales and at least forty cubits in length. The long neck tapered to a thin, earless head, and the beaked mouth looked large enough to swallow a horse in one bite.

"KALIYAAAAA!" Sulmar backed into the bedroom, then ran forward. He leaped, planted a foot on the ledge, and hurled himself off the balcony. He flew through the air and crashed into the limbs of a tall birch. He bounced and rolled and tumbled through the leaves, landing on the ground in a loose tuck.

The vorpal blade had been twisted from his grip, and it fell to the ground next to him. Ignoring it, he drew his black sword and charged for the clearing.

Bone was already aboard the dragon's back. He pointed with his wand, and a stream of raw power shot toward the Tengarian.

Sulmar dived to the side, barely avoiding the magical bolt. He rolled to his feet and started running again, but the dragon was already lifting into the air.

"NOOO!" The Tengarian hurled his sword at the dragon. The blade spun through the air, spinning slowly end over end. It passed beneath the dragon's belly and fell, plunging into the soft dirt of the garden.

Flames blazed along the length of the Thunderwood. A'stoc took aim at the flying beast, then reconsidered. The Earthpower faded as he pulled out his *mandril* wand instead. A jet of hot flame shot from the wand and sizzled against the dragon's wing.

The beast's only response was to dip its long neck and open its mouth. Vile liquid sprayed from its maw, arcing toward the company.

A'stoc jumped backward, using the Staff to push Chentelle and the Legionnaires into the bedroom.

Dark acid splashed on the balcony behind them. It hissed and bubbled. The stone terrace disintegrated and tumbled to the ground.

Far above them, hollow laughter faded into the distance.

❧ 15 ❧

WESTLANDS

Father Marcus lay motionless in the bed where they had placed him. Chentelle put a hand on his forehead. Nothing. For two days, the High Bishop had remained motionless, unresponsive to the touch of hand and Gift. His eyes and mouth were closed only because the local healer had shut them for him.

"I don't know whether you can hear me. You may not even know Gorin is dead. He sacrificed himself for you, you know, for the hope and the faith you inspire. He believed in you. We all do. We need you to come back to us, to lead us." She sat on the bed and placed a white flower into the priest's hand. "I planted some of these over Gorin's grave, but I saved this one. I thought you might like to have it. We buried him today. I wish you could have been there. Gorin would have wanted you there.

"We didn't know what kind of funeral he wanted, but we did the best we could. The local priest performed the ceremony. Then, each of them said good-bye in their own fashion. Sulmar performed a Tengarian ritual, reciting a poem and mixing some of his blood with the grave. Even A'stoc said something." Chentelle felt her tears coming again. That was all right. Gorin deserved them. "Leth and Gerruth told stories about playing quickbones and matching riddles. I hadn't even known Gorin did those things. I think that was the saddest part, realizing how much I still had to learn about him.

"Thildemar composed a song, telling about his bravery and compassion, about his great deeds and his part in the quest. I sang a song, too, only mine didn't have words. I just tried to sing what I felt. Would you like to hear it?"

Chentelle wiped a tear from her eye and brushed it across her mouth. The salt and sorrow mingled in her lips, and she sang. Her voice was low, soft, but strong and steady. It was Brother Gorin, daring everything to follow the path of his faith. The solitude of an exile, the rapture of a prophet, the courage of a martyr, the serenity of a good man: these things and more found life in her requiem.

For an instant, she thought she felt a tremor of response from Father Marcus. Had he moved? She couldn't be sure. She kept singing, pouring every part of her grief and love into the song. The Gift swelled within her, laying every part of her bare to the music. She sang emotion. She sang need. She sang until her voice cracked and her lungs strained for air.

Finally, she could maintain it no more. She slid to the floor, resting her head on the bed. Her shoulders trembled with sobbing, though her tears were long since exhausted. Though her voice was gone, the Gift was still strong within her. It reached into Father Marcus, desperately reaching for any sign of contact.

Nothing.

⮞

The common room was empty when Chentelle came down the stairs. Dacius apparently had the Legionnaires drilling again. He had been pressing them hard since the necromancer's attack, seeing danger behind every shadow. She didn't know where A'stoc was; probably meeting with A'rullen again or checking on the Lore Books. Sulmar's whereabouts were less of a mystery. He spent every free moment reliving the battle.

Chentelle walked into the street and turned down the lane to the park. The streets were busy, but people moved quickly out of her path as she neared. Stories of dragons and Ill-creatures had made them all objects of fear and suspicion. She passed the locked tower that had been A'trile's. The rubble of the fallen balcony had been cleared, but the rear of the tower was scored deeply from the dragon's bile. She crossed through a line of trees and caught sight of Sulmar.

The Tengarian stood in the clearing, on the very spot the dragon had landed. His heavy breaths misted in the cold air, and sweat poured down his face. He had torn the right sleeve off of his shirt, and the dragon brand writhed darkly on his arm. Suddenly, he flipped his sword into his left hand and raised it above his head. The blade swung down, heading straight for his right arm.

"No!" Chentelle dashed forward, but she knew she would be too late.

The ebony blade sliced easily into the Tengarian's arm, but it did not cut. The dark steel merged with the dragon's mark, becoming part of the same blackness. Sulmar dropped to his knees. His back arched, and thick muscles bunched in his arms and chest. A war of shadows played out on his flesh, mirroring the dark magic that coursed through his body. A guttural scream tore from his throat, and blood trickled down his left arm.

Darkness flashed, and Sulmar's arms were thrown apart. The black sword flew from his grasp, landing in the grass more than thirty cubits away. He fell backward, arms spread wide and legs bent awkwardly beneath him.

"Sulmar!" Chentelle dropped to his side. She tugged at his legs, straightening them to protect his joints. The Tengarian neither helped nor hindered her. His eyes had rolled backward, showing nothing but white, and his breath was ragged. She folded his arms in by his side and gasped.

The brand was growing! The dragon mark swelled before her eyes, writhing upward to cover the Tengarian's shoulder. The dragon's eyes seemed alive, and she heard a faint hissing.

Sulmar jolted awake. He sat upright, knocking Chentelle backward. By the time she regained her balance, he was standing again. And the black brand had shrunk to its normal size.

"Sulmar, what's happening?"

"Your pardon, mistress. I must retrieve my sword." Without waiting for an answer he turned and jogged toward his fallen blade.

Chentelle wanted to scream. He had been like this ever since the dragon appeared: sullen, uncommunicative. The solid presence that she had come to rely on was suddenly gone, and she felt alone and vulnerable. Worse than that, she knew that Sulmar was suffering. His unflappable calm was shattered. More often than not, when she looked at him she surprised a face set in bitterness or rage. She had to do something.

Sulmar hadn't returned. Instead, he had returned to his exercises in the spot where his sword landed. She walked over and stepped directly in front of him.

The Tengarian's eyes widened in alarm. His left arm shot across and grabbed his right wrist, stopping his stroke an instant before it sliced through Chentelle's neck.

"Liegeman!" Chentelle poured every tone of command she could muster into her voice. "Do you seek to break your Oath with me?"

Agony showed in the Tengarian's eyes. The sword fell from his hands and he dropped to his knees. He bowed forward, touching his head to the ground. "Mistress, I am unworthy. I—I abandoned your side, left you in danger."

Good. He was talking at least. But he was still holding something back. "Why, Sulmar? What made you attack the dragon?"

"I have no excuse, mistress."

She put the edge back into her voice. "I did not ask for an excuse, liegeman. I asked for an explanation."

"Yes, mistress." He fell silent again, and Chentelle was afraid she had pushed too hard. Then he continued. "The beast—it was Kaliya, mistress, the dragon whose curse I bear. Our fates are tied. If I do not destroy her with my own hand, with this blade, forged from the darkness of the beast's own heart, then I am doomed. When I saw the dragon, I—I lost my discipline. I failed you."

"Stand up." Chentelle let her tone soften. She could feel Sulmar's emotional dam opening. When he was on his feet, she reached up and turned his face to hers. "Look at me. I am not dead. I am not hurt. I am here, and I'm worried about my friend. Now, tell me what will happen if you can't break the curse."

"If I die while wearing Kaliya's mark," he said, "my soul will become hers. I will be resurrected as a shade and serve the dragon for all eternity."

"By the Creator." Visions flashed in her memory. Sulmar battling the vikhor with his bare hands. Sulmar wading through a score of goblins. Sulmar pitting steel against magic in the demonspawn's lair. How many times had he risked damnation to save her life? How many times? "You should have told me! This is too much. I release you from your vow. You mustn't—"

"Mistress!" He dropped to his knees again. "Please, Lady Chentelle, do not banish me. You are my hope, my destiny. I have no other direction. Your path brought me to the Black Dragon once. It will do so again. Please, mistress, let me stay. I will not fail again."

"You didn't fail the first time!" It was horrible. How could she ask him to risk his soul? How could she let him? But how could she deny the need in his voice? She wanted to run away, to let somebody else decide. She reached down and grabbed Sulmar's arm. "Stand up. I won't send you away. You are still my liegeman. But I do not want you to protect me to the death. Do you understand? I order you not to trade your life for mine."

"Yes, mistress."

Chentelle looked into Sulmar's eyes, eyes full of strength and serenity, and she knew he was lying. She sighed. "Just be careful, please. I don't want to lose you."

"Yes, mistress."

Well, maybe that would help. Perhaps the dragon would not return. She turned and started walking down the stone path. The solid presence of her liegeman fell into place behind her.

She walked aimlessly, following the winding path. It brought her to a set of stairs. She followed them and found herself walking along the top of the outer wall. The wind whipped through her dress, but she didn't feel cold. She saw a pair of figures up ahead. It was A'stoc, his silhouette was unmistakable, and one of the Legionnaires—Drup.

She stopped a short distance away from them. "Wait here, Sulmar. I need to talk to A'stoc, and that's usually easier if I can get him alone."

"Yes, mistress." Sulmar's tone was flat. If he sensed the hidden motive in her request, he gave no sign.

A'stoc turned as she approached. "Is there news?"

"No," she said. "Nobody sent me to find you. I didn't even know you were here. This just seemed like a good place to walk."

He smiled and turned back to the wall. "I have always liked the view from this spot. It makes all of my troubles seem small—and all of my efforts."

Chentelle leaned out over the crenellations. The city of Tel Adartak spread beneath them, filled with the motion of tiny figures. Autumn leaves turned the surrounding hills into a brilliant tapestry, stretching to water. In the center of the bay, Pilot's Island shone with all the colors of the rainbow. Beyond that, the Great Sea stretched toward infinity.

"It's breathtaking," she said.

"I see that you have regained your shadow." The wizard nodded toward Sulmar. "Drup has been my own, today. Lord Gemine will not hear of my person being left undefended."

The young Legionnaire bowed to her. He smiled, and the light of Ellistar twinkled in his eyes. "I am glad you're here. The wizard has been foul company. He seems to fear that I may be hiding a slim ray of optimism."

"If you did not want to hear the answer," A'stoc growled, "then you should not have asked the question."

Drup laughed cheerfully. "We were talking about the necromancer. I made the mistake of observing how lucky we were that he didn't destroy the Lore Books when he had the chance."

Chentelle looked at A'stoc curiously. "Isn't that good?"

"Of course it is. The question is why." He nodded toward Drup. "As I was explaining to this simpleton, the only reason he would have spared the Lore is if it was not a threat to his master's plans. As A'trile, he had full access to the books."

"But he would have risked detection," Drup said. "And the books can be replaced with new copies."

"In time," said A'stoc. "But our efforts would have been set back by several months. No, he did not act because he knows that it will take years before we decipher enough of the Lore to shift the balance of power. And he knows that we do not have years."

The young elf's face became suddenly sober. "What will happen when the war comes? Can we stand?"

A'stoc met the Legionnaire's eyes. When he spoke, his voice had lost all hint of mockery. "If it came today—no. Nor if it comes soon. We need more time to gather strength. And the Dark One knows this, thanks to Bone's masquerade. I do not think he will wait."

Determination etched in Drup's face. He clapped his hand on the hilt of his vorpal blade. "He will find at least one sword ready."

"I do not doubt it," A'stoc said. "But how many more? Ten? Twenty? A thousand would not be too many. We need the weapons from A'kalendane's vault."

Chentelle heard the note of finality in his voice. "What are you saying?"

"I have spoken to A'rullen," he answered. "We leave tomorrow for Covenant's Keep."

"But you can't." Chentelle turned to Drup for support, but saw that he agreed with the wizard. "What about the quest? We can't leave until Father Marcus recovers."

"And when will that be?" A'stoc said. "We cannot afford to wait. The Dark One's forces are in motion. If the High Bishop recovers before I return, the rest of you can meet me at the vault. If not, then we will be in the same position, and the Legion will have a new treasure of weapons."

His words rang with certainty. Chentelle turned away from him, trying to understand the chaos in her thoughts. The world was spinning beneath her. She was lost. Sulmar's words echoed in her mind: *You are my hope, my destiny.* But what was *her* destiny? He was risking his soul to follow her, and she was stumbling around blindly.

"Do not worry, enchantress." A'stoc's voice held a note of concern. "I am not abandoning the quest. But we can go no further until Father Marcus recovers. In the meantime, this is something I must do. It is part of my own quest."

"I know," she said. "It isn't that. I know that you have to go. But—I just found out that Sulmar's soul will be lost if he dies while protecting me. I tried to send him away, but he wouldn't go. He believes I will lead him to his destiny. But how can I let him risk his soul for me? I ordered him not to trade his life for mine, but I don't think he listened."

"Of course not," A'stoc said. "His Oath will not let him place his life above yours, no matter what the consequences."

"But what if he dies?" Chentelle struggled to control her voice. "He's following me because I'm his liege, but I don't even know where I'm going. You have your own quests. The Legionnaires have their duty. But why am I here? I haven't had the Dream since I left Lone Valley. What if my part is over? Sulmar could forfeit his soul because I didn't know it was time to go home!"

"You are correct." All softness had vanished from the wizard's voice. "You should go home. Whatever hope this quest had fell with Father Marcus. Your part is done. Go home. We will destroy the Dark One, or we will fall. There is nothing you can do which will alter that fact."

"That isn't fair, wizard." Drup laid a comforting hand on her shoulder. "Do not underestimate yourself, Chentelle. You have proven your worth more—"

"Stay out of this, soldier!" A'stoc's gray eyes flashed with anger. "You risk a life and a soul with your prattle." He spun around and marched for the stairs. "I must prepare for the journey. If you remember your *duty*, you will follow."

Drup froze for a moment, shocked at A'stoc's outburst. He turned to Chentelle and shrugged. Then he scrambled after the wizard.

Chentelle stared out over the city. Maybe she *should* go home. After all, what was really keeping her here?

Chentelle and Sulmar walked into the middle of an argument. The Legionnaires had returned to the common room, and Dacius was squared off with A'stoc.

"—the risk!" The human lord's beard bristled, hardly a cubit from A'stoc's face. "I can't guarantee your safety."

"I am not asking for your protection," A'stoc said coldly. "Or for your permission. I am leaving in the morning for Covenant's Keep. That is not an issue for discussion."

Dacius threw up his arms in exasperation. "Creator save me from wizards and fools! Fine, you're going. Then I'm going, too. I won't have the Staff unguarded. Thildemar, you're in charge here. If the High Bishop wakes up and can travel, meet us at the keep. Otherwise, wait for our return."

"Lord Gemine?" Drup stepped forward, his eyes resolute. "I would like to accompany you."

Dacius paused, searching the young elf's face. "Permission granted. Anyone else?"

Leth and Gerruth stayed silent. A different determination burned in their eyes—they would not fail the High Bishop again.

"Sulmar and I will go," Chentelle said.

Dacius nodded, as he had expected as much, but A'stoc's head snapped around in surprise.

Chentelle smiled at him. "I still don't know what my part in this quest is, but Infinitera is my world, too. If there's any way to save her, I'll do what I can. If there isn't, I'll still do what I can."

"Fine," A'stoc said stiffly. "But you should stay in Skysoar. This mission is no part of the quest."

"No," she said. "But you are. My first part in the quest was to ensure that you, the Staff, and Father Marcus were safely united. Perhaps I will get to play that role again."

"Hel's bones, am I suddenly a child, unable to find his way home? Fine. We leave at dawn." The wizard stomped out of the common room.

Deneob's first-light found them gathered at the foot of the tower. The dawn shattered against the adartak, filling the crystal with an inferno of warm red light.

Chentelle shut her eyes, letting the heat wash over her. A slight tremor tickled the bottom of her feet. "They're coming."

"Are you sure?" A'stoc shaded his eyes and squinted into the east. "About time. I told A'rullen dawn."

Chentelle smiled, remembering a time when he had been less anxious to get an early start. The vibrations grew stronger, and now she could hear the clatter of hooves falling on stone. They would soon be in sight.

"There," Drup said, pointing down the east road. Twin columns of riders approached, each a dozen horses long. Most of the horsemen were soldiers, a mixture of men and elves all wearing the black and tan of Tel Adartak's Legion garrison. With them were two riders who wore the blue and gold robes of the council.

Two? One would be A'rullen, but who was the second? She turned to look at A'stoc and saw the tension in his jaw and brow. Of course, the First Chair had said that A'valman was the best they had for Metal Lore. With A'trile lost, they had to bring him.

She sighed. It might be a very long trip.

The riders came to a halt a dozen paces away. A'rullen and one of the soldiers detached from the group, leading a string of unladen horses. They pulled up in front of A'stoc and dismounted.

"Wizard A'stoc," A'rullen said, "honored friends, allow me to introduce Commander Kruzel. He and his men will be escorting us to the keep."

The tall human rested easily on his saddle, as though he would rather sit there than on the softest couch. Auburn curls showed from beneath his metal cap, mingling with thick muttonchops and a heavy mustache. Deep lines surrounded his eyes, though he did not seem old. He bowed to A'stoc and saluted Lord Gemine. "I am honored to have you share our road."

"I fail to see why we use the road at all," A'stoc said. "It is a hundred leagues to Covenant's Keep. We would make better time by ship."

Kruzel shook his head. "Closer to ninety, master wizard, if you'll excuse my saying so. And we have relay stations every five leagues from here to Sylvandale. If the weather holds, we'll make the keep in three days. There's not a barge floating that could wind her way up the river in less than four, and we'd still have to ride the last leg."

"A relay system?" Dacius said. "Can it handle a company so large? Normally they're only used for messengers."

"Aye, and so it was with this one. But during the war it was used for fast transfer of wizards and healers. The way houses were reinstated when Covenant's Keep became an interest." He motioned to the line of riderless horses. "Now, if your concerns are satisfied?"

A'stoc grunted, and they each chose a mount.

Chentelle went to a chestnut mare, not very tall but proud and graceful. She whispered softly into the horse's ear, telling her what she needed and how happy she was to have such a beautiful guide and companion for the road.

The mare nuzzled her cheek and neighed softly in greeting.

"Thank you. It's a pleasure to meet you, too, Gloriful." She stroked the mare's neck gently. Her hand drifted back to the saddle. It was beautiful—leatherbark, soft and light and worked as delicately as any she had ever seen. She would never have guessed to find such a treasure on an unclaimed Legion horse. Tel Adartak obviously had vigorous trade with the elves in Sylvandale.

"Does she have to wear this?" she asked Commander Kruzel. "It doesn't really bother her, but she would rather run naked."

The human looked at her curiously. "We have a long road ahead, lady elf, and we will be riding hard."

"All the more reason to make her comfortable," said Chentelle. "Don't you think?"

Kruzel laughed easily. "Aye, and no doubt you'll surprise me again ere we part. Leave the saddle by the gate. Old A'truen will guard it for our return." He spun his horse about and galloped back to his men.

As soon as Chentelle was ready, the troop moved forward at a trot. Kruzel signaled, and the garrison cavalry divided into two squads of eight. The first squad stayed at the head of the column, riding just behind their commander. The second veered off and came back into line behind Chentelle and the others. In that formation, they rode westward into the streets of Tel Adartak.

Kruzel kept their pace moderate as they moved through the city proper. They held to the center lane, swerving only to dodge the occasional cart or wagon. Luckily, the crowd was still thin. By the time Deneob was full above the horizon, they had reached the Rupthauh.

Waiting barges ferried them quickly across the river. The west bank was only sparsely settled, and the road lay clear before them. Kruzel shouted and urged his mount to a canter.

They rode into the western hills, following a wide dirt trail that had been hardened by heavy traffic. Despite the thick trees and rolling terrain, the path held to a true course. Deneob's heat remained at their backs all the way to the first relay station.

They pulled in at a two-story brick building flanked by a large stable. They paused only long enough for the men to shift their saddles onto the fresh horses. Then Commander Kruzel spurred them forward again. Chentelle had barely had time to exchange greetings with her new mount, a gray gelding named Silk.

They kept a hard pace all through the morning, trading horses twice more. Sometime after noon, they forded a trickle of stream with the grandiose name of the Shane River and came to the village of Thyan. Passing through a seemingly random scatter of thatch-roofed houses, they arrived at the square stockade of a small Legion garrison. This time, Kruzel granted them a half hour to visit the mess and stretch their legs. Then it was back to the road.

Twice more they traded horses, stopping no longer than was absolutely necessary. At the last station, Kruzel inspected them all carefully, weighing their condition against some timetable that only he knew. The men were exhausted, legs and backs aching from hours in the saddle. Even Chentelle felt the strain, though she rode lightly and was buoyed by the joy of communing with her mounts. But it was the wizards who suffered most. A'stoc and A'valman were both rigidly pale, seemingly held in the saddle only by their mutual determination not to fail before the other. Amazingly, A'rullen looked stronger than either of them. The old councilor leaned heavily on his saddle horn, but there was iron in his eyes and a smile on his face.

Without a word, Kruzel mounted and started for the road. He pressed the horses hard, alternating between a walk and a canter. Even so, Deneob started to creep below the horizon before they caught sight of the next station.

"Playtime's over," Kruzel shouted. "Now we ride!"

He kicked his horse into a gallop, and the party lurched forward after him. They raced westward, trying to catch the sun.

Chentelle rocked with Tanglehair's powerful gait. The roan gelding soared beneath her, hammering the ground with ironshod hooves, and she hummed into his ear, echoing the song of his speed. Froth gathered around the horse's mouth, and his breath formed hot clouds in the evening air. But the proud beast showed no signs of slowing. Instead, he ran faster, drawing strength from the song.

One by one, he drove by his stablemates, giving them his dust. They bristled at his passing, summoning all of their strength and speed. But none could match him. He worked his way steadily to the front of the herd, where Silverhoof ran carrying the tall human with the curled mane.

The stallion's nostrils flared in challenge, and he bolted forward. For long moments, the two horses ran side by side. The red sun disappeared behind the far pasture, and still they raced. The herdmaster had the strength of legends. His sire could outrun the west wind, and he, himself, had never been beaten. But today he faced Tanglehair, whose strength was the mountains and whose teeth flashed like lightning. Gradually, the stallion fell behind.

The gelding cried out in exultation, but Chentelle realized that it was Kruzel who had slowed the stallion—a wooden palisade was visible just over the rise, illuminated at each corner by sheltered beacons. She coaxed the gelding into a slow walk. "Easy, friend. Easy. Don't be too proud. The next day might belong to him."

Tanglehair tossed his head and started to prance beneath her, but his muscles suddenly quivered with the strain of his efforts. He blew his lips in confusion, his mood suddenly subdued.

Chentelle rubbed his neck gently. "That's all right, boy, you were wonderful. It was a race for the legends."

"It was indeed!" Kruzel reined the stallion in beside them. His cheeks were flushed and his eyes sparkled in the twilight. "I never dreamed the gelding could run so fast, nor be ridden so well. Truly, you are a creature of surprises."

Chentelle shrugged. "It isn't anything hard. I just let him carry me."

A rumbling of hooves heralded the approach of another rider. Sulmar. The Tengarian crouched low in the saddle, yelling encouragement in the ear of a dappled mare. He pulled up when he saw her, and the grateful mare relaxed into a trembling walk. "Mistress! Are you well? This horse would go no faster."

"Oh, Sulmar, I'm sorry. I just got carried away."

"Ho!" Kruzel said. "She speaks truly, warrior. Grant her no blame, for she was merely carried while the beast ran." He stood up in his stirrups, watching the rest of the company appear, still riding in formation. "Sound off!"

The two squads reported in sequence. Then Dacius answered for himself, Drup, and the wizards.

"Well done, men. You've earned your rest tonight." He pointed toward the flickering lights of the outpost. "Welcome to Goodnight. We won't be here long."

ఞ

Chentelle settled into a cot between Sulmar and A'stoc. Loud snoring already rumbled from the wizard's blankets. Like most of the company, he had chosen immediate sleep over the option of a light supper. The cook had promised them all that a sturdy breakfast would be waiting for them at dawn.

Sulmar sat on his cot. Weariness showed in his bloodshot eyes and the slackness of his mouth, but his posture was rigid and alert.

"Relax," Chentelle said. "You need sleep, too. We're in a barracks full of Legionnaires with three of the strongest mages in the world. How much safer could we be?"

"Powerful companions offer little protection while they sleep," he said. "We will be safer with a watch."

"There is a watch," she said. "They're outside on the walls where they're needed. Now, you may not need sleep, but I do. And I'm not going to get any until I see you lie down and close your eyes for at least five minutes. So, unless you want me to be dangerously tired for tomorrow's ride, you'll stop arguing, lie down, and *get some sleep.*"

He paused, searching her face impassively, then stretched out on the cot and closed his eyes.

Chentelle watched him closely. His body slowly relaxed, and his breathing became deeper and slower. His folded hands slipped apart and slid down to his side. Good! She covered him carefully with a light blanket and settled down into her own bed. Sleep came almost immediately.

When she woke, Sulmar was sitting on his cot, watching over her. He looked fresh and alert, but his eyes were redder than they had been the night before.

The breakfast was waiting as promised, and they devoured it with unfettered abandon. Their new mounts had already been prepared, and they were on the road before the winter sun had cleared the horizon.

They rode through the morning, changing horses once. Kruzel was setting an easier pace, today, for which most of the company was quietly grateful. For much of the day, they had been able to see the bulk of a great forest in their path, and they reached its border well before noon. Thick trees formed a canopy over the road, covering everything in deep shadow.

Mossenmauve. A tingle of excitement shivered along Chentelle's spine. Willow had told her stories about the great forest. It was older and more powerful than the forests of the east, full of terrible secrets and enchanting mystery. It was whispered that the lifelms here had sprung from the first seeds of the Creation.

The road narrowed and twisted as soon as it entered the forest, forcing them into a single file. Commander Kruzel called for his standard bearer to unfurl the colors and move to the front of the column. The crossed swords banner of the Legion led the way as they rode into the darkness.

Chentelle felt the life of the forest surround her. Birds and insects filled her ears in a hundred songs, some familiar, some strange. Elm, maple, tangle oak, walnut: the trees sang to her heart with their soft music. The branches closed in around her, brushing her face with leaves, tugging playfully at her clothes. It was glorious. So much like Lone Valley, yet so different. Memories of home rose within her, and she felt like laughing and crying all at once.

"You may pass, Commander Kruzel." An elven Legionnaire dressed in deep green and brown emerged from the trees and saluted. He waited until they were by, then hooted in the fashion of a barred owl. The call was echoed many times from the trees farther along the path.

Thick brambles closed in about the trail, making sure they kept to the path. Chentelle could feel the presence of lifelms nearby. They were entering the heart of the forest.

Lifelms. They called to Chentelle with a voice only elves could hear, traveling along a bond that the word 'friendship' could never hold. Lifelms, the final stage of the dendrifauns' cycle, when they rooted themselves deeply into the Creation. Lifelms, the heart and spirit of an elven forest. They provided shelter, concealment, and the leatherbark that was so useful to her people. But most of all, they provided memory. The tales of the people, the history of the wood, the lineages of the families, all of these were preserved in the minds of the great trees. Where the lifelms grew, there was home.

The path deposited them suddenly into a wide glade. Soft grass spread before them, mingled with an explosion of wildflowers. Three trails led out of the clearing, one of which continued in the same direction they had been riding. Kruzel ignored that one, turning to the north without hesitation.

The new trail wound tortuously through the thick brush and then ended in a thick wall of thorns. Again, Kruzel didn't hesitate. He spurred his stallion forward, pushing through the bramble with ease. The rest of the company followed.

Chentelle stared in amazement. The wicked-looking thorns were actually soft as down. And the dense mass which had seemed so impenetrable was hardly six cubits thick. The leaves tickled her as she passed, and she laughed with delight.

They came to a second clearing. This one was dominated by a huge structure. Vines and branches had been woven together with *rillandef* and *rillanmor* to form a large Earthhall. Several horses and a burro were hitched to posts outside the hall, and the company added their own mounts to the total.

"Stay close," Chentelle said to Rainbow. "You can graze, but don't go far."

Every elven community kept one large building on the forest floor. It was used as a common hall for large gatherings and as a guest hall for visitors uncomfortable in the heights. Chentelle pushed through the door and was immediately wrapped by the smells of roasting nuts, fresh bread, and pipe smoke. Her eyes watered, but it wasn't because of the smoke. It was just like home.

A dozen faces turned toward them as they entered the Earthhall. Most were elven, though there were a few human traders gathered at one end of a long table. A smiling young boy of about a hundred greeted them and showed them to the kitchen. Commander Kruzel excused himself, but the rest of the company happily filled bowls from the wide selection of nuts, breads, fruits, and vegetables. When they returned to the common room the size of the crowd had more than doubled.

Most of the attention was focused on Drup and Chentelle. Legionnaires and wizards were commonplace, especially since Covenant's Keep had been uncovered. But it was a rare thing for an elf from Endaleof to come to Mossenmauve, and no one remembered the last time they had a visitor from Lone Valley.

She fielded questions while she ate, telling her hosts about home: the way the grass felt between her toes, the color of the sky at midnight, the shapes of the leaves on the great trees. They knew, of course, about the excavation, but they wondered how she had become involved. She needed to be careful there; Father Marcus had stressed the need for secrecy. She told them that she was traveling with Wizard A'stoc, who had come to check on the Lore Books.

Of course, that only started a new round of questions. What Lore Books? Was this the same A'stoc who had fought in the Wizards' War? Why was she traveling with him? Was she his apprentice? How many girls were in Lone Valley? (That from the boy who had shown them the kitchen.)

Chentelle turned to A'stoc for help, but the wizard was suddenly fascinated by the contents of his bowl and didn't see her. She was beginning to give up hope when the door to the hall swung open, drawing everyone's attention.

"Everyone's full," Kruzel called from the doorway. "We're moving out."

To their surprise, there were no fresh horses waiting outside. In fact, there were no horses at all other than the few that had been here when they arrived. Kruzel walked to the rear of the Earthhall, motioning for them to follow. He pushed through a narrow gap in the vines and into another clearing.

Chentelle gasped. The clearing was dominated by a huge lifelm, the greatest she had ever seen. A trunk more than forty cubits around climbed into the air. She couldn't see how tall it was because the limbs formed a canopy so dense it blocked out the sky. Roots thicker than a lesser tree's trunk drove into the earth, digging into the very foundation of the Creation.

Kruzel walked toward the tree and started walking up its trunk. He didn't climb using handgrips and footholds. He walked. Knots and bumps spiraled up the lifelm's bark, forming a set of steps as even as any human mason could carve. There was no railing, but a sturdy limb always seemed to be in reach, as if by an act of providence.

A *rillanmor* master could have formed such a stairway, encouraging the tree to shape its growth to his design. But Chentelle knew that wasn't the case. This was the Heart Tree of Sylvandale—it could be no other. It had shaped itself to satisfy the needs of its people.

She placed a reverent hand against the warm bark. "Greetings, honored one. I am Chentelle of Lone Valley."

Greetings, Chentelle of Lone Valley. Mirabel and Ettiene named me Crookhollow when we shared together the tales of Mossenmauve. To their grandchildren's grandchildren I am Sylvanhart. What will you call me?

Chentelle felt herself being pulled into the slow song of the wood. The rhythm drew her deep into the earth, through soil and rock and rivers that knew nothing of the suns. She suckled Earthpower from the heart of the Creation and it sent her soaring into the sky. She climbed past oak and elm, looked down upon the eagle in flight, spread her limbs over the peaks of tall mountains. Her fingers touched the vault of the sky, and she held hands with the Sphere of Perfection.

"Yggdrasil."

Your touch is strong, Chentelle of Lone Valley. It echoes deep in my roots and whispers through my smallest leaves. But it reaches further than your understanding. The name you choose belongs to one far older than I, though perhaps I could carry it until you find its rightful owner.

Chentelle felt like a child again, finding all the wrong answers to Willow's questions. "I'm sorry. I don't know where that name came from."

No, but perhaps you will find out. And you need make no apologies. It is a pleasure to share a story again with one who bears the Gift. But our time is drawing short, and there is an important question that you still have to ask me.

"A question?"

Yes, Chentelle of Lone Valley. You must ask. Then I will answer, for I know many things. My roots stretch beneath all the forests of Infinitera, and my leaves hear the stories of the wind. Anything that walks or crawls or flies through any forest is known to me. Now, our stories part. There is only time for your question.

What should she ask? She had a hundred questions, but which one was the right one? It had to be related to the quest. She could ask about the Fallen Star! No, Father Marcus said that was from beyond the Creation. She had to ask something the Heart Tree would know, something about forests and elves and dendrifauns. What would Willow ask if she were here? No, that wouldn't work. She'd just ask how to tell an old story or—

"Mistress—"

Something tugged at Chentelle's attention, pulling her away from the lifelm. It wasn't fair! She needed more time.

"—where is Fizzfaldt?"

I do not kno . . .

"Mistress, can you hear me?" Sulmar was shaking her shoulder gently.

"NO!" Idiot. What was she thinking? One of the oldest and wisest creatures on Infinitera grants her an answer, and what does she ask? Idiot. She didn't even get a good answer.

She pushed off Sulmar's hand and threw herself against the lifelm. "Ygg-drasil! Sylvanhart! Crookhollow!"

There was no answer.

"Mistress?"

"What!" Immediately, she wished she could take the word back.

Sulmar jerked away as if she had slapped him. No, that wasn't right. He wouldn't have moved at all if she had hit him.

"I'm sorry," she said. "I'm sorry. It isn't you, Sulmar. It's myself that I'm mad at."

"I did not wish to disturb you, mistress, but Commander Kruzel refused to delay for more than two hours."

"Two hours?" Chentelle looked to the sky but saw only the dense forest canopy.

"Yes, mistress. Not even A'stoc could talk him into more." He pointed to the stairs. "They are waiting for us at the river."

Chentelle let herself be led up the trunk and into the elvenhome. Distracted as she was, the beauty of it still touched her. Masters of *rillanmor* had guided the growth of the city, mapping it out with graceful curves and intricate balances of shape and void. Flowers and songbirds were cultivated and arranged to yield complementary patterns in sound and fragrance. Not a leaf rustled in the wind without adding to the aesthetic harmony of Sylvandale.

To her left, the soft scent of honeysuckle was reinforced by delicate red veins on the underside of broad leaves. The whole effect was enhanced by—

"This way."

Sulmar guided her down a *rillanmor* stairway and onto a long ramp. The ramp took them to the shore of a wide river where four barges were waiting. The first held the councilors and most of the Legionnaires from Tel Adartak, while each of the others carried eight horses and a keeper. Three figures stood waiting at the edge of the dock: A'stoc, Dacius, and Drup.

Chentelle and Sulmar ran down the dock, and the five companions scrambled aboard the barge together. An instant later, all four barges cast off and headed downriver.

"Are you all right?" A'stoc asked. Had Chentelle not been distracted, she might have noted his unusual concern.

"I'm fine," she said. "I had a conversation with the Heart Tree. To me, it only seemed to last a minute. I think I had the chance to learn something important."

The wizard's eyes locked on to hers, and his voice dropped to a whisper. "What happened?"

Chentelle's face reddened at the memory. She turned away from him, shaking her head. "I guessed the wrong name and asked the wrong question."

"I have lost count of the number of times I have done that," he said. Then, remembering himself, he resolved his features into their habitual frown.

There wasn't anything else to say, so Chentelle wandered toward the front of the barge. The pilot was there, deep in the meditation of sagecraft. And Kruzel was there, too, staring intently into the depths.

Kruzel looked up at her approach. "Ah, Lady Chentelle. I am glad that you were able to join us."

"Were you worried?"

"Aye," he said. "But not for you. I have called the elves of Sylvandale friend for more than half my life. They told me you were well, so you were well. I worried because every moment we delayed made our voyage more perilous."

"Perilous?" Chentelle stared curiously at the slow-moving river.

"Don't let her fool you," Kruzel said. "The Silverflow may look tame here, close to her home, but she becomes treacherous farther on—full of rocks and rapids and swirling currents. She's hard enough to manage in the daylight. Only a fool dares her at night. I had hoped to make the outpost at Tranquillity tonight, but if darkness comes we shall have to camp in the open."

They left it unsaid that night in the open might be just as dangerous. No one had forgotten Bone.

ॐ

The Silverflow narrowed as they moved westward, becoming deeper, swifter, less placid. It turned toward the north and merged with another river, which the dwarves had ironically named Tranquil. Large rocks jutted from the river bottom, some lying just below the surface. These were joined by jagged cliffs which rose from both banks, looming above them like the teeth of some giant beast.

Their pilot was pushed to his limit, now. He chanted furiously, his sagestaff locked in unity with the planks of the barge. He kept them close to the south bank most of the time, drifting farther out into the current only when absolutely necessary.

The other boats followed his path so closely that they might almost have been trying to float on the same water, and their faith was soon proven. The rocky coast gradually gave way to forested hills, and they encountered fewer and less dangerous boulders in the river. They had made it safely through the rapids.

Commander Kruzel stared at the red disk of Deneob, already hanging low in the western sky. "We aren't going to make it," he announced. "Pilot, there's a bridge up ahead that marks the Old Westland Road. Put ashore there; we'll have to finish the trip overland."

"I know it, commander," the pilot answered. "It's just around this—By the Creator!"

A mass of rubble blocked the river just in front of them. The bridge had collapsed. The barge lurched to the side, narrowly missing a huge granite slab. Chentelle was thrown sideways and slammed into the rail. The boat spun wildly in the current, and water washed over the side. Chentelle's feet were swept out from under her, and she slipped to the deck. She grabbed on to a railing support and clutched it as hard as she could. Her legs dangled over the side, twisted and tossed by the cold current.

A strong arm reached under her waist and pulled her back to the deck. "Mistress, are you hurt?"

"No," she said. "I'm fine, Sulmar. Thank you."

The craft steadied as the pilot managed to regain control and guide them to the west shore. They grounded softly on the narrow.

The second barge wasn't so lucky. Its pilot hadn't seen the rubble until it was too late. The wooden craft split in two against the rocks. Horses and boatmen alike were thrown to the mercy of the Silverflow. Luckily, they were close to the west bank. Mounts and men alike managed to scramble to the safety of the shore.

The last two barges put in to shore without incident, warned by the screams of their predecessors.

"Blood and bones!" Kruzel swore, watching helplessly as the panicked horses scattered into the woods. "All right, everyone out. Squad leaders, keep those mounts under control. We don't need to lose any more. Bargemen, I suggest you detach your skiffs and carry them beyond the obstruction. You will be safest following the river to Trothgard. Everyone else is on retrieval detail. We need to—"

"Commander Kruzel?" Chentelle interrupted. "You don't need to do that. I can bring the horses back."

He stared at her curiously, then shrugged. "Anything you can do will be appreciated. The sooner we're under way, the happier I'll be."

Chentelle turned away from him and started to sing. Her voice echoed through the river valley, mingling with the rushing water and the cool wind. She filled the song with harmony and peace and the joy of belonging. She reassured the frightened horses, reminding them of the safety of the herd and the friendship of men. Then she accompanied it with the joy of companionship, the thrill of a run shared, the comfort of a soft brush.

The forest rang with a chorus of neighs. The lost horses came bounding toward her by ones and twos. They pranced playfully and nuzzled against her.

The amazed Legionnaires stared at her in awe, then hurried forward to harness the returning mounts.

"Incredible!" Councilor A'valman stepped forward and took her hand. He bowed low, brushing her fingers with his lips. "I can hardly believe what I just saw—what I just heard!"

"Of course not," A'stoc said bitterly. "You have never been one to allow fact to override your opinions."

"Excuse me, masters." Kruzel stepped between the two wizards. "If I may interrupt your bickering for a moment, I would appreciate your opinions on the matter of the bridge."

A'stoc's eyes turned hard, but he spun around and stalked toward the ruins without answering.

"Have a care, Kruzel," A'valman said softly. "Not everyone shares your opinion of what is humorous."

Chentelle walked after A'stoc and found him squatting beside the ruined bridge. Vines and moss had overgrown much of what remained on this side of the river, just as trees and grass had encroached on the road that led from it. But as she drew near, she began to appreciate the marvels of its construction.

The stones were fitted together so tightly that the covering vines could only cling desperately to the rough surface; not a crack or a sprout showed from between the bricks. The surface of each stone was engraved. At first, she could make no sense of the carvings. Then she realized that they were part of one large pattern. It was difficult to be sure, but she thought it might be an open hand, reaching for the far shore.

"It was a marvel of construction." Councilor A'valman stood on the road above them. "Dwarven work, of course."

Chentelle looked around her at the empty land and the neglected road. "Why did they build it here?"

"It was built before the Wizards' War," A'valman answered. "The Old Westland Road used to link the eastern kingdoms to the Giant Nation."

"The giants." Chentelle remembered the stories Willow used to tell her, stories about a peaceful folk who loved long tales and huge feasts. "Were they really as the legends say?"

"They were happy," A'stoc said suddenly, "full of love and hope. Now they're dead." He picked up a ruined stone that had fallen near the bank and tossed it at her feet. "What do you think of this?"

The brick was pitted scored deeply. The scars were smooth, as if worn down by long years, but too uneven for natural weathering. She had seen identical scars on the wall of A'trile's tower. "The dragon."

A'stoc nodded agreement. "The last time I saw this road, ten thousand men marched along it. They found death at its end."

"Are you saying that the necromancer destroyed the bridge?" A'valman asked. "Why?"

"Why, councilor?" A'stoc sneered. "Has your godlike wisdom finally admitted its boundaries? Perhaps he was simply making sure the Realm could not use this road to send troops against his master. Perhaps he wanted to force us to follow this particular path to the west. We will know the answer soon enough."

The wizard climbed up the bank and walked to the waiting horses. Without another word, he mounted and started to ride down the Old Western Road.

Kruzel didn't call for a halt until only a thin sliver of red showed above the horizon. More than two leagues lay between their backs and the dwarven bridge, and the forest had yielded to rolling grassland with only scattered trees. He led them to a hilltop a few furlongs off the road, and they made a hurried camp.

Neither fires nor orb-lights were lit. They pastured the horses on the slope shielded from the road, and then settled on the ground with their cold rations. The wizards established passive wards along the perimeter, and Commander Kruzel set up a schedule of watches. No one spoke of the danger they feared.

Most of the company fell immediately asleep: the Legionnaires from practiced necessity and the wizards from the unaccustomed physical exertions. But Chentelle tossed and turned without relief. Her conversion with the Heart Tree kept spinning through her mind. There was so much she could have learned! And why didn't the lifelm know where the Wanderer was? He had to be in a forest somewhere. Even if he was dead, his passing should have been known to the wood.

It was no use. Chentelle threw off her blanket and sat up. The sentries stood alertly at either side of the camp, and two figures sat in quiet conversation near the center. At least she wasn't the only one who couldn't sleep.

She stood up and walked over to the men, shaking her head in resignation when she heard Sulmar's quiet footfalls behind her.

Dacius looked up at her approach. "Good evening, enchantress, Sulmar. Commander Kruzel and I were discussing the likelihood that Bone will attack."

Chentelle shuddered as the memory of the necromancer's eyes rose unbidden. She thought about the ruined stones of the bridge. "It is certain."

"Our thoughts exactly," Kruzel said. "The question is when. We will be two days on the road, now. And he can hit us either night. Or he might wait until we reach the keep, imagining our guard relaxed. He might even wait until we have opened the vault, hoping to take the treasure for his own."

"I don't think so," Chentelle said. "I mean, the vorpal weapons are only useful *against* creatures like him. And if we get into A'kalendane's laboratory, then all of your men will be armed with them, too. Right now he only has to worry about a few of us."

"Exactly." Dacius nodded encouragingly. "So we must expect attack on the road or soon after. And we should expect him to come in force. Three swords will be little protection, I fear. Our defense must rely with the wizards." He drew his vorpal sword and planted it into the hard ground. "The blade will glow if Ill-creatures are near. Should that happen, tell your men not to engage. Their weapons will be useless. The first priority is to awaken A'stoc. He is our best hope."

"Understood." Kruzel stood and saluted. "I will inform the sentries."

Dacius returned the salute, then turned to Chentelle. "Was there something you needed to talk about?"

"Huh? Oh, no, I just couldn't sleep."

He smiled and nodded. "You aren't alone, but I suggest we both try. Fatigue will only make the road harder."

From the corner of her eye, Chentelle thought she saw Sulmar's mouth twitch in a fleeting grin. Well, it served her right. She should listen to her own advice. "You're right. Come on, Sulmar. Time for bed."

To her surprise, she felt slumber coming almost as soon as she lay down. The dream came later.

❧

She creeps along the ground, sliding between the dark places. Prickling fences circle the prey, trying to keep her out. But she's too clever. The fences reach only to the ground. A hole opens into the hill, and she flows into it.

The tiny warmthing squeaks in fear and skitters away, but it can't escape her fingers. She wraps around its selfglow and squeezes. Careful! It's fragile. She makes herself very small and slides into the warmthing. Its selfglow quivers and then fades, surrendering to her shadow.

She rides the warmthing upward, scratching her way through dirt and grass. The warmthing climbs to the surface inside the prickly fence, near the middle of the prey's camp. She squeezes the last of its selfglow and leaves it behind.

Prey is everywhere: quickfast man hatethings and longsteady elf hatethings. Purelight screams from the center of the camp, burning her with its rays. Two of the hatethings start to move.

Fast. She has to be fast. She stretches long fingers, grabbing at the hate-things' selfglow. Ahh! It's hard. She has to reach so far to touch them both. She has to reach through the purelight, and it scalds her. But she can't let go. The hatethings are trying to scream. She feels it in their throats. Ignoring the pain, she wraps around their selfglows, surrounding them with her shadow. She squeezes as hard as she can, suffocating them with her darkness, drawing their warmth into herself. When their glows fade completely, she pulls out of their husks.

Quickly, she retreats from the burning purelight. She hates it. She drifts toward a cluster of selfglows. There are strange tastes among them, things she doesn't understand. She doesn't like them. Prey is all hatethings, but she doesn't like them. They will be first.

She reaches toward a man hatething. Her fingers slide into him, reaching for his quickfast selfglow. It pulses very strong, very warm. But something is wrong. Another shadow is there, bigger than hers, colder. She snatches her fingers back. *Don't hurt, don't hurt.* But the other doesn't come. Maybe the other didn't feel her.

It isn't fair. Master promised; prey is hers. Bigcoldshadow other shouldn't be here. It isn't fair.

She creeps over to next prey: longsteady elf hatething, strong selfglow, very tasty. Her fingers stretch out—

＆

"NO!"

Chentelle's eyes snapped open. A cloud of blackness floated above her bed-roll, illuminated by the fierce glow of Dacius's sword. Tendrils of shadow shot forward, piercing her chest and head.

Cold! Ice formed around her heart. She couldn't move, couldn't scream. The cold ripped through her, filling every part of her flesh. She was sinking into a frozen lake, a lake of death.

Without interest, she noted a flash of light and a roar like thunder. It didn't matter. All was numbness. The world was ice.

Ahh! Something hot burned into her forehead. It hurt! It was bright and hot and—wonderful! She grabbed hold of the glow, willing it to spread through her body. The icy darkness retreated, unable to withstand the light.

The shadow fled Chentelle's body, pouring out of her mouth and her eyes. It hovered above her, a seething hole in the midnight air. A glowing sword leaped from her forehead, tearing through the darkness. Blue sparks crackled through the void, and the Ill-creature vanished with a childlike wail.

Sulmar crouched in front of her, eyes searching the darkness.

"Wraiths!" A'stoc stepped toward the center of the camp, surrounded in the green flame of Earthpower. "Beware! We are under attack!"

Chentelle scrambled to her feet. Orb-light erupted all around. She heard the panicked neighs and the rumble of hoofbeats. Someone screamed from the other side of camp, but the sound cut off in a gurgle of blood. Misshapen dark forms with gleaming claws and pale yellow eyes slouched into the camp. Vi-khors!

Kruzel's Legionnaires retreated before them, using spears and swords to ward off the Ill-creatures' claws. One man parried too slowly, and a gleaming claw sliced and ripped his arm from its socket. He collapsed in a fountain of blood, screaming horribly until a second claw removed his throat.

"Drup! Sulmar! Follow me!" Dacius charged forward, grabbing his sword as he passed.

A'stoc was there before them. He waded into the vikhors, wielding the flaming Thunderwood like a quarterstaff. The Ill-creatures burned to ash at the Staff's touch.

Growling with rage, four of the vikhors hurled themselves at the wizard. But they could not penetrate his fiery shield, which he moved with considerable mechanical skill. It was actually a better weapon than a vorpal sword! One by one, he obliterated them with the Staff.

Sulmar and the Legionnaires met the remaining vikhors with glowing steel. They drove through the Ill-creatures' center, relieving the pressure on the cav-alrymen.

But the defenders were still outnumbered five to one. The vikhors sur-rounded them, howling and slavering in anticipation.

A chain of yellow lightning shot around the perimeter, tearing through the orb-lights. The round crystals exploded, plunging the hilltop into darkness.

A pillar of fire shot into the air, filling the countryside with light. A'stoc swept the Staff before him, and an arc of flame scythed through the vikhors, destroying half of them.

Chentelle heard a strangled cry behind her. She spun around.

A shadow of absolute darkness was driving into Councilor A'rullen's chest. The old wizard was withering before her eyes, becoming a shriveled, lifeless husk. Three more of the wraiths were flickering toward them.

Chentelle called on her Gift. She sang a song of warmth and light, a song of nature and growth. She filled her voice with the joy of communion and the heat of the Golden Sun.

All four wraiths instantly charged her.

Councilor A'rullen dropped to the ground, discarded in the Ill-creatures' lust for her warmth.

Chentelle cut off her song, frozen with sudden terror. What could she do? The shadows closed like lightning, much faster than she could run. Tendrils of ice reached toward her heart.

She screamed. A single note tore from her throat, driven by desperation. She filled it with the one thing that had saved her before, the burning brilliance of the vorpal sword. She latched on to the memory of that light and poured it into her song.

The wraiths stopped. They floated less than an arm's reach away from her, neither advancing nor retreating. Shadowy fingers danced in front of her eyes, searching for an opening in her barrier of sound.

Chentelle knew it was only a matter of time. This was not a melody she could renew and sustain. She was holding a single desperate note. Already she could feel her voice faltering.

One of the wraiths pressed forward, sensing her weakness.

A glowing star slashed through the darkness, striking the center of the wraith. The Ill-creature exploded in a shower of sparks.

The star hung in the air, spinning rapidly. Then it shot sideways, destroying another shadow. The last two fell in quick succession, vanishing just as Chentelle reached the limit of her air.

Councilor A'valman ran forward to check on A'rullen, and the vorpal star drifted back and hovered obediently above his shoulder.

Hollow laughter rang through the night. The necromancer stood on a hilltop behind them, leaning against the trunk of a solitary oak.

A'valman pointed, and the vorpal star shot through the night like a miniature comet.

A crackling bolt of yellow lightning met it halfway, shattering the blade into a thousand fiery slivers.

A'valman clutched his head and fell to the earth.

"Bone!" A'stoc waved a hand contemptuously, and the last vikhor was consumed by a jet of flame. He marched to the crown of the hill, still surrounded by the pillar of green flame.

The Ill-creature didn't move. His eyes gleamed evilly from beneath the tree's branches, as if daring A'stoc to attack. Once again, the necromancer's laughter floated toward them.

Suddenly, the pillar of flame disappeared, casting them into darkness. A moment later there was a flash of light. A sphere of flame shot through the air and crashed into the far hilltop. The oak burst into flames, casting a flickering light over the prairie. There was no sign of Bone.

A'stoc muttered a spell and a teardrop of flame dripped from the *mandril* wand. It fell to the ground and burned brightly, illuminating the hilltop.

The smoking remains of vikhors littered the camp, but they had not died alone. Two of Kruzel's cavalrymen had died beneath their claws. A'valman and A'rullen would recover quickly with rest, but the two sentries were not so lucky. Their bodies were desiccated husks, drained of life by the wraith.

"They were good men. Good men! They didn't deserve this." Commander Kruzel stared at the bodies, rage trembling in his hands and voice. He turned to A'stoc. "Pry open the vault, wizard. Give me a weapon that can kill that bastard!"

Drup knelt beside one of the bodies. "I think this one sounded the alarm. Without him, we might not have beaten back the attack." He reached down to close the sentry's eyes. The flesh crumbled to dust under his fingers, and he jumped away.

"This was not the attack," A'stoc said. "He was only testing our strength."

The others stared at him. This had been a mere preliminary? Chentelle felt despair. How would they ever survive the serious siege, when it came?

❧ 16 ❦

COVENANT'S KEEP

Shortly after noon on their third day on the road, the company reached the fringe of the Desecration. It was visible a half league away, a black scar stretching into the horizon. The sight sent a mixture of dread and relief through the party: relief because it meant they were near to their destination, dread because the barren landscape seemed to promise that the worst lay yet before them.

For Chentelle, it was a vision of sadness. From a mile away, desolation screamed to her. The Desecration Fault was a gravestone, marking the death of the land itself. She had seen too many graves since she left home, too many funerals. Captain Rone, Alve, Simon—the images rose in her mind, a grim procession of death. Lilies grew around the rich soil of Brother Gorin's grave; prairie grass around the simple holes they had dug for the Legion cavalrymen. Yet they were the same. She had seen wonders and horrors and mysteries beyond counting since she set out to follow her Dream, but it was the graves that haunted her most.

And now she was riding into the largest grave of all. The agony of the land hit her as soon as she crossed the threshold. Worse than the pain of the *Treachery*'s wood, worse than the dust of *Kennaru*'s ancient city, this was the death of the world. No plant, no bird, no beast or bug could live on this land. Water neither fell here as rain nor existed hidden below the surface, not even if one sank a shaft to the center of the world. The ground was bare rock, covered by the chalky dust that had once been fertile soil.

A wave of dizziness threatened to topple her from Sundancer's back. She clutched the mare's mane desperately, terrified of falling to the ground. She couldn't face that, not yet. She stifled a cry, focusing all her will on Sundancer's solid presence. The dizziness passed, and she pulled herself back to a secure seat.

"Mistress, are you all right?"

She was suddenly the focus of dozens of concerned eyes. "Fine. I'll be fine." Her voice was weak and full of tremors. She knew she had to regain control.

Chentelle ordered herself to let go of Sundancer's mane. The scream of the Desecration grew louder as her attention left the mare. She ignored it. She clamped down on her Gift, locking it inside, shielding it from the pain. She forced herself to see only with her eyes, hear only with her ears. The scream faded into nothingness.

She bounced awkwardly on Sundancer's back, and the mare snuffled in surprise at her clumsiness. She felt very alone. She could *see* her friends, but she couldn't feel them. She had no idea what they were feeling or needing. She scanned their faces, trying to deduce what should have been obvious.

The Legionnaires seemed edgy, especially Dacius and Kruzel. They kept turning their heads and scanning the wasteland, as if expecting a hidden foe to materialize from the dust. Councilor A'rullen looked exhausted. He had not yet recovered all of his strength from the wraith's attack. A'valman stared intently at A'stoc, but his expression was unreadable. And A'stoc didn't notice; his eyes were focused far in the distance. It wasn't difficult to guess the subject of his thoughts. That left only Sulmar, who met her gaze calmly and without expression.

The horses stepped nervously through the dust and broken stone, and Kruzel kept their pace light. He veered northward, leaving the Old Western Road and leading them toward a ridge of bare rock mountains. Within minutes, the ruins of Covenant's Keep came into view.

The remains of shattered battlements littered the hillside. Not a wall remained more than a few cubits high, as if the fortress had been swept aside by a giant hand. Dry dust smothered the rubble, painting the scene in monochrome gray.

"Stand and identify yourselves!"

Kruzel snapped upright in his saddle. "Lakey, is that you? Thank the Creator, I was afraid the necromancer had been here."

"Necromancer? What are you talking about, Commander?"

"Not now." Kruzel kicked his mount forward. "Spread the word, I want a command meeting in the main tent as soon as possible."

They rode through an opening in the foundation that might have been a gate. Several large tents dominated the interior, painted boldly in the black and tan of Tel Adartak. The largest tent had open ends and was obviously being used as a makeshift stables. They quickly dismounted and secured the horses.

"All men are on stable duty until further notice." Kruzel motioned for the rest of them to follow him. "Feed, water, and loving care are the order of the day. Treat them well, boys, they deserve it."

Chentelle had not dismounted with the rest. She cringed, now, at the thought of touching this earth. Slowly, she lowered her feet to the dust and stone. Her feet tingled slightly, but that was all. She still had her Gift contained. Sighing with relief, she hurried after Commander Kruzel.

He led them to the entrance of the next largest tent and paused. "Councilor A'rullen, the command is yours, now. My charge was only to deliver you safely. But I strongly suggest you listen to the counsel of Lord Gemine and his fellows."

"I thank you, Commander," A'rullen said. "Both for your wisdom and valor in bringing us here and for your sage advice, which I will certainly heed."

They entered the tent and were greeted by three figures. The first was a young human with dark skin and an easy smile. The other two were dwarves, little more than two cubits tall and nearly as wide. They wore mirrored suits of green and gold silk, embroidered with threads of spun platinum. Each had a belt of silver link from which hung a large pouch and a small, flat drum. Like the colored silks, the arrangements of pouch and drum mirrored each other. Rubies sparkled in the green-dyed beard of one, while emeralds shone in the stiff red whiskers of the other. Both wore caps of finely worked gold, which they removed respectfully as they bowed to the newcomers.

"May I present the brothers Fel and Fen," A'rullen said. "They are the engineers in charge of the excavation. Yeoman Jarl commands the mission guards."

A'rullen made quick introductions and then told Jarl and the dwarves about Bone and the attack on their camp. The dwarves were horrified to learn of the destruction of the bridge, but it was the news of Bone's impersonation that stunned Jarl.

"How long?" the yeoman said. "How many times did I stand next to him and never see him for what he was?"

"Do not blame yourself," A'rullen said. "More experienced eyes than yours were taken in by his deception. Now I suggest a short rest to recover from the road before we examine the vault."

"No," A'stoc said. "We must attempt the opening immediately. The necromancer will attack tonight."

"How can you be certain?" A'valman asked. "How do you know that his earlier attack was only a test?"

"Do you think that he would sacrifice his entire force just to destroy your toy star?" A'stoc sneered. "Think. Where was the dragon? Why did the necromancer hold back from the battle? Because he was gauging our strength. The true attack will come tonight. He does not dare wait longer."

"But why did he wait at all?" Chentelle asked. "Why didn't he attack again while we were on the road? It doesn't make sense. We'll be stronger if we reach A'kalendane's workshop, but the vorpal weapons are no use to Ill-creatures."

"Perhaps he has human allies."

All eyes turned to Sulmar, surprised at his sudden loquaciousness, but he did not elaborate further.

"Why does not matter," A'stoc said. "The fact remains."

A'rullen nodded. "Master A'stoc is right. We must be prepared for the worst." He turned to Fen and Fel. "Please take us to the vault."

"I will stay here," Jarl said. "I must prepare my men."

The brothers led them to the center of the keep's foundation. A gaping shaft opened into the rock, cordoned off by a rope barrier. More ropes dropped down the center of the shaft, attached to large winches. A set of narrow stairs spiraled down the edge of the pit, and the dwarves paused at their head.

"There's no rail," Fel said, or was it Fen?

"So don't fall," the other completed.

That said, they marched quickly down the stairs.

Chentelle had no great fear of heights, but the stairway made her uneasy. She stayed close to the wall, yet the gaping emptiness to her left kept pulling her eye. The stonework was magnificent, hard granite polished as smooth as marble and lit with orb-light, but the narrow steps and shallow drops matched poorly with her stride. After one turn around the shaft, the stairway was covered by the bottom side of the steps above. The ceiling was actually high enough for even A'stoc to stand erect, but Chentelle's eyes were not convinced by such logic. She had to fight the unreasoning urge to duck her head.

After several turns down the shaft, the stairs ended in a circular chamber. Several large buckets sat in the center of the room, attached to the ends of the ropes from above. A dark tunnel branched from the room, supported by huge stone buttresses.

A basin in one wall held a collection of flattened adartak circles. Each of the dwarves grabbed one and fitted it into a brace on his cap. A quick incantation later the crystals glowed with orb-light. It illuminated everything, but the gold caps somehow focused the light particularly to the front. One of the brothers led the way down the tunnel, while the other took the rear.

The tunnel ran for perhaps forty cubits and then ended suddenly at a large hole in the floor. An iron ladder poked up through the hole, and the lead dwarf scrambled quickly down it. One by one the company followed him, illuminated by the shaft of orb-light from his helm.

Chentelle found the ladder unwieldy. Like the stairs, its drop was too short for her to step smoothly and too long to take two rungs at a time. Despite the shallowness of the steps, she was surprised to count more than thirty of them before she reached the bottom. The climb took all of her attention, so it wasn't until she stepped down onto the floor that she took note of her surroundings.

They were in a large, rectangular chamber. The stonework here was coarse and uneven, nothing at all like the smooth, straight sides of the tunnel and stairs above. These walls seemed to have been chiseled with rough, almost savage strokes. Something on the far wall gleamed in the orb-light: chains. Large iron fetters, covered with rust, hung from the stone. Two of them held skeletons.

The bones were manlike but twice the size of any human. No, they weren't really manlike. The massive jaws were elongated and filled with the sharp, widely spaced teeth of a carnivore. And the hands had four fingers, two of which seemed to be thumbs. There were three bones in the forearm, and other differences in the rib cage and legs.

"What are they?" she asked.

"Trolls," Fen said, or maybe Fel. "The keep was theirs before Lars Covenant took it during the war. This room was walled up from the outside. Old Lars probably didn't even know it was here."

"We think it was a ritual burial chamber," continued the other brother. "Haven't figured out what the chains were for, though."

Chentelle stared at the skeletons. "And you just left them here?"

"Sure."

"They aren't good for anything."

They passed through a hole in one wall and turned left at the passage beyond. The masonry here was cleaner, but still rough-hewn compared with the dwarven tunnels. Iron doors lined both sides of the corridor, locks and hinges secured by rust. The hallway opened up into a large, marble-tiled gallery.

Parts of the gallery's ceiling had collapsed, and the fresh supports which lined each wall were obviously new, as was the archway carved out of one wall. The arch opened into another circular shaft, and a metal ladder attached to the near wall took them deeper into the mountain. The stone within a cubit of the ladder had been scrubbed clean, but the rest of the shaft was cloaked in a thick layer of black soot.

They dropped off the ladder and found themselves standing inside a huge furnace. A thick layer of ash covered the edges of the floor, but a wide path from the ladder to the thick stone door had been swept clear. An irregular hole near one wall sank even deeper into the stone, but the brothers led them through the door and into a large smithy.

A dozen smaller forges lined the walls next to the great furnace. Hammers and anvils and tongs of every size lay scattered about the room. Metal bars and rods littered the floor: iron, gold, silver, steel—and others that Chentelle didn't recognize. Weapons were strewn haphazardly in one corner, their blades tarnished and pitted with age and neglect. A wide metal door stood on the center of the far wall, looking as if it had been polished yesterday.

"Here we are, gentle beings."

"The workshop of A'kalendane."

The three wizards stepped up to the door and examined it in great detail.

Chentelle wanted to go with them. But without her Gift, the metal of the door would just feel cold to her fingers. Without her Gift the magical runes would just be carved letters. And she couldn't use her Gift without opening herself to the agony of this dead land. She stayed with Fen, Fel, and the Legionnaires.

The wizards conferred for a moment. Then A'rullen and A'valman backed away from the door.

Chentelle remembered what had happened when A'stoc forced the door to Boemarre's workshop. "We'd better find cover."

They crouched in the shelter of the kilns while A'stoc called green flame from the Thunderwood. It was strange to see it without *feeling* the tremendous rush of Earthpower. Surrounded in the aura of his power, the wizard tapped the Staff lightly against the portal.

The metal rang like a mammoth bell. Sparks of blue lightning crackled along its surface. The power exploded from the door, engulfing A'stoc and flashing through the workshop beyond.

But A'rullen and A'valman had been standing ready. The lightning splashed against their wards and dispersed harmlessly.

The brunt of the assault, though, still snapped and hissed around A'stoc's shield of Earthpower. The green flame started pulsing. With every surge, it became a little brighter, a little stronger, and the blue lightning diminished. As the last spark vanished, a clap of thunder blasted through the room.

Darkness. The green flame flickered and died. The orb-light disappeared. The deafening roar seemed to echo forever in the closed chamber.

"A'stoc!"

Suddenly, vision returned. Fen and Fel looked around in confusion as their orb-lights returned to life.

A'stoc stood absolutely still in front of the doorway. Slowly, he raised the Staff and tapped the door again. It swung silently open.

"Wait!" Dacius stepped forward, drawing his sword. The steel shone coldly in the orb-light, but it did not glow. "Drup and I should go in first, just in case."

A'stoc shrugged. He mumbled a quick spell, and orb-light filled the chamber beyond the door.

The two Legionnaires moved cautiously into the room. A few moments later they called out that the room was clear.

A'kalendane's workshop was a smaller version of its neighbor. Forges and smelting cauldrons lined one wall. Another was the home to a dozen varieties of metalworking tools. Buckets of raw ore sat beside sword blanks and barrels of refined metal. But there were several differences between this shop and the larger one: the tools and material here were in perfect order, the forges were stocked with wood and ready to be fired, and there were no weapons of any type, vorpal or otherwise. There was also another door.

The party had missed it at first. It was unadorned stone and nearly indistinguishable from the walls of the chamber. But the sharp eyes of the dwarves had spotted it immediately.

One of the brothers ran his hand along the stone. A panel slid aside, revealing a keyhole. "Number three, Fen?"

Fen reached into his pouch and pulled out a small granite cylinder. "Number three, Fel."

Fen put the cylinder next to the lock and started a slow, rhythmic chant. Fel accompanied him with light taps on his drum, which had an amazingly deep and full timbre for so small an instrument. As the music built, Fen started kneading the granite cylinder. The stone shaped like clay beneath his fingers, taking on the shape and configuration of the keyhole. He inserted and removed the key several times, making small adjustments to match the tumblers.

Fel stopped his drumming. "Done?"

"Done." Fen turned the key.

The lock clicked loudly. Fen pushed on the door. Nothing happened.

"Aaa—"

Chentelle spun around. Commander Kruzel lay on the ground, his face contorted with a frozen scream. A gelatinous sphere hovered above his body, reaching out with long, transparent tentacles. On the far wall, a panel had dropped open to reveal a hidden alcove.

One of the creature's tentacles brushed A'valman's neck. The wizard dropped to the ground, his open eyes staring lifelessly into the distance.

"A guardian!" Dacius charged forward, sword in hand.

But Councilor A'rullen was closer. The creature floated toward him with deceptive speed. Its body undulated as it moved, as if it were swimming through the air.

A'rullen lifted his cane. Lightning crackled around the wood, and he thrust it toward the guardian.

The creature retreated from the attack, but one of its tendrils whipped forward, wrapping around the wizard's wrist.

A'rullen crumpled to the ground.

" 'Ware the tentacles!" Dacius' blade cut deeply into the guardian's trunk, cleaving through the soft flesh easily.

The stroke left a deep gouge, which sealed itself instantly. The creature's only reaction was to lash out at the Legionnaire with a half-dozen thin tendrils.

Dacius dropped to the ground and rolled, barely avoiding the deadly sting.

Drup moved in behind him, sword flashing in a horizontal arc. The vorpal blade sliced through the extended tentacles, which continued to reach forward as if nothing had happened. Drup twitched once when they reached his chest, then fell.

No! This shouldn't be happening. Chentelle stared in horror as the creature drifted toward her.

Sulmar stepped between them, his black sword whistling through the air.

The guardian reached forward, and two of its tentacles fell to the ground, severed by the dark blade. The creature retreated to the ceiling, limbs flailing wildly. It tried to circle around the Tengarian, but Sulmar moved to intercept it.

The black sword sliced through the air, flicking another tentacle to the ground. The creature retreated, and Sulmar followed. With careful precision he backed the guardian into a corner from which it had no retreat.

Chentelle watched the silent combat, doubt rising in her mind. What was it? It couldn't be an Ill-creature; the vorpal blades weren't glowing. And if it was a guardian placed here by A'kalendane, then it wasn't evil. It was just protecting its master's home.

"Sulmar, no!" She ran forward, placing herself between her liegeman and the guardian. "Don't kill—"

The tentacle touched her face.

She drifted in a sea of tranquillity. Drup was there, so were Kruzel and the wizard Councilors. They understood now. All was peace within the union. But her friends were still apart, still isolated. She had to help them.

The body that had once trapped her collapsed in a heap. She didn't need it anymore. She reached out to Sulmar.

"Chentelle!"

A'stoc was pointing at her with a wooden rod. Fire burst from the wand. It burned! The union screamed with agony. Her hands shriveled and fell away. The tranquillity bubbled and churned under the assault. Peace was lost. The union was dying. There was only pain and isolation.

"No!" Chentelle sat upright.

"Chentelle!" A'stoc lowered the *mandril*. He started toward her.

"You killed it!" Tears welled in her eyes. "It wasn't evil! You didn't have to kill it!"

A'stoc froze. His mouth opened, but he made no sound. Slowly, he turned and walked away.

"Everyone, please give me your attention." Councilor A'rullen levered himself to his feet. "Obviously A'kalendane took steps to protect his secrets. I should have anticipated that. But there must be another door somewhere. We have to find it."

Chentelle stayed sitting on the floor while they searched. She knew she should be helping, but she didn't have the energy. Nothing felt right. The smell of the burned guardian caught in her throat. Why did there have to be so much death?

Her friends scoured the room, tapping walls to find hollow chambers, brushing fingers against the stone to detect hidden seams. But they found nothing.

Chentelle startled to giggle. It was so absurd. They ride like the wind for a hundred leagues, tunnel through a thousand cubits of rock, undo a spell of forbidding that withstood the breaking of the world, murder an innocent creature, and what do they find—nothing. It was too cruel.

"What is it?" A'stoc said. "Why are you laughing?"

Chentelle struggled to regain her composure. "I was just thinking. What if there is no other door?"

"There must be!" Councilor A'rullen pounded his cane against the floor. "We have the histories! We know that A'kalendane had a hidden stockpile of weapons and Lore. It must be here! There has to be a second door!"

"No," A'stoc said thoughtfully. "There does not."

He walked to the stone door and turned the key back to its original position. The tumblers dropped loudly into place, hiding the muffled scrape of the panel pulling shut to conceal the guardian's alcove. Then he turned it again in the same direction. The door clicked softly and swung open.

The room beyond was filled with gleaming metal: swords, spears, lances, armor. Hundreds of weapons were stacked neatly on metal racks and shelves, and every one was forged in the blue-hued steel of A'kalendane's vorpal Lore.

"Thank the Creator." Councilor A'rullen walked slowly forward. "Fel, Fen, get your workmen down here, and the Legionnaires, too. I want these weapons moved to the surface as quickly as possible."

"Yes, councilor."

"We're on our way."

Moving slowly, almost reverently, the party entered A'kalendane's vault. Treasures of destruction and war surrounded them. On the far wall, a small shelf held five thick tomes.

"The Lore!" A'valman rushed forward and grabbed one of the books. He flipped through it, finding page after page of blank paper. "No!"

He grabbed the next book, then the next. All five volumes were the same. "It can't be. There must be more books, maybe even another room."

He began searching the rock walls.

"No, A'valman." A'stoc pulled the other wizard gently away from the wall. "Remember how it was: the jealousy, the fear. Knowledge was hoarded, encrypted in magic runes. There are no more books. A'kalendane took his Lore to the grave."

Councilor A'rullen set a comforting hand on A'valman's shoulder. "He speaks the truth, my friend. I will have searchers explore every part of these chambers, just to be certain. But in my heart, I know they will find nothing."

"Look at this!" Dacius stood before a wooden figure which was draped in armor. A cuirass of full plate covered the torso, and a pentagonal shield hung off one shoulder. There were no arms or leggings, but metal gauntlets sat on the stand. The full helm was cylindrical in back but came to a sharp angle in the front. It was featureless and lacked either eye slits or a faceplate. "Surely this was destined to be worn by a great warrior."

"One of the greatest," A'rullen said. "The histories say that A'kalendane promised a suit of armor to Lars Covenant, as repayment for the use of this workshop. It was never delivered, because it was never finished. But this can only be that armor. Do you wish to take it?"

"What?" Dacius stared at the old wizard. "Do you jest?"

"No," A'rullen said. "Our agreement with the men who worked to open this vault was that each would be free to take one item should we succeed. I deem that the agreement holds for you as well."

"But I had no part in the opening," Dacius protested.

"No?" A'rullen said. "Perhaps it was another whose sword I saw flashing on a dark hill. But if you do not want it . . ."

"No," Dacius said quickly. "I am simply overwhelmed by your generosity. I shall do my best to bring the armor the honor it so obviously deserves."

"Master wizard," Kruzel asked, "does that also apply to me?"

"Of course, Commander. You as much as any."

"Thank you." Kruzel snatched a long, leaf-bladed spear from the nearest rack. Both shaft and point of the weapon were forged from vorpal steel. "I name you Bonesplitter, and I vow that you will live up to your name!"

"Does anyone else wish to choose?" A'rullen asked.

Chentelle looked at the collection of shining blades and shook her head. She wanted nothing from here.

A'stoc also declined to take anything.

A'valman searched for a throwing blade to replace the one he had lost, but did not find one. He finally settled on a lightly curved saber. Drup selected a quiver of vorpal arrows. And Sulmar surprised everyone by selecting a bracer of vorpal steel. He immediately rolled up his right sleeve and slid his forearm into the band.

By the time they had finished, Fen and Fel were back with their fellows. The work of hauling A'kalendane's hoard to the surface began immediately. The dwarves coordinated with seamless precision: sorting, bundling, and loading the weapons into wheeled carts. The rest of them did draft duty, ferrying the carts to the furnace and unloading them into a waiting bucket. Legionnaires at the top of the ladder worked the pulleys to lift the weapons to the next level.

In less than an hour, the vault was cleared. Everyone headed back up the ladder to help carry the hoard on its next step, but Chentelle lagged behind.

She found herself drawn back to the guardian. Whatever magic had sustained the creature through the long years had vanished now. Its charred flesh was decomposing rapidly, vanishing into the stale air. It wasn't right. The creature deserved better.

"The guardian served well," Sulmar said from behind her shoulder. "It was charged to defend this store until the weapons were needed again, and it succeeded in that duty."

"But it didn't have to die," she said. "I knew it wasn't evil. I could have used my Gift to communicate with it, to let it know we were friends. I could have saved it! But I was afraid. If I were half as brave as you or Dacius the guardian would still be alive."

"You judge yourself harshly, mistress. You do not react like a trained warrior, because you are not one." He pointed to the decaying husk. "Lord Gemine and I both attacked the creature. Neither of us had the insight or wisdom to recognize its nature. I would have been the one to kill it, had you not stopped me. Do not chastise yourself for who you are not, mistress. Find the strength in who you are. Anger does not help you, whether directed inward or toward a friend who acted only to save you or avenge your death."

"A'stoc?" He was right, of course. Chentelle felt the truth of his reasoning. "I know. I owe him an apology. I just lost my head." But she felt that maybe she was getting it back now. She pointed to the bracer on Sulmar's arm. "Will that help?"

The Tengarian smiled grimly. "It will not harm Kaliya or affect the curse, but I think it will make her angry."

As soon as the last load of vorpal weapons reached the top of the excavation shaft, Councilor A'rullen called everyone together. "You all know our situation. I have sent a message to Tel Adartak-Skysoar, but we cannot expect help for several days. We expect the necromancer to attack tonight. Because of the danger, I will not order any man to stay. All workers are released from their contracts. Any dwarf who wishes to select his share of the treasure and leave may do so without disgrace. Master A'stoc and his party are also free to choose their own path."

No one moved.

"Thank you," A'rullen said. "Now, I yield all authority to Commander Kruzel so that he may direct our defense."

"No," Kruzel said. "Your pardon, master wizard, but I must refuse. Lord Gemine is the senior officer."

A'rullen turned to Dacius. "Will you undertake this, Lord Gemine? I have no authority to call on your service."

"Nor am I free to give it, for I am committed to another quest. But in this, all our interests lie together." He turned to Kruzel. "What is our strength?"

"I have twelve horsemen left in my command, though they fight well afoot, too," Kruzel said. "Jarl has ten more in the outpost guard, and the dwarves number fifteen, including Fen, Fel and the cook. Then, we have the wizards and your own comrades."

"Wait!" A'valman walked forward and turned to face A'stoc. "You must not stay. The weapons are a treasure we sorely need, but losing them will be nothing compared to the danger of the Staff falling into the necromancer's hands. You must leave here before nightfall!"

"Your fears betray you, Councilor," A'stoc said calmly. "The Staff will not be safer if I am caught unprotected on the open road. I will stay."

"Good. We will need your power." Dacius' eyes scanned the ruins of the keep. "The outer wall is useless. We are too few to hold it. The inner battlement will be our first line. With luck it will blunt their charge. Jarl, take your men and have them plug those holes; scavenge whatever material you can from the outer keep. Then track down every adartak crystal and scrap of wood you can find. I want fires readied along both sides of the wall and orb-lights placed throughout the perimeter."

He grabbed two spears and marched off forty paces from the edge of the pit. He planted the spears in the ground with about three cubits between them. "Fen, Fel, I need new walls. Anchor the ends to the mountainside, there and there, and angle them forward to these points. If I give you Kruzel and his men to assist, how high can you raise it by an hour before sunset?"

Fel examined the distance. "Four cubits if we sacrifice aesthetics and permanence."

"But we will have to scavenge the buttresses from the excavation tunnel," Fen added.

"Do it," Dacius said. "And take whatever material you need from the outer wall. How many arrows do we have?"

"One hundred and seventy-eight."

"Plus the twenty your man selected."

"Okay, give me six archer stands, three on each wall." Dacius turned to Drup. "Find the five best bowmen here and place them under your command. Distribute the arrows as you see fit. That's all. Move out, people! We'll meet again one hour before sunset."

The camp exploded into activity. Legion horses were used to haul stone from the excavation tunnel and the outer walls. The odd scraps went to patch the inner battlement, while the best pieces were handed over to Fel and Fen.

The dwarves were a marvel of efficiency. Each brother took a crew of six miners and worked on one wall. The last dwarf, the cook apparently, sat in the middle of the camp and pounded a slow cadence on a large drum. The dwarves matched the beat with a deep, rumbling chant and set their work to the rhythm. They shaped the granite easily, using strong fingers and the power of their chant. *Drum*—accept a stone from a Legionnaire. *Drum*—flatten and smooth the bottom. *Drum*—the right. *Drum*—the left. *Drum*—the top. *Drum*—set the brick in place. Fen and Fel came behind the miners, using their Lore to bind the stones in place. Wherever their fingers passed, the bricks joined together, forming a seamless wall.

Chentelle joined the Legionnaires in hauling the stone. The work seemed endless: lift, carry, drop, return. Her muscles trembled with strain, but she took comfort from the steady chant. The droning rhythm seemed to lend strength to her back and legs.

As tirelessly as the dwarves worked, they could not keep pace with the influx of stone. By the time the wall was two-thirds complete, enough granite had been stockpiled to readily complete the fortification. Kruzel kept three men with him to assist with the final stages and sent the rest to join Jarl at the inner battlement.

Chentelle placed her last load of rock onto the pile and stretched her back gratefully. It felt as if she had carried the entire mountain single-handedly. She massaged the back of her neck with one hand and noticed someone staring at her from beside the field stables: A'stoc.

He turned and started walking away when she looked up.

"A'stoc, wait!" She told Sulmar to stay where he was, then rushed over to intercept the wizard. "I want to apologize. I shouldn't have yelled at you. You were only doing what you thought was right. I'm sorry."

His eyes searched her face for several moments before answering softly, "No, Chentelle. I acted foolishly. You were right to be angry. Now, please excuse me. I must prepare."

Chentelle watched him walk away, unable to decipher the strange emotion she had heard in his voice. Despair? Was the coming battle truly hopeless? She heard nervous whinnying from inside the tent. *Even the horses could feel it!* She felt blind and stupid.

The horses! She ran to the center of camp and burst into the command tent. "Dacius!"

The Legionnaire looked up from conversation with Councilor A'rullen.

"Oh, I'm sorry."

"That's all right, Chentelle. We were just finishing." He nodded his head to A'rullen. "Thank you for your help, councilor."

"Now," he said as the wizard left the tent. "What can I do for you?"

"I was just wondering," she said. "What are you going to do with the horses?"

He shook his head sadly. "We can't use them, I'm afraid. Our force is too small to fight a battle of maneuver."

"But what are we going to do with them? There isn't room for them inside the wall, and if we leave them tied outside they'll be slaughtered."

"I know," he said. "But they can't survive loose in this wasteland, and I can't spare a man to lead them away."

"Let me do it." Chentelle fought down a surge of fear. "I don't have to go with them. I can use my Gift to send them east."

Dacius smiled and nodded assent. "Fine. But wait until the construction is complete and don't send them all. Move the four fastest horses inside the new fortification. Face them into the mountain and make sure they're hobbled and wearing blinders. Grab one of Jarl's men if you need help."

"I will." She started to back out of the tent.

"Wait," Dacius said. "Will you do me a favor before you leave?"

"Of course."

Dacius walked to the corner of the tent, where the armor of Lars Covenant was laid out neatly. His face flushed with embarrassment, and he shrugged. "There aren't any squires here. Would you . . . ?"

Chentelle grinned and bowed deeply. "I would be honored."

While Dacius lifted the breastplate and held it to his chest, Chentelle struggled to lift the back plate. *By the Creator, it must weigh three stone.* Groaning with effort, she raised the armor and pressed it against the human's back. The molded shoulders and waist slid into place as if the cuirass had been forged precisely for his body. But how was she supposed to attach it? There were no straps or buckles.

Dacius shifted the frontpiece slightly, and the two halves slid into alignment. The metal rang with a high, clear tone, and soft blue light glowed along the lines of joining. When the glow faded, the seams were gone. Nothing remained to show that the armor had ever been more than one piece.

"Amazing," Dacius said. "It's nearly weightless."

Chentelle blinked. The armor had changed. The skirt of plates that had hung only from the bottom of the breastplate now circled the Legionnaire's hips completely. And new plates dropped from the shoulders, protecting his upper arms. She pointed. "Dacius, look."

His eyes followed the line of her finger, then grew wide in surprise. "More wonders!" He picked up the gauntlets and slipped them on quickly. He flexed his fingers experimentally, seeming pleased at the ease of movement. Then he picked up the five-sided shield and slid his left arm through the braces.

As soon as his hand closed around the grip, shield and glove both flashed with brilliant blue light. "Look." He spread his arm to show Chentelle the inside of the shield.

The steel gauntlet had extended upward to cover the inside of his arm to the elbow. More astonishingly, the glove itself now showed neither fingers nor thumb. It had fused with the grip of the shield.

Chentelle reached out and tilted the shield so that Dacius could see its face.

"By the Creator." Dacius grabbed the shield with his right hand and pulled. There was a muffled pop, and his arm slid free of the braces. The left gauntlet showed no signs of its earlier transformation. He flipped the shield around so that he could see it better. "Even now. By the beard of my father, this A'kalendane was truly a wizard."

The face of the shield now bore the twin suns of House Gemine.

Dacius picked up the solid-faced helm. "I had thought this unfinished. But now . . ." He lowered the casque onto his head.

Once again, the steel shone with blue light. The headpiece joined to the cuirass forming a segmented gorget that completely protected the Legionnaire's neck.

"CHENTELLE, THIS IS MARVELOUS." Dacius's voice resonated from the helm in all directions. It filled the tent with deep, rich sound. "I CAN SEE CLEARLY, BETTER THAN CLEARLY. I THINK I COULD SEE IN COMPLETE DARKNESS."

"You look . . ." Chentelle struggled to find the right words, "very fearsome."

"WELL, I—"

Sulmar came crashing through the door to the tent, sword in hand. His eyes searched the tent for any threat. Seeing none, he relaxed and sheathed his blade. "I heard yelling, mistress. Lord Gemine, is that you?"

Dacius reached up and slipped off the helmet. "Hello, Sulmar. I'm sorry to have startled you. The helm seems to amplify my voice."

Sulmar nodded and ducked out of the tent.

Dacius stared through the open flap, eyes fixed upon the new construction. All mirth vanished from his face, replaced by iron determination. "It won't be long, now."

As soon as the walls were complete, Dacius called everyone together again. He had spread out the bundles of weapons and armor on the ground, and he stood behind them, helmet resting on his arm. He waited quietly while everyone settled into place.

"Order of Battle!"

The Legionnaires present snapped instantly to attention. Everyone else became silent and attentive.

"Commander Kruzel," Dacius called, "you have the right flank. Yeoman Jarl, you are the left. Both units minus the archers Drup has selected. The wizards will deploy as follows: A'rullen—left, A'stoc—center, A'valman—right. Fen and Fel, you and your miners will be our reserve. Determine authority however you wish, but let me know who commands before nightfall.

"Both flanks and their magical support will deploy at the inner battlement. We will hold that position as long as possible. Reserves and bowmen deploy within the inner walls. Archers, you're too few for volley fire. Select targets and make each shot count. If there are shadow knights among the enemy, target them first. Sulmar, you and I have no fixed position. We will provide immediate support for any position that is pressed. Pay particular attention to A'stoc. He will be unsupported in the center. Chentelle, the mountain guards our back, but the enemy may have forces that can cross it. I am trusting you to find your own path, as you have done before, but keep an eye on that slope as well."

Dacius paused, then continued in a softer voice. "Most of you have never seen the kind of enemy we will face today, but by now you have all heard tales. Make no mistake, the necromancer is a terrible foe, but all of the advantages are not his. We have the high ground and a fortified position, and the enemy cannot maintain his attack past the hours of darkness. We have three of the mightiest wizards in the Realm at our side, one of whom commands the power of the Thunderwood. And we have one thing more. I tell you now, the enemy made a fatal error when he allowed us time to retrieve A'kalendane's hoard, for he has given us the power to destroy him."

Dacius stepped back and donned his helm.

"FRIENDS." A flutter of astonishment rippled through the crowd at his voice. "BEFORE YOU LIES THE POWER OF WHICH I SPEAK, THE WEAPONS OF A'KALENDANE. BY CONTRACT, YOU ARE EACH ENTITLED TO ONE ITEM FROM THE HOARD. I TELL YOU NOW, TAKE TWO, TAKE THREE. I COMMAND EACH MAN TO TAKE WHATEVER WEAPONS HE CAN USE EFFECTIVELY, WHATEVER ARMOR HE NEEDS. THIS IS NOT GREED. IF THERE IS NO BATTLE, YOU WILL RETURN ALL BUT YOUR SHARE. BUT IF BATTLE COMES, WE MUST MEET IT WITH ALL THE STRENGTH WE HAVE TO BEAR. THEN, EVERY SWORD THAT FINDS ITS MARK BECOMES PROPERTY OF THE ARM THAT WIELDS IT. EVERY SHIELD THAT TURNS A BLOW BELONGS TO THE LIMB THAT IT SAVED. WE FIGHT TODAY FOR THE HOPE OF THE WORLD. WE WILL NOT FAIL."

Dacius drew his sword and thrust it into the air. "FOR HONOR! FOR LEGION! FOR CREATION!" The shout thundered off the mountain, echoed by the voices of every warrior in camp.

Quickly, the men filed through to select their arms. Most of the Legionnaires chose a sword and a light shield. Some also selected a spear or dagger. The few helmets and bits of armor were snatched up quickly. Fen, Fel, and one other dwarf chose large shields, nearly as tall as themselves, and heavy daggers which they could use as swords. The others all took long spears and the same type of dagger.

Chentelle headed for the stable. She couldn't put it off any longer. The horses that were staying had already been moved. Now it was time to send away the others. Sundancer was waiting for her by the entrance of the tent. She pushed open the makeshift gate and swung onto the mare's back. The other horses milled behind her, free to leave but too well trained to bolt.

Chentelle wrapped her arms around Sundancer's neck and slowly reached for her Gift. She focused every ounce of concentration on the mare, on her feel, her heat, her strength. She needed to open up only a tiny bit, just enough to communicate a simple idea. She wasn't even touching the ground, only Sundancer. Even so, the dead scream assaulted her, twisting her world into a spasm of pain and despair. Her body shuddered uncontrollably, giving a vibrato to her voice.

"Go east," she sang into Sundancer's ear. "Guide the herd. East is food, east is water. Go east. Go."

She felt a chord of understanding in the mare and clamped down her Gift immediately, blocking out the scream. Sundancer twitched nervously, and Chentelle slid off of her back. She pushed her way through the tent, prodding the other horses to leave. With Sundancer's help, she managed to get them all under way. She watched long enough to be satisfied that they were heading in the right direction, then headed back to the fortifications.

The Legionnaires were already in place along the inner battlement. With a feeling approaching awe she realized that many of them were sleeping. Dacius and Councilor A'rullen were deep in conversation on the left flank, and A'stoc and A'valman were arguing about something on the right. She walked toward the right.

"Enchantress!" A'valman called. "I'm glad you are here. Perhaps you can help me talk sense into him. I am trying to convince him that if the battle goes poorly he should leave the rest of us and escape with the Staff."

She turned to A'stoc. "It does make sense. We can't afford to lose the Thunderwood. Don't forget the—the other mission we're on."

"Exactly!" A'valman said. "Remember your other mission, whatever it might be. It serves nothing for you to throw the Thunderwood away. If we are all going to die anyway, you should save yourself and the Staff."

A'stoc looked at Chentelle strangely, then turned to the other wizard. "I do not think that will happen."

A'valman threw up his arms in disgust. "I give up. If you are determined to risk the destruction of the Creation, I cannot stop you."

"Wait," A'stoc said as the councilor turned to leave. "Do you know how to focus through a *mandril?*"

"What?" A'valman raised his brows at the unexpected question. "Yes. It is not my specialty, but I can use one."

A'stoc pulled a thin wooden rod from inside his robe. "This was your father's. It may serve you better than that sword in the coming battle."

A'valman stared at the wand. His jaw trembled, and tears welled in his eyes. Slowly, he extended his hand. "I—I don't . . ."

"It's all right. You don't have to say anything. Just use it well, brother." He placed the wand in A'valman's hand and walked toward his place in the center.

Chentelle stared after him. He wasn't acting at all like himself. She hurried to the new fortification, a knot of fear twisting in her belly.

The dwarves had taken a position just inside the gateway. They squatted in a circle, facing inward. Each of them had a small drum between his knees, on which he was beating a soft, slow tattoo. On the walls, Drup's archers ranged their bows, firing Legion arrows at fixed targets on the hillside. Quivers full of A'kalendane's vorpal shafts were stacked neatly at each one's feet.

Chentelle found a position in the corner near the horses, and sat down with her back to the mountain. Sulmar appeared from somewhere and stood beside her. If he was frightened, or even anxious, he gave no outward sign. They waited.

Just before dark, a Legionnaire rushed by and dropped two loaves of bread and a canteen at their feet. Chentelle had no appetite but she forced herself to eat some of the bread. It was heavy and slightly bitter, but it seemed to settle her stomach a little. She washed it down with water from the canteen, then sat back to wait some more.

Twilight faded into night, and Dacius called for orb-light. Scores, maybe hundreds, of adartak crystals sparked into life, illuminating the hilltop with a soft white glow. Chentelle's eyes were drawn to the fringe of the radiance, to the gray shadows and the black curtain beyond. She searched the darkness, expecting at any moment to see the foul yellow eyes of the enemy.

Time passed: minutes, hours. Nothing came.

She began to wonder whether A'valman had been right. Maybe Bone didn't have any more Ill-creatures to throw at them. After all, they had forced the necromancer's hand when they showed up at Skysoar. He might not be able to mount a large attack so quickly. The ways of the enemy were often inscrutable, but surely it, too, suffered the strictures of logistics. Her eyes burned from fatigue and the stinging dust. Blinking didn't help, so she shut them for a moment.

"THEY COME!"

Chentelle jerked awake. What? She jumped to her feet. The dwarves stood solidly between her and the gap in the wall, arranged now in a phalanx five deep and three across. When had that happened? She squeezed past them and peeked through the opening.

Pale shapes lumbered through the darkness. Fleshless bones gleaming in the orb-light, pinpricks of yellow light floating in empty sockets, bodies clicking grotesquely with each step, the skeletons marched toward them. Ancient weapons twitched in their fingers, and scraps of tattered uniforms hung from their bones.

By the Creator! Bone had raised the bodies of those killed in the Desecration, torn them from the womb of this dead land. Logistics? This was the formation of an entirely new and terrible force! They surged up the hill, hundred or more for every man on the walls: skeletons of humans, goblins, elves, and other creatures she didn't recognize.

Cries of panic sounded from the left flank.

"They are too many! We have to fall back!"

"Yes! To the vault, we'll be safer there!"

"No!" A'stoc slammed the Staff against the ground. Green fire engulfed the wood. "There is no safety belowground. The necromancer commands power enough to collapse the tunnels around us."

Indecision rippled through Jarl's men. Nothing in their short service had prepared them for the dread foe before them.

"HOLD YOUR POSITIONS." Dacius' voice thundered through the confusion. "THE FEAR YOU FEEL IS THE ENEMY'S WEAPON. DO NOT SURRENDER TO IT. REMEMBER YOUR CAUSE."

The men steadied, discipline and courage rising to fight back the terror.

Six flashes of blue light arced through the sky. They fell among the skeletons. Two missed their mark, and three more passed harmlessly through cloth and hollow ribs. The sixth shaft landed solidly in the ball of a shoulder. Blue flames flared from the wound. The skeleton's arm and part of its chest were reduced to cinders.

The Ill-creature staggered sideways for an instant, then resumed its march.

"Hold your fire!" Drup shouted. "Save your shafts for more rewarding targets!"

The skeletons shambled up the hill. Already, they were past the outer battlements.

"WIZARDS, READY."

The Ill-creatures reached the colorful Legion tents.

They attacked the canvas as if it were a living foe, ripping it savagely into scraps.

"NOW."

Earthpower blazed forth in a flaming shaft. A'stoc swept the blast through the center of the attacking line. An arc of skeletons five deep and twenty abreast burst into flame like dry twigs in a campfire.

An explosion of red flame demolished a half dozen of the creatures on the right flank as A'valman brought the *mandril* to bear.

A'rullen's magic was less visually spectacular. He simply pointed with his cane. Wherever he pointed, a skeleton collapsed into a pile of loose bones.

The barrage of magic continued. A score fell before A'rullen's spells, then a score more. Blasts of green and red fire tore wide swaths through the enemy, littering the field with ash and charred bone.

The skeletons came on, uncaring. Why should the dead be concerned about death? The hillside crunched beneath their feet as they marched over the bones of the fallen. Their eyes held no fear, no rage, no pity.

Chentelle looked into those eyes and saw the future, Sulmar's future. These men were enemies of the Dark One once, and now they danced helplessly on the strings of his minion. And what awaited Sulmar was even worse. These bodies were just empty shells. If her liegeman died while bearing the curse, his *soul* would be corrupted. "Sulmar, I want you to stay by my side."

His eyes widened in surprise. "But, mistress—"

"That's an order! I want you here."

"Yes, mistress." His face set in a hard mask, and he turned to watch the battle.

The skeletons had penetrated to the inner battlement. A'stoc still denied them the center, but by sheer numbers they had pressed through on the flanks. They hit the wall in waves, driving the defenders backward.

The Legionnaires fought bravely. Glowing swords sliced the night with ribbons of light and destruction. A hundred skeletons fell on each flank before the first scrambled over the wall, but come over they did. The lines bowed dangerously inward.

"SULMAR, SUPPORT THE RIGHT."

The Tengarian turned to Chentelle, eyes hard, muscles tensed for action.

She looked down, unable to face his stare. Her hands trembled uncontrollably and she felt ill, but she kept silent.

Dacius crashed into the skeletons on the left flank. He waded through their ranks, rallying the Legionnaires to his side. Not claw nor sword nor ancient spear could pierce his glowing armor. His shield turned every strike. His helm resisted every blow. And his vorpal blade carved a tireless pocket of destruction.

Ill-creatures swarmed around him, trying to overwhelm him with their mass.

A'rullen stepped forward and tapped a skeleton with his cane. Lightning erupted from the wood, shattering the creature. Then it jumped to another, and another. Then lightning chained through a score of Ill-creatures, leaving fractured bones in its wake.

Jarl rallied his men into the opening. They fought their way to Dacius' side, and together they drove the skeletons back to the wall. Two Legionnaires lay dead among the bones, but they had repelled the assault. And the ranks of the enemy were thinning.

The right flank was not faring so well. Kruzel's men had been forced back from the wall. They gave ground slowly, struggling to maintain the integrity of their line.

A'valman anchored the pivot. He stood beside A'stoc and rained fire upon the Ill-creatures. But there were hundreds of skeletons, and he dared not strike too close to the Legionnaires.

Kruzel was a marvel of harnessed rage. Bonesplitter howled through the air, decimating its foes with shaft and blade. He held the far end of the pivot, preventing the skeletons from turning the flank.

But the Legionnaires' line was stretched thin. A man dropped, his back exposed an instant too long and his comrade a step too far away. The second man fell an instant later as skeletons surged through the gap. Before the Legionnaires realized their peril, two more men had died.

Their screams rang like an accusation in Chentelle's ears.

"FEN, PLUG THAT HOLE!"

The dwarves ran forward, voices raised in a wordless chant. Their feet fell in perfect unison, and four ranks of long spears snapped forward as one. They hit the breech like a juggernaut, crashing through the line of skeletons without slowing. The shieldmen drove forward, pressing against the mass of Ill-creatures. The rear ranks skewered the enemy with a mass of glowing steel points.

The dwarven phalanx drove the skeletons from the breach, then continued to press forward. But they were too successful. They gained ground faster than the Legionnaires could support them. They found themselves isolated, surrounded by enemies on three sides. They struggled to realign their long spears.

Kruzel fought like a madman. Heedless of risk, he pressed through the melee, fighting to the dwarves' side. His men struggled to stay with him.

A dwarf died, his throat opened by a skeletal goblin's claw. The others dropped their spears and fought with their heavy vorpal knives.

Two of Kruzel's men reached his side. Together they solidified the dwarves' right.

But the outcome was still in doubt. The skeletons pressed the dwarves' left, trying to drive between them and the Legionnaires. Another dwarf fell.

Then Dacius arrived, charging from the now secure left flank. He slammed one skeleton at a full run, crushing its skull with his shield. His blade severed another through the waist. A curved blade glanced harmlessly off his shoulder, and he dispatched its owner with his backswing. He drove into the center of the attackers. A dozen blows rang against his armor without effect, and his sword answered with sweeping arcs of blue destruction.

The skeletons concentrated their attacks on the human lord, leeching strength from their forward thrust.

Kruzel and the dwarves took advantage of the break to solidify their lines and organize a coordinated counterthrust. In minutes, they had succeeded in pressing the enemy back to the battlements.

A'stoc held the center by himself. Surrounded by an unassailable inferno of Earthpower, he stood against the horde of Ill-creatures. Hundreds vanished under his storm, and still they kept coming. He decimated thousands, and they kept coming. The power raged around him. He waved his arm, and three score of the creatures exploded in green flame. He swung the Staff, and a cyclone of fire swept a hundred more into oblivion.

The skeletons, answering to some hidden call, abruptly abandoned the center, committing all of their numbers to the flanks.

A'stoc let more power flow into his storm. Roaring walls of flame sprang up behind the Ill-creatures. The flames swept forward, crushing the skeletons between the defensive line and certain destruction. The air crackled with the sound of exploding bones.

Chentelle felt a twinge of panic. The wizard's face twisted with strain, but was it from the effort of summoning the power or the effort of keeping it in check? If he lost control . . .

The wall of flame surged toward the battlements, consigning hundreds of Ill-creatures to oblivion. Then they stopped, again answering to the hidden command, and tried to re-form their line. But the power of the Staff caught them, and they soon flickered into nothingness.

Roaring in triumph, the Legionnaires drove forward and quickly dispatched the few remaining skeletons.

"WELL DONE, WELL FOUGHT. BUT HOLD YOUR POSITIONS; THE BATTLE IS NOT DONE. RESERVES, GATHER THE FALLEN AND RE-TURN TO THE DWARVEN WALL."

The rush of elation faded. Soberly, the Legionnaires returned to the walls.

The dwarves ferried bodies with solid efficiency, laying them neatly in one corner of the fortification. Two of their fellows and six Legionnaires joined the line.

To Chentelle, it seemed each pair of lifeless eyes stared straight at her.

Suddenly, a chain of dark force ripped through the orb-lights. One after another, the adartak stones exploded into sparkling fragments. The shrapnel glittered on the hill like a thousand twinkling stars, then they faded into darkness.

A'rullen shouted a spell and touched his cane to a nearby crystal. Gold radiance shot forth to combat the Ill-Lore. The two chains twisted about each other and flashed into nothingness. Orb-light still glowed within the perimeter, but the hillside was now swallowed by night.

"LIGHT THE OUTER FIRES."

Flames leaped along oil-soaked lines of timber, driving the darkness farther down the hill.

Hollow laughter dropped from the sky. A flash of lightning seared the air. For an instant they caught a glimpse of the enemy. Companies of vikhors gathered at the foot of the hill. Shadow knights ranged behind them, scurrying back and forth on segmented legs. In the rear, a half-dozen demonspawn towered above them all, iron staves clutched in their claws.

That army remained motionless at the bottom of the hill, but already the second wave was moving into the firelight: more skeletons. There were many fewer than in the first wave, but these were not the remains of goblins or elves. Giants marched toward them, and misshapen trolls like the ones below. Twice the height of any human, the huge skeletons wielded great hammers larger and heavier than any man. Some carried chunks of stone that they had ripped from the outer walls.

But most terrible of all were the four smaller figures that led the assault. No skeletons were these, but fresh bodies clothed in flesh not two days cold—bodies clothed in the black and tan of Tel Adartak's Legion companies. The necromancer had raised the bodies of their fellows against them.

Stunned silence gripped the Legion ranks as the horror of what they faced became clear. Then a single arrow flashed through the distance. It struck one of the Legion corpses in the center of its stomach. Blue radiance surrounded the shaft as the zombie flesh disintegrated.

The corpse never broke step. It marched toward them, the bones of its spine and ribs glistening in the flickering light.

Rocks filled the air, propelled by arms that had long since lost flesh and sinew. Legionnaires ducked for cover as the stones crashed into the fortifications. Walls shook with the impact, and an archer dropped to the ground near Chentelle's feet. His skull and chest were crushed beyond recognition.

"No!" Terror and rage whirled through Chentelle's heart. So many deaths, so many graves, and even that was not the end. The necromancer would defile everything. She ran forward, letting the Gift swell within her. She didn't care how much it hurt. She had to do something.

"Chentelle! Stay back!"

She ignored A'stoc's call. Agony burned through her. She had to release it. She crashed into something hard—the battlement. Grimacing in pain, she scrambled over the low wall and dropped to her knees in the dust and bones beyond. Death surrounded her, reaching through her Gift with icy fingers. She threw back her head and screamed.

Death! Her voice ripped through the air, filled with the power of her Gift. She didn't sing; she wailed. The anguish of this dead land poured through her, and she shaped it into a keen of mourning. Her cry rang through the animated bodies, filling them with echoes of dry bones and cold graves.

The skeletons were the first to fall. The hand of death had been long upon them, and the memory returned quickly. The Legionnaires' bodies crept onward, clinging desperately to their last vestige of life. But Chentelle's lamentation would not be denied. It pierced the shield of Ill-Lore that drove them. One by one, the bodies fell. The field was empty.

Chentelle let her howl fade. She had released much, but the torment of the Desecration was endless. The world spun in a haze of anguish, and she was cold, very cold. She lay down on the cushion of bones and curled into a ball.

A high-pitched whine filled the air. She knew that sound—shadow knights, calling to their vikhors. A chorus of roars and yelps followed. They were coming.

Strong arms lifted her from the ground. Immediately, the pain receded. "Mistress, we must move."

Sulmar carried her back inside the dwarven wall. The instant he set her down, the agony returned.

"Oooh!" She swooned against the wall. Sulmar reached forward to help her, but she held him away. Her mouth trembled uncontrollably, but she made herself speak. "No. Go on, Sulmar. Fight, die, do whatever you must. I'll be fine."

Indecision showed on the Tengarian's face. The roar of combat filled the air, but he hesitated, searching her face. Then he spun and ran toward the walls, his vorpal sword shining like a steel sun.

Chentelle forced herself to stay upright until he was out of sight, then she slumped to the ground. It would be so easy to shut the pain away, to suppress the Gift again. But that was like denying a part of her soul. She couldn't do that again. Already, too many good creatures had paid the price for her cowardice. Sulmar was right, she had to find the strength in who she was.

She opened herself to the Gift, letting the pain wash through her. She was dimly aware of the battle: screams of rage and pain, magic thundering in the night, the ground trembling beneath her. But these things faded into a haze. The Desecration filled her world.

The gray agony was endless. It extended to the core of the world. The Creation was shattered; no life remained. No, that was wrong! The dwarven wall pulsed steadily at her back, giving warmth to push back the chill of the land. *There is life, our life.*

She grabbed onto the revelation, fixing it in her heart. The cold gray of the Desecration was endless, but not hopeless. As long as life remained, hope remained. Slowly, the pain dissipated. She still felt the torment of the land, but it no longer consumed her.

She climbed to her feet, searching the battlefield for Sulmar.

Vikhors snarled through at the perimeter. The inner battlements had been overrun, and the retreating lines were in danger of collapse.

The center was dominated by an inferno of Earthpower and Ill-Lore. Four demonspawn were arrayed against A'stoc, their iron staves joined together to counter the power of the Thunderwood. The wizard's green flames were slowly gaining ascendancy, but he could offer no help to the flanks.

A'rullen and another demonspawn dueled on the left, but the old wizard was obviously overmatched. He did not attack. All of his energy went into maintaining a shield, but even that was failing. The demonspawn's magic ripped into his wards, creeping ever closer to the exhausted mage.

Vikhors and shadow knights harried the retreating Legionnaires. Without magical support, the line could not hold. Only steady fire from the archers kept it from becoming a rout.

"FOR LEGION!" Dacius waded into the mass of attackers. He cut the legs from under a shadow knight and severed the creature's head as it fell. His armor glowed like a beacon in the chaos as he strove to rally the line.

He leaped forward, sword sweeping in a great arc. Two vikhors flashed into oblivion.

Another Tenebrite rose before him, and he took its blade on his shield. His own counter found only air as the monster danced backward on insect legs.

A vikhor crashed into his flank. His shield blocked the creature's fangs, but a long claw raked his leg. He staggered to one knee, then pivoted and thrust upward. The vorpal blade drove through the vikhor's chest, and the Ill-creature vanished with an earsplitting howl.

A glowing red blade sliced through the air. It struck Dacius in the back, driving him face first to the ground. Vikhors swarmed over him as the shadow knight moved forward for the kill.

A bolt of lightning shot through the melee, incinerating three of the vikhors. It caught the Tenebrite full in the chest. For an instant, the Ill-creature withstood the assault, burning with blinding intensity. Then sword and master both exploded into flames.

A'rullen spun back to face the demonspawn, but he was too late. His protective shields collapsed as the Ill-creature took advantage of his distraction. A bolt of force splintered the cane in his hand and hurled him backward against the inner wall. He slumped to his hands and knees, unable to stand.

The demonspawn marched forward, lightning crackling around its iron staff.

"FOR HONOR!" Dacius pressed past a vikhor and charged the demonspawn. The Ill-creature brought its staff crashing down against his raised shield. Lightning surged around the glowing steel, then vanished. His sword radiated into brilliance, leaving a trail of blue flame as it cleaved the air in an overhand stroke.

The demonspawn raised its staff to block the blow. The sword sliced through the iron stave without slowing and buried itself in the demonspawn's skull. The Ill-creature fell, swallowed by blue fire.

"FOR CREATION," Dacius shouted, crashing back into the mass of vikhors.

Chentelle turned to the right flank, searching the madness for signs of Sulmar.

Kruzel's men fought desperately against the tide of Ill-creatures. The dwarven reserves stood next to them, already committed to the battle. Together, they were managing to hold the retreat, but the line was thin. Every man who fell threatened to strain it beyond hope, and too many men were falling.

A'valman stood alone on the extreme right, *mandril* thrust before him in trembling hands. Ball after ball of wizard-fire roared from the wand, flying through the air to crash into a demonspawn.

The Ill-creature took the assault on its staff, the iron glowing red with heat as it absorbed the magic, then white. Lightning flashed around the Ill-creature, ripping through the ranks of its own army. It was trapped. It had no safe place to redirect the assault.

A'valman pressed his attack. His body shook with effort, but the *mandril* stayed pointed straight at the demonspawn's heart.

The iron rod flared brightly and exploded into flame. The demonspawn followed an instant later.

The wizard staggered and let the *mandril* drop to his side. A vikhor leaped into the opening created when the magical flames died.

A'valman jerked the wand upward. A trickle of fire sputtered from the *mandril*, vanishing long before it reached the Ill-creature. The wizard let the wand fall from his fingers. He stood unmoving as the Ill-creature approached.

The vikhor dashed forward, howling in anticipation.

Two arrows flashed into the monster's chest, reducing it to ashes.

More vikhors rushed into the gap, but a swordsman interposed himself in front of the wizard. It was Sulmar! He fought defensively, holding the Ill-creatures at bay while A'valman regained his strength.

Luckily, the bulk of the attackers remained engaged with the dwarves and Legionnaires. Less than a dozen turned to harry Sulmar. The vikhors snarled and snapped just beyond reach of his blade, but any who came closer vanished in a flash of blue steel.

Vikhors! Chentelle searched the battle lines. It was only vikhors. Where were the shadow knights? She spun around. A dozen shapes were scurrying down the side of the mountain, clinging to the rock face like giant spiders. "Drup, behind you!"

The young Legionnaire whirled. His bow came up as he sighted and loosed in a single motion. "Archers, guard the rear!"

Blue light sparkled in the abdomen of one Tenebrite. It staggered and fell from the wall in a rain of ash.

More arrows shot through the air. Three more shadow knights fell.

The others burst into frenzied action, closing the distance with unbelievable speed. Two of them simply jumped from the wall. Their legs buckled as they crashed to the ground, but they started to rise again immediately.

Vorpal shafts took out the leapers before they could regain their feet, and more Tenebrites fell from the rock face. The others made the perimeter. Three of them went to the walls, their legs and abdomens blurring as they stepped onto the narrow walkway wearing the bodies of armored men. The other dropped in front of Chentelle, its yellow eyes glowing maliciously.

She summoned her Gift and opened her mouth to sing.

The Tenebrite tilted forward. Its back legs scraped together in a blur of motion.

The shrill whine drove through Chentelle's ears, drowning out her own voice. Her Gift could not save her.

The Tenebrite shuffled forward, sword raised to strike her down.

Drup leaped at the creature, a vorpal arrow clutched in his hand. The Ill-creature dodged sideways, but the gleaming tip still scraped a shallow gouge across its abdomen.

The shadow knight sent its blade whistling toward the Legionnaire's exposed back.

Drup dived out of the way and rolled to his feet. His vorpal sword scraped from its scabbard.

He barely had time to raise it before the Ill-creature was upon him. Steel crashed against steel as the shadow knight forced him backward. Every touch of swords leeched power from the vorpal blade.

He needed help. But the Tenebrite's screech still drowned Chentelle's voice. She searched the walls. Three of the other archers had already fallen. The last was fighting a desperate duel on the walkway with the last remaining shadow knight. He looked young, even for a human.

The walkway!

Chentelle ran to the wall and pressed her face against it. She extended her Gift, feeling the firm threads of dwarven Stone Lore. She latched on to those threads and sang. Her voice had to reach only to the stone wall; the whine couldn't stop that. The threads of dwarven magic vibrated with her voice, carrying her need to the walkway underneath the shadow knight. The bricks released their hold on each other, and the Ill-creature tumbled to the ground in a shower of loose rock.

But was she in time?

Almost no radiance remained in Drup's vorpal blade. He was being herded steadily into the corner by hammer blows of the shadow knight's sword. He ducked under a cut and tried to roll free of the trap.

One of the Tenebrite's legs shot forward. It struck the Legionnaire in the chest and hurled him back against the wall. The red sword shot downward.

Drup raised his blade to block. The vorpal sword shattered and dropped from his limp hand. He scrambled backward, but his feet tangled in the row of bodies and he went down.

The Tenebrite scuttled forward.

A bowstring thrummed. Light whistled through the air. The Tenebrite staggered, blue flame spouting from its back. The red sword fell to the ground, landing mere moments before the ashes of its master.

Chentelle looked behind her. The young archer was already stringing another shaft and turning toward the front. His sword vibrated in the ground near the foot of the wall, embedded in a pile of ash.

Laughter rang down from above. A great shadow swept over the battlefield. The dragon roared, and acid spewed from its mouth, splattering their right flank.

A score of vikhors fell, howling in agony as the vitriol burned through them. But they were not alone. Five dwarves and three of Kruzel's Legionnaires went down with them.

Ill-creatures surged through the hole. The lines collapsed. All sense of order disappeared as the battle dissolved into a dozen individual melees. The left flank disintegrated as the vikhors attacked their rear.

A'valman came hurtling over the wall. He landed hard, but scrambled immediately to his feet.

Chentelle gaped at him. "What are—"

He drew his vorpal sword and threw it past her shoulder. The blade spun through the air, then it stabilized. It floated in the gap between walls, lashing out at any vikhors that came near. An instant later, the archer's blade sprang from the ground to join it.

Drup scrambled onto the wall and retrieved his bow. His hands moved in a blur, sending bolts of blue flame into the swirling chaos.

Dacius formed a rallying point on the left flank. His armor shone through the mass of Ill-creatures, and his sword carved through their ranks. His voice thundered over the field, but it gave no rousing cry to battle, only the guttural grunts of a man pushed to exhaustion.

The right flank was hopeless. Vikhors swarmed without check. Defenders were isolated, surrounded, and torn to pieces.

Suddenly, the pressure eased. Vikhors streamed away from the walls, charging back down the hill.

What was happening? Chentelle climbed onto the wall and searched the field. It was Sulmar!

The Tengarian was halfway down the hill, charging toward the Black Dragon. Vorpal swords glowed in both of his hands, and his path was littered with smoldering ash. He chanted a one word battle cry like a mantra. "Kaliya!"

Kruzel was only a step behind him. The Legionnaire matched Sulmar's deadly grace with a berserker fury. He laid about him with the vorpal spear, Bonesplitter. Blood flowed from a dozen wounds on his chest and legs, but he gave them no notice. His battle cries were incoherent and terrible.

Vikhors poured down the hill, swirling around the two warriors, trying to cut off their advance.

Bone gestured. Lightning shot from his wand, sizzling toward the humans.

It shattered against a wall of green flame. A'stoc had finally dispatched the last of the demonspawn. The Thunderwood blazed in his hands, but he didn't attack. He couldn't as long as the necromancer sat astride a living creature.

Bone's cackle roared over the hilltop. "You are exhausted, fool. You can barely stand. I will pry the Staff from your dead hands and then raise your corpse to serve my whim."

Lightning shot from the necromancer's bone wand. A'stoc blocked it with Earthpower, but it penetrated far into his shield before dying.

Dacius drove his sword through a vikhor. The Ill-creature fell, and none jumped to replace it. The hilltop was clear. "FALL BACK. FORTIFY THE INNER WALLS."

What about Sulmar and Kruzel? Chentelle watched the weary Legionnaires stagger through the gate. Not one was uninjured, and most seeped blood from a half-dozen wounds. Dacius was right. These men had no strength to pursue the vikhors. But Dacius himself was absent.

She turned back to the field. There! The human lord stalked purposefully down the hill. Beside him were Fen, Fel, and two of their brethren, marching to the steady beat of a war chant.

But they were too far away. Scores of vikhors surrounded the two humans. Kruzel's spear still flashed with manic energy, but as often as not, now, it missed its mark. The human flailed about, trying to react to a dozen threats at once.

Sulmar was halted, too. The vikhors ringed him completely. He spun in a continual circle, blades whirling without cease. The Ill-creatures could not penetrate the defensive web of his steel, but he could not press forward without exposing his back. And the spinning blades were slowing.

A'stoc was paralyzed. He could neither attack the necromancer nor turn his attention away long enough to help the warriors.

"Necromancer!" Kruzel shifted his grip on the vorpal spear. "Die!" His arm shot forward. Bonesplitter sailed through the air, piercing Bone through the rib cage.

The necromancer dropped from the dragon's back.

A'stoc took advantage of the reprieve to gather his strength. Earthpower ripped through the vikhors, reducing scores of them to dust. But the wizard dared not strike too close to the humans. The vikhors closed around the defenseless Legionnaire.

Arrows shot through the air, destroying two of the vikhors. A sword followed, whistling through the air to reduce another of the Ill-creatures to ash. A second blade whirled and hung in the air before Kruzel's face. Howling in triumph, he seized the blade and lashed out at his attackers. He slashed about wildly, holding the monsters at bay until Dacius and the dwarves arrived to relieve him.

Sulmar jumped into the opening created by A'stoc's blast. He sliced a sword through a vikhor's neck and let it fall to the ground with the creature's ashes. The second he left in one of the Ill-creature's chests. Now nothing lay between him and the Black Dragon. He bolted down the hill, drawing his black sword as he ran.

The dragon leaped, huge bat wings beating furiously against the air. The ground fell away beneath it.

Sulmar jumped, dark blade thrust over his head in both hands. The sword bit into the dragon's shoulder and sank to the hilt. He pulled himself onto the dragon's back, using the sword as a grip.

The beast screamed and beat its wings faster. Dragon and rider sailed into the darkness.

Lightning flashed into A'stoc's shields, driving the wizard backward. Bone stood at the bottom of the hill, Kruzel's spear still driven through his ribs. The necromancer advanced on A'stoc, Ill-Lore crackling in the air around him.

A'stoc steadied himself and called on the power of the Thunderwood. Green flame shot forth to meet the necromancer.

Magic dueled in the air. The glare was blinding. Earthpower and Ill-Lore flared and pulsed, ripping chunks of stone from the earth in their fury.

The center of the storm raged back and forth between A'stoc and the necromancer. But through it all, Bone advanced up the hillside. Step by step, he drew nearer to the exhausted wizard.

Suddenly, the necromancer screamed. In a moment, Chentelle saw why. Bonesplitter glowed fiercely and lifted the Ill-creature into the air. The spear thrashed back and forth, ripping through Bone's leathery flesh.

The twisted wand dropped from Bone's hand. The aura of Ill-Lore vanished, and Earthpower ripped through the necromancer. Flesh and bone flaked away into glowing embers, and the embers faded to nothing.

Chentelle felt a rush of freedom and joy. She was suddenly conscious that the necromancer's eyes no longer touched her soul. By the Creator, all this time! She hadn't even realized the connection still existed, but now she knew it was gone. And she knew something else. Father Marcus would be free, too.

Bonesplitter hung in the air for a second, then dropped to the ground.

The few remaining vikhors offered little resistance. Those who did not fall under vorpal steel turned and fled into the night.

"It's over," A'valman said.

A wave of relief rippled through the defenders. A few even managed to raise a weary cheer.

"Wait," Chentelle cried. "What about Sulmar?"

⬱ 17 ⬱

REUNITED

W e have to find him!"

Dacius pulled the helm from over his head. His face was pale from exhaustion and blood loss. "I'd like to, Chentelle, but how? We don't know where to look, and we don't have the strength to search. Look around. I have a dozen wounded and no healer. There aren't three men in camp who could walk farther than the bottom of the hill."

"But—" She cut herself off. He was right. One look at the battered and exhausted soldiers told her that. The wizard councilors had set up a first aid station, but their skills were quickly overwhelmed by the demand. Broken bones sat unattended while they struggled to bind wounds and control bleeding. Some of the wounded were closer to death than life.

She glanced at the deep red blood that still seeped down Dacius' leg. "You'd better go see the wizards yourself."

He followed her look. "You're right. As soon as I check the perimeter." He turned and limped off.

But she couldn't just give up. She had to find Sulmar. He might be in trouble. Might? He had been carried away by a dragon!

She spotted A'stoc poking through the rubble on the hillside and ran toward him. Maybe the wizard could help?

"Be careful where you step," A'stoc said as she approached. He was using the Staff to sift through the piles of broken and charred bones that littered the hill. The gnarled wood trembled in the wizard's hands, and his breath came in heavy gasps.

"A'stoc, I need your—"

"Wait!" He flipped part of a giant's femur out of his way with one end of the Staff. "Ah, there you are."

Bone's wand lay exposed on the hillside. The twisted rod was hardly distinguishable from the remains that surrounded it. She shuddered, remembering what its touch could do. "Is it still dangerous?"

A'stoc raised his Staff overhead with both hands. The Thunderwood crashed down, splintering the bone wand. "Not anymore. Now, what do you need?"

"We have to find Sulmar." She stared into his eyes, letting him see her need. "The dragon flew off with him. You have to help me find him!"

A'stoc winced and looked away from her. His shoulders slumped, and he leaned heavily on the Staff. "Where is he?"

"I don't know!" Chentelle took a deep breath. She had to stay calm. But Sulmar needed help. She could *feel* it! They had to find him. "He was on the dragon's back. I don't know where they went."

A'stoc looked at the night sky. "We have an hour or more until first-light. We can organize a search then."

"But that might be too late!" She grabbed the wizard's arm, pleading with him. "Don't you see? If he dies, his *soul* will be lost forever."

A'stoc's arm quavered under her fingers. "Chentelle, please, try to understand. I will help, but we have to wait. There are still vikhors out there. They will not attack the camp, but alone in the dark we will be vulnerable. Whatever strength I had has been spent already. I could not protect you."

"Oh, no, he'll be helpless." She tried to catch the wizard's eyes with her own. "Please, we can't leave him out there alone!"

A'stoc turned away and rested his head against the Staff. "I'm sorry, Chentelle."

"Fine." She spun on her heel and stalked off. The wizard called something to her back, but she didn't really care what he said right now. If no one would help her, she'd find Sulmar on her own. The question was, how?

Find the strength in who you are. Sulmar's words; maybe they held the key. She walked to the edge of the ruined battlements, far away from the others. The distance would make it easier. She sat down on the cold rock and shut her eyes, closing out the world of her senses. She had reached a peace with the torment of the Desecration. Now she needed more; she needed a boon. Breathing deeply and slowly, Chentelle let her awareness expand into the tortured earth.

The land screamed at her, but it was the old scream. She knew it, now. She could go beyond the pain. She became aware of other notes, faint buzzes of warmth underneath the land's cold dirge. They were touches of life on an ancient grave. These were close, dotting the hillside above. She allowed herself a slight smile.

But she had to go further, had to ignore the close presence of her friends. She opened herself to the Desecration, letting the song of cold agony fill her. It seemed to go on forever, the grave of the world, endless, eternal. But there had to be more. Somewhere, there had to be warmth, life. Somewhere, there had to be the touch of Sulmar. She just needed to find it.

The scream was everywhere. It roared through her, drowning everything. The cold was terrible, final. There was no resisting it, no denying it. She could only sink into the icy grave, surrendering all hope of warmth. She just had to let go. It would—wait!

Chentelle's eyes snapped open. Her body was shivering violently, and a horrible scream burned through her throat. Her jaws ached and her head throbbed, but she couldn't make herself stop. Finally, her exhausted lungs gave out. The scream ended, and she gasped desperately for fresh air. More shouts drifted down to her from the top of the hill.

Drup was running toward her, vorpal sword bare in his hand. He covered the distance in fast, easy strides. Behind him, A'stoc stumbled down the slope. Even with the Staff for support, he barely managed to keep from falling.

"Chentelle, what's wrong?" Drup's eyes flicked restlessly through the shadowed hillside.

"Nothing," she said, trying to stop her teeth from chattering. Her strength was returning swiftly. "Everything's wonderful! I found him." She grabbed the Legionnaire's arm and started pulling him back up the hill. "Come on. Let's go."

A'stoc lurched to a halt as he saw them approaching.

"I found him," Chentelle called as she and Drup ran past. "Hurry! He's very faint."

She dashed into the camp, unconcerned with the commotion she was causing. "Dacius! Where are you?"

"Here." The human lord lay facedown across a slab of rock, naked below the waist. A jagged rip extended nearly the length of his left thigh, spilling blood onto the stones. A'rullen stood behind him, weaving the wound closed with a tendril of shimmering light.

"I found Sulmar!" Chentelle said. "I know where he is. I need one of the horses to go get him."

Drup walked up beside her. "I'll go with her, to keep her safe."

"As will I." It was the young archer from the wall. He picked up his bow and swung it casually over one shoulder.

"Very well." Dacius turned to Drup. "You're in charge. No unnecessary risks, turn back if you're challenged seriously."

"Let's go!" Chentelle ran to the corner and ripped the hobbles and blinders off three of the horses. She swung immediately onto the back of a brown mare, not even pausing to remove the saddle.

"Wait." A'stoc shuffled through the gateway. "Hel's blood, girl, give a minute."

Chentelle dropped to the ground and readied the last horse. She bristled at the delay, but part of her also smiled. It would be good to have the wizard along.

As soon as they were mounted, Chentelle led them northward. The horses stepped nervously across the shattered landscape, dropping each hoof carefully through the dust. Chentelle's heart pounded with the need for speed, but she kept their pace to a walk. It wouldn't help anyone if a horse came up lame.

A'stoc mumbled a soft spell, and soft orb-light shone from between his fingers. "Here." He tossed her the adartak.

Chentelle grabbed the glowing crystal gratefully. She leaned over her mare's neck, letting the orb-light illuminate their path. She closed her eyes and rocked with the motion of the horse, blending her body into the mare's rhythm. Then, confident that her seat was secure, she cast her Gift into the north.

She knew where to look, now, and the mare's strength shielded her from the Desecration. She found Sulmar's presence almost immediately. But it was weak, a dying ember fading to ash. She sang softly into her mount's ear, touching her with the sense of Sulmar and the urgency of their need.

The mare snorted and broke into a run.

Chentelle held Sulmar's spark in her mind, willing it to survive. *I'm coming. Hold on, Sulmar, hold on. We're almost*—There!

Chentelle was on the ground before the mare could come to a stop. Sulmar's body lay in the dust at the base of a hill, like a discarded doll. His legs were twisted horribly, and points of white bone poked through the torn fabric of his trousers. A crust of dried blood covered one side of his face and neck. His eyes were open but unfocused, and his right arm was completely covered with a writhing shadow.

Chentelle dropped to her knees and pressed her face to Sulmar's. Immediately, her Gift pressed into the darkness. Black tendrils floated through the agony of shattered limbs and blood-filled lungs, but a hard light blocked their progress. Despite his injuries, Sulmar's will remained strong, resolute. But his body was dying, and the flame of his spirit grew weaker with each ragged breath. It was only a matter of time until the curse claimed him.

NO. Chentelle drove her Gift toward the light, blending her own will with Sulmar's. The instant she made contact, a feeling of peace flushed through her. The pain faded, the sorrow disappeared. There was no fear, no rage—only focus, discipline. A shimmer of warmth carried Sulmar's recognition of her presence. He welcomed her into the struggle with a surge of satisfaction, almost joy. What more could a warrior ask than to enter his final battle at his liege's side.

No. Chentelle refused to accept that. Sulmar had the will but not the strength, so she gave him hers. The Gift rose within her, and she shaped it into a song of hope and power, a song of life. She poured her music into Sulmar, filling him with the dance of butterflies and the laughter of children. The light of his spirit steadied and grew. They could not banish the darkness. But, together, they could press it back.

With that contact of spirit, Chentelle found also Sulmar's memory of the most recent events. It focused on the struggle that had brought him to this state. His spirit had been injured as well as his body, and in her effort of healing she became part of both. To understand it and help mend it, she had to relive the struggle with him. She joined him on the body of the Black Dragon.

The wind howled in Sulmar's ears as he crawled across the creature's back. His fingers gripped the scant purchase of the rough scales. Their metallic plating overlapped, making the armor as effective as any worn by man. Now he understood why his sword had not penetrated deeply. The dragon had been injured, but the wound was far from mortal.

The great head whipped back and forth on the sinuous neck, trying to locate the nuisance that rode the body. But the neck flexed mainly down and to the sides, where the prey usually was, rather than up or back. Perhaps on the ground the dragon could have twisted its body tightly enough to snap effectively at the encumbrance, but in flight it had to maintain an extended position. It couldn't reach him. Yet.

The head oriented on something to the side. Sulmar looked. There was a faint outline of a shape in the distance. It seemed to be a truncated mountain with a roughly level plateau on top. That would be an ideal place for a dragon to land, so that it could then coil and dispose of whatever clung to it. The wing beats strengthened, and the flight pattern changed. The mountain plateau was now ahead.

Sulmar knew that he could not afford to wait on the Black Dragon's convenience. He had to act now. Stretched flat, he worked his way to the base of the neck, where the necromancer had been seated. From here he might be able to control the dragon's flight, the way Bone had. If there were any spurs or reins or other devices to compel its compliance as a steed—

Aware of the motion, the dragon also acted. She raised a hind leg and clawed at the vorpal sword wedged in her side. The sword came loose and fell away.

Sulmar cursed under his breath. He should have tried to recover that sword first! Now he had no chance to use an effective weapon.

The dragon swung its head around, trying to bite, but the saddle region was out of its reach. The jaws snapped just shy of Sulmar's leg. It occurred to him that if he had gone for the sword, the dragon's leg could have caught him and dislodged him as readily as it had the sword. So maybe his mistake had avoided a worse mistake. That could even be why the dragon had waited to scratch out that sword; she had expected the man to go for it.

Nevertheless, Sulmar knew he was at a serious disadvantage. The dragon was at home in the skies, while he was not. Every time he lifted his head, the freezing wind threatened to rip him away. He saw the dragon's neck writhe as the head tried once more to get at him. Any slip, any misjudgment on Sulmar's part, would give the dragon that marginal leeway to catch at some part of him. The moment that happened, it would be over. But for the moment, they were at a stalemate.

It would last only until the dragon reached the plateau. Yet why was it still trying to snap at him now? Why didn't it simply wait until it could more conveniently dispatch him on the ground? That suggested that it knew something he didn't. That it had a vulnerability it feared he was about to exploit. But what could that be?

Then the dragon changed tactics. It bucked and twisted in the air like an unbroken horse, trying to pitch him from his precarious perch. Sulmar held on, knowing that it would be folly to let go. Fortunately this saddle region had places for hands and feet to grip, though he found no reins or other mechanism of control. Probably Bone had used magic for that.

When it was apparent that the effort wasn't effective, the dragon tried a new ploy. It climbed up into the heavens. Sulmar was amazed as it moved so high so fast, seeming to leave the whole of Infinitera behind. Higher and higher, it sailed through the darkness of night. The air became thin. Sulmar dug his fingers into the fleshy crevices of the beast and hung on. If it could breathe here, so could he!

The pale luminescence of the earth below and the overbright stars above became a swirl as the dragon spiraled on upward. Was it trying to use centrifugal force to dislodge him? That wasn't sensible, because though his legs dangled out over empty space, the neck of the creature was between him and that space; he was actually more firmly anchored than before.

Then the dragon folded its wings and dropped like a stone, plunging toward the earth with terrific speed. The wind increased, threatening to tear him away, but still he managed to hang on, hoping the monster was not aware how close it was coming to success. The thing was using everything to throw him off. Eventually, it would succeed.

Sulmar, uncertain whether his life would continue more than a few moments, considered the alternatives. If the dragon didn't bite him or throw him off, it would soon land and finish the job more messily there. Without a sword, he could not hope to fight it. So he had to stop it very soon. But even if he found a way, it would be only half a victory, because when the dragon fell out of the sky, Sulmar would fall, too. Still, he was determined to do something. He had vowed to put an end to this evil creature and the curse. If it meant dying in the process, then so be it. At least he would not be tormented after death.

Yet it seemed to be hopeless. There was no clear way to kill the beast without a weapon. Was he to do it bare-handed?

Bare-handed. Abruptly he had an idea.

The dragon spread its wings and leveled out from its dive, almost grazing the ground. Sulmar left his relatively safe perch in the saddle region and began inching his way forward. Now he was scaling the creature's massive neck. The dragon thrashed its head around, trying to gore him with its horns, but this was another vain effort, because of course the motions carried him with them. He realized that the creature wasn't all that smart; it was proceeding mostly on instinct and viciousness.

But the mountain plateau was coming uncomfortably close, and that was a kind of deadline. Had the dragon simply flown straight toward it, instead of trying the fancy maneuvers, it would have had him at its nonexistent mercy by now. Would it kill him outright, or cripple him and play with him for a while, prolonging his torture and its entertainment? He would soon find out, if he didn't deal with it very shortly.

He worked his way forward until he reached the back of the giant head. Here he found that the armor was of rigid bone, rather than scales, impenetrable. He sighted down the long snout and saw the dull gleam of the monstrous teeth, the darting red tongue, and closer in, the burning right eye.

That eye swiveled in its socket until it focused directly back on him. The effect was eerie; he had had no idea the dragon could do that. It was watching him!

Suddenly Sulmar heard a booming voice in the wind. "Accursed, I will destroy you!"

He was so surprised that he almost let go of his grip. The Black Dragon was speaking in his human language!

But it didn't matter. He had a job to do, and it had to be done now, or he would be lost. So he didn't answer, once again denying the creature knowledge of how close it had come to unseating him. Instead he leaned forward as far as he could without falling, and stabbed the rigid fingers of his hand into the bright globe of the dragon's immense eye.

There was a scream of outraged anguish. It wasn't Sulmar's. He felt the tissues parting and the fluid shifting. Ooze squirted, flowing along his arm. But he drove his hand in deeper, then clenched his fingers into a fist inside the eye, ripping the jellylike substance asunder.

The dragon roared as never before, a howl of utter pain. The sound deafened Sulmar, who was so close to the trumpet of its throat. But it was immensely gratifying. He had found his weapon, and its target. He was truly hurting his ancient enemy.

The Black Dragon veered as if losing control of its flight. It dipped down close to the ground before recovering, and then its flight was unsteady, because it was hardly concentrating on it. It was simply suffering the pain. But soon enough it would realize that though one eye was injured, the prey had not escaped. The dark slope of the mountain was just ahead.

Sulmar attempted to draw his hand free, and could not. The eyelid was clasped tightly down on his wrist. It was an involuntary reflex on the part of the dragon, but effective. He was unable to free his hand. He had been caught.

Then the dragon's head snapped back, dislodging Sulmar from his precarious seating. His hand sucked out of the eye, and he went sprawling down the length of the creature's back. The creature had inadvertently freed him even as it reached the base of the mountain.

Sulmar groped for a hold, but the slime that covered his arm prevented him from getting a grip. He slid off the dragon's back and slammed into an outstretched wing. He tried again to catch hold, but rebounded over the moving wing, rolling. Unable to recover, he plunged into the emptiness below.

Chentelle recovered her perspective. Her body was shaking from the horror of the savage encounter and the near death of Sulmar. "But you survived!" she cried. "You did not die! You were very close to the ground, and your fall was short, and you lived. The dragon is injured and gone. Now I have you safe, my friend. Safe!" But was it enough?

Sulmar's iron discipline shielded them both from the pain of his body, and they drifted in the harmony of Chentelle's Gift. Dimly, they were aware of other voices. A horse rode off. Later, one returned. Words floated around them. Gentle hands lifted them and set them down again. The ground moved, sliding beneath a makeshift travois. When it stopped, there were more voices and more hands. The travois gave way to a large bed, and coarse pillows materialized to support her back. Sulmar's body was straightened, and his wounds were cleaned.

Time passed. The song had no words, now, no images, no shape. It was life, passing through her lips as naturally as her own breath. The music flowed into Sulmar, taking her strength with it. Occasionally, she listened to the voices, riding the waves of worry and concern that carried the words. But most of the time she just drifted in the song.

Exhaustion claimed her several times, and she was forced to rest. Whenever that happened, A'stoc or Drup would be waiting nearby with food and water. She accepted the sustenance mechanically and dozed fitfully, never letting the contact with Sulmar disappear. The slightest waver in his spirit brought her instantly to alertness. Twice, she woke to the sound of her own song.

Her muscles twitched with the strain of inactivity, and she became aware of deep pains in her knees and hips. Eventually, the sensation melted into a numb tingle. Then it vanished altogether as her body moved past fatigue. She let the world fade away. Existence was a defiant glow and a single chord that enfolded two souls in desperate harmony.

She was not surprised when a third spirit joined in the song. She had felt it approach, and dismissed it as unimportant. But something in the new voice touched her: notes of worry and concern, pain and self-recrimination. The voice trembled with a spiritual depletion that echoed her own physical weariness. The other spirit pulled away and she allowed herself to follow it back to the physical world. Words drifted into her awareness.

". . . no response since she found him three days ago." It was A'stoc. He gave no sign of noticing her. Perhaps she hadn't opened her eyes after all.

"Her song is the only thing keeping him alive." The other voice belonged to Father Marcus. That was the one that had brought her back. "His injuries are beyond healing. I haven't the power to bring him back."

"You must!" Urgency rang in A'stoc's voice. "It will crush her if he dies after all her efforts."

Sadness flared in the High Bishop. "It is worse than that. Their spirits are so closely bound that when he dies it may kill her as well."

Chentelle listened without alarm. It was only proper. When the song ended, life would fade. The tension she felt in the two humans seemed strange and unnecessary.

"We have to break the connection!"

"After so long?" Father Marcus' hand brushed lightly against hers. "They balance on the edge of a precipice. Sundering their bond could send them both toppling over. No, you were correct the first time. I must heal him."

"How? You said that you could not."

"I said that I lacked the power." There was silence, punctuated by a flicker of shame. Then Marcus continued. "The Staff of Life has more than enough. I can save them, but only if I possess you once again."

Emotions poured from the wizard: anger, fear, bitterness. His spirit shivered with tension. "Do it."

Father Marcus began to chant. His voice formed a bridge to A'stoc, a bond similar to her own song but so very different. There was no sharing, no peaceful harmony. The chant jangled harshly against the wizard's will. The music dissolved into cacophony and discord. Then the wizard surrendered. The chant poured into him, echoing through body and spirit. One will drove both bodies now, Marcus' will.

Earthpower blazed into being. It danced around the two bodies that were Marcus, wrapping them in the warm radiance. A hand reached out and touched Sulmar's chest.

Life. Chentelle sucked greedily at the power, pulling it into her Gift. Sulmar's spirit flashed in response. Light filled their union, driving the dragon's shadow deep into hiding. The Earthpower thrummed with vitality, swallowing their song in its own cadence.

Sulmar's bones shifted and knit together. Veins mended and ruptured tissues became whole. Blood-choked lungs emptied, then refilled with air. The healing rhythm pulsed through them, replenishing body and spirit. In its wake came peace and safety and an exhaustion filled with satisfaction and accomplishment.

Sulmar was saved! Chentelle wanted to shout and leap and dance for joy, but sleep called to her with a voice too lovely to ignore. She felt herself fall into the drowsiness.

A'stoc's hand touched her face.

Earthpower swept through her, washing away self and identity. The High Bishop's chant resonated within her, but the commanding tone had altered, softened. It sang through them, binding the four into one circle of harmony. All barriers disappeared. She *was* Marcus, battling the weight of uncertainty and despair with faith and a hope that stretched thinner each day. As Sulmar, she knew iron determination and devotion to a beautiful vision that she hardly recognized as Chentelle. In A'stoc, she churned under the pressure of a dozen contradictory emotions: hope and despair, arrogance and insecurity, selfishness and—

By the Creator! Could it be?

The music vanished as suddenly as it had begun. The world spun dizzily as Chentelle snapped back to her single self. Already the perfect nature of their communion seemed a distant dream.

"You have saved my life." Sulmar's voice was thick with sleep. "All of you did. I am in your debt."

"There is no debt," Father Marcus said. "I heal what I can. We all act as the Creator guides us."

Chentelle tried unsuccessfully to stifle a yawn. Her eyes burned with the need for sleep, but she forced them to remain open. "A'stoc, we—"

"High Bishop, I believe you owe us an explanation." The wizard talked over her, refusing to meet her gaze. "What is the dark stain that mars your soul?"

"A secret," Father Marcus said, "a most terrible secret. I carry the seed of Infinitera's destruction, the knowledge of evil which will allow me to destroy the Fallen Star. It is a burden I thought best to keep for myself, but now I realize that such mysteries were driving our fellowship apart. What hope remains will not be served by lone sacrifices or solitary heroics. We must place our trust in each other. That is why I brought us all into communion."

"And did it never occur to you," A'stoc growled, "that some secrets are better kept than shared?" The wizard spun around and stalked out of the tent.

"A'stoc, wait." But he was gone. Chentelle leaned back against the pillows, surrendering at last to the siren's call of sleep. She was dimly aware of warm hands lifting her and placing her into a bed of her own.

⪚

Sulmar was standing beside the bed when she woke. The belt at his waist hung low with the weight of his black blade, and the vorpal bracer once again covered the dragon's brand.

"What are you doing?" she asked, clambering stiffly to her feet. "You shouldn't be up."

"I am no longer injured," he said calmly. "My full strength has not yet returned, but I have recovered enough to resume my duties."

"Your duty is to get well!" Chentelle looked around, trying to shake the cobwebs from her thoughts. The tent was filled with orb-light, but a glance toward the entrance told her that night was full upon them. "What's happening? Is it another attack?"

"No," Sulmar said, "the Ill-creatures have not returned. The High Bishop has spent the day ministering to the wounded. Now he and Lord Gemine make plans for their departure. They mean to leave at first-light, without us."

"What?" Chentelle sucked in a deep breath and stalked toward the doorway. "We'll see about that."

The camp was brightly lit and silent. The tents had been repaired, or else new ones had been erected. Shadows moved inside several of them, but the only figures outside were the sentries near the wall. Chentelle marched for the command tent.

The Legionnaire at the entrance saluted and waved her through. Father Marcus, Dacius, and the wizards were gathered around a central chamber, deep in conversation. They did not seem to have noticed her arrival.

"... less than a day behind me," Father Marcus was saying. "They will certainly arrive tomorrow."

"Thank the Creator," Councilor A'rullen said. "I will rest much easier once the vorpal weapons are safe in Skysoar."

"As will the Realm," Dacius said. He turned to Father Marcus. "Still, I would be happier if we waited until the reinforcements arrive, just to be safe."

"No! I cannot say how much the necromancer drew from my mind. Any delay could prove fatal." Marcus' voice nearly trembled with intensity. She remembered the despair she had felt during the communion. Bone's attack had shaken him deeply, as had the loss of Brother Gorin. "The enemy may already know the location of the Fallen Star. We leave at first-light."

"And just when were you going to tell me, or had you planned on sneaking off without saying good-bye?" Chentelle was rewarded by a chorus of surprised starts.

Only Dacius didn't jump. The human lord smiled, his blue eyes gleaming in the orb-light. "Good evening, Chentelle, Sulmar. It's great to see you on your feet again."

Chentelle bowed politely. "It is a good evening, Lord Gemine, though it seems less so when I hear that my friends have made plans to abandon me."

"Chentelle, please," Father Marcus said gently. "No one wants to leave you, but we must travel quickly. Sulmar's wounds are healed, but his spirit was sorely taxed, as was yours. You both need time to recover."

"I see." Chentelle stared at the assembled faces. "And you saw no need to consult us about this decision?"

"You were unconscious," Marcus said. "We had no idea when you would awaken. We—discussed it among ourselves. You have sacrificed much for our quest; no one could ask more."

The hesitation in his voice told her everything she needed to know. *Oh, A'stoc.* With effort, she managed to keep her voice even. "No one did ask. That's the point. But we will be joining you anyway, unless you drive us off. The Gift brought me to you, and I don't think that my part is finished."

"Of course," Father Marcus said quickly. "The quest would have been poorer without you. It was only concern that motivated us."

There was a general murmur of agreement.

"I know." Chentelle smiled, letting them see that she was not angry. "And I understand, but I am not a child in need of protection, and neither is Sulmar."

"Good! Then that's settled." Dacius grabbed a parchment and spread it across the table. "I got this map from Fel. It isn't complete, but he swears that the distances are true to within five cubits."

Chentelle worked herself around the table while the humans consulted the map. She found a place beside A'stoc and spoke softly toward his ear. "We need to talk. Shall we do it here or in private?"

The wizard winced as if she had slapped him. Slowly, he stepped away from the table. "You will excuse me, gentlemen, but I have some arrangements to make before we leave."

Chentelle moved to follow him. "I think we should go, too, Sulmar. Father Marcus was right. We do need rest."

Once they were outside, she turned to Sulmar. "I want you to go back to the tent, and sleep as much as you can. There's no danger here tonight, and I'll need you to be strong tomorrow."

To her surprise, he didn't argue. "As you wish."

Chentelle watched him leave, then turned to find A'stoc. The wizard was waiting for her beyond the battlements. She picked her way toward him, stepping carefully between the fragments of bones and debris that still littered the ground outside the camp. She used the time to try to gather her thoughts.

A'stoc stood rigidly while she approached. His face was a mask of iron. But she could feel the emotional turmoil underneath, and the unmistakable tinge of—fear. *Oh, A'stoc.* The discovery threw her off balance, and her carefully prepared speech vanished from memory.

"I love you," he said.

"Wh—what?"

"I love you. That is what you wanted to hear?" His voice rose, becoming almost a snarl. "But you already knew, didn't you. You found out when Marcus drew us into communion. Still, you wanted me to say the words. Well, now I have. Are you happy?"

His anger washed over her. Something was wrong. This wasn't how it was supposed to happen. She tried to speak, but the words wouldn't come. The world was spun crazily under her feet. "Stop it! Stop it. Why are you doing this?"

"Chentelle?" A'stoc's voice softened. He grabbed her arms, keeping her from falling. "Are you all right? I—I'm sorry. I didn't mean to hurt you."

"I don't understand." The dizziness was passing, but she still felt unsteady. "Why are you so angry?"

"Why?" A'stoc stepped back. He towered over her for a moment, staring into her face. Then he dropped down to his knees. In this position, their heads were almost level. "You don't know. You haven't worked it through."

He met her gaze with eyes that pleaded for something indefinable. "I love you, Chentelle. You are the most beautiful creature I have encountered. You are more kind, more caring, more generous and understanding than anyone I have ever known. You possess in abundance all the gentle qualities I lack. Your eyes shine like a rainbow and your voice touches the heavens. I love you, and we can never be together. Every time I look at you, hope swells in my heart. But it is a hope that brings only pain."

"But—" Chentelle struggled for the right words. "You haven't even asked me how I feel?"

"There is no need," he said. "I know."

"How? I wasn't even sure until just now."

"Then you are not as adept at reading your own emotions as you are at deciphering another's. I felt it in you the same way you found it in me." He hesitated, turning his eyes away. "I was—looking for it. I knew it was foolish, but I couldn't stop myself."

"Then you know!" Chentelle grabbed his face and turned it toward her. "A'stoc, it isn't hopeless. I—"

"No!" He jerked away from her. "Don't say it. Please, don't say it. I—I don't think I could bear it."

"But why?" He wasn't making any sense. Chentelle wiped the tears away from her eyes. Her face felt hot under her hand. "Why are you pushing me away?"

"I have to." He turned back to face her. His eyes were red and moist, but they held hers firmly. "You have the Gift. Touch me with it. Touch yourself. Touch the world and listen to what it says."

Chentelle reached out and brushed his cheek. Emotion swept through her, raging out of control. Bitterness, hope, joy, despair, they assaulted her, filling her with passion and then leaving her empty for the next wave. She tossed helplessly in the storm, unable to retain her bearings.

No. She wouldn't surrender. She had to understand what was driving him. She searched through the storm, seeking for an emotional anchor. *There—love.* She latched on to it, refusing to let it go.

Joy bubbled through her: happiness, warmth, ecstasy, desire. Her heart echoed the feelings and returned them manyfold. *This was the answer.* Love, what could overcome it. She sang, wrapping her love and herself in a song of rapture. The love surrounded them, filled them. It was perfect.

Images came to her. The two of them standing among the trees of Lone Valley, delighting in the wind and sounds of children playing. She smiled. They were beautiful. She reached out to stroke the girl's hair, but there was no one there. The children had vanished. *No offspring, our union is sterile.*

Chentelle felt suddenly ill. Lifelms were the heart of an elven forest, but children were the soul. To be cut off from that, isolated from the circle of birth and renewal—no, it didn't matter. If they could not have children of their own, they would take joy in the families of others. Love would sustain them.

The children returned, laughing and dancing but now somewhat apart. Still, it was good to share with them. She wrapped her arm around A'stoc, finding deep pleasure in the simple gesture. His body was warm and welcoming, but it withered under her fingers. He aged before her eyes, shriveling and twisting into a wrinkled graybeard. His skin flaked into dust and blew away on the wind.

It doesn't matter! He will age before me, but he's a wizard. We'll have centuries together before he dies.

A'stoc reappeared at her side. She grabbed on to him, clinging with desperate intensity. They were together. That was all that mattered. No one was guaranteed an eternity. She felt his love embrace her, warming her, filling her with light. Nothing could stand against that. She threw back her head and sang, letting Lone Valley echo with her joy.

Something was wrong. There was no answer. She felt the Gift rising within her, reaching out to the harmony of nature, but she felt no response. She tried again, seeking rather than sending. She called out to the trees and the grass, to the birds nesting around them. Nothing.

She was being denied, shut out. The Creation itself rejected her.

"No," A'stoc said. "It does not reject you, or me. It rejects only our love. The original Creation made it impossible for different species to love or breed. Only the fact that the present Creation is flawed makes it possible for us to love. Restoration of Creation will extirpate any notion of love between us. Therefore what we feel is pointless, and can lead only to the subversion of our mission."

"Nooo!" She staggered away from A'stoc. Her foot slipped and she fell to the ground, landing in a cloud of dust and bones.

A'stoc reached down and lifted her easily into his arms. She buried her head against his shoulder, trying to stop the flood of tears. How could the Creator be so cruel? "It isn't fair."

"No," A'stoc said gently. "But it is the truth. The Sphere of Creation has no place for our love."

Chentelle wanted to scream. It couldn't be true! But she knew that it was.

The vision had left no doubt. She let A'stoc carry her all the way to her tent. Part of her soared, even now, to be held in his embrace. Somehow, that made the pain even sharper.

A'stoc laid her softly onto the rumpled blankets of her bed. She started to speak, but he pressed his hand to her mouth, silencing her. A drop of water splashed against his fingers. "There is nothing more to say. Tomorrow, we ride out to save the Creation that damns us. Perhaps that means something."

Chentelle watched him walk away. He paused at the door, mumbling a spell. The orb-lights died.

She rolled over in darkness, tasting the salt of his tear on her lips. It was a long time before she fell asleep.

๛

Ellistar was still only a sliver on the horizon when they gathered near the battlements. The entire company was mounted, and an extra horse was laden with extra supplies and a large tent. Most of the camp still slept, but the two wizards were there to see them off. Councilor A'rullen was saying something to Father Marcus, but Chentelle couldn't hear what. She reached down and stroked Sundancer's neck absently, grateful for the mare's solid presence. She wondered whether she had come back on her own or been rounded up by a patrol. She could have asked, but it didn't really matter.

A'rullen stood before the company with a small pile of vorpal weapons. He handed out bundles of arrows and parrying blades to each of the Legionnaires. "I do not know the exact nature of your mission, but I know that it is urgent. Without Wizard A'stoc we would never have recovered A'kalendane's treasures. Without Lord Gemine's leadership we would not have held them against the necromancer's assault. Take these to help you in your quest, and may the Creator smile on you all."

"Thank you, Councilor," Dacius said. "We will wield them with pride and in honor of those who have fallen."

A'valman cleared his throat loudly. "As long as we are bestowing gifts, I have one to give as well, or perhaps I should say 'return.' " He reached into his robes and pulled out the *mandril* wand. "This is the wand of a Wood Master. It belongs in the hands of one."

He extended the wand to A'stoc. "Take it. The master was not wrong when he left it to you. Perhaps when you complete your quest you will come to Tel Adartak-Skysoar. Your wisdom would be welcomed in the Collegium."

A'stoc smiled and took the wand. Then a strange shadow passed over his features. "No. I wish you well in your work, A'valman. But I do not think that day will come."

Without waiting for a reply or further formalities, A'stoc spurred his mount forward. The others had little choice but to mouth hurried good-byes and ride after him. They headed east until they were clear of the Desecration, then turned northward. They skirted the edge of the broken lands, staying just inside the fringe where water and forage were, while not plentiful, at least possible.

The hours crept wearily by. Chentelle rode without joy, without passion. Sundancer surged beneath her, as steady and powerful as ever. But she felt it only vaguely, as though she were a great distance away. The constant scream of the Desecration was gone now. In its place was a pain that was colder and far more personal.

A'stoc avoided her throughout the long ride. He avoided everyone. The wizard rode on their flank, staying just within earshot. When they broke or stopped for meals, he would join them but sit without speaking.

On those occasions, it was Chentelle who turned away. She knew her tears would just increase his suffering.

"May I join you?"

Chentelle patted the ground beside her. "Of course."

Father Marcus sat, legs folded neatly underneath him. "I fear that I have made a grave mistake. I opened our spirits to each other hoping to forge new bonds of sharing. Instead, I have driven two of you further apart. Is there anything I can do to help ease your burden?"

His voice was steady, but tinged with a need that bordered on desperation. She let his words bounce through her. *Was there?* "Tell me, Father, can the laws of the Creation be changed?"

"Changed?" He seemed almost shocked. "No. We struggle to heal the Creation, to restore it to its true form. Any change from that would be a scar, an imperfection. That is how evil originally came to the world, when the Abyss was torn in the fabric of the Sphere."

She grabbed the High Bishop's arm. "But do all changes have to be evil? What it we could make it better?"

"Chentelle!" Now he was shocked. "You, of all people, should know better than that. With your Gift, you touch the Creation more closely than any of us. You have felt the Creator's plan, the Truth that binds us all together. You know its beauty, its perfection. When the world is healed, there will be no strife, no conflict. All things will live in accordance with their nature, distinct but in absolute peace. There is no better world."

Chentelle dropped her eyes and let go of his sleeve. "You're right. The plan sings to me: all things in their place, all creatures balanced in harmony. It's— it's too exquisite for words. I can touch it, *feel* it, but I don't think I'll ever understand it. And I know that I will never love it again."

Father Marcus stared at her, alarm and confusion churning behind his eyes. "But, Chentelle, how can you not love it? It is perfect."

Chentelle nodded. "I know. The problem is, I am not."

There was nothing else to say. She rose to her feet and climbed back onto Sundancer's back. As if waiting for her cue, Dacius called for an end to their rest. In moments, they were back on the road. Chentelle and A'stoc continued to avoid each other, and now Father Marcus was withdrawn as well. The company rode in awkward silence until only a sliver of Deneob remained above the horizon. Then they stopped and set up a hurried camp.

The supper was cold and tasteless. Chentelle swallowed as much of it as she could stomach, then wrapped herself tightly into her blankets. Dacius had set up a watch schedule, but neither she nor Sulmar was on it. It was just as well. The night was not cold, but she couldn't stop shivering. She shut her eyes and surrendered to the numbness of sleep.

Morning came almost immediately. Chentelle fought free of the bedroll and climbed to her feet. Half consciously, she rolled up the blankets and stowed them in her pack. Then she pulled herself awkwardly onto Sundancer's back.

She let the mare set her own course, trusting her to stay close to the other mounts. Chentelle's own eyes were closed. She felt Ellistar's light on her face, but it didn't warm.

They halted at midmorning for a light meal. Dacius pulled out the dwarven map and spread it on the ground. "We have a choice to make. I mark our position to be here, just shy of the Desecration's boundary." He pointed to a spot on the map. "Our destination is the Erietoph Forest, right, Father Marcus?"

"Beyond the forest," the priest replied. "But that heading will serve us for now."

"Of course." Dacius ran his finger in a straight line to the northwest corner of the map, which was dominated by a densely colored forest. The path he indicated took them straight through an area marked only by the word "waste." "As you can see, the direct route takes us straight into the Trollskin Desert. We should be able to make the crossing in two days. If we skirt it to the north, it will take at least three, maybe four. But we'll be fresher when we reach the other side."

"We should go through," Marcus said, "speed is vital."

Thildemar pointed to the map. "I thought that I knew all the forests of the Realm, but this Erietoph is new to me. Do any of you know it?"

"There is a verse in one of the Prophecies of Jediah," Father Marcus said absently. "It speaks of sanctuary and trial in a forest beyond the mists. The verse might refer to the Erietoph, but it is impossible to be certain."

"Strange." The old elf stroked his jaw thoughtfully. "Still, it is well beyond the western frontier, that land is seldom traveled. Father Marcus, do you know what we will find beyond the forest?"

There was a long silence, then Dacius stepped in with an answer. "The Mountains of Time begin on the other side. Fel told me that there used to be a dwarven settlement there, Marble Falls. It hasn't been in contact with the Realm since before the Wizards' War, and he wasn't certain of its location, but it's our best bet to find help and resupply."

"A new forest and a forgotten city." Thildemar smiled. "There's a song in this, or I'm no poet."

A strange look passed over Dacius' face. "I just hope it has a better ending than your last creation."

As if responding to an unspoken signal, the Legionnaires started stowing their gear. Minutes later, they entered the grim wasteland of the Trollskin.

Chentelle had never seen a troll's skin, but if it resembled this desert then they were ugly creatures indeed. The hard ground had a grayish-brown tint and was webbed with sunbaked cracks. The terrain was scarred, forcing them to wind their way through a maze of deep pits and gullies. Occasionally, a thorny bush managed to scratch a bleak existence from the waste, but there were no grasses or forage for the horses.

As evening neared, a wall of black clouds closed in on them from the north. Lightning flashed in the distance, and the roar of thunder was unmistakable.

Dacius ordered an immediate halt. Hurriedly, the Legionnaires erected the tent and tied it down with extra supports. Everything went inside: people, horses, equipment. The shelter was barely secured before the first splatter of rain pounded angrily at the canvas. The company huddled together, sharing silence and cold rations.

Chentelle found herself staring at A'stoc. She wanted to go to him, to wrap herself in his arms and ride out the storm. Frustration roared in her soul, echoing the thunder outside. She took a deep breath and let it out slowly. She refused to give up. There had to be a way.

Sighing quietly, she stood up and moved over to the horses. The poor creatures shifted nervously at each clap of thunder. She reached out to them, touching them softly with her Gift. She was tired and angry and empty inside, but she let the music fill her. She sang to herself as much as to the horses, wrapping them all in a melody of warmth and safety.

A'stoc stared at her as if entranced. The emotion swelling behind his eyes mirrored her own heart exactly, but she wasn't sure whether it was torment or joy. Maybe it was both.

ॐ

Morning was cold. The lightning had passed beyond them, but heavy clouds still hid the suns, and steady rain beat down on their backs. Murky water swirled around the horses' hooves, running swiftly over hard ground in some places and forming deep pockets of mud in others. They were forced to dismount often and lead the horses over treacherous stretches of terrain. The gray mud clung to their clothing, smelling powerfully of decay and seemingly impervious to the cleansing effect of rainwater.

Shortly after midday, the storm finally broke. The clouds scattered and then vanished as if they had never been. Deneob's light beat down on them. The warmth was welcome, but the humid air was soon heavy with putrid odors. No one objected when Dacius pushed onward without stopping for a noon meal.

Just before nightfall, they halted and made camp. Dacius parceled out supplies for the evening, including the last of the oats they carried for the horses. As soon as they were settled, he brought out the map again.

"The storm slowed us too much. We're a long day still from the edge of the desert, assuming we don't find more delays. That's if we hold to our present course." He turned to Father Marcus. "If we turn due north, we'll reach the boundary sooner."

"That takes us out of our way," the priest said. "It will slow us down."

"Yes, but not as much as if we lose our mounts." Dacius nodded to the horses. "If we don't find them decent forage soon, they'll suffer. Some may even die."

Father Marcus hesitated, then nodded. "You are right, of course. Haste is important, but we must not let it blind us to other needs. What do you suggest?"

Dacius jabbed a finger at the map. "There's a town here, Sutan Marr. If we turn north now, we'll be less than three days' ride from it once we clear the desert. We can replenish our supplies and follow the open plain all the way to the Erietoph."

"Then that is our course," the High Bishop said. "I yield to your wisdom in this."

ॐ

The next day's travel was even slower. The ground had solidified. Indeed, it gave no hint that there had even been a storm. But the horses were exhausted. The party alternated between walking and riding until midday, then simply led the horses the rest of the way. By the time Ellistar set in the west, the terrain had begun to change.

The gray clay gave way to a layer of soil, not rich but still fertile. Clumps of grass began to appear, along with other sprouts which the horses eagerly devoured. The landscape before them flowed into gently rolling hills covered with lush grass and the occasional patch of wildflowers. To their right, a spur of mountains thrust in their direction. The slopes were blanketed with the deep hues of juniper and pine, while the peaks glistened with snow.

Dacius took them only a short way into the hills before calling a halt. He removed his helm. Chentelle realized that he must be very tired in that armor, but he would never admit it. "We'll stop here. Give the horses free range and then let them rest. They need it, and so do we."

"Do you know where we are?" Father Marcus asked.

Dacius pointed. "That's the western reach of the Pretgard Mountains. If we turn back to the northwest here, we should make Sutan Marr in three days of easy riding."

"Excellent," the priest said. "So we will be on the road again at first-light."

"Not unless we're forced to," Dacius said. "These horses will make it to the village, but they won't go much farther unless we give them more rest. I'd rather keep them healthy. Even if we can find replacements at Sutan Marr, they would be poor substitutes for Legion steeds."

The High Bishop nodded agreement. If he bristled at the new delay, he gave no outward sign.

For once, they ate a leisurely meal, neither too hurried nor too exhausted to enjoy their rations. Of course, the rations themselves were much depleted, but the atmosphere remained buoyant.

Chentelle took advantage of the time to groom the horses. Drup volunteered to help, and together they set out to give each mount a good brushing and hoof trimming. The young elf tried his best to engage her in song and pleasant conversation, but her heart wasn't in it. She kept laughing an instant too late at his jokes, and her own attempts at humor fell woefully short. By the time they were finished, it was nearly dark. Chentelle thanked the Legionnaire for his help and settled in for a good night's sleep.

She woke to the warm glare of both suns full above the horizon. She scrambled quickly to her feet, certain that she had overslept. If so, she was not the only one. A'stoc, Father Marcus, and most of the Legionnaires were still in bed, too. Only Dacius, Drup, and Sulmar were up.

Chentelle smiled and repacked her bedding, then she walked over to join them. They spent the morning easily, sharing interesting tales and stories of home. To her delight, Chentelle found that she was able, even eager to join in. The morning just had an optimistic feel to it.

Dacius let the company rest until midmorning, then led them to the northwest. They spent two days riding without incident over gentle hills. On the third, they spotted smoke rising from the west.

"Cooking fires!" Drup called excitedly. "Oak and ash, it will be good to taste warm food again."

They turned toward the smoke and almost immediately ran into a worn trail rutted with wagon tracks. By midday, the small hamlet of Sutan Marr came into view, resting on the crests of twinned hills. It took only a glance to see that something was terribly wrong. The smoke was rising not from chimneys, but from the remains of the buildings themselves. Burnt timbers and blackened stone were all that remained of the small shops and farmhouses. Only the large hall in the town center was still standing, and its doors had been battered down.

"Leth, Gerruth, check the perimeter. Everyone else is with me. Keep your eyes open for survivors." Dacius spurred his horse into a gallop.

They charged up the hill and into the village square. Carrion birds scattered at their approach, squawking in protest and moving just out of reach. The smell hit them a moment later, removing any doubt. There were no survivors.

"Thildemar."

The old elf dropped smoothly to the ground and examined the field. "The fires are mostly out, but the deep embers are still warm. Call it two days." He examined a series of tracks. "Wolves, northern grays from the size, but no natural animal fired these buildings."

Chentelle stared at the tracks. They were huge, twice the size of any wolf's paw she'd ever seen. "What are you saying? Wolves don't attack people. They must have come after the attack."

"No, enchantress." Thildemar pointed to scratch marks on the door of the hall. The wood inside the scratches was charred, indicating that it had been fired after the wolves tried to force it. "I fear these are dire wolves."

"Dire wolves?"

"He means they are possessed, Chentelle." A'stoc stared intently at a point just past her shoulder. "This pack is subjugated to the will of wraiths, shadows like those that attacked us on the road."

She shuddered, remembering the horrors she had seen in her dream.

Leth and Gerruth rode up to join them. "The perimeter is clear," Leth said. "There are wolf tracks leading north, but they are at least a day old."

Dacius nodded and swung out of his saddle. "Everybody down. Forget about supplies; anything here will be spoiled. Gather the bodies and move them into the hall. We can't stay long, but I won't leave these people for carrion."

They moved through the rubble, collecting whatever remains they found. Chentelle's stomach churned at the carnage. Body parts were thrown randomly through the village, many of them half-eaten. This was no natural pattern of feeding, it was deliberate desecration.

There was no hope of sorting out individual remains, so they simply laid the pieces into a communal pile. Father Marcus said a quick blessing, and they left the hall. Then Dacius nodded to A'stoc. Flames shot from the *mandril*, so hot that the stones themselves caught fire. In seconds, the hall was transformed into a funeral pyre.

No roads led westward from the town, so they took to the open plain. Dacius pushed their pace much harder, now, though he still took care that the horses were not overtaxed. The company traveled until past sunset and then made a hurried camp. They had barely finished their evening ration when the first howl split the night.

It was a mad and maddening sound, tortured and cruel at once. But, fortunately, it was faint and far off. The silence that followed it stretched for long minutes. Then came the second cry, no less jarring and much nearer.

"Stand ready," Dacius said.

Swords slid from their sheaths and arrows slid onto readied bows.

"Wait," Chentelle said. "If it is wolves, let me try first."

Dacius raised his sword. The steel shimmered with a faint blue aura. "You can try, Chentelle, but stay behind us. These are no ordinary animals. Archers, fire on my mark, not before."

The howls grew louder and more frequent. The vorpal blades glowed brighter. Chentelle steadied herself, marshaling her Gift and preparing a song.

The wolves appeared, a dozen of them or more. They were huge, tall as ponies and nearly as thick. Their eyes shone yellow, and their coats shimmered with pale silver light. They charged the company, baying wildly in anticipation.

Chentelle called out to them, shaping her song into a message of peace and coexistence. She sang of brotherhood and packs and the bonds that went beyond hunger. Her music danced with friendship and sharing, and it would not be ignored.

The lead wolves skidded to a halt, yipping in surprise and pain. Behind them, their packmates milled in confusion. One of the leaders tried to advance again, then howled in agony. He turned and bolted back the way he had come, followed closely by the rest of the pack.

"You did it," Dacius said, surprised. "You drove them off, and most effectively."

"But it shouldn't have happened like that." Chentelle stared into the empty darkness. "They should have welcomed the Gift, not run away in pain."

"It is the influence of the wraith," A'stoc said. "It twists them from within."

A chill wind blew across Chentelle's back. "Can we have a fire, now? They already know where we are."

"No," Dacius said. "The wolves know, but there may be other eyes searching for us."

Other eyes. Chentelle wrapped herself in a blanket and tried to suppress a shiver. She knew the watch that night would be particularly alert, but sleep was still a long time coming. She wished she could have close company, but knew that was neither likely nor wise.

Dacius had them awake and mounted before first-light. There had been no more trouble in the night, but he wanted to put distance between them and the pack.

The land beyond Sutan Marr flattened out into a wide prairie. Looking at the horizons, Chentelle could see that it climbed steadily to the northwest, but the grade was shallow enough that it did not strain the horses. They made good progress, but the wind grew colder with each league.

They stopped that night near a narrow stream. The water was fresh and clear, but bitingly cold. Gratefully, they refilled canteens and washed away the dirt of the trail. Then they ate and settled in for another cold and fireless night.

Chentelle dreamt that she was cold and wet and hungry. She traveled a long, hard road, but a hot meal waited at its end. Then she could find a warm bed. It would be paradise.

She woke to screaming.

"Wolf! Wolf in the camp!"

Her eyes snapped open. Bared fangs snapped and snarled only a few cubits from her face.

An arrow whistled and buried itself deeply into the wolf's side. The beast staggered sideways, but showed no sign of pain. It righted itself instantly and charged for Chentelle.

She scrambled backward, trying to escape. But the blankets were still wrapped tightly around her legs. She stumbled and went down.

The wolf leaped.

Desperately, Chentelle sang out with the Gift, hoping to drive the beast away. It had no effect. The creature was rabid with blood lust and frenzy. There was no will for her music to touch.

Long teeth sank into her shoulder, and her song became a scream. The wolf thrashed its head. Water splashed her face and hard fangs ripped through muscle and sinew. The jaws released her for an instant, then flashed toward her throat.

Sulmar slammed into the beast, driving it off her. They wrestled together on the ground. Sulmar wrapped his arms around the wolf's neck. He twisted and wrenched, but the wolf was too powerful. It broke free and rolled to its feet. It paused for an instant, yellowed fangs hovering a hand's breadth from the Tengarian's face. Then it whirled and ran for Chentelle.

"No!"

A sphere of magic exploded around the creature. Flames roared in the darkness like a thousand furnaces. Flesh burned away, leaving only a charred skeleton to clatter at her feet. A'stoc ran forward, *mandril* wand still thrust out before him. "Chentelle, are you all right?"

She tried to answer, but the world spun into gray numbness.

She drifted on warm and blissful music. The song washed through her, filling her with wellness. She felt the flesh of her shoulder knit together, and she accepted it without surprise. How else could it be?

"She will be fine," Father Marcus said, letting his chant fade away. "But she needs rest."

A'stoc still hovered over her, his eyes wild. "Why was *she* the target? Why did the wolf single her out?"

"Because she was the one who drove them away last night," Dacius answered calmly. "They perceived her as a special threat. What I want to know is how it came this close without being discovered. Leth? Gerruth?"

The brothers winced and exchanged a helpless glance.

"Perhaps I can explain it." Thildemar was crouched near the bank of the stream. "Chentelle, was the wolf wet when it attacked you?"

"Wet? I don't know—wait. Yes. It splashed me with water as it bit."

"I thought so." Thildemar walked back to the camp. "The wolf swam up the stream and emerged on the bank once it was past the sentries. The signs are clear."

"The stream!" Leth cried. "Lord Gemine, I beg for your pardon. We never thought to watch the water."

"And why should you?" Dacius said. "Who expects a wolf to slither upstream like a moccasin? But we must all be more wary. The enemy has many weapons to use against us."

"By the Creator." Father Marcus's voice was hushed. His eyes were wide with surprise and discovery.

Dacius's hand slapped against his sword hilt. "Where is it, High Bishop? What do you see?"

"An answer." He laid a hand on the Legionnaire's shoulder. "Relax, my friend; there is no new danger. It is your wisdom that has opened my eyes. You give good counsel."

The priest knelt down beside Chentelle. "You have suffered much, enchantress, but time is not our ally. Can you ride?"

Chentelle nodded. "I think so."

"Excellent." The High Bishop turned to address the company. "These wolves do not know the nature of our quest, but we must escape them before the enemy turns his gaze in this direction. Do not lose heart. Despair is but another of the Dark One's weapons. The Creator has not forgotten us. He still guides our steps, if we remember how to listen."

They mounted quickly and rode hard. The High Bishop led them unerringly to the northwest, following his inner sense of the Fallen Star's location. The twin suns rose and chased each other across the sky, but Father Marcus only pushed their pace even harder. Late in the day, a deep shadow rose on the horizon before them, a thick haze that obscured all vision.

"The Erietoph," said Father Marcus. "We are close."

But the forest was still two leagues away, and Deneob was already vanishing into the west. Chentelle stroked Sundancer's neck gently. The poor mare was exhausted. Her head hung low, and foam gathered around her mouth. Chentelle guided her over to the High Bishop's mount. "Can't we stop? The horses need to rest."

Father Marcus looked down at his own horse. If anything, his young gelding looked even more spent than Sundancer. He kicked himself out of the saddle. "We must continue, but we will lead the horses. They can rest once we reach the shelter of the trees."

"Lord Gemine, look!" Leth stood upright in his stirrups, pointing back to the southeast. A dozen silver-hued shapes coursed along their trail, perhaps half a league away.

"The wolves," Dacius growled. "A'stoc, can you stop them?"

The wizard considered. "They are living flesh, so the Staff is useless. But with the archers help I should be able to defeat them with the *mandril*."

"And the second pack?" Thildemar gestured to the north. Another group of wolves ran toward them, many times as large as the first.

❧ 18 ☙

⟨ **ERIETOPH FOREST** ⟩

Father Marcus swung himself onto the gelding's back. "Ride! We must make the forest."

They surged into a gallop, begging one final burst of speed from their weary mounts. A memory of pain throbbed in Chentelle's shoulder, and her legs ached from fatigue. She rocked with Sundancer's motion, feeling the tremor of strain in the mare's gait. She reached for her Gift, trying to ease the horse's burden, but the song was a feeble whisper, swallowed by the wind. Her head spun dizzily, and all she could do was cling desperately to Sundancer's mane.

Suddenly, Thildemar's mount went down. The horse's left foreleg snapped audibly, and it plowed into the earth with a frightened whinny. Thildemar launched himself from the saddle and landed in a smooth tuck. The old elf rolled several times, letting the ground absorb his momentum. Then he hopped to his feet and started to run. The lead wolves were less than two hundred cubits behind him.

"Ride on!" Dacius shouted. "Head for the trees!" His own mount spun under his command, arcing around to circle behind the running elf. Dacius matched Thildemar's course and hung low in his saddle. His arm hooked under Thildemar's shoulder and swung the elf easily onto the back of his saddle. Simultaneously, he kicked the stallion's ribs, urging the beast into a full gallop.

But the wolves were closing fast. A few of the leaders paused by the fallen horse. They fell upon the helpless creature, ripping and tearing at the poor beast's flesh while it screamed and kicked feebly. The rest of the pack charged after the fleeing Legionnaires, growling and yipping in anticipation.

Thildemar faced backward on the horse's rear. He had to clutch Dacius' shoulders with both hands, but his feet remained free. As the first wolf approached, snapping and biting at the horse's legs, the elf kicked. His worn boot landed solidly on the wolf's snout. The beast yowled and stumbled, but as quickly as the one fell behind, three more surged forward to attack. The two weren't going to make it.

Warm air blasted Chentelle's cheek.

A jet of green fire roared toward the Legionnaires. The Earthpower forked around Dacius' terrified mount and rejoined itself on the other side. Then the magic grounded itself into the hillside and flashed sideward in both directions. The flames formed a wall, six cubits high and a hundred wide.

The first wolves were too close to avoid the barrier. Driven by their vile hosts, they leaped into the flames. The Earthpower let the living creatures pass through, but it latched on to the wraiths, ripping them from their shelters of flesh. Three wolves landed awkwardly on the near side of the wall; their fur was singed, but they were not seriously hurt. Three black shadows hung suspended in the wall. Deneob's last rays caught them there, fracturing them into a thousand shards. Their pitiable wails echoed through the hills.

A low moan caused Chentelle to snap her head around.

A'stoc's horse was stopped. The wizard stood rigidly in the stirrups, his arms shaking violently. Earthpower seethed along the length of the Staff, but it also raged through the wizard himself. The growl from his throat became louder and less coherent, and tremors spread outward from his arms. Suddenly, A'stoc's entire body rocked in a great spasm. He was thrown backward out of the saddle and landed heavily on the hard ground.

Chentelle gasped and reined in Sundancer's flight. "Sulmar! Help me."

They raced back to where A'stoc lay. Chentelle called to the wizard's mare and held her steady while Sulmar lifted A'stoc and set him across the saddle. Wisps of smoke rose from the dazed human's body, carrying the scent of burned hair. The Thunderwood was grasped in his hand, inert now but still hot to the touch.

"Hurry!" Dacius reined his stallion in beside them. The horse snorted and kicked at the earth, tearing large clumps from the hillside.

Chentelle risked a glance beyond the Legionnaire's shoulder. The wall of flames had vanished. More than that, the pack from the north had joined their brethren. Nearly a hundred wolves now charged after them.

Sulmar slammed A'stoc's right foot into the stirrup and wedged it into place. "Go!" He dashed for his own horse and leaped smoothly into the saddle.

They ran. The shrouded forest lay just before them, but the snarling wolves seemed only a few steps behind. Chentelle's back itched, and she imagined she could feel hot breath on her neck, wet saliva dripping from glistening fangs. Her fear would not let her turn around; the howls grew louder, closer.

Finally, they passed into the mist. Chentelle's skin tingled; the moisture seemed to fall through her rather than on her. The mists were thick, almost tangible, but they were through them almost immediately.

A tangle of large trees loomed suddenly before them. Sundancer veered sharply, barely avoiding one of the trunks. Chentelle twisted on the mare's back, reaching to catch hold of one of the limbs. Pain throbbed in her shoulder, but she forced herself to ignore it. Slowly, she pulled herself into the branches.

"Quickly," Father Marcus called from his own perch. "The wolves are coming!"

The tree shook. Chentelle looked over and saw Sulmar swinging himself into the heights. The Tengarian climbed as quickly and freely as a child. In seconds, he was above her, reaching down to lift her to safety.

Dacius and Thildemar found refuge in their own tree, but A'stoc was still moving in a daze. He climbed slowly, hampered by the Thunderwood Staff gripped in his left hand. He was barely out of the saddle when the first wolves emerged from the fog.

The frightened horse reared as they approached and ran deeper into the woods. A'stoc reeled, nearly falling from the tree. He hung upside down for a moment, his legs and right arm clutched around a low branch.

Two wolves leaped. The first snapped at A'stoc's back, but its teeth caught only a scrap of hanging robe. The jaws of the second clamped around the Thunderwood, ripping the Staff from the wizard's hand.

A'stoc screamed with rage. His eyes grew wide, and he wrenched himself onto the top of the branch. Still lying prone, he started chanting in harsh syllables. The *mandril* appeared in his hand, and he leveled it at the running wolf. A jet of hot flame caught the beast in midstride, reducing flesh and bone alike to ashes. Even after the wolf was gone, A'stoc poured power into the blaze. A raging fire grew, surrounding the untarnished wood of the Staff.

Then A'stoc shifted his focus. Scores of wolves were now weaving in and out of the trees, leaping and snapping in futile attempts to reach the company. One by one, he began to pick them off. Spheres of fire shot through the trees, swallowing wolf after wolf.

Chentelle felt the anguish of their deaths, both the helpless rage of the wraiths and the confused pain of the wolves. And she felt something else, an ancient presence waking slowly and becoming angry. "A'stoc, stop!"

But the wizard was beyond counsel. The *mandril* flicked back and forth, finding and tracking new victims. Fireballs flashed from its tip, roaring in chorus to A'stoc's guttural spell. Another wolf fell, then another. Then one of the spheres missed its target. The flames burst against a massive tree. Half of the trunk exploded into burning fragments, and the tree crashed to the ground.

"Nooo!" Agony stabbed through Chentelle's mind. It was not just a tree, it was a lifelm. *Beltis*, the name echoed in her thoughts in a woman's voice. Memories flooded her, the recollections of a millennium vanishing into smoke. She pressed her face against the tree that sheltered her, letting her tears run down its trunk.

"Chentelle?" A'stoc shook his head in confusion. "What are—" His eyes went round as he saw the burning tree. "Oh, no. I'm sorry, it was an accident."

A wordless moan filled the forest around them, throbbing in their ears and vibrating through the marrow of their bones. The dire wolves started whining and slinking submissively.

Suddenly, huge roots burst from the ground. A dozen wolves were wrapped in wooden coils and dragged under the earth. As soon as they vanished, a fierce wind blew through the trees. Some wolves were lifted into air and dashed against hardwood trunks. The rest were blasted back onto the plain in a tempest of twigs and flying leaves.

Chentelle wrapped her arms around the trunk, ready to fight against the wind. But no wind came. Slowly, she forced herself to relax. Amazingly, a hurricane whistled across the forest floor, but six cubits above not a branch was stirring.

The last of the wolves disappeared into the mists, and the night became suddenly very still and very silent. The only sound was the crackling of flames around the Thunderwood and the fallen lifelm. Father Marcus chanted a quick prayer, and orb-light pressed back the darkness.

A'stoc swung down to the ground and walked over to the Thunderwood. He passed the *mandril* slowly over the flames, and fire swirled upward and disappeared into the wand. Then he reached down and picked up the Staff. The wood remained whole and perfect, as if the flames had never touched it. Smiling thinly, the wizard turned and walked over to the burning lifelm.

Chentelle started to climb down from the tree, but Sulmar's hand closed on her wrist. She started to voice a protest—then froze. She heard it. Shifting branches and a slow, heavy thudding, like the tread of some huge beast.

Soon everyone heard it. Swords slid from their sheaths, and arrows slapped against taut strings. But the vorpal metal glowed only with reflected orb-light. Whatever was coming was no Ill-creature.

A'stoc stood exposed in the clearing. He spun to face the noise, but made no attempt to run. He was at least a dozen cubits away from any tree large enough to provide shelter, and the sound was close. He planted the Staff against the earth and raised the *mandril* wand.

A huge figure pressed through the trees and into the small clearing. It was a giant! He stood at least nine cubits tall and nearly half that wide. He strode forward on gnarled legs, and his massive hands clutched an oaken staff as thick as a human's chest. His gaze locked on to A'stoc, and he lifted the staff above his head. His voice was a deep rumble that easily filled the clearing. "Stand aside!"

A'stoc moved cautiously to his left.

As soon as he was out of the way, the giant started to chant. The language he used was strange, almost harsh. Syllables scraped against each other like slabs of stone, but the rhythm was steady, tranquil. Wind gusted around the giant's feet, then swirled forward to surround the lifelm, Beltis. Frost formed on her bark, and a thick blanket of snow materialized to smother the flames.

Chentelle felt the pull of the giant's song. The winter wind wrapped Beltis in a tender embrace, easing her into a painless death. The lifelm's relief and gratitude poured into Chentelle, and she sang.

Her voice twined through and around the giant's chant, warm life blending with cold death. It was Beltis' song, a song of deep roots and falling rain, of long tales and windblown leaves. It sang of joy and family and profound contentment, of patience and understanding as fathomless as the underground sea. It sang good-bye and fare well. It sang peace.

The two songs ended as one, and the giant let his staff rest against the earth. He turned to face Chentelle, his nearly bald head level with hers as she stood in the tree. His eyes were stark blue rings surrounding deep circles of emptiness. They latched on to hers with a need that bordered on desperation. Pain lived in those eyes, and sadness beyond words. But they held hope, too, and surprise. "What magic is this? Your song captures grief and turns it to love."

"It is my Gift," Chentelle said, "I am an enchantress. But the song was not mine. I was only the messenger."

The giant nodded. His eyes closed and he lifted his head as if he heard the music still. Large tears slid freely down his weathered face.

Tension eased from the company. Swords were sheathed and arrows replaced in their quivers. Dacius dropped to the ground, and the others were quick to follow. Even A'stoc relaxed, letting Staff and *mandril* drop to his sides.

"Well," the wizard said, "what do we do now?"

The giant's head snapped down and his eyes fixed on A'stoc. A finger larger than Chentelle's wrist jabbed toward the wizard. "You are the one, the murderer of Beltis. Your life is forfeit for destroying one of the ancients."

"What?" A'stoc's mouth went wide in surprise. "Surely, you are not serious? It was an accident. I meant no harm to the tree." His knuckles went white on the Thunderwood, and the *mandril* twitched in his hand, though he did not raise it.

"Nevertheless—"

"One moment." Father Marcus stepped forward, interposing himself between A'stoc and the giant. "Your pardon, sir, but this company travels under my authority. If any blame is to be leveled, it is mine to bear. I am Father Marcus Alanda, High Bishop of the Holy Order in Talan. May I ask with whom I speak?"

If the giant was impressed by the priest's title, he gave no sign. "I am Glathrel Geodimondan, Last of the Giants, Keeper of the Erietoph."

"Keeper?" the High Bishop asked.

"Servant, if you prefer." The giant shrugged. "The words are identical."

Chentelle sensed confusion in the priest. "Father Marcus," she said softly, "this forest is aware. It knows we are here."

Glathrel nodded. "The singer is correct. The Erietoph has a will, and I am the voice of that will."

Father Marcus opened his arms in the sign of harmony. "Truly, the Creator has blessed us. The wonders of his Creation are infinite. My heart warms to speak with a giant when all were thought lost, and it soars to learn of a new spirit that joins in the circle of harmony. But I must put those things aside, for our need is urgent. We are on a quest of terrible importance. If we fail, Infinitera will be destroyed. I beg of you, please allow us to pass without hindrance. The Creation itself depends upon it."

Glathrel's expression wavered. He cocked his head as if listening to a voice on the wind, then his eyes became firm once more. "The Erietoph has no quarrel with you, High Bishop of Talan, nor with any of your other companions. You may pass freely through the forest, but the murderer must pay for his crime."

A'stoc slammed the Thunderwood against the ground. There was a gust of wind, a hushed whisper that seemed to spread through the forest. "Enough! Listen to me, Keeper. I will not submit to trade my life for a tree. I regret the accident. It was never my intention to harm the forest, but I acted only to defend our company from the wolves."

"Not true." The giant's voice had a hard timbre of finality. "You were consumed by rage. The anger made you careless."

"I—" A'stoc faltered, unable to deny the truth in the accusation. "I'm sorry. But it was only one tree."

"Stop saying that!" Chentelle was surprised at the vehemence in her voice. "It wasn't a tree. It was a lifelm."

He stared at her, shock and incomprehension mingled on his face. "What are you saying?"

"Oh, A'stoc." She forced herself to keep her voice calm. "Lifelms aren't just trees. They're dendrifauns that have gone through the change—metamorphosized like caterpillars into butterflies."

"Dendrifauns." Understanding spread slowly across the wizard's face. "I have heard legends, but . . . I'm sorry. I did not know."

"Such ignorance," Glathrel said. "And unless my eyes deceive me, that robe proclaims you as a Master of Wood Lore."

A'stoc turned away from the accusation in the giant's eyes. "Much knowledge was lost during the war. We are only now beginning to recover it."

"Inexcusable," the giant growled. "It requires no special knowledge to know that wood burns and you must be careful with fire in a forest, especially magical fire. You should have considered the possible consequences *before* you murdered the ancient."

"It was not murder!" A'stoc shouted.

"It was," Glathrel answered coldly. "And so it shall remain until you have paid the penalty for your crime."

"Gentlemen, please." Once again, Father Marcus moved to place himself between the two. "Wizard A'stoc, I must ask you to remain silent for a moment. The strain of your ordeal has made you intemperate. Glathrel, we all share your grief. Some of us are only now coming to understand how great was your loss, but we all felt the power in Chentelle's song. But I ask for your understanding. You have lived through the massacre of your people; you understand the Desecration. I say to you now that if we are not allowed to complete our quest, the entire world will suffer such destruction. And we cannot succeed without A'stoc. He was the apprentice to A'pon Boemarre, and he bears the Tree of—"

The giant moved with astonishing speed, pressing past the startled priest and snatching A'stoc off the ground. One huge hand surrounded the wizard's arm, holding him suspended in the air. The other raised the oaken staff, preparing to deliver a crushing blow.

The company exploded into action. A chorus of swords scraped from Legion sheaths. As if by magic, an arrow appeared in Drup's bow, and he began to draw back the string. Sulmar charged forward, aiming a lunging punch at the inside of the giant's leg. But they were reacting too late. Glathrel's sudden attack had taken them by surprise.

"Stop!" Chentelle screamed the word, backing it with all the power of her magic. It rippled through the clearing, freezing everyone in midmotion. But she knew it wouldn't last. Already, the delicate equilibrium was shifting back toward violence. She had to do something.

"Please." She concentrated on the Keeper, using her Gift to let the giant feel what was in her heart. "Glathrel, I can't pretend to know the pain you have endured, but I do know the Desecration. I know the emptiness, the desolation. I have felt it in my own heart and in the memories of one who lived through it, and I feel it now in the rage that consumes you. It's horrible; the world shouldn't hold such pain. But A'stoc didn't cause the Desecration. He doesn't deserve to be the target of your vengeance."

The giant did not answer, but he did not strike either.

Chentelle walked forward. Sulmar started to protest, but she waved him to silence. "Glathrel." She laid a hand gently on the giant's knee. "I have been told that the giants are a magnanimous people, that you love long feasts and longer tales. The legends call you gentle and noble and peaceful of heart. Please, do not turn those stories into lies. Don't become a murderer in the heat of rage, as you accuse A'stoc of being."

Pain misted in the Keeper's eyes, and he lowered A'stoc to the ground. Then he dropped heavily to his knees and threw back his head. A cry of raw misery tore from his throat, and a cold wind howled through the trees in sympathy. He rocked forward until his head almost touched the ground.

Chentelle trembled under the force of his sorrow, a grief as deep and vast as the sea. A scream burned through her throat, joining in the chorus of lamentation. The wail echoed through the forest and then faded slowly into the wind. After it ended, Chentelle wrapped her arms around Glathrel's neck and hugged him tightly. Locked in embrace, she shared the giant's silence and his tears.

She wasn't sure how long they stayed that way. But when the giant finally pressed her away and stood up, the company had moved off to the far side of the clearing.

Father Marcus must have been watching for any movement, because he walked immediately toward them. "Your pardon, Keeper. Now I must apologize to you once more. I had not meant to awaken such pain within you."

"That guilt is not yours," Glathrel said, "for the pain never slept. But perhaps now it will. The old ones told that sorrow shared is sorrow diminished."

"Such is the lesson of harmony," the priest agreed. "May it be so with you. But, again, I must insist that you allow Wizard A'stoc to pass freely. We are on a quest to destroy a great evil."

"You speak of the star," Glathrel said, "the one that fell beyond the Mountains of Time."

"Yes!" Father Marcus cried. "Did you see it?"

"Only for a moment, while it was in the sky above. The Erietoph sensed its malevolence, but then it passed beyond the mists."

"Then you understand the importance of our mission," Marcus said. "You know that the star must be destroyed."

"I know that the forest must be protected, and its laws must be obeyed." The Keeper's voice started to regain its former edge. "Retribution is due."

"Glathrel." Chentelle spoke the word gently. "Please, we are trying to protect the forest, and everything else in Infinitera. Help us."

The Keeper looked at Chentelle, his expression slowly softening. Then he closed his eyes and knitted his brows in concentration. After a moment, he spoke again. "The Erietoph must consider. For now, the forest will let you pass freely. Follow the path; it will take you where you must go. I will return to you when the Erietoph has reached a decision. The wizard must not attempt to leave the forest before then."

Father Marcus shifted uneasily. "I thank you for your efforts, Keeper, but I pray that your forest decides quickly. We must move with haste."

"That does not matter." Glathrel turned and started to walk away.

"Um, excuse me," Drup said. "But what happened to the horses?"

"Your mounts were hard-used," Glathrel called without turning. "The Erietoph has given them shelter and a place to rest. If you would travel these paths, you will do so on your own legs. Make no fire and bare no steel. There is nothing in this forest that will harm you."

"What about our equipment?" Dacius called. "Our supplies are still on the horses."

There was no answer, and the trail the Keeper had walked down so easily now seemed an impenetrable wall of brush.

"This is an ill omen," Father Marcus said. "We make enemies where we should have found friendship."

Hot emotion flashed across A'stoc's face, but the priest continued before he could make a retort.

"No, wizard, I do not blame you. But this delay serves only the enemy." He paused, surveying the tired faces of the company. "I know that we are all weary, but I would like to travel a little farther. I fear this clearing will make a poor campsite."

No one objected.

A single pathway led out of the clearing, heading almost due west. Father Marcus led the way, lighting the trail with orb-light, and the rest of them followed in line. The pathway was wide and even, but Chentelle's legs trembled with every step. She wasn't sure when she had been so tired. Sulmar tried to offer her support, but the moment they touched she felt his own exhaustion. She would make her own way.

After nearly an hour, the trail opened into a wide glade. There were no paths out, and a neat pile in the center held all of their supplies. They made camp quickly and without comment, as if nothing unusual had occurred. Drup prepared a simple meal of bread and nuts, but Chentelle was too tired to think of food. She found her blankets and dropped immediately into a deep and dreamless slumber.

⌒

She woke to the splash of raindrops on her face. The weight of her soaked blanket testified that the rain had been falling for some time. It was light, but she couldn't see either of the suns. The daylight seemed to emanate from the omnipresent blanket of mist.

Most of the others were still asleep, but Leth and Gerruth stood alertly in the center of camp. She stood up to go join them, but as she threw back the cover she saw A'stoc huddled in the shelter of a gnarled oak. The wizard's eyes were bloodred and deeply shadowed. If he had slept at all, it had not been restful.

He looked up as she approached and rolled stiffly to his feet. "Good morning," he called loudly. "The suns are hidden, but it must be nearly dawn."

By the Creator, the man could be infuriating sometimes. But his ploy had worked. The whole camp was stirring now, and Father Marcus would waste no time in urging them onward. She sighed and turned back to her bedroll. Maybe she could squeeze some of the water out of the blankets.

Dacius called for everyone's attention. "Pack carefully and lightly. From now on you'll be carrying the weight yourself." He grabbed his helm and lowered it onto his head. The metal glowed briefly and melded seamlessly with the steel of his breastplate. Then he tossed a large pack over his shoulder and hefted his shield. "REMEMBER, THE MOUNTAINS BEGIN AS SOON AS WE LEAVE THE FOREST."

Chentelle wrung her blanket one last time and then rolled it neatly. Besides her bedroll and an extra blanket, she had only the clothes she wore and a heavy traveling cloak. She stowed these neatly in her pack along with a portion of their supplies. Then she was ready.

A wide trail now led into the west, though the ring of trees had been solid not an hour before. Thildemar started to take the lead position, but Father Marcus motioned him back. "I do not think your skills will be needed. It is evident that the Erietoph guides us where it will."

Chentelle hung back in the rear of the company with Sulmar. A'stoc was immediately in front of them, but the wizard rebuffed or ignored all her attempts at conversation. The rain stopped almost as soon as they were under way, but the wet ground still made travel slow. The path seemed to reveal itself step by step, never visible more than three paces in front of them and disappearing entirely once they had passed.

It was curiously quiet. Not a bird chirped, nor an insect buzzed. Chentelle could feel the life around them, but it remained distant. It wasn't natural. She had never felt so isolated and uncomfortable in a forest. She was tempted to reach out with her Gift, to force some kind of contact with the creatures of the Erietoph, but something held her back.

They marched on in eerie silence, and finally Chentelle could take it no more. Just because the forest was hushed didn't mean she had to be. She started to sing, choosing a song Willow had taught her when she was barely fifty. It was a merry tune about the adventures of a drop of water, and it ran up and down the scales like splashing rain. She sang with her natural voice, not using the Gift, and smiled at the simple pleasure the sound brought.

A delighted chuckle drifted toward her on the wind, and she cut off her song. Immediately, the laughter disappeared. She eyed her companions, but though her song had lifted their spirits, none showed any sign of such levity. In fact, they seemed not to have heard the tittering at all. *Of course.* Chentelle smiled. If there were lifelms, there must be dendrifauns. She started to sing again, using her Gift, now, to let the listeners feel her joy at their presence.

A rich tenor blended into her song—Thildemar. Soon Drup joined the chorus, then Leth and Gerruth. Even Father Marcus hummed along, though he could not follow the words. The other humans looked confused, unable to understand the deep joy that filled the elves. But even they responded to the nature of the song. Their steps grew light, and the furlongs fell away behind them.

Suddenly, the trail vanished. Chentelle stopped her song in midmeasure. Trees pressed in all around them, branches swaying in a steady breeze. There was no path ahead and no retreat behind. They were trapped. Deep laughter echoed through the woods.

Dacius's hand snapped to his sword, but he drew only the first hand width from the sheath. The vorpal steel remained cold and lifeless.

"Easy, my friend," Thildemar said. "There is no danger."

"WHAT IS IT?" Dacius's voice rumbled through the forest. He reached up and pulled off his helmet. "Sorry. It's easy to forget I'm wearing it."

Thildemar smiled. "No harm done, but you may have scared them off. The forest spirits are shy. I do not think one has shown itself to a human in more than a century."

"That's about to change," Chentelle said. Curious eyes turned her direction, and she nodded toward the forest.

A dozen trees had come to life and intertwined their limbs, forming a great circle around the company. Wind whistled through leaf and branch, surrounding them with the same melody that the company had been singing. Roots kicked loose from the earth, dancing across the ground and beating a steady percussion.

"Dendrifauns?" A'stoc asked, cocking an eyebrow at Chentelle.

She nodded. The warmth of the song bubbled through her. And she could hear other sounds, now, birdsong and the rustling feet of squirrels. The forest was finally welcoming them.

Suddenly, the song ended. The dendrifauns scurried away, cloaking themselves once more with the illusion of trees. Only three remained behind: a female with rose-colored buds and two males who hovered together a little farther off.

"Hello," Chentelle said. "Thank you for the song."

The dendrifaun answered in her own tongue, which was also the tongue of elves. "We found it floating through the forest and thought we should return it. But who are you, elf girl, who sings so charmingly in the forest language?"

"I am Chentelle," she said, "daughter of Dalen and Eudora, child of Lone Valley Forest where the restless unicorns roam. It is far to the east, near the Quiet Sea."

"I am pleased to meet you, Chentelle, child of Lone Valley Forest. It is a joy to hear the old tongue spoken by youthful lips. The only travelers we usually see are dwarves. They make good songs, though the subjects are strange, but their manners are atrocious."

"Your pardon, elder." Thildemar stepped forward and bowed respectfully. "But are you responsible for hiding our trail?"

The dendrifaun wiggled her twigs in amusement. "No, the trees move when we ask them, but they sometimes set their own path. Still, perhaps I can restore it." The wind gusted, carrying the rustle of leaves and the scent of spring blossoms. Then a cricket chirped three times and the pathway reappeared before them.

"Thank you," Thildemar said.

A'stoc shuffled noisily forward. "I don't suppose one of you would care to translate? Do these creatures speak for the forest?"

The dendrifaun bristled, sharp thorns shifting along her branches. "You are the killer of Beltis," she said in the language of the Realm. "You have the manners of a dwarf."

Chentelle jumped in hastily. "Perhaps introductions are in order." She presented the company one by one, giving their names and homelands. The elves each bowed respectfully when mentioned, and the humans mimicked their etiquette.

"Well met, wanderers. I am Prickly-Ash." The dendrifaun dipped her trunk gracefully until her branches swept the ground. Then they straightened and motioned for the two males to join her. "The handsome one with the gray bark is Ironwood, and the youngster is Laurel. Say hello, fellows."

The two males bowed in unison. Then the younger one spoke to Prickly-Ash. "Are you sure we should be talking to them? The Keeper has forbidden it."

"The Keeper cannot forbid, dear, only suggest." Prickly-Ash winked a knotted eye at Chentelle. "Besides, it has been three thousand years since the elves left the Erietoph; would you have us ignore their return?"

Laurel waved a branch at A'stoc. "But he killed an ancient!"

Ironwood reached out a limb and moved the branch away from the wizard. "Don't be impolite, Laurel. It is not our place to judge or condemn. The Erietoph will decide his punishment. Our business is of another nature." He turned to face Chentelle. "Did I hear you say that you come from Lone Valley?"

"Yes, elder."

"This is surely a sign." The dendrifaun rippled his bark meaningfully. "Gnarlroot has told me many tales of that fine forest, and it is because of him that we come to you."

"Gnarlroot?" Chentelle asked.

"Yes," Ironwood said. "He dipped his roots into Lone Valley for many centuries before coming to join the Erietoph. I believe he used to be called Fizzfaldt."

"Fizzfaldt!" she exclaimed. "Oh, this is wonderful. Can you take us to him?"

"That is the reason we are here," Ironwood said.

"Enchantress?" Father Marcus touched her arm gently. "I am sorry, Chentelle, but I do not believe we have the time for this."

Ironwood turned to the High Bishop. "You are a healer?"

"I am a priest," Marcus said. "I heal when I am able."

"Then you will understand. Gnarlroot's time is near, but the change does not go well with him. The Keeper cannot help him, and he has ordered us not to seek your help." His branches twitched in agitation. "I cannot explain further. You must go to him. You are his only hope."

"Please, Father." Chentelle gripped the High Bishop's hand. "He's a legend in Lone Valley. We have to go see him. There may be something we can do to help."

Sadness welled in the priest's eyes, but he shook his head. "I am sorry, Chentelle. It grieves me to turn away from a creature in need, but we must keep moving. All of Infinitera depends upon us. There's no time to spare."

"Time?" Prickly-Ash wiggled her twigs. "We have all the time in the world!"

"Perhaps you do," Father Marcus said, "but we do not. We must be on our way."

"Perhaps I can ease your mind," Ironwood said. "The path you follow will lead you to Gnarlroot. Whether you stop or ignore him is up to you. As to Prickly's comment, she is essentially correct. Time within the Erietoph flows differently from that beyond the mists. Less than an evening passes in the world outside for each two days in the forest. I do not understand why this is so, but it is. Perhaps Gnarlroot can explain it to you."

Father Marcus shook his head. His shoulders slumped as in defeat, but there was a smile on his face. "It seems our path is set, then. Lead on, forest spirit. But I make no promises. We can't afford to antagonize the Keeper further."

The dendrifauns moved ahead of them, gliding down the trail on sinuously writhing roots. The motion looked deceptively slow. Chentelle knew from experience that they could keep pace with the swiftest walk and hold it tirelessly through the day.

Dacius dropped back to Chentelle's side. "I heard them mention dwarves. Do you think they might know where Marble Falls is?"

"Marble Falls?"

Dacius started at the voice. He wasn't used to the keen hearing of dendrifauns.

"I've heard some of the dwarves mention it," Prickly-Ash continued, "but I don't know where it is. Someplace cold and hard, I imagine. Maybe Gnarlroot can help. He knows more about the world outside than any of us."

Chentelle smiled. So they had yet another reason to go see Fizzfaldt. Now Father Marcus would surely let them stop.

They walked for hours, stopping only once for a brief meal. The dendrifauns entertained them on the journey, sharing stories about ancient oaks and hidden streams. Ironwood did most of the talking, keeping courteously to the tongue of the Realm. Prickly-Ash and Laurel were mostly silent. When they spoke, it was only to keep up a running argument about the wisdom of approaching the company and what the Keeper would do if he found out.

They marched along steadily until the light began to fade from the sky. Then the dendrifauns started to slow and become halting in their movements.

"Is something wrong?" Father Marcus asked. "Do we need to stop?"

No one answered. The dendrifauns were gone, vanished back into the dark forest. Father Marcus muttered a quick prayer and called for orb-light.

The trail before them opened into a small clearing. A lone figure occupied a knoll in the center of the glade. It had to be Fizzfaldt. A shaft of sunlight poured down through the mist, bathing him in red warmth. But his branches were bare of leaves, and patches of bark had fallen away from his trunk and limbs. Much of what remained was coated with a layer of white fungus, like barnacles on an aged whale. The old dendrifaun remained fully in tree form, not acknowledging their arrival. He looked dead.

Chentelle ran to Fizzfaldt's side. She felt the disease within him immediately, but she also felt life. He was not gone yet! She reached into him, singing softly with the Gift. She sang of Lone Valley, of the taste of its soil and the scent of its wind. She sang of Willow and the Heart Tree she had longed to have in Lone Valley, and she heard a soft echo rise within the dendrifaun.

A face materialized slowly in the bark of the trunk. The knots of his eyes were deeply shadowed, and the crack of his mouth shifted constantly. His lower limbs quivered slightly, but his roots remained embedded deep in the hilltop. It was apparent that Fizzfaldt would wander no more. "Who are you, that sings sweetly of home and calls me by a forgotten name?"

"I am Chentelle of Lone Valley, daughter of Dalen and Eudora," she said. "But your name is not forgotten. I have heard tales of your exploits ever since I was a child. Fizzfaldt the Wanderer is a name of legend."

"A legend! Is that what they call me?"

"Of course!" She stroked his face tenderly. "Your story is one of the greatest—no, the greatest mystery of the dendrifauns. Willow sang of you many times, of your driving curiosity, your desire to taste the sea and travel to all the forests in the world. Most people think that you succeeded in your quest, that you found paradise and never wished to return."

"Paradise, eh?" Fizzfaldt made a rasping sound that may have been a laugh. "Well, perhaps I have found it now, to hear that I am still remembered. In truth, I had imagined that I was long forgotten in Lone Valley."

"Never!" Chentelle said. "No one has forgotten. Everyone will be so happy when I return and give them the end of your story. They will rejoice to learn of your journeys."

Again, the rasping laugh. "All they will learn, dear child, is that I have become Gnarlroot the Old. I traveled the world and tasted many strange soils, but such a life was not meant for dendrifauns. We are creatures of the forest, and in forests we should remain. Each land I wandered sapped more of my strength. I have grown weak, and my roots are withered. I can't even make the change. Death is the end of my story. Carry that back to Lone Valley."

"No. You aren't going to die." Chentelle was surprised at the vehemence in her voice. She motioned to the High Bishop, pleading with her eyes. "This is Father Marcus, a great healer. He's going to help you."

The priest stepped forward, all doubts banished by the sight of Fizzfaldt's suffering. "I will do what I can."

He closed his eyes and started to chant. The peace of sanctuary surrounded him immediately, and reached out to touch the dendrifaun. His hands roamed over Fizzfaldt's face for several minutes, then he opened his eyes and let his chant fade. "I'm sorry. I can sense the illness within you, but your body is so different from anything I have known. I do not have the knowledge, the understanding required to correct the damage. I have stopped the disease from spreading, but that is all."

"Then I am still going to die," Fizzfaldt said.

"No!" Chentelle cried. "There has to be a way. Please, Father Marcus, isn't there anything you can do?"

The High Bishop sighed thoughtfully. "Perhaps the knowledge of Wood Lore is what's needed. Wizard A'stoc, if you would allow me to possess you once more?"

"No."

Chentelle stared. "What do you mean? You have to! He'll die otherwise. Don't you see? This is your chance to pay back the forest, to replace the life that you took."

Pain showed in A'stoc's eyes. "You misunderstand. I meant that my knowledge of Wood Lore will not help. I did not even know that dendrifauns existed before yesterday. I know nothing that will help."

"Oh." Chentelle turned away from his eyes. She should have known better. "A'stoc, I'm sorry. I shouldn't have—Wait. Father Marcus, I can help. I know *rillanmor*, the Lore of Living Wood. I can guide you."

"Are you certain?" the priest asked. "You would have to open yourself to possession. It is not a pleasurable experience."

"Of course," she said. "If that's what it takes to heal Fizzfaldt, then that's what I'll do."

"One moment." The dendrifaun's words were becoming slower, more labored. "Before you heal me, I want to know. Will I be able to move again, or will I make the change and become a lifelm?"

"I—I don't know," Chentelle said. "Let me see."

She reached into Fizzfaldt with her Gift, searching now with her knowledge of *rillanmor*. She drifted through fibrovascular bundles and sap-filled arteries. The trauma of disease was everywhere. Some of the tissue was dead, much of the rest had already made the transformation to lifelm. Those parts that were still vital and dendrifaun balanced in uneasy equilibrium: too strong to die, too weak to make the change.

She pulled herself back to her own body. The tears in her eyes probably gave Fizzfaldt his answer, but she had to say it anyway. "The change has already started. Your roots are set."

"I see." His voice was weak but steady. "Do not cry, child of my home. This is the natural course. I have been preparing myself for death. It feels much better to look forward to experiencing the millennia from this warm roost. But the healing must wait until morning. It grows late, and there are still things which must be said."

The dendrifaun's face vanished back into featureless bark. Father Marcus looked at her, questions obvious on his face.

She waved vaguely at the twilight. "Dendrifauns go dormant at night. It takes too much energy to stay active without sunlight, especially for the very old."

"So we wait until morning," he said, "and more time passes." Exasperation was plain in his voice, but it soon vanished, replaced by quiet serenity. "Still, we can take comfort in Ironwood's words. If time truly passes more quickly here, then we will lose little. The Creator has blessed us with a safe haven and long night. Let us make the most of both."

They set up camp quickly. After a simple meal, Father Marcus insisted that everyone go to bed. He allowed no watch to be posted and ordered only that the first person to awake in the morning rouse the others.

Chentelle needed no special urging to retire, but she found sleep elusive. The fatigue of her body was countered by her racing mind. So much had happened. To stumble across Fizzfaldt here, so far from Lone Valley, who would have believed it? Something nagged at her, though. Why hadn't the Heart Tree of Sylvandale known where he was? It was connected to all the forests of Infinitera, and the Erietoph was certainly a forest.

She sighed. It was no use. She threw off the blanket and stood up. Everyone was asleep except A'stoc and Father Marcus. The priest was deep in meditation, but the wizard was simply standing by himself, leaning on his Staff and staring at Fizzfaldt.

She walked over to him. His eyes were red with fatigue, but they stayed locked on the dendrifaun with manic intensity. "A'stoc? How are you feeling?"

His gaze shifted, slowly coming to rest on her. "It does not matter."

"It does! It matters to me." She wanted to reach out to him, to hold him in her arms. She ached with the need to make promises she couldn't keep. "Oh, A'stoc, don't be afraid. I won't let them hurt you."

"I am not afraid." The words spoken were devoid of emotion. They hung in the air as his eyes slid away from her face and back toward the hilltop.

Chentelle spun away in frustration. There was no talking to him when he was like this. She stamped back to her bedroll and jerked the blankets over her shoulders. Her thoughts chased each other late into the night, but sleep came at last.

ᐁ

She stands next to Fizzfaldt, touching him with Father Marcus' hands. A voice challenges her. It is A'stoc.

"You cannot heal what you cannot comprehend."

She sees the High Bishop's pain, and brushes his cheek with a withered branch. "Don't cry for me. Change is much better than death."

"You know better than that," Father Marcus answers. "The Creation is perfect."

His words stab her like a knife. "But how can I love it? I'll never understand it."

A'stoc sweeps her into his arms. His eyes are warm and full of love. "There is no hope, only pain."

ᐁ

Chentelle's eyes snapped open, and she barely stifled a scream. The images of the dream echoed in her mind, and the cold wind whispered pain and despair. She pulled the blankets tightly around her, trying to stop her shivering.

Soft voices drifted toward her: one calm, the other strained. A'stoc and Father Marcus were talking on the far side of the clearing. The High Bishop was shaking his head vehemently. Finally, he threw up his arms and stalked back to the camp. A'stoc stayed where he was, leaning against a tree, staring thoughtfully into the night.

Something about his posture reassured Chentelle. She took several deep breaths, letting the trembling subside, then she rolled over and closed her eyes. Sleep came quickly this time, and it brought no painful dreams.

🙠

The morning was bright and full of hope. Father Marcus led them in a hymn of thankfulness, reminding them all of the wisdom and guidance of the Creator. When the song ended, Drup laid out their breakfast. It was the same spare rations they had eaten for several days, but this morning it seemed fresher, more satisfying. They ate heartily and with many satisfied sighs. Then they packed up the camp.

Chentelle stowed her blankets quickly and hurried to the top of the hill. Fizzfaldt was still asleep, and gave no sign of noticing her approach. She sat down beside him, forcing herself not to disturb his rest. She was anxious to get started, but they couldn't begin until Father Marcus got here anyway.

The High Bishop waited until everyone had secured their gear, then led them all up to the dendrifaun. The impatience of the last few days was gone, and his face had recovered the quiet serenity she had noticed when they first met.

Fizzfaldt stirred as soon as they were all present. His condition had not changed, but his voice was steady and quick, strengthened by the warm morning. "Greetings. It is a glorious day that has come to mark my passage. I could not ask for better. But you have not come to hear me ramble. You have questions to be answered."

"We have come for both," Father Marcus said. "We seek answers, but we also come to mark the last day of one of the Creator's beloved children."

"Ah, you have learned patience in the night." Fizzfaldt chuckled softly. "We shall make a proper forest-dweller of you yet. Ask your questions, I will answer if I can."

"We are on a quest," the priest said. "We seek the Fallen Star. Can you give us any guidance?"

"Yes, leave it alone." Fizzfaldt's branches fluttered weakly. "It does no good to wander around searching for things. It's better to stay at home and care for your soil."

Father Marcus smiled. "I am afraid we do not have that option. We must destroy this evil before it spreads. It is very important."

"Of course," the dendrifaun said. "I know that, and so does the Erietoph. That is why the forest will allow the Tree of Life to leave, though every trunk quivers with the need to hold it here. But I can't help you with that. This forest was the end of my travels, I know little of the lands beyond."

If Father Marcus was disappointed, he hid it well. "We have heard of a dwarven city, Marble Falls. Do you know where it lies?"

"Where? No. But I can tell you how to get there." The dendrifaun waved a leafless limb. "Head north once you leave the forest. You will come to an eight-sided stone marker. A mountain will be carved on one face, a tree on another. Head in the direction of the mountain. If you follow the mountain at every marker, you will find Marble Falls."

"Thank you." Father Marcus glanced at Dacius, making sure the Legion commander had noted the directions. "Then I have just one more question. Ironwood told us that time flowed differently here, but he could not explain how or why. Can you?"

"Yes."

The silence stretched for long minutes.

"Fizzfaldt?" Father Marcus said. "Are you well?"

"You said that was your last question," the dendrifaun growled.

The priest's eyes widened in surprise. "But—"

"Heh heh heh." Fizzfaldt's rasping laugh scraped through the clearing. "Forgive me, it was only an old tree's last joke. What Ironwood told you was true. Time flows swiftly in the Erietoph, but it rests lightly on those who live here. If you stayed for a century, less than a score of years will have passed beyond the mists. But if you returned to your home, you would seem hardly a year older than when you left."

"But how is this possible?" A'stoc interjected. "It was proved long ago that the flow of time is impervious to magical alteration, even for the forces of Earthpower."

"Ah, now you are asking for a story." Fizzfaldt's bark rippled with glee. "Sit, sit, this will take some telling."

The dendrifaun paused, trunk furrowed in concentration. When he spoke again, his voice resonated with new depth. "The Children of Erietoph are old beyond your reckoning. Only four generations of ancients have taken root here since time began to flow. You all know the stories of the Perfection, the time when the Sphere of Creation was unblemished and all things were Pure. Let me tell you, now, a story that you have not heard.

"The forest Erietoph was awake even then. It sang with the music of the Sphere and filled its place in the Perfection of Creation. But one day, one day more terrible than any other, the Creation was shattered. The Erietoph did not know where the Flaw had come from, or how it had been born, but the evil of its nature was clear. Change rippled through the Sphere. Death entered the world. The balance of harmony gave way to the balance of opposition. And the Eternal Time of Perfection yielded to the time of entropy.

"But the Erietoph had its roots deep in the Foundation. It resisted the waves of decay. The forest gathered the Eternal Time into itself, forging a barrier against the Abyss. At first, the Erietoph was successful. The barrier held; one pocket of the Creation was preserved. But the Foundation continued to erode. The Eternal Time grew thin, strained. Entropy entered the forest.

"And the story continues. There are two Creations, now, the Erietoph and the world beyond, and there can be only one. The Erietoph is a shadow of what it was. It has forgotten much, and each day entropy claims a little bit more.

Eventually, the forest will fail. Then the Abyss will swallow Creation and the world will die."

"No." Determination resonated in Father Marcus' voice. "The Creation can be saved."

"Perhaps," Fizzfaldt said, "but only if the Foundation itself is repaired. Then the Erietoph will have the strength to resist the Abyss."

"Then the Foundation shall be healed," the High Bishop said. "What must we do?"

Fizzfaldt shrugged his branches helplessly. "I don't know. The ancients believe that the Erietoph once knew how to heal the Foundation, but the knowledge was lost long ago."

"Then we shall find it again," Father Marcus said, "or create it anew. The world shall be healed. The Creator has not abandoned us to despair."

"No, He has not," Fizzfaldt said. "He has even sent new hope to a foolish vagabond of a tree. But now I think it is time for me to put down roots. Shall we begin?"

Father Marcus reached for Chentelle. His hand touched her neck, and an electric shock ran through her spine. She was filled with a powerful rhythm, a music which could not be denied. She panicked, and her Gift rose up, trying to fight off the invasion. *No.* She forced herself to relax, surrendering to the priest's chant.

Her hand moved, reaching out to touch Fizzfaldt. The Gift swelled and poured into the dendrifaun, but she felt no contact. It was answering someone else's call. Healing power flowed through her and into the wood, following the trail of her Gift. The chant pulsed with life. Scarred tissue became whole; disease vanished; roots drove into the earth with renewed vigor. And she watched it all through eyes that were no longer her own.

Fizzfaldt's bark hardened, and his limbs became rigid. The holes of his eyes covered over, and the rough slit of his mouth closed for the last time. A moment before the transformation was complete, a deep voice rumbled from the lifelm. "The soil here is good, my friends. Thank you for coming."

A great chorus of wood and wind spoke in answer. The hillside was surrounded by dendrifauns. The forest spirits had crept up silently, but now they raised their voices in joyous welcome to the new ancient that had joined their home.

Father Marcus removed his hand, and Chentelle staggered as the body suddenly became *her* again. She reached out a hand and steadied herself against the lifelm. Fizzfaldt's bark was smooth and whole, and his branches were covered with tiny green stalks that would soon be leaves. She touched him with her Gift, but felt no response. His mind was consumed with the process of change. It would stay that way for a season more. *Good-bye, Fizzfaldt. You will not be forgotten in Lone Valley.*

The company moved back down the hill and collected their packs. Most of the dendrifauns had vanished back into the wood. Only the three companions from yesterday remained behind.

"Thank you," Ironwood said. "You have made the forest richer today."

"SO." The great voice roared through the clearing. Glathrel emerged from the trees, his great staff resting over one shoulder. "The deed is done."

"Keeper!" Laurel's leaves fluttered nervously. "We were just—um—that is—"

"Hush, Laurel." Prickly-Ash thrust her branches out to their full extension. "I brought them here to see if they could help Fizzfaldt, Keeper. And they did."

"I know," Glathrel said, "and the forest is glad."

The dendrifaun's branches drooped slightly. "But you ordered us not to go near them."

Glathrel smiled broadly. "Of course, dear sister. What better way to insure that you would seek their help? The Erietoph wanted to see whether they would show compassion despite the risk. It would have shown nothing if they had helped the elder to please the forest."

Chentelle stared at the giant. "Then, this was some sort of a test?"

"Yes," he said, "and it is not finished yet. The Erietoph agrees that the threat of the Fallen Star is grave. It is more dangerous, even, than the Tree of Life in the hands of the evil or the ignorant. The killer of the ancient will be allowed to leave the forest, provided he swears an oath to return and accept punishment once your quest is complete."

A'stoc looked up to meet the giant's eyes. "So, you want me to save the world and then return for my execution."

"No. If you return, then you will have shown honor, and the penalty will not be death. The Erietoph is just. It will listen to your defense before passing judgment." The Keeper's jaw clenched, and his voice took on a hard edge. "But if you forswear yourself, I will hunt you down and destroy you."

A'stoc smiled. "I give you my word. If I survive the High Bishop's quest, I shall return to settle our dispute."

Glathrel nodded, and the tension disappeared from his face. He lifted his staff and swung it in a wide arc. A ripple of motion passed through the forest, and a wide path materialized leading straight into the west. "Then you are free to leave. The Erietoph wishes you good fortune in your quest and awaits your speedy return."

"I am certain it does," A'stoc said softly.

❧

They made excellent time on the broad trail, covering several leagues in a few hours of steady walking. The forest floor seemed to help them, lending extra spring to every stride. The dendrifauns stayed with them until they reached the wall of gray mist that marked the Erietoph's boundary.

"This is where our paths must part," Ironwood said. "May your journey be a safe one."

"Thank you," Father Marcus said. "And may the Creator smile upon you and your forest."

Laurel waved his branches in a shy farewell, but Prickly-Ash slid forward and wrapped her limbs around Chentelle and Father Marcus. "Thank you so much for helping Fizzfaldt. And thank you for sharing your songs with us, Chentelle of Lone Valley, daughter of Dalen and Eudora. Please come back and sing for us again, sometime."

Chentelle glanced at A'stoc, but the wizard was lost in thought. "We'll be back."

"Oh, that's right." Prickly-Ash wiggled her buds in embarrassment and retreated back to the forest.

The company pushed through the veil of mist and emerged on a rocky plain. Ellistar was overhead, coloring the world with golden first-light, but Deneob had not yet risen. It was early morning. Rain clouds dropped a light shower on the eastern horizon, and Chentelle wondered if it was the same rain that had fallen on them the first night in the forest.

Father Marcus checked Ellistar's position, then turned the party to the north. Thildemar moved a little way ahead, and the other Legionnaires took up positions around the edge of the group. They could not count on the Erietoph's protection now.

An hour of walking brought them to a steep ridge. A winding path led up to the heights, and at the top was an octagonal stone pylon. The angles were aligned to the cardinal directions, and the northwest face bore an elegant carving of a two-peaked mountain. They were on the road to Marble Falls.

❧19❧

◄ **Marble Falls** ►

The road led them steadily higher. The Mountains of Time stretched before them, league after league of stark, cold beauty. Low clouds flowed over and around snowcapped peaks of sharp granite. Though they were still below the timber line, few trees decorated the bare slopes, and the unbroken wind swirled crisply through the mountain passes.

They stopped shortly after noon. Gathering what dead wood they could find, the company built a small campfire. They huddled gratefully around its warmth and enjoyed their first hot meal in several days. Though Deneob was high overhead, their legs complained of a full day's worth of hiking. Full bellies and fatigue soon carried them into drowsiness.

"We need to rest," Dacius said. "The Erietoph has thrown off our sense of time."

Father Marcus nodded. "Agreed. But we must make it brief—two hours, no more."

Chentelle found a level section of road and unrolled her blankets. She was tired and heavy and deliciously warm. She closed her eyes and let her thoughts drift, waiting for sleep. But it did not come. Despite her weariness, or perhaps because of it, she could not find rest. No matter how she twisted, the rocks of the road seemed to seek out her spine, and the cold ground swallowed any hint of comfort from the fire. She willed herself to relax. All she had to do was concentrate on her breathing, ignore the sharp edges poking into her back, pay no attention to the frigid earth.

It was hopeless. She sat up and looked around. Everyone else was settled in peacefully. Even Dacius was asleep. Only A'stoc was still up, standing watch beside the dying fire.

She rolled up her pack and went over to join him. There was no more deadwood to add to the flame, so she shifted around what was there, trying to coax more strength from the blaze. "I'll stand guard, if you want. There's no sense in both of us going without rest."

"Thank you," he said, "but I do not need to sleep."

She looked up at the wizard's face. How long had it been since he slept? His eyes were clear, but there was a glassiness, almost a blankness, about them. "Is something wrong? Are you worried about the Erietoph?"

"No." He smiled thinly. "I do not fear the judgment of the trees."

"Is it—is it my fault? Because of—of what you told me before?" How she wished he would cast aside his reservations in that respect! He was such a good man, behind that forbidding wall of cynicism.

This time his mien softened perceptibly. "Nothing is your fault. The notion of you lends nothing but pleasure to an otherwise barren existence."

"Then what is it?" She stepped around the fire and stood in front of him. "I know you haven't been sleeping. I heard you talking with Father Marcus last night."

"Did you?" A'stoc planted the Staff on the ground between them and leaned against it. "I fear the High Bishop found little comfort in my words."

"Why? What did you say?"

The wizard shrugged. "I told him that I felt his mission was doomed."

"What?" Chentelle searched his face, but she saw no bitterness there, no anger, no despair. "What do you mean? Has the Dark One already found the Fallen Star?"

"No," he said calmly. "No, I was not speaking of our quest, though that will probably fail also. I meant that the mission of the Holy Order is futile. The Time of Perfection will never be restored. The understanding that such a healing would require is beyond us. We no longer belong to that world."

His voice was flat, expressionless—and each word shocked like ice in Chentelle's ears. She wanted to deny them, to scream out that he was wrong, but the truth of them echoed in her heart. "Then, it's all for nothing. There's no hope?"

His eyes softened then, just for a moment. But when he spoke, his voice was cold and distant. "Hope? You may find some, if you wish. The Flawed Creation has existed for centuries; we are unlikely to live long enough to witness its end. It is far more probable that one or the other of us will perish on Father Marcus' mad quest, or that I will be sacrificed to the vengeance of the Erietoph. If we survive those perils, perhaps hope will be in order."

Something trembled in A'stoc's voice, just beyond the threshold of hearing. Hope? Could it be? Emotion flashed briefly in his eyes. Chentelle chased after it with her Gift, but the feeling vanished into the wizard's blankness. She came back to herself just in time to catch the wizard turning away.

"You know something," she said. "You have a plan."

"What?" He turned back, and the emotion in his face this time was easy to read—fear. But it, too, soon disappeared into the calm. "No. I have no knowledge, no plan, only—a suspicion. But I will keep that burden for myself. I doubt that I will live to see it realized."

He turned away after that, and Chentelle returned to watching the fire. The flames were burning low, so she stirred the embers. The dry wood hissed and snapped and burned with renewed vitality, but the effect was transitory. Soon, the exhausted blaze was fading again. Sighing, she checked Deneob's motion and decided that it was time to wake the others.

The company assembled quickly and resumed the journey. The dwarven road was not wide, but it was well marked and laid out with geometric precision. A stone pylon appeared at each forking of the path, insuring that they never strayed from the road. They made good time through the rugged terrain, climbing ever higher into the Mountains of Time.

The air cooled after Ellistar set. Chentelle's breath swirled before her in wispy clouds, and she huddled gratefully into the warmth of her traveling cloak. Even within its folds, she could feel the bite of the wind. The cold air whipped through the hem of her dress, making her wish for warm trousers as well. Clutching the spidersilk with one hand, she forced her aching legs to keep moving.

A long line of gray clouds closed in on them just before twilight. Deneob was disappearing rapidly behind the mountains, and they started hunting for a place to camp. Thildemar spotted a nest of tall pines, standing a short way off the road. The trees backed up against a sheer rock face, providing a perfect clearing for lean-tos, and the ground was littered with dead wood.

They set up camp quickly, taking advantage of the last light. Then they built a large fire and cooked supper. The day's climb had left them all famished, but Drup kept their portions small. There was no forage in this forbidding country, and no one knew how long their slight supplies would have to last. The air grew steadily colder, and they gathered closer around the campfire. The flames might betray their presence to watchers, but they desperately needed the heat. The snow started to fall just as they were retiring for the night.

Chentelle pressed herself against Sulmar. The lean-to sheltered them from the snow, and their blankets were a barrier against the cold ground, but the cold still made her tremble. She pulled the Tengarian's heavy arms around her, trying to surround herself with their warmth. Of them all, Sulmar seemed least affected by the cold. She supposed it reminded him of his mountain home. Eventually, the icy chill dulled to a tolerable level, and she slept.

In the morning, the world had changed. Half a cubit of snow covered the mountain. The sky was iron gray, casting the world into a cold gloom. No new snow was falling, but the hard wind raised powder from the ground and sent it swirling madly through. The white wasteland extended for leagues around them, obliterating all traces of the road.

They gathered their packs and swallowed a sparse meal. After a brief search, Thildemar was able to verify the path of the road, and they continued their march. Dacius and Sulmar took the lead now, followed by A'stoc and Father Marcus. The humans drove a trail through the fresh snow, clearing a path for the shorter-legged elves to follow.

If not for the precision of the dwarven road, they would surely have lost their way. The path was invisible. They could only hold true to the direction of the markers and pray they were not being led astray. Their hearts lifted each time a stone pylon appeared in the distance.

Shortly after noon, they encountered another obstacle. An avalanche had obliterated the pathway before them, cutting a swath of gray stone through the white snow. The rock slide was nearly two hundred cubits wide and extended far up the mountainside.

"IT'S RECENT," Dacius said. His amplified voice boomed through the mountains, followed by the sound of stones shifting high above them. Quickly, he pulled off his helmet. "And apparently not too stable. Suggestions?"

"We can detour around it," Thildemar said, examining the terrain, "but we'll have to backtrack half a league or more."

"No," Father Marcus said. "If we leave the path, we could hunt for days trying to find it again. We must cross."

"I agree," Dacius said. "Thildemar, take the point. Check each step; remember, it has to hold my weight, too."

The old elf climbed nimbly onto the rocks. He crept slowly on all fours, keeping his weight distributed. He wound his way across the stones, working slightly downslope during his traverse. The other Legionnaires tracked his course, pointing out landmarks that would help them all retrace his steps. At last, Thildemar reached the far side. He climbed to his feet and stood balanced on the edge of the slide, waving for the rest of them to follow.

"All right," Dacius said. "Chentelle, you're next."

Me? But it made sense. She was the lightest. Trying not to look afraid, she climbed out onto the rocks. The beginning was easy; she had seen exactly where Thildemar had set his hands and feet. But soon she was out into the center of the slide. She placed her hand on a rock, and it tilted suddenly underneath her. Panic surged through her, but the rock steadied, resting firmly at a new angle. Chentelle forced herself to resume breathing, then moved forward again.

Thildemar called encouragement from the far side, and helped her to find the secure path. Soon he reached out to help her climb to her feet.

They stood balanced on a large boulder at the edge of the slide. The rock was cold, but the unbroken snow beyond looked even colder. Chentelle decided that Thildemar had the right idea, and she settled in beside him to watch the others cross.

They came one at a time, the elven Legionnaires first and then the humans. It took time, but they made it without mishap. Thildemar's path held even Dacius' solid bulk. At last, they all stood together on the solid ground beyond the fall. The road was a short distance above them, but the climb did not look difficult.

"Lord Gemine, look." Drup waved for their attention. He was pointing to one of the rocks in the slide. A thin crust of ice remained on one face of the stone, outlining a clear footprint. The print was short enough to be a child's, but far too wide. Deep indentations showed the clear mark of thick, bare toes.

"Gnomes," Thildemar said.

Dacius nodded gravely. "Stay sharp, people. They may still be around. String your bows and keep them ready. Thildemar, keep an eye on our back trail." These orders given, he slammed his helm back into place and drove a trail up to the road.

They marched for several hours without sight of gnomes or any other creature. As evening neared, they began searching for a good campsite. The ground sloped sharply on either side of the road, making their choices slim. In the end, they settled for a shallow cave slightly downhill from the path. It scarcely had room for them all, but a thin ledge by the entrance provided shelter for a fire.

They gathered what wood they could find, but waited until Deneob had set to light it, lest the smoke betray them. Once the blaze was going, Drup assembled their rations and started portioning out a meal. The look on his young face was uncharacteristically grim.

"How long will it last?" Father Marcus asked.

"Three meals," Drup answered. "Five, if we spread them thin."

The High Bishop closed his eyes for a moment, deep in thought or prayer. "Three. Make us hot meals now and at dawn. We'll need them to fight back the cold. Hold out only enough for a light lunch."

Chentelle felt a surge of excitement at his words. "Are we close? Will we reach the city tomorrow?"

Father Marcus shook his head, but his calm smile never wavered. "I do not know where we are, Chentelle, or where Marble Falls lies. But I believe we will reach it."

"Then let us hope," A'stoc said without emotion, "that your faith is rewarded."

They ate a large meal and set up camp. In the morning, they reversed the ritual. The day greeted them brightly. No new snow had fallen, and the dome of dull clouds showed signs of disintegrating under the twin suns' light.

Dacius and Sulmar plowed a path up a long series of switchback trails. Around noon, they rounded the edge of a long ridge and stopped in their tracks. A long valley lay below them, closed on its southern end but extending for leagues to the north. A downward trail wound northwest into the valley, and a dwarven pylon stood beside it. The northwest face was engraved with a shepherd's crook, while the southwest bore the sign of the mountain.

Their eyes searched the snow of the ridge line. Gradually, the signs of the trail became visible. It ran all the way around the closed end of the valley, staying nearly at a level. On the far side, it tacked back and forth, climbing into the saddle of a twin-peaked mountain—a mountain identical to the carving on the marker.

"Praise the Creator," Father Marcus said, his tone possibly hinting that his faith had been uncertain.

They lunched where they were, within sight of their destination, and then resumed their trek. Less snow had fallen on this side of the ridge, and the little that had was already melting under the Sister's warmth. They walked easily through the hand's breadth or so that remained, stretching their legs gratefully into long strides. Nightfall was still an hour away when they started up the last of the switchback trails to the city.

Dacius motioned for a stop and pulled off his helm. "Father Marcus, these people have been separated from the Realm for a long time. We don't know what kind of a reception we'll receive. Do you wish to announce yourself?"

The priest considered. "No, not unless it becomes necessary. It would be better to keep our mission secret. I will let you take the fore. Make what arrangements you can for supplies and information, but it must be done before morn. We dare not stay longer."

Dacius nodded and tucked his helm under one arm. He took the lead, motioning for Leth and Gerruth to flank him. Drup and Thildemar fell to the rear of the company, and they began the final ascent to Marble Falls.

A wall of stone loomed above the road to their right. To the left, the mountain fell away in a sheer drop to the last leg of the trail, forty cubits below. The bricks of the wall were polished smooth like river rock, and the lines of their joining were thinner than hair.

"Halt!" A small figure jumped into the road before them, appearing from a door that had been invisible a moment before. He wore steel armor and wielded a shield in one hand and a loaded crossbow in the other. A clatter of metal above them announced the arrival of several more dwarves at the top of the wall. "State your business!"

"We are travelers," Dacius said, extending an empty hand. "We are in need of lodging and provisions, and we seek the town of Marble Falls."

The dwarf's eyes remained hard beneath his spiked helm. "Are you merchants?"

"No," Dacius answered, "though we may have some objects to trade. We are merely passing through."

"Passing through to where? And what are elves and humans doing in these mountains? Your lands are far away."

A red flush came to Dacius' cheeks. "As I have said, we are travelers in need of lodging. We seek the hospitality of Marble Falls, if such a thing exists."

"Have a care, human!" The dwarf pounded his shield against the wall, raising an impressive clang. "You will find only a hard road unless I am satisfied about your business. Now, identify yourselves."

Dacius lifted his helm and lowered it slowly into place. The vorpal steel flashed brightly as it bonded to the mystic armor. "I AM LORD DACIUS GEMINE, LEGION COMMANDER OF THE FIRST MARK. MY COMPANIONS AND I TRAVEL UNDER THE BANNER OF THE REALM, THE FREE JOINING OF THE COMMUNITIES OF MEN."

The dwarf took a startled step backward, but then he steadied himself and raised his crossbow. "Very impressive, but you'll forgive me if I don't accept that on faith. Anyone can—"

"Grimdel!"

The shout was punctuated by a drumbeat that echoed like thunder off the valley walls. An elderly dwarf had appeared from farther up the road. He was tall for his race, nearly two cubits in height, and dressed quite conservatively. His pale pink robe was accented only by a pointed green cap and an emerald studded belt, into which his long gray beard was tucked. Platinum threads were woven through both hair and whiskers, but the ruby chips they held were used only for highlights. He held a small drum in one hand, and a small golden rod in the other. "What do you think you're doing?"

"I—I'm guarding the road, Uncle, like you told me to."

"Yes, against bandits and gnomes!" The old dwarf waved his hands wildly through the air. "Do they look like gnomes to you? Do they look like bandits? Do you see them charging up the road with weapons drawn? In fact, do you see them doing anything other than looking like weary travelers trying to find shelter from the cold?"

Grimdel hung his head meekly. "No, Uncle."

"Good, then why don't you and your boys go back to your mead and let me greet our guests properly." The old dwarf waved the guardsmen back into their hiding places. "Oh, and Grimdel? Your vigilance is laudable. Just remember to temper it with wisdom."

Grimdel perked up and straightened his shoulders. "Come on, boys, the mead's getting cold."

The old dwarf waited until the guards disappeared, then bowed deeply to the company. "I beg you pardon for Grimdel's enthusiasm. We have had some trouble with gnomes, lately, and it has put some of the warriors on edge. I am Hammond, one of the Elders of Marble Falls. On behalf of my fellows, I welcome you and offer you the hospitality of our Home."

Dacius slipped off his helm and returned the bow. "Your apology is as gracious as your greeting, and I accept them both in kind. I can well understand your warriors' caution. We saw signs of gnomish activity just yesterday, near an avalanche that covered your road."

"What? Again?" The gold rod twitched agitatedly in Hammond's fingers. "Blast their hides. Now we'll have to divert workers to clear the road and additional guards for safety. It will put us way behind in our work."

"Your work?" Dacius asked.

Hammond looked at him strangely. "Why, building Marble Falls, of course. Creating the Home is every dwarf's first job, as well as his greatest love. What is your work?"

"At the moment," Dacius said, "my job is finding a path for my companions into the lands to the west. We need lodgings for the night and supplies for the journey. Also, if you can give us any information, or especially a map, I would be most grateful."

"Of course, of course." Hammond smiled genially. "I have already promised you our hospitality. The information, though, is a bit trickier. Perhaps if I knew the nature of your journey?"

Dacius hesitated. "We are—searching for something."

"Ah, no matter." The dwarf shrugged. "None of my business anyway, I'm sure. Well, follow me. We can talk once you're settled in."

He led them through a succession of wide streets. Square buildings lined the road, constructed with characteristic precision and care. Seamless walls formed a perfect grid on a plateau of polished granite. Every building was immaculate, every thoroughfare spotless, but there were no people. The wind whistled through empty corridors of stone.

"It's so cold," Chentelle said. "How can you live here?"

"It is in our nature. Dwarves have always been explorers, seeking out new lands, new beauty. Where you see a forbidding wilderness, we see a landscape of stone and soil and precious minerals. The earth speaks to us, when we listen, and Marble Falls sings in rare and wonderful fashion." Hammond paused, and laughed softly. "I sound like one of your elven poets, don't I?"

The dwarf led them to a huge building in the center of the town. The hall was built to a giant's scale, with stone doors ten cubits high set in walls twice that height. A stable sat beside, filled with neatly stacked hay and empty of horses. Hammond pressed on one of the doors, and it swung silently inward. "This is our Earthhall. It is the only building large enough for everyone to be comfortable. You will find rooms upstairs with beds to accommodate several species."

Chairs of various sizes ringed a large table which dominated the interior of the hall. The table was perfectly level, but chairs sat in tapered channels so that a giant at one end could speak comfortably with a dwarf seated at the other. Smaller tables lined the walls, each designed to a different scale. Evidently this hall had been designed before news of the demise of the giants reached this isolated region.

"By the Creator." Chentelle ran her fingers across the table built for elves. The stone was cool and perfectly smooth. It whispered to her of loving care and skilled hands, but the touches were old. It had been decades, perhaps centuries, since anyone had sat here. "Beautiful, but it's so lonely. The whole town is. Where is everyone?"

"Why, in Marble Falls, of course." A look of comprehension swept across the old dwarf's face. "Ah, I see the source of your confusion. These meager dwellings are not Marble Falls. The Home lies within the mountain. This is just the temporary camp we raised while the construction got under way. Now, they serve as lodgings for newcomers until they earn a place in the boroughs. But winter is nearly here; we are unlikely to receive settlers this year. In fact, very few families have joined us in recent years."

"That's because no one knows where you are!" Chentelle said. "I mean, the dwarves told us a town had been settled, but they didn't know where it was or whether it still existed. Isn't that right, Dacius?"

The human nodded. "It's true, Hammond. Marble Falls is little more than a memory to the peoples of the Realm."

"I see." The dwarf frowned thoughtfully. "Disturbing, but it makes sense. We have been too busy to maintain regular contact with the other homes, and the Erietoph is a forbidding boundary." He shuddered, then shook his head and smiled. "I thank you for this news. I shall take it up with the council. Now, what information can I give you in return?"

"Tell us about the lands to the west," Dacius said. "What can we expect to find and what advice can you give us?"

"Advice?" Hammond said. "That's easy. Don't go. The Mountains of Time are harsh landlords, and this is going to be a hard winter. The first storm has already hit. Soon, the passes will be blocked for good. You will be lucky if you make the Long Lake before it freezes."

"Long Lake?" Dacius said. "Where is that? Do you have a map?"

"A map?" Hammond smiled. "We don't need one. It's in the mountains. The Long Lake is just past the western range. Either of the main passes will take you to it. As for what's beyond it, well, it's the edge of the world."

"What?"

Confusion rippled through the company.

Hammond waited while they regained their calm. "Ten leagues beyond Long Lake lies Karsh Adon, the Barrier Ridge. It is a sheer cliff, more than three thousand cubits high. No one knows how far it extends. Our scouts have followed it for a hundred leagues in either direction without reaching its end. Some say that the Creator lives beyond it and that he raised Karsh Adon to keep us from discovering his mysteries. Personally, I do not believe that. The rocks are formidable, but they are rocks. Eventually, we will scale their heights, but we must secure the Home first. If the object of your search lies beyond the Barrier, then your task is hopeless."

All eyes turned to Father Marcus.

The priest closed his eyes in concentration. When he spoke, his words rang with finality. "We must go beyond."

"So," Hammond said. "The leader makes himself known. Well, holy man, you are either a lunatic or on a mission of great importance."

"The latter," Father Marcus said. "Our quest is urgent, and it requires both caution and secrecy."

"Obviously," the dwarf replied, "but I urge you to reconsider. The Barrier Ridge has never been climbed, and your party is ill-equipped for such a trial."

"Nevertheless, we must undertake it." Father Marcus' tone was calm but firm. "You mentioned a lake. Is there a boat to ferry us across, or must we circumnavigate it?"

"Have you heard a word I said?" Hammond threw up his arms in frustration. "It can't be done! Go home!"

"No." Iron sounded in the word. "If you cannot guide us farther, then we will continue on our own. I thank you for your hospitality. We must leave in the morning. If you can give us supplies and direct us to the quickest pass, we will be grateful."

Hammond laughed heartily and slapped his chest. "Such determination! It does you proud, holy man. You will have your supplies, and what other help I can offer. But first, you will have a proper welcome to the Home of Marble Falls. Come. Tonight you dine under the mountain."

They stowed their gear and followed Hammond back out into the settlement. Both suns had set, now, but lines of adartak shone softly along each side of the street. The dwarf led them northward along one of the avenues, and they soon left the walled square of the surface city.

The path curved gracefully westward, winding around the twin peaks and sloping downward on the far side. Half a league or more of walking brought them to a towering fortress, built back into the face of the mountain. Crenellated walls guarded a pair of nested iron gates, and slits in both walls and ceiling told of dangers that would meet any attackers.

A thick-limbed dwarf hopped up onto the battlements as they approached. "Who approaches the gate to Marble Falls?"

"I do," Hammond shouted. "I have invited these travelers to dine with me inside the Home."

"And I refuse to admit them."

"What?" Hammond glowered and hefted his drum and golden rod as if they were weapons. "I'm in no mood for nonsense, Pontale. These people have been met too rudely already."

"Do you call the safety of the Home nonsense, Elder?" Pontale jabbed an accusing finger toward Sulmar. "No Tengarian will pass through these gates while I am Master."

Chentelle looked a question at her liegeman.

"Blood has been spilled between Tengar and the dwarves," Sulmar said. "The Small Ones have started mines in mountains that have long been claimed by the Great Kings."

"You see!" the Gate Master yelled. "He admits it. They claim to own a mountain because they can see its surface. I might as well set out in a boat and claim right to all the fish in the sea."

"But Sulmar isn't a Tengarian anymore," Chentelle said. "He was—he's with us, now. Doesn't that make a difference?"

"No."

"Pontale, you fool." Hammond's hand twitched and two sharp beats roared from the drum. "These are the first humans and elves ever to visit the Mountains of Time. Will you have it echoed through the Seven Ranges that the dwarves of Marble Falls throw decent folk to the winter? Use your eyes! This is a holy man. These are Legionnaires. Have you forgotten that the veins of our people stretch back through the Realm?"

The Gate Master bristled but did not back down. "I know our history, Hammond, and I know our laws. I will not allow a Tengarian spy into the Home, and not even an Elder can overrule me in this."

"You are right," Hammond said softly. "I can't overrule you, but I can convene the council and make a motion to remove you from your post."

Once, twice, three times the Gate Master opened his mouth only to close it again without speaking. "All right," he said finally, "everyone except the Tengarian can enter, but they have to leave their weapons here."

"No!" Chentelle cried. "I'm not going to leave Sulmar out here alone. If Sulmar can't go, then I won't either. I don't think I want to see Marble Falls anymore."

"Chentelle speaks for us all," Father Marcus said. "It is sad, for I would have loved to have beheld the beauty of your Home and hospitality. With your permission, we will return to the Earthhall."

"A moment, friends." Hammond sounded one firm retort on his drum. "Your decision is unsatisfactory, Pontale. Since when do we demand that guests render themselves defenseless? And do you expect them to dine in comfort while their comrade squats outside the gate like a scavenger? Detail some men to escort them back to the topside dwellings. I will assemble the council immediately. I suggest you prepare your oration."

The Gate Master shuffled his feet nervously. "Uh, just a minute, Elder. Perhaps I was too hasty—Yes, I think I was. They can keep their arms, and if you will speak for the Tengarian, I will let him enter."

"Of course I'll speak for him," Hammond said. "What do you think I've been doing? Now, open the gates!"

"At once, Elder."

The front gate opened and Hammond led them through. A closed passageway thirty cubits long led them to the inner gate, which slid upward as they approached. Beyond it lay a vast courtyard.

"Oh, my." Chentelle gaped in surprise. The thirty cubits between gates represented the total depth of the fortress, which was really just a gatehouse. And the courtyard was actually a huge natural cavern. The dome of the chamber was polished obsidian flecked with adartak, simulating a star-filled sky. The floor was a startling mosaic of semiprecious stones.

Chentelle stared at the pattern, trying to make sense of it. It reminded her of someth—By the Creator. The map! Part of it looked like Fel's map. There was the Erietoph and the Pretgard Mountains. But the pattern was larger, much larger. It showed the Great Sea and the Isle of Rennock, the Highlands of Balt and the Istagoth Forest, even Lone Valley was there. But it didn't show the Desecration; a gentle swirl of tiger-eye hills sat where the Great Fault should be.

She traced the path of their journey across the waste and through the Erietoph. There were the Mountains of Time, represented in stark alabaster, and an oval of lapis that had to be Long Lake. So the big dark patch must—

She froze. The floor ended abruptly in a jagged chasm. Chentelle looked down, but if the fissure had a bottom she couldn't see it.

The rift spread the width of the cavern, spanned only by a narrow jut of crystal. At a word from Hammond, the adartak bridge blazed into life. On the far side, a sheer wall of polished marble glimmered in the orb-light like flowing water. The bridge led to the base of that wall, where battlements seemed to grow naturally from the rock. A woman's face had been carved beneath the battlements, and two huge granite doors stood below the face. The doors stood open and inviting.

"Magnificent," Thildemar said. "It reminds me of the gate into Rockhome."

"You flatter us," Hammond said wistfully. "There is no matching the glory of that ancient Home." He led them across the glowing bridge and into Marble Falls.

Wind whipped around them as they crossed the chasm. As they passed through the doors, it whistled through the open mouth of the carving, forming airy syllables. *Welllcommme.*

Hammond guided them through the entry hall and into an orb-lit tunnel. They passed dozens of dwarves going about their business, and each one greeted Hammond respectfully. A steady rhythm pulsed through the Home, vibrating just below the level of hearing, and everyone they saw seemed to be moving to that subliminal cadence. Even their own steps were soon falling to the same beat.

They descended a long ramp and turned into a series of natural chambers embellished with intricately carved doors. The deeper they went, the warmer it became, and they were soon loosening and removing their cloaks. An underground stream trickled through the stone, collecting in a chain of shallow pools. Children splashed and laughed in some of these, playing under the watchful eyes of an ancient couple.

"These are the boroughs," Hammond said. "The heart of the Home. One day, the children raised here will set out to explore new lands. Infinitera is filled with wonders, and there are many yet to be discovered. Perhaps the object of your search is one of them?"

Father Marcus only smiled in reply.

They passed through the boroughs and into a large hall. More than two hundred dwarves were here, seated around long, low tables. On a platform in one corner, a group of musicians was filling the air with a delightful combination of laughing drums, exotic horns, and tinny harps. Their song was joyous and filled with exuberance.

Hammond took them to a serving line where they selected food from long stone troughs. Much of the food was strange to the company, but the old dwarf guided them. There were mutton stews and roast spiders for the humans, while the elves found a good assortment of lichens, mushrooms, baked mosses. Hearty breads and excellent mead helped round out the meal for everyone.

The food was delicious, and they ate with relish. Conversation was kept to a minimum. Gradually, they noticed that the other tables were growing quiet, too. No one approached them, but their presence in Marble Falls was definitely being noted. Soon, a second round of mead was delivered to the table. In fact, new glasses were being delivered to every table.

Suddenly, two hundred dwarves stood as one and raised their glasses. "WELCOME."

At Hammond's signal, they lifted their own glasses and joined the community in drink.

"There," the Elder said, "now it's official. The doors of Marble Falls are open to you. Now, to arrange provisions." He set his drum on the table and pounded out a rapid series of beats, taps, and scratches. The sound carried powerfully through the hall, cutting easily through the rhythm of the music. A few moments later a chubby dwarf in a well-used apron and an impressive white cap walked up to them.

"These friends need rations," Hammond said, "at least two weeks' worth.

They're on foot, so make sure you keep them light and compact. And no meat for the elves."

"Yes, Elder." The cook nodded and scurried back to the kitchen.

Once he was gone, Hammond turned back to Father Marcus. "Now, technically, since you are not going to become part of the community I should ask you for some form of recompense."

"I understand," Father Marcus said. Dwarves often bartered goods based upon estimated values for jewels or precious metals. The humans of Odenal used a similar system. "Perhaps I can repay you with information. There are things of great importance that I should share with—"

A heavy drumbeat rumbled like thunder through the cavern, silencing all conversation.

"The warning," Hammond said. "It's probably a gnome skirmish clan."

The drum sounded again, pounding with desperate urgency. Silverware clattered against stone tables as the dwarves surged to their feet and charged for the doors.

"That's no skirmish call!" Hammond called over his shoulder. "Wait here. I need to check on the gate."

"Absolutely not," Father Marcus said. "We may be able to help."

They raced back toward the surface, keeping the fastest pace the dwarf could manage. The climb seemed to take forever, and the drum calls became harder and more frenzied. At last, they reached the entry hall. Several phalanxes of armored dwarves were assembling in the huge chamber, but there was no sign of any foe. The main doors were still open.

Dacius' helm and armor were glowing violently. His blade whistled forth in a flash of blue steel. "THE BRIDGE!"

They charged through the open portal. Beyond it, the adartak bridge illuminated a grisly scene. Dwarven soldiers filled the gatehouse battlements, locked in combat with hulking, black forms. The dwarves' weapons rose and fell with uncanny precision, only to bounce ineffectually off of their targets. Pulsing red blades flickered in return, slicing easily through flesh, armor, and even stone. The defenders were being slaughtered.

"Prepare the bridge!" Hammond shouted.

A tremendous click echoed through the cavern, and the bridge shuddered. A thin line crevice appeared in the crystal's far end.

Suddenly, the inner gate slid open. A dozen dwarves fled through the gate, running for the bridge. One of them, Pontale, remained behind to close the gate and jam the mechanism. He had hardly finished when a mob of vikhors slammed into the bars. The portal held, but just barely.

The Legionnaires charged forward, moving to support the dwarves' retreat. But they were too late.

A half-dozen Tenebrites launched themselves from the top of the battlements. Their bodies shifted as they fell, forming insect thoraxes and six segmented legs. Hard claws gouged pits in the stone as they landed. Then they were running, closing distance as if the dwarves were standing still.

Drup, Gerruth, and Leth stopped and took aim with their bows. Three arrows blazed through the air, sailing over the dwarves' heads. One of them took a Tenebrite full in the chest, reducing it to smoking ash. The other two hit at shallow angles and ricocheted off armored torsos.

A shadow knight loomed over the Gate Master, its sword lifted high in preparation for a strike.

The dwarf spun around, warned by some sound or instinct. He planted his spear against the ground and braced himself for the impact. The spear's tip caught the Tenebrite full in the chest, driven by the Ill-creature's own power and strength.

It made no difference. The metal tip bent, and the shaft shattered. The Tenebrite reared, its momentum briefly countered; then the red sword swung toward Pontale's head.

A jet of green flame shot across the chasm, incinerating the Tenebrite in midstroke. A'stoc stood on the inner battlements, Thunderwood Staff blazing in his hands. Smiling grimly, he redirected the Earthpower, sending an arc of flame toward the other shadow knights. One by one, they vanished into the fire.

Dacius and Thildemar guarded the far end of the bridge while the dwarves hurried across. The first wave made it safely, but Pontale was still a dozen cubits from the chasm when the stones of the gatehouse exploded apart.

Scores of vikhors surged from the rubble, driven to a frenzy by the Tenebrites behind them. More blasts of Earthpower met them, but they kept coming, heedless of the cost. A few managed to slide through the wizard's barrage.

Dacius and Thildemar met them with mystic steel. The human's armor was glowing like a blue sun. His shield countered every attack, and his blade cut wide swaths through the Ill-creatures.

Thildemar was equally impressive, in his way: graceful and efficient rather than flamboyant and powerful. He fought with sword and dagger, using the shorter blade to parry. He fought as if the battle were choreographed, wasting no energy on unnecessary motion.

Together, they cleared the last of the vikhors from the field. Then they backed slowly across the chasm. A few Ill-creatures bolted after them from hiding places in the rubble, but A'stoc's magic struck them down easily.

Once the warriors were safely back on solid ground, the crystal bridge began to move. The adartak shrunk in on itself, retracting into some hidden chamber in the stone wall. Soon, only a tiny spur was visible, spanning less than a tenth of the deep rift.

Tense silence fell upon the chamber. A hundred eyes scanned the rubble, searching for any new threat. Long moments passed, and nothing moved. They were safe, for now.

Suddenly, Pontale's voice cut through the quiet. "You!" His angry gaze pierced each of the company in turn. "You brought those monsters here. What were they? And why are your weapons the only things that can kill them?"

A murmur of suspicion rippled through the dwarven guardsmen, a murmur that became louder as A'stoc emerged from the stairwell to the battlements. Steel weapons twitched in nervous fingers.

"What is this?" the wizard said. "Will you reward your saviors with treachery?"

"You dare to speak of treachery?" the Gate Master shouted. "It was you who led those monsters to the Home!"

"The fault is mine," Father Marcus said calmly. "It is I who led us here. I am deeply sorry for the loss you have suffered. I did not expect the Ill-creatures to attack us here. We had not seen any for several days."

"You're sorry!" Pontale roared. "That's not good enough. I hereby place you under detention. Surrender your weapons at once!"

"Wait!" Hammond slapped a single beat on his drum, sending a deep note of calm through the assembled soldiers. "Pontale, you were but a child during the wars. You do not realize the magnitude of what the holy man is saying." He turned to Father Marcus, concern plain on his furrowed brow. "Do you say that the Dark One has returned to Infinitera?"

"Yes. His Ill-creatures are active throughout the Realm and beyond. That is the news I was going to share with you when the attack interrupted us."

The Elder winced. "I will convene the council immediately. We must discuss these matters."

"No." Pontale lifted a small drum from his belt and pounded three hard beats. "They have endangered the Home! I call for immediate exile, and I demand that the matter be settled by assembly."

An excited ripple ran through the soldiers. "What about the gates?" someone called. "What if the monsters return?"

"I have placed wards around the chasm," A'stoc said. "We will have warning before any new attack."

"Excellent, wizard," Hammond said. "I thank you for your caution and concern."

"Nevertheless," Pontale said, "I want two full phalanxes on watch and a third in reserve. Speak to your brothers, so that they may know your mind at assembly."

Hammond raised his voice to address the crowd. "You have heard the call, and the cause is just. Let the summons be sounded. Marble Falls will decide."

The hall erupted into activity. Soldiers ran about, some heading for the walls, others disappearing into a myriad of passages. Somewhere, a huge drum pounded the same pattern of three hard beats that Pontale had played. A moment later, it sounded again, and then again.

Hammond turned to the company. "I must speak with the other Elders before the assembly. Do you remember the tunnels to the communal hall, or should I assign you a guide?"

Father Marcus said something to Dacius in a hushed tone, then spoke to the dwarf. "No guide is needed. We will meet you there."

"Speak for yourself, High Bishop." A'stoc raised himself to his full height. "I do not intend to waste my time listening to the bickering of small minds." He spun about and marched back toward the battlements.

Dacius called Drup and Thildemar to his side, and a moment later the two warriors were following A'stoc into the stairwell.

Father Marcus led the rest of them back into the winding tunnels. He retraced their path confidently, as if he had lived below the mountain all of his life. In a few minutes, they were back in the boroughs. The High Bishop paused for a moment outside the hall, bowing his head in a quiet meditation. Then he pressed open the door.

The hall was filled with dwarves. Men, women, children, the entire population of Marble Falls was coming together. The long tables and benches were gone, secreted in some hidden compartment. Everyone sat cross-legged on the floor, arranged in neat rows facing the corner podium. Each dwarf had a small drum tucked between his or her legs. The chamber was quiet. Not a word was spoken as new people filed in and took their places in the crowd.

The company moved to a spot away from the door and waited, uncertain where they should be.

The quiet procession continued for several minutes. Then the mighty drum sounded again, pounding once, twice, three times. A hidden door swung open behind the podium and four figures emerged. Each one carried a drum and a thin golden rod—and Hammond was the third in line. The four dwarves took their seats on the platform. Then the first Elder motioned for the party to come forward.

They filed down the long aisle between dwarves and stood in the open area before the dais. Chentelle wondered if they were supposed to sit, too, but no one gave any sign.

"Who makes the charge?" the fourth Elder said.

"Pontale, Master of the Gate, Defender of the Home." The burly dwarf marched forward, holding his drum before him like a pennant.

"Who speaks for the accused?" the Elder said.

"The company is under my charge," Father Marcus said.

Hammond stood up suddenly. He set his drum and rod down on the stage, and hopped off to stand next to the High Bishop. He pulled a smaller drum from under his robes and held it at the ready. "He is a stranger to the ways of the Home. I will sound his voice."

If any of the dwarves were surprised by his action, they gave no sign. The fourth Elder lifted his rod and struck three beats on his drum, filling the chamber with echoes. "Marble Falls is assembled. Let the parties speak."

Pontale immediately established a rhythm on his drum. His playing was soft, but powerful, punctuated by angry beats and accusatory pauses. "Kellior is dead; his wife is a widow; his children are fatherless. Tamar is dead; his father has no heirs. Forn is dead; his wife mourns; his brothers weep . . ."

The litany continued, gaining power with each name. In the crowd, a dozen drums joined Pontale's beat, then a hundred. The music swelled, pounding at the company with rage and grief.

"The strangers caused these deaths, as surely as they harbor a Tengarian in their midst."

"That isn't fair!" Chentelle cried. "Sulmar—"

The fourth Elder pounded his drum. The beat was deafening, crashing against their ears like an open hand. "There can be only one voice! Who speaks for the accused?"

Hammond turned to Chentelle, his eyes filled with warnings, and she shrank quietly back into the company.

Pontale resumed his rhythm, drumming more powerfully than before. "They knew they were being followed. They knew that the Home was defenseless against the Ill-creatures. Only their weapons can kill the monsters. Still, they said nothing. They entered the Home; they led the Ill-creatures to our gate. They invited death into Marble Falls, and death came. If they remain, or if they return, death will come again. The Home must be protected. My voice is clear, and the word it screams is exile!"

The chamber roared to the Gate Master's cadence. Five hundred drums sounded as one. *Guilt!* said the drums. *Exile!*

Hammond nodded to Father Marcus.

The High Bishop spoke into the din, phrasing his words like a chant. "I am Father Marcus Alanda, High Bishop of the Holy Order in Talan, and I have made many mistakes. The first was in not trusting the people of Marble Falls to be wise and good. I concealed my identity and the nature of my quest, but such mistrust serves only to help evil gain a foothold in our hearts."

Hammond beat his drum, matching his measures to the priest's words. He pounded a counterpoint to the Gate Master's rhythm: understanding instead of anger, inclusive rather than accusatory. His cadence was strong, steady, but it was lost in the chorus of rage.

"My second mistake," Father Marcus continued, "was not realizing that the Ill-creatures had tracked us here. I believed we had lost them in the Erietoph. I believed that secrecy would shield us from rediscovery. I was wrong, and Marble Falls has paid the price for that mistake. I cannot repay you for your loss, but I can help to insure that it does not happen again." He nodded to Dacius.

The Legionnaire stepped forward and laid a pile of weapons on the floor before the platform. It held all of the Legionnaires' parrying blades and half of their vorpal arrows.

"These weapons," the priest chanted, "are part of a store that was recovered from A'kalendane's workshop. They can destroy Ill-creatures. Give them to your best swordsmen and archers, and Marble Falls will never again be defenseless against this evil."

A few drums joined Hammond's rhythm, strengthening it slightly, but Pontale countered with a note of renewed outrage. "Bribery! My voice will not be swayed. Exile! Then we can confiscate all of their weapons."

Father Marcus continued his chant, keeping any anger he felt out of his voice. "Should you do that, you would be making a mistake as grave as my own. Hatred is a tool of the Dark One. It serves him as ably as any demonspawn. If we are driven into the wilderness without weapons, without supplies, then our quest will surely fail. If that happens, then Marble Falls will die. The Realm will die. All of Infinitera will die. This is truth.

"I am Father Marcus Alanda, High Bishop of the Holy Order in Talan, and I come here searching for the star which fell from the sky before the First Season of Light. This star does not belong in the Creation. It comes from beyond the Abyss and carries an evil which will consume us all if it is not destroyed."

The mention of the Fallen Star sparked a response in several of the dwarves. They added their numbers to Hammond's cadence, bolstering his rhythm.

"Marble Falls has paid a high price for this mission, but it has not paid alone. A score of men died before the quest had even begun, their bodies strewn across the shores of Larama. More died in the vastness of the Great Sea, battling goblin hordes. One companion died under a mountain called Hel's Crown in the land called Kennaru, defending us all from Ill-creatures far more terrible than those you have seen. Another gave his life to help us escape from that dread island. In Tel Adartak-Skysoar a friend more dear than I had realized sacrificed his life to thwart a necromancer, and among the bleak wastes of the Desecration brave Legionnaires and stout dwarves laid down their lives to save these weapons from a host of living death.

"All of this is truth. Death follows this quest, and it has claimed far too many good souls. But there is hope yet. We recovered the weapons of A'kalendane, and now brave men can defend their homes. We have traveled across the Great Sea and returned bearing a talisman of power. We have reached the edge of the world, and the end of our quest is now close. But the greatest cause for hope lies elsewhere. You see, the men who made these sacrifices did not act out of fear, or anger, or compulsion of any type. They acted for love: the love of friends, the love of family, the love of Creation. As long as that love exists, we have cause for hope.

"Those are my words. The quest has brought us here. We have no guide. We have no supplies. We are beset by enemies and alone among a people strange to our experience. And we place our trust in your goodness and your hospitality. The future of our quest lies in your hands."

As the High Bishop fell silent, the war of rhythms escalated. Drum beats clashed in the air, resounding off the stone walls and ceiling. Cadences and counterpoint swirled through and around each other, swelling and diminishing as new drums joined in or old drums shifted allegiance. At last, the issue was resolved. One rhythm emerged from the chaos, slowly absorbing all voices of opposition—Hammond's rhythm, Father Marcus' rhythm.

The three Elders raised their rods. As one, they joined in the song, driving the measure of unity to new levels. Then, responding to some unspoken signal, every drum fell silent.

The Elders stood. The fourth Elder pounded out two slow beats with his rod. "Marble Falls has spoken. This assembly is dissolved."

The Elders filed quietly out through their hidden door. Some of the other dwarves stood immediately and left the room, but many remained seated, deep in thought or meditation. A few gathered in groups, conversing quietly among themselves.

Pontale walked over to the company and bowed formally. "We will help you however we can. Please forgive me for my suspicions. They were unjust and unwarranted."

Father Marcus smiled and returned the Gate Master's bow. "There is no blame. I cannot fault you for your grief or for your fierce love of this beautiful Home. I believe that you were correct. This assembly was necessary."

"You are gracious," Pontale said. He nodded to a corner of the room, where several dwarves were busily shaping stone benches. "It is not safe to return topside. We will provide accommodations here, though they may be spartan. Once Ellistar rises, you can return for your equipment."

"Thank you," Father Marcus said. "The day has been long. I think we will all welcome some rest."

"Then I must apologize to you, High Bishop." Hammond shrugged and smiled wanly. "I'm afraid that the council would like to meet with you for a while. We still have many questions."

"Of course," Father Marcus said. "I will be happy to come with you."

Pontale led them over to the corner once Hammond and Father Marcus had left. The dwarven workers had created nine beds of stone, each one sized and shaped to fit one of the company. Soft pillows rested inside the stone, waiting to welcome them all into restful sleep.

Chentelle rolled herself into her bed, letting the soft mattress envelope her.

It was wonderful, like floating in a cocoon. Already, her eyes were becoming heavy. She forced herself to sit up. "Someone should go tell A'stoc and the others what happened."

"Good idea," Dacius said. "Any volunteers?"

She smiled. "I'll go."

The path to the entry hall seemed shorter this time, and she and Sulmar retraced it easily. They found A'stoc standing on the ramparts, standing apart from both dwarves and elves. The wizard looked gaunt and worn, though his back was unbent. He glanced toward her as she approached, but did not speak.

"Father Marcus cleared everything up," she said. "The dwarves are going to help us."

"I know," he said. "The dwarves here heard the drums."

"Is there anything I can get for you? Food? Drink?" Chentelle searched for any response. There was none. "The dwarves have made us some wonderfully comfortable beds in the boroughs."

"I think I'll stay here," he said. "The solitude is refreshing."

Chentelle turned away. Drup, Sulmar, and Thildemar stood waiting near the stairs. She joined them, and together, they returned to the communal hall.

❧ 20 ❧

⟨ KARSH ADON ⟩

Father Marcus awakened them at first-light. If the priest had gotten any sleep, it didn't show on his face. "Lord Gemine, I must return to the council chamber. Please lead a party back to retrieve our supplies. We will be continuing our journey from here. The Elders have agreed to let us use their secret tunnels."

"Excellent," Dacius said. "Leth, Gerruth, stay with the High Bishop. Thildemar, Drup, you're with me."

"I'll come, too," Chentelle said. The dwarven caverns were beautiful in their way, but she already longed to see the open sky.

An escort of dwarves was waiting for them in the entry hall, as was A'stoc. The crystal bridge was extended back across the chasm, and they marched out to the ruins of the gatehouse. Two squads of dwarves fell out from the phalanx and stood guard while workmen came to clear the rubble and retrieve the fallen. The rest marched with the company back to the topside settlement.

They arrived to a scene of carnage. Not a building was left standing. The Earthhall lay in ruins and the protecting wall had been razed. Everywhere, fragments of stone showed the ragged tears of vikhor claws. Body parts were strewn randomly through the wreckage, mutilated beyond recognition.

Chentelle remembered the brash young figure of Grimdel, challenging them on the road. Tears welled in her eyes. Hammond would be crushed.

Dacius trembled with rage. Slowly, he turned to the dwarves. "I'm sorry. We should stay and help you, but we have to go."

The dwarves just nodded and began silently sifting through the chaos.

"Lord Gemine," A'stoc said. "Do you think this amount of damage could have been delivered before the attack on the gates last night?"

"What? What are you—Blood and Hel." Dacius' eyes went wide. "There's another band of vikhors about!"

A'stoc nodded. "Or else refugees who fled from the battle at the gate. Either way, we should find them and destroy them while the suns are up. It will be safer for us and our new friends."

"Agreed," Dacius said. "Can you find them?"

"No, but Chentelle can."

He wanted her to use her Gift. Her eyes drifted over the ruins, stopping for a moment on a bloody scrap that might have been an arm. She nodded and closed her eyes.

The mountain spoke to her, telling old, slow tales of thrusting plates and shifting earth. It told her of hard winds and the slow death of rainfall. She listened to its stories and moved beyond them, searching for knowledge of the present. The mountain understood. It knew the warm touch of the dwarves and the deep rhythm of their love. And it knew something else, the vile darkness that buried itself under the stone. Chentelle felt the shadow's presence, and understood. "I have them."

She opened her eyes and scanned the mountainside, trying to match the landscape to the sensations of the stone. Jaw set in determination, she led them out of the settlement and up a natural ridge line on the near peak. The path wound beside a frozen stream and ended near the foot of a deep gouge in the granite. Shadow filled the cleft, and the outline of a cave mouth was barely visible in the rocks above. "There."

"Are you certain?" A'stoc asked.

She nodded. "Of course I am."

Dacius' sword whispered from its sheath. Grimly, he lifted his helm and set it into place.

A'stoc put a hand on his arm. "No, Lord Gemine. I will deal with this alone."

The Legionnaire shook his head. "YOU ARE NOT GOING IN THERE ALONE."

"Who said anything about going in?" He planted the Thunderwood against the mountain. The heel of the Staff blurred and joined with the stone like a sagestaff to a ship's deck. "Stand back."

They moved away cautiously.

A'stoc chanted in low, guttural tones. Earthpower flickered around the Staff. But instead of bursting forth in brilliant flame, the magic flowed into the hard stone. Green radiance pulsed through the stone, gathering slowly around the cave.

A'stoc screamed, and the mountainside ripped open. The line of the gorge ripped upward. Huge flaps of pulsing stone peeled backward, opening the cave to Ellistar's light. Hideous screams erupted from inside the cleft, rising into the air on clouds of foul smoke. It wasn't the movement of the stone that killed them; they were impervious to any natural force. But they could not bear the direct sunlight.

The few dwarves present stared. They understood the kind of force required to move rock in this manner.

After the last cry faded, the earth fell back into place. Only a thin scar of cracked stone remained to mark the mountain's ordeal.

By the Creator, how much power could he control?

A'stoc pulled the Staff from the earth and turned back to the company. "Now, let us be on our way."

They returned to the communal hall, pausing briefly at the inner gate to report the attack on the topside settlement. The stone beds and mattresses had been cleared away. In their place was a long table with chairs of various sizes.

Father Marcus and Hammond sat in two of the chairs, engaged in an animated discussion. They hopped to their feet as soon as the others arrived.

"Please follow me," the Elder said. "The council has agreed to grant you access to the secret tunnels. It will make your journey much swifter."

There was a note of weariness in the old dwarf's voice that Chentelle had never heard before. He must have learned about Grimdel.

Hammond led them out of the boroughs and into a series of mining shafts. The tunnels here were narrower and curved irregularly, following the natural veins of ore. After several branchings, they turned into a tunnel that looked much like the others, except that it held no miners or equipment. The passage twisted along for a few dozen cubits and then ended in a partially worked wall. This vein had apparently been exhausted quickly.

Hammond hummed softly to himself and ran the fingers of his left hand across the stone. After several passes, he zeroed in on a lump that seemed indistinguishable from any other on the wall. He tapped the spot once with his golden rod, and the blank wall split down the middle. Orb-lights sprang to life, revealing a cramped passage beyond.

"I'm afraid that you will have to stoop," the Elder said, grabbing an adartak torch. "These tunnels were designed to discourage pursuit by large creatures."

He wasn't exaggerating. The ceiling was so low that even Chentelle had to duck occasionally. The poor humans had to bend nearly double, often choosing to scramble along on all fours. Luckily, after a confusing series of switchbacks at the very beginning, the tunnel ran perfectly straight. Despite the humans' awkward gaits, they made excellent time.

They stopped once each hour. Father Marcus would summon the power of his order as soon as they did, and use it to ease sore backs and tired muscles. Unfortunately, the healing power could only be applied to another. The High Bishop himself had to suffer his pains without help.

As the day dragged on, the priest became more and more worn. His breath came in heavy gasps, and he groaned audibly whenever his spine changed alignment. But he would not let the company slow their pace. At his command, Hammond pressed them to move even faster.

At last, they came to the end of the tunnel. The door on this side opened at a simple push. Cold air blasted into the passage, and the orb-torch illuminated a small cavern. A handful of stars glittered in the night sky beyond the cave's mouth.

"Be careful; the ceiling here is not much taller." Hammond led them up the brief slope and out into the open air.

"Uhhhhhnnn!" Dacius stretched out his arms and shoulders. "By all that's holy, it feels good to stand again."

"I agree," Father Marcus said, straightening up much more slowly. "Hammond, how far have we come?"

"This is the north face of Sawtooth, on the far side of the western range. The lake is less than half a league away."

"The Creator be praised." Father Marcus extended his arms in the sign of harmony. "We are close, my friends, and our steps are guided by providence."

"Providence *and* dwarven ingenuity." Hammond raised his torch and chuckled softly.

A narrow path wound through the trees and brought them to the shores of Long Lake. Hammond turned northward and led them around the thin strip of beach. Before long, they reached a rocky cliff that jutted a dozen cubits out into the water.

The dwarf paused, as if taking his bearings. Then he stooped down and picked up a rock from the beach. He started a hum and began shaping the stone, molding its edges easily with strong fingers. Then, satisfied, he ended his spell and slapped the rock against a depression in the cliff face. A hidden door revealed itself and swung gently inward.

Bile rose violently in the back of Chentelle's throat, and she barely kept from retching. The pungent odors of fish and brine blasted from the door.

Hammond stared perplexedly at the grimaces on the elves' faces. "What's the matter? I told you that this was a fishing cabin."

"It's all right," Chentelle gasped, trying to regain her breath. "We're just— surprised at how strong the smells are."

"Hah, what did you expect, perfume?" He grinned and pressed through the door.

A huge oven dominated the interior, flanked by a round table with stone chairs. Wooden barrels filled racks all along the outer walls, some closed, some open. Great bags of salt sat in a far corner, along with a generous pile of firewood. A low opening led to a smaller chamber furnished with two large dressers and five small beds. Another door, this one shut and barred, sat in the wall facing the lake.

"Please start a fire," Father Marcus said, "and put out the orb-light. Some Ill-creatures are sensitive to magic."

Hammond hurried to comply. Soon, the interior of the stone cabin was filled with warmth from the fire. The burning wood also masked some of the fish smell, to the great relief of the elves. They ate a quick supper and cast lots for use of the beds. Dacius, Drup, Thildemar, Hammond, and Father Marcus drew first shift, but the priest surrendered his lot to Chentelle, saying that he wished to meditate.

The beds were short, but comfortable. Even so, Chentelle found herself tossing and turning, unable to sleep. The quiet snoring that filled the room was sure testimony that none of the others shared her problem. Sighing, she stood and walked out to the main room.

Sulmar was standing just inside the doorway. He fell quietly into step beside her, ignoring her offer of the empty bed. Leth and Gerruth sat by the stove, deep in conversation about the forests of Inarr. They, also, chose to delay sleep until later. Father Marcus sat with his back to the wall, surrounded by the aura of sanctuary. Of the wizard, there was no sign.

"Where's A'stoc?" she asked.

"He wished to stand by the shore," Sulmar said, "and he actively discouraged any suggestions of company."

She remembered the rocky coastline near the wizard's caves on the Quiet Sea. No wonder he wanted to stand by the shore. It was so similar to his own home. Her thoughts turned to the trees and kinfolk of Lone Valley. She drifted in the memories, awash in love and sadness.

Time passed, and she became aware of other thoughts, other emotions impinging on her homesickness: anger, fear, doubt, reproach. The feelings weren't hers. They came from outside. At first, she thought they were A'stoc's. She could easily imagine them pouring from the turmoil of the wizard's heart. But he was too far away, and shielded from her Gift by a wall of cold stone. The emotions came from Father Marcus.

Her eyes snapped into focus. The priest still sat against the wall, but the aura of peace had disappeared.

"Father Marcus," she said softly, kneeling down beside him. "Are you all right?"

"Eh?" He jumped, as if he had not seen her approach. "Oh, Chentelle, I'm fine. I was only lost in thought."

"But they were dark thoughts," she said. "I can feel how heavily they weigh on your spirit."

He smiled wearily. "Bless you, child. Yours is such a precious Gift. The knowledge I carry gnaws at me. I feel the evil stirring, just below the level of thought. I can't understand it yet, but it frightens me. I know that if I fail Infinitera will die, but I am worried that even if I succeed, the seeds of destruction will find life in my own mind."

"But you are the High Bishop," she said. "Surely, your faith can contain the evil."

"Perhaps, but I am also a man, and I have all the frailties of men. Sometimes I am plagued by doubt, and I wonder whether I have the strength my task requires. Already, so many people have paid the price for my mistakes. So many have died." He stopped, reacting to her expression of shock. "No, I have not surrendered to despair, Chentelle. My faith is still strong. But these thoughts are in my head, and I dare not ignore them. Faith in ignorance is a brittle thing. Only by facing our doubts can we move beyond them."

She sensed the steadiness return to his spirit. "You are a good man, Marcus Alanda. Without you this quest would have been lost long ago. Your wisdom has been our guide, but it is your faith that holds us together. No one else doubts your strength. Remember that when your thoughts grow dark."

"Thank you," he said. "I will. Now, if you will excuse me, I think I could use some sleep."

Chentelle watched him leave, a slow smile building on her face. When the time came to exchange sleeping shifts, she made sure the priest was not disturbed. There was an extra bed anyway, since A'stoc still refused to rest.

Chentelle woke to the smell of roasting oats and nut muffins. A quick glance told her that everyone else was already up. Only Sulmar was still in the room, standing alertly beside her bed. The others were waiting for them in the common room.

After the morning meal, Hammond took them through the barred door into the boathouse. A pair of sailboats floated in the water, as did several small rowboats. The Elder pressed on the rock facade opposite the door, and the stone wall pivoted around its center line. "The sailing skiffs are yours for as long as you need them. I will leave these doors unlocked. When you return, simply press on the cliff face near the water."

The dwarf swept off his cap and bowed deeply. "I wish you fortune on your quest. You will always be welcome in Marble Falls."

Father Marcus returned his bow. "We are grateful for your help, and for the help of your people. But most of all, we are grateful for your friendship. Thank you, Hammond, and may the Creator smile on all of your days."

The company quickly removed the nets and fishing tackle from the sailboats, replacing them with their own supplies. The boats were built for dwarves, but they were sturdy and had room enough for the party. Chentelle and Sulmar boarded one boat with A'stoc, Drup, and Thildemar. Father Marcus and Dacius rode in the other with the brothers Leth and Gerruth.

They used paddles to push themselves out into open water, then raised the triangular sails. The water was calm, but a light wind from the east drove them steadily across Long Lake.

Father Marcus glanced at the sky. Ellistar was well above the mountains, and the first rays of Deneob's red dawn were already poking over the peaks. "Wizard A'stoc, can you increase our pace?"

"Of course." Standing in the small boat was precarious, so the wizard knelt in front of the mast. His face relaxed into an easy smile as the Thunderwood Staff melded into the wood. He began a soft chant, and the boats darted forward on a strong wind.

Chentelle trailed her fingers in the water, watching the tiny wakes swirl around each other. Before long, the far shore came into view. A long line of gray clouds hung in the distance behind it. No, not clouds, it was a line of snow-covered mountains that stretched the length of the horizon.

She let her eyes shift to the other boat. Father Marcus looked better after a good night's sleep, but he was still a worn shadow of his former self. Deep hollows ringed his eyes, and his tattered robes reflected the ragged emotions that she knew still raged within him. In many ways, he looked more like the A'stoc who had confronted her near the Quiet Sea than the solid priest who had first greeted them in the Holy Land.

"Alert!" Dacius jumped into a crouch, causing the other skiff to rock perilously. His eyes shifted back and forth, scanning the horizon.

Chentelle stared. What was he doing? Then she saw it. Faint blue light shimmered around the human's armor. Ill-creatures were near. But where? And how? The twin suns were both high in the sky. The icy water tickled her fingers. Of course! She extended her Gift into the lake, searching beneath the surface. Something was coming toward them from the dark depths. Something large. "Behind us! It's in the water."

Vorpal swords sang from their scabbards, glowing fiercely even in the light of day. But the tiny boats were too unsteady for the Legionnaires to stand securely, much less fight.

"A'stoc," Father Marcus called. "We need more speed. We have to outrun it."

The wind gusted ferociously. The little skiffs leaped forward, tilting dangerously to starboard. Swords slammed back into sheaths as the Legionnaires rushed to find secure holds. They threw their weight to port, trying to balance the force of the gale.

Chentelle thrust her Gift back into the water. It was working. The follower was falling behind.

"Brace yourselves!"

The skiffs slammed into the far shore, driving far up the rocky beach. Chentelle was thrown forward, clearing the low rail and landing roughly on the hard ground. Before she could recover her feet, strong hands captured her arms and lifted her into the air.

Sulmar carried her well away from the water, then set her gently on her feet. The rest of the company was just behind them, scrambling for the safety of solid ground.

A wake appeared on the surface of the lake, following behind a huge swell of water. The wave rushed toward them, growing larger as it neared. Finally, it crashed against the beach, lifting the boats off the beach and throwing them several cubits inland. Water splashed violently through the air, then ran quietly back into the lake. Then everything was calm again.

"Is that it?" Chentelle asked.

Dacius shrugged, his eyes never leaving the water. "You tell me. Can you still sense it?"

She extended her Gift toward the water, but she felt nothing out of the ordinary. "No. It's gone. It must have retreated from the light."

"Perhaps, but it didn't go far." Dacius tapped his breastplate meaningfully. The vorpal steel still glowed.

It didn't make sense. If the Ill-creature was that close, she should be able to sense it. But there was nothing active in the shallows, not even a school of fish.

The ground exploded under their feet. A giant hump of slimy flesh burst into the light, driving them backward with a shower of rocks and flying sand.

Father Marcus was closest to the eruption, and he was tossed high into the air. He landed badly, falling flush on one shoulder and the side of his neck.

"Mikahi!" Thildemar shouted. Mudworm.

Normally, mikahi were harmless creatures, scavengers of refuse and decay. They ranged throughout Infinitera, delving through solid rock and soft silt with equal ease, but they preferred to stay in deep waters. They usually came to the surface only during the Seasons of Light, to mate and lay their eggs. But this worm was driven by other needs. Its liquid eyes gleamed with malignant intelligence, and the red skin peeled back from its face, revealing a circular mouth rimmed with razor teeth. The mudworm's head reared more than twenty cubits into the air, then lurched for the High Bishop.

Father Marcus was too stunned to react. He screamed as the mouth closed around his leg and lifted him into the air.

Dacius jumped forward, thrusting his sword at the worm's neck. The vorpal blade sliced easily through the soft flesh, burying itself to the hilt.

The worm screamed, dropping the priest from its gaping mouth. The dark shadow of a wraith oozed from the worm and crackled into smoke under the light of the suns.

The mudworm thrashed wildly, slamming Dacius to the ground. Only the binding force of A'kalendane's gauntlets kept his vorpal blade from flying out of his grasp.

Leth and Gerruth stepped forward, driving the worm away from their commander with a series of deep cuts.

The mikahi writhed under their assault, its vast body tearing up great chunks of earth.

"Stop it!" Chentelle yelled. "You're killing it. Look at your swords!"

The Legionnaires paused, and comprehension came to them suddenly. The blades no longer glowed. The Ill-creature was destroyed; only the natural worm remained.

But the pain-maddened beast was still a danger. Chentelle sang out with her Gift, soothing the terrified creature. There was little intelligence in the worm, only a driving instinct for self-preservation. She nudged at that instinct, guiding the animal toward flight. The mikahi dived back into the earth, burrowing toward the safety of the lake. In seconds, it was gone.

She let her enchantment fade.

"Chentelle, come here." Dacius was kneeling beside Father Marcus, cradling the High Bishop's head in his lap.

She ran to the priest's side. He was still conscious, but his eyes were glazed with pain and shock. She placed a hand on his chest, reaching into him to inspect his injuries.

His shoulder was badly bruised, but the injury was not great. She was able to soothe the nerves and adjust the flow of blood to the area, bringing at least a little relief. She did the same for the contusion on his neck, but the damage to Marcus' right leg was more serious. The force of the mikahi's bite had broken both of the bones in the lower leg, and the sharp teeth had lacerated the flesh of the calf in a dozen places.

"He needs a healer," she said. "This is more than my Gift can handle."

Father Marcus placed his hand over hers. "You must do what you can. I can't heal myself, and there is no one else."

She nodded. He was right. "This is going to hurt," she told him softly. Then, louder, "Sulmar, help me. We need to set his leg. Drup, bring me something clean to bind his cuts. And splints, we'll need splints. Scavenge something from the boats if you have to. Hold him steady, Dacius. Thildemar, give him a hand."

She reached into the priest once more, using her Gift to pinpoint the location of the breaks. "Now." Sulmar pulled on the leg, stretching the bones apart. As he released the pressure, Chentelle made minor adjustments to the angles, making sure the breaks set properly.

"Good, now hold the leg steady. Drup, where are those splints?"

The young Legionnaire placed two sections of oar and several strips of cloth into her hands.

She used the cleanest of the cloths to cover the lacerations. Then she placed the splints and tied them into place. "That's the best I can do for now. How does it feel?"

Father Marcus' face was flushed with pain, but he managed a thin smile. "It hurts. But it would be much worse if not for your ministrations. Thank you."

"We should return to Marble Falls," Dacius said. "They will certainly have a healer."

"No." The priest's voice was faint but firm. "There is not enough time. We must continue the quest." His tone admitted no argument.

Dacius' eyes turned to the boats. "Chentelle, can you use your wood shaping to turn the oars into stretcher poles? Good. Drup, take down one of the sails. We'll use it for a sling. Leth, make sure that both boats are tied down and secured for our return."

The oars were sized for dwarves, so Chentelle blended two of them together to form each pole. It felt good to use her *rillandef* again. The simple act of wood shaping reminded her of gentler days.

In less than an hour, the stretcher was complete, and they were on their way. They all took turns bearing the stretcher, rotating positions frequently. Though they were still leagues away, the massive wall of the Barrier Ridge dominated the horizon. Fortunately, the terrain between the ridge and Long Lake was a plateau with only the gentlest of upward slopes.

They made almost five leagues before Deneob's disk vanished behind the massive stone cliff. Darkness came quickly, and with it a sudden drop in temperature. They searched for some shelter from the driving wind, and at last settled on a small clutch of boulders. It was not a perfect windbreak, but it was the best available. Even if they had chosen to risk a fire, the barren plain offered little in the way of usable wood. So they huddled together around the priest's stretcher, faces turned inward, backs to the wind.

"Father Marcus?" Drup said. "What are we going to do when we reach Karsh Adon? We can't carry you up it, and you'll never be able to make the climb with that leg."

"You are right," the High Bishop said. "But it was never my intention to climb the ridge. Hammond was correct; we do not have the necessary skills or equipment. Luckily, the Creator has provided us with another way."

"What do you mean?" the Legionnaire asked.

"Is it not obvious?" A'stoc said. "He means me."

"Of course!" Chentelle exclaimed. "A levitating platform, like the one at Tel Adartak-Skysoar."

"I am glad you remember," the wizard said, "because I will need your help. Integrating the wood to contain the power of the spell is a simple matter. Constructing the platform itself is not. It takes great skill in *rillandef*."

Chentelle nodded thoughtfully. The disk at Skysoar had been shaped into a single mass, even down to the level of the wood fibers. She wouldn't have the time to do something like that, but she had to make it solid enough to both contain the spell and support their weight. "I can make the platform. Can you really levitate us all so far?"

A'stoc smiled. "It has been decades since I tried to move anything larger than a jug of wine, but what I lack in finesse I make up for in power. If we leave the ground, then we will make it to the top."

"I do not doubt it," Father Marcus said. "We have come too far to be turned back by a wall of rock. The Creator is with us. We shall not fail."

ᐒ

They huddled together through the night, grabbing what fitful sleep the biting wind allowed. Dacius ordered double rotations of the guards, so that no one had to stand exposed to the cold for too long. Shortly before dawn, a distant roar rumbled across the plain.

"Kaliya," Sulmar hissed, waking from a sound sleep. He jumped away from the others, drawing his black blade in a lightning motion. "I am here, dragon! I am here!"

"Sulmar," Dacius growled. "Be quiet."

But the Tengarian's eyes gleamed with madness. He opened his mouth to scream another challenge.

Chentelle grabbed her liegeman's arm. "It's all right, Sulmar. The dragon is out there, but now is not the time. Don't let the rage consume you. It only makes you careless."

He hesitated, sanity slowly returning to his eyes. "Yes, mistress, I beg your forgiveness. I will be patient. The dragon will come to me. Our destinies are joined."

Dacius scanned the eastern sky, where the pale hints of first-light were already beginning. "Well, since we're all awake anyway, we may as well get moving. We can cover a league or more before stopping for breakfast."

No one argued the point. The dragon's roars were still audible in the distance.

They made good time through the early morning, but after breakfast they met increasingly difficult terrain. The slope was steeper, now, and the ground wildly uneven. Concealed holes and loose rocks made the footing difficult, and more than once a stretcher bearer's stumble nearly dumped the High Bishop on the ground.

Karsh Adon loomed ever larger before them, always seeming to be just past the next rise or around the next hill. But this was an illusion of scale. The Barrier Ridge towered over the landscape, reducing everything else to comparative insignificance. At Father Marcus' insistence, they pressed on without stopping for a noon meal. But it took the company three more hours of marching to reach the massive cliffs.

They stopped inside a cluster of rocks just a few cubits from the ridge. Some of the boulders were as tall as A'stoc, but they seemed mere pebbles beside Karsh Adon. Chentelle tilted her head back until it seemed she was looking straight into the sky. Still, she could not see the top of the cliffs.

Dacius gave them scarcely a minute to rest before setting them to work again. "All right, we need wood for the platform, and this land isn't exactly rich in timber. Everyone split up and search, but stay within earshot of each other."

It took Chentelle several minutes of wandering to collect her first armload of deadwood. When she returned to the camp, she saw that several of her companions had had better luck. A pile of wood awaited her, containing several fine pieces, including a large section from a lightning-struck tree.

She immediately started sifting through the pile, arranging branches in an approximation of the disk she would try to shape. The lightning section was her center, and she laid the other boughs around it like pieces of a puzzle. When the rough outline was complete, she called upon the Lore of *rillandef*. She sang softly as she worked, using the music as a focus for her will. The wood melded together under her sure fingers. The first joinings she created were artless, crude welds of bark to bark useful only for maintaining the form. Once she had fit together a basic framework, she retraced each seam.

Now, the wood flowed like a living thing. Wherever her fingers touched, branches flowed into each other like tributaries to the same stream. Bark mingled and re-formed as a single whole. Fibers of cedar and pine twisted around each other, forming a new wood stronger than either of the first. New wood found its way into her hands, ferried by one or another of her friends, and she added it to the shape. Layer by layer, she thickened and reinforced the disk, building it into the shape of her song.

As the last piece melted into the whole, Chentelle let her music fade. It was smaller than the platform at Tel Adartak-Skysoar, but it would do. She felt a pleasant weariness and the warmth of exertion. But the latter disappeared almost immediately under the cold wind. She glanced around her. It was dark already! But how? Time sometimes drifted when she used the Gift, but building the disk couldn't have taken so long. Then she understood. They were at the foot of the ridge, covered by its long shadow. Deneob was not four hours past midday, but it was hidden behind the monumental cliff.

A'stoc reached down and lifted a chunk of wood that she had discarded as too brittle. He held the branch in an open palm and chanted an incantation. The wood floated slowly into the air and turned a stately pirouette.

"It's beautiful," she said. She so rarely saw him use magic that was not destructive.

He smiled broadly. "Yes, it is one of the more graceful spells. Of course, the platform will be somewhat heavier. Are you finished with it?"

"Almost," she said. "I just need some more branches to make the guardrail."

He flipped his wrist and the floating wood dropped to the ground. "Forget the rail; there isn't time. I need to integrate the wood. If the flow of magic is not perfectly modulated, the platform will tilt and sway during flight."

A'stoc set aside the Thunderwood Staff and dropped to his hands and knees by the platform. He crawled slowly over every part of the disk, whispering a spell to the wood. Then he crawled over it again, retracing his route exactly. This time, his right hand hovered just above the surface. Radiant magic flowed from his fingertips, seeping into the platform. Wherever it touched, the wood sparkled and then settled into a glossy sheen.

His spell complete, the wizard climbed to his feet. His knees trembled and the blood rushed from his face. He staggered sideways, unable to keep his balance.

"A'stoc!" Chentelle jumped to her feet and grabbed the wizard around the waist, trying to steady him. The instant they touched, his weakness and fatigue hit her like an electric shock. She understood immediately. Days of exertion, hiking through mountains, battling Ill-creatures, and the wizard had never slept, never rested. But always, he carried the Thunderwood, drew upon its power. Now, he had had to use his own strength, and he had precious little left.

She guided him to a clear area next to the High Bishop's stretcher and helped him to lie down. "You're exhausted. You have to rest."

"No," he rasped. "There is no time. Bring me the Thunderwood Staff."

"No!" Chentelle turned desperately to the High Bishop. "Father Marcus, please, he has to sleep."

The priest's eyes grew distant, and he seemed to stare through them. "It's so close, Chentelle. I can feel it. It—pulls at me. Only a few leagues more, just beyond the Barrier Ridge."

"Father Marcus!" Chentelle waved a hand in front of his eyes, and they came suddenly into focus. She pointed to the wizard. "Look at him. Now, look at the cliff. Do you really want him to try the ascent?"

"Eh?" Father Marcus looked momentarily confused. "Of course not, Chentelle. We have learned already that undue haste can be our enemy. Let him rest. We will continue when he is able."

"Thank you, Father." She turned back to A'stoc. "Did you hear that?"

But the wizard was already asleep.

Chentelle turned back to the platform. There was not enough wood left to make a guardrail, and she didn't want to upset the balance. But they should at least have something to hang on to. She grabbed a few of the remaining branches and molded them into curved handles. She couldn't blend them with the wood of the platform—A'stoc's spell would not permit it—but she could push the ends *through* the disk. The fibers penetrated without joining and stuck fast when she released the touch of her *rillandef*.

Father Marcus called to her when she was finished. "Beautiful work, Chentelle, as we have all come to expect. Tell me, do we have enough wood left to fashion a pair of crutches?"

She started to protest, but the ache in his eyes stopped her. He needed at least the option of moving about on his own. "I'll see what I can do."

There were a few good branches left, and an assortment of scraps. She measured these against the priest's body and decided that they would suffice. The crutches she made were crude and indelicate, but Father Marcus thanked her exorbitantly when she handed them to him.

The night grew quickly colder and darker, punctuated occasionally by strange growls and high-pitched calls. A'stoc slept through it all, but tension sat heavily on the rest of them. The platform sat tantalizingly in their midst, already laden with the company's packs and supplies. They understood the need to wait, but they felt the need to leave.

Chentelle shivered. "Can we build a fire? Anything that can sense magic already knows where we are."

Dacius shook his head. The blank mask of his helm seemed suddenly strange and menacing.

"Not all Ill-creatures have that sense," Thildemar explained. "We don't want to give them another means of detecting us."

Chentelle nodded. She had known what the answer would be before she asked. She just wanted to *do* something. This silent waiting was terrible.

Suddenly, Dacius' head snapped toward the south. He froze, searching the darkness. "WAKE THE WIZARD."

"What is it?" Chentelle asked. Her eyes followed the path of his attention, but the night revealed nothing to her elven eyes.

"NOW."

She shook the wizard gently. "A'stoc, wake up."

His eyes fluttered briefly, but they did not open.

Then she saw it. A faint blue nimbus was barely visible around the human's armor. "Wake up!" She grabbed A'stoc's shoulders and shook him firmly. "Illcreatures!"

His eyes snapped open. "What is it? Where?"

Dacius pointed. "TENEBRITES. I COUNT AT LEAST TWO SCORE, TRAVELING UNDER THE SHADOW OF THE CLIFF."

"Are there demonspawn among them?" the wizard asked.

"I SEE NONE. WHY?"

"With demonspawn I would be forced to spend my strength in battle," A'stoc said. "Without them, we can escape on the platform."

They scrambled to the disk, squeezing together near its center. A'stoc raised the Thunderwood Staff and set it gently against the wood. The end of the Staff merged with the disk, and a gentle green glow poured from the wood. The wizard started to chant.

Nothing happened.

A'stoc chanted louder. Green flames roared around the disk. The platform bucked and started to rise. The wood trembled slightly under their feet, then shook violently. The wizard cut off his spell and yanked the Thunderwood free from the disk.

The platform dropped, plummeting two or three cubits and slamming against the ground. The companions staggered wildly, struggling to stay upright.

"WHAT HAPPENED?"

"It was too much power," A'stoc said. "The binding spell could not contain it. I will have to begin again."

"THERE'S NO TIME."

Chentelle looked to the south. A wave of chitinous black scurried toward them on segmented legs.

Dacius jumped off the platform. His armor glowed vibrantly, and the twin suns of House Gemine were ablaze on his shield. "GERRUTH, DRUP, USE YOUR BOWS. EVERYONE ELSE FORM A SKIRMISH LINE. A'STOC, GET THIS THING AIRBORNE."

The human lord centered himself between the Barrier Ridge and a large boulder. Thildemar stood at his left, and Leth held his right. "SULMAR, BE ON GUARD FOR A FLANKING ACTION THROUGH THE ROCKS."

Chentelle nodded, and her liegeman hopped down from the platform, adding his sword to the defense.

"FIRE!"

Two shafts flew through the air, then two more, then two more. The archers were a blur of motion: draw, fit, pull, sight, release—draw, fit, pull, sight, release. A score of arrows shot through the air in less than a minute, sparking more than a dozen explosions of blue flame.

The Tenebrites charged forward, their lines fragmented but undeterred. One of the shadow knights reared up on four legs, a bloodred ring glowing in one hand. The Ill-creature's arm shot forward, and the crimson circle flew through the air with an eerie whine. It sailed past Drup's shoulder and blasted a deep hole in the side of the cliff.

Several more Tenebrites paused, reared, and threw.

Dacius took three of the rings on his shield. The magic drained from the circles and they crumbled into gray dust. Power crackled around the Legionnaire's sword, leaving a glowing trail in the air.

Two more disks ripped gouges in the Barrier Ridge, barely missing the dodging archers, and another embedded itself in the boulder less than a hand's span from Thildemar's head. The last was headed directly toward A'stoc's chest before Sulmar's blade deflected it into the ground.

The wizard never even noticed the danger. His eyes were closed in concentration as he slowly channeled Earthpower into the platform.

Then the lines crashed together.

Dacius jumped forward, swinging his sword in a vicious cut toward a Tenebrite's chest. The shadow knight parried, and power exploded around the clashing steel. The Ill-creature's sword shattered, filling the air with glowing red shrapnel. Dacius' blade dulled to its original glow, but the force of his cut carried it halfway through the Tenebrite's abdomen. The Tenebrite flashed into ash.

The Legionnaire pivoted and directed his return stroke at the attacker to his right. Again, the Tenebrite parried, but this time its sword held. The red blade pulsed greedily, sucking power from the vorpal steel.

Leth darted forward, taking advantage of the Ill-creature's distraction. He severed two of the beast's legs with a sweeping slash, then impaled the Ill-creature as it fell.

Thildemar blocked the charge of a third shadow knight, vorpal sword in one hand, wooden battle stave in the other. He feinted with the sword, then jumped back, dodging the counterstroke. The battle stave lashed out, striking the trailing edge of the Ill-creature's blade and driving it out of position. Thildemar lunged into the opening, dispatching the shadow knight with a long thrust.

But new Tenebrites surged forward to replace the fallen. By sheer mass, they began to drive the Legionnaires backward.

Gerruth and Drup tossed their bows onto the platform and drew their swords.

The rear rank of Tenebrites divided and broke for the flanks. Three of them circled around the left, weaving through the cluster of boulders. The other four scurried up the face of the cliff, arcing above the line of defenders and dropping down again behind the platform.

Drup and Gerruth raced back to meet the new threat. They managed to catch one Tenebrite as it was still in the air, skewering it with a double attack.

But the other Ill-creatures had time to set themselves. Two of them engaged the Legionnaires, while the third broke off to attack the platform.

Chentelle sang out with her Gift, projecting a pure note of peace and harmony. Neither the shadow knights nor the Legionnaires were able to attack while her note held.

The nearest Tenebrite raised its rear limbs. The legs flashed together, creating an earsplitting whine that shattered the peace of her song.

Drup dived to his right and rolled smoothly into a crouch. In the same motion, his vorpal blade sliced through the Tenebrite's exposed thorax. The shadow knight burst into flame, its legs falling silent forever.

But Drup had exposed his flank. One of the other Tenebrites kicked out with a clawed foot, knocking him to the ground. It raised its sword, preparing to finish the young Legionnaire.

Chentelle sang out again.

The four combatants faced off in a precarious equilibrium. No one could attack while Chentelle used her Gift, and the Tenebrites couldn't disrupt her song without exposing themselves to the Legionnaires.

Then four new attackers came scuttling down the cliff. One of them stopped in the distance and countered her spell with his shriek. The others charged forward unimpeded.

The platform shot suddenly into the air. Chentelle stumbled, caught by surprise. She grabbed one of the handles, barely avoiding sliding off the edge. By the time she regained her footing, they were hovering thirty cubits above the ground.

The Tenebrites flicked their swords angrily through the air beneath the platform. One of them raised a glowing ring and hurled it at the platform. The projectile slammed into the wood in an explosion of sparks, but it did no damage. The Earthpower flowing through the wood was proof against it.

Sulmar jumped from one of the boulders, attacking one of the Ill-creatures from the rear. Five piles of ash smoldered in the rocks behind him, and he quickly added a sixth.

The other two spread out, trying to flank him. Then the last Tenebrite joined them, no longer needing to counter Chentelle's song.

Sulmar dodged and weaved through his attackers, keeping them off balance with lightning counters and uncanny reflexes. But the open ground worked against him. Without the shelter of the rocks, he was unable to control the Tenebrites' positions. They harassed his flanks, threatening to surround him, and he was forced farther and farther away from the Legionnaires.

Everywhere, the story was the same. The defenders were being slowly cut off from their fellows. The Legionnaires fought valiantly, but every clash of steel leeched power from their weapons. Only Dacius' sword still blazed at full strength, replenished from the magic absorbed by his shield. Slowly, inexorably, the tide of the battle was turning.

"GO. TAKE THE HIGH BISHOP TO SAFETY. SAVE THE QUEST. WE WILL HOLD THEM AS LONG AS WE ARE ABLE."

"No!" Chentelle turned to the wizard. "A'stoc, don't you dare."

She had to do something, but what? Her eyes roamed around the platform and came to rest on Drup's bow. But what good was it? Even if she could draw it, she didn't have any arrows. "A'stoc, can you move us laterally?"

The wizard nodded without breaking his chant.

"Good, move off ten cubits north and then take us back down to the ground."

The platform drifted slowly sideways, then dropped rapidly.

They hit the ground near Drup. The Legionnaire was locked in a duel with a shadow knight, and his vorpal blade was nearly extinguished. His flicked toward the platform, the Tenebrite stood between them.

Chentelle waved frantically and started to sing.

The Tenebrite reacted quickly, backing away to counter her spell. But that gave Drup the opening he needed.

The Legionnaire dived for the safety of the platform.

"Go," Chentelle shouted.

The platform soared twenty cubits into the air.

Chentelle helped Drup to his feet and thrust the bow into his hands. "Hurry."

The Legionnaire needed no prodding. He grabbed for his quiver and counted seven shafts remaining. He nocked one, and chose his target carefully.

A shadow knight burst into flame seconds before it could launch an attack at Gerruth's rear. Two more died as they circled around Thildemar's flank. One of Sulmar's attackers vanished, as did three members of the pack that had surrounded Dacius and Leth.

"RALLY TO THE PLATFORM! FOR LEGION! FOR HONOR! FOR CREATION!"

Dacius drove into the ring of attackers, hacking furiously with his sword. He opened a wedge through the Tenebrites' lines and charged through it, Leth following close on his heels. They battled their way to Thildemar's side, then joined up with Gerruth as well. They formed a new line, a defensive arc anchored against the Barrier Ridge.

Sulmar had managed to dispatch his remaining attackers. He was no longer being threatened, but he was caught on the far side of the field, isolated from the other defenders.

A'stoc guided the platform over to the Legionnaires' position and brought it low to the ground.

"GO!"

Gerruth and Thildemar broke formation simultaneously, diving for the platform.

Dacius jumped to his left, driving his sword into Thildemar's foe as it lunged after the elf. The human's own opponent scored a clean cut across his ribs, but A'kalendane's armor turned the blow easily.

Leth covered his brother's retreat in similar fashion, though he neither dispatched the Tenebrite nor received a wound in return.

But now the two Legionnaires were alone against over a dozen attackers, and they had no hope of holding the line.

"GO!"

Leth jumped for the platform.

Again, Dacius slid to his side, blocking the blows of the elf's attackers. Again, he left himself open to attack from his own foe.

But the Tenebrite shifted its attack as well. Instead of capitalizing on Dacius' exposed flank, it lunged forward, driving its blade into Leth's back. The sword pierced the elf completely, erupting through the front of his chest.

The Legionnaire's body dangled in the air for a moment, suspended from the glowing metal. Then it fell to the ground.

"Noooo!" Gerruth jumped from the disk. His sword flashed in a wide arc, decapitating the Tenebrite. He landed in a crouch and charged toward the mass of Tenebrites.

The shadow knights retreated, luring him farther away from the platform.

Dacius lashed out with a foot, tripping Gerruth. As the Legionnaire fell, Dacius dropped to a crouch and drove his shield into the base of the elf's neck. Then, he stooped and picked up the unconscious Legionnaire. A vicious cut slammed into the human's helmet driving him to his knees, but he regained his feet quickly. Shielding Gerruth's body with his own he ran for the platform.

A shadow knight moved to cut them off, and Chentelle sang out again. Her Gift was quickly nullified, but the slight delay was enough for Dacius to reach the platform.

"GO!"

The platform shot into the air.

"Wait!" Chentelle screamed.

The disk stopped, hovering ten cubits above the ground.

Sulmar raced toward them. Two Tenebrites moved to intercept him. The Tengarian swerved around the first and ran straight toward the second. He rolled under the shadow knight's thrust and came up behind it, severing one of its legs in the process.

The Ill-creature staggered, and Sulmar jumped. He planted one foot on the broad thorax and the other on the armored back. Using the Tenebrite as a platform, he launched himself into the air. His left hand caught the edge of the disk, and he hung from the rim.

Dacius and Thildemar grabbed his wrist and pulled him quickly on board. "Go!" Chentelle shouted.

The platform shot upward, climbing toward the unexplored heights above Karsh Adon.

❧ 21 ❧

FALLEN STAR

The platform climbed slowly up the side of Karsh Adon—four hundred, five hundred, a thousand cubits into the air, and the top was nowhere in sight. The pale flickering of A'stoc's spell illuminated the sheer wall of the Barrier Ridge; all else was darkness.

Chentelle was strangely disoriented. Her ears ached, and the frigid air trickled through her cloak. They floated above mountains, but she felt as if they were diving deep into an icy sea. Was it water or wind that made her shiver? The throb of her own heart beat painfully in her skull. Finally, the pressure vanished, and welcome relief flooded through her. The world snapped back into focus.

A'stoc remained frozen in concentration, eyes closed, rhythmic spell flowing slowly through tense lips. The Earthpower shimmered in time to his chant, carrying them steadily upward in a nimbus of flame.

Gerruth moaned softly, and his eyes flickered open. He stared blankly for a moment, then lunged for the side of the disk.

"No!" Father Marcus grabbed the Legionnaire and pulled him into a firm embrace. They tumbled together to the floor of the platform, less than a cubit from the rim. "Don't give in to it. Remember the love. The pain will pass."

Gerruth screamed, drowning out Father Marcus' soft words. Tears crystallized on his face, and he struggled to escape from the priest's clinch. "Let me go! I have to save him! I have to—"

"GERRUTH." Dacius' voice cut through the tumult. "REMEMBER YOUR DUTY. YOUR BROTHER IS DEAD. DO NOT LET HIS SACRIFICE BE IN VAIN."

The Legionnaire froze. Color rose in his face, and his hands clenched into trembling fists, but his eyes slid into focus. He sat up slowly, disengaging himself from Father Marcus' loosened grip. "Thank you, Lord Gemine. I will carry out my duty."

"THAT'S ALL I ASK. LETH WAS AN EXCELLENT LEGIONNAIRE. WHEN THE TIME COMES, WE WILL MOURN HIM TOGETHER."

Gerruth nodded and turned away. He stood facing the cliff, his eyes turned slightly upward and his right hand twitched on the hilt of his sword.

The gray face of Karsh Adon floated silently by. Cubit after cubit of blank stone disappeared into the darkness below, broken only rarely by a shallow cave or a craggy ledge. The expanse seemed endless.

Then one fact became clear. Their ascent was slowing.

Chentelle's eyes snapped toward A'stoc. Sweat beaded on the wizard's brow, and the muscles along his jaw twitched with tension. The Thunderwood Staff trembled slightly in his hands, and an answering tremor shook the platform.

"CAN YOU MAKE IT, A'STOC? WE PASSED A LEDGE NOT LONG AGO THAT SHOULD HOLD US WHILE YOU RECOVER STRENGTH."

The platform kept rising.

A'stoc's spell grated from between clenched teeth, but his voice never faltered. Their pace slowed. The cubits crawled by, each one surrendering its height more grudgingly than the last. But surrender they did, and soon the summit came into view.

Suddenly, wind whipped against Chentelle's face. The platform lurched sideways and dropped away from her feet. Her stomach twisted wildly, and she scrambled for a handhold. As her hand closed around the wood, the disk jerked to a halt. She tumbled to the floor, slamming her head against the wood. Pain blurred her vision, but her right hand kept a firm grip on the handle.

Something brushed against her other arm, and she grabbed it reflexively. Her hand closed around leatherbark, and a sudden weight tore at her grip.

It was Gerruth! The Legionnaire dangled over the edge of the platform. A loose pack slid off of the disk, barely missing the elf's head. His hand closed around her forearm and squeezed tightly.

New strain burned in her shoulders, and the fingers of her hand started to slide across the wooden handhold.

"Mistress!" Sulmar's hand locked around her right wrist. His other hand kept an iron grip on his own handhold.

Then, the pressure of Gerruth's weight disappeared. Father Marcus had both arms wrapped around the Legionnaire's chest. Dacius anchored the priest's legs while he pulled the elf back onto the platform.

"Wizard A'stoc," the High Bishop said once Gerruth was secure on the disk, "please lower us to the ledge. We have come too far to risk disaster now."

The platform didn't move.

"Wait." Chentelle understood. Determination screamed in the wizard's stance, fueled by a desperate fatalism. He had set this task before him as a test, a trial to see if he was ready for the challenge to come. To turn back was tantamount to surrender. "It's all right, A'stoc. Keep going. We trust you."

The platform began to rise again. It moved slowly, but without any hint of trembling. This time, there was no sudden lurch when they left the lee of the cliff. The platform held steady in the wind and continued to float upward. Finally, the top of the ridge slid into view, revealing a wide cleft covered in ice and snow.

"GRAB YOUR PACKS. PREPARE TO JUMP."

The platform halted its rise and drifted toward the cliff. It bumped against the stone, perhaps two cubits from the top.

"GO!"

One by one, the Legionnaires sprang onto the summit. Father Marcus followed, levering himself into their waiting arms with his crutches. Then Dacius nodded to Chentelle and Sulmar. The Tengarian vaulted easily onto the ridge and turned back to lift her.

"No." She turned to Dacius. "You go on. I'll ride with A'stoc."

The human stared at her, or at least she thought he did. The blank mask of his helm was unnerving. It seemed to shield him even from her Gift. Without another word, he turned sharply and pulled himself onto the ledge.

The platform moved away from the stone, quivering slightly. A'stoc's eyes were open, now, but they drifted without focus. His face was pale, and his cheeks hung slack as he chanted his spell. The trembling in his hands was growing steadily.

Chentelle grabbed his forearm with both hands. Emotion raged through her Gift: fear, anger, love, recrimination, but most of all weariness. "Just a little farther, A'stoc, and the platform is so much lighter. You can do it."

Resolution flowed through the wizard. The disk steadied and rose the last few cubits. It glided laterally until they were securely above solid ground, then settled heavily into the icy snow. A'stoc pulled the Staff free of the wood and reined in the Earthpower. The instant the flames vanished, he collapsed in a heap.

Chentelle held on to his shoulders, barely managing to keep his head from hitting the wood. The wizard was unconscious, but his breathing was steady and regular. With Sulmar's help, she managed to drag him off the platform and settle him in the shelter of a large boulder.

Dacius motioned to his men. Together, they carried the platform to a nearby drift. "COVER IT WITH SNOW. WE DON'T WANT THE ILL-CREATURES TO FIND IT. WE'LL NEED IT FOR THE RETURN TRIP."

The Legionnaires used their blades to smooth snow over the disk. Then Thildemar used a blanket to mask any tracks leading to and from the drift.

"EVERYONE MARK THIS SPOT. YOU NEED TO BE ABLE TO FIND THE PLATFORM ON YOUR OWN, IN CASE WE BECOME SEPA-RATED."

"An excellent suggestion," Father Marcus said. "Now, we should find shelter as soon as possible. We need rest, and the cold will kill us if we stay in the open. Put A'stoc on the stretcher. I can walk with the crutches."

They worked their way out of the cleft and emerged onto a wide plateau. An unblemished blanket of snow stretched for leagues around them. Mountains rose in the distance, sheathed entirely in ice. The cold wind blasted against them, stinging hands and faces with its fury.

Father Marcus pressed forward without hesitation, hobbling unsteadily on the frozen turf. He kept their course set firmly to the northwest, following his inner sense of the Fallen Star.

They marched for an hour or more, driving through the snow until the numbness of cold and the numbness of exhaustion were indistinguishable. They were less than halfway to the first mountains, and no other shelter was visible.

Sulmar pressed his face close to Chentelle's. "Mistress, we should stop here."

"We can't," she said. "We need shelter."

"Yes, mistress, but we will not find it. We will have to make our own." His voice held both certainty and urgency.

"Father Marcus!" she yelled. "Wait!"

The High Bishop paused and turned to face her.

"Sulmar says we should make camp here!"

"You will not make the mountains, but this snow is deep enough for shel-ter." The Tengarian drew his sword and began digging an angled tunnel into the frost. Then he paused, seeing incomprehension on the other's faces. "My people know the mountains. The snow will protect us from the cold and wind. Make each hole large enough for two people to share heat, but no larger. And do not dig too deeply; the weight will make it collapse."

The party hesitated, turning to Father Marcus.

The priest hesitated in turn, turning back to look at the mountains. "We are so close. I can feel it."

"HOW CLOSE?" Dacius asked.

"Tomorrow," the priest said, turning back to the company. "We will reach it tomorrow. For tonight, do as Sulmar says. I trust his knowledge no less than his sword."

They carved four warrens into the snow, with Sulmar supervising each construction. By the time they finished, fresh snow had begun to fall. Father Marcus had them place A'stoc with him, so that he could help the wizard regain his strength. The Legionnaires paired off among themselves, and Chentelle shared the last den with her liegeman.

"The snow is good," Sulmar said, "so long as it does not fall too heavily. It will hide our tracks and keep the night from becoming too cold."

Chentelle shivered under the layers of blanket and pressed herself against Sulmar's warmth. If this night wasn't already too cold, she didn't want to know what was. Her hands and feet stung as if she had been running through brambles, but at least sensation was returning. She started to compliment Sulmar on his ingenuity, but yawned deeply instead. Sleep came for her suddenly, carrying dreams of endless glaciers.

She snapped alert at the pressure of a hand across her mouth. It was Sulmar. The Tengarian pointed to his bared blade. The vorpal metal shone with soft blue light. Ill-creatures! They watched the faint glow grow slowly brighter, then fade into cold steel again. They hadn't been discovered.

Chentelle steadied herself and tried to relax, but the rest that had come so quickly before was now elusive. She lay awake for a long while, searching the darkness for any hint of vorpal light.

⮑

Father Marcus woke them at first-light. Snow was still falling, or falling again, though it was not as heavy as it had been the night before. Heavy clouds covered the plateau, shrouding the landscape in shades of gray. Despite the cold and the gloom, a hopeful mood pervaded the company. Father Marcus rested firmly on his crutches, showing no signs of discomfort. A'stoc stood beside him, apparently fully recovered from his exhaustion. Even Gerruth's anger and pain had been tempered by the night's rest.

"This is the day," Father Marcus said. "Please, join hands and help me welcome this morning. We have come so far, and today our quest reaches its conclusion."

They formed a circle, and the High Bishop guided them through the First Meditation.

> *"In peace, there is harmony.*
> *In harmony, there is unity.*
> *In unity, there is healing.*
> *In healing, there is peace."*

The chant rolled across the icy plateau, driving back the gray clouds. The mists did not vanish entirely, but Ellistar's light seemed to shine a little brighter.

"Thank you," Marcus said. "Now, let us be off. With the Creator's blessing we can complete our mission before the Ill-creatures find us."

"It does not matter," A'stoc said. "The Ill-creatures already know where the Fallen Star lies."

"What? Are you certain?" Marcus' eyes bore into the wizard.

"Of course. Do not delude yourself. How else has it been possible for them to hound our path so effectively? The attack at Marble Falls, the mudworm, the assault before the Barrier Ridge—at each stage they were able to anticipate our destination. Obviously, they have found the Fallen Star, or at least discerned its general location."

"Why didn't you say something before?" the priest asked.

"It would have made no difference," A'stoc said. "Our path would have been the same. This confrontation has long been inevitable."

The High Bishop's calm certainty suddenly vanished, replaced by grim determination. He grabbed his pack and slung it over a shoulder. The motion disrupted his balance, and he teetered unsteadily on his crutches. He righted himself, and paused for a moment, struggling visibly to regain his composure. Finally, he turned and limped away into the falling snow. "It is time to leave."

A'stoc grabbed Chentelle as she turned to follow the company. He pressed something into her hand—the *mandril* wand. "Keep this with you. I implanted a levitation spell when I bound the wood of the platform. If I die, use your Gift to activate the *mandril*. It will trigger the spell. The platform will levitate for two minutes before it descends. Use that time to push it clear of the cliff."

"A'stoc, I—"

"Don't argue! Listen carefully. Tie yourselves securely to the disk. Lowering is easier than lifting, but it still requires power. The platform will drop very quickly until it is three hundred cubits from the ground. Then it will slow. You may land hard, but you will survive." He closed her fingers around the wand and squeezed tightly. "Do this, Chentelle. It may be your only hope to see Lone Valley again."

He spun away before she could answer, and fell into the line of march. Chentelle hesitated, then realized that she had no choice. She tucked the *mandril* into her cloak and hurried after him.

Father Marcus refused all entreaties to moderate his pace. He drove relentlessly through the deep snow, his wounded leg dragging uselessly behind. After several hours, they reached the foothills of the frozen mountains. The snow had stopped falling. But the clouds remained, and the rocky ground was treacherously slick.

Father Marcus attacked the slope. He slipped almost immediately and crashed to the snow. Without hesitating, he tossed away his crutches and started to crawl. He would neither stop nor allow himself to be carried. "I will make the climb," he said plainly, and the passion in his voice could not be denied. All the others could do was collect his discarded crutches and follow.

The High Bishop scrambled up the mountainside, driving his hands through ice and snow and pulling himself at last over the crest of the summit. He collapsed for a moment, letting his face rest in the cold powder. Then he sat up. A narrow circle of level ground formed the apex of the hill, and a hill it was compared to what lay before them. A grim mountain sat directly ahead, its steep granite slopes vanishing into the clouds.

A narrow pass curved southward, driving between the mountain ahead and its neighbor. The priest oriented on the opening and started crawling forward.

"Father Marcus, wait." Chentelle ran up and put a hand on the priest's shoulder. Her arm tingled under the desperate need that drove him. "Please, I know the quest is urgent, but I'm exhausted. Can't we rest for a minute? We may need our strength once we find the Fallen Star."

The priest's eyes stared blankly through her for a second, then pulled into focus. "Of course, Chentelle. Forgive me. The proximity of the Star calls to me. Its pull grows stronger the nearer we get. But you are correct; I must maintain control. We shall rest here."

The company ate a hurried meal of cold rations. As they finished, the cover of the clouds parted momentarily, allowing the red light of Deneob to shine through clearly. The Winter Sun was already well past zenith.

"Gather your things," Father Marcus said. "We must be on our way."

"HIGH BISHOP." Dacius nodded to Drup and Thildemar, who unlimbered the stretcher. "WE WILL MAKE BETTER TIME IF YOU ALLOW US TO CARRY YOU."

A protest rose behind the priest's eyes, but he didn't give it voice. Instead, he hobbled over and sat down on the litter. He pointed toward the downward slope. "Follow the southern pass until we clear the mountain."

The descent went quickly. The floor of the pass was wide and relatively smooth. Dacius led the way, and the Legionnaires followed, dragging Father Marcus' stretcher across the ice like a travois. They cut between the towering mountains and emerged on the verge of a steep valley.

The cut was nearly a league across and bounded by peaks a thousand cubits high. A frozen river ran through its center, and sparse pines dotted the snow near the water. On the far side, a blackened crater the size of a small village marred the pristine landscape. Fresh snow struggled vainly to hide the dark scar, and bright light flashed like a beacon from its center.

The company stood in silence. They were too far away to make out details, and the object itself was obscured by snow and a recent landslide. But one thing was clear. The Fallen Star was immense.

They began the climb down the valley wall. The slope here was far more treacherous than the gentle pass. They abandoned the stretcher, and Father Marcus allowed himself to be carried over Dacius' shoulder. Thildemar led the way, picking out a careful path and testing each rock and ledge to make sure they were stable. The valley was less than five hundred cubits high, but it took most of an hour for them to reach the bottom.

Father Marcus accepted his crutches from Gerruth and stood gratefully erect on the level ground. But his eyes tracked the position of the suns nervously. His conclusion was obvious in his manner: the descent had taken too long. It would be night before they reached the Fallen Star.

The High Bishop headed across the valley floor, covering ground steadily in long, slow swings. The company followed, stretching their strides over the flat terrain. They made excellent progress, but even so Deneob was hardly a sliver above the mountains when they reached the river.

The stream was completely frozen, as solid as rock beneath their feet but far more slippery. Chentelle smiled with delight and kicked herself onto the ice. Her leatherbark soles slid easily across the surface, then caught slightly as her momentum ebbed. She pushed off at an angle and continued across. It was just like skating on the winter ponds back home.

The others seemed far less comfortable. Apparently water seldom froze in the southern forests. Still, they managed the crossing well enough, and soon they were gathered on the far side. They pressed through the final patch of trees and stared over the lip of the crater.

The Fallen Star was half-buried by rock and snow, but what was visible gleamed coldly in the twilight. It was solid metal, shaped into strange curves and angles that couldn't be natural; they jarred the eye harshly. A thousand cubits of broken ground lay between them and the Star, but it was so large that it seemed close enough to touch.

"BEWARE!" Dacius' sword slid from its sheath. The metal blade glowed softly in the fading light, as did the armor and shield of A'kalendane.

A dark shape detached itself from the shadows below the Fallen Star. It walked out onto the snow and halted, black wings twitching outward into a familiar silhouette. Throm.

"SPREAD OUT. FATHER MARCUS, STAY BEHIND US. A'STOC, ARE YOU READY?"

"I am." A'stoc walked forward, planting the Staff firmly in the snow with each step. "Keep your men behind me, Lord Gemine. This trial is mine."

They made their way across the crater, the wizard in the lead and the others following cautiously behind. The Ill-creature waited motionlessly as they approached.

When A'stoc was thirty cubits away, he lifted the Staff and called forth the Earthpower. Green flame blazed along the length of the wood.

SO, YOU HAVE BROUGHT YOUR TRINKETS DIRECTLY TO ME. I AM GRATEFUL. I SHALL GRANT YOU A MERCIFUL DEATH IF YOU SURRENDER THEM NOW.

"Your jests are tiresome," A'stoc said. "As is your existence. The time has come to end them both."

SUCH BRAVADO! AND YET YOU HESITATE. CAN IT BE THAT YOU REMEMBER OUR LAST BATTLE? THERE IS NO POOL OF EARTHPOWER TO SAVE YOU NOW, LITTLE APPRENTICE. I WILL PULL THE THUNDERWOOD FROM YOUR IMPOTENT FINGERS AND USE IT TO CRACK OPEN THIS METAL EGG. THEN THE DARK ONE HIMSELF WILL TREMBLE BEFORE ME. The Ill-creature took a lumbering step forward, and lightning crackled between his talons. COME FORWARD, WIZARDLING, AND I WILL SHOW YOU THE MEANING OF DEATH.

A'stoc stepped forward, Thunderwood Staff raised high above his head. As his foot came down, a glowing iron rod burst upward from beneath the snow. It struck the wizard full in the chest, slamming him backward in an explosion of power. A'stoc flew a dozen cubits through the air and landed limply in the snow. The Staff slipped from his hand and fell near his side.

"A'stoc!" Chentelle bolted to the wizard's side. Her Gift reached out to him instinctively, searching for life but afraid of what she might find. Praise the Creator! He was alive. The Earthpower had shielded him from much of the blow. He had a mild concussion, but he was unhurt otherwise.

Dacius launched himself forward. His vorpal blade sliced into the demonspawn before it could climb free of its hiding hole. The Ill-creature's head tumbled from its neck and dropped to the snow in a shower of ash.

Four more shapes climbed from ambush sites around the company—Tenebrites, not demonspawn. Their insect legs danced lightly across the surface of the snow.

Suddenly, Father Marcus screamed and fell to the ground. He clutched his skull with both hands and writhed with uncontrollable convulsions.

HA HA HA HA HA. SUCH EVIL YOU HOLD, PRIEST OF WEAKNESS. HOW SIMPLE TO SET IT FREE, TO LET IT RUN LOOSE IN YOUR FEEBLE SOUL. PERHAPS YOU WILL THANK ME LATER, IF I LET YOU LIVE.

Dacius charged the demon, his armor gleaming like the sun. "GUARD THE HIGH BISHOP. THROM IS MINE."

Lightning flashed from Throm's claws, crackling across the snow to obliterate the Legionnaire. But Dacius caught the blast on his shield. The mystic metal flashed blindingly as power transferred to his sword. A trail of blue flame arced from the blade as it cleaved through the Ill-creature's outstretched wrist.

AAAAHHHHH! Throm staggered backward, staring at the burning stump of its arm. Its wings flailed wildly, and a massively taloned foot shot out at the human lord. Dacius again took the blow on his shield, but the impact drove him a dozen steps backward. **YOU WILL SUFFER FOR THAT, LITTLE MORTAL. I WILL RIP YOUR SOUL TO SHREDS AND FEED IT TO THE VIKHORS.**

Steel clanged against steel just beyond Chentelle's head. She crouched over A'stoc's body, trying to shield it with her own.

Sulmar turned aside the Tenebrite's thrust and shifted his weight into a lunging counter. But the snow slowed his movements and the shadow knight danced easily out of the way.

The Ill-creature circled and struck again, aiming not at Sulmar but at the fallen form of the wizard. Again, Sulmar was forced to parry the strike. Metal rang sharply and power leeched from Sulmar's blade into the Tenebrite's.

"Mistress, run!" The Tengarian reached down and grabbed A'stoc's collar. Parrying desperately, he dragged the wizard back toward the company. He managed the retreat, but it cost him dearly. By the time he deposited A'stoc's form next to Father Marcus's, his vorpal blade barely glowed at all.

But now the companions could shield each other. The Tenebrite attacking Sulmar was forced to yield ground as Thildemar thrust toward his exposed flank.

The defenders arrayed themselves in a tight perimeter, coordinating their tactics. They avoided direct confrontation whenever possible, using flank attacks and leg cuts to fend off the Tenebrites.

But the shadow knights had the advantage of maneuverability. They circled endlessly, skittering easily over the crust of snow that hampered Sulmar and the elves. When they attacked, the thrusts came unpredictably from any or all directions. They struck at A'stoc and Father Marcus whenever possible, forcing a parry that served only to strengthen the Ill-creatures.

IT IS OVER, LITTLE MORTALS. YOUR DEATHS ARE HERE. Throm's flesh was a crisscross of flaming blue cuts. Dark ash poured from its wounds like blood. But triumph echoed maliciously in its mental voice. Lightning flashed from the demon's remaining claw, striking not at Dacius, but at a large boulder near his feet. The stone shattered, blasting the Legionnaire with a thousand fragments.

Dacius' armor was scored and dented in a dozen places. It held up to the assault, but the shrapnel battered him mercilessly. He staggered backward, and his foot slipped on a patch of ice. He fell to his knees, and his shield dropped momentarily out of position.

Throm darted forward. The Ill-creatures claw crackled through the air, catching the human's head cleanly. A clap of thunder echoed through the valley, and Dacius' helmet tumbled through the air, split down the side with a jagged tear.

Dacius crumpled to the snow, his eyes staring blankly into the air and blood trailing from his ear.

HA HA HA HA HA. SURRENDER, GNATS. YOUR LEADERS HAVE FALLEN. THE BATTLE IS OVER.

"No!" Gerruth threw himself to the ground, rolling across the snow and sliding under the belly of a Tenebrite. His move caught the Ill-creature by surprise, and his vorpal blade thrust cleanly into its abdomen. The Tenebrite vanished in a flash of dust.

But Gerruth was exposed. Another shadow knight darted forward. A sharp claw drove through the Legionnaire's side, pinning him to the ground. A blood-red sword sliced downward in a vicious arc.

Thildemar jumped forward, deflecting the cut with a combat baton. His vorpal blade slashed in a lightning counter that neatly decapitated the Ill-creature.

A gaping hole opened in the Tenebrites' formation. Drup lunged forward, engaging one of the remaining Ill-creatures.

Sulmar attacked the other, thrusting into its exposed chest, and then slicing through the legs of Drup's foe on the backswing.

The young Legionnaire waited until the Ill-creature fell, and then drove his blade into the exposed side. The last of the Tenebrites dissolved into ash.

SO, THE GNATS HAVE STINGS. NO MATTER. NONE OF YOU HAS THE POWER TO HARM ME.

Agony ripped through Chentelle's mind. Her brain was on fire! She clapped her hands to her head. The pain was incredible. A whimper escaped from her throat, and she heard an answering cry from one of the Legionnaires.

Throm stalked slowly toward them, lightning crackling around his ebony skin. **GOOD RIDDANCE, FOOLS! YOU SHOULD NEVER HAVE CHALLENGED YOUR MASTERS. I WILL AAAAAHHHH!!!**

Steel erupted from the demon's heart. Blue flame shot outward, enveloping the Ill-creature even as he fell.

Dacius had recovered, and run the monster through from behind. Now the Legionnaire lurched forward, pulled off balance by the demon's weight. He landed heavily in the snow, vorpal sword still locked in the grip of his mystic gauntlet.

By the Creator! Chentelle shook her head, trying to clear the memory of pain. Was it really over? She glanced around the crater. A'stoc groaned softly as his awareness returned. Drup moved to Dacius' side, helping the lord to stand. Father Marcus still writhed on the ground, and Gerruth lay in a growing

pool of his own blood. The vorpal blades were dark. There were no more enemies, but had they won or lost?

A'stoc stumbled across the snow until he reached the Staff. His hands closed
around the Thunderwood, and his posture steadied immediately. His eyes remained
glazed and unfocused, but he walked back to the others with slow, firm strides.

Chentelle put a hand on Marcus' brow. The skin was hot and strangely dry.
She reached out with her Gift, trying to comfort him.

Her arm jerked backward, burning as if she had plunged it into a flame.
Nausea flooded through her, carried on a wave of ugliness beyond imagining.
She saw a world swallowed by metal and dark glass. Not a cubit of grass or
forest remained. Even the oceans were covered with islands of desecration. Nox-
ious fumes choked the air, killing everything that flew or breathed. People
moved aimlessly through strange cities of metal cliffs and black roads. There
was no music in their world, no love, no life.

Chentelle fought down the urge to vomit. It was horrible! How could the
Creator allow such a world? But she knew the answer. This was the knowledge
of the Fallen Star, knowledge from beyond the Creation. The world she glimpsed
had never known the Creator's touch.

And now that could happen to Infinitera! Fractured images coalesced in
her mind: Father Marcus sitting on a mighty throne, an army of twisted mech-
anisms swarming through the Realm like steel insects, mountains being shaped
like clay by ribbons of cold light. It was a vision of the future. Father Marcus
spoke, and his voice echoed around the world like that of the Creator Himself.
The Heresiarchs of the goblins knelt in reverence, surrendering to the power of
the High Bishop's faith. Gnomes and dwarves came together in unity, and giants
and trolls were restored to the world. The Dark One was bound in chains of
light and banished forever beyond the Abyss.

The vision continued. Death became unnecessary. The Creation was made
whole again, and the people praised Marcus in joyful song. He let no being
suffer or know need. Hunger, pain, illness, strife, all vanished in the new Creation. A vast city rose from the plain, providing its inhabitants with every need
and luxury. It was a place of perfect peace and perfect safety. Anything wild or
dangerous was locked away behind impenetrable bands of force. The people
spent eons in rest and contemplation, surrendering their world piece by piece
to the cold metal walls.

Chentelle shuddered. She knew that she had felt only the tiniest part of
what ran through the High Bishop. Strangely, that thought brought her hope—
she had been shielded from deeper contact by Father Marcus himself. The priest
had rejected her touch, protecting her from the evil he suffered. That meant
that he wasn't lost entirely; he still struggled for control.

Chentelle called upon her Gift again, weaving a quiet song around the High
Bishop. She didn't try to force her magic into his mind; she couldn't fight the
raw power of the evil in his mind. Instead, she called to his body. Her enchantment opened the priest's senses to the music of Creation. Life sang to them
from the frozen peaks: fish swimming deep under the icy river, tall pines reso-
nating strength and resilience. Chentelle worked the music into Marcus' flesh,
filling him slowly with harmony and truth.

The priest's mind seethed with conflict, torn between hymns of glory and the quiet music of Creation. But his faith was strong. His spirit swelled in answer to Chentelle's song, answering it with love and joy and communion. The balance shifted, and the evil slowly surrendered its hold. Marcus' body twitched in one final spasm. Then his eyes fluttered open and his limbs relaxed.

Chentelle helped the priest to stand. "Are you all right?" The question was rhetorical; she knew his condition was desperately mixed.

"I think so. Thanks to you." Marcus squeezed her hand softly. "The Creator was generous when he sent you to us."

Chentelle shrugged off the compliment. "You're the one we need, now. Are you strong enough to heal? A'stoc's concussion isn't serious, but Gerruth and Dacius might be badly hurt."

Marcus took a slow, deep breath. "Where are they?"

Dacius had regained his feet. The human still clutched his vorpal sword in one hand, while the other held the ruined remains of his shield. Blood trickled from the ruin of his left ear, matting in the lighter red of his hair and beard. He dragged himself through the snow with stiff-legged steps, but his deep blue eyes were clear. He waved them away before they had taken two steps. "I'll keep! See to Gerruth first!"

The elf lay where he had fallen, conscious but deep in shock. The Tenebrite's claw had driven entirely through his body. Steam rose from the jagged tear. Thildemar had stanched the wound, but not before a large pool of bile and blood had stained the ice.

"Blessed Creator." Marcus dropped to his knees beside the Legionnaire. His eyes closed in concentration and he started to chant. The peace of sanctuary glowed into life around him.

But something was wrong. Marcus' chant faltered, and strain laced his voice. The shimmering aura flickered and died. "No! Creator, we follow your wisdom and walk on your path. Give me the strength for this."

Father Marcus began his chant again. Once more, the strain told in his voice, but this time he didn't falter. The rhythm of the meditation was perfect, the meter exact. It made no difference. The aura was even fainter this time, and it vanished more quickly.

The priest continued his meditation, but it was no use. There was no harmony in his soul. The evil in his mind was contained, but it was not conquered. He was cut off from the power of the Holy Order. After several minutes, he broke off his song. There were tears in his eyes as he met Gerruth's gaze. "I'm sorry."

"Don't be," the Legionnaire said softly. "Just don't let them win."

"I won't." Father Marcus pulled out the Sphere of Ohnn and discarded the rest of his pack into the snow. He turned to look at A'stoc. "You and I will make the final journey alone."

The wizard glanced over his shoulder. The gleaming metal of the Fallen Star lay less than fifty cubits away. "So far?"

"Do not be dense!" the High Bishop snapped. "The quest is not done. We must travel inside the Star to destroy it."

"Inside?" Chentelle asked. "You mean it's hollow?"

"Of course it's hollow!" Father Marcus spun to face her. His face twisted into a sneer, but the expression disappeared almost immediately. "I'm sorry, Chentelle. You did not deserve that. None of you deserve anything but praise.

Without you, the quest could never have come so far. But the rest of the journey is for A'stoc and me alone."

"I do not agree," Dacius said. The human swayed slightly on his feet, but his voice was firm. "Who knows what dangers lurk inside the metal. You should not go unprotected. Thildemar can stay to guard Gerruth. The rest of us should go with you."

"No!" The protest came from both Gerruth and Father Marcus.

"No one comes with us," the holy man insisted. "The danger that awaits is the danger of knowledge. No one must learn the secrets of the Fallen Star, not even you."

Chentelle looked back and forth between A'stoc and the priest. The humans stood in nearly identical postures. Iron determination straightened their spines, but their eyes were hollow. Cold certainty ran through her. They weren't coming back. "No! Father Marcus, this is wrong."

The priest's eyes bore into her. "Do you speak with your Gift?"

Should she lie? He might listen if she gave her words the weight of prophecy. "I speak from my heart. Remember your own words. Our hope lies in love, in harmony and cooperation, not solitude and desperation. We have to stay together. You were never meant to make this trip alone."

"Listen to Chentelle," Dacius said. "Her wisdom has never led us astray before."

Anger flashed behind the priest's eyes, but it quickly subsided. "Very well, but I must have your oath. Not one word will be spoken of what you see or learn, not to comrades, not to family, not even among yourselves. The knowledge must vanish forever. Swear it!"

One by one, Father Marcus bound them to the oath. He bypassed Gerruth initially, but the Legionnaire growled in protest.

"I will not be left behind! What, shall I honor Leth's memory by cooling myself in the snow while great deeds are done." Gerruth grabbed hold of Thildemar's arm and jerked himself to his feet. Fresh blood seeped from his wound, and he doubled over in pain. But not a sound escaped his clenched lips. Slowly, he straightened up, loosening his grip on Thildemar's arm. "I can walk."

Dacius stepped in front of the elf, blocking his way. "Are you trying to kill yourself? I've stopped you from doing so once already."

Gerruth met the human's eyes with a hard stare. The message was clear. Without healing, he wouldn't survive the night. He would not wait meekly for the end to come.

Dacius stepped out of the way. "Stay with him, Thildemar."

Father Marcus led Gerruth through the oath. Then he spoke it for himself. "So, we are ready. May the Creator guide us through this final test."

"Lord Gemine." Drup stepped forward, holding the helmet of A'kalendane outstretched in one hand. A flip of his wrist sent it spinning toward the Legionnaire.

Dacius caught it smoothly and examined the damage. The helm was split along one side nearly to the crown, and the entire surface was blackened. Smiling ruefully, he shrugged and placed the helmet over his head.

Arcs of blue radiance shot from the metal. The sparks coursed around Dacius' body covering every inch of A'kalendane's armor. Wherever they passed, rips mended and scars disappeared. In seconds, the armor gleamed like new.

Even the shield welded itself together, and the twins suns of House Gemine blazed proudly on its argent field.

"Amazing," Father Marcus said. "But we must hurry." That said, he turned and began to limp toward the Fallen Star.

"I have seen worse omens," A'stoc said blandly. Then he shrugged and followed after the High Bishop.

Marcus' eyes scanned the smooth surface intently. He took them close to the curved metal, then circled around until they reached the rock slide. He scrambled up the loose stones, dragging his injured leg behind him. When he reached the top, he pointed to a small oval protuberance. "Clear away the rubble on either side of that bulge."

Dacius and Sulmar set to work quickly, tossing stones to the side and scraping away ice and snow. Soon, bare metal showed for several cubits in both directions.

Marcus ran his fingers along the oval swelling. A hidden door snapped open. Behind it lay a glowing red knob. The priest pressed against it with his thumb, and a hexagonal crack appeared in the metal. Air hissed angrily as the hexagon sank away from them. Then the door snapped to the side, revealing a dark tunnel into the Star. Something hummed deep within the metal, and a walkway pressed toward them. It came to rest on the stones near Marcus, an invitation into the Abyss.

"What magic is this?" A'stoc muttered. "I sense no power here, no spells or talismans."

Chentelle reached out with her Gift. A'stoc was right. There was no flow of magic within the metal, but it went deeper than that. The Fallen Star radiated nothing at all. It was an emptiness, complete and absolute void. Not even the Desecration was so blank. The land there felt pain and retained the memory of life. The Fallen Star was an utter null. Her Gift slid off of it without making contact.

"Hold your questions," Father Marcus said, stepping onto the ramp. "The answers are dangerous."

The walkway took them to a small, dark chamber. Father Marcus touched a square tile on the far wall, and the door slid shut behind them. Immediately, light sprang from strips that ran across the top of the walls. It was white, like orb-light, but harsh and very bright.

Again, Chentelle sensed no magic.

Father Marcus touched another tile. A six-sided door hissed open and disappeared into the wall.

Dacius' hand snapped to his sword. The vorpal metal remained quiescent, but he drew the blade anyway. Cautiously, he stepped through the open portal.

As soon as his foot crossed the threshold, light strips burst into life, revealing a curved tunnel carved from a smooth, beige material. Twisted tubes draped the ceiling and ran along the walls. Some of the tubes were metal, others seemed to be glass.

Father Marcus pushed past the Legionnaire and hobbled down the corridor, using one wall for support. He led them deeper and deeper into the maze of tunnels that riddled the Fallen Star. He took each junction without pausing, as if he knew the path intimately.

Dacius and A'stoc followed just behind the High Bishop. Chentelle and

Sulmar were next, followed by Drup, Thildemar and Gerruth. The old elf supported most of Gerruth's weight. His soft voice drifted forward, counting doors
and passages and repeating their turnings over and over in a rhythmic chant.

Father Marcus turned down a short tunnel that ended in a huge six-sided
door. A flat oval of dark glass was mounted on one wall, surrounded by rows of
red and white knobs. Each knob was decorated by a strange rune. The priest
ran his fingers quickly over the knobs, pressing some and twisting others.

More runes appeared, glowing in illish green from the black glass. Father
Marcus twisted a knob and the runes slid quickly upward, replaced by new ones
from below. The priest scanned the writing for several minutes. Then he pressed
another knob and the door slid back into the wall.

The hexagonal chamber beyond was a junction for three tunnels. Large
doors still blocked the other two exits. Marcus' fingers moved again, and one
door across the left passage hissed open. Then the priest touched a knob and
the glass blinked back into darkness.

Marcus hopped through the first door, then froze. He turned slowly and
stared at Gerruth, worry plain in his eyes.

Thildemar had abandoned the pretense of assisting and now simply carried
the Legionnaire in his arms. Gerruth was barely conscious. His face was pale,
and his half-open eyes stared blankly at one wall. Only the quivering of his
bloodless lips revealed that he was still alive.

Father Marcus went back to the glass and called up the writing again. Then
he pressed a knob and the other door slid open. He banished the runes once
more and limped into the next passage, leading them down the right fork.

They made two more turnings and stopped before a door on the right side
of the corridor. A glowing red rune pulsed above the doorway, and a smaller
version of the same symbol decorated a tile beside the door. Marcus pressed the
tile and the portal slid open.

The room beyond was large and held several oddly shaped altars. Marcus
pointed to one and told Thildemar to lay Gerruth upon it. Amber lights above
the altar glowed into life, and a panel slid aside from the pedestal's base. Segmented metal tentacles shot from the opening, reaching up to surround the elf.
Then thin metal thorns sprang from the sides of the altar, lancing into both
sides of the Legionnaire's neck.

Dacius leaped forward. His vorpal sword clanged against one of the metal
arms and rebounded harmlessly.

"Wait!" Marcus shouted. "Leave it alone. It's trying to save his life." He
held another machine close to his injured leg, and weblike strands flowed from
it to wrap around his ankle.

Dacius stepped back. He turned to face the priest, but his blank metal helm
betrayed no expression.

The tentacles formed a bridge over Gerruth's head and snapped together
with a loud click. Then the surface of the altar slid forward, passing the elf's
body through the metal arch. When the injury was centered below the tentacles,
the altar stopped moving. Then the surface dropped away, falling open from the
center. Strands of pale white fiber shot from above and below, forming a retic-
ulate sheath that first penetrated and then sealed the elf's wound.

The altar snapped back into place, and the long thorns pulled out of Gerruth's neck. Deep punctures showed where the spikes had been, but no blood

flowed from the holes. The tentacles separated smoothly and retracted back into their home. The panel door slid shut, and the golden lights faded to darkness.

The Legionnaire's eyes opened, showing massively dilated pupils. He glanced around the room without comprehension. Then he sat up slowly.

"GERRUTH, ARE YOU ALL RIGHT?"

"Sure. I'm fine." His voice was thin and slightly slurred. He raised a hand and ran it across his belly. The long fingers passed from torn leatherbark to flesh to the pale fibrous sheath that now bandaged his injury. His eyes snapped suddenly into focus. "Lord Gemine! What—?"

"Later," Father Marcus said quickly. "We must hurry."

The priest marched into the corridor and turned back the way they had come. He walked steadily, now, with no trace of a limp, and the others had to scramble to catch up to him.

Chentelle extended her Gift. Gerruth's body showed almost no sign of his injury. The torn flesh and ruptured organs were completely healed. Even the weakness brought on by lost blood was gone. His body was whole, but the wound itself was a mystery to her. The area covered by the pale fibers was a blank, impenetrable to her Gift. She felt a similar blankness in Father Marcus' right leg.

They returned to the junction chamber and turned down the other fork. Almost immediately, they emerged into a vast round chamber. A deep throbbing filled the room, and rows of long metal cabinets lined the floor, flickering with the light of glowing glass. Columns of twinkling white knobs covered the dark walls like a host of uniform stars. In the center of the hall, a huge, transparent conduit ran from floor to ceiling. Brilliant light swirled within the tube, ranging from flame blue to molten white but emitting no heat. A wide shaft surrounded the conduit, climbing hundreds of cubits past the tall ceiling and dropping beyond sight into the depths below.

Father Marcus led them around the conduit and into the maze of cabinets on the other side. It was there that they found the first body.

It appeared to be the skeleton of a human, but it was no creature from the races of man. The bones shone like ivory and showed no signs of age. They were draped by strange robes, clean and unwrinkled as though they had just been laundered. Many of the organs had also resisted decay. They hung from the rib cage, suspended by thin hollow tubes. Liver, kidneys, heart, they were all there, partly metal and partly composed of pale white fibers. Even one of the eyes remained, staring blindly upward with a pupil held an ember of glowing red at its center.

Father Marcus paused and removed a strange wand from the cadaver's belt. It was fashioned of sleek black metal and resembled an oddly shaped bird, pointed at one end with its wings folded back. A short stock was attached to the other end, like the handle of a gnomish crossbow. The priest adjusted a tiny lever on one side of the stock and thrust the wand into his robes.

They passed several other corpses, each with a different selection of unnaturally preserved organs. Despite the bodies, there was no scent of decay. The air remained odorless, sterile. Several of the carcasses showed signs of violence, but the floor was unscarred and absent of bloodstains.

Father Marcus slid open another door and paused outside the small, bare room it revealed. "This is a—levitating chamber. It will take us to the top of the shaft. It is there that we will activate the Sphere of Ohnn."

The company crowded into the chamber, and Marcus pressed the topmost knob of a series along one wall. The walls hummed and a slight heaviness fell upon them. Though there was no visible sign, it did indeed feel like a levitating platform.

Chentelle felt a constriction in her throat. The Fallen Star remained impenetrable to her Gift, but something felt wrong. It had no source she could name, but a cold finger of fear touched her heart.

The sensation of motion stopped, and the door slid open. Corridors branched off to either side, but Father Marcus took them straight ahead. They entered a large, domed hall that sat at the top of the conduit shaft. A web of metal supports and hollow tubes connected the glowing pillar to floor, walls, and ceiling. In the center of the chamber, a metal stairway climbed toward the top of the conduit. A dais with a single gleaming cabinet sat at the top of the stairs like the throne of some unknown king.

Father Marcus walked to the foot of the stairs and then turned to face the company. "The landing is too small to hold us all. A'stoc and I will go up alone. The rest of you wait here. Once the Sphere is ignited, we will have to flee, so stand ready. Speed will be essential." He hesitated, then turned to Chentelle. "Perhaps you should come, too."

"Of course," she said, stifling the protest she had been preparing to voice. "Wait here, Sulmar."

They started up the stairs. The climb seemed interminable. They were so close to their goal, so close to the end of the quest—but each step seemed to drag slowly through time. Chentelle's thoughts turned to Leth and Brother Gorin, to Simon and Captain Rone. So many deaths, so many sacrifices, but now they would redeem them all. And they would survive. Whatever Father Marcus planned, she wasn't going to let him add his name or A'stoc's to the list.

They reached the midway point and paused on the small landing there. Father Marcus looked tired, suddenly weary beyond his years. His breath came in shallow pants, and he was muttering quietly to himself. "It will be done. Finally, it will be done."

A flicker of motion caught Chentelle's eye—a shadow passed across the dais. Blue radiance exploded from the floor of the chamber as vorpal steel blazed to life. A cold hand clamped down on her mind. She was paralyzed. She could not even turn her eyes. The dais mocked her with its emptiness, and still she had the sense of a shadow moving just beyond the edge of vision.

Desperately, she reached out with her Gift. She sensed the presence of her friends, felt their fear and rage. A'stoc was gripped by the same force that held her, as were all of those on the floor of the chamber. Only Father Marcus managed to resist it. His mind blocked the possession, trained to resistance by his experience with Bone. The High Bishop climbed the last flight of stairs, coming to a halt beside the raised cabinet.

A single vikhor loped into the chamber. It moved past the frozen company and climbed up the steps. Chentelle's skin crawled as it pressed by her, but she couldn't even flinch away. The monster bounded up to the dais and stood facing

Father Marcus. The half-seen shadow descended, then wrapped itself around the vikhor. The Ill-creature went rigid, and its features started to change. In moments, it looked exactly like Chentelle.

She recognized the effect from A'stoc's memory—the Dark One. To her eyes, it was like staring into a clear pool, but her Gift sensed a cold, dark hunger that could swallow the world and never be sated.

"*High Bishop Marcus Alanda,*" the Dark One said. Its voice was hers, dripping with all the power and persuasion of her Gift but none of the gentleness. "*Welcome to my new demesne. I have been waiting for you to arrive. The power here resists my touch, but the knowledge you hold will lay it bare before me.*"

Father Marcus snapped suddenly erect. His face twitched with tension as the Dark One's will pressed against him, but his voice remained steady. "Such knowledge is not yours to take. I am not your creature."

"*True.*" The Dark One smiled sadly, and its voice held a twinge of actual disappointment. "*But neither are you in a position to deny me. Your quest has failed.*" As if to emphasize the statement, the Dark One gestured and a clatter of steel echoed through the hall. Sulmar and the Legionnaires had cast aside their vorpal weapons. "*If you do not give me what I wish, then I will be forced to subject your friends to indescribable agony. Eventually you will capitulate. The only reward for your recalcitrance will be their suffering.*"

Chentelle screamed. Fire burned through her eyes. Flesh melted and ran down her face in scorching rivulets. The bones in her legs shattered and crashed to the stairs. She was blind, paralyzed, and a thousand insects swarmed over her body, digesting her piece by piece. Another cry tore from her throat, joining the chorus from below and beside her.

"Stop it! Stop!"

Chentelle's agony vanished. She could see again. Her legs were whole, and she was standing exactly as she had before. Only the rawness of her throat remained. The screams, at least, had been real.

"*Of course,*" the Dark One said. "*They are nothing to me. I take no pleasure from their pain; it is simply the means to my goal. But there is a better way, if you would entertain it.*"

"What way?" Marcus asked.

"*Cooperation.*" The Dark One smiled with Chentelle's face. It was a kind expression, filled with compassion and gentle concern. "*I submit to you that your cause is lost. Your Creator has long since abandoned this world to my will. I cannot be stopped. Without the Fallen Star, I will destroy Infinitera and all that lives upon it. No other outcome is possible.*"

The Dark One raised a finger, and A'stoc jerked forward. Green flames flickered briefly around the Thunderwood Staff, but they were feeble and died quickly. The wizard lurched up to the top stair and stopped. His arm thrust forward, raising the Staff as if in offering.

"*Such an interesting toy. It's really a pity that I'll have to destroy it.*" The Dark One lifted the Thunderwood from A'stoc's hand and set it casually on the dais. "*As I was saying, this world is mine. Without the Fallen Star, all I can do is destroy it. But there is power here, the power to shape rather than annihilate. You are the key to that power, Marcus Alanda. Together, we can reshape Creation. We can end the strife and the bloodshed. We can forge a new order of perfect unity. All you have* to do is open your mind to me. In return, I will grant you immortality. You will live forever, and rule the world as my most favored son."

"Perhaps you are right," Marcus said. "Perhaps there is no hope for this world. Perhaps your power is unstoppable. But I notice that you come here only in spirit, and you hide your soft words behind my own face. Where is your body?"

"*My body is elsewhere!*" Anger flared in the Dark One's voice. Its gaze drifted away from the High Bishop and locked on to A'stoc. Then it snatched up the Thunderwood and jabbed it at the wizard. Earthpower roared from the Staff, scorching the very air and halting barely a finger's width before A'stoc's face. "*Your master died before I could repay him for the pain he caused me. You shall not be so fortunate.*"

"So," Father Marcus said, "your lies collapse one after the other. You are neither as kind nor as omnipotent as you pretend. Listen to me. The power of the Fallen Star comes from beyond the Creation. You cannot control it. You may harness it for a time, but in the end it will destroy Infinitera and you along with it."

The Dark One turned back to the priest, banishing the flames from the Staff with a negligent wave. It threw back its head and laughed merrily. The sound was musical, lilting, and chilling. "*You forget, Marcus Alanda. I, too, am from beyond your Creation. My power is boundless. I can be diminished but never destroyed. I do not fear the Fallen Star. I shall master its power as easily as I control the Thunderwood.*"

"Perhaps you would like a taste of that power first." Father Marcus reached into his robe and pulled out the bird-shaped wand.

Instantly, the Thunderwood blazed to life. A thick barrier of mingled shadow and flame surrounded the Dark One.

Marcus pointed the wand and squeezed the handle. A shaft of intense red light lanced forward, piercing the magical shields as if they were nothing. The light ripped through the Dark One's body. The vikhor flashed into ash, and the Thunderwood Staff clattered to the floor. A soundless scream echoed through the hall, and a flicker of shadow fled into the depths of the open shaft.

Chentelle stumbled, nearly falling as her paralysis vanished. Sound erupted in the chamber as warriors scrambled for their weapons. A similar noise followed A'stoc as he raced to regain the Staff.

"WELL DONE!" came a shout from below. "WELL DONE, HIGH BISHOP. JEDIAH HIMSELF WOULD BE PROUD."

"We aren't finished yet," Father Marcus said, grabbing the Staff and handing it to A'stoc. He set the wand down on the dais and pulled the Sphere of Ohnn out of his robe. "Hurry! Call upon the Thunderwood."

Earthpower flared around the Staff, but the wizard hesitated. "I cannot ignite the Sphere while you hold it. You might be harmed."

"Don't argue!" Marcus shouted. "It must be done this way. Use the Staff! Now!"

Green flame shot forward, pouring into the obsidian sphere. For long moments, power poured into the Sphere of Ohnn. The black stone sucked in the power greedily, but there was no answering spark. The Sphere remained inert.

A'stoc dropped to his knees, letting the Earthpower fade. His shoulders slumped, and the Thunderwood Staff dropped to the floor. "It's no use. I am too weak." Hopelessness and shame sounded in his voice. The Dark One's possession had rocked him deeply.

Chentelle knelt in front of the wizard. He started to turn away, but she reached out and pulled his face back to hers. "Don't do this, A'stoc. You have the power. Remember the battle under *Kennaru*. Remember the storm and the ascent of Karsh Adon. Your battle isn't with the Dark One; it's with yourself. This is the reason you're here. Ignite the Sphere. The power is in you, you only have to find it."

His eyes bore into her. A dozen emotions raged behind them, balanced precariously on the edge of despair. He was so close to surrendering everything.

"Please," she whispered. "Don't give up. You have to keep trying."

A'stoc's shoulders shook, and tears trickled from the corners of his eyes, but he grabbed the Staff and pressed himself to his feet. "And whose puppet am I now? Yours? Father Marcus'?" He planted his feet firmly, and green fire roared from the Staff. He glanced toward Chentelle and smiled thinly. "Or perhaps my own."

Earthpower shot forward, striking the Sphere of Ohnn. Magic poured from the Staff, building in intensity with every pulse. A seething inferno enveloped the High Bishop as the Sphere struggled to absorb the power. A'stoc increased the flow.

Suddenly, an ember of pure light glowed from deep inside the Sphere. The radiance grew until it swallowed the dark stone. Marcus lifted the Sphere high into the air, and the flames vanished with a muted pop. Warm white light spread from the Sphere, washing everything in its purity.

A'stoc staggered backward, unbalanced by the sudden interruption of the Staff's power. "By the Creator!"

"Yes." Father Marcus was bathed in serenity. "You have succeeded, A'stoc, as I knew you would."

A flicker of darkness shot from the shaft. It raced toward the High Bishop, reaching for him with long shafts of darkness.

Father Marcus grabbed for the bird-shaped wand, but one of the dark prongs lanced into his wrist. Instantly, the priest went rigid. His hand twitched, sending the wand clattering to the floor of the chamber.

The priest's face melted, shifting as the vikhor's had done before.

A'stoc jumped forward, swinging the Staff in a great arc. Earthpower burst from the Thunderwood and smashed into the shifting shadow. Flame and darkness twisted about each other, neither side able to gain the advantage. A'stoc screamed in incoherent rage, summoning even more power from the Staff. Thunder echoed through the chamber, and the metal stairs rocked under the strain, but still the darkness held.

"You haven't the power to stop me, apprentice!" The Dark One's voice issued from Marcus's mouth, but the transformation was not complete. The priest's features shifted wildly in a state of continual flux. *"You only delay the inevitable. The High Bishop's mind will fail, and his secrets will be mine for the taking. Then I will deliver the punishments you have so imprudently earned."*

"Mistress, duck!"

Chentelle dropped to her side.

Sulmar jumped to the landing, his vorpal sword raised high overhead. His arm shot forward, and the sword flew from his hand. The blade tumbled through the holocaust of power that surrounded A'stoc and the High Bishop, flipping end over end. The point swung around and struck precisely into the heart of the shadow. The sword glowed faintly but passed harmlessly through the darkness. It bounced off the far wall and dropped to the floor.

"*You hurl stones at the ocean. A'kalendane's toys may bother my minions, but they are nothing to me.*" The darkness firmed, and Father Marcus' features began to assume a more definite shape.

A bolt of searing red light sliced through shadow and flame, striking the wall just beyond the High Bishop's shoulder. Gerruth stepped onto the landing, aiming the bird wand carefully at the priest's heart.

Panic flashed across the shifting face, but it was replaced quickly by mocking confidence. "*Fool, you cannot strike at me without killing your precious High Bishop.*"

Gerruth's lips curled into a snarl. "Do you think Father Marcus would hesitate to make the same sacrifice he asked of us, the sacrifice my brother made?" The tip of the wand dropped, but it lowered less than a hand's breadth. Red light shot out again, piercing mystic shields and lancing through the priest's thigh. The smell of burnt flesh filled the air, and Father Marcus dropped to the ground, screaming in pain.

The Dark One's shadow hung in the air. Then it flicked suddenly toward Gerruth.

The red light flashed again. The darkness howled and shattered into a thousand pieces. The fragments hung in the air, twisting horribly. Then they shot outward, disappearing into a hundred dark corners.

"Well done, Gerruth." Father Marcus' voice was tense with agony. The beam of light had burned completely through his leg. No blood poured from the wound, but smoke still rose from the charred flesh. He still held the Sphere of Ohnn clutched in one hand.

Chentelle ran forward to help him.

"No! Stay back!" The priest grabbed the dais and hauled himself upright. His hand slapped against the metal cabinet and a shimmering wall of blue light surrounded the dais and the conduit shaft.

Chentelle pulled up abruptly. She reached out tentatively and ran her fingers against the light. It felt solid, but a violent tingling shocked her hand, and her fingers clenched into a tight ball.

A'stoc stepped forward and thrust the Thunderwood against the wall. The aura of Earthpower surrounded him, but neither Staff nor flames penetrated the blue shimmer. "High Bishop, what are you doing?"

Father Marcus slumped against the dais. Sweat ran freely down his ashen face. "I am dying, wizard, but I will take this evil with me."

"Father Marcus, no!" Chentelle pressed her thoughts toward the priest, but the glistening barrier was proof even against her Gift. "Don't. Too many people have died already."

"I must, Chentelle. The poison of the Fallen Star is deep in my mind. I can never forget it." The priest tried to smile, but a wince of pain obliterated the expression. His eyes took on a faraway look. "Such power, Chentelle. I could work miracles, end warfare, banish disease. Nothing would be impossible. No one would have to suffer pain or loss. I could remake the Creation. I could . . ."

He let the sentence trail off and brought his eyes back to Chentelle's. "You see, the temptation grows ever stronger. Already I am cut off from the True Creation. That is why I could not heal Gerruth. And it will only become worse. There must be an ending. If I return to the Realm, all of the sacrifice will be for nothing."

A wave of pain swept over the priest's face. He slumped lower on the dais. "Listen, there isn't much time. This is my destiny, Chentelle. It is the path the Creator guided me to. I walk it freely and without remorse. My life has been dedicated to preserving the Creation, but you must find your own path. Listen to your heart. I have learned to respect its wisdom."

Father Marcus dragged himself upward, balancing on his one good leg. His face went even whiter, and he swayed unsteadily, but his blue eyes were clear and focused. His hand closed around a red lever and pulled it slowly downward. A circular portal spread open in the center of the conduit.

Arcs of power shot from the opening, engulfing the landing in a tempest of multicolored flame. Father Marcus opened his arms in the sign of harmony, letting the conflagration wash over him. The Sphere of Ohnn glowed fiercely through the storm, a shining beacon of pure white light. Father Marcus disappeared, swallowed by the raging inferno. "Run, Chentelle. Run and don't look back."

Chentelle watched from behind the safety of the shimmering blue shield. Just before the High Bishop vanished, a soft glow enveloped his body—the light of sanctuary. She grabbed A'stoc and ran for the stairs.

Dacius and the others were waiting at the bottom of the steps. "WHERE IS FATHER MARCUS?"

Chentelle stopped. The glare from the top platform was now blinding in its intensity. "He isn't coming."

The human lord hesitated for only a moment. "THILDEMAR, TAKE THE POINT."

A tremendous explosion rocked the Fallen Star. Cabinets crashed to the floor. Metal cables ripped apart, sending showers of lightning sparking across the chamber. They raced through the chaos, scrambling for the doorway through which they had entered. Fires chased them into the corridor, singeing their hair with fierce heat.

Dacius paused at the doorway. As soon as the last person was through, he slammed the glass tile with his fist. The metal door slid closed, blocking off the heat and smoke.

They ran to the levitating chamber. Thildemar touched the opening tile, but something was wrong. The portal didn't open. He touched it again, then smashed it with his elbow. The door stayed shut.

"FORGET IT. FIND ANOTHER WAY."

Thildemar looked down each of the side corridors. His lips moved silently as he reviewed the twists and turns they had taken to reach this spot. Then he ran down the passage on the right.

The old Legionnaire led them through a series of curved walkways, always choosing the turns that took them toward the east. The Fallen Star shook under a series of explosions, each more violent than the last. The corridor lights went out, then flashed on again, now blinking bloodred. Twice, they had to retrace their steps when a corridor ended in a dead end, but they finally found a long ladder mounted in a deep shaft.

Without hesitation, they scrambled over the edge. They climbed past a half-dozen landings. Then Thildemar stopped, glancing at Dacius for guidance. The human lord shook his head. Shrugging, Thildemar hopped off the ladder.

Again, he led them into the maze of passages. He paused at each junction, searching the side corridors, but in the absence of visual clues he always turned toward the east. The explosions sounded more frequently, now, and the tunnels were becoming treacherous. Steam poured from ruptured pipes. Strange liquids bubbled along the edge of the walls, and the red lights blinked with desperate intensity.

"There!" Thildemar pointed down a side passage. At its far end stood a heavy hexagonal portal. "It is like the one Father Marcus brought us through."

They dashed down the short hall. Thildemar pressed and twisted at the knobs on the wall until the door finally slid open. They crowded into the small chamber, stopping before an identical door on the far side.

Thildemar pressed and twisted the tiles and knobs, but the door remained stubbornly closed. He tried again, and then again. Nothing.

"Wait," Chentelle said. "Remember when we came in. The first door shut before the second one opened."

"Of course!" A'stoc lurched across the chamber and pounded the tile beside the open portal. The door swung shut, plunging the room into darkness.

"THE ORB-LIGHTS AREN'T WORKING. A'STOC!"

Flames roared from the Staff, illuminating the chamber.

Thildemar pressed and twisted. Something hissed in the walls above them, and the atmosphere changed. The sterile scent of the Fallen Star vanished, replaced by cold, vigorous mountain air. An instant later, the outer door slid open.

They were thirty cubits above the crater floor, and at least as far from the rock slide they had climbed to reach the other portal. Another explosion rocked them, and the Fallen Star shifted deeper into the crater.

"We can't go back!" Chentelle shouted. "The end will come soon."

A'stoc pressed by her and stood on the ledge of the doorway. He spun around to face them, holding out the Staff at shoulder level. "Grab hold."

The company hesitated.

"A'STOC, ARE YOU CERTAIN?"

Another explosion shook the chamber.

"Grab hold."

Chentelle latched on to the Thunderwood with both hands. The others quickly followed, though Dacius paused to disengage his shield and toss it to the ground below.

A'stoc started to chant. The Thunderwood grew warm, and tiny flames flickered around their fingers. The Staff surged upward, lifting the elves well clear of the floor and dragging Dacius onto his toes. Then A'stoc leaned backward.

They plunged out the doorway, falling steadily but not swiftly. They hit the snow with a muffled thud, sinking hardly a cubit into the crusted powder.

Hideous howls erupted from the rim of the crater. A pack of vikhors charged down the slope, their eyes glowing maliciously.

Dacius dived for his shield, but by the time he recovered it, A'stoc had acted.

The wizard flicked the Staff casually. A ribbon of green light poured from the Thunderwood, undulating slowly toward the vikhors. It spread out in a wide band as it moved, completely blocking the Ill-creatures' path.

The beasts loped forward heedlessly, reducing themselves to ash in a vain attempt to force the barrier. In seconds, the encounter was over.

"Keep moving," the wizard said. "We have no time to spare."

No one argued. They fled east, clearing the rim of the crater and then retracing their path from the river. They had hardly reached the line of pines when a blinding glow obliterated the night. A blast of wind pressed at their backs, followed seconds later by a cold gust into their faces. The blinding glow flashed once and then disappeared. Everything was suddenly quiet.

Chentelle turned around. The Fallen Star was gone, as was the crater itself. In their place was a huge shaft, perfectly cylindrical, that shot straight down toward the center of the world.

❧ 22 ❧

TRANSFORMATIONS

The company crossed the frozen river and then came to a halt. Fatigue weighed down their arms and legs. The quest was over. Infinitera was saved. Now they just had to get home again. They made a hurried camp, huddling together in the sparse shelter of the pines.

"Can we risk a fire?" Chentelle asked.

Dacius considered the sky. Already, the eastern horizon was showing hints of first-light. "I would say yes. What about you, wizard? What is your counsel?"

"Burn what you like," the wizard said absently. "The Dark One will be long recovering from this night, and I have lost my taste for cowering in the dark."

They built a small blaze and gathered close to its warmth. Their supplies were nearly exhausted, but Dacius ordered everyone to eat a full ration.

"Before a challenge, adrenaline and need drive the body onward," he said. "It is after a victory that you must stoke the inner flame. We will have only our own strength to call upon now, and we are a long way from the Realm."

There was little conversation. The magnitude of the night's events were setting in, and each of them wandered in their private thoughts. After the meal, Dacius assigned a watch schedule. They would rest until midmorning, then make for the Barrier Ridge.

Chentelle laid out her blankets close to the fire. She expected to fall asleep as soon as she closed her eyes, but her thoughts would not settle. She kept remembering Father Marcus' eyes as he opened his arms to death. She knew it had been necessary, but that didn't make it right. She was so tired of death, so tired of sacrifice. And it still wasn't over. There was still the Erietoph to deal with.

She turned to A'stoc. The wizard stood under one of the pines, leaning on the Staff. His eyes were far away and deep in thought.

What would the forest do to him? Couldn't it see that he was a good man? He hadn't even known that the ancient was sentient. Yes, he had acted rashly, but he had also made atonement. Without him, the whole world would have been destroyed.

Chentelle rolled over. It was no good fretting over it now. They didn't even know what punishment the forest would demand. She took several deep breaths, trying to clear her mind. This was maddening. She was exhausted, but she couldn't fall asleep. She opened her eyes.

Ellistar was already full in the sky, and Deneob's tip was poking above the horizon. The sky was a uniform gray, decorated only by the smoke of their own campfire and a small black speck far to the south.

She jumped to her feet. "Something's coming!"

The Legionnaires burst into action. Vorpal blades slid free of their sheaths, but the mystic metal gave no telltale glow. It was daylight. Whatever approached, it was no Ill-creature.

Chentelle heard a guttural growl. She spun and found Sulmar staring at the metal bracer that covered his right forearm.

"Kaliya." The Tengarian's eyes snapped to the south, then studied the intervening terrain. He dropped his pack and his vorpal sword. Then he drew the black blade and discarded that scabbard, too. He stretched and shifted his weight back and forth, and finally decided to throw off his winter cloak as well. Thus unencumbered, he jogged away from the camp, moving to a flat bluff just beyond the trees.

Dacius hefted his shield and donned his metal helm. "DRUP, GERRUTH, STRING YOUR BOWS. A'STOC, READY YOUR MANDRIL. STAY TO THE COVER OF THE TREES, AND REMEMBER SKYSOAR. THE BEAST'S BILE IS DEADLY." The Legion lord started out after Sulmar.

"Dacius, no!" Chentelle pulled on the human's arm, holding him back. "Sulmar has to do this alone. No one can help him."

The featureless metal helm turned toward her. "ALONE? HE'LL BE KILLED. HE ISN'T EVEN ARMORED. HE CAN'T STAND AGAINST A GREAT DRAGON BY HIMSELF."

"He *must*." Chentelle turned to watch the other Legionnaires as well. "Listen to me, all of you. Sulmar must kill the dragon unaided to end his curse. Any other outcome, even a single wound by another hand, and his soul will be forfeit."

"BLOOD AND BONE!" Dacius pulled free and marched to the edge of the trees, but he went no farther. "STAND READY. IF SULMAR FALLS, I WANT THE DRAGON TO DIE WITH ITS NEXT BREATH."

Chentelle breathed a sigh of relief. But had she just saved Sulmar—or condemned him? *Blessed Creator, not him, too. Please, no more death.*

The Tengarian took up his position on the bluff and watched the dragon's approach. He stamped back and forth, packing down the snow and testing the footing. The black blade swung slowly back and forth, keeping perfect rhythm to his steps. "Kaliya!"

The dark shape shifted course, orienting exactly on the sound of her true name. If there had been any chance that the dragon would pass them by, there was none now.

Kaliya turned in a stately circle, inspecting first the Tengarian and then the rest of the company. As the beast drew near, they could see the hollow pit of an empty eye socket. Apparently Sulmar had managed to scar her during their last encounter.

The dragon's great wings beat against the air. She rolled over and dived sharply for the bluff. Two great claws stretched out before her, reaching for Sulmar with talons larger than scimitars.

The Tengarian stood his ground until the last possible instant; then he dived sharply to his right. His body twisted, barely avoiding the dragon's claws. The black sword sliced upward, continuing the motion of his body. It ripped into the back of one foreleg. Scales parted, muscle tore, and a stream of dark blood splattered across the snow.

The Black Dragon screamed with rage and climbed higher. She pivoted at the top of her arc and swept down in another dive. This time, she stayed well beyond the reach of the black blade. As she drew near the Tengarian, her great mouth opened and dark liquid spewed forth.

Sulmar dodged backward, seeking the cover of the trees. Vitriol splashed against trunk and snow. A pine tree fell, its foundation eaten away in seconds. A second toppled a moment later. Steam hissed into the air, forming a thick cloud. When the mist cleared, Sulmar walked calmly forward and resumed his place on the hill.

Kaliya flapped her wings slowly, circling around again to regard her enemy. The dragon's head cocked to the side, as if considering alternatives. Then the beast glided to the ground, coming to rest on a rise less than fifty cubits from the Tengarian. The huge jaws opened again, and the Black Dragon spoke. "I have come for you, Prince Sulmar Coregal, outcast heir to the throne of Tengar."

"I am here, Kaliya, servant of evil, traitor to the Creation."

"Prince?" Chentelle repeated, amazed. Suddenly certain mysteries were unraveling.

The dragon hissed and moved forward, crawling slowly like a hunting cat.

Sulmar stood his ground, waiting calmly. "Kaliya, the last time we fought, I allowed my rage to consume me. That was a mistake. I no longer lust for your death. I wish only to be free of the curse you placed upon me. Release me, and I will spare your life."

"*You* will spare *my* life. What arrogance!" The Black Dragon gave a barking laugh. "Listen to me, mortal son of a mortal dam. Your soul is mine. You accepted my brand willingly, in penance for your crimes, and I will not release you. If I wished, I could simply fly away. Human lives are brief, and you would be mine soon enough. But you *marked* me, human! You scarred me and caused me pain. Now, I will return the favor. And after you die, I will place your soul into the shell of an Ill-creature and kill you again and again until my wrath is sated."

"Listen to yourself," Sulmar called out evenly. "The Dark One abhors all life. After you have served his purpose, he will destroy you without a qualm. Once, you were a noble creature, a spirit of puissance and grace. What are you now? In your quest for immortality you have chained yourself to death. Seeking power, you have made yourself a servant."

"I serve a master of my own choosing," Kaliya hissed, "one who rewards me well. The same will not be true for you." The dragon clawed at the ground, tearing loose large clumps of dirt and rock.

Sulmar raised his sword in a calm salute. "We are bound together, Kaliya. The threads of our destinies twine together. Shall we explore them in life or in death? The choice is yours."

"DEATH!" Kaliya's wings churned the snow, raising a blizzard of powder. Then the dragon surged forward in an avalanche of scale and claw.

Sulmar dived to his right, rolling smoothly to his feet. The black sword lashed out, striking scales from the beast's flank but not penetrating.

The dragon roared and lashed out with a wing and a claw.

Sulmar ducked the wing, thrusting upward to score a cut along the delicate membrane. Then he dropped to his side, allowing the claw to slide just past his

ribs. Reversing his grip on the sword, he thrust backward as the dragon recovered. The black blade sunk deep into the foreleg. The dragon flinched, and
Sulmar cut the leg again as he rolled to his feet.

Kaliya sprang upward, twisting sinuously in the air. Her jaws snapped forward, clacking together in the spot where Sulmar's head had been the instant
before.

Sulmar rolled to his right, coming up on the dragon's blind side. The black
sword swung in a low arc, slicing deeply into Kaliya's other foreleg.

Kaliya changed tactics, swinging her massive tail toward Sulmar's legs. The
Tengarian somersaulted gracefully over the first sweep, but the return swing
forced him to jump backward. Kaliya took advantage of the distance to snap
her head around and spray the Tengarian with bile.

Sulmar dropped flat, his body sinking into the snow. The acidic fluid passed
harmlessly over him, and he hopped to his feet before the dragon could press a
new attack. He raised his sword in a defensive posture and circled slowly toward
his right.

The lull lasted for less than one breath, maybe two, then the combatants
burst into motion again. The Black Dragon was magnificent, raw strength and
power personified. She swarmed over Sulmar, attacking with tooth, claw, wing,
and tail. A hundred strikes screamed toward the Tengarian, any one of which
could have killed him instantly.

Sulmar countered with measured precision. The Oath of Discipline filled
him, guiding his movements and perceptions. He parried or avoided every attack, seemingly without effort. His motion flowed with the dragon's creating a
beautiful, horrible dance of destruction, a dance that circled always toward the
dragon's blind eye. The black blade carved a dozen wounds in Kaliya's side, then
a dozen more. But none were deep, and they served only to spur the dragon to
greater ferocity.

Chentelle watched the battle with growing dread. Sulmar's style looked
effortless, but she knew that it was taking its toll. He would tire eventually, or
his foot would slip on the ice. Then it would be over. Another friend would be
dead. "No."

She had to do something, but what? Sulmar had to win the battle on his
own. If anyone else attacked the dragon, the victory would be meaningless. Fine,
she couldn't use her Gift against Kaliya, so she would have to use it for Sulmar.
She summoned her power, taking her cue from the battle drums of the dwarves.
She sang pure rhythm, wordless cadence punctuated by all the power of her
Gift. She matched it to Sulmar's motion, letting his need define the beats.

Thildemar melded his rich tones to hers, followed by Drup and Gerruth.
Even Dacius' rough voice joined the chorus, making up in power what it lacked
in finesse. The song thrummed across the frozen earth, creating a reservoir of
power for Sulmar to draw upon.

Kaliya sensed her danger. She pulled back as if taking to the air. Her mouth
opened, spitting dark acid at the Tengarian. But instead of continuing backward,
she twisted and lashed out to her left, anticipating Sulmar's evasive roll.

This time, however, Sulmar had rolled to his left. He rose up beside the
dragon's wing and thrust cleanly into her remaining eye. Without pausing, he
dropped to the ground and slid sideways.

Kaliya screamed and beat her wings wildly, trying to gain the air. Her head swung back and forth, spewing vitriol blindly across the landscape.

But Sulmar was safe, crouched below the belly of the beast. He waited calmly for his opening to appear. Then he jumped to his feet, driving the sword upward with all the strength in his arms and legs. The blade slid into the base of Kaliya's throat and buried itself to the hilt.

The Black Dragon crashed to the earth, her dark blood pouring over the snow. The massive head twitched once, twice, then fell to ground and lay still.

Sulmar staggered backward. His sword pulled free, but a cord of darkness remained, linking the blade to the dragon's body. The vorpal bracer exploded off of his arm, landing by his feet in a twisted clump.

A shadow swept through his body and down his right arm. When it reached the dragon's mark, shadow and brand together bled downward and passed into the sword. There was a flash of light, and the cord of shadow disappeared. Kaliya's body shriveled and collapsed into a pile of bones and desiccated scales.

Sulmar stared at his sword—as the bloodred mark of a dragon shifted sinuously on the black blade. Shouting in triumph, he thrust his sword into the air. His dark eyes gleamed in the sunlight, and his normally stoic expression vanished under a smile of wild joy.

Chentelle ran forward. "Sulmar! You did it!" She threw her arms around his chest and hugged him tightly. Then she jumped back and grabbed his right arm. The forearm was clear and unblemished. "You're free. Oh, Sulmar, I'm so happy for you."

"My lady." Sulmar dropped to his knees and presented his sword. "You have guided my destiny from the day that we met. My honor, my dignity, my soul, my discipline, I owe all of these to you, for they were lost until you led me back to them. My sword is yours, as is anything else you might ask."

Chentelle smiled. "I ask that you stand up. That is an unseemly posture, for a prince."

"PRESENT, ARMS." The Legionnaires clapped to attention. Dacius' sword snapped forward, then back, pommel pressed over his heart. "HAIL SULMAR, PRINCE OF TENGAR."

A'stoc raised an eyebrow and smiled sardonically. "Prince, eh? I always knew there was more to you than met the eye."

"Ignore him," Chentelle said. "He's only teasing."

She reached down and hauled the Tengarian to his feet. "Prince Sulmar Coregal, I hereby release you from your Oath of Fealty. Our quest is done, and your service is over. Your debt to me is more than paid. Thank you—dear friend."

Sulmar smiled and met her eyes. "Thank you, Chentelle."

The Legionnaires surged forward, clapping Sulmar on the back and shouting praise and encouragement. "MAGNIFICENT, I HAVE NEVER SEEN THE LIKE." "A deed for the ages." "No song shall do it justice."

Chentelle grabbed Sulmar's collar and shook him gently. "Why didn't you tell me you were a prince?"

He shrugged. "It was not relevant, and it is no longer true. My titles were stripped when I accepted banishment."

"But you've vindicated yourself," she said. "You defeated the dragon. Now, you can return and take back your rightful place. You can be with your family again."

"My family." Sulmar's eyes grew shiny with tears. "If only that were true, mist—Chentelle. But I can never return to Tengar."

"Why not?" Deep sadness washed through her as her Gift reacted to Sulmar's pain. "I thought that only the curse kept you away."

The Tengarian shook his head. "No, the curse and the banishment were separate. My soul is redeemed, but my crime can never be forgiven."

"YOUR CRIME!" Dacius yanked off his helm. The Legionnaire's eyes blazed with passionate intensity. "You spoke once of murder, and I stayed silent, for I did not know what manner of man you were. But you have proven your worth in a hundred trials. Any man who calls you a murderer speaks lies, and I will swear that before the highest court in Tengar!"

The Tengarian smiled. "Thank you, Lord Gemine. Your words echo my own heart, though, in truth, the word used was 'regicide.' "

"Regicide?"

Sulmar nodded. "I killed Mortiris Coregal, Great King of Tengar."

Chentelle gasped. "Sulmar—your father?"

"My uncle." Sulmar's eyes went suddenly hard. "He had no sons and both of his brothers died early. I was first heir until I killed him. Now, my cousin Cowan wears the Stone Circle."

Chentelle searched the Tengarian's face. "There's something you aren't telling us. Why did you kill him? And why was it called murder?"

Muscles tensed along Sulmar's jaw. "Mortiris had entered a secret pact with Bone the necromancer. He pledged Tengar's armies to the Dark One's cause in exchange for help against the dwarves. I discovered the plot and challenged Mortiris to honorable combat, but after I killed him, Cowan denounced me as an assassin. There were no witnesses to speak for me, and his voice carried the council."

"Blood and bone!" Dacius grabbed Sulmar's arm. "The alliance—does Cowan continue it?"

The Tengarian returned his stare. "I do not know, but it is possible. He values power over honor."

The Legionnaire swore and turned back to the camp.

There were no more questions for Sulmar. The company broke camp and began the long march home. The time for rest was over.

The hike went quickly. They were tired, but no fresh snow had fallen. They stayed to their back trail, taking advantage of its packed base and firm footing. Deneob was still in the sky when they reached the sharp drop of the Barrier Ridge. It took them only a moment to locate and uncover the levitating platform.

A'stoc mounted the disk and planted the Thunderwood Staff. Then he reclaimed his wand from Chentelle. Once everyone was aboard, he triggered the *mandril*'s spell and augmented it with the power of the Staff. The platform glided over the edge of the cliff and began a smooth, gentle descent.

Once they reached the bottom, the wizard summoned orb-light to drive back the deep shadow of the ridge. The remains of their earlier camp lay un-disturbed among the rocks, as did Leth's crumpled body.

They buried the Legionnaire at the foot of Karsh Adon, marking the grave clearly so that the body could be easily retrieved. With Father Marcus gone, it fell upon Dacius to give the honors to the dead.

"One day, Leth's body will return to the Inarr. He will rest, then, among the hills and forests that he loved so well. Until then, it is fitting that he lies here.

"Karsh Adon is a mighty barrier, a fitting symbol of the trials that blocked our quest. Leth never climbed this ridge, yet he conquered it nonetheless. His sacrifice kept hope alive. His sacrifice allowed us to succeed. His sacrifice pre-served the Creation. So let him lie here, marked by a stone that befits the magnitude of his triumph, the measure of our loss. He will not be forgotten."

Gerruth was excused from the watch schedule, though he might as well have taken every shift. He spent the night sitting beside his brother's grave, singing and telling stories from their childhood.

The next day took them all the way from Karsh Adon to Long Lake. The two skiffs were beached where the company had left them, but they were now lacking oars.

"That will not be a problem," A'stoc declared, climbing aboard one of the boats. "Simply push us off."

The wizard hummed a soft spell and melded the Staff into the skiff's hull. As soon as they were floating free, he summoned a gentle sagewind. He stood easily on the prow, rocking smoothly with the motion of the waves. His eyes were closed, and his face bore a look of quiet serenity.

Watching him now, Chentelle could imagine the wizard as a shipsage, spending his years calmly guiding ships through treacherous waters. He looked so happy, so much at peace. Then her smile vanished, and she looked away. What hope did they have for such a future? A'stoc still had to face the judgment of the Erietoph.

ॐ

The dwarven cabin still reeked of fish and salt. It was tiny and cramped and held few comforts. The company settled into it gratefully. A roaring fire, shelter from the wind, and soft mattresses, however small, seemed the height of luxury. They slept until dawn and greeted the morning with fresh enthusiasm.

They did not have Hammond to guide them, but Thildemar easily retraced the path to the hidden tunnel. Chentelle used her Gift to reveal the doorway. None of them welcomed the prospect of another trek through the cramped passage, but it was infinitely preferable to trying to locate a pass through the frozen mountains. They stopped frequently so that the humans could rest their legs and backs, and when they finally reached the deep mines under Marble Falls, a platoon of dwarven guards were waiting for them.

"So, it is you." Hammond tramped forward, a broad smile on his face. "When the telltales gave warning, I hoped that was the case. But where are the others?"

The smile vanished as the dwarf read the pain on their faces. "So, the sad times are not over. Come, we will find you warm food and a safe bed for the night. Tomorrow will be soon enough for bittersweet tales."

They spent two days among the folk of Marble Falls. It was a time of rest, a time of healing. They told their story a dozen times, omitting only the details of the Fallen Star. The dwarves shared freely in the tale, applauding their triumphs and grieving for their loss. Every home, every heart was made open to them, and they were sorry when the time came to leave.

It was A'stoc who finally provided the goad. "I have an appointment to keep. It does no good to delay it."

They resumed their trek, forced now to use the mountain passes. When they reached the location of the gnomish sabotage, they found that the avalanche had been completely cleared. The road stayed clear throughout the day.

They made camp high in the Mountains of Time, using a small cave that the dwarves had recommended. The night was bitterly cold, and a hard wind blew from the north. By the time they finished dinner, the wind had turned into a storm. Snow filled the air, driven into a frenzy by the gale.

"Enough." A'stoc grabbed the Staff and stalked toward the cave's mouth.

Dacius grabbed his arm. "Wizard, are you sure that's wise?"

A'stoc pulled his arm away. "Don't worry, Lord Gemine. The Dark One will not recover soon, and no Ill-creature will dare to usurp their master's vengeance. I, for one, do not relish the prospect of another cubit of fresh snow to trudge through come morning."

The Legionnaire smiled and released A'stoc's arm. "Point taken. Please, continue."

The wizard pressed out into the storm. As soon as he was clear of the cave, the Thunderwood roared to life. Great arcs of Earthpower shot into the sky, shifting winds and breaking apart the clouds. In minutes, the blizzard had been reduced to soft wind delivering only the lightest sprinkle of snow.

A'stoc returned to the cave, brushing frost from his shoulders. "Now, let's get some sleep."

Chentelle smiled and curled up near the fire. Her stomach was full, and the warmth pulled her toward drowsiness, but she did not fall asleep. Instead, she watched A'stoc.

Despite the wizard's seeming levity, he did not relax with the others. He unrolled his blankets near the wall of the cave, but soon abandoned them. He walked softly toward the cave's entrance and stood motionlessly at the threshold. The wind whipped gently at the hem of his robes, and a thin coat of ice formed around his unruly white hair.

Chentelle sensed the battle raging in his heart. He yearned to return to his studies. The seclusion of his seaside home called to him, as did the crystal halls of Skysoar. But the wrath of the Erietoph loomed between him and his desires. There was anger in his soul, outrage that he should be judged so after all he had done. Part of him wanted to run, to avoid the forest and never look back, but he wouldn't. He had given his word, and (was there a twinge of surprise here?) that was enough.

Chentelle felt her own ire rising. It *wasn't* fair. A'stoc deserved praise and gratitude, not retribution. She forged her anger into iron determination. Whatever happened, he would not have to face it alone. She would not abandon him to the mercy of the Erietoph.

Weariness followed in the wake of her resolution. Her course was set. Now she could relax. Sleep came quickly, and she dreamed.

🙠

A'stoc stands in a forest clearing, holding one end of the Staff. Glathrel stands opposite him, gripping the other end. They tug and pull, each trying to seize the Staff for his own.

The Thunderwood starts to pulse, filling the glade with white radiance. The wood shifts and grows, transforming itself into the Heart Tree of Sylvandale. The lifelm reaches out, brushing her with its branches. A single word echoes in her soul.

Remember.

🙠

Someone shook Chentelle's shoulder, jolting her awake. It was A'stoc.

"It is time, Chentelle." The wizard's eyes were red, and his face was lined with fatigue.

Chentelle rubbed the sleep from her own eyes and looked around. Everyone else was already up and packed. The remains of a light breakfast sat next to her in a wooden bowl. She ate hurriedly and packed away her roll, embarrassed to be delaying the others.

They climbed down from the mountains and started across the rocky plain. The shadow of the Erietoph loomed before them, shrouded in its perpetual mist. They followed the markers for the dwarven road, and by the time Ellistar dropped behind the peaks, they had reached the edge of the fog.

They hesitated for a moment, remembering their earlier visit. The forest was not evil, but it was strange, almost eerie. And they were about to enter its power once more.

A'stoc walked forward, plunging into the mist without a backward glance.

Chentelle and the others hurried after him.

A wide trail awaited them, leading deep into the heart of the Erietoph. They marched along it, content to follow the forest's guidance. Behind them, the path vanished into a wall of brambles. The wood was taking no chances.

They walked for hours, though whether such measures had any meaning here was doubtful. No sun was visible through the thick canopy and the overhanging mist, but it seemed to be twilight when the trail finally disgorged them into a hilly clearing.

Chentelle smiled, recognizing both the glade and the silhouette that rose from the crest of a small knoll. "Fizzfaldt!"

She ran forward, throwing her arms around the ancient's trunk. "It's good to see you again, wise one."

She extended her Gift into the tree, feeling a warm rush of greeting. Fizzfaldt could not speak to her—he was still too new to the transformation, but he knew she was there.

"Look, it's Chentelle of Lone Valley." Prickly-Ash moved into the clearing, followed closely by Laurel and Ironwood. "Have you come to sing with us again, child of Lone Valley?"

"Now, Prickly," Ironwood chided, "you know that the wanderers have other concerns."

"Of course," Prickly-Ash said. "I meant after the judgment."

Chentelle hugged the dendrifaun. "We'll see, elder. Is this where the trial will be?"

Ironwood nodded his trunk. "It was Gnarlroot's request. His roots do not extend far, yet, and he wanted to listen to the judgment."

The sound of chimes blew into the clearing. A ripple passed through the trees, and there was a sudden *presence* to the forest. A new path opened into the glade, and Glathrel Geodimondan stepped into view.

The Keeper stopped a dozen cubits in front of A'stoc and leveled his oaken staff. "You have returned. Do you now submit to the judgment of the Erietoph?"

"Pronounce your sentence," A'stoc said. "Then I will decide whether I find it acceptable."

The Keeper's eyes narrowed, and his voice grew hard. "Impudence will not serve you here, tree killer. Your crime is known. What have you to say in your defense?"

A'stoc met the giant's gaze and said nothing.

"Very well." Glathrel raised both arms, holding his staff high overhead. When he spoke, his voice thundered through the trees. *"A'stoc, for the murder of the ancient, Beltis, you are—"*

"Wait!" Chentelle called on her Gift, filling the cry with all the urgency she felt in her heart. "I want to speak in A'stoc's defense."

The Keeper glared at her, lowering his staff. "It is too late. The Erietoph has decided. Judgment will be given." The staff rose again.

Chentelle's mind raced. She had to find a way to make him listen. "Glathrel, what harm can it do to hear me out. If the Erietoph is firm in its will, then nothing will be altered. If the forest changes its mind, then justice will be served. All you risk is the time it takes to hear a story of triumph and tragedy. Tell me, has the last giant lost his love for a tale?"

The Keeper cocked his head, listening to the silent voice of the forest. His hard expression did not change, but his arms lowered to his sides. "Tell your tale, enchantress. The Erietoph will listen, and so will I."

Chentelle took a deep breath, gathering her thoughts. A flicker of movement caught her eye. The clearing was suddenly surrounded by dendrifauns. Most were in their tree form, though a few, like Prickly and her friends, were animate. How had they come up so quickly? Or had they been there all along, hidden by the magic of the Erietoph? Somehow, their presence reassured her. They made the forest seem more natural, more like home.

Chentelle sang. She built her song slowly, letting it grow from a tiny seed. The core of her tale was the company itself, so she introduced each member one by one, those who were present and those who had died along the way. Then she introduced the quest—the grim danger of the Fallen Star and the slim hope that guided them. Her Gift touched every syllable, every note, filling them with emotion.

She sang of the meeting in the Holy Land and the journey across the Great Sea. She sang of Tel Adartak-Skysoar and the vault of A'kalendane. When she came to the point where the skeletons of the Desecration were raised by Bone, Glathrel cried out in grief and rage.

She recounted every triumph, every struggle, every moment of joy or desperation, leaving out only the nature of the Fallen Star. She sang of great deeds and terrible sacrifice, stressing always the important part that A'stoc played, the invaluable service he had given to the world. And she sang of love—the love for Creation that inspired the company, the love for each other that held them together and allowed them to succeed.

She ended her song with a plea for mercy, a single note of hope that hung in the air and faded slowly into a deep silence.

"Magnificent." Tears rolled down Glathrel's face, and his voice was hushed with reverence. "Never have I heard such a tale—or such a telling. I thank you, Chentelle, enchantress of the forest children. You have given me a new understanding. I now feel the proper remorse for what must be done."

Remorse? Chentelle was stunned. Her song hadn't made any difference. The forest was still going to punish him.

The Keeper raised his staff once more. *"Wizard A'stoc, the will of the Erietoph is clear. You have taken a life from the forest, and you must replace it with your own. Never again will you be allowed to pass through the mists. Your days will be spent among the trees, so that you may come to understand the nature of your crime. Such is the judgment of the Erietoph. Do you submit, or must you be compelled?"*

A'stoc turned to his companions. His eyes met each of theirs in turn, coming to rest finally on Chentelle's. He lingered there for a long moment, letting her see his pain, his regrets, but also his acceptance. Then he turned back to the giant. "I submit to the forest's judgment. The Erietoph is now my home."

Glathrel lowered his arms. "It is good. The Erietoph is pleased. Now, there is one final matter."

"Wait!" Chentelle stepped forward and stood beside A'stoc. "I'm staying, too."

The wizard turned to face her, fear and hope warring on his face. "Chentelle, you can't—"

"I can! And I will." She grabbed the human's hand and squeezed it in both of her own. "A'stoc, I love you. I'm not going to leave you here alone."

A murmur of shock ran through the dendrifauns and the Legionnaires. Only Sulmar seemed unsurprised.

"I will stay also," the Tengarian said.

The feeling in his voice touched Chentelle deeply. "Sulmar, are you certain? You have no obligation. Maybe you should think it over?"

"I have been considering it for several days, Chentelle. I knew that you would not leave the wizard."

"You knew?"

Sulmar smiled, but it was a smile of sadness. "I know the pain of a love that is forever out of reach. I recognized it in your face long ago."

"Enough!" Glathrel's voice boomed through the clearing. "The Erietoph has no objection to Chentelle's presence, and neither do I. But Prince Sulmar Coregal must leave."

"What?" Chentelle exclaimed.

"I am the master of my own destiny," Sulmar declared. "I will choose my own path."

The Keeper shook his head. "No. The threads of destiny are determined for us. Your own lie outside the mists. The Erietoph sees this. It will not allow you to remain."

"Sulmar." Chentelle caught his eyes with her own. "He's right. You don't belong here. This is where my heart takes me. You need to follow your own."

Slowly, his gaze softened and he nodded acceptance.

Chentelle hugged the Tengarian tightly. "I'll miss you, Sulmar." She paused, a troublesome thought suddenly occurring to her. "Oh, no. I promised Fizzfaldt that I would carry his story back to Lone Valley. Sulmar, if your travels should take you that way . . ."

He smiled. "It will be my first destination."

"Thank you. And tell my mother that I'm all right. She worries about me."

"I will." He turned back to the giant. "I will leave, but one day I will return, and it would be unwise to bar my way."

The giant nodded his head. A chorus of whinnies sounded from the wood. Seconds later, a string of horses clopped into the clearing. "The Erietoph wishes you all well in your destinies. These mounts have been healed and well cared for. Take them to speed you on your way."

The horses walked up and waited docilely to be mounted.

"Just a minute." Dacius pushed past the horses and locked gazes with the Keeper. "Call me suspicious, but I seem to remember you saying there was one more matter. I'm not going to leave until I'm sure everything is settled."

Glathrel nodded. "Of course. What remains is simply a question of propriety. A'stoc must surrender the Thunderwood Staff. The Tree of Life must be returned to its own."

"Impossible."

Stunned eyes turned toward the wizard.

"It is not a matter of choice!" The Keeper's eyes went hard, and he raised his staff menacingly. A sudden stillness gripped the clearing.

"You misunderstand," A'stoc said. "I do not refuse. I state a fact." He handed the Staff to the giant. "Here, work your magic."

Glathrel placed his own staff on the ground and took the Thunderwood. He closed his eyes and began a deep chant. The song filled the Erietoph, echoing in the wind and the rustling leaves. It built in intensity until every word pounded like a thunderclap. But the Staff stayed dormant.

The Keeper broke off his spell, confusion plain upon his face. "I don't understand. The Tree of Life should not refuse my call."

"You are not holding the Tree of Life," A'stoc said gently. "You are holding the Thunderwood Staff. It is a tool, a weapon created by the Lore of my master. It was forged from the essence of the Tree, but shaped by the mind of A'pon Boemarre. And only his Lore, or its equal, can command it. Now, *give me the Staff.*"

The last words were spoken with such authority that Glathrel surrendered the Thunderwood without protest.

"Thank you." A'stoc's voice was quiet again, but his eyes were filled with determination. He thrust one end of the Staff into the ground and began to chant. The Thunderwood melted into the earth like a sagestaff joining to a ship. Fire burst from the wood. The Staff shifted and grew. Branches pressed toward the sky. Roots spread out from the base. But the shoots were fuzzy, indistinct. The roaring flame grew louder, brighter, more ferocious. Then the Earthpower vanished. The Thunderwood Staff slipped from the wizard's hand and fell to the ground, returned to its original form.

"So, once again the apprentice is less than his master." A'stoc dropped to his knees next to the Staff. Quiet tears ran freely down his face, and he turned to look at Chentelle. "I'm sorry. I thought that if I could restore the Tree of Life . . . It doesn't matter. I don't have the power."

Remember.

Understanding dawned in Chentelle. She knelt beside A'stoc and picked up the Staff. "You do have the power. What you need is the understanding." She pressed the Staff into his hands.

A'stoc stared at her, and new hope rose in his eyes. He grabbed the Thunderwood and planted it into the ground. Earthpower burst from the Staff.

Chentelle reached out with her Gift, forging a bond between her spirit and A'stoc's. Memories poured through the bond: roots that touched the Foundation and sucked water from rivers that had never seen the suns, limbs that cast shade over mountains and touched the vault of the sky. As one, she and A'stoc gave sound to a word and shape to a world.

"Yggdrasil."

This time the roots and branches did not fade. They grew and strengthened, expanding rapidly up, down, and outward, reaching what seemed impossibly far. But that was only part of it.

Change swept through the Erietoph, riding the crest of a thunderclap. The world wrenched, and the mists vanished. The red light of Deneob poured into the clearing, falling upon the trunk of a mighty tree—the Tree of Life.

Chentelle climbed to her feet. Yggdrasil towered above her, climbing fifty cubits or more into the sky. The World Tree lived once more. Her hand found A'stoc's. "Can you feel it?"

The wizard spun her around and wrapped her in a warm embrace. His kisses were gentle, salty, and more precious than anything she had ever known.

Gradually, she became aware of music. Glathrel and the dendrifauns had formed a great circle around Yggdrasil and the companions, and the forest rang with their joyful paean.

"What happened?" Awe and incomprehension mingled on Dacius' face.

Chentelle disengaged herself from A'stoc with a twinge of regret. "Something wonderful. The World Tree is alive once more, and her roots have reunited the Erietoph with Creation."

The human's eyes grew even wider. "Do you mean that the Creation is healed? Are we entering a new Time of Perfection?"

She shook her head. "No. I don't think that will ever happen. We have drifted too far from that place. We no longer belong there. Remember Fizzfaldt. The only way to heal him was to help him change into something new. It is the same with the Creation. It has to transform, or the Flaw will consume it. Yggdrasil will be the instrument of that transformation.

"Right now, she is still young. Her roots are not deep, and her influence extends only to the borders of the Erietoph. But she will grow. One day, her roots will reach the center of the world, and they will find a seed there, a core of pure Earthpower planted by Father Marcus."

"The Sphere of Ohnn!" Dacius shouted.

"Yes. And when the Sphere and the Tree are united at last, the Foundation will be healed. The Flaw will be closed and the Abyss will vanish. Then, the New Creation will sweep across Infinitera."

Dacius' eyes tracked from Chentelle to A'stoc and back again. "I had thought A'stoc was the true power behind our mission. But now I see that it was you, Chentelle, always you. So gentle, yet without you, none of it would have been possible."

"No—" Chentelle demurred. But she saw the others nodding. Even the dendrifauns, in their fashion.

"And in the New Creation . . . ?" Dacius inquired.

She turned to face A'stoc. "In the new Creation, love will transcend boundaries. It will not reject us, and our love will not be barren. One day, that will be true throughout the Creation. For now, it holds only within the boundaries of the forest."

A'stoc smiled and swept her into his arms. "I love you, Chentelle. And I have sworn never to leave the forest."

AUTHORS' NOTES

JAMES RICHEY

The quest to complete the novel was indeed a difficult one. It took six years to write and two years of attempts to sell it. But all along I never gave up hope. I *knew* it would find publication. I believed it adamantly even through the worst of its trials. I didn't know exactly how it would come together, but I knew it would. For me, it was an utter act of faith to see this work through.

This story began with a boyhood dream of becoming a novelist. One day, I sat down in front of an ancient manual typewriter and began hammering out a beginning. Quickly, I graduated to the electric typewriter, then to the computer. Struggling all the while, I rewrote the manuscript three times, and in the process taught myself how to write. Eventually, the story was completed to my satisfaction. But I found this was only half the fight.

A new battle was before me. The battle for publication. I figured a couple of rejections, then I'd get accepted. It was just a matter of playing the odds and finding the right editor. I had a great novel! No one could turn it down! But after thirteen rejections, the light of hope grew dim. They say most writers suffer the fate of not being able to sell their first story. And this work was my very first. Fortunately, despair did not win out. I refused to quit, and kept searching for an opportunity to present itself.

During its creation and solicitation, I followed other writers and their successful careers. I kept my hope alive by reading of their successes, and pictured myself among them. I read their fantastic novels with a measure of wonder and envy. Would I ever achieve my desire? Then one day, I was at a friend's house who caught one of our favorite writers on videotape. Piers Anthony! Advertising his Xanth novels and newsletter on the TV! Of course, I had to get the newsletter. And one of the things I ordered was the ninety-minute video interview, *Conversation with an Ogre*. It was inspiration for a writer-ling such as I! I even braved writing him a letter of praise, which I actually got a curt response to. (I had touched the hand of one of the literary gods!) Eventually, we got a little correspondence going after I had indicated my status of Struggling Writer. I told my woes of trying to get the story published. And something wonderful and unexpected happened.

Piers not only responded kindly, but offered to read the first chapter of my story! Without hesitation I sent it to him. He gave me pointers on tightening it up so that it might not get rejected. He suggested some changes, and I did them, improving the text considerably. He made mention he would ask his agent if any other agents were taking on new writers. Instead, his agent offered to read my story. And after doing so, the agent concluded it was worth soliciting. Suddenly, I realized there was a chance it could actually be sold. Time went by as despair gathered within my soul. The story accumulated more rejections.

Fortunately, Piers stepped back in. Unable to accept my story's fate, he offered to collaborate with me on it. I of course jumped at the prospect! But, he explained, present circumstances wouldn't allow him to get to it for at least another year or two. He gave me a few alternatives, one of which was to bring in a third party to shorten the wait. Piers had a research analyst who could do the major overhaul in short order, and was looking to credit a novel to his name. At first, I was reluctant to bring someone else into this. But once again, I relied on faith. I decided to open the story to them both not only because I was desperate to have it published, but knew I would be given invaluable knowledge and experience. I acceded to the three-way collaboration, and was introduced to Alan Riggs.

Alan and I became acquainted over the phone, and I instantly found him likable. He made me feel comfortable in his ability to handle the work. Soon we exchanged numerous phone calls hammering out the details of the novel. Slowly, the story took on a new shape. His contribution included modifying the point of view—the major weakness in the novel—and adding flavor to the weaker scenes. But what I consider his greatest accomplishment was turning the Ill-creatures into more heinous, foreboding monsters. He brought their dark forms to life. I am more than grateful for his part in this.

During Alan's course in the novel, I had the chance to catch a ride with a group of friends to Florida from Texas. I visited with Alan and Piers, and had a conversation with them in Piers' study about the manuscript's future. Alan offered his hospitality for a night before I went back to my mundane existence. For me as an unpublished writer, I felt as though I had stepped into a writer's Holy Land, then been forced to return to the outside world to continue my quest as Struggling Writer. But my hope to make a writing career was rekindled.

Now under the name of three collaborators, *Quest for the Fallen Star* is more than it was when I first wrote it. The story is considerably improved and better written. It has the added imagination of Alan Riggs and the storytelling finesse of Piers Anthony. This collaboration is an example of what happens when we open ourselves to the harmony of mutual cooperation.

Sometimes I wonder what inspired me to write this story. But there isn't any definite answer to that. Simply put, I took a journey into writing and into myself, pouring my heart into a tale. I have always believed that life should not be despairing; I believe people can love one another without the need for conflict; and that we can minimize suffering by doing our part to care for one another. As in the Holy Land, we can harmonize with each other, joining our hearts together in the Creation which we are all a part of. Each one of us has a sanctuary of peace within, and we can allow ourselves to share this with others, letting the harmony grow. I truly believe that human beings will eventually achieve a peaceful, loving society. It will encompass everyone. I don't see it happening a hundred years, or even a thousand years from now. But I know it is in our future. The world is becoming a better place. And all I can encourage anyone to do is embrace life joyfully—no matter what trials are set before you in your quest within our creation.
James Richey can be reached at: WWW.JAMES-RICHEY@USA.NET

ALAN RIGGS

This is the second collaborative novel that I have been involved with, but it is the first to be completed. The difference lies entirely in the nature of the people involved. (I miss you, Drew. You're still an asshole.) When Piers brought me into this project, we knew what we could expect from each other. Richey and I were strangers. A two-way collaboration is a delicate beast; try to balance three creative personalities and the words "potential nightmare" spring instantly to mind. Thankfully, in this instance they were just as quickly dispelled.

Imagine, if you will, my first conversation with Richey. [*Ring. Ring.*] "Hello, James, this is Alan. I read your novel, and I like it very much. You don't mind if I change the viewpoint and kill one of your major characters in the second chapter, do you? James? James? Operator, I think there's something wrong with my phone."

Actually, Richey responded to these requests, and many others, with equanimity and aplomb—a statement which should not be confused with "he rolled over and let me do whatever I wanted." When we disagreed, he listened to my reasoning, expressed his own position, and worked with me to find the solution that best fit the needs of the story. It was an excellent way to begin. In the end, he even got his character back (sort of).

This was a completed story before I ever laid eyes on it. My part was simply to polish the pieces and smooth the edges. I expected to take about five months to do the job. It took me eleven. As so often happens, concerns of life and family intruded and delays mounted. It was a frustrating and trying period for me, one which was eased considerably by the patience and well wishes of my collaborators. So, if the good reader will indulge me for a moment, I'll take advantage of this spotlight. Thank you, Richey. Thank you, Piers. It was a long detour, but we seem to have ended up in the right place.

Richey mentioned the work I did to embellish his Ill-creatures. As I think of the book now, it is other details that stand out for me: an old man, a dream, a thread of music. No matter. When I read the story again, the focus will be different. That's the thing about stories.

Long ago, I had a debate with a dear friend. We were trying to determine the most hopeful experience a man could have. He argued for the first bloom of love. I believed that it was the beginning of a true friendship. Soon after, he killed himself. And as I write this, I am about to be married. That's the thing about life.

I'm not sure what that story has to do with this one. Maybe I'll read the book again and find out.

PIERS ANTHONY

Actually, I first heard from James Richey's wife, which gave her a kind of priority. I have been averaging 150 letters a month in recent years, and at present I use no secretary (1-800 HI PIERS hired her away from me), and this really crowds my time, so I try not to waste words. Thus my "curt" response he mentions; sometimes folk think I'm mad at them, when I am merely trying to be efficient. Sometimes they think I'm a personal friend, when I am merely trying to be relevant. So I try to be reasonable and responsive and brief, with imperfect success. It's not always an easy line to draw. When I mentioned to one young woman that I had a daughter slightly older than she was, she replied that I had just ruined her crush on me. Sigh; so high, then so low. Each letter is a window to the life of another person, and every person is real and feeling and worth knowing. So I thought of Richey as the spouse of a correspondent, which in my twisted awareness is a lesser state.

Nevertheless, I do pay attention, and when I saw that he was serious about writing, I decided to take a look. Many of my readers—maybe twenty-five percent—are hopeful writers, but most are not really serious. Some are age twelve or younger, and they simply need more time in life, though I once wrote two pages of advice to an eleven-year-old girl whose letter showed that she really might make it as a writer. Some are dedicated, but have little knowledge of the basics, such as paragraphing, syntax, and plotting. Some are truly ambitious, but their prose is impenetrable. There are a thousand ways to fail, and very few ways to succeed. When the other factors check out, I may be able to pinpoint the problem by a look at the text.

Richey's text seemed good. He had a very nice protagonist in Chentelle, good pacing, and depth of description and characterization. He seemed to have a good story to tell, and a clear vision of his objectives. In fact, he seemed to be of publishable level. So why wasn't he getting published?

Well, there are a number of dirty little secrets (and some dirty big ones) in the realms of writing and publishing and bookselling, and every so often I get in trouble by blabbing one of them. I have been blacklisted in the past for insisting on honest dealings. I'm a slow learner, so here we go again. While you might think that there is an eager market for good new fiction, Parnassus (that is, the formidable literary establishment centered in New York) is largely closed to hopeful writers. Many editors will not even look at unsolicited manuscripts; they return them unopened or throw them away. Editors will, however, consider agented material. But a hopeful writer can't get a good literary agent unless he has already been published, or has some independent claim to fame. Thus there are bad agents and vanity presses preying on the dreams of innocents, leeching their money as well as their hopes. It's an ugly business, and I hate the bad aspects while loving the craft of creative writing itself.

So I figured that it could simply be the lack of a competent agent that was balking Richey. I tried to find one for him. Fat chance! I could get any agent I want for myself, but I may not even get an answer when I query for others. It seems that most agents, like editors, don't read amateur manuscripts, and some do bounce them unopened. If I ruled Parnassus, such folk would be expelled for arrogance. But I don't govern this infernal realm of ignorance and greed. In due course this quest got my own agent involved. He's not in New York, so his streak of decency has not yet been obliterated. He read the full novel—I had seen only fifty pages—liked it, and marketed it. With no better success. Parnassus remained impervious.

I am known in some circles as The Ogre. It is true that I don't just turn the other cheek when wronged, and by similar token, when I feel something is worth doing, and it falls within my compass, I do it regardless of the resistance. Ogres are justly famous for their stupidity; I don't know when to quit. I had set out to get *Quest* into print, and Parnassus wasn't listening. So I considered the next escalation of the effort to get a decent novel published: collaboration.

Now I have done a fair number of collaborations, more than twenty novels, but I don't do them lightly. For one thing, I was having trouble placing several prior collaborations. I was also conscious of the potential for abuse. Could an established writer steal the notions of unknowns whose work he sees? Could he make easy money by collaborating, when the other writer might have been able to make it on his own? It is said of the other countries in the American continents that dealing with the United States is like sharing a bed with an elephant; they tend to get pushed around, and may even get squished without the elephant even noticing. An unknown writer collaborating with an established author could feel like that, and I have always tried my best not to be an ogre when it comes to individual rights. I never liked having editors tread all over my fair prose—sometimes I managed later to get my books restored to their original state—and I don't like doing it to anyone else. Usually I try to change the collaborator's work as little as possible, not to save my energy, but as a matter of courtesy. I try to make the text as good as it can be, without changing its nature. So my collaborations do not read the same as my individual novels; they are good stories in their own right, true to their original distinctive types. I try to fix their flaws, not to remake them in my own writing image.

But *Quest* had been rejected something like twenty-six times. I realized that editors might not even consider it as a collaboration, unless it was substantially revised. Editors occasionally strike me as exotic birds: they all take flight at the same time, sometimes for no apparent reason other than the fact that the first one spooked over a falling leaf. If an editor knows that a piece has been rejected before, he is likely to reject it, too, for no other reason. Ask any writer, if you don't believe this. So this would require a solid overhaul. So I was cautious, wanting to be sure that Richey understood. This would be heavy treading. I knew this, though I had not yet read more than fifty pages of the novel.

He agreed, and my agent sent me the manuscript. That was when I discovered that it was about nine hundred manuscript pages long. I judged it would take me two and a half months to rework it, and I had allowed for only about one month. I didn't have time to do it then. *Quest* was a good novel, but its problems, though subtle, were not simple to fix. For example, viewpoint; it is best that it be unified, while this had a number of different ones. That meant changing several views. But telling the same story from the perspective of a different character is likely to mean changes in almost every sentence, and some scenes can't be done at all, while others must be added to cover the material the way the new character sees it. It can be like repairing a house that has suffered structural damage in an earthquake: every part has to be tested and shored up. The casual reader may not notice the difference, but a whole lot of detail work has been done. Chentelle was the strongest character in the story, for all that she saw herself as the weakest, and the novel would stand much enhanced if she had the viewpoint wherever she was present. But all other major characters were male, which meant converting male-perspective adventure to female-perspective adventure. To the Flaw with political correctness; the difference between male and female is qualitative as well as quantitative. In other words, you don't just give Lord Dacius' dialogue and thoughts to Chentelle and figure there's no difference. You have to rethink the whole scene. Much work loomed.

I discussed the problem with my researcher, Alan Riggs. I didn't want to make Richey wait yet longer, but neither did I want to disrupt my own schedule to that extent. Alan inquired whether he could help. And thus came the surprising notion: to make it a three-way collaboration. That would get the work done, while enabling me to keep my schedule. Alan would rework the novel, and then I would go over it last. It seemed feasible because Alan has worked with me several years and knows the way my mind works. I am thoroughly experienced in writing and in collaborating, which means that he has a fair notion how to do these things, too. So I suggested it to Richey, and he, ever the soul of amity, agreed. Alan took the manuscript and started work.

But we had not anticipated one thing. Alan did know how to do it, and I was there to advise him when he needed it, but he has not had the three decades of general and collaborative writing experience I have. In those decades I have not necessarily gotten better, but I have gotten faster. Alan was good but slow. In addition, at that time he lost several family members and suffered illnesses, interfering with his concentration as well as his available time for working. So what might have taken me two and a half months took him eleven months, and I took a month going over his work. This resulted in a worse disruption of my schedule than the one I had sought to avoid. I had been working on one of the GEODYSSEY historical novels, and Alan's research notes together with my individual research kept me going for a couple of months, but then I ran out. I didn't want to do all my own research, because Alan is better at it than I am—I am a slow reader, and just can't get through the voluminous necessary material rapidly—and even with Alan's research, those novels take me twice as long as regular novels do. So I filled in by revamping my schedule to do a no-research Xanth novel early, and to learn a new operating system and word processor, Windows and Word. Those proved to be ogres of their own type, powerful but user unfriendly. I also had interruptions of my own, as my father fell and fractured his hip; my daughter Penny and I traveled to see him for several days and see what we could do to help. Later he visited us, too. In this same period, Penny got married, and that wasn't exactly a ceremony I could ignore. I also wrote about 50,000 words of the sequel to my autobiography, *How Precious Was That While*, updating my life by a decade; if you think this Author's Note is candid, that book is off the wall. Dirty little secrets galore. I also worked on a special movie-related project. But all that time, the project I longed for was GEODYSSEY, and so did Alan. It wasn't that *Quest* wasn't worthwhile, just that we had had no idea that we'd be in it for a year.

So now at last it's done, and the full package is about 240,000 words. About seven years' work, split quite unevenly between the three authors. Was it worth doing? Of course. What a fantastic experience!